P9-CRJ-413

A MERGER OF
EQUALS

A Novel by
DEBRA SNIDER

MJS
Publishing
Group, LLC

MJS Publishing Group, LLC

Printed in the United States of America.

Published by:
MJS Publishing Group, LLC
950 6th Street
Del Norte, Colorado, 81132
www.mjspub.com

This book was typeset in Sabon which was designed in the 1960s by Jan Tschichold (1902-1974), and is based on Garamond types.

ISBN: 0-9764336-4-8

Cover art by: Jeff Bowers
Cover Design by: Jenny Kruse
Interior Design by: Ignite Communications & Design Inc.

OTHER BOOKS BY DEBRA SNIDER:

The Productive Culture Blueprint:
A Business Driven Model for Corporate Law Departments and Their Outside Law Firms,
(American Bar Association Career Resource Center, 2003)

Working Easier: A Toolkit for Staff and Board Members of Nonprofit Arts Organizations,
(Illinois Arts Alliance Foundation, 2005)

FedEx is a trademark of Federal Express. Technicolor is a trademark of Thomson SA. "Organizational ambition" is a term used in James O'Toole, *Leadership from A to Z: A Guide for the Appropriately Ambitious* (Jossey-Bass, Inc., 1999).

For Annie—my fan, my critic, my daughter.

ACKNOWLEDGMENTS

Thanks to Karl Androes, Jane Cody, Jane Keane, Joan McCarthy, Kathy Morris, Carrie Ohannes, Ruth Olsen, Pamela Pepper, Audrey Rubin, Sandra Sexton, Susan Sneider, Charlie Snider, Mark Snider and Jeanine Zook for their enthusiasm and their interest in reading early drafts. Thanks also to Jeff Bowers for the perfect cover artwork and to Jenny Kruse for the glorious cover design.

I am especially grateful to Anne Snider for her honesty, her great ear for dialogue and her superb editorial contributions, to Jane Pigott for her prompt, eager and insightful reading and her supportive coaching for my every endeavor, and to Mona Syring for loving the book and deeming it important to put it out in the world.

The part-time schedule described in the book is not a pipe dream. I did it happily and successfully as a transactional lawyer at a large law firm (with a reputation for being a sweat shop) for several years, and I'd like to acknowledge Jerry Penner and Dave Shevitz at what is now Katten Muchin Rosenman for clearing the way to make it possible for me to prove it could be done—to the powers that be, as well as to other women. The resort off the coast of Venezuela also exists; it's called Petit St. Vincent and it's extraordinary. The restaurant that looks like a dive and has some of the best seafood around is real, too; it's called the Half Shell, it's in Chicago and it truly hasn't changed (in a good way) in the 29 years since I first enjoyed the grilled shrimp and vegetables.

I hope my characters are a fraction as cool as the people from whom I appropriated their names: my son Charlie and my friends Jane Cody and Jane Pigott. Finally, thanks to Mark for cheerfully living with these characters (who were at times nearly as real to me as he is), for reading aloud with me, and for still thinking, nearly 34 years later, that just about everything I do is wonderful.

A MERGER OF EQUALS

PROLOGUE

Jane

In a man's world, a woman at work is an imperative but perilous proposition.

Long before I learned this, I decided to become a huge success in the traditional business world. I developed my goal in junior high and I had a detailed plan for achieving it. I'm not sure what originally made me want this so passionately and set about accomplishing it with such determination, but my ambition was certainly fueled by my particular history.

I grew up a very smart and not especially pretty girl in a family composed of a distant father who seemed to think girls had a lesser need than boys for education and worldly success, a smart mother who saw no benefit in displaying her intelligence and spent her adult life hiding it behind more traditional "feminine" attributes, and a beautiful younger sister who bought hook, line and sinker into Mom's whole "look pretty/don't be threatening/snare a man who will keep you comfortable and treat you decently" game.

As for me, I would be damned before I'd let being a girl keep me from accomplishing what any mediocre male could accomplish—and more.

Instead of following their rules and attaining the things men admired in women, I decided to attain the things they admired in themselves. Relying on finding one of them to take care of me—and having to pretend to be an idiot in the process—struck me as a very dubious strategy. I figured I'd just follow the male path myself and buy my own goddamn comfort and security, thank you very much.

I have no desire to be a man, but you can't argue with their freedom or their ability to make themselves successful. Under the circumstances that had been normal for at least the century preceding my arrival in the business world, it's highly doubtful that they would have been inclined to make room in their cozy little boys' club for the likes of me. Usefully, however, by the time I graduated from college, their need for women in their ranks outweighed their disinclination to include us.

You need to know a few extra things if you're a woman and you plan to make it big in the traditional corporate world. The game being played in the office buildings and dinner clubs around town is not the one you probably think it is. The game actually being played has rules that don't sit well with excellence, plain speaking, nonconformity or diversity. Integrity can also be dicey. You don't have to play by these rules, but you do have to know what they are. You also have to appreciate that most of the people around you will be playing by them.

The rules of the game include, among many others, the following categorical imperatives:

- ✓ One size fits all—and it's basically a 42 Regular (well, until you get to the executive suite, where it's OK to be a fatter cat). If you want to win and you're not that size, do a great imitation of someone who is
- ✓ Preserve the status quo
- ✓ Don't call a spade a spade if the important people are calling it a shovel
- ✓ The important people are the important people whether you think they deserve to be or not. They're the ones who get to define success—if you want it, pay attention to them
- ✓ Figure out who can help you and suck up
- ✓ It's a zero sum game—don't let anyone get ahead of you
- ✓ Excellence need not apply—it makes others nervous and will be quashed

Work is not about producing results, and it's not organized around the customers or the markets or the employees or any other "centric" bullshit you may have read about. It's a hotbed of human intrigue, propelled by each individual for himself. And with very few exceptions, each individual's game is personal gain.

The people who stay low on the corporate ladder define "gain" as relative comfort, keeping their jobs, managing their misery. They will never stick their necks out, even to get a promotion.

Middle manager types typically get there by separating themselves from the herd in some way—often by focusing on individual performance in the moment at the expense of organizational performance over time. Down deep, they know they got in their elevated positions via the sheerest of luck, no matter how talented they might be. They haven't admitted this top of mind, however, so middle managers tend to focus on a mixture of doing the job at hand (just in case that actually turns out to be relevant to staying employed and getting ahead) and making sure they don't lose their advantage.

Most senior executives reach their lofty positions by being adequate or better (up to, but definitely not including, intimidatingly excellent) in their performance of the job at hand and—here's the important part—by being masters at not unduly upsetting anyone in a position to hurt them. A few get there via utter ruthlessness. Once at the top, both types of senior executives rewrite history and place innate quality and competence at the heart of their promotion track. In a Calvinist "my very getting here means I deserve to be here" sort of way, they shift their efforts 100% to preserving the status quo and keeping themselves in power.

It's really rather remarkable that services get delivered and products get designed and manufactured at all. Such work as gets done apparently does so thanks largely to a momentum/inertia principle—the company delivers services or produces products because that's what it's always done. Like an ocean liner, business once started is evidently hard to stop. It's also nearly, but thankfully not quite, impossible to change.

So why is a woman at work a perilous proposition? Because she has fresh eyes. She's not who the rules were written by or for, so they don't make natural sense to her. No matter how much of a conformist or panderer she may seek to be, she still has to think about the rules in order to understand them.

Like mist, these rules are hard to see when you look at them directly. Like a house of cards, they collapse completely when you poke at them. Unless you're hardwired with them and can just play by them without thinking (which you can't do unless you're a certain sort of male or a very unusual something else), the whole fabric of rules becomes a tissue of meaninglessness.

Long ago, the prototypes of the boys in charge today developed the rules of the game by and for themselves. Without all the path-smoothing assumptions those rules create in their favor, many of today's boys couldn't be where they are. This, of course, whether deliberately or unwittingly, is why big companies—all of which are run and have always been run by that certain sort of male—are terrified of diversity in the workforce. "Women don't get it" or "Minorities never seem to succeed here" are code phrases for "They don't understand the game, and preserving the game is Job 1."

Do the mediocre white male fat cats and wannabe fat cats act this way because they know they're dead in the water if they let original or even alternative thinking in? Do they do it because they truly believe they're the chosen leaders, best able to make the business world tick? Are they totally oblivious—so lacking in self-awareness and strategic vision that they simply do what they do without motive?

Who knows? Honestly, who cares? The point is that the woman seeking to succeed has a Hobson's choice: she can play to win and in the process be forced to hide—and risk losing—big chunks of what makes her herself or she can eliminate herself from the game.

Eliminating ourselves from the game is out of the question as far as I'm concerned. Where's the sense in leaving all the independence, all the power, all the money, and all the other advantages in the hands of white men, many of whom will *never* willingly share those goodies with the rest of us?

Not on my watch. There was no way I was going to *let* them win. All they have is home field advantage. That's powerful and intimidating, but it's not conclusive. And it's by no means the game's only available advantage. Win or lose, I was going to give them a run for their money.

It's been a decade since I officially joined the game. Unexpectedly, both the world and I proved to be less carved in stone than I imagined. Quite a few so-called "truths" turned out not to be true at all. And to my ongoing amazement, among the ranks of the enemy I met my match—an equal whose perspective and partnership, like a fresh and determined wind, blew open my guarded inflexibility and inspired me to rearrange the pieces of my puzzle.

Here's our story.

CHAPTER 1
LET THE GAMES BEGIN

Jane

I started my career at the Firm fresh from college, with the ink barely dry on my *summa cum laude* diploma and the applause from my valedictory speech still ringing in my ears.

The Firm is a big-time investment bank. I had been recruited while still in college by the standard good-looking white guy team, mouthing the standard "we're the best" approach commonly used to hook top students. Like nearly all large and well-known companies, the Firm was comprised predominantly, almost exclusively, of these guys. (Actually, there weren't that many good-looking ones. The beauties on the recruiting team had evidently been hired at least in part for that purpose and, sadly, they weren't representative.)

Because of its lack of diversity, the Firm was finding itself at a disadvantage with clients and prospective clients who were—or had found it good for business to pretend they were—more progressive. The Firm needed women and minorities badly. Those of us who were strong candidates for hire in traditional terms (that is to say, those of us who had achieved in the ways powerful white men found impressive) were finding ourselves deluged with offers of employment.

My plan for making it in the business world required a start at a company that would impress others and look good on my resume. I was reassured (if also a little disgusted) by the Firm's recruiting pitch, which seemed to assume that I was or wished to be male, and it was hard to argue with the "we're the best" point the recruiters made. The Firm struck me as absolutely the right next move, so I accepted the offer.

I viewed the Firm as a critical stepping stone—just as I'd viewed college. I had worked hard to achieve the grades and test scores that would get me into the top colleges and then I'd gone to the best college

I got into (as defined by *U.S. News & World Report* and the male college counselors at my high school). I majored in Economics and minored in Business. I was often the only girl in those classes and I had no trouble consistently outscoring my classmates.

Economics and Business classes also taught me how to relate to men as a peer. In college, this was mostly a matter of developing an interest in sports and steering clear of being seen as someone's girlfriend. At only 5'4" tall and slightly built, I'm too small to play football or other mainstream men's sports, but I learned the rules and how to converse intelligently about all of them. And I did learn to play golf.

(It turned out to be lucky that I found golf so hideously tedious that I couldn't make myself play very often. Once in the business world, I quickly learned that no one is very good and it doesn't pay to be able to beat your male colleagues and clients. I knew how to behave on the golf course and I was never the worst player in any foursome, which is all that's really necessary where golfing for business benefit is concerned.)

I joined the Firm because it was the best, most prestigious and most widely recognized as such of the many excellent opportunities I was offered. I didn't know if I would like working in investment banking or not, nor did I particularly care. I was sure I could do well and parlay the experience into the next rung on the ladder to the top.

Enjoying my work on a day-to-day basis was a luxury that could wait until I had climbed into the stratosphere. I would not be derailed on the way up by giving top priority to something of such relative triviality as interesting or enjoyable work. For me, it was the destination that mattered, not the journey, and I poured all my passion into reaching that destination ASAP.

The way to get ahead at the Firm was to be seen by powerful people senior to you as unusually brilliant at reeling in clients, getting deals done (so hefty fees could be collected) or, preferably, both. Other aspects of your behavior or performance, including your ability to manage, lead or even tolerate rookies, were basically of no consequence whatsoever.

Well, to be fair, it was usually a problem if you were such a complete asshole or moron that people flat out refused to work with you, but even those deficiencies could be overcome if you had a powerful enough senior supporter or client connection. As a result, the environment was not a nurturing or coddling one, particularly for rookies. We not only had to sink or swim, we also had to locate the pool and dive in pretty much on our own.

The Firm did, however, take its financial investment in new professional hires very seriously. Right from the beginning, we were significantly overpaid, even taking into account that we were expected to work sixteen-hour days and to live in one of the most expensive cities in the world. We were also given dazzling amenities like offices and secretaries and expense accounts.

In short, we cost the Firm a bundle and the Firm wanted to maximize its return on the investment. Management had come to believe, with the coaxing of some persuasive consultant, that the key to maximizing that return was successful assimilation and long-term retention of fresh blood—and, in turn, that the key to successful assimilation and retention was to provide each new professional hire with a more experienced mentor. The same consultant offered to sell the Firm the tools to implement a mentoring program, and the Firm—apparently without questioning the purity of the consultant's motives—bought the tools and instituted the program.

I was among the beneficiaries of the Firm's mentoring program in the third year of its existence—that palmy time in the lifecycle of corporate initiatives after most of the more egregious bugs have been worked out, but before true results can be measured. (The measurement phase is, for most initiatives, the one that immediately precedes the death phase.)

In the first year of the mentoring program, the only senior people who volunteered to be mentors were the executive who bought the program from the consultant (his sole contribution to the diversity committee he chaired) and the hapless head of Human Resources. It's obvious why the exec who purchased the program volunteered. While the head of HR may have had honorable motives, at most companies that position carries no real power and is senior only on the organization chart. Seeing that nobody important was interested in the program after the introductory fanfare, the mid-level suckers who volunteered in the first year did basically nothing but hold the initial mentoring meetings mandated by the consultant's rulebook for successful mentoring programs.

The second year saw some improvements. Thanks to some lobbying by the executive who bought the program, some whining by the head of HR, and a nod to the importance of the mentoring program as a way to increase diversity in the Firm's ranks by the CEO in his annual letter to employees, a few additional senior executives were strong-armed into volunteering.

Those who were agile enough to avoid volunteering personally did so by volunteering their up-and-comers, who were made to see being mentors as a new way to suck up to their bosses. Inevitably, some of these "volunteers" ended up being good mentors to their assigned rookies and anecdotal results started to flow.

By year three, the CEO was feeling heat from the marketplace on diversity issues. He was impressed enough by the anecdotal results to get himself solidly behind the mentoring program, which naturally caused every other senior executive to join enthusiastically in the talk about its merits. Of course, these executives still felt strongly that it would be best to avoid actually interacting with rookies on a set schedule. Fortunately for them, they had wised up enough by year three to realize that the whole program would work like a charm if being selected as a mentor were presented as an extra nod of recognition for the truly up-and-coming—a sort of divine right of kings.

The divine-right-of-kings strategy offered all sorts of potential benefits. Those selected as mentors would work much harder to make their mentoring relationships successful so as to get good reviews and be chosen again the next year (proof that they were still A-listers). Rookies would be exposed to and guided by the people the Firm viewed as the *best* of its younger employees—as opposed to the mopes who became mentors because they were too timid or slow to avoid being roped into the program. It was genius, really—one of those mysterious and intriguing confluences in corporate life where mere form transforms itself, apparently alchemically, into actual substance.

My rookie year at the Firm was the first year in which each rookie was assigned to a young king. Of course, there were no young queens (or, in any event, no females). It was much too soon in the Firm's history for any women to have reached the exalted level of acceptability required to be selected as a mentor.

Leaving all cynicism aside, the mentoring program had become a hell of an opportunity to learn from someone six to eight years ahead of you who was succeeding spectacularly. Even holding your cynicism close, it was a great chance to hitch your wagon to a star. New hires looked forward to meeting and wowing our mentors with an eagerness matched only by the zeal with which we collected and cashed our outsized paychecks.

Before I met Charlie, my assigned mentor, I figured he was the usual C-plus player able to succeed at an A-plus level thanks to being a white male in a package that other white males envied and revered in equal measure. Charlie had all the attributes that make it possible for mediocre men to succeed, and he had them in world-class form and style.

He was 6'3" and built as if designed specifically for the purpose of looking terrific in a business suit (strong and slim, but not scarily muscled or inelegantly lanky). He was a beauty, but in a manly and unself-conscious way. He was good but not too good at golf and tennis, funny but not too funny, smart but not too smart, ambitious and hard-working but not obsessed. He even had a father who was a top executive at a prominent company.

Charlie was only in his fifth year chronologically, but he had been skipped up and was treated as a sixth-year in the Firm's class hierarchy. Despite the acceleration in status and compensation represented by this elevation, nearly everyone liked him. He didn't seem overly impressed with his superstar status and he had a nice way about him—he was easy-going and very charming.

In short, Charlie was exactly what many, many men wished to be. In a rather telling coincidence of evaluation scales, this assembly of physical, parental and personal attributes was also what many, many women wished to snare. Charlie was the embodiment of the "great catch" breathlessly articulated in so-called women's magazines, and he had quite the following among the ladies.

After listening to my secretary tell me that she and all her friends thought he was "just a doll" and I should consider myself lucky to have been assigned to him, I figured he would be insufferable. I spent most of my prep time for our first meeting deciding how I would sidestep him if he made a pass at me without derailing the chance to use him to further my career.

I met Charlie in mid-July. The first thing I learned from him was the obvious (but not well-followed) lesson that it doesn't pay to judge a book by its cover. While he was certainly on a turbo-charged career path thanks in part to his golden boy attributes, Charlie was no lightweight. He was, in my judgment, an A-minus player with frequent flashes of brilliance, not a C-plus player at all.

He was also a truly decent guy who became a real friend as well as a first-rate career counselor and supporter for me. We kept meeting monthly even after our mentoring year ended, and Charlie remained committed to helping me succeed. He never doubted my competence or my commitment to my career. From our first meeting, he took me seriously and treated me like a colleague.

This was bizarre to me in the beginning, like a category mistake. It was as if one of the popular boys in high school had suddenly and inexplicably decided to use his eminence to elevate the status of a smart, serious girl instead of spending his time on a ditzy cheerleader or his jock entourage.

I spent our first few meetings doubting Charlie's sincerity, patent though it was. He so looked the part of the golden boy—you just knew he had been one of the popular kids in high school, in college, probably in every single thing he'd ever done in his whole goddamn golden life— that it was hard for me *not* to have the smart, serious girl's disdain of him and even harder for me to believe there was more to him.

There was, as it happened, a great deal more. In fact, when I eventually told him how I'd initially misjudged him based on what he so stereotypically seemed to be, his response was, "I'm surprised that someone so harmed by stereotyping, first of smart women and then of career women, would be willing to stereotype anyone else." Touché.

It turned out that Charlie's mother was a college professor. He also had two sisters—one a practicing internist, the other in medical school— as well as an intelligent and successful brother. Unlike me, he had grown up in a family where women were viewed no differently than men vis-à-vis brains and career choices.

Charlie was completely comfortable around smart, ambitious women. He considered my gender to be merely one factor, and not the most important one, relative to my chances for—and my right to—career success. He didn't offer me any sexist bullshit nor did he let me get away with any as we planned my future at the Firm.

I learned a lot from him during our mentoring year. Possibly the most important of these lessons was that not every member of the existing power structure automatically considered me an inappropriate, incompetent interloper simply because I was female—and that I did myself no favors by treating people as if they did think that.

Both directly from Charlie's advice and indirectly from the example of his own behavior at work, I learned that one of the reasons white men stick together in business and other settings is that they don't make each other uncomfortable. Of course, some of this is certainly thanks to the discriminatory crap that excludes the rest of us and should have been stripped of its "business as usual" status long ago: shared upper-middle-class backgrounds; patronizing view of women as sex objects; constant sports talk; and the blithe assumption that white and male and American is the way to be.

To my surprise, though, it became clear that plenty of the comfort men feel with one another is due to an unspoken behavioral code that minimizes discord and embarrassment and maximizes feeling convivial and "in it together." This behavioral code is available, albeit with some effort, to everyone.

Men develop jargon as a shorthand way of speaking—nicknames for themselves and for bosses, clients, projects, types of deals, what have you—and then use the jargon to feel clubby with one another. They join in each other's football and basketball pools and contribute to each other's charitable causes for the same reason.

They are very competitive, but they typically express this in impersonal "raise the bar" language, not in "I'm better than you" personal threats. They joke with and kid one another constantly, but lightly—almost gently, despite the often crude language—and only on mutually acceptable topics. Sexual or sports prowess, political leanings, girlfriends, minor work flubs, amusing habits are all OK; personal appearance, religion, serious political issues, and wives are not.

They really do have a code of silence, too. Obviously, this can be—and sometimes is—taken too far. More often, though, it's harmless. They are simply careful not to put one another in difficult or embarrassing positions relative to bosses, each other, women, etc. Maybe because the possibility that they *aren't* right never occurs to them, they care more about fitting in and getting along than about being right. So long as the problem caused by a *compadre* is relatively minor, they consider it bad form to point it out and make an issue of it.

It's all rather like a frat party, if you ask me, where the idea is to overlook the vulgar realities—the truly terrible beer, the silly drunken behavior, the people vomiting in the garbage cans, the banality of what conversation there is, even the sexual harassment—and just go along with the general pretense that everyone is having a wonderful time in this, the best of all possible worlds.

Still, Charlie helped me see that the game was the game whether or not I approved of it or thought it was the right game. He made it plain that if I wanted to win, I would improve my chances enormously if I learned how to fit in and play like one of the frat boys.

I absolutely wanted to win. I wanted that much, much more than I wanted to rub people's noses in the actual fact of my superiority as a woman who'd had to be better, work harder, and achieve more to get to the same place as my male peers. So I choked down my sense of superiority (and occasionally my better judgment) and played their game.

There are three keys to playing this game. First, you have to understand it. Second, you have to hide any sense you may have that it's a stupid game or the wrong game. (There will be plenty of time to use that insight to change the game *after* you've won.) Third, you have to make the fact that you're a woman irrelevant—or at least incidental—to how others view you.

The hardest part turned out to be part two. It was a daily challenge and a nearly constant frustration to hide my sense of how wrong and stupid the game often was. But understanding the game was easy (which, considering who routinely plays and wins it, shouldn't come as a surprise to anyone). And making my gender a non-issue required vigilance, but it wasn't all that difficult either, and it worked beautifully for me at the Firm.

This was not assimilation in a bad sense. It was not necessary for me to give up anything I considered important. And many of my more stereotypically feminine skills and characteristics—multi-tasking, listening, strategic planning and being underestimated, to name a few—were precisely what made me so successful.

Taking gender off the table as an issue involves nothing more than operating—by which I mean performing and behaving—in a way that causes people to think when they see you of well-done work rather than of gender. You want them to look at you and see a brilliant idea or great analytical skills or a strong work ethic or ease in relating to and handling clients—preferably, all of the above.

You don't want them to look at you and think about women in general, women they know or sex or romance. It isn't any better to remind sexist pigs of their wives, daughters, mothers or sharp little sisters than it is to make them think about actually having sex.

There is one exception to this rule. It can be helpful to remind some older men of their daughters. Many of them think protectively, but not in a sexist way, about their daughters, especially if those daughters are trying to make it in the work world and have complained to daddy about the discrimination they have to deal with.

Using this strategy judiciously with carefully selected senior men can pay off in a big way.

Tactics for taking gender off the table are straightforward. They fall into three categories: overt, subtle, and work-related.

Overt tactics include looking presentable, but not sexy, and wearing a little makeup (so as not to appear unfeminine in a bad way), but not very much (so as not to appear feminine in a bad way). Never cry. Never run your hands through your hair or lick your lips. Be careful about how you take such actions as crossing your legs, reaching for things, etc. Never refer to or blame anything on cramps, PMS or anything else gynecological.

There are many, many subtle tactics. The point here is to fit smoothly and without raising hackles (or anything else) among men. Join intelligently in conversations about things men find interesting or important—sports, business and cars, primarily. Use their jargon and join them in developing new jargon. Don't make speeches to general audiences about sexism or diversity or day care or other so-called "women's issues."

Don't carry around a ton of stuff, even work stuff—men never do. Don't be moody—men can get away with this; women cannot. Don't flinch when someone swears or tells an off-color joke. Be sure to swear yourself—but do use caution with the word "fuck." "That guy is so fucking smart" is fine. "Fuck!" or "Fuck you" may not be fine, depending on the context. You don't want to cause men to think about actual fucking.

Work-related tactics are obvious for the most part. Do a great job. Be organized, not scattered. Consider numbers, financial models and the bottom line to be of critical importance. Be strategic and focus on the big picture; make sure the details are right, but don't get bogged down in them. Think ahead and be prepared so you don't have to say "I don't know" too often. Do say "I don't know" when you really don't or people will assume you never really do.

Most importantly, never make a mistake. The specific becomes the generic awfully fast with women—make a mistake and people will feel justified in doubting not only your competence, but every other woman's, too.

One great day toward the end of my second year at the Firm, Charlie told me that I was going to be invited to join Corporate Finance's Mergers & Acquisitions group as an associate—a position that represented a significant boost in status and reputation for me. Here's what Charlie reported they had said about me: "Superstar potential, easy to work with, great sense of humor, smart, strategic, and really fits in."

I knew I was now well on my way.

❖ ❖ ❖

Charlie

At the end of my sixth year at the Firm, I was right where I wanted to be: a star on the fast track to the top.

I already had a few terrific clients and was working connections for several more. I got staffed on the best projects when I wasn't working on my own deals. I had developed solid relationships all over the Firm that facilitated getting my deals approved, my work prioritized, even my packages mailed. I traveled an enjoyable amount, made a ton of money, and felt more like an expert with every closed deal.

I had officially been one of the Firm's "young kings" for two years. At the beginning of my fifth year, Jim (the head of Corp Fin's M&A group) called me into his office and told me I'd been selected as one of the mentors for the Firm's mentoring program—a kudo that, up to then, had been reserved for people at least a year ahead of where I was at the time.

I knew this was something of a left-handed compliment. Because the mentoring program was the CEO's baby, we all pretended we thought it was important. But not very many people really believed in it and no one wanted to bother with taking on a rookie who might not succeed. Still, only A-listers were asked to be mentors, so it was a request we all hoped to get.

Being the youngest person ever to have been asked was a big thing— something destined to become part of Firm lore. As the news got out, congratulations poured in and I suddenly had a crowd of new volunteers who wanted to work on my deals. At the Firm, it's always wise to get close to stars and hope some of the stardust rubs off.

I planned to get to the top, but I tried not to take the adulation—or myself—too seriously. I knew that a fair amount of what led to success at the Firm was meaningless. Talent and drive were important, but the place was far from a meritocracy. Success resulted from a complex mix of talent, aptitude, personality, ambition, being in the right place at the right time, not making any powerful enemies, and looking the part.

I fit the profile that was thriving at the Firm and I wanted to ride that as far and as fast as I could. Despite its impressive staying power up to that point, I was sure my profile wouldn't be the only right one forever—it was long past time for change. My goal was to be one of the senior executives in the power structure who would determine *how* things changed. I wanted to end up in charge of the Firm.

I was honest enough to admit that this desire stemmed in part from pure ambition and self-preservation. I liked calling the shots and taking charge of deals and people, and I intended to keep collecting ever-bigger paychecks. I also had another motivation, though, and it was at least partly altruistic. I had a more open-minded view of the world than many of my peers, and I was sure I could make the Firm a more successful force in the market and a better place to work.

My reasons for thinking this stemmed from my family and the way I was raised. My dad was then a senior executive at the big, well-known company he'd worked for his entire career. My mother was a math professor at a prestigious university. They instilled in all four of their kids (I'm the next to last) a strong sense of self-worth and also of responsibility to others.

Basically, they thought the four of us were smarter and far more advantaged than the vast majority of other people and, accordingly, that it was incumbent on us to use our good luck to make the world a better place. My mother and father didn't apologize for our advantages nor did they feel undeserving. Theirs was also not a knee-jerk "serve soup at shelters" sort of reaction to good fortune or a penance designed to keep the evil eye at bay.

They simply believed there weren't very many intelligent, capable people in the world who could end up in influential positions. As my mother lovingly but pointedly told my brother and me every chance she got, big, smart, easy-to-get-along-with white men have an unparalleled opportunity—and, thus, a bigger obligation—to use their blessings for the forces of good in the business world.

Speaking from a more financial bottom-line perspective, my father was certain that the reason his various business units always dramatically outperformed other units was that his were always more inclusive—of women and minorities, and also in general operating terms. Most of his results were produced before companies started worrying about and measuring diversity or teamwork, and you couldn't argue with them. He had been very, very successful.

Based on my experiences after I left home to go to college, I knew this was an unusual way to be raised. I was a big fan of it—it felt great and it worked. My sisters, my brother and I had great childhoods and grew up into happy, productive, successful people. The four of us were self-confident, but not full of ourselves—probably because we were told over and over that our good fortune was far more a matter of the random luck of having been born where and to whom we were than a matter of personal entitlement or even reward for personal effort.

We were also raised in a way that made us comfortable with different people and well aware that talent and brains come in all sizes and shapes. We often had hard-working exchange students from exotic, usually under-privileged, places living with us, and my mother was by far the smartest person in the family. (She's incredibly smart—the kind of math she teaches is so abstract it barely involves numbers at all.) If you had grown up in my family, you would have found the negative assumptions that people at the Firm routinely made about women and minorities not just inappropriate and offensive, but also completely absurd.

These were the reasons I thought I belonged in charge of a place like the Firm. I knew it would be a better business if it learned to take institutional advantage of a much wider range of resources and opportunities, and then to deploy those for the benefit of its clients and, in turn, its employees and owners.

My mother often observed that the handsome white guy disguise was the best protective coloration imaginable for someone seeking to be a change agent in the business world. She was right. Even at that relatively early stage of my career, I'd already had quite a few opportunities to put my protective coloration to good use. The camouflage was important, though—you had to be careful who you talked to about changing the game. I kept my goals pretty much to myself and just did what I could to operate in accordance with them when I staffed my deals or talked to recruits or otherwise had a chance to move the ball forward. I intended to keep doing that, win the game, and then use my power to change it to a better game.

Given all this, I had to laugh and consider the place of design in the universe when I met Jane, my first mentee. Tiny, fierce, defiant and brilliant, she was as sure the world was out to make it all but impossible for her to succeed as she was determined to succeed anyway. I was the perfect mentor for someone like her, but it took her several meetings even to be able to listen to me, so certain was she that I was the enemy.

It was actually hard not to laugh at her at first—the chip on her shoulder was bigger than she was. Jane has told me since that she isn't freakishly small and I only think of her that way because I'm freakishly big. She's probably right, but she really did seem too small to contain the brains, the strategic savvy and the determination—not to mention the indignation—that she had in spades. She always seemed to me to be about to burst.

Jane's background was very different from mine. Her father didn't value her brains and grit the way he would have if she'd been a boy and her mother found it more expedient to appear compliant than intelligent. Jane was too ornery to buy into her father's view of things and too independent to settle for her mother's life.

She was also not a girly girl (as she said) in any way, being bony, blunt, brainy, and totally unwilling to pretend she was anything different. I'm sure she scared the hell out of her family and the kids she went to school with. People at the Firm found her plenty intimidating, too. She might have scared me if we'd met under different circumstances.

As it was, the first thing I offered her in the way of advice was a strong and plainly stated suggestion to lose the attitude and quit acting as if she thought she was somehow above the game she was trying to win. I told her she was doing herself no favors by scaring people and that she would move up faster and further if she knocked the chip off her shoulder and relaxed.

Jane was stubborn as hell, but she had a strong desire to make it big and she took my advice. She never got as far as relaxing that first year (nor has she since), but she started playing the game as if she were entirely certain it was the most important and compelling game on earth. This attitude adjustment was all it took to put her firmly on the Firm's fast track. She is truly brilliant and she was a sophisticated strategic thinker even as a rookie. Her skills made her a shoo-in so long as she didn't rub people the wrong way.

Jane's success was one of the best testimonials the mentoring program had in its favor. Had she not been given a mentor who could stop her from being an irritant and, accordingly, self-destructing, her brilliance and determination would all have come to nothing despite the Firm's acute need for women on its fast track and in its senior ranks.

Our mentoring relationship evolved just the way these things are supposed to—I got as much out of the relationship as she did. It didn't hurt me any that my mentee showed signs of becoming a superstar in her rookie year or that she was hand-picked to join M&A as an associate at the end of her second year. I got a lot of credit for Jane's success, far more than I actually deserved.

We even avoided the raunchy rumors that attended the other male/female mentoring match-ups. There wasn't anything sexual or romantic in our relationship, but that was also true of all but one of the other mixed relationships and the rumors flew anyway.

Jane simply disappeared so completely and convincingly into her role as brilliant up-and-comer that no one thought of her primarily as a woman. This protected her from a good deal of the sexist garbage that other professional women at the Firm dealt with constantly, no matter how capable they were.

Jane hated being seen first as a woman instead of as a professional and she took great care to avoid creating that impression. She wasn't soft or stereotypically feminine anyway, but it wasn't that she seemed unnaturally male or not female. She just very effectively made her gender a non-issue. While this may have been a grossly unfair thing for her to have to do, it indisputably super-charged her success.

CHAPTER 2
LIFE AT THE FIRM

Jane

There were four other women in my rookie class at the Firm. We rarely got to work together because only the biggest deals were staffed with more than one rookie analyst. As for hanging together at the office, I had my doubts about the wisdom of appearing to be connected at the hip with other women. Given my strategy of taking the gender issue off the table, they didn't seem like the best entourage for me.

But they were terrific and our mutual need for solidarity and support overrode our disinclination to look like a girls' club. After meeting at orientation and bonding during bathroom breaks ("How male of us!" Lynn exclaimed), we started getting together outside the office for drinks and sometimes dinner once or twice a month.

One such cocktail hour occurred about six months into our rookie year. It was a Friday night and we'd all worked like pack animals all week. It was a testament to how much we needed to debrief that we got together at all instead of going home to sleep—especially since we would all be going into the office to log some Saturday time the next day.

Cheryl and Katherine had been traveling, in both cases with senior people for whom they were working. The stock market was hot and several of the Firm's deals had priced, so Anna, Lynn and I had spent one or more of the previous nights at the financial printer, hobnobbing with lawyers and proofreading prospectuses. (That also meant we'd eaten basically nothing but candy and salty things and were, as a result, a weird combination of buzzed, exhausted and greasy.)

Our second round of drinks had just been delivered when Lynn yawned and then declared, "We need a worst week contest. I'll start. I'm working with that asshole Howard who can't be bothered to get to work before eleven and puts all conference calls off until after his leisurely lunch."

She rolled her eyes in resigned abhorrence. "Then around seven, he sticks his head in the conference room where the rest of the so-called team is slaving away and says, 'Any questions, kiddies, before I leave? I want those numbers on my desk in the morning. Oh, and make sure the damn lawyers get the revised docs over here by morning, too.' Then he hits the road and we work all night! He did that three of the five nights this week! What a dick!"

"At least you have Matt between you and Howard," I said. "He's decent, isn't he? I've got Jim at the top of my deal, but he's not really involved unless someone important from the company shows up. Most of the time, I'm stuck with 'let me check every comma' David." I pantomimed shooting myself in the head. "He argued with the printer flunky for ten minutes last night about whether the centered text on the cover page was really centered!"

"Matt *is* decent, quite decent," Anna confirmed, her hands cupping her brandy snifter. "I enjoyed working with him on the auto parts company deal. And I have no complaints this week either. I'm working with Jordan and he's brilliant."

By "brilliant," Anna meant "wonderful" or "excellent." She was from England and she had a European reserve that set her apart. She was someone you noticed even before she spoke, then when she did speak, the combination of her intelligence, her composure and her accent was killer.

"Brilliant and beautiful," Katherine said appreciatively. She actually licked her lips. "That guy is gorgeous! It's been very taxing to have him as my mentor—I can barely concentrate when I'm with him."

After exchanging her wolfish look for one of displeasure, Katherine added flatly, "I win, guys. Wait until you hear this. We're flying back from New Orleans yesterday. Mr. Team Leader sits up in first class with the client, so I'm squashed into coach next to—are you ready?" She paused dramatically before she said tragically, "Michael!"

We all groaned except Anna, who said, "Hang on. Who's Michael? What am I missing?"

"That intense, weird-looking guy who gave the orientation talk on corporate bonds?" Lynn prompted. "The one who apparently thinks the Firm hires women to provide a dating pool for him?"

"I remember the talk, but a dating pool?" Anna asked, her brow still furrowed.

Cheryl piped in. "That's right. He missed you during the break where he approached us serially to check us out."

Anna smiled. "Should I be offended, then?"

"No, love," Lynn said, in a try at Anna's accent and inflection. "Your aristocratic bearing probably intimidated him. Anyway, he was horrible. His pitch is basically 'I can do great things for you, chickie, if I decide it would be worth my while to take you on.'"

"*Anyway*," Katherine said emphatically, reclaiming the floor, "the fucking flight was delayed *after* we were shoe-horned into the plane— weather, we were informed, but it must have been some internal plane weather because you could look out the window and see pretty blue sky everywhere. The airlines should really consider bringing in those Hollywood rain machines to make their lies more believable."

As always, Katherine's face perfectly accompanied her narrative by running fluently through a variety of expressions—this time, expressions of annoyance, confusion, surprise, and derision. She really should have considered being an actor or a comedian; she's animated, hilarious and bigger than life.

After chewing and swallowing a small handful of cashews, she continued, "To get back to the point, I had to spend hours and hours ducking personal questions and listening to the horrible Michael tell me how great he is, all the while sitting about two inches away from him and pretending I don't find him completely revolting."

"She does win, don't you think?" Cheryl said, with a gentle and sympathetic smile for Katherine.

Lynn started to say something, but Katherine beat her to it. "Wait. You haven't heard all of it. At one point, Michael wants to see something in the presentation. It's in my briefcase, which is properly stowed under the seat in front of me as required by FAA regulations for takeoff and landing," she spoke and gestured like a flight attendant, "so I'm all contorted—ever so gracefully, of course—trying to get the damn thing out when the hook on the front-close bra I'm stupidly wearing pops open!"

We all gasped or laughed and Lynn said, "No way!"

"Way," Katherine said sadly. "So I'm paralyzed for a second, thinking 'now what?' But, what are you gonna do? I get the presentation. I carefully—oh, so carefully—sit up. I find what Michael wants. Then, for at least an hour, I discuss important matters with him in a manner that befits the competent professional I am—sitting, the whole time, like a fucking statue.

"He *finally* gets up to go to the bathroom. The minute he's out of sight, I yank my blouse out of my skirt, stick my hands under it, and hook the bra. God knows what anyone looking at me must have been thinking."

We were all laughing by then, even Anna. "Did he notice?" I asked Katherine.

"I don't think so. I'm sure he would have taken it as a come-on if he had. But, fuck, can you even believe that happened? I'm going to shitcan every front-close bra I have, even though they're the only ones that are even halfway comfortable. Oh, the special delights of being a woman." She sighed theatrically and polished off her Scotch.

"Cheryl, my dear," Lynn said sweetly, after we had all stopped laughing and ordered one last round, "you're awfully quiet. Was it a fruitful husband-hunting week? Don't I recall that you're working with the sublime Charlie?"

Cheryl blushed. In a moment of weakness, she had told us that her goal was to find a husband and use her brains and energy to help make him rich and successful so she could leave all the work aggravation behind and instead sit in a beautiful home, raise kids, and help make her husband even more rich and successful.

We had given her a lot of grief, obviously, but you couldn't fault the originality of her strategy. She figured the best way to meet and then snag the kind of man she wanted would be to qualify for and get the same kind of job he would have. That way, she could scout the prospects while also displaying her own skills and desirability.

Time would tell, but I was betting it would work. Cheryl was smart, pretty, deferential and willing to be in the background in that way men like, but she was obviously nobody's fool. She would make the perfect wife for a guy savvy and secure enough to put her considerable skills to work to help *him* look good.

"Yes, I am working with Charlie," Cheryl said. She grinned. "He *is* sublime—glorious, really. It's hard to imagine better scenery! He does have a rather terrifying steely side, though. When we got to L.A. on Tuesday, the client's financial guys hadn't finished the numbers we needed to value the new product lines for the sale book. Finishing the book was the purpose for the meeting and the CFO was the one who set the date and insisted we go out there. Charlie was furious."

"The perfect man has a flaw? Do tell," Lynn commanded. Her face was a picture of gleeful curiosity—head tilted, eyebrows high, expectant grin on her lips.

"I don't know that it's a flaw," Cheryl said, smiling. "It's obvious that he has a temper, but he can control himself. He got all icy and determined, spoke privately to the CFO, and people started hopping to. It was kind of thrilling, but I was really glad I wasn't the one who'd screwed up."

She turned to me and touched my shoulder lightly as she said, "Jane, I thought again on the flight back that he must be a great mentor. We had the most interesting conversation, and there's just none of that outsider feeling when you talk to him."

"That's the best thing about him," I agreed, nodding. "He really seems to see women as people and colleagues, not as interlopers or dates or prey. I'm not entirely sure he's for real—I keep waiting for the other shoe to drop—but he's been terrific so far."

"Well," said Lynn categorically, "sorry to be shallow, but I think the best thing about Charlie is the way he looks. He is magnificent. There isn't nearly enough scenery of that quality at the Firm."

Lynn fascinated me. She was a very bright woman from a ritzy suburb of Cleveland. Highly ambitious, she nevertheless was not willing to compromise her personality or her behavior one iota. She never for a moment considered that she might not succeed—or that she might not be *entitled* to succeed—just as she was.

Lynn was totally at ease with herself and totally unapologetic about being female. In a conference room full of people, she was as comfortable reapplying her (usually red) lipstick as she was giving a presentation or explaining a complex revenue projection model. She figured people could take her or leave her; when they were inclined to leave her for sexist or other unacceptable reasons, she dealt with them head-on.

I doubted her strategy would work in the long run, but I wished more than once that I had the guts to try it her way. Lots of people considered her arrogant and didn't like her, but I thought that was unfair. Lynn was simply the female equivalent of the blithe, sure-he-should-prevail white male. Also like that sort of man—and unlike any other woman I'd ever met—she considered the opposite sex to be little more than eye candy or sex toys.

"Lynn," Cheryl said reproachfully, "here's one guy who evidently thinks women are actually fellow human beings and you want to reduce *him* to object status?"

"Oh, please," Lynn scoffed. She flicked her perfectly manicured fingers as if to brush away the very idea. "I'm sure under that façade of decency he's a pig like the rest of them."

"I bet he's a great fuck, though!" Katherine said, her whole face vivid and joyful. "He's so hot! Jordan, too. And that Patrick guy—do you remember him, from the orientation talk on Public Finance? There's something about the way those three guys wear their suits that really turns me on." She grinned at Cheryl and me as she added, "And the ability to consider me actually human would be a real nice plus!"

"Ladies," Anna said, her nose slightly wrinkled, "wouldn't we be very annoyed indeed to learn they were discussing *us* in this sexual and objectified fashion?"

After a chorus of "As if they aren't!" exclamations, we reluctantly finished our drinks, said goodbye to one another and headed home to catch some much-needed sleep.

❖ ❖ ❖

Charlie

Just before the end of her first year, Jane came to my office for one of our regular meetings looking very downcast. She didn't refer to whatever was bothering her; instead, she picked up a couple ongoing topics where we had left them at the end of our last meeting.

We had been having useful, enjoyable—and candid—conversations for months, but she still seemed to be holding on to some lingering doubts over how far she could trust me. I couldn't tell if this had something in particular to do with me or was just the result of her characteristic disinclination to rely on anyone but herself. In any event, she was obviously dejected, so after not too long I said, "Is something wrong, Jane?"

She looked at me quizzically, as if unsure either why I asked or whether she should answer. After a moment or two of silence, during which I tried my best to look receptive, she said, "I don't know if this is something I should talk to you about or not."

"I consider our conversations confidential," I assured her.

"Oh, it's not that," she said quickly. "I'm worried about sounding whiny or silly."

"It's hard to imagine you sounding either one," I said, with a smile. "Come on—if you think I might be able to help, tell me."

"It's just that I've been feeling so disillusioned," she said slowly. She crossed her arms as if to shield herself. "I assumed once I was working at a place like this, I'd be surrounded by people who were more results-oriented, more self-confident, less like people trying to win a popularity contest or something instead of trying to do a great job. I thought it would all be more—well, more *rigorous*, I guess." She stopped talking and looked at me, again quizzically.

"I'm not sure I know what you mean," I said. "Can you give me some examples?"

"Well, yeah, sure. Last week, I made a suggestion in a drafting session that solved a problem. I got a compliment from the client and the senior Firm guy. That totally pissed off the manager, who had a fit the minute the senior guy was gone." She sighed. "Lots of people don't seem to push themselves very hard or care very much about doing a great job. They seem to do the minimum or whatever will keep them out of trouble, but that's it. And then they have a problem with anyone who does work harder and might show them up.

"Or you're in a meeting and the presentation makes no sense, but everyone sits there and pretends it does because they're afraid of the presenter or they don't want to admit they don't get it by asking a question." She uncrossed her arms and held them out in a gesture of bewildered frustration. "Like it never occurs to them that maybe it really doesn't make sense! It seems like people would rather *be* stupid than risk looking stupid. Or let something stay wrong rather than risk offending someone by trying to fix it."

Jane paused, but it was obvious she had another example and was deciding whether or not to offer it up. I waited.

"And then there's the 'kill the messenger' type thing," she finally said, looking down at her hands. "When people blame you for some shortcoming you make them feel in themselves? After a meeting the other day, a guy told me I didn't have to use such big words all the time because everybody already knew I was smart." She looked up with a very defensive expression. "I just wanted to look at him and say, 'I know you are, but what am I,' you know? I use words because they're in my vocabulary, not because I'm trying to show people I'm smart! Why can't people focus on the point instead of thinking everything is about them?"

I wasn't sure exactly what I wanted to say in response to all this, so I bought some time by asking her why it made her feel disillusioned.

"I guess I thought I'd be done with this kind of adolescent, zero sum game behavior when I left high school," she said. "And college actually was better. People seemed more focused on what was going on, what

35

they wanted to accomplish or whatever, and less worried about how they looked or what other people thought. They were less judgmental or less *comparative* somehow. Do you know what I mean?"

"I think so," I answered. "I have a few thoughts in response, but I doubt they'll be very helpful." I smiled again, but she still didn't smile back. "I'm sorry you're feeling disillusioned, but it was probably inevitable. You have to know that you're in the top tier where brains and drive are concerned. *Most* other people are going to strike you as less capable and less driven—not in a judgmental way, but as a simple matter of fact. If you let that get you down, you're going to be down all the time."

I put my forearms on my desk and leaned toward her. "Also, don't forget that it's useful to know what other people are thinking. Even when it's stupid or offensive or the people are people you don't think much of. You have to work with them, so knowing what they're thinking and how to deal effectively with them is useful intelligence for you. If you have to dumb down a little to deal effectively with the guy who's intimidated by your vocabulary, that's a good thing to know, right?"

"I guess," Jane said doubtfully.

"This is another aspect of the same thing we've talked about before," I tried to persuade her. "The game is the game. If you want to win it, you can't waste your time or effort wishing it was a different game—or wishing it had different players."

"I know you're right," she said, sounding both weary and annoyed. "It's just so lame! And so time-consuming and beside the point. I mean, should I not have made the suggestion in the drafting session? Was it more important for the manager not to feel undermined than for the problem to get solved? Should I have to sit in a presentation wondering if I should let flawed logic go because I've spoken up in the last three meetings and it's probably not the best idea to speak up yet again? I hate all this interpersonal bullshit! Why can't we all just focus on getting the job done?"

As they always did when she was worked up, Jane's hands betrayed the intensity of her feelings. She continued to sit very upright, even stiffly, but her hands moved fluently and emphatically throughout this speech.

"Your last question is rhetorical, I assume, but you know the answers to the other questions as well as I do," I said. "Of course solving the problem and fixing the logic are more important. The issue isn't what you should do in situations like those, but how to deal with the fallout when you do it. Right?"

"OK, yes."

"I think you have to focus on your goal." I leaned back and put my feet up. "Look, there are always going to be people who have a problem with you or who want to take shots at you for one reason or another. Sometimes that will have nothing to do with you at all—and, when it doesn't, there's nothing you can do but ignore it. You can't care about whether people like that approve of you. It's always worth considering whether you can do things differently to make working with them easier, but your goal at this stage is to get the job done well, not to make people like that happy or to get them to like you."

"So you just feel attacked or distrusted and pull arrows out of your back all the time?" she asked skeptically, as if that couldn't possibly be the answer.

"Pretty much, yeah," I said, shrugging. "You're a 'have' as opposed to a 'have not' around here. The 'have nots' are always going to resent you or be intimidated by you. You can't get distracted trying to placate them. Don't rub their noses in it, don't gloat or make it worse, but their problem isn't really you. They know they look bad by comparison, so they blame you. It's a pretty understandable reaction, don't you think?"

"For a ten-year-old, maybe," Jane said, disgusted. "That's why I'm disillusioned, I guess. I thought work would be more adult."

"You thought wrong. Some people never get past thinking like ten-year-olds. We all deal with that. When I started here, there were a few people who resented my connection to my father's company. Instead of seeing it as a lucky thing for me, they viewed it as a way I was trying to show them up. Like I'd arranged to be born into that family just so I could come to the Firm someday and have a leg up on them."

Jane finally smiled. I smiled back and said, "It's ridiculous, right? But what could I do other than try not to make it worse—you know, by talking too much about the client or acting like I thought it actually did make me a better person. Otherwise, I ignored it. It's not like there was any way to change their minds or stop them from feeling inferior because they didn't have a similar connection."

"But," she said, and then stopped. She looked at me uncertainly.

"But what?"

"I'm just whining, I think," she said, looking frustrated again. "But it's just so disappointing! It irritates me and makes me impatient. Sometimes, it's hurtful. Work is hard enough as it is. It's so exasperating to have all this crap to cope with, too. I expected it to be better."

"It is what it is, Jane. Sorry to sound glib or unsympathetic—I am sympathetic—but there's no choice other than finding a way to deal with it so it doesn't drive you nuts." I smiled again and offered, "If whining to me helps, I can take it. I'll listen."

To my surprise, she didn't laugh. She looked grateful and said seriously, "I really appreciate that—thank you. I do feel slightly more optimistic now, actually. It helps to think about my disillusionment in the context of my goal. I'm not going to decide against working here or winning the game because of this bullshit."

"Exactly! Find a way to deal with the exasperation it causes you, and you'll be fine."

"You know, Charlie," she said, "this isn't that different from dealing with the negative assumptions people make about me because of my gender—be a good sport about it at work, try not to play into it or make it worse, and find some humane equivalent to going home and kicking the cat."

"Good analogy. You're right." I put my feet back on the floor.

Jane looked at her watch. The mentoring program rules included one about not using more than the allotted time and she was always meticulous about this. "I should go," she said. "Thanks again."

As I walked her to the door, she looked up at me and asked, only half-joking, "You're not going to make a note that says 'whiner' in some file about me, are you?"

I laughed and assured her that I wasn't.

CHAPTER 3
SIGNIFICANT OTHERS

Jane

By the middle of my second year with the Firm, it had become obvious that I needed a reliable and highly presentable male friend to show up with at corporate social functions.

There are two kinds of corporate social events: the all office people variety and the all heterosexual couples variety. There's no in-between. If you're a man in his 20s, you can bring a different babe to every couples event without raising eyebrows (except in envy), but if you're a woman, you need someone appropriate and consistent.

You can't have people thinking you're promiscuous or unstable. You can't have your colleagues' wives worried that you're looking to replace them and, accordingly, telling their husbands nasty little things to discredit you. You also can't have people thinking you're gay if you're not. (It's probably not the best career move even if you are.)

And, unfortunately for people who work essentially all the time, you absolutely cannot date someone from work—not if you want your colleagues to keep thinking of you as a colleague instead of as a woman/potential date/sex object.

During my first year at the Firm, this wasn't a problem. There weren't that many command social performances, and the ones there were usually didn't include spouses or dates. The only social functions rookies really had to attend were work-related events, like golf outings and closing dinners. (There were also the office holiday parties, but the less said about what goes on at those bacchanalias, the better.)

Golf outings and closing dinners were social events in name only. They never included spouses. In essence, they were business meetings held at golf clubs or restaurants instead of in conference rooms.

Golf clubs did present some awkwardness, since many of them had only recently (and no doubt reluctantly) opened their doors to women. Even if we could get past the front door, they never had decent facilities for us. Worse, the people in the clubs—members and staff—always looked truly horrified to see women in their midst. (I wondered more than once exactly what it was they were so afraid of. Distraction? Higher-pitched voices? Tampon wrappers in the garbage?)

Similarly, closing dinners often presented the awkwardness of being the *only* woman present. If it hadn't been so dispiriting, it would have been funny to watch the men as they separated into their two camps: the ones who scrambled to sit next to you versus the ones who appeared to think you had a particularly nasty infectious disease. Closing dinners also offered the incomparable cigar presentation dilemma—that moment watched by everyone when the poor cigar steward dithered over whether it would be worse to offer you a cigar as if you were a man or to skip you as if you weren't.

I was always able to neutralize the golf club and restaurant situations. It was only marginally more difficult than the day-to-day challenges, which I was very adept at meeting, of making my gender a non-issue. Defusing this kind of social awkwardness never required anything more than being a gracious good sport and smoking the occasional cigar. Smoking cigars was not actually as bad an experience as I'd feared. I much preferred it to smiling politely at sexist pigs while I labored to put them at ease.

Being a single woman at a couples event, however, triggered awkwardness of the sort that was impossible to defuse. It threw off table seating arrangements. It created great discomfiture all around when dancing was involved. (Some of these ghastly events were dinner dances, actually called "proms," as if the Firm really were a fraternity or even a high school instead of an investment banking outfit.) And it prompted way too much questioning—some catty, some pitying, some predatory—about one's lack of a suitable social life.

In short, attending couples events "stag" was out of the question. Of course, there was no one to tell young women about this in advance, so the only way to learn it was to live through the nightmarish experience of showing up alone at the first such event and quickly ascertaining that it would have been far less awkward to have shown up naked.

To preserve your "professional colleague" status, you absolutely had to stay below the social radar and avoid being labeled "woman."

In the social context, "woman" could only mean spinster or slut, both of which were labels very detrimental to your continuing ability to be seen by your colleagues as a peer. The only effective strategy (and it was by no means foolproof) was to have a spouse or its functional equivalent. "Wife" was a demeaning label, too, but at least it put you out of range of all but the most odious wolves.

That's how corporate life works—as before, not unlike that frat party it always reminds me of. On the surface, we pretend everyone's life should be—and is—wholesome and upright and clean-living in a Norman Rockwell painting sort of way. We slavishly maintain this pretense even though, in fact, we all know X is sleeping with his secretary and Y prefers handsome young men to his wife and Z's wife has gotten drunk and propositioned one or more of her husband's better-looking colleagues at each of the last few events.

Like the frat party, the substance of corporate life doesn't really matter all that much. What's important is that we all act like we admire the form. And of course the form we're all supposed to admire is the conservative, traditional, heterosexual white male template. It's disgusting, but it's how the game is played.

As I mentally reviewed the candidates for "Jane's usual corporate date," I had to admit I didn't really have any very good ones. My male friends were all people from work or people who lived in other states, so none of them would do. I needed a man whose company I could stand, which narrowed the candidate list considerably, and who was also a non-scary outsider from the Firm's standpoint. Jazz musicians and blue-collar workers need not apply (not that I knew any).

Even though I was not at all inclined to reopen the potential Pandora's Box he represented, I decided the best option was Tyler, my college boyfriend. He lived in town and would probably be willing to do it. He was also close to perfect for the role, at least on paper—rich and well-known family, prestigious college degree and boarding school background, similar line of work, preppy appearance, and first-class social skills (including dancing, dressing properly, chatting with dowagers, and using the correct flatware—all critical for Firm functions).

I met Tyler my sophomore year of college when we both lived in the same coed dorm. It was before colleges decided it was too dicey for men and women (as they coyly called us) to live on the same halls and use the same bathrooms, so Tyler lived four doors down from me. I ran into him in the hall or in the bathroom occasionally during the first semester. He seemed like a nice enough guy, but we didn't pay any real attention to each other until we ended up in the same calculus class second semester.

Tyler is not stupid, but calculus was his Waterloo. He just couldn't get it. After class one day, we walked back to the dorm together and he asked me to help him, by which he meant either tutor him successfully or help him find some other way to get a passing grade so he wouldn't have to retake the course or take something else awful to satisfy his course distribution requirements.

His timing was good. My roommate, Nina, had fallen in love. She spent most of her time in our room having sex with the object of her affections. Nina was normally a sensible person, but she had become positively gooey over this guy. I found it hard to be around her without wanting to gag. Also, I couldn't study in a room where people were having sex no matter how oblivious to me they seemed to be.

So I said OK to Tyler and told him we'd have to study in his room since mine was otherwise engaged. Trying to turn on the calculus light in his brain was quite instructive. It showed me that people aren't just smart or stupid, but rather that there are multiple layers and many different kinds of intelligence.

Tyler is actually pretty smart and he did very well in college overall. His life path will always be a smoothed one, thanks to his family's money and connections, so he's already more successful than he deserves to be on merit alone. Still, he's intelligent enough and he's shrewd, too—plenty capable of actually doing his job, which is in banking (the real money kind, not the investment kind like me).

All that said, Tyler simply could not learn calculus. If we did problems together, he could follow along and he seemed to understand. Leave him alone with a problem and a pencil, though, and he was utterly lost. The light bulb in his brain steadfastly refused to go on.

This frustrated him for a while, but he's not one to worry much about his weaknesses. Why should he, he figures, when he has so many strengths to float on? About a month into our little tutoring effort, he gave up trying to understand and just copied my work. I also helped him cram enough into his calculus-thick head to pass the midterm and the final, which he did—barely.

Perhaps more importantly from my standpoint, Tyler introduced me to sex. By my sophomore year in college, I was pretty curious and also anxious to get some experience. A couple weeks into our tutoring sessions, Tyler was already bored with trying to understand something he found incomprehensible and so he started flirting with me instead of concentrating on related rates problems.

He didn't find flirting incomprehensible at all. He was very good at it—natural and light, but not frivolous, and he left no room for confusion about what he was after. I felt pursued and desirable. I knew I could handle him and I didn't need to review related rates problems for my own benefit, so I figured what the hell and let him take me to bed.

It was nice—not breathless or overwhelming or life-changing or any of the other ridiculous clichés promised by books, movies, and certain besotted friends, but nice. Tyler liked it a lot. He was also uninhibited and willing to talk, so he was a good first partner and teacher. To this day, he tells me I'm the best kisser ever, but if that's true, it's totally thanks to him. I didn't have much of a clue before I started making out with him.

To be honest, I had better orgasms on my own, but Tyler occasionally made me catch my breath and I liked having sex with him. I liked the physicality of it, and I liked him well enough, too.

I'm not sure whether all the fucking that was always going on in my room made me more or less interested in an actual relationship, but the bottom line was that Nina and her boyfriend were incorrigible and I often needed a place to sleep. Tyler had a single room, as befitted the rich boy he was, so our relationship worked out nicely for everyone.

It continued to work out nicely for two more years until the day Tyler told me he wanted to break up because he didn't think I took him seriously. He said I always seemed detached, and he was tired of being in a relationship where he cared so much more than I did. He was right about all that, so we broke up. I was sorry to see him go and I missed him, too. I didn't love him, but I had enjoyed his company.

We stayed in touch after graduation. Sometimes we talked on the phone; sometimes we got together for dinner or he took me to his family's box at the opera or the symphony; sometimes we spent the night together. Every time, he started out by saying we should get back together, then ended up by telling me I didn't love him like he loved me. I never denied that and I always reminded him that he knew what our deal was—friends and occasional sex partners. I'd even offered to stay out of the picture altogether for him, but he kept coming back.

Given all this, I knew that asking Tyler to be my reliable corporate date wasn't the kindest thing in the world to do to him. I also knew that he might misinterpret my goal no matter how plainspoken I was. But I was desperate.

A "prom" was coming up. It wouldn't do to invent a reason to be "out of town." Going alone was out of the question, and I had probably just about exhausted my ability to show up with a new guy without occasioning the wrong kind of comment. The guy I took to this event would need to accompany me to the next few events, too. So I swallowed my reluctance, laid my dilemma on the line for Tyler, and asked for his help.

He surprised me. He understood completely—and told me I could return the favor by accompanying him regularly to similar events held by his bank or his family. Tyler said he was tired of squiring a different trophy to each of these occasions, sleeping with her (usually), and then having to dash her hopes of becoming his permanent date (as in wife, preferably with a favorable prenup). It's hard to be wildly eligible, he complained.

The very rich really do live differently than the rest of us. It wasn't only the chauffeurs and household servants; I was also surprised to learn that a great deal of what Tyler's family did was public and horribly tedious. Don't even get me started on museum exhibit openings or "the" ballet—the combination of uncomfortably formal clothes and shoes, stuffy people, and pretentious art forms is excruciating. Ditto on dinner parties at Tyler's parents' house in the city, although they were at least excellent for business networking purposes.

There's no question that I benefited—a lot—from returning the favor and being Tyler's reliable official date, but I was often bored. I also gained a new understanding and appreciation for the obligations and requirements that came along with his family's loot.

As "Jane's young man," Tyler worked out spectacularly. The senior people at the Firm all knew who he was the minute he was introduced and, in several cases, the minute they saw him. He was totally at ease and appropriate as he told people we had known each other since college and were great friends.

Without ever actually saying so, Tyler also skillfully left open the possibility that we might one day be more than friends. He knew the corporate game well, and this was a huge gift. The Firm's executives and its snobs (mostly the same people) practically drooled at the thought that Tyler's family and the Firm might end up with such a tight connection. My star rose significantly.

Even better, I became sort of inviolable. It would not do for the Firm to offend or in any way mistreat someone who might end up with Tyler's father as a father-in-law. For all the people at the Firm knew, I might already have an ally in that august and powerful gentleman. (In fact, he and I got along well. He got a kick out of me, thought I was "spunky.")

Once I started attending Firm events with Tyler, wives who had previously considered me invisible suddenly wanted to tell me how much their husbands enjoyed working with me. Their husbands sought to staff me on deals and then treated me like a colleague when we did work together. Whatever catty or bawdy or unfavorable comments any of them may have had they kept to themselves.

It irritated me, of course, to find myself for the first time treated like an insider instead of an interloper thanks to the possibility that I might *marry* well. But the insider treatment itself was terrific. Work was so much easier, so much less frustrating, when the assumptions being made about me for irrelevant reasons were positive instead of negative— exactly, I presumed, what being that white male template must feel like.

So I went along with it and soothed my irritation with the knowledge that I had no intention of marrying Tyler.

❖ ❖ ❖

Charlie

The Firm is too short-sighted to recognize that the value of first class air travel far outweighs the cost, and so it has implemented a complex jumble of rules for when it will pay that cost and when it won't. Instead of sorting through all that, my secretary simply makes sure I always have a first class ticket. When the Firm won't pay for it, she uses some of my thousands of frequent flyer miles instead.

Given the potential clients you can meet and the additional room you have, first class offers a much better opportunity to get some work done on the plane. One of my best client relationships (and one of the Firm's most lucrative) started during a conversation I had with the guy in Seat 2A when I was seated in 2B. Even when I don't meet any potential business or have any paperwork to do, there's a decent chance that I'll catch up on some sleep when I'm in a seat with almost enough legroom.

I also met Annemarie in first class. She wasn't seated next to me, but, like everyone else, I noticed her the second she appeared. She was one of the last people to board the plane and the only woman upfront.

As the guy next to me said, she looked like a lingerie model. Nearly six feet tall, with a spectacular body, great hair, a beautiful face—she attracted all our eyes like a magnet.

Annemarie seemed somehow cloaked in her beauty, too—as if it were armor. She had to have been aware that everyone was staring at her, but she ignored it. She might have been alone on the plane for all the attention she paid to the rest of us as she sat down, stashed her bag under the seat and buckled her seat belt.

The flight was cross-country—the long way, going east to west against the jet stream. About an hour into it, Annemarie got up, stretched and headed toward the back of the plane. I imagine everyone who could see her stared at her; I certainly did.

She reappeared quickly, having apparently walked the length of the plane and back to stretch her (long, long) legs. Instead of returning to her seat, she stopped in front of me. Smiling down at me, she said, "You're the only person on this plane more beautiful than I am. Would you mind sitting with me to deflect some of the attention?"

It was a solid pickup line, but not just anyone could have gotten away with it. Annemarie brought it off perfectly. She was beautiful enough not to make the statement about her beauty ridiculous, and she said the line with complete matter-of-factness as if her appearance were no more remarkable than the fact that she had brown hair or was from Philadelphia. She also said it very lightly and with some irony.

We arranged the seating switch and spent the rest of the flight getting to know each other. The first thing she said, with a self-mocking smile, was that she really didn't need me to deflect attention from her because she had learned long ago to ignore all the eyes that were always on her. I assured her it wouldn't have worked anyway, regardless of who might be sitting next to her. Her looks were impossible to miss or ignore.

Annemarie waved away the compliment. Laughing, she said she wasn't above using her looks to pick up handsome men, but in general she disliked being classified by her physical appearance. After a couple very uncomfortable and self-conscious years as a teenager, she reported, she realized she needed some sort of invisibility mechanism to defend herself emotionally from the constant staring. She had learned to consider her beauty inconsequential, a random happenstance—and also how to act accordingly. She knew that didn't stop the scrutiny, but for years she had noticed or been bothered by it only rarely.

Not surprisingly in light of all that, Annemarie was not a model. She worked in an advertising agency on the creative side. She traveled a lot, which she enjoyed. Unlike many of her colleagues, she said, she was not a frustrated poet or novelist or songwriter. She had no problem with developing jingles and slogans for cream cheese or cars or cough syrup— in fact, she found it entertaining. She liked her job.

When I told her I was in investment banking, she nodded as if that were OK with her. Then, after remarking that she was terrible with money and didn't really understand or have any interest in "high finance," she changed the subject.

Annemarie was pleasant to talk with. She had a combination of self-confidence and self-mockery that was very attractive. Her looks were spectacular, and she made it very plain that she was available. We spent that night together in my hotel room and had a great time, so we made plans to get together again when we were both back home.

We don't actually get together all that much since we both travel frequently and, except for that first flight, not to the same places. This is probably a good thing since we have very little in common other than liking to have sex with each other.

In addition to being great in bed, Annemarie is easy to get along with and evidently no more interested in a serious relationship with me than I am in one with her. It's a good arrangement that will likely last until one or the other of us finds someone we like better.

CHAPTER 4

PROMOTIONS AND COMPLICATIONS

Jane

Lynn, Anna, Cheryl and I met for one of our regular "girls' club" dinners a week or so before the end of our second year with the Firm. Katherine had a conflict, but planned to join us later. Intriguingly enough, she had promised it would be worth our while to wait for her even though she might not be able to make it before dessert.

Promotion to associate or possible alternatives thereto had been the principal topic of conversation throughout our class at the Firm for several weeks. Analysts were considered for promotion at the end of the second year. Some made it; some left the Firm either because they didn't get promoted or because they were instead going on to law school, business school or "real jobs" somewhere in the corporate world; a few stayed in the analyst program for a third year.

Formal performance reviews (and official offers, if those were forthcoming) were scheduled for the coming week. Thanks to advance info from Charlie, I knew I would be invited to join M&A as an associate. The rest of the women in my class were well-regarded, too, and the Firm continued to need women at all levels, so I was confident the others would have similar opportunities.

Sure enough, it appeared that we would all have the chance to stay on at the Firm as associates, although only Lynn and I already had definite information. Cheryl and Anna had assurances from their mentors, but wouldn't know the specifics until their formal reviews. No one had heard anything yet on this topic from Katherine.

Like me, Lynn would be joining Corp Fin's M&A group. Cheryl was hoping for a spot in the Public Offerings group. Anna wasn't as interested in financial products; she wanted to specialize in the global technology or media and telecom industries. Her longer-term goal was to work in London—possibly for the Firm or another investment bank, possibly directly for an industry player. She was also mulling the value of getting a U.S. business school degree before she went back to Europe.

We kicked all this around through drinks and dinner, still with no sign of Katherine. We knew she would have called if she'd gotten hung up and couldn't come at all, so we ordered dessert and kept talking.

Katherine finally waltzed up to our table halfway through dessert, looking like she might just have won the lottery. Perching on the seat we'd saved for her, she said, "Hello, all!"

"Something up, Katherine?" Lynn asked dryly.

"We need to have a 'most unexpected tale to tell' contest," Katherine announced, "and no one else need bother to play. I definitely win today."

She settled back in her chair, looked at each of us to make sure she had our full attention, and then crowed, "I've quit my job at the Firm and gotten a new job! And I'm going to marry Jordan!"

While the rest of us gathered our wits—we hadn't known she and Jordan were even dating—Lynn sipped her coffee, then asked, "Has Jordan heard?"

Katherine elegantly flipped her the bird (if such a thing is possible). Lynn laughed before she demanded, "Start at the beginning, please, and tell us every detail."

"Well," Katherine said, signaling the waiter, "you all know I've always thought Jordan was hot. Very hot. Having him as a mentor that first year was really quite trying for me. Whenever we met, he was always doing that thing where he slouches out of his jacket, loosens his tie, unbuttons the top button of his shirt, rolls up his sleeves..."

"I've seen him do that!" Cheryl exclaimed as I thought about how much more freedom men had to do things like fiddle with their clothes at work. "When I worked on that employee leasing company IPO for him, he did it every time we got out of a meeting."

Katherine ordered a drink and some calamari *fritti*, then said to Cheryl, "Apparently, that little striptease doesn't have the same effect on you that it has on me. It always makes me want to take off my own clothes. I had to restrain myself from actually reaching for buttons a few times."

After an illustrative little shiver, she continued, "Anyway, we were all appropriate and professional for the whole fucking mentoring year. For all I could tell, he never even noticed I'm a girl." She tossed her head in exasperated disbelief, then pushed away the curls that had fallen in her eyes. "*Finally*, the end of the year arrives, and we decide to celebrate by going out to dinner. It's not a date or anything—I've just had a good performance review and Jordan's all excited because he's been invited to be a mentor again, so he knows he's still on the A-list. The dinner is just a little event to mark the end of the year."

Her drink arrived (Irish whiskey that night) and she took a healthy gulp. No one said a word; the floor was clearly Katherine's.

"The dinner is great," she resumed, smiling happily. "Jordan leaves his clothes on for a change, which makes it possible for me to concentrate and converse intelligently. There's champagne, the food is delicious and the conversation is even better. It's all very appropriate, too—had the people on the Executive Committee been sitting at the next table, they would have found nothing to disapprove of."

She took another good-sized gulp of her drink. "When dinner's over, we decide to split a cab. In the cab, we suddenly look directly at each other and it's totally obvious we're thinking the same thing. I don't know if it was the champagne or what, but the next thing you know we're all over each other. I think I jumped him, if you want the honest truth, but he caught up pretty fast."

She breathed deeply, reminiscently, her face radiating pleasure. "This delightful activity goes on for several blocks—until we hear the cabbie bark out Jordan's address in that disgusted 'For God's sake' tone cabbies have. Jordan flings some money at him. (We assume he figures out for himself that a stop at the second address is no longer necessary.) Jordan and I make our way into his building and up to his apartment, no longer behaving appropriately at all. In his apartment, we rip off each other's clothes and go at it."

At this point, Katherine's calamari arrived. She thanked the waiter kindly. Then, with obvious relish, she ate several pieces, sipped some water, grinned, and contemplated our rapt, slightly shocked faces.

"I can't tell you if we should be thanking the champagne again or the entire fucking *year* of foreplay," she continued merrily, "but it is sensational. Really incredible—the best ever! When it's over, we're lying next to each other, staring at the ceiling. I don't know about him, but I have no clue what to say. Suddenly, he remembers he's supposed to review some risk factors disclosure for a call with a guy in California. He rounds up the papers, climbs back in bed, and starts reading."

I burst out laughing—couldn't help it. "I'm sorry," I choked. "I'm just trying to picture it."

Katherine chortled. "It was pretty hilarious. And it gets even funnier. He's reading and making notes with a pen that appears out of thin air. At least I hope that's where it came from—I like to think my husband-to-be doesn't actually keep a pen under his pillow. As for me, I still can't think of anything I might want to say, so I figure a snack will help."

Lynn snorted and Cheryl started giggling. Katherine was always hungry; it was impossible to spend 30 minutes with her without hearing at least twice that she was starving. Anna wrapped her hands around her teacup and looked as if she were observing a bizarre and unfamiliar, but fascinating, phenomenon.

"Well, I was hungry after all that excitement!" Katherine said. "So I'm foraging in Jordan's kitchen and what do I find in the freezer but a pristine carton of premium chocolate ice cream with an expiration date that's in the future. I ask you—what kind of man who works 24/7 has fresh ice cream in his freezer? I fall in love with him on the spot. Now I have something to say to him, too, so I collect a couple spoons and head back to the bedroom with the carton."

Katherine stopped to eat more calamari. Cheryl was still giggling, and I was tempted to join her. Lynn rolled her eyes and said, "Katherine, you're killing us here. Let me amend my demand. Please skip a few details—the boring ones, if there are any—so we can get past that night before this night is over."

"You need this level of detail to understand the outcome," Katherine clarified haughtily. "Don't worry. It fast forwards soon. OK, so I'm now standing just inside the bedroom door. Jordan looks up and I toss him one of the spoons, which he catches neatly—a nice trick that makes me like him even better. 'I've fallen in love with you,' I tell him, nodding at the ice cream. Incredibly, he understands."

Katherine shivered blissfully. "We eat ice cream companionably—in his case, while still revising risk factors. Then it happens again, just like in the cab. We look at each other and have the same thought. This time, it's 'ice cream and naked bodies.' So we spread the stuff around. It's very cold, but also very hot, if you get my drift. We're eating it off each other when the phone rings."

After a dramatic pause during which she delicately patted the corners of her mouth with her napkin, she went on. "Jordan tries to resist, but he's not strong enough. It's the guy from California and he has to take the call. He picks up the phone and commences discussing risk factors—intelligently as far as I could ascertain—while I'm licking ice cream off his..." She stopped and then said demurely (a tone somewhat spoiled by the exuberant directness with which she met our eyes), "Well, I fear that to continue would be indiscreet."

"Katherine," Cheryl giggled, "you blew past 'indiscreet' quite a while back."

"Well before you arrived this evening, I daresay," Anna said, looking amazed for the first time since we'd known her.

I was speechless. Uncharacteristically, so was Lynn. I figured she was probably doing the same thing I was: trying to picture Jordan in this outrageous situation. All of us but Katherine had worked with him. She was right—he was very, very good-looking. He was also exceptionally bright and, we'd thought, quite serious. At the time of this astonishing development, he was in his seventh or eighth year with Corp Fin's IPO group.

Picturing Jordan discussing risk factors was easy. Picturing him discussing risk factors in bed after having sex was doable, if harder. But picturing Jordan discussing risk factors in bed after having sex and while doing unorthodox things with ice cream was impossible.

I began to laugh helplessly again, which started everyone but Katherine doing the same. Katherine munched contentedly on calamari and signaled the waiter for another drink. When the drink came and we had all calmed down slightly, she inquired serenely, "How could I do anything but marry a man like that?"

"We'll all have to make adjustments, won't we?" Anna said wryly. "I can't imagine working with Jordan will ever be the same."

"Certainly not if there's any ice cream around," Lynn said, apparently having found her voice, but sounding rather desperate. "Kath, how did the two of you ever manage to keep this under wraps for nearly a year?"

"Oh, well, that," Katherine said breezily. "It doesn't pay to titillate the people at the office, does it? Plus, who knew how this sexy little story would end? We decided that night we had to keep it quiet. Then, when it got serious, we had to get our ducks in a row before anyone found out or even suspected.

"We never worked together. We never left the office together or came in together. We ignored each other in the few meetings we both had to attend. We took other dates to last year's prom. We never went anywhere we thought there might be the slightest danger of running into someone we knew. We were very, very careful."

She glanced around as if checking for spies and then confided conspiratorially, "Honesty compels me to admit that there were a few clinches in his office and one thrilling late night conference room fuck, but otherwise we were above reproach or suspicion." She made a sad face. "The hardest thing was not telling you guys. That's why I ditched a couple of our sessions."

"Understandably," Cheryl said, leaning over and giving Katherine a hug. "We forgive you."

"What's the story on the new job?" I asked.

Katherine named one of the Firm's competitors and told us she had lined up an associate position in the Public Finance group there. She had finalized the details the week before and given the Firm her notice that afternoon, which was why she and Jordan were finally able to go public.

"We couldn't both have stayed at the Firm—there actually is a no-nepotism policy," she explained. "It makes more sense for me to leave since Jordan is so much further along and such a star already. Anyway, we all know that after this he can still be a professional at the Firm, but I will forevermore be a scarlet woman. Or—worse—a wife."

❖ ❖ ❖

Charlie

One of my regular meetings with Jane was scheduled for the day after the news about Jordan and Katherine broke. I was willing to bet that Jane would have a problem of some kind with the news or people's reactions to it—and I couldn't wait to hear it.

By that time, Jane and I were friends as well as colleagues. We still met monthly as we had during her first year, but our conversations ranged far beyond the usual mentoring subjects. I'd noticed that her take on things, while always interesting, was predictable, too. She saw sexism and inequality everywhere. I liked debating and brainstorming with her—and also trying to knock off or at least further dent the chip she persisted in carrying on her shoulder.

I couldn't resist saying, as soon as she sat down, "Interesting news about Jordan and Katherine."

To my surprise, Jane immediately started laughing.

"What's so funny?" I asked her, but she was laughing too hard to reply. Jane wasn't giddy at all, but I'd noticed before that when something struck her as funny, her response was spontaneous and lively.

When she was able to talk again, she said, "I'm sorry. I was with Katherine and some other people last night. You know what a riot she is—her description of the whole thing was completely hilarious." Jane looked a little blown away, even as she grinned. "I really can't repeat it— I'm pretty sure I was told in confidence. Even if not, though, I honestly don't think I know you well enough to repeat it. I'm not sure I know *anyone* well enough to repeat it!"

"Sounds entertaining," I commented, wondering what Katherine could have said. "I actually don't know what a riot Katherine is. I worked with her once—she did a great job, but I don't recall that she was particularly funny."

"See, that's one of the things about work that bugs me," Jane said, slicing the air in front of her with her hands. "Katherine is uproarious— really, really funny and irreverent and outrageous. She has a bigger-than-life personality that she has to keep completely under wraps at work for fear of being considered unprofessional. Even with someone like you."

"Why does she have to keep it under wraps? I mean, we do have to be professional, but that doesn't mean bland. There's room for humor, personality."

Jane shook her head. "For you maybe. Those of us who don't fit the profile so perfectly have to be very careful. It rarely pays for us to stand out or draw attention by being unusual—even in a good way."

"So this is another facet of the usual 'not a white male' problem?" I asked to goad her as I leaned back in my chair, shoved some papers aside and put my feet up on my desk.

"Don't try to sound so oblivious, Charlie!" she said, rising to the bait. She leaned forward and started waving her hands around. "You know exactly what I'm talking about. You know perfectly well that Katherine and I—and others of 'our ilk'—have to climb uphill against negative assumptions all the time. In a way that you, Mr. Golden Boy, do not. No one assumes going in that *you* aren't sufficiently committed to your career. No one worries that *you're* going to be a distraction to a young king like Jordan. No one thinks the likes of *you* doesn't belong at a place like the Firm."

"OK, OK, relax." I held up my hands in surrender. "But not everyone shares those negative assumptions about women, even if they are in the air around here. Quite a few people don't share them, including me. Wasn't Katherine making the same kind of uncalled-for negative assumptions by assuming she had to hide her real personality from me?"

Jane looked exasperated. "You're being naïve. Katherine has developed a work persona. It works well for her. So have I. We can't just put those on and take them off when we feel like it or when the coast looks clear. They have to be consistent.

"Also, there's no way to tell if the coast is clear. If you take a chance and you're wrong, you're dead. You have to play the percentages and take the route that will most probably protect you—and make it possible for you to achieve your goals. And, for a woman, that route does not include letting yourself be uproarious, except very selectively and only when you're absolutely sure of your audience."

"You didn't answer my question," I said mildly.

"Yes, Katherine was making an assumption about you," Jane said, scowling. "And, yes, it was unwarranted. But, no, it was not the same kind of negative assumption. There was no career downside for you in the assumption she made about you."

"I guess not," I conceded. "But, Jane, part of your goal is to change the game. How will it ever change if people like you and Katherine—people who are unquestionably good enough, who really are succeeding—still feel you have to pretend you fit some arbitrary accept-able profile? Aren't you just perpetuating that profile? If you aren't being your real selves, how will anyone learn that talent really does come in a wide variety of exteriors and personalities?"

"Good questions," she granted. "But isn't it a lot to ask of people like Katherine and me that we be willing to go down in flames for the cause? That we sacrifice or potentially sacrifice our success to teach a bunch of sexist pigs a lesson they should have learned in elementary school?"

Jane got up and walked over to the window, where she perched on the sill, facing me. "Lots of these guys aren't like you," she said. "This isn't a lesson they want to learn. They're just mediocre white guys who have learned to play the game. They need the status quo to remain the status quo because without the assumptions in their favor, they wouldn't be succeeding—and they know it."

"I don't disagree that there are men like that here, but there's still the question of how it will ever change if you succeed the same way—by playing their game in a way that they've defined as acceptable."

"It's lucky I don't have anything handy to throw at you right now!" Jane pointed at me threateningly. "There *is* no other way for me to succeed in this environment, and you know it! They're the ones with the power to *define* what succeeds!"

Slightly more calmly, she continued, "You also know as well as I do how it will change. It will change when people like me are in power. Not just powerful individually, but really in power, so that we can stop being so vigilant about seeming acceptable to a bunch of hacks without fear of losing everything we've worked for."

"'People like you' as in women?" I asked. "Or as in people who believe in inclusivity and in judging talent based on merit and contribution instead of appearance?"

Before she could answer, I grinned and added, "You do believe in those things, right?"

"Of course I do," she said as she walked back to her chair and sat down. "But I wonder if the pendulum has to swing too far the other way before it can settle in the right place. I'm not sure it will be enough for *more* women and minorities to be powerful within the existing power structure. Maybe parity isn't enough to correct this imbalance. Maybe we need hegemony the other way first before we can really achieve inclusivity."

"That means domination?" She nodded and I said, "So we white males are just supposed to trust that you'll be more even-handed with your hegemony than we've been with ours?"

Jane smiled wickedly. "Now *that's* a sweet situation to contemplate!"

"Depends on where you're sitting." I smiled back at her as I picked up my letter opener, turned it in my hands, and ran my thumb and forefinger along its length. "You can see, I hope, why the existing power structure finds the likes of you terrifying."

"Oh, yeah, I've never had any confusion about that," she laughed. "Do you think I'm wrong? About the parity thing, I mean?"

"I hope you're wrong," I said. "And, yeah, I do think so. Fewer of the men in power are on the wrong side than you suspect. Plenty of them are just followers. I think the balance can be tipped by more right-thinking and diverse people in powerful positions. Look what my father has accomplished by being that kind of thinker—and not only since he's been powerful. That's how he became powerful."

"Well, I hope you're right," she said doubtfully. "I just have a hard time believing it. Not that you could be right," she clarified, with a small smile, "but that it could work out that well."

"I think the only viable option is to work toward the right result and trust that your efforts will pay off. Exchanging one power imbalance for another seems worthless."

"That's easier to say from where you're sitting, don't you think?"

"I admit that. But that doesn't make it wrong."

"No, it doesn't." Jane sighed. "But trust is a very hard thing to have unless it's reciprocal. I don't know that I can make a decision to have faith that my efforts will pay off relative to a power structure that doesn't have faith in me."

"Come on—that's overstated."

"Not really." After quickly saying this, she tilted her head slightly, seeming to think the better of it. "Well," she admitted, "it's probably overstated with respect to me personally because I now have a context here. You know, by getting to know people and doing good work in a way they can appreciate and be comfortable with, I've overcome some of the negative assumptions originally made about me because of my gender.

"But vis-à-vis me as part of a category, it's not overstated. Here's an example: Katherine said a striking—and I think true—thing last night. She was telling us why she instead of Jordan would be the one leaving the Firm. In addition to the good reason that he's much further along and already established as a star, she made the point that she wouldn't be able to stay even if their positions were reversed. After this news, Jordan can still be seen as a professional here, but she will, as she put it, 'forevermore be a scarlet woman or, even worse, a wife.'"

My inclination was to scoff at this, but, thinking about it, I had to agree that there was some truth to it. Katherine could have overcome it, I thought, but it was true that the circumstances gave her—and not Jordan—something to overcome.

Jane waved her hand. "Are you still here? Do you see the point?"

"Yeah, I was just thinking about it. I don't think Katherine would have been labeled forever, but it's true that she'd have to overcome a perception that Jordan won't."

"Exactly!" Jane said. "It's incidental to Jordan—a good story he'll get kidded about—but not something that will affect anyone's ability to see or admire him as a professional. Even if someone thinks he might not have behaved completely appropriately given their mentoring relationship, it will be OK because he's marrying her. 'Doing the right thing,' if you will."

She said this last bit very sarcastically, then added in a more normal tone, "For Katherine, though, the story is not incidental. It's defining. It already *has* affected people's ability to see her first as a professional."

"I knew you'd have some problem with the news," I teased her.

She laughed, but sounded serious when she said, "I'm very happy for them, but I do think this sort of thing sets women back. It feeds right into the perception that we're distractions or we're at the Firm to find husbands instead of for the same reasons men are here. You know, to get the job done, make money and succeed."

I put my hands behind my head and stretched my neck and shoulders against them as I asked, "You're not suggesting professional women shouldn't have personal lives, are you? That *would* be sexist."

"No," she drew the word out. "No, I'm not suggesting that, but it doesn't seem possible to avoid the negative impact when we do have personal lives—or at least when they become known at the office. Neutralizing the impact of the whole gender thing is part of how we succeed. And 'romance'"—Jane put the word in sarcastic quotes—"seems to put our female-ness squarely, and prominently, back on the table."

My secretary stuck her head in my office to tell me I had a call in ten minutes. Jane looked at her watch, jumped to her feet and exclaimed, "God, I had no idea I'd been in here so long! I'm sorry— I should go."

"Not a problem," I smiled. We calendared our next meeting and went back to work.

CHAPTER 5
FAMILY TIES

Jane

I worked on a deal for Jordan late in the fall of my third year at the Firm. I hadn't worked with him since my rookie year, and it was interesting to see how he'd changed. He was still a pleasure to work with, but he also seemed energized and a bit dreamy, rather as if he'd been struck by a completely delightful bolt of lightning. Not a bad way to describe Katherine, when I thought about it.

He reported that she liked her new job very much, but—she had instructed him to tell me—the new office's male scenery didn't begin to compare with the Firm's. Jordan looked relieved to have heard this, but pained to have been forced to repeat it.

Luckily, there was never any ice cream in the vicinity while we worked together. I managed to behave normally around him, although I did have several shaky moments while we worked on the risk factors disclosure for the prospectus. The worst of these was one day in a conference room when he appeared to have conjured a pen out of thin air to make notes on his copy of the draft we were discussing. I thought I covered my burst of laughter with a cough, but Jordan gave me a very suspicious look.

He and Katherine got married in January. Their wedding was the most fun of those I'd attended (which wasn't saying much, but theirs really was terrific). I went with Tyler and we had a great time, in part because we weren't at his parents', required to behave, and so were free to respond like naughty children to the sniffing noses and raised eyebrows of Jordan's appalled relatives.

Jordan turned out to be from an uptight upper-crust family. Like Jordan, the rest of his family looked rather as if they'd been struck by lightning. Unlike him, they didn't appear to have found the experience delightful. Their demeanor reminded me of the snootier people I'd met at dinner parties at Tyler's parents' house. It always amazes me when snobs convey their disapproval so clearly without saying a word—and also evidently without realizing that their behavior reflects far worse on them than on their usually oblivious targets.

Katherine was from a family of people just like her. Her parents and younger brother were as irreverent and outrageous as she, and this set the tone for the whole event. The wedding wasn't outrageous, but it had an informality and a humor to it that were the complete opposite of stuffy. Also, Katherine and Jordan were euphoric—and unmistakably crazy about each other. Their manifest chemistry and a great deal of general hilarity and high spirits were apparently too much in the way of physical and emotional display for Jordan's stiff-upper-lip relations.

My invitation to the wedding had included a surprisingly delicate note from Katherine to the effect that she hoped I would use my "Guest" spot for Tyler. Katherine and Tyler had become buddies at the various Firm functions he attended with me while she was pretending Jordan was nothing more than her former mentor. She wrote that she would have invited Tyler directly, but hadn't wanted to put me in an awkward spot.

I was happy to take him to the wedding even though it wasn't an official Firm function. He had shown himself to be a genuine friend, as well as a charming ex-boyfriend—and it would be hard to quantify the value of the favor he did for me. Our "business arrangement," as he called it, also seemed to have given balance to our relationship. I no longer felt I might be taking unfair advantage of his feelings for me. He no longer told me I was breaking his heart every time he felt lonely. We continued to enjoy each other's company. We still occasionally slept together, too, and that was also familiar and agreeable.

For the dinner, Katherine had seated Tyler and me at a table with Lynn, Cheryl, Anna and their respective guests. Better company was impossible to imagine.

True to her belief that men were best considered eye candy or sex toys, Lynn was with a great-looking guy named Paul. He didn't say much, but he seemed pleasant enough and he was certainly a pleasure to look at. A certain loose physical ease made it easy to believe he was probably a good sex toy, too.

Anna was with her brother, James, who was visiting from London. Anna had decided to stay in the U.S. and at the Firm for another year, while at the same time attending an executive MBA program. She hadn't had time to get back to England before all that got underway, so James was spending part of his vacation with her. Like Anna, he had a killer accent and was very bright; unlike her, he was also quite gregarious.

Cheryl brought Richard, a lawyer she'd met on a deal and started dating when the deal closed a couple months before. Richard was terrific—smart, funny, self-confident. I thought he fit Cheryl's "perfect husband" profile very nicely even if he was a lawyer instead of an investment banker. Lynn whispered the same thing to me; I whispered her out of saying so aloud on the spot.

Since there were no truly heinous Firm people in attendance at the wedding, we women were able to sit together without occasioning—or worrying about occasioning—unfavorable commentary. We did hear a few comments from our male colleagues about how we must be plotting to take over, but that was to be expected, if tiresome and disappointing.

As we were all finding our places and getting seated, there was suddenly a buzz in the room. Tyler spotted her first. He clapped his hand to his heart dramatically and said, "Holy shit! That is the most gorgeous woman I have ever seen!"

We all turned in the direction he indicated. Sure enough, the woman who had just walked into the room was sensational. Taller than most of the men around her, she seemed to radiate beauty. Most of the people in the room were staring at her. I laughed aloud when I saw she was with Charlie. He always had a good-looking date at Firm events, but this one easily eclipsed all the others.

"Where does he find them, do you suppose?" I marveled, shaking my head in wonder.

Cheryl frowned ruefully. "You know," she said, "maybe it's not so surprising that Charlie seems to see all of us as people instead of as women. If she's his definition of a woman, we're not even in the same game."

"I think you are plenty beautiful," Richard said to her, resting his palm for a moment on the back of her neck. "She's a star player, but really, you are completely qualified to be in the game."

"Thank you for that," Cheryl said, beaming at him. "Honest enough to be believable, but still flattering. Nicely done!"

Turning back to the rest of us, she said, "Whenever I see a beauty like that—not that I've seen many like her before—I always feel a little like I've had the wind knocked out of me. I think I've gotten past wanting or expecting to be gorgeous, but there must be at least a few remnants of that teenage desire left in me."

"Being gorgeous is such a double-edged sword for a woman," Lynn said. "Her options have to be limited. Can you imagine her in our shop, for instance? She'd be a terrible distraction. Her looks are probably a big part of her identity, too—what's going to happen when she gets old? And inside that beautiful wrapping, she's probably a regular person dealing with regular things. Only she has to do everything with people staring at her."

"And probably making assumptions about her, too," I chimed in.

Lynn laughed. "Well, we can only hope she's a half-wit. It would be too annoying to find out she has an advanced degree in physics."

James, who was a research scientist, said plummily, "I can confidently assure you that people with advanced degrees in physics tend to be anything but fabulously beautiful women who are nearly one meter eighty-five tall."

"I knew there was a reason I shied away from physics," Tyler mumbled, his eyes still glued on the woman.

"The reason you shied away from physics," I reminded him, poking him in the side, "was calculus."

"That, too," he said, smiling at me. "But great as it was to meet you thanks to calculus, it would be very depressing to find out I could have met someone like that babe if I'd almost failed physics instead."

"I think I'm offended!" I teased indignantly. "To think that all this time you've been pretending to prefer scintillating conversation to beauty."

"No need to be offended, Jane." Tyler patted my hand. "You know you're cute as well as scintillating."

"Cute?" I said, retrieving my hand and waving it in protest. "Now I really am offended!"

"'Cute' is not a word I ever thought I'd hear applied to Jane," said Cheryl, with a wink for me. "She's too serious—and much too prickly—to be cute, don't you think?"

Anna had, as usual, been listening and observing. Now she said, "I had an experience recently that made me think of your point, Jane, about how we are always being categorized based on surface attributes. I was working with a new client—new to me, not to the Firm. We spoke on the telephone several times before we met in person. He was initially very dubious about me—curt, brusque; seemed doubtful that I could know what I was talking about—but we overcame that and were getting on quite well by the third or fourth call.

"Then we met in person. He looked surprised when he saw me and said he never expected me to be pretty. I'm sure he intended it as a compliment, but I thought the comment inappropriately personal. I was also insulted by his evident belief that a smart woman would not likely be attractive."

"There you go," Lynn said, sitting up straight and looking nearly as imperious as Anna. "That's the flip side of my point about that gorgeous woman's options being limited."

"The either/or aspect of all that makes me nuts!" I said, a little more heatedly than I'd intended. My vehemence got everyone's attention, but I toned it down before continuing. "So does the negativity of both assumptions. The notion that a woman would only bother to be smart or accomplished if she doesn't have looks to rely on is just as limiting as the notion that a beautiful woman is probably a half-wit."

"Especially since neither brains nor beauty is exactly a voluntary choice," Cheryl said.

"Ladies," James said, his knife and fork poised over his plate in that efficient European fashion, "aren't you making a bit much of all this? Surely it's possible for a gent to compliment a woman's looks without implying any sort of negative agenda or insulting belief."

This comment produced a chorus of impassioned voices raised in rebuttal. James looked taken aback and a little alarmed; his fingers went from holding the flatware to clutching it.

"You've disturbed a hornets' nest now!" Richard told him, laughing.

Cheryl, with another smile for Richard, took up the gauntlet. "Here's the problem, James. Of course, it's possible to compliment someone's looks without an underlying negative agenda. But the client surprised to find that Anna is attractive wasn't doing that. He was telling her he was surprised to discover she was attractive as well as competent. Just as he had earlier communicated his surprise that she was competent as well as female."

"Well said," I agreed. "Also, commenting on Anna's looks in a business setting calls into question her standing as a professional. It wouldn't be done to a man and it's the kind of thing that really hurts us. We're not 'the norm' in our line of work and we don't enjoy the same presumption of competence that men do. We already have to prove ourselves over and over."

"Men have to do that too, Jane," Richard argued. "Nobody gets a pass. We're all justifying our continued existence."

"That's not the same," Lynn said, shaking her head. Her shiny hair swung around her face, then settled back into its perfectly cut shape.

"You may be justifying your existence, but you're doing so from firmer ground. Also, that's an ongoing value point, not a baseline competence point. With respect to competence, you are assumed to be competent unless and until you demonstrate otherwise. We are assumed *not* to be competent until we prove that we are—over and over."

"She's got you there, Richard," Tyler said. "But isn't beauty more of an issue for women because you're too focused on it yourselves? Seems to me it's just a random thing, like any other personal strength or weakness. You can use it to your advantage or not, but you don't have to let it define you, as Jane would say."

"Spoken like a true rich kid," Lynn teased, saluting him with her champagne flute. "You're right that it's random, but we aren't the ones—or the only ones, anyway—letting it define us. Our point is that both beauty and the lack thereof seem to prompt negative or at least limiting assumptions about women. Your illustrious family ties are a positive for you. They make your life easier."

"Not wholly true, Lynn," Tyler countered. "People wonder all the time if I'm a half-wit coasting on family connections."

"This all falls in the category of interpersonal bullshit or maybe self-protectiveness, doesn't it?" I said, remembering what Charlie had said about how people responded to *his* illustrious family connections. "I mean, Tyler didn't choose his parents any more than that woman chose to be gorgeous or Anna chose to be brilliant and also attractive. But people make negative assumptions about all of them as if they not only chose those advantages, but did so for the specific purpose of making others feel envious or inferior."

"You're mixing two points, Jane," said James. "You're right, I think, that we tend to blame others for showing up our own shortcomings. That's human nature and I venture to say it affects men and women similarly, if not absolutely equally. But weren't you arguing before that women are more adversely affected by negative assumptions where work is concerned?"

"I was, yeah." I ran my finger and thumb down the stem of my water glass as I struggled to articulate my point. "And I might be reaching to see a pattern here, but couldn't all this be because the status quo—the 'norm,' if you will—at work is male, just like the status quo for looks is not that gorgeous woman and the status quo for families is not Tyler's family? For that matter, disgusting as it is, I suppose one could also argue that until fairly recently the status quo for women was that beauty eliminated the need for brains or accomplishments."

"I see what you're driving at!" Richard said. "What prompts the negative assumptions is variance from the accepted norm. Just like with large groups of numbers deviating toward the mean, the attitudes of large groups of people tend to do the same."

"And since the accepted norm—institutionally speaking—is typically white and male and not gorgeous or wealthy, anything other than that is generally viewed with suspicion or even hostility," Lynn wrapped up.

In the break before dessert was served, Katherine and Jordan circulated among the tables and there was some general milling around. The gorgeous woman sent another wave of excitement through the crowd by standing and heading for the ladies room. She was one of at least 20 women doing the same, but the effect was rather like a queen and her ladies-in-waiting. All eyes were on the queen.

Katherine joined us on her own, having left Jordan a few tables away with some of his Firm buddies. She perched on Anna's vacant seat next to Paul, draped her arm over his shoulders in a familiar way and said, "You're awfully good-looking, aren't you?"

Paul looked startled, but recovered quickly, smiled at her and said, "So I've been told."

"Hands off, Katherine," Lynn said, her expression long-suffering. "This is your wedding. Behave!"

"I'm tired of behaving," Katherine griped, but she let go of Paul. "Jordan's relatives are so fucking stuffy! I feel like I've been behaving for weeks. I'm *dying* to do something totally outrageous."

"Is there ice cream for dessert?" Cheryl asked wickedly. She, Lynn and I laughed, while the men looked confused.

Katherine looked wounded. "It seemed essential to me that we have ice cream for dessert—chocolate, of course. But for chocolate ice cream, we might not be having this shindig at all."

Then, she chortled and looked tickled. "You should have seen Jordan's face when I suggested we put it on the menu. He went nuts. I innocently told him it would be our private little secret to enjoy while everyone else thought about how delightful it was to have ice cream with wedding cake. He looked at me very darkly and said he was quite certain the two of us weren't the only people in on that so-called secret."

Frowning severely, she demanded, "So which of you gave me away?"

We all protested our innocence. Cheryl added, "Your husband just knows you, Kath. And, FYI, he's on his way over here right now."

"Mum's the word," Katherine warned, with a stern look around the table. She stood up, turned to Jordan, threw her arms around his neck and kissed him very passionately on the lips. The passion was plainly sincere, as was the pleasure I'm certain she took in knowing she had caused yet more aghast expressions among her new in-laws.

After dessert (which did not include ice cream, chocolate or otherwise), there was dancing, the music for which made further conversation difficult. Like the people at other tables, we all got up and either danced or mingled in the farther areas of the room where conversation was still practical.

Finally, Tyler said he couldn't wait another minute to meet the gorgeous woman. People were starting to leave and he couldn't bear the thought that she might get away before he saw her at close range. I wanted to say hi to Charlie, too, but given the incessant crowd his date drew as if she were bait, it hadn't yet been possible for us to get anywhere near them.

Thanks to their height, they were easy to spot and we headed their way. When we got close enough to see their expressions, Tyler commented in a low voice that both Charlie and the woman looked glazed and in need of rescuing. Charlie did greet Tyler and me very gladly.

Tyler used some of his social magic to move the crowd along. (I had watched him pull off this trick many times, but could never figure out how he did it. It must have been one of those finely-tuned skills honed from birth.) Charlie introduced Annemarie and we all talked for a few minutes before Tyler—again skillfully—drew her aside to talk to her himself.

"Nice-looking date, buddy," I teased Charlie. "You've really outdone yourself. I think everyone in the room has spent at least some of the evening staring at her."

"She does cause a stir, doesn't she?" he said, with a somewhat weary smile. "I'm reconsidering the wisdom of appearing in public with her. Annemarie knows how to ignore it, but I'm finding all the adulation and commentary she generates exhausting."

"What did you expect? She's extraordinary. At our table, we were hoping she doesn't also have an advanced degree in physics."

Charlie laughed. "No, she's in advertising."

"That's a relief." I grinned up at him. "Hey, I've accumulated quite a list of things to talk with you about. I stopped by last week to see if you had time, but Pam said you were traveling. Where have you been?"

He told me about a deal he was doing in Denver and a new client prospect he was working in Chicago. Just as we were finishing up on these topics, Tyler and Annemarie rejoined us.

Annemarie took Charlie's arm and said, with a slightly desperate expression on her gorgeous face, "Unless there are more people here like this lovely man, who tells me he and Jane are leaving soon, we should get going, too. I don't think I can stand any more compliments or boring talk about investment banking."

"Let's go," Charlie agreed, smiling at her. "Jane, I'll be in most of next week. Give me a call and we'll set up a time to talk about your list."

I said I would and we all said good night. It took Tyler at least fifteen minutes to stop marveling over Annemarie and significantly longer than that to get the stars out of his eyes.

❖ ❖ ❖

Charlie

My father called a month after Jordan and Katherine's wedding to talk about the divestiture of one of his company's business units. President and Chief Operating Officer of the company at the time, Dad was thinking about retiring and wanted to get the unit successfully sold first, preferably to a strategic buyer who would pay a premium for it rather than to a financial buyer who probably wouldn't. He thought market conditions were good for the right kind of sale on favorable terms, and wanted to know if I agreed. I did, and the Firm took on the project.

As I thought about how to staff the deal, it occurred to me that it offered a great opportunity for Jane to use her strategic skills on an important matter for an important client. It was always a good idea to introduce bright Firm people to the team at my father's company (especially now that he was thinking about retirement), and I'd been looking for a chance to work with her.

The rules of the mentoring program didn't permit mentors and mentees to work together during the mentoring year. Jane had done some financial modeling and analysis on one of my deals during her second year, but she'd worked with the associate managing that deal, not with me. She was now more than halfway through her third year at the Firm—and her first year as an associate—and she was still getting uniformly superior reviews on everything she did. I decided to staff the new deal unusually to give her an unusual opportunity.

The usual route for this kind of transaction would have been to designate someone a couple years behind me to take on the day-to-day management role and a rookie or second-year analyst to assist. The leadership/relationship management role was always played by the person who brought the client to the Firm. For most clients, the originator was a very senior person; when it wasn't, there was typically a sharing arrangement. I originally shared the responsibility (and the origination credit) for my father's company with Jim, the head of the M&A group. For the last couple years, though, I had been handling the senior role on my own and so the staffing decision was mine to make.

I decided to give Jane the management role instead of getting someone more experienced. This would mean taking on more day-to-day oversight myself than would normally be necessary, but I stayed close to my father's deals anyway and I wanted to see what Jane could do with the role. If she aced it, she'd be a superstar; she might even be able to skip a class. If she didn't, she wouldn't lose much—just a little face. I thought she was up to it, and wanted to give her the chance.

I also wanted to see her face when she heard this news, so I decided to tell her in person. Jane was always sure that the world in general and the Firm in particular were intent on filling her career path with as many obstacles as possible. I liked giving her a hard time about the still sizeable, if now effectively cloaked, chip on her shoulder.

Before I talked to her, I stopped by Jim's office to let him know what I was doing. I wasn't inclined to change my mind, nor did I think he'd have a problem with my plan—he'd done the same thing for me a few years before—but putting Jane in the manager role would inevitably lead to talk around the Firm. It never pays to let your boss get blindsided.

Jim was on the phone in his office, but he motioned me in and indicated he wouldn't be long. I flipped through his new *Business Week* while I waited, searching for something obscure. Jim's knowledge was legendary, and there was a sizeable ongoing pool payable to the first person who could surprise him with some business or political news. I was still looking for a tidbit to try with when he got off the phone.

As I expected, Jim had no problem with giving Jane the manager role. He'd worked with her a couple times and had a very high opinion of her abilities. After he assured himself that I planned to supervise her more closely than I would a more experienced manager, he said, "Fine. Good," and turned to make another call.

I walked to Jane's office. Her secretary, who seemed flustered, told me Jane was working alone behind her closed door, so I knocked and went in. "Jane? Got a minute?"

She looked up, took her pen out of her mouth, smiled and said, "Sure. What's up?"

"I've got a new deal, and I want you to work with me on it."

"Great!" she said enthusiastically. "Good timing, too. I'm just finishing up the last loose ends on this one, and there's not too much else on my plate. What have you got?"

"It's a divestiture for my father's company. A non-core business unit that we'll ideally sell at a premium to a strategic buyer." I handed her a folder containing the info we had on the unit to be sold. "We'll get details later this week, then it'll start moving fast."

"Cool," Jane said. "Who's managing?"

I leaned against the wall and grinned at her. "You are."

She looked shocked. "Are you serious?"

"Yeah, I am. I stay pretty close to this client, so I'll be there to help you when you need it, but from everything I hear, you're up to this. Here's your chance to prove it."

"Charlie, this is huge!" She put the pen down and sank into her chair, as if pressed back by the enormity of the news. "Thank you so much. Wow!"

"You're welcome." I looked at her pointedly, but couldn't help smiling as I said, "Remember this the next time you're inclined to complain about how the world is out to make your life difficult, OK?"

Jane smiled, her eyes still wide. "I'll never forget it," she said. "I'm thrilled—really. I can't wait to get started!" She sat up straight. "Other than getting myself up to speed on the company, is there anything else I can do before we get the details?"

"Look at the info in that folder and the recent SEC filings and press releases, then let's talk. Take a look at the closing binder from the company's last deal, too, and get familiar with the names, the way they disclose things, the form docs. Oh, and think about who you want to staff to assist."

Jane looked even more than usual like she might burst. "Will do," she said eagerly. "I'll also get on your calendar for tomorrow afternoon to go over staffing and any questions I have after I read everything."

"Take a few extra hours, OK?" I teased her. "I'm traveling tomorrow, so let's talk Thursday instead."

As I turned to leave, she said, "Charlie, wait. I recognize that this is a huge break for me and I promise I won't let you down. I want you to know how much I appreciate it and your vote of confidence, too. Thank you very much."

"You're welcome," I said again, smiling. "I'm looking forward to working with you finally. See you Thursday."

I walked back to my office thinking about how great it felt to give someone an unexpected opportunity. Given the chance and, as Jane had said, the vote of confidence, most people rose to the occasion—and everyone felt like a million bucks and gave it his or her best shot. At least that had been my experience.

I felt like a million bucks myself, and the feeling lasted through the rest of what turned out to be a very productive day. This will be fun, I thought that evening as I packed up the things I would need for the next day's meetings.

❖ ❖ ❖

BY THE TIME we met late Thursday morning, Jane had developed perceptive questions about the company and insightful thoughts about the potential financial and strategic impacts of selling the unit. She had done some research on possible buyers and outlined strategies for getting their attention. She had also assembled starting point templates and samples for the timeline, the due diligence questionnaire and the contact sheet. She was all over it. I'd never worked with anyone so organized.

She had also decided to recommend a rookie named Eric to assist on the deal. She told me she'd wanted to give the job to a woman, but of the four in each of the classes behind her, none was available. Jane had checked out the available analysts, and Eric seemed to have the best background. She had talked to him and found him bright and easy to get along with. She had also talked with the managers from the two other deals he'd assisted on, both of whom gave him positive reviews.

A little blown away by all this activity, I said Eric sounded fine. After a short pause, during which she was obviously deciding whether or not to continue, Jane smiled and said Eric did have one drawback.

Apparently, he was also very tall and she was a little concerned about feeling like Gulliver among the Brobdingnagians.

I laughed and told her to wait until she met my father. I also told her that if she kept up the impressive level of insight, activity and organization, no one would have any question about who was managing the deal.

The company's Strategic Planning EVP called on Friday. Joe was a smart and bottom-line-oriented guy, but not a great manager. He was a pleasure to work with personally, but there were always problems with his people on information flow and follow-up. I made a mental note to mention this to Jane so she and Eric could troubleshoot.

Joe said he could assemble the necessary troops on Monday, so we set the organizational meeting for Monday afternoon. He then alerted me to two potential problems—an HR issue with one of the executives of the unit being sold and an employee benefits plan funding issue—and promised to messenger over the info he had available.

Once the messenger package arrived, I summoned Jane and Eric and went over everything with them. Jane asked a few questions, all of them again perceptive. Then, she outlined how Eric would incorporate Joe's information into our materials for her review and she would find out which in-house employee relations and benefits lawyers had the right kind of expertise and were available, all before Monday. She also asked Eric to pay particular attention to Joe's people at Monday's meeting and to think about how to stay on top of them.

I felt a little sorry for Eric. He did seem bright—once he caught up and managed to insert a couple questions and comments of his own—but he was working at about half Jane's pace.

As for her, I knew she was still relatively inexperienced and would need my help once we got to the meat of the deal. So far, though, she was far better than the more experienced managers I'd worked with. I couldn't think of a single additional thing to suggest to her.

❖ ❖ ❖

THE DEAL got underway at Monday's meeting, but the most interesting development of the day was the interplay between Jane and my father.

I had told her that he was a masterful corporate diplomat worth watching for ideas and tips on how to negotiate the highly political waters of corporate life like a pro. When he stopped by Joe's conference room about ten minutes before the meeting was scheduled to start, I saw

Jane note his arrival and watch him carefully. (I also noticed with amusement her widened eyes when she first saw him—even in his 60s, he was still the tallest member of my family.)

His timing and his demeanor were little masterpieces. He made it plain that he was the senior executive, the real player, but also that Joe was the top company man for the meeting and the deal. As he was always careful to do, Dad also identified and defused his and my personal relationship. This time, he did both by shaking my hand, as he did everyone else's, then resting his arm around my shoulders while he told Joe and me—in a voice heard by all—that he had every confidence we would complete this deal as successfully as we had all the others.

Finally, he worked the room. Relaxed, informal, and in fewer than five minutes, he walked around, said hello or introduced himself, and chatted briefly with every person present. As usual, it was a virtuoso performance. Also as usual, I had to struggle not to laugh out loud. Both my brother and my mother did dead-on parodies of this meet-and-greet routine in which they made charming and sincere comments to ficus trees, furniture, the art on the walls, etc. Of course, I thought of the parodies every time I witnessed the real thing.

When my father got to me on his walk, he leaned in—manner still relaxed, genial smile in place—and muttered, "Not so much as a goddamn snicker, do you hear me?" It could have been worse. Sometimes he actually quoted from the parodies. I managed to keep a straight face, but it wasn't easy. He asked me (in his normal voice) to stop by his office when the meeting was over, and continued on his rounds.

The meeting went well. The people from the company's various departments looked to be a group that could gel into an effective team. The two top executives of the unit being sold—both of whom would likely be retained by the buyer after the sale if they played their cards right—were intelligent and cooperative. Their cooperation (and the orchestrated absence of Ron, the executive who'd caused the problematic HR issue) would streamline the deal process considerably, particularly in connection with preparing a first-class sale book and conducting the dog-and-pony shows—two of the keys to getting a premium price on the sale.

Jane did a good job in the manager role. She was proficient and appropriate, and she demonstrated that she could listen and put people at ease as well as take charge. Her skills, organizational and otherwise, spoke for themselves and she let them. I was also pleased to see that she cleverly created a couple opportunities for Eric to shine and that he recognized and made the most of them.

As the meeting was breaking up, I spent a few minutes debriefing with Joe, then turned to find Eric schmoozing with Joe's two sidekicks and Jane talking with Bill, one of the unit executives. I wanted to take Jane with me to my father's office, as I usually did with managers. He liked to meet them, and it was always interesting to see what they made of their time with him.

I told Eric we would meet him back at the office, then joined Jane and Bill as they finished up their conversation. Bill said he looked forward to working with us, shook both our hands, and hit the road. Jane said, "Ready to go?" and started putting her folders back in her briefcase.

"We have a meeting with my father first," I told her. "Eric's going to stay with Joe's people for a while, then meet us back at the office."

"Great! Do I need our files?"

"Maybe, maybe not, but bring everything along so we don't have to come back here when we're done."

The walk from Joe's conference room to my father's suite of offices took a few minutes. As soon as we were out of hearing distance of the meeting room, Jane asked, "Do you think the meeting went well?"

"Yeah, it was good. I'm particularly glad Bill and Roger seem cooperative. People in those positions often get paranoid about losing their jobs and have a hard time keeping their eye on the ball. The numbers seem to be shaping up to support the kind of price the company wants, too. Oh, stay on top of that Finance guy—the one with all the papers? He's been slow in the past."

"Will do. What's this next meeting about?"

I grinned at her. "It's a chance for the big man to assess you— and probably give me a hard time about something—while he keeps himself informed."

"He was impressive," Jane said, smiling, "if ridiculously tall."

When we reached his offices, it took some time to make our way past his receptionist and his secretary. Both these women had been working with Dad forever. Each treated me like one of her own children, and it was always nice to see them. I spent a few minutes talking with them and introducing Jane before we were ushered into the big corner office.

Dad was sitting on his couch, leafing through a presentation book. He stood when we came in, shook Jane's hand again and, this time, hugged me.

"Please," he said, gesturing to the easy chairs facing the couch, "sit down." To Jane, he added, "And please call me Alex."

He also sat, saying, "Still think we can get the premium, Charlie?"

"Yeah, I do." I leaned toward him, resting my hands on my knees. "We don't have all the numbers yet, but the ones they showed us today are in the range we were looking for. Sales on the new product line are ahead of forecast, which is good strategically as well as financially. Bill and Roger were a relief, too."

Dad chuckled. "They're both smart enough to know what's in their best interests. You won't have any problem with them, but watch out for Ron. Joe warned you about that?"

"Yes, he did. But this still looks like a pretty straightforward deal. At this point, the only challenge I see relative to getting the premium you want is interesting a decent-sized number of the right potential buyers and then getting two or three of them into a bidding war."

"As I understand it, that's what you do to earn the Firm's enormous fee," he said dryly. "I assume you have some brilliant ideas on the subject?"

I grinned and leaned back. "Actually, Dad, you can badger Jane about that instead of me. She has already suggested several brilliant ideas."

Dad turned to her, smiled far less sardonically than he had been smiling at me, and said, "I would be very interested to hear them."

Jane handled it like she'd been advising corporate executives effectively for years. She summarized her research on likely buyers and, handing Dad a copy of the list of names she had compiled, she broke down the potential buyers into three categories. She succinctly enumerated the strategic benefits and our best approach to getting the buyers interested. She spoke articulately and confidently. She even called him Alex once, although I'm pretty sure she swallowed hard before she did it.

I got a kick out of watching Dad while we both listened to Jane. His eyes widened a couple times, a sure sign that he was impressed. He asked her several questions. Some of these probed her assumptions—to see how solid they were and also how strong her convictions were. Two signaled doubt about the efficacy of the suggested approach—sincere enough questions, but also designed to see how she responded to being challenged. Jane handled all his questions with aplomb, including the one she dealt with by saying, "I don't know how to answer that," and turning to me for help.

Dad then offered his insights and opinions on our potential buyers. The three of us kicked all this around for 20 minutes or so, at the end of which Dad handed the list of names back to Jane. With a congratulatory smile, he said sincerely, "Excellent work, Jane—I'm impressed. It's been a pleasure to meet you and I'm sure it will continue to be a pleasure to work with you."

He turned to me, eyes twinkling, and said, "Jane may be the smartest person you've introduced to us yet, Charlie. Good job!"

We were obviously being dismissed, if very graciously. Jane and I both stood, as did Dad. After saying, "I'll look forward to talking with you again as the deal progresses," he shook Jane's hand warmly.

As he walked us to the door, he slung his arm around my shoulders and said, "I have to get home tonight or I'd take you to dinner. Your mother teaches that bizarre graduate seminar on Mondays now—you know, the one that always attracts such peculiar students? This year, she thinks they may all be visiting from other planets. Several seem entirely unable to speak." He shook his head as if bewildered. "In any event, she counts on me to rescue her precisely at 7:30."

In the taxi back to the office, Jane slumped against the seat and said, "Whew! I feel like I just ran a marathon."

"You did great," I told her. "Both at the meeting and with your new friend, Alex. He was sincerely impressed."

"He's really amazing!" she said. "So smart and bottom line-ish, if you know what I mean, but also so smooth and in control without being at all arrogant or unpleasant. It was obvious that he was grilling me and seeing if he could trip me up, but in a way that I didn't resent at all. In fact, I wanted to please him and make him like me, not just impress him." She smiled. "Probably because he treated me like a colleague and a professional—you know, as if I could take it. Like you do. I also liked the way he comfortably talked about your mother as we were leaving—as if it's OK to have a personal life. He's kind of hypnotic!"

"He *is* hard to resist," I said, grinning. "And he's always smooth. Like, you never see him look at his watch, but somehow you're always leaving his office just before the hour or the half-hour. He's incredibly focused, too. He can listen to or read reams of material in practically no time and then hone in on the two or three critical things or point out the important mistake everyone else missed. And he never keeps anything you bring to him—papers, problems, whatever. He always gives them back to you along with what you need from him to go out and deal with them yourself."

"Was he a terrifying father to have growing up?" Jane asked. Looking a little stricken, she quickly added, "You don't mind if I ask you that, do you?"

"Not at all," I said, surprised by her concern. "No, he wasn't terrifying. He expected a lot from us, but he always seemed to think we were up to any challenge." I smiled. "He doesn't take himself too seriously. And he's very funny. So is my mother. There was always a lot of laughing at our house. Still is."

"Sounds wonderful," Jane said enviously. "As long as I'm asking personal questions, may I ask one more?"

"Shoot."

"I noticed you called him 'Sir' in the conference room and 'Dad' in his office. That's because your roles in the conference room are client and service provider, not father and son, right?"

"Exactly." I nodded. "As you saw, he doesn't deny the personal relationship in front of others, but it's important for both of us to defuse it and not let it become a distraction or an issue."

"Kind of like the issue with my gender, isn't it?" she said. "I've always assumed people like you just get to be who you are all the time in a way I don't. I guess to some degree we all have to play different roles in different situations."

I was tempted to call her on the "people like you" label, but figured her day had already been rigorous enough. Instead, I smiled, agreed with her point and went back to talking about the deal.

❖ ❖ ❖

A MONTH LATER, we were putting the finishing touches on the sale book. It had taken more time than it should have to get it done. This was due partly to delays in getting final numbers from the company and partly to disputes over how best to disclose the two issues Joe had identified at the beginning.

The HR issue with the executive was a delicate equal opportunity violation, but the company had already handled it, so we were able to present it as a closed matter. Unfortunately, it had caused too many ripples for us to leave it out altogether.

The benefits plan funding issue was far more difficult. In addition to being a real money issue, it occasioned the usual frustrating impasses among the various lawyers weighing in on it. This time, we had the company's and the Firm's in-house and outside lawyers, all of whom felt obliged to discuss the issue interminably and none of whom seemed to have the same view.

Complicating the issue further, I couldn't deal at all with the Firm's inside lawyer. Frank and I were at odds from the moment we met. He barked questions at me as I tried to describe the issue and our client's goals for the sale. Taken aback and aggravated by his attitude, I made it clear—forcefully—that I expected an uninterrupted chance to lay out the facts and his assignment.

Frank listened grudgingly. When I finished, he asked sarcastically if it was finally time for questions. His questions seemed beside the point and legalistic to me—like he was trying to show off his expertise rather than make sure he understood the issue. He didn't bother to hide his contempt over my ignorance of the niceties of ERISA and the other laws governing benefit plans.

After putting up with this for a (short) while, and despite the presence of Jane and Eric, I finally told Frank it was his job—not mine—to solve legal problems and suggested he debate legal issues with his opposite numbers at the company and the law firms instead of wasting my time. I then stood and asked him if he had any other non-legal questions. With a glare, he said he didn't. I told him to coordinate with Jane on timing and language, and he left.

"What an asshole!" I muttered, walking around my office to dispel the aggravation.

"He was nothing like that when I talked to him before the org meeting," Jane said, sounding horrified. "Suppose he's just having a bad day?"

"I hope so. These fucking ERISA issues are agonizing enough without having to deal with a pain in the ass lawyer."

Eric looked wide-eyed and I realized how angry I sounded. With an effort, I sat back down and said calmly, "Sorry, guys. I'll relax. What else do we have to cover today?"

A few days later, Jane and I met to review status. Among other things, she reported that she'd had a very productive meeting with Frank. I told her I was amazed to hear it.

"I knew you would be," she said, looking smug, "but really, he was quite pleasant. Impressive, too. He's very smart and, as far as I can tell, he did a great job. Wait until you see his list of suggestions—it's detailed, but he also told me the pros and cons of each one, and prioritized them in order of best cost-benefit to the company."

"Great! So what's your secret for dealing with assholes like him?"

"I don't have a whole testosterone thing going on with him," she said, with a small smile.

"Huh?"

She sat back and crossed her legs. "Frank was fine with me," she said, "just like the first time he and I talked. So I knew his problem wasn't with me. Since he barely noticed Eric the other day, and the tension between you and him was so thick it was practically visible, I figured you were his problem."

"Me? No way." I shook my head. "He was an asshole from the minute he showed up."

"Your golden boy reputation had preceded you," Jane said. "Remember you told me once that there will always be people who take shots at you for reasons that have very little, if anything, to do with you personally? Well, that's sort of what this is. Instead of dealing with his real problem, Frank's decided to loathe people like you."

"Yeah? What's his real problem?" I asked, feeling antagonistic. "Can't stand people taller than he is?"

"You're not far off." She still looked smug, even as she eyed me warily. "Don't get mad again, OK?"

"OK," I agreed, curious now.

Obviously choosing her words carefully, Jane explained, "I got the impression that you're everything Frank resents not being—a star instead of a supporting player, on the inside track with the client and, yes, tall, too. He thinks he works a lot harder than you do for a lot less reward. It also drives him crazy that you're the big shot when he considers himself much smarter."

"He told you all that?" I asked her, incredulous.

"Of course he didn't," she said impatiently. She uncrossed her legs and leaned forward. "He told me he resented your high-handedness. He also made a few comments about people who do nothing but schmooze with clients, don't have to see anything but the big picture, and get treated like kings anyway. I listened carefully and drew my own conclusions."

"I wasn't high-handed, was I?"

"Actually, Charlie, you were. I was surprised and I think Eric probably was, too. It was very unlike you, at least in our experience with you. You don't get disliked or challenged much, do you?" She eyed me warily again. "Frank showed up with an attitude, determined to dislike you, then he goaded you, and you responded by being high-handed and asserting your superior rank. That's why I called it a testosterone thing."

I thought about this, remembering how provoked I'd felt.

"I told you the truth and my opinion because I thought they would be useful for you to know," Jane said after a short silence. She looked uncertain. "I hope my bluntness isn't why you're frowning and holding that pen as if you might stab someone with it."

"No, that's not why—don't worry." I smiled at her and put the pen down. "I appreciate your bluntness. I was frowning because I don't like to think that's really what was going on. Just in case, though, how about if you keep dealing with Frank?"

"No problem." Jane pulled her chair up to my desk, opened the folder she'd been holding, and said, "Now, let me show you how we can deal with the funding issue."

❖ ❖ ❖

OUR SALE BOOK generated interest on the parts of most of the likely strategic buyers we had identified. A couple financial buyers were also interested. Things were shaping up well for the kind of bidding war we wanted as we headed into the dog-and-pony shows. Working with the company and the lawyers, we had developed a good script for these show-and-tell presentations to potential buyers. We also had a pretty good cast of characters in Bill, Roger and most of the unit's other managers, as well as in Joe and the Finance people at the company.

Thanks to all that, the presentations went well. As usual, they generated a lot of follow-up questions and requests from the buyers. Several of these required the Firm to do additional modeling or otherwise help the company figure out what to offer in response or how to offer it. Other follow-up requests were specifically financial or legal and could be handled directly by those experts, but I'd learned it was wise to preview the responses before they were given to the buyers. Experts often got sidetracked from the big picture goal—that is, to sell the unit for a premium price—by the chance to show off their expertise.

In her role as manager, Jane coordinated all the responses. She did a great job keeping information organized and flowing, and she was also able to suggest quite a few insightful ideas for responding effectively. Because of her lack of experience, though, she frequently needed my help on substance and strategy. We essentially co-managed this stage of the deal. This was not bad or unforeseen—I expected we would do the same when we got to the negotiation phase.

One night around 8:30, Jane, Eric and I were going over the day's requests and responses. We had commandeered a conference room near my office, which looked that night as if a tornado had blown through it. The containers and leftover food from the dinner we'd ordered in were pushed off to one end of the conference table. The rest of the table was covered in a multilayered jumble of papers, marked-up sale books, spreadsheets and the like.

I didn't think the assumptions underlying one of the spreadsheets Eric had run were quite right. After explaining why and outlining the assumptions I wanted, I sent Eric off to redo the model. As soon as he left, Jane put her head in her hands and groaned in frustration.

"What's wrong?" I asked her.

"Hang on," she said, holding up a palm. "Let me organize my thoughts."

I shoved some of the clutter aside and put my feet up on the table.

When she looked up, she said, "The problems you just pointed out with the assumptions are problems I could have caught and fixed before you ever saw the results. I can't seem to consistently make the right call on when to bird-dog Eric's work. Either I over-review or under-review." She frowned. "I hated it when managers overdid it with me when I was an analyst, and I didn't want to subject Eric to that. But my decision to step back and let him work more independently seems to have created more work for you. I'm really sorry you had to do it."

"Relax, Jane," I said. "First of all, it wasn't that much work and it's one of the things I'm here to do. Second, everyone has a hard time learning how to delegate and review effectively. Like the rest of us, you got used to knowing the work was right because you did it yourself. It's hard to make the transition to knowing it's right because you gave the right instructions and eyeballed the results. Most of that comes with experience."

"It's nice of you to say that," she replied, looking both frustrated and unconvinced, "but I think my problem is more than inexperience. I've always been paranoid about making a mistake and I know how to check my own work to make sure it's as right as I can make it. That sort of check seems to be the only kind I can really do effectively."

She frowned again. "I've watched you and others delegate to me and not check every decimal point, and I see the difference between that and the bird-doggers who drive me nuts, but I can't seem to get the hang of how to do it when I'm the person delegating instead of delegated to. How do you do it?"

"There's no secret to it. I think about what we're trying to accomplish and what the result should look like—substance and, depending on what we're talking about, form too—and then I review what I get to see if it's right."

"How do you define 'right'?"

"Really, a lot of it is experience," I reiterated. "I knew those assumptions were wrong just now because the results looked off. You couldn't have done it that way at this point, right?"

"Right. I would have figured it out by reviewing all the assumptions and recognizing what was wrong or missing in them."

"Yeah, and that would have been inefficient, given that I was here to do it the shortcut way. So give yourself a break." I smiled as I gave her the advice she always needed. "Lighten up, Jane."

"OK," she said, "but it can't all be experience. There must be something I can do while I'm waiting around to get experienced."

I tried to think of something useful to tell her. "The only other hint I can think of is to make sure you're reviewing to assure the work is done well—not to assure that it's done your way. It only needs to be right. Even if your way is better, the incremental benefit is not going to be worth the incremental cost most of the time."

Jane looked intrigued and even a bit hopeful. "*That's* helpful. I do tend to look for how the work differs from what I would have done. Also, not that I achieve it, but my standard for measuring work is how close it is to perfect."

"You could also be more trusting," I suggested. "Both of the person in Eric's spot and of the reaction to a fixable mistake of the person in my spot. It's not the end of the world to make a mistake—so long as it's not a stupid one and it's fixable."

"Me? More trusting? What, are you kidding?" Jane said, her face a picture of exaggerated incredulity. "Seriously, though, I can't stand the thought of a mistake on my watch—not one I could have avoided."

I smiled, but said, "You have to get over that or you won't be able to move up. Perfection isn't the standard—it isn't cost-effective. Once you're responsible for the big picture, you have to rely on other people for the details. That means you have to be tolerant of little mistakes—and able to recognize and fix them before they cause problems. Mistakes happen all the time. They're part of the process. If your people get so afraid of making one that they get paralyzed, you're dead."

Jane was silent. She looked thoughtful. Finally, she said, "I definitely want to move up and be responsible for the big picture, but I'm going to have to think about how to aim for less than perfection and how to get comfortable with mistakes. The whole idea gives me the shivers."

"Almost as bad as having to trust someone, right?" I teased her.

She grinned. "Almost," she said shamelessly as Eric walked back into the room, "but not quite."

❖ ❖ ❖

THE BID PACKAGES came in on a Tuesday evening, most of them within a few minutes of the 6:00 p.m. deadline. There was no real reason to rush reviewing the bids, but as usual we assembled the lawyers in one of our conference rooms that evening to digest the submitted materials.

The bids were good—all in the range we wanted, price-wise, and not too much hair on any of them, condition-wise. I was somewhat concerned that the best potential buyer—the one for which we thought the benefits were most compelling—was number 3 in terms of price. Given what we knew about the respective buyers' motivations and the less than stellar financial capacity of number 2, our best bet for getting the premium price looked to be a bidding war between the buyer who'd bid top dollar and the number 3 bidder.

Jane and I left Eric in the conference room to ride herd on the lawyers as they prepared the bid summaries and comparisons to present to the company. We went back to my office to kick around the benefits plan issue and the best way to spark the bidding war we wanted, stopping on the way to give Jane's secretary some documents to type.

Back in my office, Jane sat down, slipped off her shoes and some-how managed to tuck her legs under her in the relatively small chair. She didn't look uncomfortable, but the sight made me stretch out my own legs under my desk as she asked, "Now that you've seen the bids, is there anything you think we should have done differently with the sale book or the show-and-tells?"

"Good question," I said, thinking about it. "The prices are fine— well, the top four, which is all we need. We always knew the benefits plan would be a problem. It is interesting that only one of the bidders discounted the price materially over it."

"Yeah," Jane said gloomily, "but it's the best potential buyer."

"Yeah, it is. They also seem to have the most legal comments—and not just on the plan issue. There's some real beside-the-point garbage in their documents. You appreciate, I assume, the extra execution risk that presents?"

"Yes. That's come up on other deals I've worked on. But we might be able to clear out some of that nitpicky crap in the second round after we narrow the field."

"Maybe." I shrugged.

"Do you have any brilliant suggestions for addressing the plan funding issue?"

"Nope. Do you?"

"Sadly, no." She shook her head. "I used up what I had on the disclosure."

"Well, it worked for five out of six. Why don't you round up your buddy Frank tomorrow and see what the two of you can come up with?" Seeing her amused expression, I added, "I'll stay out of the way. He and I still don't seem to be able to talk without ending up at odds."

"At odds?" Jane repeated, her eyebrows raised. "That's euphemistic. He hates your guts. And you always look at him like you're thinking about picking him up and tossing him through the window."

"Come on, Jane. It's not that bad, is it?" I asked, laughing.

"Yes it is," she said firmly. "Luckily, you've got me to deal with him."

"Luckily."

Jane's secretary knocked, then came in and handed us papers to review.

"Thanks," Jane said to her. "Would you mind hanging around outside here for ten minutes or so? We'll look at these right now and give them back to you so you can start copying and assembling packages."

"Feel free to sit at Pam's desk," I offered.

Jane's secretary nodded, but didn't say a word. As usual, she seemed very flustered to me. After she left, I mentioned this to Jane and asked her if it was a problem. Jane peered at me as if she couldn't believe what I'd said, and then she laughed.

"What's so funny?" I asked.

"She's only flustered around you," Jane said, still snickering.

"Around me? Why? And why is that funny?"

"It amuses me that you're so oblivious. She has a crush on you, you idiot."

"For God's sake," I said, rolling my eyes. "That's all I need."

I started reading the new papers, then looked back up at Jane as what she'd said sunk in. "Wait a sec. Did you just call me an idiot?"

"I meant it in the nicest possible way," she said, grinning. "And with all due respect, of course."

"Jane, is it possible that you've finally decided you can actually trust me?" I asked her in not wholly mock amazement.

"Looks like it," she said glibly. "Can you believe it?" She put her feet on the floor and back into her shoes. "Come on, let's review this stuff and let my poor secretary get on with it before she's in a complete tizzy. And then we have to figure out how to start the bidding war."

❖ ❖ ❖

JANE AND FRANK did come up with an innovative idea for resolving the benefits plan issue. It required the company to put some money on the table, but Joe saw the advantage of keeping the number 3 bidder in the game, so he did what he had to do to round up the extra scratch.

Thanks to that, the bidding war worked just the way bidding wars are supposed to. The number 1 bidder turned out to be determined to buy the unit. That buyer's second and final round bids were obviously set so as to remain the highest. Because of the strong interest of numbers 2 (through the second round) and 3 (all the way), number 1's final price ended up right at the top of the range the company had specified—even after netting out the extra money ponied up for the benefits plan issue. The final negotiations and the closing also went smoothly and quickly.

I couldn't have been more pleased about the whole transaction. My father and Joe were satisfied, the Firm had collected a sizeable fee, and the winning buyer's CEO had made noises to the effect that he'd like to work with the Firm again.

On top of all that, Jane had aced the manager role.

As I collected feedback from Joe and others and thought about Jane's performance, I realized that thanks to her first-class organizational and strategic thinking skills, the whole process had been much smoother than usual. Her approach was reactive only where it had to be; she handled in advance everything that could be handled that way. Her attention to things like templates for documents and forms, preparing for foreseeable eventualities and scheduling proactively had streamlined the process enormously.

We hadn't felt behind the eight ball or pressured for time on the deal except where that was unavoidable. Deals always have surprises and crises, events and circumstances that can't be predicted and planned for. We'd had plenty of time to think about and take care of those because there was never any underbrush blocking us. It had all felt more relaxed somehow, despite the usual complement of late nights, financial and legal concerns, interpersonal squabbles, slip-ups, etc.

I decided to recommend to Jim that Jane officially be skipped a class. That would mean more money and better opportunities for her and a big boost to her already stellar reputation. It would also mean the Firm would finally have a woman in its young king ranks, an important—and personally gratifying—milestone.

The timing was good. The deal closed about a month before July's formal performance reviews (and the end of Jane's third year). Jim agreed enthusiastically with my recommendation, which was also good since he was the one who would have to sell it to the compensation committee.

A couple weeks later, Jane and I had one of our regular meetings. We hadn't had a chance to talk since the closing dinner—I'd been traveling and she'd been busy on another deal. She showed up (as usual, at the exact time we'd agreed on), pen and portfolio in hand, and practically before she sat down she asked, "So, how did I do?"

"Hello, Jane," I teased. "How have you been?"

She laughed and set the portfolio down on the front edge of my desk, then laid the pen on top of it. Sitting back in a decent imitation of someone prepared to be patient, she said, "Fine, thanks. And you?"

"Can't complain."

"I'm so glad." Raising her eyebrows, she asked, "Is that enough small talk or shall I ask if your trip was productive?"

"Don't bother. I know you wouldn't listen to the answer anyway," I said, smiling. "You did great on the deal, Jane—really great. We've talked about most of the highlights already—client-handling, identifying and dealing with issues, financial savvy, great strategic thinking. But I do have a few new things for you. I had lunch with Joe last week, and he told me how impressed he was both with your work and with how smooth the deal process was. He plans to ask for you the next time we do a deal for them."

Jane smiled happily. "That's great! I really liked working with him."

"His comment about the deal process got me thinking about that. This deal did seem smoother and more organized than they usually do.

You approach the process as strategically as you approach the business issues, don't you?"

"I haven't thought about it that way," Jane said, looking very pleased, "but, yeah, I guess I do. So many hard or time-consuming things come up as the deal progresses. It's much easier for me to focus on those if I already have a sense of the whole and I've gotten the basics done and out of the way as early as possible."

"It's a great approach. I've always concentrated on the client and the issues and pretty much let the process play out on its own," I told her. "You're right, though—spending some time and effort on shaping the process actually created more time for the big items. We were all less hassled and I think our work was probably better, too."

"I'm glad you think so," she said. "Sometimes I wonder if it's nuts to figure out the format and do a template for a presentation or draft the cover letter before I've got even a clue about the actual substance. But the time it takes to conceptualize the template so I know what the final product needs to look like—or to get the letter done and typed while there's still a secretary around—always seems so worth it, so much better than trying to figure all that out at 3:00 a.m. *after* the hard part is done."

"It's not nuts at all. It really made a difference. It was also a good learning experience for Eric. You did a good job managing him, by the way. I know you were struggling with how to review effectively, but you didn't drive him crazy or leave him unsupervised."

"Thanks."

"And here's the big highlight," I said, grinning. "I've recommended to Jim and he's going to recommend to the comp committee that you be skipped up."

"That's fantastic!" Jane exclaimed, her eyes wide. "Thank you so much!"

"Hey, you earned it."

"Yeah, but you gave me the opportunity. Without that white boy break…" She broke off abruptly.

"Charlie, I'm so sorry," she apologized before I could say anything. "I can't believe I said that out loud. Please don't think I'm being flip or ungrateful. The opportunity to manage a deal is the kind of thing that can make such a difference for someone at my level. I've been thinking about it as a white boy break because that's who it more commonly happens for. Truly, though, that makes me appreciate it—and your vote of confidence in me—even more."

"Relax, Jane," I said, smiling at her. "You haven't offended me. I know how things work around here. It's fair enough to call it a white boy break. I don't doubt that you appreciate it—and you really did make the most of it."

"Thanks again," she said, looking relieved. "I'm very grateful, despite the sarcastic label. I'm just so used to climbing uphill all the time that I can't help thinking in those terms."

"Some day you're going to have to knock that chip off your shoulder," I reminded her. "How many white boy breaks is it going to take before you do?"

"At least one more, apparently," she said, shaking her head ruefully. "Before that unfortunate slip of the tongue, what I was going to say was without this opportunity, I wouldn't have had even a shot at skipping a class, regardless of my talent. I really owe you one. More than one, actually—you've offered me great advice and support right from the beginning."

"My pleasure," I smiled. "I'm glad to be able to help you succeed. Leveling the playing field is one of my goals."

Jane contemplated me, looking undecided or maybe puzzled. "You really are the real thing, aren't you?" she said. "Someone who fits the established profile perfectly, but isn't dedicated to making sure that profile remains the status quo forever."

"Why is it so hard for you to believe that?" I asked her, leaning forward to see her expression better. "You see the benefits of diversity and you find them compelling, not just because it suits your purposes, but because they *are* compelling. Why shouldn't I?"

"You should—definitely. I'm just too used to people defining their own best interests narrowly and in a way that affects me negatively. You're right that I have a chip on my shoulder. It's a predictable response to the sexist garbage I've spent my life dealing with, but I'm not proud of it." She smiled contritely. "Especially not when it makes me appear to be doubting someone who's done nothing but help me. I really am sorry."

"You're forgiven. At least that chip is getting slightly smaller. It used to be bigger than you are."

"I know, I know," she said, laughing. "Not that that's saying much, right?"

"Exactly." I leaned back in my chair and smiled at her. "So how does it feel to be on the brink of being the first female young king? Or would you prefer 'young queen'?"

"Hell, no!" she said. "I want to be a young king. I hate that business about changing the title when a woman finally gets a high-falutin' position. You know, it's always been 'chairman,' but suddenly it becomes 'chairwoman' or 'chair'? The language may be sexist, but it is what it is and I want the real thing.

"And," she concluded with a grin, "it feels fantastic!"

CHAPTER 6

DEFINING WOMEN

Jane

Lynn, Anna, Cheryl and I met for dinner the week after I learned I was being offered money instead of the status of skipping a class. We started as usual with a round of drinks and some catching up and griping about everyone's current aggravations.

I wanted to kick the whole money/status thing around with the others, but wasn't sure it was a good idea. It was easy to foresee the awkwardness the increased compensation might create among peers. As it turned out, though, I didn't have to bring it up nor did it cause any problem among us.

Lynn took advantage of the pause after we ordered food to say, "Jane, I heard the Firm suddenly decided that class-skipping isn't such a good idea now that a woman has qualified for it. Convenient for them to make a policy change now, isn't it?" Her expression was as indignant as her tone. "I think this really blows. Did they offer you more money at least? Are you totally pissed off?"

"God, nothing's a secret over there, is it!" I exclaimed, surprised. "But I'm glad you already know. I wanted to talk to you guys about it, but I felt a little weird bringing it up."

"Please, Jane," Anna said. "We support you completely. You're our best hope for breaking into the young king ranks."

I smiled at her gratefully.

"So what happened?" Cheryl asked.

I leaned back and shook my head dolefully. "It's a very depressing— if typical—story. The manager opportunity really was the huge white boy break we thought it would be, despite the disappointing ending. It was a great deal to manage. We got the company the premium price it wanted for the unit, and the working group was fun all around, even the lawyers and accountants."

I sipped my water while I figured out what order to put the facts in so they made the most sense. "Charlie was terrific to work with—there when I needed him, but didn't babysit. He gave lots of real-time feedback, too. Eric—the rookie—did a great job. I had a chance to show how I can think. One of our lawyers and I figured out how to resolve the one serious issue, and Charlie made sure we got the credit we deserved, both with the client and with Jim.

"Even the closing dinner was a pleasure instead of the usual 'Yikes! There's a woman present' thing." I smiled as I recalled how welcome Alex had made me feel. "I told you Charlie's father is a complete charmer, right? Well, he treated me like the most important person at the dinner. Since he actually *was* the most important person there, of course everyone else fell in line."

"Sounds wonderful so far," Cheryl said.

"Yeah, it was! The whole experience was the best one I've had at the Firm. And I *loved* managing. It was just as satisfying as I'd imagined to be the one in charge and to control the process instead of always playing catch-up because the manager was just letting stuff happen. I learned a lot, too, including more about how to delegate effectively."

"That's a very different experience from the manager standpoint than the grunt standpoint, isn't it?" Lynn nodded. She had been designated manager for a deal a few weeks before. "I was surprised by how naturally I fell into the 'check every number' mindset even though, as a grunt, I always really resented it."

"Exactly," I agreed. "So, the deal closed and a couple weeks went by. At one of our regular meetings, Charlie told me he had talked to Jim and they were in agreement about recommending that I be skipped a class. Obviously, I was thrilled."

The waiter delivered our food—beautiful and comforting bowls of pasta all around. After we all sampled our own and each other's, Lynn said, "So then what happened?"

"Well," I continued, "a month or so later, I was called into Jim's office. Charlie was already there, looking like he might have to be restrained from murdering someone. Jim explained that the Executive Committee had decided as a policy matter that class-skipping was disruptive and not the best way to run a railroad—I'm paraphrasing—but there was no question that I was doing a superior job and, while he couldn't offer me the status of skipping a class, he was pleased to offer me a ton of money."

"The money might have worked if you hadn't been aware it was a consolation prize," Anna said, somehow managing to use her knife and fork to eat long noodles quickly and without dripping. "I imagine Charlie got dressed down for telling you about the recommendation, didn't he?"

"He didn't say so, but you're probably right," I said. "Still, even if he hadn't told me, I might have guessed. It's not like anyone doesn't know class-skipping is a possibility after doing well in a situation like that. Almost half the young kings were skipped, I think."

"What a bunch of insular morons those Executive Committee bastards are!" Lynn exclaimed. "Could you tell from what Jim said whether they really did this to hold you back?"

"Not from what Jim said, but Charlie told me later what he knew. Honestly, I don't think that is why they changed the policy. Charlie reviewed a paper trail going back nearly a year, including some HR consultant's analysis and recommendation. Apparently, they really had been considering a new policy since reviews last year." I shrugged. "I doubt they were brokenhearted that the change kept a woman back, but it really does seem to have been a coincidence. It also kept two guys back."

"You're very calm about this, Jane," Cheryl commented as she reached for a piece of bread.

"I am now," I told her. "I was outraged and really disappointed at first, but what can I do except take the fucking money and be a good sport? I'm not going to quit over something like this."

"I heard about it a few days ago from someone who overheard part of a *very* heated discussion between Charlie and Jim," Lynn said. She looked impressed as well as conspiratorial as she leaned forward and reported, "Word is that Charlie almost did quit over it."

"I don't know about that, but he was livid," I said, feeling my eyes widen as I remembered how ferocious he'd been. "He really does have a temper! Cheryl, wasn't it you who told us he got furious on some trip?"

"It sure was," she said. "I remember being very glad I wasn't the person he was mad at." Her eyes widened, too. "It was scary—if also kind of exciting. And you know, as I recall, he was very frustrated and basically in the right then, too."

"Well, ditto on this," I said. "I think the combination of believing he was right and not being able to compel the result he wanted made him wild. I doubt he's had much experience with being stymied and he's got no patience for it. The barely contained fury *was* scary—it was hard to talk to him and I was kind of worried about what he might do. It didn't take him too long to calm down, though, and he's been fine since."

Anna had been looking thoughtful and now she said, "It's excellent that he's such a strong supporter of yours, Jane. Assuming he doesn't quit in a fury over something, it appears that he will be one of the people in charge of the Firm one day."

"That would be good for all of us," I said with confidence. "Charlie's the real deal—a guy who truly believes talent and brains should be recognized and rewarded irrespective of the package they happen to show up in. He's also someone willing to fight for what he thinks is right. I was impressed—and grateful, too."

Lynn had taken off her earrings, which looked heavy, and dropped them in her briefcase. Looking back up, she grinned and said, "And, as I always say…"

"We know, Lynn," Cheryl interrupted, surprisingly firmly. "He's beautiful, too, but let's not objectify him tonight. We owe him better than that."

"Fair enough," Lynn capitulated. "Let's order dessert instead."

We decided on three desserts to share all around. While we were waiting for them, Cheryl said, "Speaking of the real deal, Richard and I are thinking of moving in together."

"I really like Richard," Lynn said warmly. "I'm not a big fan of lawyers, but he's great—and so normal."

"I like him, too," I agreed. "He's smart and funny." I smiled at Cheryl. "And he seems to adore you."

"I adore him, too," she said, smiling back. "He makes me very happy. He *is* smart and funny. Also, he's very self-assured, which I like a lot, but he's not arrogant or domineering."

"Just what your perfect husband profile calls for," Lynn teased, tilting her water glass in Cheryl's direction.

"Have you told him about your plan to leave work behind once you marry?" Anna asked.

"We're not really talking marriage yet, but yeah, I have. He's OK with the idea, but I'm not as sure as I once was about the wisdom of quitting at that point." Cheryl laughed. "There's something about having had to cross out 'investment banker' and write in 'lawyer' that's caused me to rethink my whole plan."

"That plan could use some rethinking, in my opinion," Lynn declared. "You are too good at the job—and you seem to like it too much—to give it up in favor of sitting around and reading decorating magazines or whatever you'd be doing."

Cheryl smiled at her indulgently. "Thanks—I think. I do like the job. I can't see hanging around and doing it forever—I look at those senior guys who still work all the time and I can't imagine being enthusiastic enough to keep up this pace for decades. But I really don't feel ready to give it up any time soon."

"Then you shouldn't," I said. "No reason to be a slave to a plan you developed when you were a teenager."

Our desserts arrived and we spent a few minutes tasting them all, then placing them where we could each reach our favorites.

"You know, I have a different idea about marriage than I used to," Cheryl said meditatively, wiping a fleck of chocolate off her lip with her fingertip. "I never envisioned it as essentially a friendship that also includes romantic love and sex. My original conception assumed a certain distance between the husband and wife, I think. And it was sort of more about *what* the people were than *who* they were. I think that's why I figured I'd have to quit working—so I could 'be a wife.' Do you see what I mean?"

Anna looked deep in thought and Lynn didn't jump right in, so I answered, "I think so. My parents have a marriage sort of like your original conception. They get along fine and I think they love each other—whatever that might mean—but they're very separate in terms of interests, responsibilities, spheres of influence. Also, it's always seemed to me that they have personas they use with each other, instead of just being who they are."

"Quite the opposite of Katherine and Jordan, isn't that?" Anna remarked.

"Yes, exactly!" Cheryl said. "I was so surprised at first by how Katherine is always herself around Jordan. I remember thinking, 'Well, *that's* cool,' which made me realize I apparently had some weird notion that you had to play a part to be a wife—you know, that you couldn't just be yourself. Ever since, I've been wondering why on earth I'd think that."

"It's because the 'wife as a role to play' notion is what we grew up with, don't you think?" I said. "My mother wants my father to keep supporting her, so she hides her intelligence—I assume so as not to threaten or intimidate him or give him any idea that she could actually take care of herself."

Lynn finally spoke. Her fork was poised halfway between her plate and her mouth, and I found myself hoping she wouldn't gesture with the fork—there was a piece of lemon tart speared precariously on its tines. "Let's not be naïve, girls," she said. "Men don't like the idea of being outshone by women under any circumstances. Where their wives are concerned, they seem to prefer someone they can confidently feel superior to—either legitimately or because the little woman is willing to play the inferior role. That's one of the reasons I've never wanted to get married."

"Certainly that's not inevitable, Lynn," Anna argued as Lynn (to my relief) ate the bite wobbling on her fork. "Marriage isn't required to be a contest or a power struggle even if societal conditions or specific situations sometimes turn it into that. I like to think of it more as a pact— a deal where each person loves the other for his or her contribution, his or her true self. Katherine and Jordan seem to have that sort of marriage, don't they?"

"Well, it's only been six months," Lynn said, "but, yeah, they seem to."

"I really think it's possible," Cheryl said. "That's how Richard and I are, too. We're very real with each other, and what's connecting us definitely relates more to identity than to status or relative power. We admire and like more fundamental things about each other than what he does for a living or whether I work or not—or, for that matter, who does the dishes or pays for dinner. Those things all seem like personal decisions that are somehow independent of who we are to each other."

She laughed and picked up her cappuccino. "Obviously, I guess, right? Otherwise, I'd never have been able to overlook his having the wrong job."

"Marriage hasn't historically been about love or companionship, has it," Anna said. "It's been about propagation and physical comfort for men and about security for women. It's not surprising that women sought a powerful husband—or played roles to keep him—in that sort of scenario. It's also not surprising that they were often willing to be subservient.

"The point for the woman was to assure that she and her children were provided for in a society where she couldn't take on the provider role herself. She wasn't looking for a companion or a lover so much as a meal ticket and protection against the cruel world. He wasn't looking for a companion or lover so much as someone to bear his children and assure that he had a well-run household."

"Sounds awful, doesn't it?" Lynn said with disgust.

"Yes, it does," Cheryl said. "But only because we don't need men for that now. At least for those of us who can provide for ourselves, now the goals really are love and companionship."

"Do you think those are men's goals, too?" I asked. I pulled the plate with the chocolate mousse cake closer. (Unless Katherine was present, it always fell to me to finish the desserts.)

"Well, I don't," Lynn said. "They may start out there, but I think they end up expecting their wives to be like their mothers and take care of household and other dreary things for them, all the while making them feel like big shots. Then, they end up demeaning or disdaining their wives just like they do their mothers."

"God, Lynn, you're so cynical!" Cheryl protested. "They can't all be like that. I can't imagine Richard transforming from someone who loves and admires me as I am into a sexist pig who expects me to cook dinner for him and then disdains me for doing it, all so he can feel superior."

Giggling, she added, "And can you even imagine Katherine's reaction to Jordan expecting her to behave like a Victorian or a 1950s housewife in any respect whatsoever?"

"He wouldn't dare," Anna said, as we all laughed.

"I'm as skeptical as you are, Lynn, about men's motives and their attitudes toward women and wives," I said, "but maybe our skepticism is more applicable generally than specifically. I mean, it's obvious that Jordan loves Katherine for her actual bigger-than-life self. She's about as unlike his mother—or, for that matter, a wife from central casting—as someone could be. Richard seems equally progressive. Maybe with the right connection, the sexist marriage bullshit just goes away. Or do you suppose Jordan and Richard are just exceptional?"

"Richard is clearly exceptional," Cheryl said, with an impish smile. "But, no, I don't think he and Jordan are the only two men in the world who want real companions instead of subservient drones they can feel superior to."

"I certainly hope not," Anna said fervently.

❖ ❖ ❖

Charlie

One night, Annemarie and I ran into my sister Claire and her husband at a restaurant. Seeing Claire anywhere but at my parents' house at family events was a rare occurrence. She's an internist and Stephen is a lawyer; they both work most of the time and don't go out much.

Claire and Stephen were leaving as we were arriving, so I introduced Annemarie and we talked briefly. Claire and I agreed that it had been way too long since we'd seen each other and made plans to get together for lunch the following week.

Claire is usually late for things, thanks to patients who arrive late for their appointments with her or require more time than her standard for office visits. Lunch was no exception, but it wasn't too bad. I only waited about ten minutes for her. She breezed in, apologized for being late, reached up to kiss my cheek and said, "Hello there, little brother!"

"Your apology for being late sounds too automatic, Claire," I teased her. "You need to up the sincerity a few notches."

She laughed. "It's not automatic because I'm insincere. I just have to recite it too often. You look terrific, toots. What's been going on with you lately?"

I brought her up to date after we were seated, and she did the same in return. After we ordered, Claire leaned back and said, "OK, enough with the generalities. What's the story on that unbelievably gorgeous woman you were with the other night? Stephen exclaimed over her all the way home! He'd probably still be waxing eloquent if I hadn't glowered at him and told him I didn't want to hear any more."

I laughed. "She is a looker, isn't she? I told you about her—she's the one I met on a plane about a year ago. She's in advertising."

"She is spectacular. Honestly, I was as riveted as Stephen was when you introduced her. And I noticed that she seemed unaware of our dropped jaws, which interested me. What's that about?"

"Annemarie says she's been stared at for as long as she can remember. It drove her crazy—made her feel exposed—so she found a way to ignore it. She really is unaware of the stares—and she's not vain herself, either."

I laughed again and told Claire, "She said once that her situation was not unlike having a visible deformity. She felt permanently self-conscious and on display and had to develop a coping mechanism."

"Pretty high-class dilemma," Claire said. "I get the point, but I'm betting beauty offers a lot more upside than deformity."

"Well, yeah, obviously. I think Annemarie gets that point, too. She was just trying to explain the exposed feeling. She asked me if I ever felt that way, which I took as a compliment, even though I had to tell her I never have—except on her behalf when I'm out with her."

Claire gave me a look meant to be withering. "I'll admit you're good-looking, baby brother, but frankly you're not in her league. I doubt people even notice you when you're out with her."

"Thanks," I said sarcastically.

"Any time," she said airily. "What are big sisters for?" She sipped her iced tea. "Actually, even if you were in her league, you might not feel the same way. Men and women react differently to beauty in themselves—or maybe it's that beauty has a different impact on them."

"What do you mean?" I asked as I straightened my legs under the table and put my feet on the floor on either side of Claire's chair. Her toes were already resting on the bottom rung of mine so there was plenty of room on her side.

"Well, appearance is important for everyone, but I think it's more central to how women think about themselves and about one another. I'm sure Annemarie's looks have always figured more prominently in her sense of self than yours have in yours." Claire grinned. "I've spent my life surrounded by pretty boys, you know. I've had plenty of opportunity to observe how differently you react to how you look. You and Andy—Stephen, too—all of you seem heedless or, I don't know, unimpressed by your conspicuous good looks. None of you seems to think it's a very big deal."

"It's not."

"You wouldn't say that if you were a woman, sweetie," she said, patting my cheek condescendingly. "Probably because it's one of the things we get prized for in this sexist world, it is a bigger deal to us. We're very judgmental about appearance—in ourselves and in one another. It's more...more defining of us somehow."

"It's so interesting that you would use that word, Claire," I said, surprised that she had used it. "I have a friend at the Firm who uses the same word all the time about the different impacts of personal things like that on men and women. She made the point a while ago that being married is viewed as incidental for men, but defining for women."

"She's right." Claire took her pager, which had evidently vibrated, out of her pocket, glanced at it, and put it back before she asked, "How did you happen to be talking about that?"

"Oh, a couple of our colleagues got married earlier this year. The man is older and more established, so it made sense for the woman to be the one who found another job. My friend felt, though, that even if their positions were reversed, the woman would still have been the one who had to leave. You know, because once people knew about the relationship, they would still think of him as a professional, but she would be perceived first, and maybe even primarily, as a wife."

"Right again. The Firm's moldy old halls must be scandalized to have such subversive insights being said right out loud!" Claire said gleefully. "And the moldy old gents in those halls must be reeling. What a good thing it is that you finally have some women at that stodgy place, Charlie!"

"I agree. It doesn't seem to be changing the status quo very fast, though. Jane—my friend—was complaining about that, too. She sees sexism and inequality everywhere."

"They *are* everywhere."

"Come on, Claire." I gave her a "get real" look. "Everywhere?"

"You have no idea, really no idea, if you think otherwise," she proclaimed. "I spent my entire internship and most of my residency listening to people assume I was the nurse, not the doctor—and more than a few of them were none too pleased to find out I *was* the doctor. One guy actually told me he wanted a 'real doctor,' then clarified that he meant a man, in case I was too dense to get his point."

She rolled her eyes in disgust. "And have you watched TV lately? Practically every commercial you see says or suggests some sexist thing— like women care deeply about cleaning products or are the only ones capable of raising kids or doing dishes. If they're not categorizing us as maids or mommies, they're using our bodies to sell beer. It's disgusting! You should talk to your gorgeous girlfriend about that. Didn't you say she's in advertising?"

"Well, she…"

"Hold the phone, small fry," Claire instructed. "I'm not done. I remember Hannah asking Mom once why you and Andy had nicknames and Hannah and I didn't. That's such a Hannah question, isn't it?" She smiled. "Anyway, Mom told her that boys weren't diminished by nicknames, but girls were, and girls had enough obstacles to negotiate around without having to be undermined by their own names."

I'd never heard this story before. "No way!" I said. "They deliberately named you and Hannah so you wouldn't have nicknames?"

"Yes, they did," Claire said, with a smug smile. "Who knows whether Alex thought it was a big deal or not, but Mom wouldn't have been swayable on something like that."

I laughed, remembering how Claire had started calling Dad "Alex" after she heard the "please, call me Alex" routine when she was a teenager. Trying to get her to go back to "Dad," he explained to her that he did it to put people at ease. Claire thanked him sincerely and told him she felt more comfortable already. She's referred to him that way ever since. Even to his face, she calls him "Dad" only, as she says, on very special occasions.

"What's so funny?" she demanded. "I thought we were talking about sexism and inequality."

"I'm just remembering the 'call me Alex' episode," I explained. "I heard him say it for real in a meeting not too long ago. As usual, it was hard not to laugh."

"Uh-huh. You're just ducking the real issue, I think. While you're ducking issues, here's another one for you. What are you doing with Annemarie? Are you serious?"

"Nope. Just fooling around. So is she. Probably not for much longer. We don't have a lot in common."

Claire shook her head mournfully. "You young people," she lamented. (She is three years older than I am.) "I had this same conversation with Hannah a couple weeks ago. She is similarly dissolute, although her current flame isn't quite as eye-catching as yours. You'd think someone planning to be a psychiatrist would have better judgment about her personal life."

Claire looked gravely disappointed as she again shook her head. "It's really too bad about you and Hannah," she said sadly. "Andy and I are so solid. Mom and Alex should have stopped while they were ahead."

"Yeah, I'm sure we're a terrible disappointment to them," I said, grinning at her. "Actually, Claire, Hannah's flame, as you call him, isn't so bad. I thought he was interesting. And he's crazy about her."

"Charlie, please. Does he even have a job?"

"I don't know. I wasn't interviewing him, for Christ's sake. But who cares? Hannah has a job."

"Oh, you are quite the modern man, aren't you?" she scoffed.

I had a great time at lunch. It was entertaining to talk to Claire and it was relaxing, too—she always chose the topics and ran the conversation. As we left the restaurant, we agreed not to wait so long to get together again before we hugged and went our separate ways.

CHAPTER 7
THERE MUST BE MORE TO LIFE

Jane

My fourth year at the Firm started out normally enough. Thanks to the boost in reputation and (unofficial) stature I got from my work on Charlie's deal, I had my choice of deals to work on, all at the manager level. I was still being squired by Tyler to the Firm's social events and, thanks to that, still enjoying the benefits of insider status.

The women in my class continued to meet often enough to provide a solid cushion of comfort and support. Katherine joined us whenever she could. She consistently reported (always with a leer) that marriage was sensational. She also reported that moving laterally into a new job had some very attractive aspects.

According to Katherine, not only did you get to start with a totally clean slate, but everyone seemed to think you'd had better training and experience—in that "grass is always greener" phenomenon that characterizes competitors. You also evidently benefited from what Katherine called a certain "new toy" quality. People seemed to think you were more interesting and talented than even the most highly regarded of their more familiar colleagues.

I had a chance to work on another deal with Jordan that summer, too. He was obviously as delighted with being married as Katherine was—the lovely "struck by lightning" energy and dreaminess that had characterized him ever since the two of them got together was still very noticeable. I also noticed that he was no longer as single-minded as he had been—and as many of the people at the Firm were. Jordan seemed to have more on his mind than before, not in a distracted way, but in a way that gave him a broader perspective.

Along the same lines, I worked that fall with Katherine's old buddy, Patrick, in Public Finance. It wasn't a group I normally worked with, but we had an unusual acquisition structure that involved some municipal bond financing as well as the more normal—for me—bank financing. Patrick was another of the highly regarded people four or five years ahead of me at the Firm, and he was remarkably interesting.

Like everyone else, he worked the better part of 24/7, but he also somehow found the time for a lot of outside interests. He was a voracious reader, he knew a lot about music and played a few instruments, and he played rugby with some club. He'd lived in Australia as a teenager while his dad was on a five-year assignment there. In addition to his passion for rugby, Patrick had picked up that laid-back, humorous approach to life Australians are known for. The night he joined us grunts at the financial printer was one of the most entertaining nights I've ever spent finalizing and proofreading documents.

Jordan's broadened perspective and Patrick's multitudinous outside interests prompted me to think about adding something other than work to my own life. For the almost three-and-a-half years I'd worked at the Firm, I had done very little but work, sleep and attend social functions hosted by the Firm, Tyler's bank or Tyler's family.

But committing to do something outside work on any sort of set schedule was not really feasible. My schedule was mostly spoken for in terms of hours in the day, and it was also very unpredictable. Deals have their own pace, their own ebb and flow of activity. There's always at least one crisis at some point in the process. I remained at the beck and call of senior people, and we were all at the beck and call of our clients.

I also wasn't sure what I might want to do. I had been a regular swimmer since high school, but even that had given way to my work schedule. For one thing, swimming takes at least an hour—more if the pool isn't nearby. For another, I had to choose my times carefully. I didn't want to go back to work with wet hair that needed explaining, nor did I want to give anyone unnecessary reasons to think of me as a woman. The whole swimming/bathing suit/wet hair subject was better circumvented than faced.

The people I met at Tyler's family's social events were always talking about one charitable board or another, but their involvement seemed to consist mostly of fund-raising and making sure they continued to be seen as prominent. There would come a time when that was right for me, but I wasn't there yet. Also, interaction with those people was essentially work—creating yet more occasions for it seemed misguided.

I played no instruments and didn't fancy learning any or, for that matter, taking up photography or joining a book club. I also had no interest in joining a softball or tennis league, even assuming I could have found one and shown up more than half the time. Women's issues were close to my heart, but I doubted I'd be very good as a counselor in a rape crisis or abortion clinic setting. Being a mentor for high school girls appealed to me, but the programs I looked into all had set schedules for meetings.

Despite my desire to broaden my perspective—which felt like an emotional thirst as well as an intellectual decision—my top priority continued to be executing my plan for reaching the top of the corporate ladder ASAP. Also, the deal flow at the Firm was very robust that fall and winter. I was busier than ever.

Like most people in my situation, I ended up writing a few checks to charitable organizations, feeling bad about not getting more involved in something beneficial to society, and remaining over-focused on work. I did resolve to swim more often and to revisit the charitable possibilities later down the road.

Tyler's family hosted a huge holiday bash that December. It was a major "see and be seen" event and, for a change, the guests included some celebrities from the entertainment world in addition to the usual luminaries from the business and art worlds. I felt like quite the celebrity myself as Tyler and I, in very fancy clothes, were hustled by beefy security people past a gaggle of paparazzi on our way into the ballroom.

Unlike most of Tyler's family's events, this one had a whirlwind informality to it. It was a dinner, but it had been set up as a buffet rather than an assigned-seat, sit-down affair. It was also packed. There were probably six or seven hundred people there at any given time, and there may have been a thousand in attendance overall.

Because Tyler was one of the focal points of the party, we didn't have to circulate much to enjoy a constant stream of interesting people to talk to. (Given the staggeringly uncomfortable, if utterly chic, shoes I was wearing, not having to walk around a lot was a welcome development.) We chatted with movie stars and theatre people, an artist, several writers and the mayor, in addition to the usual business and art world suspects.

There were, of course, a few ultra-senior people from the Firm at the party. They always looked the strangest combination of delighted and appalled when they saw me at Tyler's side. Even as I spoke cordially—and, I hoped, impressively—to them, I got a secret kick out of their discomfiture over being outranked at a big-shot social event by a mere girl from the office.

Much more pleasantly, I spotted Alex and later had an opportunity to say hello to him and also to meet his wife, Kate. Charlie's mother was remarkable. Even in under five minutes of conversation, it was obvious that she was brilliant and witty. She was also tall and very striking in an elegant, slightly severe-looking way. It was not difficult to picture her teaching a highly advanced and abstract mathematics seminar.

Kate's imposing presence, along with her direct and piercing gaze, initially intimidated me—I felt rather as if I had come to her class unprepared—but she turned out to be very friendly. As soon as Alex introduced me and told her I was Charlie's colleague from the Firm, she said, "Oh, yes. Jane. Alex and Charlie have both raved about you for months! It's my pleasure to meet you. I trust you're quite revolutionizing that stuffy old gentlemen's club you work in."

I responded that I was doing my best, but the pace of change remained frustratingly unrevolutionary. Kate offered a few suggestions for speeding things up, from creating opportunities for other women to staging a coup, peaceful or otherwise. I was sorry the press of people around us prevented us from spending more time together.

The most interesting incident of the evening occurred while I was dancing with Tyler's father. He asked me if I ever thought about moving from investment banking into what he described as "real business." By this, he meant a line position with profit and loss responsibility at a company that produced products or provided services directly to customers—as opposed to a brokerage business like the Firm's.

I told him that my goal was to move at the right time into just such a position, with a longer-term goal of moving into senior management, and then asked why he wanted to know.

He said that in the course of his banking business, he often came across companies with a need for "bright young people," particularly people with strong strategic thinking skills and, in many cases, particularly women, too. He would, he said, be pleased to recommend me to these companies.

At the end of our dance and with a warm smile, he gave me his business card and told me to let him know when I was ready to hear about opportunities in the world of "real work." I did the evening gown equivalent of pocketing the card, thanked him very sincerely, and let him hand me back over to Tyler in something of a daze.

"You look stunned," Tyler said. "What did he say to you?"

"He told me if I ever wanted to move from investment banking into a real business position, he'd be pleased to recommend me to companies he knew that could use someone like me," I reported, thrilled. "Can you believe it?"

"Sure," said Tyler, as if this sort of thing happened to him every day (which, as a matter of fact, it probably did). "He's always talking about how smart you are and how 'strategically sound,' I believe is the expression he used. You should take him up on it, Jane. He wouldn't say it if he didn't mean it."

"Can you even imagine?" I exclaimed. "Well, of course you can, but wow! That would be a hell of a recommendation for me to have going into some company, wouldn't it?"

Tyler grinned wickedly at me and said, "You've just got white boy breaks coming out of your ears lately, don't you?"

I laughed and happily agreed.

❖ ❖ ❖

A COUPLE WEEKS LATER, I met with Charlie for one of our regular conversations. He had been traveling, so I hadn't had a chance to tell him I'd seen his parents. I also wanted to talk to him from a career planning standpoint about moving to a company in a line business role—something I'd been thinking a lot about ever since the thrilling offer from Tyler's dad.

I'd grown used to kicking ideas around with Charlie. It was useful as well as enjoyable—his perspective was different from mine and had always proved valuable. I also knew he would keep the info confidential. But I kept going back and forth on whether it was advisable to bring up this particular topic with him.

Charlie was committed to the Firm for the long haul; he planned to run it someday. He knew my ultimate goal was to be a senior executive at a company, but I doubted he thought I would leave the Firm any time soon. Would it presume too much on our friendship to ask him to help me think about my own interests if it meant putting the Firm's interests aside?

When I arrived in his office, I still hadn't decided what I wanted to do. I figured we could talk about his parents and whatever was on his mind for a while, then I'd see how I felt.

As part of one of those office reshuffles that status-conscious outfits like the Firm indulged in annually, Charlie had recently moved to a bigger office. The frequent moves were disruptive and wasteful, even with the secretaries doing most of the heavy lifting, but no one (with any knowledge of how to play the game) wanted to turn down the explicit bump up in rank evidenced by those few extra square feet.

Charlie's new office had a whole guest area instead of the standard two guest chairs in front of his desk. His new chairs were also a few steps above standard—meaning they were comfortable—and there was a low table between them. I knew Charlie would be in heaven over the new and improved possibilities for putting his feet up and sitting comfortably.

During our mentoring year, he had initially felt constrained by the program rules to sit on the guest side of his desk when we talked. Apparently, one of the consultants who wrote the rules suffered from the bizarre delusion that putting a desk between people made it more difficult to talk honestly—as if office furniture rather than demeanor and personality governed straight talk.

The guest chairs in the office Charlie had that first year were situated so that he couldn't put his feet up on his desk. After watching him shift uncomfortably, start to put them up and realize he couldn't for about the hundredth time, I told him it made no difference to me if he sat behind his desk or in front of it. He gratefully moved to his usual spot and stretched out his legs. I risked joking that maybe now he would be able to concentrate on what we were talking about. He laughed. That turned out to be one of our breakthrough early meetings, in terms of feeling comfortable with each other.

I had seen Charlie's new office, of course—everyone checked these things out as soon as the moving signs went up; how else would we know who was on the way up and who wasn't?—but not yet with him in it. When I walked in, he was lounging in one of the comfortable chairs, feet up, leafing through some papers.

"Nice digs," I said admiringly.

He looked up, smiled and waved me into the other chair. "Sweet, aren't they? Too bad I've been traveling pretty much ever since I moved. Hang on a sec—I want to give this to Pam."

He got up and strode out of his office. After a few words to his secretary, he returned, stopping first at his desk to put down some papers and pick up his letter opener. Carved into a graceful curve from a single piece of auburn-colored wood and polished to gleaming smoothness, the letter opener was beautiful. It called to me, too—I was often tempted to touch it. Charlie played absently with it all the time; he did so then as he sat back down and said, "How have you been?"

"Fine, thanks." I looked up from the letter opener and smiled at him. "I've been wanting to tell you that I saw your parents at an event a couple weeks ago."

"You did?"

"Yeah. It was one of Tyler's family's things—a total 'see and be seen' event. Movie stars and everything." I laughed. "I spotted your father across a room with, like, seven hundred people in it. That height is handy, isn't it?"

Charlie gestured to his feet, which were back on the coffee table. "Except for all the places I can't get comfortable in as a result."

"I knew you'd be in heaven over the new leg-stretching possibilities in here," I teased him. "Anyway, I really enjoyed meeting your mother. We only talked briefly, but she was very impressive. It's obvious why you have no problem with smart, direct women."

Charlie laughed. "She wouldn't have allowed a problem like that. She's a radical feminist with very strong opinions and she can out-argue everyone I've ever seen her argue with. She leaves me in the dust routinely. Also, I have two sisters a lot like her. I wouldn't have lasted long if I'd shown any sexist leanings."

"I can't tell you how much I envy that," I said, feeling wistful. "It must have been so empowering for your sisters."

"They're certainly powerful," he said, grinning. "So what else is up? What have you been working on?"

I told him I was working on another auction sale, but with a potential buyer this time. We debated the most effective approach for getting the information the Firm's client needed from the seller in order to make the winning bid. We got a little heated, but, as usual, disagreeing heatedly with each other produced no discomfort or resentment.

Recognizing that, I decided to tell him what was on my mind. I got up and walked the short distance to the window, then turned to face him. "So, Charlie," I began. "I have a career planning topic I'd like your thoughts on."

"Shoot."

"You remember, I assume, that my ultimate plan is to move from the Firm to a company in a line position from which I can move up in the corporate hierarchy?"

"Yes," he said, drawing out the word. I could see his focus sharpen.

"Don't get alarmed," I reassured him. "I'm not here to tell you I'm leaving tomorrow. I did have an interesting conversation, though, and so I've been thinking about how to accomplish a move like that in an optimal way."

"Tell me about the interesting conversation," he suggested.

"It was actually at the same event where I saw your parents," I said, trying to gauge the tenor of his reaction. He seemed very even—interested, but unconcerned. "Tyler's father asked me if I ever considered leaving investment banking and moving into what he called 'real business.' I told him that was my goal when the timing was right. He said he frequently comes across companies looking for bright, strategic thinkers and he'd be pleased to recommend me if I was interested."

Charlie whistled. "Nice connection!" he said.

"I know! I was thrilled. How great would it be to get into a company thanks to a recommendation from someone like him?"

"It would be terrific. Congratulations, Jane! He can't have been an easy person to impress."

"Thank you," I said, touched. "What a nice thing to say!" I walked back to my chair and sat down. "So will you help me think about next steps and timing and what the right kind of job would be?"

"Of course I will." Charlie looked surprised. "Why wouldn't I?"

"Well, I know you're committed to staying at the Firm, and I thought it might put you in an awkward position to coach me about leaving. You know, it sort of requires you to put the Firm's interests aside."

He shook his head. "Not really. It would be great if you decided to stay here and help me run the joint someday"—he smiled as he said this—"but you can help serve the Firm's interests whether you stay or go. And if you really want to run a company, you do need to move into a line P&L job and follow that track. Once you do, you can help the Firm by becoming a client and also by reflecting well on us."

"Fair enough. I appreciate you thinking about it that way. I wasn't sure I should bring this up with you."

"Trust does not come easily to you, does it?" he remarked, his eyebrows raised.

"It's not that," I started to object, but realized it was that. "I just didn't want to presume on our friendship. I'm sorry. I didn't mean to imply that I don't trust you. I do."

"Good," he said, closing the subject. "Seems to me the issue is *when* you should move. Ideally, you'd move into a position that's clearly on the leadership track—you know, one where you're already distinguished from the pack instead of vying with a crowd for a position like that. Do you see what I mean? That would be a better platform for moving up. Surer."

"I do see what you mean and I agree. It can't be too senior, though, or I wouldn't qualify for it without previous P&L-type experience."

"Right. You also don't want to look unfocused or uncommitted, so leaving here too soon wouldn't be good. I think the three-and-a-half years you have now are probably a minimum; four or five would be better. After that long, it should be clear to anyone that your experience here was real and also that you can stick with something."

"Good point," I agreed again, nodding. "So I should figure out what kinds of companies I'm interested in, then look at their job hierarchies to see what age people have the level of job I'd want."

"Yeah, and also what kind of experience those people have," Charlie said. He put his feet back on the floor and sat up straight. "Some companies would probably consider investment banking experience comparable to what they typically see; others probably wouldn't. It probably varies from job to job, too, even at the same company." He grinned. "Your buddy Alex would be a good person to talk to for the corporate perspective."

"He would be a *great* person to talk to!" I said. "Would it be appropriate for me to ask him for advice on this? Obviously, I'd do my research and be prepared with specific questions first."

"Yeah, sure." Charlie nodded. "He thinks highly of you, and he looks for opportunities to help women and minorities succeed. I'm sure he'd be glad to talk with you."

"That would be fantastic! It would be incredibly helpful to have his insight on what level and kind of job would be the right one and what experience I'd need to qualify for it." I smiled. "It's just one white boy break after another for me lately, isn't it?"

"Evidently." Charlie smiled as he pointed the letter opener at me. "Do you plan to knock that indignant chip off your shoulder any time soon?"

"Doubtful. Constant vigilance still seems advisable," I said, grinning. "This is really good, though. I'm excited! I'll do some research, develop some questions, talk to your father, and then do a game plan for the next twelve to eighteen months."

I had another thought. "I suppose, depending on what kind of companies I'm targeting, I could try to work on deals in related businesses here, too."

"Good idea. Keep me in the loop and I'll let you know what I see."

"Of course I'll keep you in the loop," I said, surprised. I studied his face, again trying to gauge what he was thinking. "If you're sure it's OK, I'd also like to pull together what I find out and what I think I should be asking, then go over it with you before I talk to your father or anyone else. I'd really appreciate your help and your perspective."

"Sure," Charlie said, apparently unperturbed. "I'm happy to help." He grinned again. "Try to target companies that have a lot of M&A work, OK?"

"Absolutely," I promised.

❖ ❖ ❖

Charlie

Right after the first of the year, I got together with Jeff, a college friend who'd spent the eight years since college steadily moving up at a Fortune 500 company. He'd started as a lowly trainee, become an account executive after a couple years, then moved onto the business management track. He was at the time Chief Operating Officer of one of the company's smaller business units.

Since college, Jeff and I had been getting together three or four times a year, usually for drinks or dinner. We were also both part of a loose, extended group that played softball in the summers, so we saw each other at games on the (increasingly rare) occasions when both of us showed up to play. Jeff had gotten married a couple years before; his wife wasn't a softball fan, so he hadn't been to more than a few games during the last two summers.

"So what's up?" I asked him after we settled into a booth with a couple bottles of beer.

"I've decided to be a teacher," he announced, grinning broadly. "Starting next fall, I'll be teaching junior high math here in the city."

"No kidding! That's new!" I was astonished. I put down my bottle and stared at him. "How come?"

"I've always kind of thought I'd like to teach, but coming out of college, that was not appealing—just more school and shitty money to boot, right? The corporate job, particularly the salary, looked a lot more attractive. And, for a while, it was."

Jeff took a sip, then said, "About a year ago, though, I found myself wondering what the point was. Nothing seemed to make much of a difference one way or the other. After listening to me complain for months, Susie finally told me to find a new job or shut the hell up. So I looked into teaching, found I could get a job in the city schools—they're desperate for teachers—and went for it."

"I thought you liked your job," I said. "What changed?"

"You know, Charlie," he replied, leaning back with his bottle in hand, "my job, the company, the people—it all got so fucking boring. Every meeting I went to seemed like a repeat of something that had already happened. I felt like I knew what people were going to say before they even started talking. No one ever had or seemed to want any original ideas. Everything just seemed the same—and mind-numbingly dull."

He grimaced. "Being bored was bad, really bad, but I was making a ton of money and I could do the job pretty much in my sleep, so for a while I figured what the fuck, why not stick around and collect the dough? But I started really hating it last year. I couldn't imagine doing it for thirty more years. Scared me even to think about sticking around that long."

"Yeah, I can see that." I nodded. "Thirty years of the same of anything sounds bad."

"It wasn't just that," Jeff said. "The whole thing started to seem so *pointless*. All these people running around, covering their asses, pretending they give a shit about the company's customers or employees or anything at all except getting more power and hanging on to it. It was basically impossible to get much of anything done what with all the politics and self-serving bullshit."

He looked disgusted as well as bewildered as he said, "And it didn't really seem to be about getting anything done either. I finally just couldn't stand all the lying."

"What do you mean—what lying?" I frowned as I leaned against the cushioned back of the booth and straightened my legs under the table.

"You must have this at your shop, too," Jeff said. "People get this idea of how they think things should be and they start ignoring how things are. Their idea is usually self-serving, but they act like it's the truth and just ignore or deny anything that doesn't fit. Then the idea somehow *becomes* the truth for corporate purposes and the real truth becomes politically incorrect. The fiction only works if everyone buys in, right?"

I must have looked confused because he explained, "You know, some asshole gets promoted and suddenly he's a great guy. Or somebody comes up with a new product idea and it's obviously based on a pile of bullshit assumptions about markets or buyer behavior or whatever, but the somebody is too important to offend, so everybody acts like the product is the best thing since sliced bread and the company pours money into it. Or the opposite—some business line that got introduced last year with a ton of fanfare as if it *was* the best thing since sliced bread runs into static this year. Suddenly, everyone always knew it was snake-bit and people are distancing themselves from it as fast as they can.

"It's like there's an elephant that no one's acknowledging in every room. Practically everything I heard was spun, if not totally fabricated. And there was no percentage in trying to cut through the crap. When everyone around you is pretending red is green, you become the problem if you insist on calling it red. I felt like I was drowning in bullshit—and for what?"

Jeff paused, then demanded, "Do I sound nuts?"

"No," I told him, signaling the bartender for another round. "You sound like you'd had it—and like you were in a bad situation. Did you consider a different job or a different company?"

"Briefly," he said, leaning forward. "But my problem wasn't job-specific or company-specific. I just couldn't get excited about any of the products or value propositions. Even streamlining operations, which I used to find worth the effort—rewarding even—started to seem pointless. I got so sick of people's resistance to change, their unwillingness to try anything new even when what they were doing wasn't working. I was just totally burned out."

"What do you think changed—you or the company?" I asked.

"I've wondered about that myself," he said, frowning. He absently peeled the label off his empty bottle. "It all seemed more valid when I started, you know? The company's mission statement and long-term goals seemed meaningful, even inspiring, instead of like so much baloney to print on mouse pads. Back then, people also seemed more interested in accomplishing something worthwhile—and not so obsessed just with getting ahead at any cost."

He shook his head as the bartender put two fresh bottles on the table. "Maybe it really was better and it all changed. Maybe it was always this bullshit game and I just didn't see it clearly until recently. Or, I guess, maybe it's fine and it's just not for me any more."

"It doesn't seem likely that the game or the people changed all that much," I said, thinking aloud. "Although as people move up the ladder, they do seem to get less interested in taking risks and more intent on preserving the status quo. I've noticed that, too. I don't think it's inevitable, but it seems to be fairly common."

"Your dad isn't like that," Jeff said. He had done an internship at my father's company one summer during college.

"No, he's not, but the more people at his level I meet and work with, the more I realize how unusual he is. He doesn't mind rocking the boat. He doesn't make unnecessary enemies, but, unlike a lot of guys in positions like his, he doesn't think pleasing other people is the top priority. He believes doing the right thing is an absolute, not a luxury to be put off when it's not obviously expedient. And he expects other people to get with the program."

"That's incredibly rare. Jaded, cynical and self-serving are the prevailing attitudes."

"Come on, Jeff," I challenged. "Aren't you being too hard on people? The game is the game. Having power is the only way to get things done. At least some of your people must have good intentions, good motives."

"So you think the ends justify the means?" he demanded. "No matter how slimy the means?"

"No, I don't think that. I'm just saying the people around you may care more than you think for getting the job done and about right and wrong, despite how slimy or misguided their methods look to you."

"Maybe. They're pretty indirect about it, if that's true." He drank some beer, then acknowledged, "You could be right. I tend to assume people think objectively about things, then make decisions about how to act, but lately I'm not so sure about that. A lot of people seem to do what they think the environment demands without thinking about it at all. I guess they're assuming you have to play the game even when it's slimy— or, for that matter, even when it's obviously wrong."

"Or they don't see what they're doing as slimy or wrong," I suggested. "If the environment seems to demand it, they might figure it's right and be doing it for that reason."

"But to what end?" he asked combatively. Then, with a "hey, what can you do?" shrug, he leaned back and said, "Anyway, that's why I had to get out. Who wants to work with a bunch of robots who evidently don't think for themselves at a company producing products you can't get excited about and in an environment where right and wrong have expedient or bendable meanings? Once I stopped getting off on the power and the money, the pointlessness and the bullshit drove me nuts."

"Well, there's nothing meaningless or pointless about teaching disadvantaged kids," I said, grinning. "Even if it doesn't offer much in the way of power or money to get excited about."

Jeff laughed. "Yeah, that's for sure," he said. "But I've felt great ever since I made the decision. I'm doing a teacher training program this summer, then starting at a school in the fall. I'm still working at the company in the meantime—told my boss I'd stay on until we hired my replacement and got him up to speed. You can bet I'm saving most of what I make these last few months."

He smiled. "Susie's still got her job, and we have a decent amount socked away, but, you're right, the cut in pay is huge. At first, I didn't see how I could give up the corporate salary, but then we started thinking about what we really need. I realized we could live pretty well on a lot less money—and that it would be a good trade-off, money for satisfaction."

"That's a smart way to look at it. Money's great, obviously, but not if what you're doing to earn it is making you miserable." I meant this, but I did wonder how he'd manage on a tenth, if that, of what he'd been earning before. "Living on a teacher's salary, though—that's going to be different."

"It'll be harder, but I've earned a lot in the last few years and we haven't been buying yachts or anything. Also, Susie and I really aren't big spenders. A lot of what we've spent above and beyond the basics was actually related to my job—clothes, cars, vacations, all that shit you think you need to keep up with everyone else. Or, as Susie says, to console yourself for feeling crummy because you hate your job."

"Sounds like she's happy about this, too," I said, smiling.

"She's been great," Jeff said. "For one thing, I'm no longer driving her crazy by complaining all the time. But, also, she figures it's more important for me to be happy about what I do than for us to accumulate more possessions. And she's glad to be done with the corporate wife thing, which she never liked. Although"—he rolled his eyes—"she's got lots of ideas about how to use all the free time I'll have."

"That's ominous," I commiserated. After drinking the last of my beer, I grinned and said, "Well, congratulations! I can't believe you're really heading back to junior high, but it sounds great for you."

He laughed. "Yeah, I know, but I'm confident that I'm going to prefer twelve-year-old kids to the corporate bozos I've been playing among for the last eight years. And not just because I'll be doing them some good, either."

❖ ❖ ❖

JANE CALLED late one afternoon in February to see if I had time to talk about what she characterized as a very exciting development. We agreed to meet at 6:00 and she burst into my office right on time.

"Are you ready for me?" she asked.

"Yeah, sit down. Just let me finish this." I made some corrections on the last of the slides I'd been reviewing, then got up and walked around my desk toward her. She was sitting on the edge of one of my guest chairs. I sat in the other, smiled at her and said, "You look like you might explode. What's up?"

"Wait until you hear this!" she said excitedly, grinning from ear to ear. "Tyler's father—who, by the way, I'm now at his insistence calling Walker, which is not easy—called me today to give us—the Firm, that is—an opportunity to pitch one of his banking clients.

"It's a smallish commercial finance company, and the CEO realizes he needs to make some strategic decisions about its future. The company's size and its cost of funds make it a relatively weak competitor, given the consolidation in that industry. To survive, it will have to grow fast, presumably via acquisitions, or get itself acquired by someone.

"Walker—God, just saying that makes me feel pretentious!—told the CEO that he needed an investment banker and recommended that he interview three or four firms, including us. Then he called me to tell me I'd be hearing from the CEO to set up a meeting to 'strut our stuff.'"

Jane paused to take a breath, which, as far as I could tell, she hadn't done since she started talking. I took the opportunity to say, "That's fantastic, Jane! Congratulations—and way to go! Recommending someone to your clients isn't something anyone does lightly—too much downside potential. You've really impressed a hell of a big shot."

"I know! It's amazing, isn't it? Tyler's dad knows plenty of old guys here, but he said he wanted to give this chance to me because he thought his client would respond well to me. Apparently, he's smart, but not all that sophisticated, and Walker thought he might be intimidated or put off by someone very senior. Walker also said careers get built on client development opportunities and he wanted me to have this one!"

She beamed. "Once I finished peeling myself off the ceiling, I decided I'd like our team to include Lynn, who's done a lot of work with financial services companies, and of course I want you to be the senior person."

Finally sitting back in her chair, Jane rested her hands, which had been flying around, smiled with satisfaction, and said, "Interested?"

"Absolutely!" I said, matching her smile. "Sounds great! When do you expect to hear from the CEO?"

"Sometime in the next week, then the pitch will probably be scheduled within a week or two after that. I've already pulled some info—there isn't much; the company is privately held. I'm planning to read it tonight and think about how to sound intelligent when he calls. Once I hear from him, I'll put together the info I have and whatever he provides and get it to you and Lynn, then we can meet and decide how to handle the pitch."

"Did you also pull what we have on other commercial finance companies?" I asked.

"Yeah, I ordered a couple recent presentation books and asked the library to find me SEC filings for the public competitors and also articles, if there are any, on issues facing the industry. And Lynn had some good stuff from deals she's done."

"Great. The last financial services deal I did was a while ago, so send me copies of anything that will help me get back up to speed, OK?"

"Sure," Jane said, nodding. "I'll get a file to you tomorrow. I'd really like to pitch this in a way that makes it clear we're interested in solving his problem—not just selling what we have. Whenever I've sat in on a pitch, it's always seemed like the clients lose interest when we start going on about what the Firm can do instead of talking about their needs."

She leaned forward again. "From what Walker said, it wasn't clear whether this CEO would prefer to be acquired or to stay independent and grow. It also wasn't clear whether he has the skills or the team to do the latter. There's going to be a real strategic decision for him to make—and we'll have to really understand the company, the industry, and the available options to give him the advice and recommendations that will help him make it. I'd love to get a head start on conceptualizing all that. Do you have time to kick it around for a while tonight?"

"Yeah, sure," I said after a glance at my watch. "It's a little premature since we don't know much about the company yet, but we can certainly kick around the likely options." I put my feet up, further loosened my tie and unbuttoned the top button of my shirt. "The issues are high cost of funds and small size of the company, right? Is the size issue separate from the cost of funds issue? If so, what's it about—volume, sales coverage, market penetration, asset diversification?"

Jane and I brainstormed for an hour or so. We came up with more questions than answers, but identifying the right questions was a good start and would help us review the background info more effectively. I had no doubt that Jane would do a great job on the call with the CEO, and told her so.

"Thanks," she said, looking delighted again. "This is just so cool! I love thinking about doing this for a client of my own. Not that I don't do the best job I can for all our clients, but this feels different."

"I know what you mean," I said, smiling. "There's something about the client being yours that heightens the experience, makes it more personal. I'll warn you, though—it also makes you feel more accountable for how it all works out, even for things you have no control over. You'll feel even more responsible for slip-ups and problems."

"It's hard to imagine feeling *more* responsible than I already do," she sighed. "You'll tell me if I start overdoing it, right?"

"You bet. Thanks for bringing me in on this, Jane—I appreciate it."

"Please." She waved her hand. "You're obviously a good choice for it and you're one of my favorite people to work with." She grinned slyly and added, "Also, I owe you at least one white boy break, even though I know you can easily get those on your own."

"Thanks again," I said, with a laugh. "Be sure you tell Jim about this opportunity and where it came from. He may still be around tonight—if not, catch him as soon as you can. He should know what a big shot you're becoming. Tell him how you've decided to staff it, too. He'll be fine with Lynn and me, but make sure he feels in the loop."

"Will do," Jane said as she stood to go. "Me, a big shot—I like the sound of that!"

❖ ❖ ❖

AFTER TALKING a few days later to John, the CEO of the commercial finance company, Jane had a much better idea of the strategic and survival issues his company faced. Late one afternoon, she, Lynn and I met to plan and prepare for the pitch, which Jane had scheduled for the following week.

I was away most of the afternoon. When I returned a little before the meeting time, I was amused to find that Jane had arranged with my secretary for the planning meeting to be in my office. There were information folders and bottles of water for Jane, Lynn and me on my coffee table.

I took my usual chair and started leafing through the folder in front of it. When Jane and Lynn came in, I looked up, smiling, and said to Jane, "I see you've co-opted my office. Are you planning to take it over altogether if we bring in this client?"

"No, you can keep it," she said, laughing, as she and Lynn sat down. "I haven't co-opted it for today either. I just knew you wouldn't be able to concentrate if we met in my tiny office or in some conference room where you couldn't put your feet up." Turning to Lynn, she explained, "It's a height thing, not a status thing."

"I understand completely," Lynn said, nodding. "I have a similar issue with pantyhose. I've often wondered if they were actually invented for the precise purpose of making women stupid. By about 5:30 in the evening, it's difficult to concentrate on anything but getting them off."

Jane rolled her eyes. "Don't embarrass him, Lynn," she chided.

"It's OK, I can take it." I laughed. "I've worked with Lynn enough to be immune to that strategy."

"I think I better exert some control over this meeting," Jane said cheerfully. She recapped her conversation with John, and described what she had included in the folders.

"Here's the thing," she then said. "I think everyone he interviews will talk about the pros and cons of two options—embarking on a growth-by-acquisition program and seeking an advantageous acquirer for the company. Obviously, we have to cover those, too, but it occurs to me that there's a third option—or, really, sort of an offshoot—that might end up making the most sense.

"From what John and Walker told me about the company, it's clear that a big part of the problem is lack of infrastructure—technological and human. Because it costs a lot to set up the right infrastructure and it costs even more to maintain it over time, the company has limited its volume. That in turn limits market penetration, diversification of assets, and growth.

117

"It's also part of why the company can't reduce its cost of funds. And because *that* cost is so high, the company can't afford to build infrastructure without cutting too deeply into its profit margins and having to either charge borrowers more, which would make it uncompetitive, or earn less, which is—ultimately—a survival issue.

"But the company does have the credit evaluation, portfolio management, and workout expertise to support more volume and more kinds of loans. What it lacks isn't the specialized skills, it's the workhorse stuff—the systems and the people necessary to process and monitor more assets and more asset diversity. So I'm thinking—what if, instead of building and having to manage the infrastructure, the company contracted with someone who already has it?"

Jane picked up, but didn't open, her bottle of water as she asked, "Couldn't we suggest a strategic outsourcing or partnering type program *to go along with* a strategic acquisition program? Wouldn't the combination of both programs increase and accelerate the benefits of the acquisition program—and, at the same time, also do a lot of other beneficial things for the company that an acquisition program alone wouldn't?"

"That's a very cool idea!" Lynn said, leaning back and putting her feet on the edge of the coffee table. "It might also make it more feasible financially for the company to stay independent instead of being acquired, if that's what it would prefer. Outsourcing can be very chancy, though. Companies seem to be leery of it, maybe because it's so often a disaster for them."

"I don't think that's inevitable," I said. "In my experience, when there's a problem, it's because the companies approach it wrong. They aren't careful to figure out exactly what they need, so they pick the wrong vendor. They also frequently try to micromanage the outsourced functions instead of specifying deliverables upfront and then getting the hell out of the way."

"So," Jane said after she swallowed a mouthful of water, "if we helped the company figure out exactly what it needs and which vendors have the ability to get the job done, and then structured a contract with the right vendor, the company would be positioned to support more volume and more kinds of loans, but would be bearing only the contractual expenses of the outsourcing instead of all the expenses of building and maintaining the actual infrastructure. That would have to amount to both less money and less distraction of management time, don't you think?"

"Yeah, definitely," I agreed. I walked over to my desk and leaned against it. "Also, the infrastructure would likely be better than if the company built and managed it directly, even assuming it could afford to do that. The company's expertise is commercial finance, not infrastructure management. In fact, there might be other functions they should also be outsourcing to reduce costs and distractions. That could improve the bottom line significantly."

"And," Lynn added, "in addition to getting rid of functions they shouldn't be handling in-house and contracting for infrastructure now, somewhere down the road they might want to vertically integrate by acquiring the infrastructure vendor, as a business and income diversification play, if that looked profitable. Depending on the vendor, we could even consider structuring a favorable purchase option into the outsourcing contract."

"This *is* a cool idea, Jane!" I said, smiling at her. "It's got a lot of potential strategic benefits. And I agree that a combination acquisition and outsourcing program would likely be financially better than an acquisition program alone. The additional costs of the outsourcing component should be offset by increased loan volume and earlier financial results. Let's make some assumptions and run numbers both ways to see where the breakeven and benefit points are."

"I'm so glad you both agree!" Jane said. "I think we can ace the pitch if we go in with a compelling presentation on the two options everyone will cover *and* a compelling alternative that's innovative and unexpected. Even if the company doesn't go for the alternative, I'm betting they'll respond well to our ability to think differently."

"And if they do go for it," Lynn said, grinning, "we'll have even more projects to do for them!"

We discussed the idea for a while longer. I outlined the assumptions I thought we should use to run numbers for both the acquisition program and the outsourcing/acquisition alternative; Lynn said she'd pull the models together. We also spent some time talking about how to present the two obvious options and how much work to do at this preliminary stage on identifying and evaluating potential buyers for the company.

Jane looked very pleased as she offered to rough out our script for the pitch and think about who should cover which aspects.

❖　❖　❖

THE PITCH went beautifully.

Walker's assessment of the CEO was right on target. John was smart and, I thought, on the ball, too, but he would have been put off by what Jane had called the "smoothness and high-society demeanor" of the Firm's customary pitch people. John was informal, unpretentious and very bottom-line oriented. He had his male CFO and female General Counsel with him when we met, and they were similarly informal and business-focused.

Lynn mentioned after the meeting that the General Counsel noted while saying goodbye that Jane and Lynn were the first women she and her colleagues had met in the process of interviewing investment banking firms. I smiled to myself as I recognized how savvy it was of Walker to have given this break to Jane. By calling her, he had done a favor for both her *and* the Firm.

He must have known that it would pleasantly surprise John and his people to be pitched to by a woman even if he hadn't guessed that Jane's team would include another woman as well as the more "usual" white male. I was sure Walker was sincere in wanting to help Jane succeed, but by giving the opportunity to her, he had simultaneously made it more likely that the Firm would win the beauty contest. Using the client opportunity to try to kill two birds with one stone was clearly an example of the shrewdness he was known for.

Jane did a great job presenting the three of us as a team. After characterizing herself as the team and relationship manager, she described my role as the senior position—there to provide experience, oversight and the clout to assure that the Firm's resources would be available to the company as and when needed. She presented Lynn as an expert day-to-day deal manager with significant financial services industry experience. The script we had developed gave us all the opportunity to demonstrate our suitability for these roles. Because the meeting proved to be interactive and informal, we also had plenty of opportunity to show off our communication and other skills—and our personalities, too.

As she had during the meetings for my father's deal, Jane let her strategic savvy speak for itself. It became clear that she would provide sophisticated strategic thinking as well as attentive management of the team and the Firm's work for the company. I wasn't sure quite how she achieved this without undermining my senior role, but she did. I didn't feel undercut or like a token during the pitch, despite the obvious leadership role Jane took.

This intrigued me and, to be honest, surprised me a little. I had never before been in the position of being the senior person, but not the team leader and principal client contact. I'd wondered if it would be difficult or awkward to split those roles between two people, even two people who worked together as well as Jane and I did. But it wasn't at all difficult or awkward, and it reflected very well on the Firm. It was evident to John and his people that Jane, Lynn and I understood collegiality and would work effectively as a team.

As far as I could tell, it never occurred to Jane that her leadership role relative to this prospect could be seen as conflicting with my more senior position at the Firm. She recognized the need for both roles on the team. And while she willingly took on the leadership opportunity she'd been given, she knew she didn't have enough experience or power to handle the senior role. Accordingly, she not only included me on the team, she also left me plenty of room to do my job well. As she would probably have said, there was no "testosterone thing" going on.

Jane was able (and determined) to see relationships for what they were instead of what they were typically assumed to be or what they might be in the worst possible construction. And she didn't feel obliged to follow conventional paths, such as, in this case, assigning both the senior and the leadership roles to the same person or splitting the roles between two people and then engaging in a battle for power.

I realized that her objective, behavior-based take on relationships was also why our mentoring relationship had been so collegial and our friendship was so comfortable, even though both existed in the context of a junior/senior working relationship. Jane insisted on being seen and treated as the capable, talented person she was. As a going-in proposition, however, she was sure people were disinclined to see or treat her equitably. She approached people and relationships with a great deal of apprehension and skepticism—and no trust at all.

Paradoxically, this prickliness and distrust seemed to be what made her objectivity possible. It surprised her when people saw her for what she was and treated her fairly, but when it happened, she recognized it and offered the same courtesy and respect in return. Jane didn't look for ulterior motives in those of us she had come to trust based on our behavior toward her.

We left the pitch meeting feeling very positive about our chances of getting the client. Our optimism turned out to be justified. John called Jane a week later to tell her he wanted to retain the Firm.

As we had hoped, John and his people were interested in exploring the outsourcing/acquisition alternative. In a series of meetings with his team over the next few weeks, we developed a solid and impressive plan, complete with goals, strategies, tactics, timetable and responsibilities. It was extremely stimulating work and we and John's team had a strong sense of purpose, given that the survival of the company was on the line.

It was also a great working group. Because John and his people were straightforward and smart, we were able to work at a fast clip and in real time. Meetings were short and to-the-point, without the usual needless repetition and posturing. Post-meeting memos and recaps were limited to what was actually useful—as opposed to what was often deemed necessary to show the client how much work we were doing.

During meetings, everyone spoke spontaneously, floated ideas, thought aloud and articulated apprehensions and concerns, all without worrying about (or actually creating) tension or any other problem among the group. I wasn't sure exactly why this was—some combination, I guessed, of the open and receptive approach John and his people were taking and the personalities on our team.

Jane, Lynn and I talked about this one afternoon on our way back to the Firm. They both agreed that our working group was an exceptionally enjoyable and effective one, and that the people at the company were a big part of the reason for that. Jane felt, though, that even a stuffier group of clients would likely have responded well to the three of us. She suspected the pleasure we took in working with one another was infectious.

Whatever the reasons, it really was a great experience, and we did a great job. About two months after John retained the Firm, we had put in place a strategically sound blueprint that we all felt confident would transform the company into a formidable—and financially solid—competitor.

At that point, I turned to negotiating the business terms for a couple outsourcing contracts and also took charge of the acquisition of a small niche player John had had his eye on for several months. Lynn managed that acquisition and led the search for additional acquisition targets. Jane worked with the company to review the desirability and feasibility of outsourcing additional functions; she also continued to manage the relationship and keep her eye on the big picture.

Since the work for John's company was no longer taking as much of our time, we all picked up or got involved on matters for other clients, too. Lynn mentioned to me one afternoon that she was finding it a letdown to work on "regular work for regular clients." All the other work and working groups, she said, seemed so much less interesting and fun in comparison to her experience working with Jane and me on real survival issues for John, his people, and their company.

I couldn't have agreed with her more.

CHAPTER 8

THE NATURE OF POWER

Jane

I hadn't expected to leave the Firm quite as soon as I did, but circumstances and events conspired otherwise. A few months before the end of my fourth year, the Firm hired a lateral with seven years of experience into the M&A group. In an example of the "new toy" treatment Katherine had described for lateral hires, Ian was lionized and offered every advantage.

One of the advantages he was offered was me as manager on an important deal for a client he'd brought with him to the Firm. I was both flattered and offended to be considered a perk for a lateral hire. Given what I'd heard, I also approached working for him with some trepidation.

Ian arrived at the Firm with a reputation for being very driven, very effective and totally ruthless. There had been some controversy over his hiring. Apparently, his ability to bring in the kind of clients the Firm liked best—those with lots of deal flow—and to keep those clients loyal to him was admirable, even enviable. The same was not said about his working style.

Sure enough, the people who worked with him on his first deals for the Firm did not enjoy the experience. Within a couple months, he already had a reputation for being demanding, inflexible and an asshole to boot.

I took an immediate dislike to him.

Ian had crammed into his too-short frame enough arrogance for someone twice his size, as well as all his bitterness over not having grown taller. He was one of those men who say they're 5'11", but are plainly at least two or three inches shorter. He worked out like a maniac, and he loved to demonstrate his strength. One of his favorite feats (to be fair, a pretty impressive trick) was to conduct conference calls attentively and without sounding the slightest bit winded while he did bicep curls with the gigantic free weights he kept in his office.

I also disliked him for his demeaning attitude toward women—in general and with specific respect to me. He used sexual terminology and told sexual jokes frequently. He referred more than once to getting laid (with an eye on me to see how I reacted). Either oblivious to or unmoved by my attempts to discourage him, he constantly opened doors or held chairs for me while saying "My dear" in a mocking tone. He always introduced me as his "beautiful and brilliant colleague," also in an ironic tone.

And he touched me way too much. He stopped short of anything I could realistically complain about at a place like the Firm, but I always felt crowded and *pushed* by his physical presence. He stood too close. When we walked together, he placed his hand on the small of my back or looped his arm casually across my shoulders. He bent over the back of my chair so as to encircle me, his left hand resting on my shoulder, his right pointing to something in the document we were working on. He grasped more of my arm than was necessary when he (altogether unnecessarily) assisted me out of a taxi—and he held on for too long.

Aggravating as all that was, Ian was not difficult to work with where the actual work was concerned. He was a demanding delegator, but also an excellent and generous one. And he was truly effective with clients. I learned quite a bit watching him steer his clients through choppy waters to the desirable landing he had in mind for them.

I'd worked with assholes and sexist jerks before. I deplored and resented the position they put me in—and the extra effort they required—but they were part of the job. I figured Ian would simply be one more to add to my already lengthy list. As it turned out, though, he was the reason I left the Firm a few months after the end of my fourth year.

❖ ❖ ❖

AFTER MY TALKS with Tyler's father and Charlie about moving from the Firm to a corporate position, I had done quite a bit of research. It looked like the smartest move would be into a brand manager position at a conglomerate of some sort, preferably a company with a diversified mix of consumer products. For the companies I researched, brand management was the high visibility track and the one that many of the senior executives had taken to reach their top positions.

Brand management is essentially running a business. Brand managers head teams responsible for delineating and implementing strategies and tactics for continuing the success of their brands. They run the P&L, develop new product ideas and advertising concepts, and coordinate supporting business systems. To excel, a brand manager must be a leader able to aim high—to establish bold goals and then to achieve them via teamwork and team management. Brand management requires and further develops marketing, business, financial, general management, and leadership skills—all the prerequisites for senior executive positions.

As I thought about what kinds of industries to target, I was inclined against the ones traditionally associated with women. I disapproved of the sexist way products such as apparel, cosmetics, cleaning and household products, and the like were typically advertised. In some cases, the products themselves seemed inherently demeaning to women, too, in that they implied that we had limited intelligence or needed enhancement in order to be presentable or some other degrading thing.

Charlie and I argued about this at length. He saw no reason not to take advantage of the relatively higher incidence of women in management positions at these companies and the relative ease of getting hired into the right position at one of them. I found this higher incidence unpersuasive given that, despite it, the companies still had no women in senior executive positions. I doubted these companies were progressive; in fact, I suspected their lack of women at the top might well be evidence of their determination to hold women under the so-called glass ceiling in just those positions I was targeting.

As with other topics we'd argued about over the years, Charlie placed far more stock than I did in the relative importance of talent and performance where promotions were concerned. He thought I could distinguish myself and move up anywhere simply by doing a great job so long as I also figured out the culture and worked to fit in.

I felt pretty confident that most companies—whether apparently progressive or not—were both more likely to view women as tokens in their management ranks and less than wholeheartedly committed to promoting on the basis of merit (even assuming they could actually recognize merit in an atypical package). Accordingly, I wanted to have the benefit of being a scarce resource.

This was not as sexist or queen bee-ish as it seemed (or as Charlie accused me of being). I had no desire to be a queen bee. I deplored those dreadful women I occasionally ran across who had made it to high positions and seemed to think there was some honor and glory in remaining alone there. They didn't try to help other women succeed; instead they reveled in their exclusive status.

Women like these were just as bad as conventional men. By setting themselves apart and making the paths they had taken look narrow and akin to climbing Mount Everest in a blinding snowstorm (without a Sherpa), they did as much, if not more, to mask opportunity and hold other women back than the mediocre men who had nothing but the pressure of the status quo on their side.

The reason I wanted to be one of very few women wasn't that I preferred working—or competing for promotions—with men. And I certainly didn't think companies were right or better if they promoted fewer women into management. On the contrary, I already had plenty of (mostly unpleasant) experience with being one of too few women among masses of men, and I thought companies without women in management were ripe for change.

It was rather that I felt sure the companies with fewer women managers would be under more pressure to promote women. I didn't dispute that it might be harder for me to get a job at a company less familiar with women in its management ranks, but I was betting that, once hired by such a company, I'd be in a much better position to distinguish myself and move up.

Just as I had chosen to accept the Firm's offer of employment without considering (or much caring) whether I would like the work, I now figured there would be plenty of opportunity to change the corporate culture once I made it to the top. The goal at this point was to position myself to *make it* to the top as quickly as possible—not to choose the most comfortable or progressive working environment.

The best bets looked to be in the food, beverage, media, and housewares industries—the larger and more diversified the company, the better. Due to consumers' ongoing need for their products, these companies would likely be around for the long haul. Due to their size, they would more likely be acquirers than acquisition targets.

And due to the large percentage of women in their customer bases, it made sense for the companies in these industries to develop and showcase some women executives. Nevertheless, while they didn't appear to be entirely unfamiliar with the concept of women in middle management, none of these companies had crowds of women already working—and perhaps stuck—in those ranks.

Armed with this conclusion, and prepped by lengthy conversations and debates with Charlie about the research and assumptions that had led me to it, I made appointments to talk with Alex and Walker. They were both amazingly generous with their time and their insights.

Alex told me a great deal about corporate life, particularly the ways in which he thought it differed from the more autonomous, individual-effort-driven investment banking environment. He also asked me a number of questions that tested the validity and strength of my reasons for wanting to move into a corporate setting. Several of these were impossible for me to answer, and I realized I needed to think more about my expectations.

Alex was frank about pros and cons. On the plus side, he spoke glowingly of the thrill of making a positive and long-term impact on a company and the thousands or tens of thousands of people working there. He talked about the many operational and lifestyle benefits of working at a company that generated revenue from selling products rather than (like the Firm) selling the time of its people. These included, among other things, a more consistent focus on merit and results when making spending, hiring and other important decisions. Alex also noted the much greater opportunity to build significant personal net worth.

On the minus side, he described the considerably more ponderous pace of corporate initiatives and projects, compared to the fast pace of a transactional business like the Firm's. He also discussed the dead weight that built up in companies, which, for morale and other reasons, was often allowed to cause problems for years before it was finally dealt with. Sounding very much like Charlie's father, Alex stressed the necessity of being patient and having a long-term definition of success. At the same time, he warned that business success was often its own worst enemy, given the stranglehold it could create on operations and innovation.

We spent a lot of time talking about corporate politics and how I would have to take them into account and use them to shape both my performance and my behavior if I wanted to be effective. In his experience, Alex said, women frequently kept their heads down and counted on excellent work performance to get them to the finish line. He assured me this never worked. Results did not speak for themselves, and *how* one went about accomplishing something and publicizing the accomplishment was every bit as important as the result itself.

As if all his insight and perspective weren't gift enough, Alex also offered to arrange for me to talk with his company's HR director about possible employment. I was very grateful, but I declined this generous offer. Although his presence would have been a big plus at any company, Alex was planning to retire soon and his company wasn't in one of my target industries. Also, I felt skittish about leaving the Firm for one of its clients.

Nor was I ready to leave the Firm at all. When I met with Alex, I had only been working with John and his commercial finance company—my first personal client—for a little over a month. I didn't want to leave that behind me until we had completed the strategic planning and gotten implementation of the outsourcing and acquisition program well underway.

My meeting with Walker was equally useful. We talked about particular companies in the industries I had targeted. Walker's perspective was more external than Alex's had been. As it turned out, quite a few of the companies banked with his family's bank in one way or another. Of course, Walker also knew all of their CEOs and many of their other officers thanks to his position in the business community.

He helped me cull my list considerably. He, too, was very candid; he told me a few of the companies had senior management that would never seriously consider promoting a woman into their ranks. Walker suggested I take those companies off my list unless and until there was a change in senior management. He then prioritized the remaining companies and told me where he could make effective recommendations for me.

My head swimming with all this input—and, I have to admit, somewhat swelled by the willingness and enthusiasm with which these two very prominent big shots gave me their time and their support—I sketched out a plan and a timetable for making my move. That done, it was clear I needed to do more research and more thinking.

It was also clear that I needed a sounding board to help me sift through all the input. Fortunately, Charlie was as good as his word. He always made time to talk with me, despite his constantly busy schedule, and he continued to provide a useful perspective—one that, among other things, consistently questioned my assumptions and made me focus on my goals.

He and I talked and brainstormed and argued over the next few weeks. In the end, I knew I had in place a well-informed game plan for moving into the kind of corporate position that would propel me sooner rather than later into the top ranks of the business world's hierarchy. All I needed to do was execute against the plan—target and do the right work at the Firm for another year or so and then, with Walker's help, pull the trigger on the move.

I was thrilled.

❖ ❖ ❖

IN ONE OF THOSE lucky timing breaks that occasionally occur when you're doing deal work and juggling multiple projects, Ian's deal solidified and headed into the home stretch just as things were heating up for me on implementation of the program we had developed for John's commercial finance company.

Ian's deal was an acquisition for a privately held company, and the target (also privately held) had proved amenable to being acquired. As a result, the terms of the purchase came together smoothly and we reached the documentation stage quickly. At that point, we handed the heavy lifting over to the lawyers and there wasn't much more for us to do.

Ian's clients decided to celebrate by hosting a dinner for the principals from the target company and all the investment bankers. This was premature and it seemed to me to be nothing but an excuse to have two closing dinners. I doubted there was much chance the evening would be anything but wearisome for me, and I was sorely tempted to beg off.

I was once again very busy working with Lynn, Charlie and a few analysts on the projects for John's company. Also, given the working group on Ian's deal, I would be the only woman at the dinner. It was bad enough dealing with Ian's presumptuous sexism and his pushy physical presence in work settings. I had serious misgivings about joining him in a social situation.

After briefly indulging a pleasing little fantasy about skipping the dinner, I bowed to the inevitable. I knew I couldn't realistically do anything but attend. It's part of the game.

The dinner was held in the private room of a very posh restaurant. To my surprise, it wasn't as bad as I'd feared. The food was remarkable and there was less drinking than there normally is at these things, possibly because the wines were so excellent that they demanded appreciative sipping rather than inebriated guzzling. There was even interesting conversation on a variety of topics, none of them uncomfortable for me.

I didn't kid myself that the conversation topics that night were appropriate in deference to me. It was just a lucky fluke. Ian's clients were rather like him—aggressive macho guys, very full of themselves. Ditto with the target company's guys. But they had all gotten used to me over the course of the deal, and they treated me as if I were one of them. My strategy of keeping my gender off the table had worked well, despite Ian's constant attempts to highlight the fact that I was female.

There was one of those natural breaks in conversation right around the time the room was at its foggiest with cigar smoke. It seemed like a good time to make my exit, so, referring to my busy upcoming day, I stood and started shaking hands. A couple people offered "It's early; don't rush off" protests, but they were halfhearted. It occurred to me that the guys might have made plans to head to a strip club as soon as I left.

After a blessedly brief round of thanks and goodbyes, I escaped and went into the little room down the hall where we had hung our raincoats. I don't know how he managed it without making any noise, but Ian appeared behind me just as I was reaching to take my coat off its hanger. He startled me and I whirled around, which was a mistake.

In what seemed like a split second, he seized the tops of my arms, just below my shoulders, pulled me toward him, and kicked closed the door to the little room. Shocked as I was, I did manage to twist my head as he kissed me, causing him to miss my lips. I jerked away—or tried to; his hands were squeezing my arms tightly. "What the hell are you doing?" I demanded.

Still gripping me, he muttered, "I know you want me, too." His mouth was horribly close to mine.

"You're crazy!" I breathed, my voice barely above a whisper, but intense and furious. I continued to struggle to get out of his grasp. He kept coming at me. When he let go of one of my arms to grab the back of my neck, I tried to push him away. He backed me against the wall, his hands pinning my arms, his legs pressing against my legs (making it impossible for me to knee him in the balls, which I dearly wanted to do).

He started talking again. His words seemed to fill the air around me; I heard fragments rather than whole sentences. He hissed something about getting off on the challenge of firing up remote girls—how hot we got, and how grateful. "You'll love fucking me," he murmured in a soft, throaty voice that was somehow even more aggressive than his grip on me. "You're so aloof—I know you have no idea how good it can be."

There was more, but I stopped trying to listen and started figuring out how to get away from him. Ian noticed pretty fast that I was no longer paying attention. He quit talking and started roaming over my body with his hands. I used my freed arms to shove him, hard. "Leave me alone!" I said, my voice low and tense with rage. "I mean it! Or I'll scream. And I'm sure you don't want your clients in on this scene."

He didn't lunge at me again, but he stood his ground, still far too close. With a smug, confrontational smile, he jeered, "You won't scream, Jane. You can't let them all see you as a helpless, uptight *girl*, now can you?"

Luckily, he then backed off, apparently having decided I wasn't worth the effort after all. He sneered at me in a very aggressive, superior, belittling way—as if he'd won. "It's your loss," he said casually, patronizingly. Then, he opened the door and sauntered away. As I watched to be sure he was really leaving, he smoothed his hair.

I looked at my watch. Barely five minutes had passed since I'd left the dining room. No one would even ask Ian where he'd been.

I stood in the coat room trembling, furious, my heart pounding in my ears, and realized that he was absolutely right in assuming he was safe from me. My choices were either to put on my coat and get the hell out or to enact some sort of outraged virgin scene in front of our dinner companions.

I put on my coat and got the hell out.

In the cab home, I started shuddering in earnest. I was frightened, horrified, angry, disgusted, and totally thrown by my own powerlessness. I felt unnerved and demoralized.

Once at home, I took a hot shower and started thinking. Figuring out how to deal with Ian was more than I could handle right away, so I put it aside. Instead, I agonized over the futility of all the excellent work I had done and all the care I had taken to assure that my gender wasn't a distraction at the Firm.

The standing and reputation I had so painstakingly built hadn't protected me from Ian. Nor would they protect me from anyone else inclined to take advantage of me sexually or otherwise by reason of my gender. They were reduced to trivialities when set against predatory intentions, superior strength and a willingness to cross the line.

My standing and reputation also wouldn't protect me from being damaged—fatally damaged—if this incident became known. The consequences of my calling Ian on his loutish and unacceptable behavior wouldn't be great for him, but they would be disastrous for me.

If I made this public, I would be perceived as a victim, a snitch, possibly a tease, a hysteric or even a spurned would-be lover. In the minds of everyone, I would primarily and irrevocably be seen as a *woman*. And, worse, a woman who could be victimized, who had been forced to resort to tattling to punish her aggressor, who should be approached with caution and maybe even distrusted.

It was obvious that I had built nothing, created no foundation of reputation or respect to rely on. I had no power at all. All my work at the Firm had yielded precisely zero in the way of status or personal clout that I could use to overcome the inherent negatives of being a woman in a situation like this.

This made me furious, but I also felt heartbroken and a little panicky and queasy, too. Curled into my most comfortable chair under a cozy blanket, I sat, still shivery, and contemplated my options.

When Alex and I talked about the pros and cons of corporate life, he had spoken of something he called "position power." In a corporate hierarchy, he'd said, managerial positions carried a certain degree of inherent power, irrespective of the person in the job at any particular time. This position power was what made it possible for even the most timid of managers to spur his troops into action. It could also turbo-charge the effectiveness of good managers.

I realized I had no position power at the Firm and I almost certainly never would. In a transactional brokerage business, the players change with every deal. Even the senior people in deal situations enjoy only a pale imitation of position power. Their power is temporary and subject to client whims. It's of a much shakier nature than the power that comes along with being president or another officer of a company.

There were certainly powerful people within the Firm's own hierarchy, but their power extended only to running the Firm—essentially an administrative job—and it was precarious, too. Senior people at the Firm could be undermined or even toppled by anyone with an impressive client base and a willingness to exert his influence. In addition, powerful Firm people had little, if any, sway over how deals or other people were managed on a day-to-day basis. Their position power was minor-league.

Even if I ran the fucking Firm, an eventuality about as probable as pigs flying, I would still not be protected from the downside of being viewed as a woman and a victim in circumstances like the ones I faced now. A leadership position might reduce the likelihood that anyone would try to flaunt his power over me as Ian had. But if someone did, I'd face exactly the same issues—and the downside would be even bigger because I'd have more to lose.

It was obvious that I needed to leave the Firm as soon as possible. I needed to put my skills and energy to work in an environment where they would yield me not just a reputation for excellence, but also a power base comprised of significant position power in addition to all the personal power my talents could muster. I needed a power base that would make me bulletproof vis-à-vis the negatives associated with being a woman at work. That kind of power was the only kind that could protect me in, as well as from, a situation like the one Ian's behavior had created for me.

The heartbroken, sick feeling brimmed up again as I thought about having to leave the Firm because of what Ian had done. I closed my eyes to blink away a couple tears and involuntarily relived a few of the moments in the coatroom. His hands on my body, his breath on my cheek, his words in my ears—it was all horribly real.

I opened my eyes and tucked the blanket more securely around me. I made myself breathe slowly, calmly. I reminded myself that I already had a game plan for moving to a corporate job. All I had to do was speed up the timetable and make the optimal decision on where to go as quickly as possible.

The only significant Firm matter on my plate was the work for John's company. I would concentrate on assuring that John was comfortable with Charlie and Lynn, so when the time came I could extract myself smoothly and without hurting either the client or its relationship with the Firm. This wouldn't be difficult. John and his team already viewed Lynn as the acquisition manager and Charlie as the overall lead on all the specific projects we were handling for the company.

Deciding to leave the Firm as soon as I could, but on my own terms, made me feel better, stronger. So I turned my attention to what to do about Ian. There was no way I was going to let the asshole get away with it. If I couldn't expose him publicly, I'd have to find some other way to sink him.

It occurred to me that while I didn't have the personal power to survive publicly exposing him, I did have a few staunch and powerful supporters at the Firm. Maybe Ian had underestimated my options after all. Couldn't I bury him by using my standing to get someone who *was* powerful enough to wield *his* power on my behalf?

There was, of course, the Firm's information leak problem. The place had proven more than once to be a complete sieve for information—the more secret and explosive the news, the more certain the leak. I could not risk confiding in anyone I didn't trust first to keep the whole thing quiet and then to handle Ian effectively, all while keeping me out of it.

As I thought about this, the complexities and risks seemed to pile up. I couldn't make it public myself. I couldn't use the Firm's confidential mechanisms for reporting misbehavior because they were actually less confidential than broadcasting the info in the main reception area. I couldn't tell anyone who might repeat it for any reason. I wanted Ian held accountable, but I needed some way to assure that he, too, said nothing to damage me—not much of a risk at the moment, but a big risk if he felt threatened.

I also needed him to know he had tangled with the wrong person. Unless I planned to spend the rest of my life feeling vulnerable to assholes like him—which I most assuredly did not—I needed to bring Ian down in a way that left no doubt in his mind that I was the one who made it happen. That way, I would have my equanimity back and he would know he'd made a serious miscalculation. Maybe he'd even stop and think before he tried it on someone else.

If I exposed him publicly and was believed, he would most likely be fired. Sitting in my chair that night, I felt I could settle for nothing less. Ian would have to lose his job. That wouldn't ruin his life by any measure, but it would be inconvenient and embarrassing. It would also be awkward for him to have to explain to prospective employers why he'd worked at the Firm for only a few months.

Perhaps I was more unsettled by the experience than I recognized—it took me almost an hour to come up with a plan to deep-six Ian. It took me no time at all, however, to decide who to get to help me. There was only one person I trusted who also had enough power at the Firm to take care of this. He would do it for me, too, I thought.

I left a message on Charlie's phone mail at work, saying I had something urgent to discuss with him and asking him to call me as soon as he got the message, either at home or at work. After I hung up, I realized it was after 2:30 in the morning, which his phone mail would tell him was the time I'd called. Sighing, I figured he might as well know sooner rather than later that this was something unusual.

I went to bed not long after leaving that message and, surprisingly, I slept pretty well. As I got ready for work the next morning, it occurred to me that the office wasn't the best place to discuss the situation with Charlie. The chances of being overheard were small, but it wasn't out of the question. And he would be angry—if he decided to stalk off in a fury to confront Ian, it wouldn't be easy to stop him.

Fortunately, Charlie checked his messages on his way in to the office. He called me at home around 8:30, just as I was about to walk out the door. Also fortunately, he had no morning meetings. He agreed to meet me at a coffee shop not too far from my apartment. I called my secretary to tell her I would be in later, and then walked to the coffee shop.

I had time to get coffee and settle at a table in a far corner before Charlie arrived. He breezed in, looking strong and wholesome and familiar, and it was incredibly reassuring to see him. Putting his brief-case down next to the other chair at the table, he looked at me curiously and asked if I was OK. When I told him I was (hoping my face looked normal, despite my anxiety), he went to get coffee for himself.

"What's up?" he asked when he came back.

"I need your help with something—something that has to stay completely confidential," I began. "I know how to handle it, but I can't do it myself."

"Sure. What is it?" Charlie looked relaxed, but puzzled. He lounged in the chair, his legs stretched out straight, his hands around his coffee cup. "And why the mystery? The middle of the night phone message, meeting outside the office—are you sure you're OK?"

"I'm fine. You'll understand in a minute." Looking directly at him, I said evenly, "Last night, I went to that dinner with Ian's clients. After dinner, I went to get my coat. Ian followed me into the coat room and completely crossed the line. He behaved totally unacceptably—said offensive, lewd things and tried to overpower me physically."

Charlie sat up straight, looking horrified. He started to say something, but I held up my hand and kept talking. "Really, I am OK. He didn't assault me. He manhandled me and was incredibly vulgar, but he backed off pretty quickly after I shoved him and threatened to scream for our dinner companions, who weren't far away."

"Seriously?" Charlie said, anger and consternation in his voice and on his face.

"Seriously. It was awful—scary and demoralizing." Unexpectedly, I suddenly felt frightened again—a very visceral feeling. I took a couple deep breaths and got hold of myself, then said, "One of the worst parts was realizing he was right when he told me he knew I wouldn't scream because, if I did, I would look like a scared, helpless girl in front of the clients."

"What a bastard!" Charlie looked tensed, like he might spring out of his seat. "What do you mean he was right? He was totally in the wrong. You had every right to protect yourself by calling for help."

"That's not the point. There's no way for me to expose him for the bastard he is without hurting myself as much, if not more than I hurt him. He knows that—he exploited it last night and he's surely counting on it to keep him safe from me now."

Charlie's face had the murderous look I'd seen two or three times before when he was enraged. I touched his forearm and talked fast. "Charlie, please listen to me. I have no intention of letting him get away with it. But I refuse to damage myself in the process. This is important, but I am not willing to go down in flames over it."

"What are you talking about? You have to report this and get him thrown out on his ass!"

"I intend to get him thrown out on his ass, but I will not report it. I will not be labeled a victim. I refuse to become the topic *du jour* at the Firm and endure everyone talking about me in this context." I met his eyes with what I hoped was a very resolute stare. "You know how it would be. At best, I'd be a harassed woman, put upon by an aggressive asshole. At worst, people would wonder if I was hysterical or lying—you know, trying to get back at him for rejecting me or some other sexist fantasy."

"Jane," Charlie started (looking pretty resolute himself), but I interrupted him.

"Don't even try," I said, shaking my head. "I will not report this. I've come this far at the Firm by keeping my gender off the table—that's why people see me as a professional and not as a sex object. If I make this public, I might as well quit at the same time because the minute it got out, I'd become nothing but a victimized woman. Everything I've worked for, my whole reputation, the status I have—it would all turn to dust!"

I watched Charlie struggle with this for a minute or two while I tried to calm down. It was obvious that he didn't like it one bit, but couldn't come up with any viable counterargument.

Speaking less heatedly, I said, "I don't like it either. It makes me crazy that the box Ian's put me in is what he counted on to try to take advantage of me in the first place—and what he's counting on to keep me quiet now. But you can't deny it, Charlie. I lose at least as much as he does if I 'follow procedures' and report this."

"Those procedures are designed to help. Both by preventing this kind of shit and giving you recourse if it happens anyway." Charlie's posture was finally less taut, and he sounded dismayed, weary, frustrated and disbelieving rather than furious. "Are they really worthless?"

"I don't know." I shrugged. "They're probably not totally worthless. I suppose they make people more conscious of what counts as harassment. They might have some preventive effect. But they're useless as recourse—as far as I'm concerned anyway. That's why I need your help."

"What do you want me to do?"

"I want you to get Ian fired without involving me," I told him. "I have an idea for how to do it, which I'll describe in a minute, but basically I want him to pay and I want him to know he tangled with the wrong person, all in a way that makes it impossible for him to say or do anything to damage me. He won't say anything unless he feels the walls closing in, but when he does start to feel threatened, he needs to be too intimidated to try to hurt or discredit me."

When Charlie didn't immediately respond, I leaned toward him and said, "I know that's a lot to ask, but I can't let him win—either by getting away with it or by taking me down with him."

"I don't have enough power to get him fired without specifying a reason," Charlie said matter-of-factly. "Jim does, though. Would you be comfortable taking this to him?"

"No." I shook my head. "I know you trust him, but I don't want him to know."

"Jane," he said gently, putting his hand on mine, "Jim would believe you and he wouldn't think less of you. I wouldn't suggest that we take it to him if I weren't sure you could trust him, too."

Charlie's natural and automatic use of the word "we" struck me forcefully. It was so reassuring, so heartening to know I had not just an ally, but one who trusted me without question. My throat felt thick. I knew my voice would quaver if I said anything, so I sat silently for a minute or two, feeling soothed by his hand on mine. Then, I moved my hand back to my coffee cup, looked up, and said, "Let me think about it. Maybe it would be OK for Jim to know. I've decided I have to leave the Firm ASAP anyway."

"Why have you decided that?" Charlie asked sharply, looking argumentative.

"Because I need to put my time and effort to work building a power base," I explained. "I'll always be vulnerable to something like this if I stay. There's no way for me to accumulate enough power at the Firm to overcome the inherent negative of being perceived primarily as a woman there."

I repeated what his father had told me about position power and described my own thought process on how to build the kind of power base that would best protect me in a situation like this. Charlie listened quietly. His palms were flat on the table and he was holding them very still.

He didn't say anything for a minute or two after I stopped talking. He looked dismayed and frustrated again, but when he finally spoke, his voice was gentle. "I'm so sorry about this," he said. "I can't argue with you—you're obviously right. But it stinks. I don't think I really understood until now how there's a brick wall just about every direction you turn in a situation like this."

My throat felt thick again. I sipped some now cold coffee dregs to buy a little time. When I was fairly certain I could speak levelly, I looked at him and said, with what I'm sure was a very weak smile, "It's not so bad that I have to leave ASAP. I was planning to go anyway—and, thanks to you and your father and Walker, I already have a great game plan for that. I'm just speeding up the timetable."

"You'll be a success whenever and wherever you go, Jane. There's no doubt about that," Charlie said. His tone was firm, but his expression was very kind. "I'm just sorry you feel so powerless."

"Thank you," I said softly, unsure I could say anything more without sounding tremulous.

"But you're not powerless," he said briskly, as if he could tell it was time to move on. "You have built some very strong support for yourself. I'll do everything I can to help you resolve this. Jim will too, if you'll let him. I know that's not as good as personal power, but it's not bad—and it's definitely something you've earned for yourself."

Gesturing at my cup, Charlie asked if I wanted a refill. When I nodded, he took both our cups and headed for the counter. I used the time to pull myself together and think over the pros and cons of bringing Jim into the loop. By the time Charlie returned, I was back to thinking (and acting) unemotionally and ready with questions and ideas about next steps.

It had occurred to me the night before that at least some of the negative press about Ian from the Firm people who had worked with him might have resulted from the same sort of aggressive sexist behavior he had demonstrated toward me. It was a good bet that I wasn't the only woman with whom he'd behaved inappropriately, even if he had stopped short of last night's behavior with anyone else.

If someone very powerful made Ian believe that an investigation that would sink him was about to be initiated under the Firm's sexual harassment policy with several women as complaining witnesses, might he not be coerced into resigning without making a fuss? Ian was no fool. I thought there was a good chance he would grab the opportunity to leave quietly rather than be the subject of such an investigation—particularly since he knew he was guilty.

I was no more interested in hurting the standing of other women than I was in hurting my own, but Ian wouldn't necessarily know that. If he believed that I had assembled damaging stories from other women and disclosed the whole thing to someone powerful, I was betting he wouldn't call the bluff.

My original thought was that Charlie could have the necessary talk with Ian. The combination of the investigation bluff, Charlie's position in the M&A group and at the Firm, and Charlie's ferocious demeanor when he was angry seemed to me to be plenty intimidating—more than menacing enough to get rid of Ian and keep him quiet.

Charlie liked the idea and agreed that it was likely to produce the desired result. We both recalled that at least a couple other women had worked with Ian since he'd been at the Firm, and that would be easy enough to verify. Although it was clear that Charlie would have loved to be the one who got to threaten, intimidate and get rid of Ian, he (somewhat reluctantly) made the case that we needed Jim.

Charlie pointed out that if he had the talk with Ian, we wouldn't be certain of success even if Ian did feel sufficiently menaced to leave quietly. Because of Ian's client relationships, Jim and other senior people at the Firm would want to know why he was leaving. Who knew what Ian would say in a confidential conversation with Jim? Charlie was sure that no matter how intimidated he felt, Ian wouldn't hesitate to say whatever he thought might help him—or hurt me—to someone whose power exceeded Charlie's.

Also, while people at the Firm didn't really have bosses, as head of M&A Jim was the closest thing to Ian's boss in a work environment like ours. Jim was also the group's decision-maker. He would not have to justify Ian's departure to anyone else. Even if someone wanted an explanation, Jim could offer up a generic "disruptive; not worth keeping" justification and the inquiry would end there.

After some discussion, Charlie persuaded me that the plan was very risky if we didn't involve Jim and practically risk-free if we did. He insisted that I could trust Jim to believe me and to handle Ian without damaging me. According to Charlie, Jim thought very highly of me and had also felt rather as if he owed me one ever since the class-skipping recommendation came to nothing. This last point was what tipped the balance for me. Thinking highly of me was all well and good, but, in my opinion, neither Jim nor anyone else senior at the Firm was likely to go out on a limb for me unless doing so would even a score or offer him some other benefit.

Charlie reproached me a bit for my cynicism, but much more gently than usual. I was impressed, actually, by everything about the way he acted. He comfortably and, as far as I could tell, instinctively treated me the way he always did—like a good friend and colleague. I had expected him to be a helpful ally and to be angry, both of which he was. I had also worried a little that he might be pitying or overly concerned or unmanageable in a way that would offend or degrade me, no matter how well-intentioned.

But he wasn't. He was definitely gentler than usual, but in a way that made me feel supported rather than pitied or weak. I would have resented any sign that he was acting out of a spirit of benevolence or superiority, but there was not so much as a speck of either in his demeanor. Charlie made it clear that his power was mine to tap because of his high regard for me—a huge gift to someone in my situation.

Before we left the coffee shop, we decided that he would arrange for us to meet with Jim, preferably that evening after the office had more or less emptied out, and I would verify that other women at the Firm had worked with Ian. In the cab to the office, we talked—to my relief—about our work for John's commercial finance company.

I felt very close to calm by the time I sat down at my desk—and very thankful for Charlie.

❖ ❖ ❖

Charlie

There were a couple urgent matters waiting for me when I got in to the office after meeting Jane at the coffee shop. I asked Pam to arrange for me to meet with Jim at 6:30 or later that evening, then turned my attention to the emergencies.

It was mid-afternoon before I had a chance to think again about the plan Jane and I had developed. I was confident it would work, but I was troubled by it. Thinking about why, I realized that it seemed wrong institutionally. Our plan would solve this particular problem for Jane, but it wouldn't really improve the Firm much, other than by getting rid of Ian.

I had to admit that Jane was right about using the Firm's procedures for handling this kind of thing. As well-intended as the policy was, it offered her no protection from the damaging talk that using it would occasion. Still, while I couldn't dispute it, I hated to think that the policies designed and put in place to assure civility and equal opportunity at the Firm were essentially worthless.

I also understood Jane's unwillingness to set an example if it required her to go down in flames for the cause. That was too much to ask of anyone. But I was stuck with my ongoing question about how anything would ever change when those who could set a compelling example were never willing to because the sacrifice was too great.

And what about someone held in less regard than Jane? Someone who wasn't a star would have no recourse at all in a situation like this one. The Firm's policy would be just as useless, but a back-door approach wouldn't be available either. Someone who wasn't a star apparently had no choice but to pay a big personal price—either by taking the fall or keeping quiet and letting an asshole like Ian victimize her and get away with it.

Had we as an organization really made no progress at all toward assuring a civil and inclusive place to work? Jane had said that her repu-tation and status were worthless in the face of predatory intentions and a willingness to cross the line. That seemed overstated to me where Jane was concerned, but it could validly be said about Firm policies—and also about the code of behavior generally viewed as acceptable.

Unless he got caught, someone willing to cross the line could get ahead or secure some advantage for himself relatively easily. We had certainly seen our share of examples of this at the Firm—from violations of the insider trading policy to squabbling over client origination points to taking credit for someone else's ideas or work.

Getting caught for over-the-line behavior was by no means a sure thing, and sometimes even getting caught resulted in little more than a slap on the wrist. Basically, to keep us from total chaos, we seemed to count on good faith and people's general willingness to keep their behavior on the right side of the line—either because they believed it was the right thing to do or because they were afraid of getting in trouble.

I recalled what my friend Jeff had said about corporate life in his shop. He'd been frustrated by the apparently prevalent beliefs that might equaled right (bad enough, but hard to overcome) and that power was all that really mattered. He'd said that policies, truth and good behavior all seemed to have become meaningless, nothing more than naïve ideals that could be ignored by those with enough power.

What was bothering me about Jane's and my plan was that using it perpetuated and maybe exacerbated the belief that enough power could turn wrong into right. Weren't we verifying that policies were meaningless, that they existed to be ignored if you had enough power to get yourself a better result by ignoring them? Our ends were more justifiable, but were our means really much better than Ian's?

This troubled me enough to want to talk it over with my father. He was a good person to talk to about work-related moral issues. Not only was he thoughtful and dedicated to acting honorably, he also knew most of what there was to know about corporate power and politics.

He was in town and in his office. After I spent a few minutes talking with his secretary and a few more holding while he finished another call, he was also available. Leaving Jane's name out of it, I outlined the situation and my problem for him.

He asked a few questions and listened carefully to the answers. Then he sighed and told me situations like these were among the worst, in part because plans like the one I had in mind were the only plans that worked. Somewhat to my surprise, Dad said that even in well-run companies policies were typically implemented for, and used primarily by, people without power.

Powerful people or people with powerful supporters were usually able to get what they deserved in the way of fair treatment, he explained, but policies were necessary to assure that those without power were treated fairly by those inclined to treat them otherwise. Policies were used to control or deal with thugs; the occasions on which they came into play were the breakdowns in the system. Dad used time-off policies to illustrate his point. These, he said, were necessary to assure that the rank and file actually got the time off they were entitled to for vacations, medical situations, deaths in the family and so forth.

With some anger, Dad agreed with Jane's assessment of the realities of sexual harassment situations. He also confirmed that no one with a better option ever "followed procedures."

He believed the relevant policies had what he called a "chilling effect" on the behavior of people inclined to behave badly, but verified that their enforcement was frequently as damaging to the person complaining as it was to the person accused. In his experience, even when the guilt of the accused was clear and indisputable, the complaining person still got labeled in a negative way as a victim and a whistle-blower. Often fatally from a career standpoint, this person became someone others thought they would be wise to take care around, perhaps not to trust at all.

Dad grumbled that he always wondered what it was people had to hide. What were they doing that they didn't want someone disposed to report bad behavior to know about? After he was done grumbling, though, he admitted the phenomenon was a real and damaging one, even if it made no logical sense.

Feeling better about going forward with Jane's and my plan, I nevertheless asked him how he, as a senior executive, justified side-stepping his own policies. I also asked how he expected any real cultural change to occur. His answers intrigued me, in part because they were so similar to Jane's.

In Dad's view, the overriding goal was to assure an open, high-performing and inclusive work environment, one that prized and rewarded those who acted honorably in accordance with this goal and, importantly, one that also dealt decisively with those who did not. He felt strongly that when power was held by people who fell in the first category, the environment automatically improved—over time, in significant ways.

The problem, he said, with attempting to better the environment with policies, even well-intentioned and well-designed ones, was that they failed to account for the realities of where power was held and how it was used and abused. Enforcement sometimes provided a cathartic opportunity for everyone to feel something good had been done to address a problem, but it rarely addressed the underlying issue of misuse of power. In fact, by damaging the whistle-blower, enforcement often made the underlying power issue worse instead of better.

What was needed was the judicious and targeted use of power to achieve the right results. In the case of sidestepping policies, Dad admitted dryly, he supposed he was saying the ends justified the means. With respect to transforming the culture, he said that while you had to work day-in and day-out to promote change, you also had to have a long-term, legacy-focused view of the results.

In his opinion, the best way to create lasting change was to tip the balance of power—to work at all times so as to assure that power was moved to and held only by those who used it to further achievement of the overriding goal. The check and balance on each individual's use of his own power was that goal's requirement of open, performance-oriented, inclusive and honorable behavior.

In short, what truly prevented people from behaving like thugs—and, over time, made it impolitic for the environment to tolerate thugs—was the appropriate and goal-oriented use of individual power. Dad encouraged me to use my power to right Ian's misuse of power, just as I had described. He also warned me not to let my temper get in the way of achieving the right result, and wished me luck.

It turned out that Jim was in the office that day, but he wasn't available until 7:00. I knew this would be OK with Jane; we'd figured the fewer people around, the better.

When I called to tell her the meeting time, she reported that Ian had worked with four other women during his months at the Firm. Two of these women were first-year analysts—likely to be particularly vulnerable—and one of them was both extremely attractive and, Jane said, known to be extremely scathing on the topic of Ian. So the plan was a go.

Jane also told me she had decided to approach the women who'd worked with Ian to let them know there had been complaints about his behavior. Without disclosing her own situation or inquiring into theirs in a way that could make them uncomfortable, she wanted to give them someone to talk to if they chose to talk and to assure them that they did not have to tolerate sexual harassment. She didn't plan to do this until Ian was gone, but, even so, I felt better about the institutional benefits of our plan.

She then mentioned that she hadn't seen Ian all day. She thought he might be out of the office, but hadn't been able to think of a risk-free way to find out. She did not want him to see us with Jim for fear of what Ian might say or do if he got nervous. This seemed overly cautious to me—there were several good and unrelated reasons for Jane and me to meet with Jim—but I agreed to see if I could find out whether Ian was likely to be nearby when we got to or left Jim's office.

There wasn't much we could have done differently had he been around, but as it happened, Ian wasn't in the office at all. Jane was very relieved, so much so that her relief, along with her stubborn insistence on taking this precaution, made me doubt that she was really as calm and unafraid as she seemed. I wondered how much it was costing her to maintain her composure.

I had taken her at her word that she was OK. Except for a few tense moments, her behavior at the coffee shop had borne that out and I'd been too angry to wonder then if she was sidestepping the question. I knew she would hate to be cross-examined, so I decided to say nothing more to her, but instead to keep my eyes open and give her all the support I could during the meeting with Jim.

At the meeting, Jane laid out the facts and outlined our plan for dealing with Ian. She sat unusually still and spoke in a very calm, controlled manner—and as if she were talking about someone other than herself. Her approach had two desirable effects: despite the sensitivity of the subject, Jim felt comfortable asking questions to get the information he needed; and our plan sounded reasonable in addition to well thought-out.

As I expected, Jim believed Jane's account and was both concerned for her and willing to help. He did spend a few minutes talking about the potential benefits, to Jane and to the Firm, of following the procedures under the Firm's harassment policy. Jane listened politely. When she replied, she still spoke calmly, but she categorically refused to file a report. Jim caved pretty fast, convinced either by Jane's stubbornness or by his own pre-existing agreement with her objections.

When he learned that Ian's deal was at the documentation stage and within a month of closing, Jim told Jane he would take care of getting her off the assignment right away. He guaranteed that he could do this without alerting Ian that anything was up simply by saying the work for her own client had heated up and required her attention, while Ian's deal no longer did.

Jane looked hesitant. I told her it wasn't uncommon for someone with her client responsibilities to be given a break like this when all that remained on the other deal was to close it. I also pointed out that Ian would assume she'd used her other work, rather than the real story, to get Jim to relieve her and, accordingly, he'd figure she planned to keep the real story to herself. Jane considered this silently for a moment, her eyes steady and her lips pursed as Jim and I waited, and then she agreed to it.

Jim felt strongly, however, that it was necessary to delay having the talk with Ian until after his deal was closed. Jim thought it would be unfair to the client to create a disruption that could derail the deal so close to the finish line. He also noted that it was unnecessary to make it more difficult for the Firm to collect its commission.

I thought Jane might jump out of her skin in response to this, but she didn't. She simply continued to insist that it was necessary to deal with Ian immediately, that we rather than he had to make the preemptive move. She was completely inflexible and, as we discussed the pros and cons, increasingly irritated and impatient.

I would have argued with Jim if I'd thought he was wrong, but I agreed that doing it his way was better from both Jane's standpoint and from the Firm's. We tried to persuade her that a three-to-four-week delay wouldn't hurt and might even help to make the investigation bluff more credible. We got nowhere. Finally, Jim suggested that we reconvene the next day after we'd all had a chance to sleep on his proposal. With a meaningful look at me, he said he was certain we would come to a resolution that was acceptable to all of us, and then again expressed his dismay and concern to Jane.

As serious as the situation was, still I smiled to myself over Jim's frustration. He was now familiar, if he hadn't been before, with how intransigent Jane could be and, as she would say, how prickly. Jim's meaningful look plainly requested that I do what I could to bring her around to his way of thinking.

By the time we left Jim's office, it was nearly 8:00. I suggested to Jane that we go out to get some dinner and debrief. She said no—she was tired and wanted to finish up a couple things in her office, then go home.

To my surprise, she called about ten minutes later to say she'd reconsidered and wanted to get something to eat after all. We left a few minutes after that. As soon as I gave the taxi driver the restaurant's address, Jane leaned her head back on the seat, closed her eyes, and said wearily, "You're going to try to talk me into the delay, aren't you?"

"I was planning to tell you why I think it's a good approach and get a better sense of your problem with it, but no, I'm not going to try to talk you into it. I think this is your decision to make."

"Very nicely put," she said, her eyes still closed, "but I'm not sure I see the difference between that and trying to talk me into it."

"Are you dead set against doing it Jim's way?"

"No," she sighed. She shook her head and opened her eyes. "No, I'm not, but I'm very skittish about the delay. Seems like there are a million ways for it to get fucked up if we wait. I want it handled and over with."

"I'm sure you do. We all do," I assured her. "But, honestly, I don't see how the delay makes it more likely to get fucked up. Ian has to be expecting either all hell to break loose or nothing to happen. When Jim tells him you're going to focus on the projects that have heated up for your own client, he'll assume you decided to keep quiet about the harassment and use those projects as your excuse to get away from him. That's totally believable, so he'll believe it. And Jim will act normal when they talk, so it will be in Ian's interest to say nothing to give himself away."

Jane looked at me doubtfully, but said nothing. She looked so small, and pale and worn-out, too. "I thought you handled the meeting very well," I told her. "You being so cool and calm made the plan seem all the more reasonable—and easy for Jim to go along with."

"Thanks," she said, sounding listless. She turned away from me to look out the window.

After a couple minutes of silence, I laid my hand lightly on her shoulder and asked, "Are you sure you're OK, Jane?"

"Yeah, I'm OK," she muttered. Then, still looking out the window, but with a lot more energy, she said, "But I'm tired and demoralized—and I feel out of control. I feel like I've been doing nothing but accommodating men and their goddamn personal agendas. I'm so sick of being pushed around!"

"I'm sorry you feel that way."

"Oh, I didn't mean you," she said quickly, finally turning back to look at me. "That's why I changed my mind about dinner. At first, I thought here's another one telling me what to do, trying to take over, *maneuvering* me, but then I realized that wasn't fair. You were just being nice—and helpful, too, just like this morning. You've listened to me and supported me, and you haven't made me feel victimized or weak or like this whole thing is somehow about you or the Firm instead of about me. You're a good friend, Charlie. Thank you."

"You're welcome," I said, taken aback by how emotionally she said all this. "You don't deserve to be in this mess. I'm glad I can help make it right."

The taxi pulled up to the restaurant I'd picked. It was a favorite of mine—more of a bar than a real restaurant, totally casual, with a very eclectic clientele and some of the best seafood around—but it looked like a dive from the outside. Once out of the taxi, Jane looked around and frowned. "Where the hell are we?" she demanded, sounding much more like her usual self.

I smiled and told her she was in for a surprise. The place was crowded, but I'd been coming in for years so Rick, the bartender who handled seating, knew me. (He'd told me he was sorry I'd stopped bringing Annemarie with me, but he was still attentive, perhaps in the hope that I would eventually bring her again.) Rick steered Jane and me to a couple seats at the far end of the bar and took our drink orders—wheat beer for her, dark lager for me.

Jane looked around dubiously. Even in the dim light, our surroundings were shabby. I told her nothing had changed, including some of the yellowing signs on the walls, in the ten years or so that I'd been eating there. She said she didn't doubt it and was relieved it wasn't any lighter, then looked down at the short, photocopied menu.

"If you don't mind getting messy," I said, "the grilled shrimp and vegetables are great. The shrimp are in their shells, though, so you have to peel them with your hands and, after that, using a fork to eat them is pointless."

"That sounds great," Jane said with relish. "I'd love to rip something apart with my hands. Better shrimp than, say, Ian, right?"

For the first time all day, she laughed. Maybe it was the dim light, but she looked less tired, too. We both ordered the shrimp and while we ripped it apart, I told her what my father had said about power and policies. From that topic, we went back to kicking around Jim's modification of our plan. By the time we finished eating, Jane seemed a lot less stressed and she had decided she could live with executing the plan Jim's way.

❖ ❖ ❖

THREE WEEKS LATER, Ian's deal closed. There had been plenty to do for John's company during the intervening three weeks, which was a good thing. Jane was fine when she was in meetings or busy with client work. Otherwise, she was incredibly nervous, more so than I would have guessed it was possible for her to be.

She felt it was important to maintain her cool, distanced demeanor with Jim, so I was the only person she could talk to about how heavily the situation was weighing on her. She continued to claim she was OK and that her nervousness was over the delay, not over what had happened. I had my doubts about that, but Jane was as definite about refusing to discuss any impact the harassment may have had on her peace of mind as she had been about refusing to file a report.

There was one M&A deal review meeting while we were waiting for Ian's deal to close. It was the only meeting Jane, Jim, Ian and I all had to attend, which was also a good thing. Jane and Ian ignored each other in a very noticeable way, and I had a hard time hiding my anger around him, too. Jim somehow managed to be his usual business-focused self. To Jane's and my (and probably Ian's) relief, he also ran the meeting efficiently and concluded it in record time.

The Firm's fee on Ian's deal was paid when the deal closed. Jim informed Jane and me that he planned to have his conversation with Ian two days later—a Friday—and to tell him to pack his office and leave over the weekend. Jim assured Jane that her name would not be connected publicly with Ian's departure in any way, but that, as she had requested, Ian would know she had started the ball rolling on his termination—and why.

Jane was suddenly very composed. I had thought her anxiety would increase once Jim scheduled the conversation, but evidently the delay really had been her concern.

Friday came and went without incident. The following Monday, there was a memo to Corp Fin announcing Ian's decision to leave the Firm. Because the memo cryptically specified no reason for his departure, an entertaining variety of rumors immediately started circulating. Ranging from sleazy business practices to sexually trans-mitted diseases, the rumors were all disparaging to Ian and none was even close to the truth.

Ian made no attempt to talk to Jane before he left nor did he say anything about her later that reached the ears of anyone at the Firm. She and I were both very curious about exactly what Jim had said to produce this ideal result. Jim, however, was close-mouthed. He confirmed that he'd followed the plan as we had discussed it. The only other thing he disclosed was that Ian had signed a separation agreement that imposed significant penalties on him for failing to comply with any of his obliga-tions, including the obligation to stick to the agreed-on story.

Jane was experienced enough to know that Ian had to have been paid some consideration to make the agreement enforceable, but this didn't bother her. Her goal, she reminded me, had been to cause Ian to lose his job in a way that left no doubt in his mind that she was responsible. She felt this goal had been achieved and she didn't care at all that he probably received a decent severance package.

In fact, she was amused by my anger over Ian getting anything at all positive out of the termination. She thought my thirst for a complete, scorched-earth triumph was understandable for someone accustomed to winning and to having every assumption working in his favor, but that "non-golden people" more likely to be victimized were obliged to define victory more realistically. With a hug, she thanked me for my help and told me she considered the matter satisfactorily closed.

A little over two months later, Jane announced her resignation from the Firm to take a brand manager position at a very prominent global diversified consumer products company. It was exactly the kind of position she'd wanted to move into and it was a brilliant career move that brought her nothing but congratulations. No one connected her departure with Ian's.

Sorry as I was to lose her as a colleague (and despite my continuing wrath over an asshole like Ian having received so much as a dime in severance), I felt confident that Jim and I had used our power to achieve the right results—and that the right overall goals had been served.

CHAPTER 9
NEXT LEVELS

Jane

Starting a new job was very strange. My job at the Firm was the only "real" job I'd ever had and I equated its rhythms and routines with those of working life more generally. From the corporate cafeteria, the stellar benefits package, and the other luxuries bestowed bountifully on its employees to its intricate politics and woeful lack (in terms of both quantity and quality) of administrative assistance, the Company was a whole new ballgame.

I felt exactly as if I had arrived in a foreign country, complete with unfamiliar locales, confusing customs and an incomprehensible language. The Company's air was thick with acronyms and jargon. Speakers of this language could craft an entire (and apparently coherent) sentence with only one recognizable or recognizably used English word. After hearing things like "LBG's NPIs have skeletal PMs," it occurred to me that a glossary would have been incredibly useful.

I made a mental note to suggest that one be developed and given to new hires. The right group to which to make this suggestion was Human Resources, but I had already learned that the people in that group had to be approached and handled with extreme delicacy. The HR people at the Firm had been a pain in the neck, too, but I had assumed that was because they were so downtrodden.

It's possible that I was just unlucky or perhaps HR people everywhere are awful, but the ones at the Company weren't any better than the ones at the Firm. They were sticklers for protocols and rules, apologists for senior management, and resolutely opposed to thinking or acting unusually in any respect whatsoever.

I learned this immediately at the Company. My resume had arrived in the office of the Chief HR Officer together with a note from the CEO recommending that I be interviewed. That was enough to assure that the Chief HR Officer viewed me with suspicion and enmity.

Once Ian had been fired and I felt confident that John and his commercial finance company were ready to accept my departure from the Firm, I met with Tyler's father to let him know that I was ready to move. He and I reviewed my list of target companies and decided on three top possibilities. Walker arranged lunches—in his private dining room—at which he and I met with the CEOs of each of these companies.

Both Walker and I felt the chemistry was best with the Company's CEO. We also thought the Company itself was a good career choice for me. Having had some experience with bristly HR people, not to mention intimidated colleagues, I particularly appreciated the CEO's suggestion that I go through the normal interviewing and hiring process after he gave my resume to his HR department.

I was qualified for the job and I knew how to ace an interview, so I'd figured there would be no problem getting hired via this "normal" process. I was right about that, but evidently something as simple as a resume coming from the CEO was enough to set off alarm bells in HR. The CHRO told me very plainly that I would do myself no favors by trying to trade on my "executive connections," and he advised me to keep the fact that I knew the CEO to myself.

The HR guy was really quite unpleasant. I wouldn't be surprised to learn that he tried to blackball my hire. (Or maybe not—he was obviously an ass-kisser of the highest order, so getting in the way of something he thought the CEO wanted was probably not his style.) In any event, everyone else I interviewed with was terrific, especially the person who would be my boss. Since the final decision was his, I was hired.

As the result of all this, I made a mental note to look for a politically correct opportunity to suggest a glossary for new hires instead of simply suggesting it and risking yet more hostility from the HR department. I also kept quiet about my "connection" to the CEO. Soon after I joined the Company, Alex was kind enough to invite me to a congratulatory lunch in *his* private dining room. When I told him about this experience and the conclusions I'd drawn, he chuckled and told me I had passed my first corporate politics test.

One of the first things I had to adjust to after I joined the Company was the different schedule. People considered the 9:30 or 10:00 arrival time I'd grown accustomed to at the Firm to be mid-morning. Most people showed up in the office around 7:30 or 8:00, and meetings were often scheduled for 8:30—a meeting time practically unheard of at the Firm. Nearly everyone at the Company took at least some time for lunch and then left for the day between 5:00 and 6:00.

It was very difficult for me to get up earlier in the morning and even harder to leave the office by 6:00. I'd gotten used to being in meetings most of the day and then buckling down late in the afternoon to think and do paperwork. I rarely left the Firm before 8:00 p.m. and there were always plenty of people still working when I left. The Company's offices were deserted and a little creepy after 6:30.

The Company was both nicer and lamer than the Firm in a variety of ways. At the Company, people stopped by my office to introduce themselves and welcome me; for the first week or two, it was a nonstop procession of pleasant people saying hello and telling me useful things. After the Firm's "sink or swim" culture, this was very surprising to me. It was also exhausting. It reminded me of being at one of Tyler's family's parties—after a while, my cheeks were sore from all the smiling and I was bored to tears with repeating my own story.

I quickly learned that the Company's lingo was more genteel, too, and that it did not include the word "fuck." The shocked looks on the faces of the (fortunately small) group in my office the first time I said something was so fucking something made that first time the last time I used the word. After its appearance in seven out of ten sentences at the Firm, this should have been a difficult adjustment, but surprisingly it wasn't, probably because I almost never heard the word spoken at the Company. Thinking about it, I realized I hadn't heard it much with the Firm's clients either.

People at the Company also demonstrated a much wider range of intelligence and work habits. Everyone at the Firm (professionals and staff) had been pretty smart and, despite what I had always thought, relatively hard-working. By comparison to the Company, the people at the Firm fell into a very narrow—and top of the scale—band of intelligence and work ethic. The Company's employees filled a much broader and more middling band. The best people were every bit as good, but those in the middle and at the bottom were much lower on the scale than their counterparts at the Firm.

As for work habits, the difference was startling. Perhaps I was seeing what Alex had described as one of the distinctions between generating revenue from the sale of products rather than the sale of people's time, but there seemed to be a lot of full-time employees at the Company with far less than full-time jobs. No matter what times of day I went to the kiosks for coffee or water, there was always a crowd chatting about last night's TV shows or sporting events. There were also frequent parties to celebrate birthdays or weddings or retirements.

People had plenty of time to stop by one another's offices; usually, although by no means always, there was some work-related reason for these visits, but they always extended into non-work-related chit-chat, too. On projects, people had a tendency to set deadlines with reference to holidays—"we want to finish this up by Thanksgiving"—rather than with reference to sensible, doable and much quicker completion dates. The pace got even slower when the resident bosses were away in meetings or traveling.

Honestly, I felt like I was working part-time when I started at the Company. My attitude, formed at the Firm, was to consider every minute of every day (including nights, weekends and holidays) to be work minutes in the event a client needed something done. This was not only unnecessary at the Company, it actually caused trouble when I didn't take care to suppress it. I rapidly learned to think about deadlines, particularly the ones I imposed on my team, more in terms of true need than in terms of ASAP.

It was also laughably easy to be considered a genius. Some of this was just thanks to the "fresh eyes" phenomenon, but the simplest ideas seemed to strike people as brilliant. One of the questions I asked as I got to know the people on my team was whether there were procedural or other problems that made it hard for them to get any particular aspects of their work done. Over and over, people identified problems with painfully obvious solutions.

Our secretary observed that it took a lot of time to file and then later to find things because all the project files looked alike, as did many of the papers in them, and the file cabinets for the different projects were nowhere near one another. I suggested first categorizing the filing, then going to each separate filing cabinet only once. I also proposed using different colored folders for each project.

She looked at me as if I'd turned water into wine, but then her face clouded and she doubtfully said they'd always used the same folders. I told her I was sure it would be OK to use different colors and promised to take the heat, if we got any, for making the change. Judging from her reaction, I'd evidently made a supporter for life.

Another group was ridiculously grateful for a simple spreadsheet on which to keep track of frequently changing information they'd been tracking manually. Nearly everyone complained about at least a few things that were easily improved by either a simple procedural fix or a similarly simple request to another department for needed information on a different time schedule. I quickly found myself with a reputation for being an innovative problem-solver.

I was glad to be able to build support and add value in this way, but I was dying to get to the actual substance of my job. What with the short workdays, the seemingly constant chit-chat and a pile of largely administrative inefficiencies to deal with, I felt very distracted initially. My first response was the obvious one of skipping lunch or staying after hours to work in a quiet, undisturbed way on learning my new responsibilities and figuring out how to succeed in my new environment.

This swiftly proved to be the wrong response. My coworkers got edgy as day after day they saw me hard at work when they were hitting the road. The people who worked for me began to make a point of telling me they'd gotten in earlier than I and explaining their reasons for leaving at 5:00. My peers started to make comments about workaholics. The cleaning staff and I regularly startled each other when they burst into my office to clean in what I considered the early evening.

After a couple weeks, I realized I had to toe the behavioral line a bit more closely if I wanted to avoid having to deal with the interpersonal buzz saw of people who felt threatened by someone doing things differently—and arguably working harder—than they were. Despite their friendliness, it didn't take long to discern in my new colleagues what seemed to be a fundamental underlying mistrust.

There were accepted ways of doing things at the Company that people adhered to rigidly. Any departure from these protocols was viewed with misgiving and sometimes even animosity. Working late prompted grumbling about what you might be trying to prove. A willingness to work on weekends or to complete a task by the next day was likewise considered out of place—and possibly fishy. Change of just about any sort was viewed as a criticism of the past—and as a very shady proposition.

This disappointed me. Apparently, the Company wasn't going to be any more purely focused on results—or any less a hotbed of personal and political landmines—than the Firm had been. As I contemplated how to deal with this, I remembered what Alex had told me about the pros and cons of corporate life. I thought carefully about my goals and what I needed to do to achieve them in this new setting.

Just as I had prudently taken my gender off the table as an issue at the Firm, I prudently toned down my work habits and developed a less directive persona at the Company. I settled on an 8:15-6:00 workday (more or less). When I took work home, I wasn't obvious about it. I made recommendations and suggestions instead of simply doing things or giving instructions. Having observed that once they knew what I thought the people on my team would not disagree, I listened and waited to express my own opinions until after they had expressed theirs.

Most of this took extra time and all of it made me crazy, but I kept my frustration to myself (and wished my girls' club and Charlie were still conveniently down the hall to gripe to). I told myself over and over that my goal was to succeed—not merely by doing my job brilliantly, but also by doing it in a way that garnered me supporters rather than detractors.

❖ ❖ ❖

A FEW WEEKS after I arrived at the Company, I got a call from Patrick, the interesting Public Finance guy I had worked with at the Firm. Patrick and I had gotten together for lunch three or four times in the year since we'd worked together. He was a pleasure to talk with, in part because he read constantly and knew all sorts of fascinating things—from the esoteric to the truly trivial—and in part because he was so lighthearted and laid-back.

Patrick's reason for calling me at the Company was to ask me out on a date. He said he was sorry he'd lost me as a colleague, but very glad he could now ask me to go out with him. I was impressed by his sensitivity regarding dating someone at work, and surprised and flattered by his interest in me. I liked him, too, so I said yes.

As I got to know him, it became obvious why Katherine had liked working with him so much. Patrick wasn't as outrageous as Katherine, but he was equally irreverent. He had a very unusual take on most things, perhaps from having spent his teenage years on the other side of the planet, and he was extraordinarily casual. He seemed to take nothing very seriously.

Despite his lighthearted attitude, Patrick was intrigued by just about everything. His intellectual curiosity knew no bounds; he was always regaling me with some engrossing new thing he'd learned. He knew how all sorts of things worked, he could recognize cars from blocks away by the sounds of their engines, he whistled entire movements of symphonies, he could even juggle. How someone like him ended up a successful—and content—investment banker (in Public Finance no less) was a mystery to me.

He surprised me by showing up for our second date with an incipient black eye. Apparently, his rugby team had played earlier that day and he'd somehow been jabbed in the eye. He said a black eye was a common injury, but assured me that rugby wasn't as violent as it looked. When I told him I had no idea how rugby looked, he rounded up a piece of paper and a pen and started drawing diagrams and explaining how the game worked.

It was largely incomprehensible. I couldn't even understand enough to formulate intelligent questions. Patrick got carried away with his diagramming—his piece of paper resembled the blueprint for a complex piece of machinery. When he looked up and saw my confused expression, he laughed and told me I'd have to come to a match. Not only would it make more sense to see the players in action, but, he assured me, I'd have no remaining questions about how he'd gotten his shiner.

The following weekend I met him at what I had learned was called the "pitch," although it looked like a normal athletic field to me. Patrick had thoughtfully provided me with a play-by-play man in the person of one of his teammates. Tim had been knocked unconscious the week before, suffered a concussion, and was sidelined. No one seemed to find this alarming. Tim was extremely pissed off about not being allowed to play, but very nice to me. He was also very into the game and, listening to him, I began to understand what was going on.

Mostly, it was shocking. The players wore no padding and spent a lot of their time in what Tim told me was called a scrum. It looked a little like the huddle in football, except the scrum was not a timeout. It was an incredibly intense part of the game that was apparently a fight for control of the ball, with rows of guys on each side bent at the waist, hanging onto each other and pushing against the guys on the other side, muscles straining, until the ball appeared in the arms of a runner for one team or the other. A couple times, I saw the entire scrum rotate, something Tim got very excited about.

Patrick was, Tim informed me, a weak-side flanker. This meant he was on the outside of the scrum, with one arm in and the other free. He was a tackler; the free arm allowed him to detach from the scrum quickly if the guy with the ball appeared on his side. Patrick was riveting to watch—his determination and concentration were fierce. I did indeed see him get knocked in the face, as well as stepped on, many times. Watching him tackle was even more painful, if also sort of thrilling. He launched himself at the ball carrier with no apparent regard for his own or the ball carrier's body.

Tim told me Patrick had good enough ball skills to play one of the "back" positions, but he hadn't been as good in comparison to the Australian teammates he'd learned with, so he'd become a flanker. According to Tim, flankers (who were forwards) were hungry to be in the thick of things physically in a way backs weren't, and Patrick fit that mold. He loved the flanker position and stuck with it, even though he could have played what Tim called one of the "less brutal" positions.

It all looked pretty brutal to me, although it was exciting to watch once I figured out enough to understand what I was seeing. Patrick's and Tim's team won (by a score that made no sense to me, but Tim had already explained it once and I was too embarrassed to ask him to go over it again). Patrick was ecstatic—it made me smile to see his joyous expression under the dirt streaking his face and caked all over every other part of him. It was obvious that he loved to play.

He had told me his team usually went to a nearby bar after matches. They graciously invited me to join them, but I suspected there would be nothing but rugby talk and also that Patrick would have a better time without having to worry about entertaining me. So he and I made plans to meet for dinner that night instead. After thanking Tim and wishing him a speedy recovery, I went to my office and worked for a couple hours.

Patrick looked like a different person when he came to pick me up for dinner—or, rather, like the person he'd been before I'd seen him play rugby. He was clean, for one thing, and he was dressed more like an investment banker than a rugby player, despite his rolled-up shirtsleeves. His eye was nearly healed—just a little greenish around his cheekbone. While he did have a few new bruises purpling impressively on his arms, it was still easier to picture him at the financial printer than on the rugby pitch.

I found the contrast intriguing, and told him so. He laughed and said the difference between rugby and investment banking was more a matter of form than of substance, more about tactics than strategy. We talked very entertainingly about this over dinner. We also talked about how I thought working at the Company differed from working at the Firm and about a biography of Henry II that Patrick had just finished reading. I had a wonderful time.

Throughout dinner, I kept picturing Patrick, the carefree and highly intelligent investment banker, launching himself with ferocious determination and pleasure at other rugby players. There was something about the recklessness with which he'd used his body that appealed to me. It wasn't sexy exactly, but it was very physical. It surprised me and made me want to know him better.

After dinner, we walked back in the direction of my apartment. Patrick had insisted he was fine to walk even though he limped a little when he first stood up. Sure enough, after a block or so, he was walking normally again. "So does your entire body hurt pretty much all the time during the rugby season?" I asked him.

He laughed. "Nah, just the day after we play. Even then, it's OK if I keep moving and don't let everything stiffen up. By Monday, I'll be fine."

"I can't get over how violent it all looked! Football looks violent too, but it seems more choreographed somehow—and, of course, there's all the padding. Rugby is so raw. I feel like I've learned a new and significant thing about you."

"And what's that?" he said cheerfully, taking my hand.

"It's such an interesting incongruity—the mild-mannered, relaxed Public Finance banker versus the relentless, intense rugby player." I smiled up at him. "And you obviously *love* playing rugby. I wouldn't have thought you—or anyone else at the Firm, now that I think about it—could be so wild or so exuberant."

"How do you feel about that?"

"I like it. I like the contrast. It's unexpected and it makes me want to know you better."

"That sounds like a great idea," he said happily, squeezing my hand.

We talked about rugby the rest of the way to my apartment. Outside my building, Patrick asked if I wanted to go to the match and out to dinner again the following Saturday. He grinned and said Tim would probably still be sidelined and available to provide commentary. I'd had a great day, so I gladly agreed to a reprise. Patrick then gently put his hands on my face, bent down, and kissed me.

After the kiss, I smiled at him and said, "That was nice—and not *too* wild or exuberant. More investment banker than rugby player."

"Don't want to scare you," he said, grinning again. "By the way, I thought you'd be a great kisser. Glad I was right. See you next week." And away he walked, whistling something classical.

My reaction to all this was complicated. I liked him very much, and I really was intrigued by the contrasting aspects of his personality. I knew he was a nice guy and I'd been exceptionally aware of him physically since watching him play. He was a good kisser, too. I'd never had sex with anyone but Tyler and he and I hadn't slept together for a few months, so I wasn't at all adverse to the idea of sex—in general or with someone new.

At the same time, the usual warning bells were ringing in my head over Patrick's and my attraction to each other. I'd always known I could handle Tyler, which was why I'd always felt comfortable having sex with him. I didn't know Patrick nearly as well and, thrilling as that athletic rugby player persona was, it could easily prove uncontrollable. A potentially wild and exuberant lover both appealed to me and made me nervous.

I was no more interested in transforming into my gooey, besotted college roommate now than I had been back in college. That didn't feel likely to me—Patrick was so casual, which made me feel similarly non-serious—but who knew how I'd react to sleeping with him? I was also uneasy over him viewing me as a girlfriend or lover instead of as a (former) colleague. He hadn't made me feel condescended to or like prey so far, but again, who knew?

❖ ❖ ❖

LYNN, CHERYL, Katherine and I met for drinks during the following week. (Anna had transferred to the Firm's London office, so we were missing her on a permanent basis.) It had become increasingly difficult to get our girls' club together since I'd moved to the Company. Four people working in three different places proved to be much harder to assemble than five people working in the same place. But we were determined not to fall out of touch, even if we did seem to spend more time making arrangements to get together than actually getting together.

I was looking forward to hearing what was up with everyone and to telling them about my first months at the Company. There were quite a few friendly and interesting people at my new office, but no women in similar positions. I missed the camaraderie the girls' club had provided when we were all at the Firm, doing similar work and having similar experiences.

Probably thanks to the shortened work hours I was now trying to adhere to, I was the first to arrive. Lynn and Cheryl showed up a few minutes later, followed almost immediately by Katherine. After hugs all around, we exclaimed over how long it had been and how good it was to see one another, then fell easily into our old communication patterns, as if only days instead of months had passed since our last meeting.

"So, Jane," Lynn demanded as soon as we'd settled into a booth with our drinks, "what's life like in the cushy corporate world?"

"Cushy," I replied, with a grin. "I think it's going to be great, but I still feel like I'm on another planet most of the time. It's different in about a million ways, some good, some not so good."

I summarized the truncated workday, the slower pace and the dizzying array of employee benefits, complained about the nonstop jargon and the dismal administrative situation, and then said, "Katherine, you were so right about the 'new toy' phenomenon of moving laterally. For the first few weeks, I had a constant stream—and I still have a good-sized trickle—of people stopping by to tell me how glad they are to have me at the Company. And they seem to find me and my background remarkably interesting."

"It's incredible, isn't it?" Katherine said, poking through the bowl of nuts on the table to find her favorites. "Only problem is it doesn't last. There's always some newer toy who shows up after you, and then you're suddenly a familiar veteran."

"I suppose so. I'm thinking it will be a relief to be familiar, though—both to other people and with my actual job, which I feel like I've spent a total of about ten minutes doing." I laughed. "I spend a lot more time managing people and projects and very little time doing actual work. There's like *no* paperwork. I'm serious—what I've done wouldn't even fill up one FedEx box! I've had to come up with a whole new definition of productivity."

Everyone laughed and Katherine said, "That sounds pretty good to me. Sometimes I think I could happily live the rest of my life without filling up another fucking FedEx box!"

"Yeah, I remember that feeling," I agreed. "It is sort of cool to be more responsible for thinking and facilitating and leading than for paperwork. It's also been nice—in sort of an alarming way—to be considered a complete genius for the lamest contributions. Honestly, you wouldn't believe it. I've made a couple suggestions that a smart third-grader could easily have made, and people are acting like I'm Einstein."

Cheryl squeezed a lemon wedge into her just-refilled soda. She wasn't much of a drinker; we could occasionally talk her into a celebratory margarita or glass of champagne, but she usually drank diet soda. "Are you giving yourself enough credit, Jane?" she asked. "You are very smart."

"Thanks, but this isn't false modesty. I'm talking about suggesting things like alphabetizing or using colored folders. Really basic and obvious stuff."

"It's hard to believe the Company is full of morons," Lynn objected. She looked fabulous. Her hair was shinier than ever and her skin was tanned and glowing. She must have been boating or something over the weekend. "It's an incredibly well-known and prominent company."

"It's not that they're morons," I said. "It's more that they're not particularly thoughtful or strategic about their jobs. People seem to show up, do the things on their to-do lists pretty much the way they've always done them, then go home. They think they've done a great job if they cross off every to-do list item, but they never stop to think about whether the items are the right ones. They don't seem to know—or maybe to care—why their work is important or how it fits into the Company's overall performance, so they don't bother to think about how to do it better—or even in a way that might annoy them less. Do you see what I mean?"

"Yeah, I do," Cheryl said. "I've seen that with clients. Someone will answer a question, for instance, without ever thinking about why you're asking it or whether some other tidbit they know might also be relevant to you. It's never been clear to me if the people just don't care or if there's something about corporations that makes it hard for individuals to know where their work fits into the whole."

"I don't think it's that the people at the Company don't care," I said, taking a few almonds and cashews before Katherine ate all of them, "but the attitude toward work is very different than at the Firm. From what I've seen so far, work isn't life for people. It's more like a necessary evil that gets in the way of what they think of as their real lives. They don't expect work to be great or particularly meaningful. They're just aiming for tolerable. People want to keep their jobs, but lots of them aren't all that ambitious or interested in getting ahead."

I laughed. "One of the guys on my team actually told me his ambition is to get to the point where he can do his job really well in his sleep and never have to stress over it or feel challenged again."

"God, I'd rather be dead," Lynn said, wrinkling her nose in disgust.

"Yeah, it sounded awful to me, too," I smiled, "but a corporation needs some people like that, I think. If everyone wanted to be CEO, it would be hard to keep the more mundane, but still really necessary jobs staffed. You know, who would handle accounts payable or run the mailroom?"

I ate a couple almonds, thinking about how to articulate what I'd observed. "I'm not sure, but I think the big difference may be that at the Firm there isn't a bigger picture. Individual deals and efforts are all there is, so naturally that's what people focus on. Also, each individual person is on the hook more at the Firm. There isn't anything except what the people do, so you can't really stay under the radar, and only people who think they can succeed in that environment choose to work there.

"The Company, on the other hand, has a huge array of products, and the big picture is about those, not about what each person does or contributes. Everyone assumes his job ties somehow to the big picture, but most people don't pay much attention to the nature of the tie or, for that matter, to the nature of the big picture. You know, they assume someone else figured it all out and knows how it makes sense, so they just show up, do their little parts, and leave the thinking to the higher-ups."

"I think the familiar also tends to take on a life of its own," Cheryl said. "The habitual or generally accepted way of doing things somehow gets equated with the *right* way to do them, as if habit or general acceptability is proof that something is tried and true." She laughed ruefully. "I'm seeing that with this goofy wedding planning, too. People are constantly telling me 'everyone does it' or 'this is how it's done' and they're appalled when I suggest I might want something different."

Cheryl sounded animated, but unlike Lynn, she looked tired and pale. She and Richard had decided a few months before to get married, and Cheryl had been running herself ragged ever since planning for their wedding the following August. Her innate good sense was at war with her desire to experience the storybook wedding she'd envisioned since she was a child. She couldn't quite let go of the fantasy, but she laughed at herself all the time.

"God, I remember that wedding drill," Katherine said, with a very indignant look. "If I'd had a buck for every time someone told me what I wanted to do was inappropriate or unusual or 'simply not done,' I could have paid for the honeymoon!"

"And for the wedding too, knowing what you probably wanted to do," Lynn teased. "I bet licking chocolate ice cream off the groom wasn't the only 'simply not done' thing you considered."

Katherine chuckled. "No, it wasn't. But even the things that wouldn't have embarrassed Jordan raised eyebrows. There seemed to be rules about everything—flowers, food, tablecloths, place cards, dresses, shoes, jewelry, you name it. It was ridiculous!"

"It's interesting, it really is," Cheryl said. "I do think this is all part of the same phenomenon. The corporate and wedding things, I mean. I've been reading about leadership recently, and the general consensus seems to be that the biggest challenge is inspiring people to do something different from what they're accustomed to doing."

"Exactly!" I nodded. "It amazes me that people want to stick with what's familiar even when it's making their jobs harder or making them miserable. It's like they think the known evil is preferable not just to the unknown evil, but to the unknown potential benefit, too. Apparently, it's not just mediocre white men who want to preserve the status quo at all costs. It seems like practically *everyone* wants to preserve it, even when it's hurting them rather than helping them."

"I think most people are basically lazy," Lynn said. She whisked the stick of olives in her martini in a way that was anything but lazy. "And either unable or unwilling to think for themselves. That's why they stick with what they know or what other people consider acceptable. They don't think. Instead, they figure if it's familiar or OK with everyone else, it's OK with them. What bugs me is their need to proselytize—as if your decision to do it a different way is an implicit repudiation of them and they're required to recruit you to their side. If *I* had a buck for every time some bimbo has told me that marriage and babies are so much more rewarding than a career and casual sex, I could retire."

She smiled. "Not that I want to retire, but you get the point. If they're so content, so fucking sure they've made the right choice, why do they need me to agree? Why do they care at all what I think or if I do it their way?"

"Great question!" Katherine exclaimed. "I was wondering the same thing after the Firm's last prom. I ran into Howard's skeleton of a wife in the bathroom. After she pretended she didn't know who I was and made me introduce myself, she said, 'Oh yes, you once worked at the Firm, didn't you, dear?' Then, in this very pitying, 'too bad your husband can't support you,' faux sympathetic way, she asked, 'Do you still work full time?'"

Katherine rolled her eyes and pantomimed sticking her finger down her throat. "Since she no doubt knows what Jordan makes down to the penny, she obviously knows he *can* support me and was either trying to imply that he wasn't willing to or to convey her disapproval of my decision to be a complete person instead of a parasite like her. I was tempted to tell the witch that I preferred a husband who liked to talk to me and fuck me, not just one who could fill up our bank account."

"You didn't, did you?" Cheryl asked, giggling, while at the same time Lynn said, "You should have!"

"I was a good girl," Katherine said, grinning. "I smiled sweetly and very politely said that I loved my job, and my husband and I loved having our work in common and being able to think things through together and give each other ideas and support."

"Ouch!" Cheryl said. "Did she get the point?"

"Hard to say. She kept her pitying, patronizing look, but, then again, she's not quick with the expression changes. That frozen, face-lifted skin must make it too hard for her." Katherine rolled her eyes again. "She nodded briskly and walked her bony butt out of the bathroom. Later, I made a point of standing very close to Jordan while he was talking to Howard and she did manage to glare at me."

Lynn laughed. "You and Jordan are always all over each other. And she's not an idiot, despite the way Howard treats her. I bet she got the point. Nice work!"

"Those Firm events are so awful! I'm so glad to be done with them!" I smiled in response to their expressions. "Sorry—didn't mean to gloat. What else is up with you guys?"

"You probably already know this from talking to Charlie," Lynn said, "but he and I are still having a great time with John and his people. The outsourced functions seem to be going well and we're in the middle of yet another acquisition, this one not so small. Did Charlie tell you about it?"

"No, he and I have traded a few phone messages, but we haven't had a chance to meet or even to talk on the phone for like six weeks. Is the new acquisition a big one?"

"Not big, but solidly mid-sized. The target does healthcare finance, so it'll be a whole new business line for the company. It's hard to tell how much integration or cost-reduction will really be possible, but the target is very profitable, with good margins, so the acquisition should be accretive for John right from the start."

Katherine had been negotiating with the waiter for another bowl of nuts, this one without the kinds she disliked. He walked away, looking like he'd gladly sort through nuts or do anything else she asked, and she sang out, "Boring! We do enough work at work. Let's talk about something juicier."

"We count on you for the juicy stuff, Kath," Lynn said, with a grin.

"Oh, I could tell you a thing or two!" Katherine crowed gleefully. Then she frowned and said, "But it drives Jordan crazy to know that people he works with have heard things that would embarrass him. He's always so nervous and sort of aggrieved when I get home after being with you guys. It might be nice for a change to be able to tell him no one knows anything new."

"I don't work with him much," Lynn said, "but I sympathize with his feelings on this. I still think about the ice cream thing every time I see him."

Cheryl giggled. "I sympathize with him, too. I work with him all the time, so I really don't think about the juicy stuff except right after I've seen you, Katherine. For a few days after that, though, it's always hard not to laugh or blush whenever I see him."

"Especially when he does one of his trademark things, like slouch out of his jacket and practically out of his shirt, too, or conjure a pen out of thin air," I remembered, laughing. "I always tried to cover laughs with coughs, but I don't think I fooled him. Poor Jordan."

"I'm confident he thinks I'm worth a little embarrassment at the office," Katherine said as if there could be no doubt about it. "Still, maybe we could give my sexy husband a break tonight. Doesn't someone else have a juicy development to report?"

"I wish I did," Cheryl said. "Richard and I are so bogged down in wedding planning and we've both been so busy at work lately that we're doing way too little that falls in the juicy category."

"I don't know if this falls in that category yet or not," I said, feeling a little hesitant, "but I've been dating Patrick for the last three weeks."

At the same time, Cheryl exclaimed "Public Finance Patrick?" and Katherine exclaimed, "*My* Patrick?"

"The very one," I said, grinning. "Although he doesn't seem to think of himself as yours, Katherine."

"No, he wouldn't," she said, unperturbed, "but that's how I think of him."

"Yeah, that's right, you liked him nearly as much as you liked Jordan when we were rookies, didn't you?" Lynn said, her eyebrows high. "Is there anything you'd like to tell Jane?"

"Not a thing," Katherine said breezily, "but I would like to hear how he is. I'll admit to a fantasy or two about him that first year."

"Can't tell you yet how he is in that regard," I said. I ran my finger around the rim of my margarita to collect the remaining salt.

"What the hell are you waiting for, Jane?" Katherine demanded. "He's so hot!"

"Give her a break, Katherine. We're not all sex maniacs like you, you know," Cheryl teased gently.

"I'm mortally wounded!" Katherine clapped her hand to her chest as if she'd been shot. "Did I or did I not wait an entire *year* before going to bed with Jordan?"

"Yes, you did, but you're still a maniac," Lynn said, smiling. "And we all admire you for it, too—the maniac part, I mean, not the waiting part." Turning to me, she said, "So, Jane, how did this start and what's been going on? Tell us all about it."

I did just that, which turned out to be fun. It was also encouraging—even reassuring—to know they considered it very cool that Patrick and I were dating. Cheryl and Katherine knew him the best, but Lynn had worked with him once, too, and all three of them thought he was a great guy. "What the hell," I found myself thinking. "Why not?"

❖ ❖ ❖

THE FOLLOWING SATURDAY, I had another terrific day and evening with Patrick. The rugby match was another good one and I had evidently learned more than I thought. This time, it looked more like a coherent game and less like a lot of chaotic, unconnected running around. Tim was indeed still sidelined. His mood was worse, but his play-by-play commentary was again extremely helpful.

At dinner, Patrick and I got into a debate about the effects of the rampant sexism at the Firm. He didn't dispute its existence, but he scoffed at the notion that it had much of an impact on what he called "ace performers" like me. He was also inclined to disagree with my assertion that I'd had to work much harder and be much more talented to get to the same place as just about any male peer at the Firm.

I didn't go into the Ian situation, but I regaled Patrick with the wide variety of significant and negative ways sexism had impacted me—from the painstaking care I'd had to take to make my gender a non-issue, to the extra effort required to deal appropriately with clients and so-called colleagues who thought my role should be getting coffee or making copies, to the psychic costs of climbing uphill day after day in a hostile environment where I felt at best like a tolerated outsider and at worst like an unwelcome interloper.

Patrick offered the usual objections and arguments. He also insisted that the freedom to behave naturally and, for that matter, to succeed was an opportunity to be taken, not given—a point I had to think hard about to rebut since I couldn't dispute its accuracy. After nearly an hour of debate, however, he shook his head, said he'd obviously had no idea, and offered his napkin as a white flag. I laughed and told him he could keep his napkin if he promised never again to minimize the damage generalized sexism could wreak.

He did so, then he looked at me curiously. "You are so smart, Jane, and such an articulate and passionate debater. Do you have any idea how sexy that is?"

"Sexy?" I repeated with surprise. "Don't you watch TV? Aren't men supposed to consider simpering brainlessness sexy?"

"Not this man. As far as I'm concerned, there's nothing sexier than a smart woman."

"Really," I said in a tone meant to convey that I didn't believe it for a minute.

"Really," he said, smiling. "You've seen me play rugby. It shouldn't surprise you that I like my hobbies rigorous."

I laughed. "If that's a line, you couldn't have picked a better one to use with someone like me," I teased him.

"Is it going to work?"

"I think so."

Back at my apartment, we almost got derailed when Patrick took off his shirt and I beheld the truly spectacular assortment of scratches and bruises, including fingerprints from the forceful fingers of other people, that he was sporting all over his chest and arms. There was also a swollen red area on his back, just above his waist, that looked suspiciously like a shoeprint.

I looked at him with horror and said I was afraid he would scream in pain if I touched him. He laughed and assured me he was fine—completely touchable and, he promised, unimpaired. A little gingerly, I took him at his word. Sure enough, he didn't flinch when I touched him—quite the opposite, in fact. And he was right about being unimpaired, too. As a lover, he was lively, considerate and fun.

I had a good time with Patrick that first night and during the nights together that followed, but it wasn't that different from being with Tyler. It was pleasurable, fine, but not breathtaking or overwhelming or intense. This both relieved and disappointed me. I was glad that I evidently wasn't in danger of losing my head, but I'd sort of hoped there would be more to it, that I would experience something more along the lines of what people always seemed to use the word "amazing" to describe.

There was a physicality to sex, to being in bed with a man—a strong, charming man—that I liked a lot. I'd thought that might be personal to Tyler, but after Patrick and I slept together, I realized that the physicality—the skin, the arms and legs and tongues, the bodies together—was what I liked about sex.

It also occurred to me that Tyler and Patrick had a lot in common. They were both fairly tall and of a similarly strong, well-built body type. They were both sure of themselves in a comfortable, sort of unconscious way, as well as interesting, amiable, appealing and, in some respects, unusual. They both wanted me in a way that made me feel pursued and desirable.

And, with both of them, my inclination to stay in control, to hold myself a little apart from the whole thing, remained stronger than my sexual interest in them. I didn't feel anything like overpowering lust—or what I imagined overpowering lust might feel like. Thinking about this in bed with Patrick one night, I also thought about how much I liked him, and this made me wonder if lust and sex were yet more experiences that in real life turned out to be much feebler than their literary and Technicolor depictions.

Maybe what I was enjoying was all there was. Maybe the pursued and desirable feeling and the physicality of sex were the things everyone enjoyed, and the difference was in the perception and characterization of these pleasures. They struck me as nice, but rather minor compared to the mind-blowing, life-changing sex I'd read about in books and seen on the screen, but maybe these exact pleasures were what other people were perceiving as amazing. Maybe my problem wasn't that I'd never *had* what other people perceived as great sex, but that I'd never *perceived* it that way.

I felt disillusioned and a bit cheated when I considered that this might be the case. It was the same way I'd felt about work when I was a rookie. I'd been truly disappointed that the Firm was so much like high school and so much less than I'd expected it to be. I hated to think that sex was more of the same, but, really, why wouldn't it be? Why wouldn't great sex be just another thing that wasn't what it was cracked up to be?

My perceptions about sex had been shaped by other people's perceptions, and other people *never* seemed to see things the way I did. From my family's definition of what was feminine, to the business world's attitude toward women, to what most of my colleagues seemed to think constituted working hard—to me, they all seemed wrong, off, illogical, incomprehensible.

My own perceptions might have been overly analytical and they were certainly out of the mainstream, but I trusted them. The swooning women portrayed in literature and movies (mostly written by men, when I thought about it), even the swooning women I'd known over the years—they were all probably having the exaggerated reaction to sex that they'd come to believe they were *supposed* to have, given the cultural messages they'd been stuffed full of since they were teenagers.

I had hoped that sex wouldn't be the same disappointing letdown that so many other life experiences had turned out to be. Was I now required to conclude that it was just one more thing that failed to live up to its reputation? Was great sex nothing but a fiction—either a willful puffing up or an overblown perception of what was in reality a nice, but relatively trifling, pleasure?

I wasn't crazy about the cynicism of these thoughts. I liked to think of myself as analytical, objective, rational—even skeptical—but not as fundamentally cynical. I also found myself remembering, with discomfort, Ian's ugly and predatory assertion that I would benefit from being "fired up." He certainly couldn't have done it, but was it possible that I just hadn't yet run across someone who could?

Patrick was a charming and attractive person, and I liked him very much, but maybe there was some mechanism of attraction—hormonal or otherwise—that I simply didn't have for him. I'd slept with him and with Tyler, too, because they wanted me, not because I'd lusted after them. I'd gone out with other guys and *not* had sex with them because they hadn't pursued it. I'd never swooned over anyone, never felt for anyone the lust that, for example, Katherine had said she felt for Jordan practically from the day they met.

Would I ever feel that strongly about someone, I wondered, or was the way I felt about Patrick as good as it was going to get? That was certainly nothing to complain about, but I did feel a little as if reality had offered up a rather pastel version of something that had been promised in rich and vivid hues.

❖ ❖ ❖

A MONTH OR SO after Patrick and I got together, Tyler called to tell me that he was in love. I didn't take this too seriously. He had called with the same news three or four times before in the years since college, and the declaration had always turned out to be premature. Tyler was a very affectionate person and he was dying to be in love, so he tended to get ahead of himself with women he liked.

Still, he'd sounded different this time. On my way to meet him for coffee late one afternoon, I found myself very curious to hear what he had to say. As soon as I saw him, I knew how to articulate why he'd sounded different. He looked dreamy and deliriously happy. His eyes were shining, he couldn't stop grinning, and he sounded even more love-struck in person than he had on the phone.

He had bought coffee for both of us and was waiting impatiently in one of two cozily arranged easy chairs. He stood, hugged and kissed me as usual, then started telling me about Liz the moment we sat down. She was wonderful, he said—smart, strong-minded, independent. She was a graphic designer whom he'd met during intermission at the opera. She was very droll, sexy, fun and, he told me merrily, sincere in preferring him to his money.

Grinning more slyly and less dreamily, Tyler disclosed that Liz had replaced me as his official date at a family event the week before. He hoped I wouldn't be heartbroken or offended. I laughed and assured him that while I would miss both him and the business networking opportunities, I'd never dreamed I would be serving as his official date forever.

But I was surprised to hear he'd taken Liz to one of his family's events. That was a bigger step than he'd taken with any of the other women he'd imagined himself in love with; maybe he really was as smitten as he looked. I told him as much, and then, smiling, asked him how she handled the event. Looking very tender, Tyler said she was totally appropriate at the event and "in your league, Jane" in terms of being hilarious afterward about how excruciatingly formal the whole scene was.

He'd told Liz "all about" me, and one of the things she said after the event was that she was betting I wouldn't be sorry about being replaced as his official date after serving in that capacity for over three years. After she let that statement sink in for a moment or two—Tyler laughed and said she had killer timing—Liz promised him she was talking about the events only. She told him she loved being with him and thought she might very much like a multi-year contract of her own. He was in heaven.

Hearing all this, I thought she sounded pretty wonderful, too. Thanks to his money and status, over the years Tyler had attracted a lot of women determined to please him by being whoever they thought he wanted them to be. He had pretty good radar for this, but I'd often worried that his longing to be in love might jam his radar. I doubted that Liz was unimpressed by who Tyler was, family-wise, but it sounded to me as if she were connecting with the real Tyler and able to hold her own with him, too.

I told Tyler this; I also told him sincerely that I was truly happy for him. He couldn't wait to introduce Liz to me. With a happy laugh, he dismissed my suggestion that she might not want to feel like she was being evaluated by one of his old girlfriends. Apparently, they'd already talked about it. Tyler said she was really looking forward to meeting me, and asked if I was available for dinner Saturday night.

I had a date with Patrick for Saturday, but it occurred to me that a foursome might be more comfortable for Liz, just in case she wasn't quite as delighted at the thought of meeting me as Tyler seemed to believe. She would probably still feel like she was being sized up, but I thought a fourth would neutralize at least some of the potential awkwardness—especially a fourth who could talk entertainingly on almost any topic.

Tyler was glad to include Patrick, whom he'd met at Firm events. When I checked with Patrick, he said in his usual laissez-faire way that it was fine with him. He also laughed and told me he knew I'd be glad to hear there was no chance he'd show up with another black eye—the fall rugby season was over. By that time, I'd gotten used to the colorful and painful-looking contusions all over the soft tissue parts of his body (chest, arms, inner thighs), but I still flinched at fresh facial bruises.

We had a great time with Tyler and Liz on Saturday. Liz was terrific and she fit right in; she was natural and friendly, sincere and fun. She was also quite obviously crazy about Tyler. She wasn't gooey—she was sharp, funny and very fast on her feet conversationally—but, whenever she looked at him, her face softened and her eyes had the same tender look his did. They seemed both excited and gentle together. As Patrick said to me later, the air between Liz and Tyler was charged.

It was evidently the kind of charged air that was infectious. After dinner, Patrick and I went home and made love very passionately—more rugby player than investment banker, we agreed, laughing, afterward. I didn't quite manage to let go and throw myself wholly into it, but it was very good. I came as close as I ever had to experiencing it solely as a participant instead of partly as a participant, partly as an observer.

This pleased me. It also made me like Patrick even more. Maybe it just took time, I thought, time and someone I liked a lot, to get to the point where I could stop feeling I had to hold myself separate and in control, where I could get carried away, where we would have the kind of feelings for each other that made the air around us crackle.

❖ ❖ ❖

Charlie

A scandal tore through Corp Fin in the spring of my ninth year at the Firm. Seven people—three from M&A, four from the Public Offerings group, and all of them senior—were discovered to have traded on inside information. The resulting investigation revealed that they had also been padding expense reports. The seven people were fired and ordered to make restitution. The head of Corp Fin, on whose watch the mess had occurred, was also fired.

The rest of us were dealing with the fallout, which included reorganizing Corp Fin and smoothing relationships with nervous clients and employees, all while federal regulators asked questions, flyspecked our procedures, and generally made their presence felt. In short order, the Executive Committee named Jim the new head of Corp Fin and Jim promoted me to his former position as head of the M&A group.

This was both expected and unexpected. I'd always assumed my career track would include Jim's job, but this was much sooner than the promotion would have occurred in the ordinary course. Two of the people caught up in the scandal were the most likely candidates, based on seniority and power, to succeed Jim as head of M&A. Their terminations cleared the way for me to get the job. Despite the circumstances, I was pleased with the opportunity and determined to make the most of it.

Jim told me he was comfortable with my ability to manage M&A and asked me to keep him posted via weekly meetings. He said he did not plan to look over my shoulder, but would be spending most of his time for the foreseeable future rebuilding Public Offerings. Robert, the former head of that group, had been the ringleader in the scandal. He was a known asshole, but he'd had a lot of clients and a long track record of successful offerings. His departure, together with his three principal cronies, left a gaping hole in the group and a great deal of concern among the remaining people.

M&A wasn't quite as shaken up, but there was a ton to do. We had to cover pending deals, some of which had been left short-staffed by the terminations. We needed to call on clients as soon as possible to give them both the personal explanation they deserved and the reassurance of the Firm's integrity and attention to their interests they required. There was also the matter of employee relations. From senior officers to associates, analysts and secretaries, everyone was worried about the solidity of Corp Fin's future—and about the form it would take.

I sat in my office one Saturday afternoon, trying to figure out how best to reorganize M&A. After a couple hours of feeling like I was rearranging the deck chairs on the Titanic, I realized I needed someone to bounce ideas off of and brainstorm with. Jim and I had talked in big picture terms, but the organizational design specifics were proving to be a puzzle that was harder to put together than I'd anticipated. Jim wasn't in the office that Saturday and, anyway, he had enough on his hands with the much more decimated IPO group—not to mention the constant reports he had to provide to the regulators and the jittery Executive Committee.

I decided to call Jane. She'd left the Firm only a little over six months before, so she was still sufficiently familiar with the players and with M&A's clients and operations. She could also offer the objectivity of someone who no longer worked in the group or at the Firm. All that plus her first-class strategic thinking and planning skills were exactly what I needed.

Hoping she hadn't changed her habit of working on Saturdays, I called her at her office. I let the phone ring several times, remembering that she'd said one difference between the Company and the Firm was the origin of important calls. At the Firm, the important calls were from outside callers; inside calls from colleagues always took second place to calls from clients or potential clients. Jane said it was just the opposite at the Company. Outside calls were more likely to be headhunters or insurance agents, and the calls you prioritized were those from colleagues.

For that reason, Jane rarely answered her phone when the caller ID told her it was an outside call. More than once, I'd left a message with her secretary or on her phone mail, only to get a return call almost immediately. She'd apologized for the runaround, but explained that it was more efficient to get messages and call back than to risk getting embroiled on a call with someone trying to recruit her or sell her something.

Evidently, she relaxed her rule about outside calls on Saturdays. After not too many rings, she did answer her phone.

"Jane, I'm glad I caught you," I said. "I need your help."

"Hey, Charlie, how are you?" she said cheerfully. I found myself smiling in response to her tone. "What's up?"

"You'll be amazed at what's up—or maybe you won't, given your opinion of some of the senior people here." I outlined what had happened and who was out, described Jim's and my new positions, then told her I was trying to figure out how the hell to organize M&A and could really use her help.

Jane was shocked by the scandal and very pleased to hear about Jim's and my promotions. She was also pleased in what she called an "evil way" that one of the M&A people caught in the mess was Howard, whom she'd never liked. We talked about all this for a little while, then she said, "I'd love to help you put your puzzle together. When do you want to meet and talk about it?"

"Now?" I suggested. "Or tonight? I'll buy you dinner."

She laughed. "Charlie, it's Saturday."

"So?"

"So Saturday night is for dates and I have one tonight. How about if I meet you at your office tomorrow afternoon instead?"

"OK," I said, frustrated at having to wait, "but I'd rather meet somewhere else. You know how the Firm is. The last thing I need is people wondering whether you're here to replace them. It's not really something I want to talk about in public either."

"Why don't you come to my office then?" Jane said. "I guarantee you there will be no one here but us and the lonely security guard in the lobby."

"That works. How about if I meet you there at 1:00?"

"Perfect. See you then. Oh, and congratulations again! You really deserve this. I'm impressed that the Firm made such a good decision. And I'm very, very happy for you."

By the time I got to the Company's building the next day, I felt as if I'd been thinking about how to organize M&A for weeks instead of days. I was glad to see that Jane was already in the lobby—and amused to see that she and the security guard were having an animated conversation. Jane always knew the names of the guards at the Firm's building, too, and they always liked her as a result. When I'd kidded her about this, she'd told me rather sanctimoniously that the guards were actually people and, in her opinion, it was rude to walk by them day after day as if they weren't.

Jane introduced me to her new friend, Ray, and then, after writing down the name of a book she'd recommended for him, she told him we'd be working on 37 for a few hours.

In the elevator, I smiled and said, "So now you're organizing a security guard book club?"

She laughed. "Just with Ray. He's the weekend guy. Around here, I'm practically the only person he ever sees. He loves books about World War II, and Patrick just finished one about the fall of Berlin that he said was great, so I was telling Ray about it." She looked me over. "You don't look as relaxed as usual. Are you OK?"

"This org design shit is driving me crazy. I haven't been able to come up with a model that covers pending deals and makes sense from an overall client service standpoint using the people we've got." I raked my hand through my hair. "And the troops get more anxious every day. I'm spending all my time either reassuring people or rejecting yet another possible structure for the group. Except for calling on a few key clients, I haven't done anything that feels like real work for two weeks."

Jane smiled. "Welcome to management. It's very weird to have to redefine productivity to mean babysitting with other people and motivating them to get the work done, isn't it? Doing the work yourself is pretty easy by comparison."

"That's for damn sure," I agreed. "Remind me again why the hell we want to be managers?"

Jane laughed as the elevator opened.

She was right—the place was deserted. She led me to a conference room, then said she would round up something to eat and drink in the nearby kitchen while I got out my org charts and client and deal lists. Grinning, she told me to feel free to get comfortable. She said she'd chosen the conference room because it had both an already-dinged table that I could put my feet on and enough room for me to "stride around angrily in."

When she came back—with two sodas and a bowl of what she referred to with enthusiasm as "the good chips"—I took her through the papers and described what I was trying to accomplish. She listened and asked perceptive questions as always, then shook her head impatiently at the answers.

"Here's your problem," she said. "You're too focused on the particular things that need to get done right now. You can't design this kind of model from the bottom up like that. You need to step back—forget about the real world and assume a perfect world for a few. If you don't think about what you're trying to accomplish in a more goal-y way first, you really are just rearranging deck chairs. Do you see what I mean?"

"Yeah, I do, but the things that need to get done right now really are urgent. I don't have time for some elaborate goal-setting process."

She shook her head again. "I'm not talking about some bullshit process. And the purpose for what I'm suggesting is to get you quickly to a model that works, not to impress some consultant—or even to get buy-in from the troops, although being able to articulate your goals will help you do that, too. We can do what I'm suggesting right now and get it done in half an hour."

She bit into a chip with a loud crunch, chewed briefly, and said, "Tell me why you think the M&A group should exist."

"Huh?"

"Work with me here, OK?" she said, with a smile. "This isn't rocket science. We're going to articulate three things: why you think the Firm should have an M&A group; what you think the ideal group would look like and do; and what skills and behaviors you think the perfect people for that ideal group would have. When we've done that, we'll know what your model needs to look like. I promise." She put her hand over her heart, then leaned forward, looked at me keenly and demanded, "So why is it important for Corp Fin to have an M&A group? What's the purpose for the group? What distinctive value does it add?"

"This all sounds very corporate, Ms. Brand Manager," I said, smiling. "But OK. I'll play."

It took us about 40 minutes to settle on an articulation of Jane's three items that felt right to me (and that she was willing to accept). And she was right about the value of the exercise. When we'd done it, it was clear how to set up the group to cover what mattered most. I quickly sketched out an org design that suited the purposes we'd articulated and the goals I wanted the group to achieve.

That done, it was also clear where my current players fit and where the holes were, so we started talking about staffing—or "resource allocation," as Jane (with a roll of her eyes) said it was called in the corporate world.

She felt strongly that it made no sense to put one group of people to work covering pending deals and a different group on making reassuring client calls. She thought everyone with a place in the group should be focused on both current work *and* client retention and development. She scorned the suggestion that people didn't have time for both and said it was a question of focus and working style, not time.

Using Lynn and me as examples, Jane insisted it was possible to do deals in a way that also retained clients and developed future business. She thought the ideal state M&A group would *only* have people who could work this way effectively. Even at the analyst level, she suggested, why not insist on people who could consider the big picture and their role in keeping clients as well as expertly crunch numbers and run spreadsheets?

This made a lot of sense to me once I got over thinking about it in terms of the people in the group I knew weren't up to it. I got over that pretty fast—the minute I expressed the thought, Jane looked disgusted and stated that great structures did not get built from crappy raw materials. Waving a chip at me, she told me I should be thinking about how to develop or hire the right people, not how to avoid difficult conversations with mopes—no matter how much I might think I needed them to cover current emergencies.

Although I gave her a hard time about the term "core competencies" and some other corporate-speak mumbo jumbo she used, I really liked what she was suggesting. If I rebuilt along the lines we'd articulated with people able to ace the tasks and functions we'd identified as the valuable ones, I'd have exactly what I wanted: a world-class M&A group able to work as a team to meet client needs efficiently, guarantee client retention and development, and contribute big value to Corp Fin and the Firm.

"And," Jane said, "a group able to regain and probably exceed the power and prestige lost because of the scandal. You'll be a hero!"

"That would be nice," I said, getting up to stretch. "We're not as bad off as the IPO group, but M&A definitely isn't the prestige place to be at the moment. That's the thing that bothers me the most about this whole fucking mess. I don't see how guys that senior could have had so little regard for the group or the Firm—or how they could have been willing to sell their integrity and their careers for a few extra bucks."

"I'm sure that's not how they thought about it," Jane said. "Those guys never cared about the group or the Firm. They were always totally focused on getting what they could for themselves. And in a non-strategic way, too—you know, they weren't nice to other people and they didn't think about the future or how to leverage their efforts. They just tried to maximize their own power and position every day, including by stepping on other people. They probably thought they were entitled to the extra money."

"Come on." I leaned against the window and met her indignant expression with a disbelieving one. "Short-selling stock after learning negative info during due diligence? Padding expenses? They had to know those things were wrong and dangerous, not to mention incredibly stupid risks to take. Hardly easy money compared to what they stood to earn from the Firm over the rest of their careers."

"Hey, they saw a score and they went for it," she snapped. "Those guys considered themselves way beyond concepts like wrong and dangerous. I bet they shorted that stock and inflated expenses simply because they could. They always thought they were too powerful for rules to apply to them. And I doubt they considered it risky at all—wouldn't surprise me if they justified what they were doing by telling themselves 'everyone does it.' They might even *believe* everyone does it. Everyone they think matters, anyway. Plenty of people like them do."

"But, Jane," I argued, taking a handful of chips (she was right; they were good chips), "they're all savvy businessmen, and their actions were just stupid. What they stood to gain wasn't as much as what they stood to lose."

She shook her head. "You're giving them way too much credit. And thinking with your way-too-trusting attitude. They didn't see what they stood to lose as years of increasing compensation and prestige at the Firm. You have to be willing to trust other people—and in the future—to see it that way. People like Howard and Robert are slime bags. Naturally, they assume other people are as slimy and untrustworthy as they are. I'm sure they figured they'd inevitably get screwed and so the right M.O. was to take what they could while they could."

"I may be way too trusting," I teased her, "but that's better than being way too cynical."

"I'm not cynical, Charlie," she said defensively (as I'd known she would). "I'm *skeptical*. I've been on the receiving end of a lot more unfairness and intolerance than you have, so I only trust people who show me they're trustworthy."

"Time out," I said, grinning and holding up my hands to slow her down. "I don't want to get into this old conversation. We're not done fixing M&A yet."

Jane smiled, but she spoke seriously. "Running the group properly is actually sort of the same conversation. You need to make it clear what the rules are—what it will take to be successful in the group—to people who are disinclined to trust, which is most people. Then you need to be consistent about rewarding the ones who do the right things and getting rid of the ones who don't. If Howard and his buddies had been forced to play by the right rules for the last fifteen years, they would either have played fair or gotten fired years ago—and before they caused this mess."

"You think they didn't know what the right rules were?"

"I think they knew exactly what the *real* rules were: get everything you can as fast as you can get it and don't let anyone get ahead of you. They put their interests ahead of the Firm's and treated people like shit the whole time I was there, and neither Jim nor anyone else made them do anything different."

I thought about this as I sat back down. "I guess that's right, but you still have to hold them primarily responsible. Short of fraud and criminal activity, it was more their responsibility to play fair than the Firm's to make them."

"It was both," she insisted. "The Firm tolerates way too much bad behavior. It's the tolerance that makes people think they can get away with it—and maybe even that bad behavior is expected or the only way to get ahead. I bet the only reason that crowd got fired this time was that this was too big to ignore. Given all the clients those guys controlled, the EC probably thought at least twice about whether it had to fire them even over this."

"They didn't think twice; they had no choice," I told her. "But there was some 'what's the big deal?' rumbling from a few people in high places."

"See, that's my point!" she exclaimed. "The Firm won't be the kind of place you want it to be until it's politically incorrect to do the *wrong* things."

This comment reminded me of what my friend Jeff had said about jaded and cynical being the prevailing attitudes, and right and wrong having bendable meanings, at his former company. I told Jane about his decision to leave the corporate world for teaching and also about what he'd said.

She recalled my father's point about how the only reliable way to transform an environment to one that didn't tolerate thugs was to work to assure that power was moved to, and held only by, people who used it to further the right goals. "Actually," she then said, "let me look at that principal client contact list again."

I found it and gave it to her. She read it, frowning. "Do you think these people are really the best ones to manage the Firm's relationships with these clients?" she asked.

"Most of them, yeah. And, in the other cases, they're the people who own the clients."

"No, the Firm owns the clients—or it should. If you want to build a meritocracy, you have to assign the client management role based on merit. It should be a prize reserved for people who are good at doing it. And it's not the only prize either. There will be plenty of prizes, monetary and otherwise, for people who buy in to your goals and act accordingly."

Jane got up, stretched, and then sat on the table with her legs folded under her.

"Client management should be a privilege," she declared, "not a perk for people who manage to stick around long enough or something that's grandfathered from the past. You can't tolerate hoarding clients and seeking to make them loyal to the person instead of the Firm, let alone reward that or permit people to consider it the only path to success."

"Good point, but not very realistic," I said. "At least not right now. Nervous senior people are not going to be willing to let go of what makes them powerful, which is their client bases. I'd have a mutiny on my hands."

She looked displeased, as if my comment disappointed her. "Their client bases only make them powerful because that's how the group worked up to now. You're going to redefine ownership—and power, too." Her face lit up. "In fact, you can make a big dramatic gesture to that effect—and show them all how serious you are—by making other people the principal contacts for all of your own clients! Now that you're in charge of the group, you don't need to hoard clients to be powerful. You won't have time to relationship manage them anyway. And you should be setting the right example."

"I'm not saying no," I said, smiling at her idealism, "but my clients are *why* I am where I am. Don't I leave myself vulnerable if I let my power base get diluted?"

"Maybe," she admitted. "I haven't quite figured that out. It does seem that bad guys willing to cheat often beat good guys who insist on playing fair. But it feels wrong to compromise what you're trying to accomplish just because somebody might cheat."

She ate another chip absently, looking puzzled. Then she asked, "Is your personal control of important clients really the whole reason you are where you are? Obviously, it hasn't hurt, but isn't it more defensive or protective than causative?"

"What do you mean?"

"It seems to me that you—and Jim, too—got these promotions not so much because you control clients, but because you act like leaders and are respected by the people who work with you. That's why I said yesterday that I was impressed the Firm promoted both of you. You're not just great rainmakers and client-handlers. You also treat people well and fairly, you're honest and you're inclusive. You're the kind of people who can put Corp Fin back on its feet after this crisis."

"Thanks, but don't forget that if Howard and Dan hadn't been involved in causing the crisis, one of them would have gotten the promotion instead of me."

"Aren't you supposed to be trying to make me *less* cynical?" Jane said, grinning. "I was giving the Firm the benefit of the doubt! Seriously, though, that may be true, but it may not. I can see Jim bypassing those guys, can't you?"

"Hard to say," I answered, thinking about it. "He would have wanted to, I think, but he might not have been willing to risk losing their clients if they decided to walk."

"See, that's why you have to change the deal on control of clients! You know I agree that power is the whole story, but it can't be allowed to result from bad behavior like hoarding clients. Client service teams have to be headed by skilled relationship managers who act in the interests of the client and the Firm—and who believe their personal interests are best served by doing that."

"I'm not arguing with that. I also agree that the senior person doesn't have to be the relationship manager or the client's principal contact. You proved that to me back when John was your client. And it makes sense for Lynn to take over the relationship manager role with him now." I smiled at Jane's pleased nod of approval for this idea. "But there's still the question of where my power comes from in a place like the Firm if I don't own my clients."

Jane was silent. She looked thoughtful. Then she said, "I think I might be able to answer that, but let's take a break first, OK? I'll meet you back here in five—and I'll get us more to drink, too. Soda or water?"

When she came back, she looked pleased. "OK," she said, handing me a bottle of water and perching on the edge of her chair. "How about this? You'll generate a lot of loyalty from the people you give your clients to and from other people in the group who already respect you and will like the way you're going to run it, right?"

"Yeah, I suppose," I said, putting my feet up on the table.

"So wouldn't you actually be far more powerful with the loyalty and support of lots of people who want you in charge of M&A than you'd be in the usual 'every man for himself' situation with nothing but the clients you can hoard? Seems to me you'd be practically bulletproof with virtually the whole M&A group feeling that their interests are best served by supporting you—and, accordingly, doing a great job of living up to your goals and making the group wildly profitable."

"Possibly. That would certainly be a more institutionally focused way to run things. I'd have Jim's backing, too. But isn't generating across-the-board loyalty and support essentially a popularity contest?"

"Like you'd have any trouble winning one of those!" she said, smiling. "But no, it's really not a popularity contest. You wouldn't be asking people to like you. You'd be counting on them to like what's in their own best interests—that is, exciting goals and lots of success for M&A, along with appropriate recognition and reward for what they contribute."

She paused, but she had her about-to-burst look, so I said, "OK, go on" instead of commenting.

"I think I'm really on to something with this!" she said, her hands starting to fly around. "Look at us for example. I like you very much, but that's not why I was a loyal supporter of yours at the Firm. I was loyal to you because you treated me fairly and helped me succeed. Or think about Frank—remember him, the ERISA lawyer on your dad's deal? He's a better example. He really *doesn't* like you, but he's loyal to you, too, because you gave him the credit he deserved on that deal. He gets that it's in his best interests to support you even though he affirmatively *dislikes* you."

At my look of distaste, which wasn't for her point, but for Frank, Jane leaned forward, tapped my knee, and said, "OK, then think about it in sports terms. The wide receivers don't play their hearts out for a quarterback because they think he's a nice guy. That helps, probably, but they play their hearts out for him because they believe that he's talented enough to move the ball down the field series after series and that he'll throw them their share of passes. They understand that they need someone in his position and they believe he can make them winners, so his and their interests are lined up."

"Very impressive, Jane!" I mocked. "You sound like one of the boys."

"Don't patronize me," she warned, pointing her finger at me.

"Don't patronize *me*!" I said, pointing mine at her. "I was frowning because you mentioned Frank, not because I need a sports analogy to get the point."

"Fair enough," she grinned. "Sorry. So are you buying it? The point, I mean? That you'll be plenty powerful—maybe even more than you are now—if you spread your clients around and run the group the way it should be run?"

"Yeah, I am," I said, realizing I was. I put my feet back on the floor, recapped my now empty bottle of water and drummed it lightly against my palm as I talked. "I'm still not sure how power like that works relative to dealing with thugs—and there are still a few of those in the group and on the Executive Committee. But I'd rather set things up the right way than compromise just to protect myself against assholes."

"Exactly!" Jane said, looking delighted. "Well said!" With an evil grin, she added, "Don't forget you now outrank the thugs in the group, so you've got position power over them. Use that to get to know their clients, who will probably like you better anyway. Once you're in with the clients, you can do whatever you want with the thugs who refuse to play your way."

I laughed. "You don't take prisoners, do you?"

"Nope," she said with terrifying relish, "and neither should you. As for the EC thugs, they may try to undermine you, but they won't do it right away. Jim can protect you for a while. All you need is time to get M&A humming along so lucratively that even the EC dopes will realize it would be counterproductive to disrupt you. Maybe they'll even wake up and try to run the rest of the Firm your way.

"God, Charlie, this is totally thrilling! You really have the chance to build a meritocracy! And how cool is it that you'll be able to deep-six assholes not by sinking to their level and crushing them but by creating an environment where their bullshit simply won't play?"

"It's pretty cool," I agreed, smiling. "I like the idea of making it clear how we're going to play and then refusing to compromise on that. I like it a lot. I may not brandish the hatchet quite as soon or as broadly as you would, though. Some of the thugs probably act the way they do because they think they're supposed to. Once the environment starts to swing the other way, they'll probably do the same."

"That's a little trusting for my money," Jane said, her eyes narrowed. "Keep the hatchet close by in case they don't, OK?"

"I will," I promised. "Any other suggestions?"

"Yeah, I meant to mention this before. Use the mentoring program to select and build the behaviors you want. It could be really powerful, much more so than it is now. Elevate some people who deserve it and create visibility for them by making them mentors. Lynn and Cheryl, for example, both deserve it based on performance and attitude. They would be fantastic mentors, and you and whoever ends up in charge of Cheryl's group would be making quite a statement by designating them."

Her expression softened as she said, "Mentoring done right makes a huge difference for the Firm and the mentee, too—not just for the mentors. I'm an obvious example of that. If you hadn't been my mentor, the Firm wouldn't have gotten anywhere near as much value from me. And there's no way I'd have had the success I've had or gotten to where I am now without your help. I'll owe you forever!"

"I got plenty of benefit from our mentoring relationship, too," I told her, smiling. "And you've made a big dent today in any debt you still think you owe me. This has been incredible! Thank you very much."

"You are totally welcome," she said, with a satisfied nod of her head. "You're going to have a world-class M&A group—I'm sure of it. I'm a little sorry I'm not there to be part of it. Actually, I kind of wish I *were* you right now. It's going to be really fun to march in there tomorrow and start doing things right!"

Later that night, I outlined what I wanted to say at the all-hands meeting I intended to call the following day for M&A. As I thought about it, I realized there were aspects of the approach Jane and I had mapped out where compromise wouldn't hurt the overall outcome and, by making and keeping people less anxious, it might actually help.

In particular, I saw no reason to ax or threaten the thugs pre-emptively. If I joined them as they called on their clients as a show of my support rather than as an outright "play my way or get fired" threat, I might be able to turn them around. As the new head of the group, I *should* be introducing myself to other people's clients. It was a good client management strategy as well as a chance to show the thugs they'd have my backing if they shaped up and played by the rules.

This approach seemed more in line with how I wanted to run M&A and be seen as its leader. I liked the idea of standing in front of the group and saying truthfully that everyone had a chance to play and win—and that the playing field would be level for everyone willing to buy in to the new model and act accordingly.

It would always be possible to deal properly with people determined to be thugs. Why not start by assuming they would all play fair once they knew they had to in order to survive, let alone to be successful in my group? The positive "here's your chance" approach seemed both fairer and more intelligent than the preemptive "you're an asshole and you're out" power play.

I didn't plan to be stupid about it. Jane was probably right in thinking that a few people were less likely to play fair than they were to sprout wings and fly. I would keep the hatchet handy and my eyes and ears open, as well as develop personal relationships with all of M&A's clients as soon as I could. I had no doubts about my ability to impress and hang onto clients even if I ended up having to fire their original Firm contacts.

I also liked the idea of getting to know all the group's clients and continuing to play a lead role in developing new ones. I enjoyed the work involved in originating clients and generating repeat business. And I had a great track record and reputation for successful business development. All but the worst thugs would be glad to have my assistance, especially in a model where they wouldn't have to worry that their clients would somehow land on my roster instead of theirs for compensation purposes.

It occurred to me that I could also cull the group's client list via this process. Like all old, relationship-based businesses, the Firm was saddled with some clients that generated pretty paltry revenue—sometimes not enough for the work we did for them to make us a decent profit.

Under the usual system, people's power resided in the clients they controlled—not irrespective of profitability, but with less attention to meeting reasonable profitability requirements than made sense for a business. People tended to hang onto clients—and the Firm tended to let them—all as if the number of clients you had were more important than the number of dollars your clients generated in annual revenues.

This un-businesslike approach had always seemed misguided to me. In my new model, we could set profitability standards and then refer the clients that failed to meet them to bankers more suitable to handle their work. This would let us concentrate on developing and handling work for clients we could serve well and make good money on, thereby improving M&A's overall profitability—probably significantly.

As I went through the client lists, I was interested and a little surprised to see that there was a fairly high correlation between thugs and less than top-drawer clients. Why had the Firm been accommodating these assholes year after year when even a total loss of their clients wouldn't have amounted to anything to get overly excited about?

I decided that question had to be either rhetorical or yet one more bewildering example of how traditionally and mindlessly the Firm ran certain aspects of its business. For that and a whole host of other reasons, I couldn't wait to do exactly what Jane had said—march into the joint the next day and start running my group right.

CHAPTER 10
VARIATIONS ON A THEME

Jane

L iz and I met for a drink one evening shortly after Tyler called to let me know the two of them were getting married. He continued to sound as love-struck as he had the first time he'd told me about her, and I couldn't have been happier for both of them.

I thought Liz was wonderful, too. We'd gotten together several times without Tyler since the dinner at which he'd introduced us, and my first impression of her as someone who was sincerely connecting with the real Tyler—as opposed to the "good catch" he represented— had solidified into friendship.

Among Liz's many sterling qualities was her complete lack of concern or discomfort with Tyler's and my relationship. Of course, he and I had quit sleeping together once he met her, but we continued to have an easy and relaxed way of interacting—a familiar shorthand thanks to nearly five years of being friends after our two years of being a couple in college. We knew each other inside out and we liked each other a great deal; even without sex, our relationship was really quite intimate.

As Liz humorously (and to Tyler's delight) described it, Tyler and I were like an old married couple. A lesser woman than Liz might easily have found this threatening. Not only was she undisturbed by it, she had told me she was relieved and impressed to know that I was the kind of woman Tyler admired—and who admired him. She'd said getting to know me made her think even more highly of him.

I was flattered by her regard for me and also tickled that she gave me credit for Tyler's non-sexist approach to women in general and girl-friends in particular. We had a very interesting conversation about this not too long after Liz first spent time with Tyler's family. Like me, she was initially put off by his mother, a lady who, at first blush, seemed impossibly elegant and entirely too conventional.

When I told Liz then how happy I was that she and Tyler were together, she said, "It's remarkable to me—I've fallen for him like a ton of bricks! I've never felt this way about a guy before. I find him totally irresistible. He's so interesting and talkative—particularly for a guy— and he's very loving. Unpretentious, too, despite his fancy family. He's not at all sexist either, as far as I can tell. Do I have you to thank for that?"

"Oh, I reeled him in from a sexist thought or two," I smiled, "but he's really not that different from the way he was when we met. Did he tell you we got together because he needed help getting through a calculus class and decided to ask me for it?"

"Yeah, he did, and that's one of the reasons I think he's so unpreten-tious and non-sexist," she said, with a laugh. "How many guys do you know who can comfortably joke about their shortcomings or tell you a woman solved their problem?"

"Not very many," I agreed. "But Tyler's always been comfortable with who he is. He doesn't stress over shortcomings."

"Still," Liz said, "I feel more confident about his not being sexist now that I've met you. I was a little worried that it was nothing but a convincing act when I met his mother."

I laughed. "She's not as bad as she seems at first. She's pretty smart and she definitely has a backbone. Her heart's in the right place, too. She knows she has power to wield as the wife of a rich, powerful man, and she sees that as a responsibility to take seriously. Walker and Tyler both listen to her and respect her opinion."

"That's good to hear." Liz sounded relieved. "The whole time I was with her I wondered if she noticed anything about me other than my shoes and jewelry—and whether she thought those were even remotely up to par. She was pleasant enough to me, I guess, but a little frosty, and there was no evidence of deep thought or backbone. Also, she looked perfect—elegant and lovely. Quite scary, really."

"I used to feel that way around her, too," I admitted. "But she never said anything that made me feel badly dressed or out of place. Even if nothing but good manners kept her quiet, I don't think you need to feel worried or intimidated." I shook my head. "She's OK, but can you imagine caring much about trivial crap like the appropriateness—or lack thereof—of shoes and jewelry? What a waste of time!"

"I really can't. I like to look presentable—and I will admit that sometimes there's nothing like a new pair of shoes to make me feel better about things." She grinned. "But I don't get women who make looks and possessions their top priorities."

"I have a friend from the Firm who says what really bugs her about women like that is their need to proselytize. She wonders why they need to try to recruit us if they're so happy with their own choices."

"We're just as bad toward them, though," Liz said, surprising me. "I mean, we may not be trying to recruit them, but we don't respect their choices. We're not any more respectful of their lifestyles than they are of ours. In fact, we probably don't try to recruit them because we think they're idiots!"

With a slightly bewildered look of disapproval, she continued, "It always amazes me that women are so hard on each other. It's not like we don't have enough adversity to deal with, given the way men treat us. You'd think we'd be natural allies able to respect each other's choices instead of rival camps fighting over who's righter or what's 'more feminine.' Really, other women hold us back and make us feel bad or unsure about our choices as much, if not more, than men do! It's very divisive when you think about it. Sad, too."

Liz's point was one I'd thought about often in the months since. She was right. Women had to fight enough battles against sexism without taking on one another. I'd decided to quit being part of the problem. The choice to be a traditional wife still seemed to me essentially a decision to be a parasite rather than a complete person—and I didn't feel any more respectful of it than I ever had—but I'd stopped undercutting other women by demeaning it aloud.

When Liz and I met for drinks after she and Tyler got engaged, we picked up on a topic we'd started to discuss once before. She'd said something about graphic design being a way to overcome resistance to change by helping people envision something new. She saw her work as a way of creating new realities, bringing ideas to life in people's imaginations.

I was intrigued by the idea of facilitating change by, essentially, pretending that something existed. I described my contempt for the widespread primacy in the business world of form over substance—and spin over truth—and asked her to tell me how she thought creating a pretense could help something real occur.

Whether because they tended not to approach new ideas visually or because they lacked imagination, Liz said, many people found it basically impossible to picture anything new, be it a product, a way of working, a new leader, even their own new lifestyle or the growth of their own children. Graphic designers worked with what Liz called "wordmeisters" to create and put out in the world the images that helped people develop their own mental pictures and see the new order.

Without a mental picture, Liz claimed, people felt lost and afraid—and, thus, unable to do something different, believe in something new or effectively change. She compared approaching something new without a visual picture to entering an unfamiliar dark house at night. It took unusual courage, she said, to feel comfortable or able to go about your business in the unfamiliar dark without a mental map. Similarly, people being asked to buy or do or believe something unfamiliar often got, if not paralyzed, then certainly very wedded to what felt familiar to them.

This fascinated me. The Company had recently "completed" a reengineering project. Although there had been a tremendous amount of hype around the project at every stage, my coworkers (even the stodgy among them) and I were in agreement that nothing had really changed operationally. A few people got new bosses, a few others were let go, but the people who remained were still doing what they'd always done the way they'd always done it.

I suspected the lack of change was due to poor communication of the purpose for and nature of the desired changes, poor thinking behind the reengineering (likely the result of consultants who didn't know what they were doing) or people's inherent resistance to change—most probably, in fact, to all three. What bothered me was the corporate-speak about the project. It was consistently spoken of by senior management as if it had been an unqualified success, and was even occasionally held up as an example of how these things could work.

Worse, any suggestion that the project had been something other than a total success was met with surprise and censure. The opportunity to learn from where the reengineering had gone off-track was utterly lost, completely swept away in the flood of positive spin. The whole thing reminded me of the Firm's pretense that everyone lived a Norman Rockwell painting sort of life, despite plenty of evidence to the contrary.

Liz's perspective made me wonder if the reengineering spin was something other than the self-serving bullshit I'd assumed it to be. It occurred to me that at least some of the happy talk might have been intended to be the kind of imagery that would help rank-and-file people throughout the Company visualize the desired changes.

Happy talk seemed to me a weak substitute for the leadership the happy talkers should have demonstrated relative to the reengineering. Actual leadership could have made the project effective and worth the effort and expense. Liz argued that visual imagery and leadership were not an either/or proposition, but rather two powerful forces meant to work in tandem. After we talked about this for a while, I had to admit it was possible the senior people sincerely believed that speaking of something as a big success might help to make it one—even if some of them did nothing to make it successful in reality *other* than talk about it glowingly.

"I can't believe I convinced you!" Liz crowed. "And I didn't even use pictures!"

"Well," I smiled, "I remain unconvinced of the merits of the Company's after-the-fact pretense that the whole thing actually *was* successful. Maybe you can work up some pictures to help me with that. Also, Liz, it strikes me as unlikely that people simply can't imagine a new way of doing their jobs without help. Don't they dream? Don't they have hopes? Don't they think ahead?"

"You have to realize how unusual you are," Liz said. "You can imagine difference, you can chart a course, and you have a great deal of courage."

"Well, thanks, but I'm not sure that's true," I demurred.

"Of course it is," she insisted. "If it weren't, you'd still be living in your hometown. You'd probably be married to someone, with a kid or two. You might not have gone to college—at all or where you did—and you certainly wouldn't have your experiences at the Firm or your fancy current job. You did something very unusual, Jane. You imagined a different way of living your own life, and you had the courage to make it happen."

"I guess," I said, thinking about it. "That felt more like escape than courage or imagination. But I get your point."

"A lot of people can't create a compelling picture for themselves, let alone set out to make it real. Even the ones who can tend not to bother unless what they're picturing is really important and personal to them. For most people, work probably isn't important or personal enough." Liz smiled. "Luckily, I guess, since otherwise I wouldn't have a job! Speaking of my job, there's something I've been meaning to ask you."

She traced the rim of her champagne glass with a fingertip, then looked up at me and said, "Do you think it's possible for me to keep doing my job after I'm married to someone like Tyler?"

"Sure. Why not?" I asked, surprised by the question.

"Well, I was originally thinking I'd handle it the same way he does. You know, by incorporating who he is into what he does. I was picturing things staying basically the same once I got used to the pace." She frowned. "But it won't be the same for me. Tyler's work is connected to all the social engagements and obligations in a way mine isn't. For me, those events and charitable boards will take up a fair amount of time that I would otherwise spend working. Also, my 'new identity' will complicate things for me at the office—with colleagues and with clients."

"Your last point is one of the things that drive me crazy about marriage!" In my haste to free my hands so I could gesture with them, I put my own champagne glass on the table with a definitive little clink that startled us both. I smiled, then said, "As far as other people are concerned, Tyler's identity won't change, but you're right—yours really will. That always seems to happen to some degree, but by marrying him, you're taking on way more than simply being married as opposed to being single."

"I know," Liz sighed. "I like to think I'll be able to continue to work for real—you know, the way I do now. I love my job. And getting married shouldn't require me to give it up. I'm hoping there will be a way to make it all work."

She smiled ruefully. "Tyler thinks I should have a personal stylist and a driver like the rest of them. But I don't see myself being dropped off at work by a chauffeur and I hope I can make myself presentable without help." She framed her face with her hands, then rolled her eyes. "Also, even if that kind of thing would make it easier for me to keep working, how am I going to do my job credibly if I never see the inside of a grocery store or have no idea what taxis cost?"

"Good question, but Tyler might be right," I said. "Wouldn't it be better to lose a little trivial normality than to have to give up your job or anything else important?"

"That's a smart way to look at it. I've been thinking I need to resist all the rich people pretensions, but maybe taking advantage of some of the less visible ones wouldn't be so bad." She laughed. "Hopefully, even with a stylist, I can avoid getting all hoity-toity or, God forbid, too much like Tyler's mother!"

"I'm sure you can avoid both," I said, smiling.

"I sure hope so!" Liz looked at her gorgeous watch (a birthday gift from Tyler), then said, "I have to get going. I'm so glad we've gotten to be friends, Jane! I don't think Tyler would have dumped me if you and I hadn't hit it off, but it wouldn't have been good."

"I'm sure he wouldn't have dumped you," I laughed. "He's crazy about you."

"Still, I'm glad we did hit it off. Thanks for being so friendly and fun." We stood and she hugged me as she added, "And thanks for not marrying Tyler, too!"

Later, as we trudged toward the subway in the rain, she said, with a wink, "It sure would be nice to have one of those limos to whisk us home tonight, wouldn't it?"

❖ ❖ ❖

I HADN'T HAD A CHANCE to talk to Charlie in person for nearly two months when we finally got together for dinner not too long after Cheryl's late August wedding. It was wonderful to see him. I knew when I left the Firm that I was going to miss our regular meetings, but I was surprised by how much I missed the *rigor* of our talks and also by how calming they were.

Charlie was always honest and direct, traits I was finding in short supply. Particularly at work, people seemed to be much more interested in promoting their own agendas than in listening and reacting candidly. When I was low on the totem pole, this took the form of trying to push me around or proselytize for one thing or another. As I gained in stature, it was starting to take the form of sucking up or telling me what the speaker presumed I wanted to hear. Charlie's candor was refreshing as well as helpful.

He was also still determined to convince me to knock what he called the sizeable chip off my shoulder. He was adept at seeing—and he loved to point out—where I was reacting out of presupposition or bias (or cynicism) instead of thinking logically or neutrally. This was a great check and balance for my more knee-jerk reactions to the various aggravations that surrounded and affected me daily.

He really had continued to provide the perspective and the outlet he'd offered during our mentoring year when he'd said if whining to him helped, I should feel free. With our now less frequent chances to talk, I found myself much more frustrated and angry about things, and it was taking a lot more effort to deal calmly with it all.

Because of my high frustration level, I had suggested we meet at the hole-in-the-wall seafood restaurant he'd taken me to in the middle of the

Ian thing. The food had been great, and the thought of once again tearing the shells off shrimp with my bare hands was very appealing.

The restaurant hadn't changed in any respect since our last visit over a year before. (Oddly, even the yellowing signs were the same. I wondered if years before they had gotten as yellowed as they were able to get and moved into some sort of paper holding pattern.) It was packed when we arrived, but Charlie talked to the bartender when we ordered drinks and somehow we were seated within fifteen minutes.

As soon as we sat down, I complimented Charlie on his multi-purpose charm and told him I'd missed both it and our regular conversations. With a smile, I confessed to being even more irritable than usual since I'd been deprived of both the sounding board and the metaphorical cat-kicking services he'd provided at least monthly for the better part of five years.

"Glad to be of assistance," he said, laughing. "I have to tell you, though, while I've always enjoyed your irritability, I don't think I want to experience any increase in its magnitude."

"You've always enjoyed it?" I asked, surprised.

"Yeah, it makes it so easy to get you ranting." He grinned. "When you rant, you always say something that goes too far and then it's easy to shoot you down. You're predictable, Jane—not wholly wrong very often and never dull, but predictable. Your irritability is your Achilles heel."

"Nice to know it has some upside for someone," I said, frowning sarcastically at him.

"Definitely," he said, still smiling. "Seriously, though, I've missed talking to you, too. I've gotten used to having both our takes on things over the years. It's useful."

"I've been thinking the same thing! In fact, there's something I want to bounce off you tonight."

"Shoot."

"Do you plan to get married some day?" I asked him.

Charlie looked taken aback. "What a weird question! Sure I do. Don't you?"

"I'm not so sure. You know that Cheryl got married last month, right?" He nodded and I continued, "She and Richard are very happy, but I was thinking at the wedding that my misgivings about marriage are stronger than ever. It's hard for me to imagine being willing to give up so much."

"What are you talking about? What would you be giving up?"

"Well, there are the obvious things, like my independence and my identity as myself instead of as someone's wife. Or people at work's ability to see me as a professional instead of as a woman—specifically, a woman liable to do some 'unprofessional' thing like have a baby or leave town because my husband gets a new job."

The restaurant was loud. I leaned toward him across our small table so I wouldn't have to shout. "There are all sorts of less obvious things, too. Like having to accommodate someone else's opinion of what I should do or who I should be or how I should act. Marriage just seems completely unequal to me and like a bad deal for women, you know?"

"No, I don't know," Charlie disagreed. "Obviously that's sometimes true, but I don't think it's inevitable or necessary."

"Really? Don't you?" I asked as he poured water into both our glasses from the carafe on the table, then drank most of his. "It seems inevitable to me. Every woman I know who's married or seriously involved has given up something I consider important. Her natural personality or how she behaves or what she expects or her power, her control over her own life, sometimes even her job or her own plans and goals." I ticked off these examples, finger by finger, ignoring his unconvinced expression. "Some of these women are really strong, too, so I'm thinking there must be something about marriage that makes compromising necessary or inevitable."

"Taking someone else's opinion into account and then adjusting your own plans or goals isn't necessarily compromising," he observed.

"No," I frowned, "but why is it that 'taking someone else's opinion into account' seems so often to mean that the *woman* gives something up? Either husbands make demands or there's something about women's sense of what marriage requires, but the bottom line is that women seem to be the ones adapting or adjusting what they want or sacrificing their independent identities when they get married."

I paused when the waiter, who was working like a dog trying to keep up with the crowd, stopped by our table. He and Charlie greeted each other like old friends and Charlie ordered the grilled shrimp and vegetables, as well as another round of drinks, for both of us. "What were you saying?" he then asked me.

"We talked about this when Katherine and Jordan got married, remember?" I said. "There's something very defining about marriage for women—not just in the way other people view us, but apparently in our own minds, too. Men seem to have more power where marriage is concerned, just like you do with so many other things. And for whatever reason, women seem to be willing to bow to that, to give stuff up, to get all malleable, even to be marginalized."

"That's a pretty negative construction," he said, his expression now decidedly skeptical. "I'm sure it's more individual than that. You, for example, would never agree to be marginalized and you know how to negotiate for what you want. It has to depend on who the people are, what they want for themselves and from each other, and what kind of deal they make."

"As usual, you're more trusting than I am," I said, smiling. "It looks more like a power struggle than an agreed-on deal to me. There always seems to be something predatory or proprietary about the man's role."

"That's ridiculous, Jane," Charlie said, with a frown that conveyed both amusement and exasperation. "Look at my parents, for example. I know you've only met my mother once, but that should have been enough for you to see that there's no way she or my father thinks he owns her or is somehow in charge of who she is or what she does."

"Well, but how hard does she have to work to maintain that sense of independence and equality? How hard does *he* have to work to maintain it, to see and treat her that way?"

"They've always been very happy together, so I'd guess not too hard." He stretched his legs out straight, so that he had a foot on either side of my chair. He often sat that way when we were in restaurants. After initially feeling a bit hemmed in by it, I'd come to find it cozy. "Seems to me it's a much more personal equation than you're making it out to be," he insisted. "It's just a matter of choosing well."

"I'm not so sure," I repeated. "I like being self-sufficient and self-reliant. I really can't imagine choosing to accommodate or depend in any important way on someone else, particularly someone to whom society gives all the cards and who probably feels if not invincible, then certainly mightier than I. Why willingly give someone so much power?"

"You are cynical, aren't you?" he said, shaking his head. "Have you heard of love?"

"Please." I rolled my eyes. "That's a big part of the problem. From what I've seen, love has a different impact on women—an aspect of surrender, for lack of a better term. I think that's probably because 'civilization' demands that we seek and prize it in a more primary way than men do. It's another one of those things that are considered defining for us, not to mention worth making sacrifices to get and hang on to.

Love seems to be the justification for giving up important things, changing in fundamental ways."

"You're including too much in your definitions of 'sacrificing' and 'compromising,'" Charlie argued. "You may think other women are changing in fundamental ways, but presumably they don't see it as that—or as a bad bargain."

"But why not? Why would being loved by someone who required that you give things up in order to love you strike someone as a good thing?"

"It wouldn't," he said, "but that's not what's going on. First, I don't think love is an intellectual thing—for men or for women. It's a feeling—a strong one that drives behavior, not one that causes people to coolly make cost-benefit decisions. Love itself is what strikes people as the good thing worth having. Second, I assume people think what they're getting is worth more—a lot more—than what you think they're giving up. It's actually a pretty powerful strategy. In your example, the woman doesn't see what she's doing as sacrificing. She sees it as doing what's necessary to get something she wants more."

"Like what?" I demanded. "It's hard to think of something that's worth giving up independence and freedom for."

"Aren't you listening?" He gave me a hard look. "That's not what people think they're giving up, you cynic! Can't you consider that they're making the adjustments they think are necessary to get what most people want—love, sex, companionship, someone to share the burdens with?"

"Yeah, I can consider it, but it's hard to buy it when women are the ones doing all the significant adjusting," I retorted, checking to see if the shrimp on the plates we'd just been given were cool enough to peel. (They weren't. Apparently knowing that, Charlie was still lounging in his chair, ignoring the food.)

"That's not true," he said patiently. "Men who get married are also putting themselves in the position of having to care about someone else's opinion. They're also giving up self-sufficiency and self-reliance. The point is that neither person *has* to be completely self-sufficient or self-reliant. Most people consider that a plus."

"But men still have more power! It seems to me that women make the bargains they make out of perceived need or maybe even out of fear. In a society where men hold all the cards, where every message says a woman is questionable and maybe even unnatural without love and marriage—and, probably, multiple orgasms and motherhood, too—she has to be pretty thick-skinned to take a different road."

"You want to stop waving that French fry at me?" he smiled. I ate the fry as he said, "So you don't think love, sex, companionship, etcetera are worth much?"

"I didn't say that. I said I don't think they're worth giving up independence and freedom and identity for. I don't see why it should be *necessary* to give up independence and freedom and identity for them. Men don't have to do that."

"Women don't have to do it either, Jane," Charlie said, now with exaggerated patience. He sat up, pulled his feet back to his side of the table, and started peeling a shrimp. "Some may—or it may look to you like that's what they're doing—but there's nothing about love or sex or marriage or companionship that requires any particular bargain. It's a matter of individual decisions, not a general requirement or an inevitability. You, of all people, should know these things aren't carved in stone."

"Nice words, buddy," I said, shaking my head, "but if what people want is to fit in, not to look unnatural or be shunned by a society that has very specific requirements for acceptable behavior, they're going to make coerced decisions, not intelligent or even heartfelt ones."

"So?" he challenged. "That's their problem. You can't reasonably extrapolate from that to yourself or use it to conclude that marriage is inevitably a bad deal for women."

"Fair enough—as a logical matter anyway," I conceded. "But if something happens most of the time, doesn't it make sense to be wary of it as a phenomenon instead of dismissing it as a series of unconnected individual bad decisions?"

"Go ahead—be wary. Like you'd do anything else, Ms. Cynic," he smiled, pulling the perfectly charred skin off another shrimp. "But that's an argument for choosing well and making a good deal, not for eliminating yourself from the game. Actually, it's just like your career decisions. You've never accepted the status quo or been limited by so-called 'standard rules' professionally. Why would you do it for your personal life?"

I considered this, my mouth full of grilled shrimp and tomato. "It's sort of the same thing," I finally said. "But I've never felt I had to give up my autonomy or anything important about my identity or personality to succeed at work. There's a different category of imbalance in romantic relationships—an inherent imbalance, I think. The crux of the issue probably relates to sex, but all of it—romance, love, sex—it all seems very categorically to put men not just in charge, but in an aggressor role that requires women to surrender *something* in order to get it and to make it work."

"That is even more ridiculous than what you said before," Charlie said, looking and sounding disgusted. "You don't trust men at all, do you?"

"Why would I? Practically all the evidence I have points the other way."

"You're extrapolating too far again," he said, his tone suggesting I should know better.

"Am I? Sex seems very predatory to me, both by its nature biologically and by how it works in our society. Even if it's not an over-the-line situation like with Ian, aren't men generally stronger? Don't you have far less to lose in just about every respect? Isn't the range of behavior generally considered acceptable much broader for you than for me? For God's sake, don't we even customarily define 'sexy' in terms that require women to be brainless and weaker?"

Charlie rolled his eyes. "Here we go again," he said. "Your delusion that sex is nothing but another way to exploit and subordinate women is still just as absurd as it was the last time you tried to make me buy it."

"That's not what I said that day!" I protested, recalling the argument about this in which I'd painted myself into a corner—and about which he'd been giving me a hard time ever since. "My point was that sex requires women to be willing to be vulnerable and to relinquish control with someone already more powerful, physically and societally."

"And mine was that the vulnerability is mutual and it isn't about control or relinquishing control at all."

"Yes, I got that," I said haughtily. "I believe I responded that that was an easier thing to say from your perspective than from mine."

He laughed. "Yes, you did. And I believe I parried that with my usual statement about that not making it wrong."

"Probably." I laughed, too. "Why do I like talking with you so much when we always seem to end up in the same place?"

"I told you you were predictable," he said lightly. "You approach things with distrust because you're certain there's sexism and inequality everywhere. You're not wrong about that, but you take it too far. There's no requirement that you be ruled by conventional views of anything—including men, women, marriage, love and even sex, despite biology."

"You make it sound as if I choose to be ruled by one thing or another and can just choose otherwise if I like. But it's not that simple. Prevailing views are prevailing views whether I like them or not. And I'm affected by them, also whether I like it or not."

"Affected by them, yes, but not ruled by them." He had assembled a bite of shrimp and green pepper, and he gestured with it to emphasize his words before he put it in his mouth. "You don't have to be limited or diminished by prevailing views. You just have to deal with them."

"I *just* have to deal with them?" I said, my eyebrows high. "If only life were as simple for everyone as it is for you, Mr. Golden Boy. It's nice being you, isn't it?"

"It is, actually," he said comfortably. "In large part because I'm willing to trust that the world is not generally out to screw me over."

I made a face of complete derision. "Since you're one of civilization's designated winners and the world *isn't* out to screw you over, that's not much of an accomplishment!"

"The world is a much nicer place than you think it is, Jane."

"Maybe," I allowed. "But it's nowhere near as nice a place as *you* think it is, Charlie." I gave his name the same pointed emphasis he'd given mine.

He laughed. "You get what you give," he said. "OK, I know that's truer at an individual level than a group or societal level, but love and sex—and marriage—are individual-level things. You can do anything you want relative to them. And you have to admit that you get what you give at the individual level, even when the cards are stacked against you. It's worked for you. Your brilliant career is the proof. Maybe you could try extrapolating from a positive like that for a change."

"I'll think about it," I said grudgingly. Having completely demolished my first, I took another napkin from the convenient (and necessary) stack on the table. (Charlie was already on at least his third.) "I'll think about the rest of it, too, but I remain edgy about marriage. It's hard to imagine liking anyone so much that I'd willingly take on all the hassle."

"Not a romantic, huh?" Charlie asked, smiling. "I'm not even going to ask what you think about having kids. I can already hear the uproar over how incredibly sexist and unequal the burdens relating to that are."

"Yeah, we should leave that for another day. I doubt I could do it justice at the moment. You've worn me out." I grinned and started peeling another shrimp. "Let's talk about something easier, like work, so I can pay attention to this incredible food. How's your M&A meritocracy coming along?"

❖ ❖ ❖

Charlie

A couple weeks after Jane and I had dinner together, I found myself in another conversation about marriage, this time with my sister Hannah. Mom and Dad were about to close up their summer home, so they'd invited all of us up for the weekend. Andy and his family couldn't make it, but Claire, Stephen, Hannah and I did go.

It was great, the way the end of the season always was. There weren't many people around, a lot of the businesses were already closed, and the whole place had an almost deserted, autumn feel to it that went with the changing leaves and the chilly night air.

Saturday night, after Mom and Dad went to bed, Claire and Stephen decided to go for a walk. Hannah and I lounged on the porch, too lazy to join them. After a few minutes of looking at the stars and listening to the just perceptible sound of the ocean, Hannah said, "Jason wants me to marry him."

Jason was the guy Claire had referred to as "Hannah's current flame" a couple years before. Despite Claire's skepticism and her comment about Hannah being as "dissolute" as I was, Jason and Hannah had stayed together. I couldn't tell from Hannah's tone, though, what she thought of his desire to get married.

"Is that a good thing?" I asked her.

"I don't know," she said thoughtfully. Hannah usually sounded thoughtful. Even as a child, she'd considered things very carefully before expressing her opinion. She'd always been completely at ease with silence, too, and she was silent then.

"Why don't you know?" I finally asked. "Do you love him?"

"I like him very much," she said, her tone even and impossible to read anything from. "And he's great in bed. I do love having sex with him."

"Doesn't seem like enough of a reason to get married."

Hannah smiled. "It's obvious why you would say that, but I'm not so sure I agree."

"What do you mean it's obvious why I would say that?" I turned my chair so I could see her without twisting my neck.

"You wouldn't think a great fuck was something to hang on to, let alone to get married for, because you've never wondered where the next one might be coming from. You're the hot commodity, Charlie, the scarce resource—a great-looking guy, not married, who's also nice and safe. Women, nice ones, have been flinging themselves at you forever.

You've never had to risk rejection or anything else to get laid. All you've ever had to do is choose someone you like."

Still in her usual calm, even tone, Hannah continued, "It's not the same for me. I don't have the constant parade of possibilities, for one thing. For another, I haven't always attracted the nicest guys, and the nice ones I have attracted haven't been great in bed. What I feel for Jason might be love and, if it isn't, I'm not convinced it makes sense to hold out for something different."

I wasn't sure what to say in response to this. Conversations with Hannah always had startling and eye-opening aspects and I was used to her, so I wasn't shocked. But I was surprised and intrigued, both by what she'd said about me and by her cavalier—or was it realistic?—attitude toward love.

This time, it was Hannah who broke the silence. "I'm freezing," she said, getting to her feet. "I'm going to go find something warm to put on. Want anything?"

I told her I was fine. She went in the house; when she returned, she was wrapped in a blanket. Sitting back down, she asked, "What do you think romantic love is?"

"Jesus, I don't know," I said. "I guess I've always thought I'd know it when I felt it. What do you think it is?"

"I'm not sure. I might love Jason. Maybe love isn't anything more than liking someone very much, thinking sex with him is terrific, and feeling very easy and comfortable together. But when Jason said he wanted to marry me, one of my first thoughts was 'What for?' So I started wondering whether I loved him or not."

"You should probably be asking Mom or Dad or Claire or Andy about this instead of me," I said, smiling. "They're presumably in love, right? They'd know more about it."

"I might," Hannah replied. "But Claire will tell me her opinion of Jason instead of answering my question and Andy will tell me marriage is wonderful and Dad will approach this as a question with an answer that we merely have to discover. I don't need advice or help making a decision. I'm just gathering information to mull over before I decide what I want to do. You and Mom are the best bets, and here we are, so I thought I'd start with you." She put her feet up on her chair and hugged her knees. "Do you plan to get married eventually?"

"You're the second person to ask me that this month," I told her. "My friend Jane asked me the same thing a couple weeks ago."

"Really? What did you tell her?"

"I said of course I did."

"Why?"

"All the usual reasons," I thought aloud in response. "It's something I've always expected I would do. I want to share my life with someone, I want to have kids, I want that feeling of partnership and mutual support that people in good marriages seem to have."

"Does it have to be a single someone?" Hannah asked.

"Yeah, I think it does. That feeling of being in something important together isn't one I think you could spread around. It's probably part of being in love." It was getting colder, and I shoved my hands in my pockets. "Anyway, I haven't felt it with any of the women I've slept with."

"That's not surprising," she said. "You choose the women you sleep with because they want to have sex with you. They're never women you take seriously—not the ones you've introduced to me anyway."

I felt a little goaded by the combination of her confrontational words and her even tone. "I can say the same things about some of them that you just said about Jason," I retorted. "I liked them very much, they were great in bed, and we were comfortable together."

"Even so, you didn't want to stick with any of them for very long," Hannah said calmly. "Do you think love is why I've wanted to stay with Jason?"

"No idea. Wanting to stay with someone for a long time could be part of being in love, I guess." I shrugged. "I know I haven't loved any of mine. I don't know why, but I assume love will be a very powerful feeling—one that I won't have any trouble recognizing when I feel it."

"That's a lovely and very romantic notion," my sister said, apparently sincerely. "I wonder, though, if we have a tendency to over-think things like love or to measure them by comparison to expectations that have been inflated for one reason or another. Jason is confident that he and I love each other, and I can't really disagree. I do know I don't want to break up with him. If what I feel for him pales in comparison to, say, Romeo and Juliet, does that necessarily mean it isn't love?"

I laughed. "I think you can confidently assume you're over-thinking this, Hannah! I'm only saying I expect love to be a recognizable and powerful feeling, not that I expect it to be something I'd be prepared to kill myself over like a couple of fictional teenagers. If you don't want to break up with Jason and you like the idea of spending your life with him, why not get married? Is your problem with marriage?"

"No, I don't think so." She looked out toward the beach. "I'm OK with the idea of marriage. I've seen some bad marriage fallout in my work, but the causes didn't have much to do with marriage. Things like clearly mismatched couples or people who don't know what they want or are trying to dominate their spouses or whatever are consequences of underlying psychological problems, not marriage issues. Fortunately, my sense of marriage is most influenced by Mom and Dad's and a little by Andy's and Claire's—all good marriages."

"Yeah, mine too."

We sat in silence for several minutes. Then Hannah said, "I didn't think this would be a decision, you know? Like you, I imagined I would know it when I felt it. Also, I'm only twenty-eight and I've been with Jason for over two years, so I don't have a lot of experience or comparison data. I'm wondering if my uncertainty is a sign that I should hold out for something stronger or just confirmation that I'm over-thinking."

"It could be both."

"That's not helpful!" Hannah laughed softly. "But it may be right."

"Here's my opinion, for what it's worth," I offered. "I'm expecting love to be an unmistakable feeling and marriage, as a result, to be an easy decision to make."

"You are a romantic, aren't you? Despite your path of least resistance approach to sex."

"What is your problem with my approach to sex?"

"I don't have a problem with it. I'm really rather envious of it," she said, reaching over and squeezing my shoulder affectionately. "I do wonder, though, if it's going to get you what you want. You approach sex purely as entertainment and you only consider women who jump in your lap. That's OK, but I doubt it's very likely to present you with a life partner of the kind you described."

"We'll see, I guess," I said. "What are you going to do about Jason?"

"We'll see on that, too," Hannah said serenely.

CHAPTER 11

THE WHOLE MAN/WOMAN DANCE

Jane

Jennifer arrived at the Company a little over a year after I did. A couple years older than I, she was also hired into a brand manager position. I didn't know if my performance (which had been well-reviewed) deserved any of the credit, but I took the Company's willingness to hire another woman brand manager as a good sign.

There were actually a number of good signs along these lines. Despite my high visibility and out-of-the-mainstream status as the only woman in the large group of men comprising my division's management ranks, I never felt as singled out or as disadvantaged by virtue of being a woman at the Company as I had felt pretty much all the time at the Firm. My gender was still outside the norm, but it seemed more beside the point at the Company, and it took a lot less effort on my part to make it a non-issue.

This interested me since both organizations were, as a matter of history and habit, predominantly male, not to mention highly political. Nevertheless, the Company was more focused on performance than on identity or "fit." It was still far from a meritocracy—there was plenty of dead weight, and the politics of getting recognized and rewarded were positively Byzantine. It certainly didn't hurt to be white and male either. But the Company offered a more level playing field than the Firm ever had.

At the Company, my gender consistently seemed to fade in the light of the results I produced. This was satisfying as well as liberating. I had no doubts about my ability to succeed when the relevant measuring stick was actual results, and it was refreshing not to feel like a sore thumb all the time.

I could also already see the effects of position power, even in a mid-level management position like mine. Alex had been right. There was a certain king-of-the-hill element to every management position, no matter how small the hill. The power intrinsic to my position was helping me establish a much more solid foundation than anything I'd had at the Firm. I was certain that I was building the kind of power base that would better protect me in—and maybe even from—a situation like the one Ian had created for me at the Firm.

All in all, I felt very positive about having made the move, and Jennifer's hire struck me as another excellent development. She appeared in my office a week or so after her start date. I had written a welcome note on the memo announcing her arrival and sent it to her; in response, she came by to introduce herself in person. I liked her immediately. She was direct, forthright and self-confident without seeming full of herself.

She reminded me of Lynn. In addition to being smart and ambitious, Jennifer was very self-assured about who she was, including being a woman. One of the first things she told me was how pleased she'd been to learn the Company featured an "onsite girlfriend." (I liked that idea, too, even if the term did make me feel prickly.)

Also like Lynn, Jennifer clearly hadn't adopted my strategy of making gender a non-issue at work. She was very pretty and she dressed in a more overtly sexy way than any other businesswoman I knew. There was nothing inappropriate about her clothes or the way she looked, but it was impossible to miss that she had a great body and what could only be called a "come-hither" demeanor.

In light of her brains and ambition, Jennifer's decidedly hot appearance intrigued me. In my experience, smart women felt undercut or demeaned by being viewed as sex objects. Not Jennifer—she courted that view. Despite this, she was taken seriously and had so far been quite successful career-wise. I looked forward to getting to know her and finding out how she'd managed to make her approach work.

We went out to lunch together a week or so after we met. With what I came to learn was characteristic outspokenness, Jennifer made it plain that she was every bit as determined as I was to make it big—and also that she was willing to pull very few punches in the process. She saw herself as a highly desirable free agent, with first-class skills and the currently in-demand gender. She planned—and expected—to succeed accordingly. In her words, they needed her more than she needed them.

Jennifer's free agent attitude was why she'd come to the Company. She'd always known she would have to job-hop to get to the top. She corroborated what Katherine and I had discovered about the "new toy" benefits of moving laterally. Jennifer observed that the obvious corollary was also true—after a few years at the same company, even the most respected employee seemed to suffer from an overly familiar and unexciting (if comfortable) "old shoe" phenomenon.

She had liked her last job, but she knew it was time to quit when she got a raise she considered too small. Sure enough, the salary the Company offered her was significantly higher. She reported with a contemptuous laugh that when she gave her notice, her old boss offered to match the salary the Company was offering. Jennifer had replied that she didn't want to work for a company without enough sense or integrity to pay a valued employee what she was worth *before* she got a new job.

We griped agreeably over how short-sighted employers could be. They so often shot themselves in the foot, whether by taking their good employees for granted, favoring people who didn't rock the boat and accordingly seemed "safe," or spending their time, effort and dollars on lame HR policies, squeaky wheels and people already halfway out the door.

Jennifer had some great dead weight stories from her last job, including one about a guy who'd already run two business units into the ground and was well on his way to deep-sixing a third. Apparently, every time questions arose about his performance, someone said, "Well, but he has six kids to support"—as if that somehow entitled him not only to immunity from being fired, but also to endless new opportunities. We laughed (ruefully) over how different things were for men. For a woman, having six kids would be the complete opposite of a helpful positive.

That first lunch was so much fun that we scheduled another one soon after. In short order, we were getting together for lunch or coffee every couple weeks. We compared notes, grumbled and debriefed, and perfected strategies for achieving our climb to the top ASAP. It was great once again to have, as Jennifer described it, an onsite girlfriend.

After three or four lunches with her, I knew it would be OK to ask her straight out what the deal was with her sexy appearance, and so I did. Jennifer grinned and, with her usual forthrightness, told me she learned two things as a teenager that had shaped her approach to work and to life.

The first was that most people had a hard time seeing her as anything but a pretty woman. The second was that she loved sex, partly for the sheer animal pleasure and partly because of the power it gave her over men. Instead of railing against her looks or trying to make people see her as something other than a "babe" (her word), Jennifer had decided to play up her sexiness and use it to her advantage.

She considered her appearance and her sex appeal to be two of the many arrows in her quiver, and she used them ruthlessly. Whether distracted by her looks or inclined to underestimate her or cut her slack because of them, men tended to fall by the wayside as Jennifer used her brains and her work-related talents to move up the corporate ladder. She reported (shocking me a little) that it had proved tremendously useful that most of the men she'd worked with were either half in love with her or dying to take her to bed.

She also confided gleefully that she loved titillating men, then taking up with the ones who appealed to her and denying or stringing along the rest. Unlike me, Jennifer was certain that sex was one arena where the balance of power favored women. "Honey," she drawled, "if you know what you're doing, they'll do anything to get you to keep doing it."

When I told her that lust had turned my college roommate into a spacey, obsessed fool and I had been concerned ever since that it might have the power to do the same to me, Jennifer hooted. She informed me that she had experienced plenty of lust—and acted on most of it—for over a decade without once becoming even remotely spacey, obsessed or foolish. She was certain the same would prove to be true for me.

She also summarily dismissed my suspicion that great sex was either a fiction or an overblown characterization of a nice, but minor, pleasure. Jennifer assured me in no uncertain terms that great sex was both possible and mind-blowing. She thought I was nuts to have had only two partners. In her (much wider) experience, really good lovers were rare and she was sure any woman needed a bigger test group than two to get a decent shot at great results.

In an attempt to illustrate that friendship with a man could actually offer more benefit, with less risk, than sleeping with him, I described my friendship with Charlie. Jennifer hooted again and told me I couldn't make a legitimate comparison of benefits without having slept with him. When I asked her why the same wasn't true in reverse, she coolly replied that she'd *had* friendships and sex with a few guys. In her view, friendship with anyone was far more intimate and fraught with peril than, as she put it, simple fucking.

Jennifer considered sex to be recreational and fun—and essentially impersonal, without the power to affect her sense of herself, her behavior or her desire or ability to succeed at work. The throes of passion, she said merrily, didn't make her feel exposed or defenseless or weak or dominated, either in the moment or in the aftermath.

She wasn't any more trusting of men and their motives than I was, but she had self-trust in abundance, and she saw no reason to hold herself or men at arm's-length sexually and thereby to deprive herself of something she enjoyed. She thought my attitude toward sex was upside-down and backwards, not to mention prudish and not very respectful of women.

This was a revelation to me. I felt quite blown away, both by her perspective and by the gleeful certainty with which she offered it. And I had to wonder if I was colder or more straitlaced than I'd thought myself to be. When Jennifer asked me why on earth I thought sex required women to be weak or doubted my ability to hold my own in bed with some guy, all I could think was "Good questions! Why, indeed?"

❖ ❖ ❖

BY THE TIME Jennifer's opinions made me question my views on the dangers presented by romantic relationships, Patrick and I had long since gone back to being friends rather than lovers. We'd been both for about four months (or, as he joked, until the spring rugby season began). But his sexual interest in me flagged once that second rugby season got underway even though the pleasure we otherwise took in each other's company remained strong, both on and off the rugby pitch.

Thanks no doubt to Patrick's laissez-faire attitude and my apparently entrenched romantic/sexual detachment, we had been able to make the transition back to a non-sexual relationship without any resentment or awkwardness. Patrick was a lively and entertaining person to spend time with, so I was glad about this, but I had to ask myself why I kept ending up with lovers whom I preferred, and who preferred me, as friends. I knew Jennifer was right about two men not being much of a test group, but I still found it curious that both my relationships had offered less than stellar results in the way of overwhelming passion and then turned easily and comfortably into (or back into) friendships.

I wasn't inclined to agree with Jennifer that friendships with men were undesirable, either in general or because they were antithetical to hot sex. Still, I had to admit that I had chosen to sleep with Tyler and Patrick more because they were friends I felt comfortable with than because I felt anything like overpowering lust for them. Leaving aside whether I was capable of feeling that for anyone, to be honest I also had to admit that *not* feeling swept away by them was a big part of why I had found them attractive.

But, obviously, in both cases it was also why, in the end and after not very long, we were happier being friends than lovers. Our physical attraction simply wasn't very strong. Or perhaps more accurately, the real nature of our attraction was intellectual and social rather than sexual.

Was this my fault, I wondered? Was I lacking the ability to feel passion or to provoke it over the long run in someone I liked and who liked me? Tyler and Patrick were both great guys, and they had both been very hot for me at the beginning. Maybe I really was cold or a prude where sex was concerned, despite what I had considered my modern and open approach to it with both of them.

This conclusion didn't feel right. I had been genuinely disappointed over not being able to let go and get carried away with Patrick, especially given how close I'd managed to come a few times. I preferred to believe that I had, however unconsciously, been self-protectively holding myself back even as I'd thought I was being appropriately receptive and interested.

Whatever the true reasons for my so far lackluster sexual experience, I wanted more. Jennifer's insistence that great sex was both possible and fantastic—not to mention no danger whatsoever to anything important about me or my identity—was fueling my interest in finding a guy with whom I could experience it. But I was having trouble figuring out how to accomplish this. I wasn't sure where to look for such a man or how to recognize him if I found him. And I seriously doubted my ability to turn off my self-protective defense mechanisms no matter how strong my desire.

I analyzed and agonized over this for a while, trying to develop a plan and some tactics for effectively lowering my defenses, but not my standards. After not too long, though, I realized that analyzing and agonizing and planning were symptomatic of the problem, not the solution. I didn't kid myself that I could simply go with the flow and trust in the future, but I resolved to do my best imitation of that and see what happened.

❖ ❖ ❖

ONE DAY about three months after Jennifer came to the Company, Charlie and I were having lunch at a restaurant near my office.

I was telling him all about the unbelievably lame and politically fraught two-day offsite meeting I'd just returned from attending. There had been a "facilitating consultant" too stupid or unprepared to use the correct Company lingo, some truly inane role-playing exercises, a couple of brutal and barely veiled interpersonal squabbles played out publicly, and the usual complement of senior people who spent most of the meeting out in the hall on phone calls.

The offsite had been a complete—and expensive—waste of time. Annoying as that was, it did provide hilarious material, and I was entertaining Charlie and myself with tales (true and fanciful) about the consultant and my colleagues. Charlie kept asking me how the hell I could stand dealing with morons and corporate-speak all the time. I finally retorted that it was preferable to the constant sexism the Firm had on tap, but I had to agree that I did often feel like Gulliver among the Yahoos.

While we were laughing about all this, Jennifer suddenly appeared at our table. "Hi, Jane!" she said gaily. "Sorry to interrupt what is obviously a very animated conversation, but I thought I'd come over and say hello."

"Hi, Jennifer!" I smiled up at her. "I didn't see you. Did you just get here?"

"No, I'm on my way out. And I'm not surprised that you didn't see me, what with your handsome lunch companion to look at." Jennifer smiled at Charlie, then said, "Care to introduce us?"

I introduced the two of them and saw sparks immediately begin to fly. I hadn't thought about it before, but Jennifer was just the sort of woman Charlie always had on his arm at Firm events—great-looking and sexy. Of course, there was no way she'd be immune to his whole golden boy thing either. I had a hard time not laughing aloud, so comical was it to watch them so predictably wow each other.

Jennifer chatted with us for a minute or two, then said she had to get back to the office. Laying her hand lightly on Charlie's shoulder, she told him it was nice to meet him. Leaving her hand there, she turned to me and said, "Call me later, OK?" She smiled at Charlie again and then she sashayed—there's no other apt word—out of the room.

"Another great-looking woman with a crush on you, Golden Boy," I teased Charlie as he watched her walk away. "Does it ever get tiresome?"

"Not really," he said, turning back to me. He frowned in mock incredulity. "You'd think it would, but it never does." He grinned, then said, "She's not what I expected from what you've said about her."

"Please don't say something beneath you, OK?"

"I wouldn't dream of saying anything like that," he said smoothly. "I'm not one of those morons you've been telling me about."

"You better not be thinking 'anything like that' either," I said in a menacing way, pretty sure he was doing exactly that.

"Never!" he protested, his hands raised in surrender. "Hey, do you have another half-hour or so? I've got an issue on a deal I'd like to get your thoughts on."

Charlie's issue was complicated and it took us a while to figure out how to deal with it. Partly because I spent longer at lunch than I'd planned to, I had a hectic afternoon. I finally came up for air around 6:00 and went to the kiosk to get a bottle of water. On the way back, I ran into Jennifer on her way to my office.

"I thought you were going to call me!" she said accusingly.

"I was—sorry. I got back late from lunch and it's been crazy ever since."

"Late from lunch, eh?" Jennifer waggled her eyebrows suggestively. "I wonder why."

"Stop it," I said, laughing. "I told you that's not my deal with Charlie."

"I can't imagine why not," she said fervently as we walked into my office. I closed the door even though the floor had pretty much cleared out by then. "Are you blind?"

"No, I'm aware that he's gorgeous," I grinned, "but he's my friend, Jen, and my former colleague, not my lover—current or former."

"So you keep saying," Jennifer said as if I couldn't possibly mean it. "But he is one of the hottest guys I've ever laid eyes on! I almost died when you introduced him. I can't believe *that's* your platonic buddy Charlie! Are you completely insane? How can you hang with a guy like that for over five years and not want to take him to bed?"

"I just don't. I've never thought of him in terms of sex. He doesn't think of me that way either. We've always been friends." Smiling at her incredulous face, I said, "Sorry to shock you, but it's true."

"Hey, it's your loss," Jennifer said. "Do you mind if I go after him?"

"Not at all," I assured her. "He's not mine. Have fun!"

"Oh, I will," she promised, with another waggle of her eyebrows.

❖ ❖ ❖

JENNIFER DIDN'T WASTE ANY TIME. The lunch at which I'd introduced her to Charlie was on a Thursday; when she and I had lunch together two Mondays later, she had already hooked up with him. She was funny about telling me—her usual forthrightness failed her for once. We were halfway through lunch before she looked at me quizzically during one of those natural conversation breaks that occur when friends talk.

"What?" I asked.

"I'm dying to tell you something, but it's about Charlie and I'm feeling hesitant," she said, actually looking a bit timid.

"Jen, I told you he's my friend. Really, I meant what I said before. I don't feel proprietary about him. Unless you're going to tell me something negative, in which case I'll probably argue with you, you can tell me anything you want."

"OK, then," she said, looking relieved. "I got together with him Saturday and he is just as hot as he looks. I'll spare you the details, but I'm telling you, he must be one amazing friend for you to prefer friendship to sex with him!"

I laughed. "He's a terrific friend, but you keep forgetting that I didn't *decide* between sex and friendship with him. Sex has just never been our deal. Ask him—he'll tell you the same thing."

"No, I don't think I will ask him," Jennifer said. "He thinks awfully highly of you. The last thing I want to do right now is put the idea in his head. I want him for myself for a while."

"I'm sure he would have come up with the idea on his own if he'd ever been interested," I said, smiling at her trepidation. "The fact that he hasn't is one of the reasons we're such good friends. I like being his buddy, and I trust his advice partly because I know he's not attracted to me."

"If you say so. But I really don't get your problem with knowing a man is attracted to you—or, for that matter, with fucking. You're so strong and direct, and you're not a fearful person at all. Why are you so afraid of sex and so distrustful of anyone who's attracted to you?"

"I don't know that I'm afraid exactly," I said, looking around to make sure no one we knew from work was nearby. "My actual experience has been pretty good, if not overwhelming, so it's not that."

I contemplated her expectant expression as I thought about how to articulate my problem. "Sex just seems to me to have the potential to be very predatory," I finally said. "It seems to subjugate women. I don't know why—whether it's men or the biological nature of sex or if women do it to themselves while under the influence of love or lust—but, whatever the reason, I hate being out of control or feeling like prey."

Jennifer had started shaking her head right after the word "predatory" and she hadn't stopped by the time I finished. "That's crazy," she declared. "There's nothing predatory about sex or, if there is, it's as possible for that to come from the woman as from the man. And they obviously have more at risk where the actual mechanics are concerned."

"OK, I get that, but why, then, do so many women get all gooey or willing to make big sacrifices, all in the name of lust or love? Why do they seem to be *accommodating* men all the time?"

"*Some* women do that," Jennifer said. "It's not a requirement! The ones who do it are probably the same ones who decide not to have real careers or who really are stupid or insecure. You can't think *all* women do that. You can't think *I* do it."

"Well, I know *you* don't." I grinned at her. "But you're hardly the most representative test case. You have self-esteem to spare."

"Why, thanks!" she said, smiling. "But so do you, my dear."

"Not so much where sex is concerned. I never feel I can be myself with sex, and I don't know quite who to be." I frowned. "It probably comes from my family."

"Elaborate, please," Jennifer directed. She put her elbows on the table, rested her chin on her hands and looked at me inquisitively.

"Well, they all think I'm crazy—crazy and unfeminine, too. My dad never really paid much attention to my sister and me, but I do know he thought the right path for his daughters was to find husbands and keep them happy. Can't tell you if he really believed it or just liked the benefits, but he seemed to think the right role for women was sweet, subservient and attentive."

I rolled my eyes and Jennifer made a sound of complete distaste.

"Exactly," I agreed, smiling. "So that's part of why I think men have a weird view of what's 'feminine.' And my mother's classic. She knows she's smarter and more capable than my dad, but she's content to keep that to herself and make him feel like the boss, the big shot, the important member of the family, all in return for her nice house and her little suburban life and, I guess, for not having to go out in the world and fend for herself."

"Disgusting how standard that is, isn't it?" Jennifer shifted in her chair and crossed her legs, momentarily (and apparently obliviously) attracting the attention of the men at the next table. "I've always wondered if the men in those situations know they're being played. And, if so, don't they care? Do they just put it out of their minds or are they really clueless?"

"I'm guessing they're really clueless. Or so arrogant they believe their own bullshit. Or, I suppose, it could be a game they're willing to play to get someone else to do all the boring stuff that makes their lives run smoothly. Who knows?" I shrugged. "The women interest me more. I don't see how my mother can think what she's getting is worth what she's doing to get it. And why doesn't she despise my dad—you know, for being so easily played?"

"You got me," Jennifer marveled. "But back to the point. Where does your problem with sex fit in?"

"I guess I'm worried that sex has the power to make someone like my mother think her compromises are worth it," I said, feeling my cheeks grow warm. "Or maybe that the whole 'give them what they want and they'll take care of you' thing applies to sex, too. You know, that there's a role you have to play because what they want is a stereotypically 'feminine' woman. So you don't get to be yourself, at least not if you're like me."

"That could explain it, I guess," Jennifer said. "But you broke away from that model without a second thought where college and your career were concerned. Why would you be hanging on to it for sex?"

"I've been thinking about that since the last time you asked me, but I don't want to tell you what I think the answer is." I fiddled with my water glass and frowned at her sheepishly. "I know you'll think I'm insane. Promise you won't hoot at me?"

"No deal," she said crisply. "You need hooting at on this topic. And you can take it. So spill it."

"I'm not doing it on purpose," I said, feeling defensive, "but I feel like I have to be vigilant and that keeps me sort of separate from the whole thing. I worry about feeling like prey or turning into a weakling. And I don't trust how guys who approach me sexually are seeing me. It makes me nervous and suspicious to be perceived primarily as a woman, and I consider being perceived primarily or only as a sex object totally unacceptable. So I can't let go and just experience it."

Jennifer was shaking her head again. "With sex, you *want* to be perceived as a sexy woman," she said sternly. "There's no downside to it. You're not trying to get ahead of them or prove something to them, Jane. You're trying to do something fun together *with* them! Anyway, it's not about how anyone appears or is being perceived."

She uncrossed her legs and leaned toward me. "You're making too big a deal about the wrong things—and doing *way* too much thinking. It's not about what goes on in your head or their heads. You don't have to become brainless or weak, but you do have to concentrate on the feelings, the physical sensations, not on who's thinking what about whom or who's winning or what the people at the office would think. It's not a political statement or a contest you'll lose if you don't win. It's just fucking."

"That's what Charlie always says. You two ought to get along great," I told her, grinning.

"Whoa, whoa, whoa!" She looked very surprised as she held up her hands and sank back in her chair. "I thought sex wasn't your deal with Charlie. You and he have *talked* about this?"

"We've talked about most things. Not as a personal matter, but as a concept. You know, someone we know gets married or some guy at the Firm sleeps with his secretary or whatever, and Charlie and I debate, among other things, whether marriage and sex subordinate women. I think they do; he thinks I'm nuts—that it's more of an individual arrangement than an inevitable power struggle."

"Although I'm inclined to agree with you on marriage, he's right about sex," Jennifer said, now looking dumbfounded. "But I cannot believe the two of you actually talk about this kind of thing and *still* haven't ever thought about going to bed together. Especially given what I now know about *his* approach to sex."

"Believe it," I reiterated for what seemed like the hundredth time. "Why is that so tough for you? You and I are talking about it!"

"That's a whole different thing, Jane," she said impatiently.

"No, it isn't. Why does the fact that Charlie's a man and I'm a woman mean that sex has to define our relationship? I got to know him as a colleague and then we got to be friends. Just because he's male doesn't mean he can't be a friend or that we're required to consider each other sexually. It also doesn't mean we have to limit our conversations to specific topics. Who's being too restrictive now?"

"I guess you're right," she conceded. "It's just not my deal, as you would say, with men. Friendship seems to me like a much more intimate and dangerous way to interact with them, not to mention nowhere near as much fun." Grinning, she added, "Just like sex seems to you apparently. I don't plan to rethink my deal, but you should seriously reconsider yours."

I laughed. "I wouldn't mind feeling the way you do about sex, but I've got a long way to go before I get anywhere close. And I'm sure not going to give up my friendships to get there!"

"That's no problem," Jennifer said with complete confidence. "There are plenty of men around."

❖ ❖ ❖

JENNIFER AND CHARLIE were apparently involved for three or four months. Neither of them said much about their affair to me. Jennifer occasionally mentioned in passing that she'd seen him; Charlie occasionally praised her brains or her sense of humor.

I assumed that Jennifer still felt somewhat awkward discussing him with me, despite my assurances that I didn't feel at all proprietary about him. And Charlie had always been reticent about his various girlfriends. They weren't a topic we had ever discussed in any detail. I didn't know if this was because he consciously chose not to talk about them with me or because the girlfriend part of his life really was as separate as it seemed from the parts we'd talked about or had in common over the years.

Whatever his reasons, I liked leaving that part out. I was hardly someone who could offer useful advice in that area—to anyone, much less to someone as experienced as he evidently was. Also, I suspected it would be much harder for us to think of each other as friends, rather than as a man and a woman, if we talked in specific terms about our personal love lives.

We continued to talk regularly about everything else. Charlie was making excellent progress with his revamped M&A group, updates about which he reported to me with enthusiasm bordering on glee. I still thought he'd been too lenient with the more egregious thugs, but I had to admit he'd apparently converted a couple of them into decent human beings and even the very worst of them were at least pretending to play his way. M&A hadn't lost any significant clients, and Charlie told me that morale in the group was better than ever.

Knowing how glass-half-full-ish he tended to be, and sure that people weren't telling him anything they doubted he'd be happy to hear, I checked this morale report with Lynn, whose opinion I was more inclined to take on faith, tinged as it was with healthy skepticism and pragmatic reservations. Sure enough, she confirmed what Charlie was saying. She also raved about what a great job he was doing. According to Lynn, the group had really turned the corner. The right people and behaviors were very visibly getting the recognition they deserved, and it was becoming politically incorrect to be an asshole in just about any respect.

Hearing this made me very proud of Charlie and also of the part I had played in helping him figure out how to organize and run M&A. It really was in some ways as if I'd stayed to help him "run the joint" as we'd once discussed. And I realized that my involvement was actually less complicated—and probably more effective—than it would have been if I still worked at the Firm.

From afar I had an objectivity I wouldn't have had as a member of the group. Obviously, I had no potentially conflicting self-interest, but there was also none of the awkwardness or the arguably unwise or worrisome appearance of impropriety that our friendship could easily have engendered were we in a formal boss/subordinate relationship. Even in a relatively non-hierarchical place like the Firm, I was pretty certain that my access to Charlie and his openness with me would have caused problems once he was in charge of M&A.

I had experienced how threatening coworkers could find a mutually respectful, honest, communicative relationship between a boss and one of his subordinates. My boss, Bill, was a unit head. He had supervisory management responsibility for all the brand managers in our good-sized unit.

The Company had dozens of units aggregated into a dozen divisions. The real power, operationally speaking, was at the division head level. Everyone expected Bill to be promoted to division head sooner rather than later. Because of his leadership skills, business and marketing savvy, and unfailing ability to get along with just about everybody, he was also judged likely to be one of the exalted few who ultimately made the leap from division head to executive management at the corporate level. The COO or even CEO positions were not considered beyond his eventual reach.

Bill was someone I would have sought to build a good working relationship with no matter how I felt about him. As it happened, though, I liked and admired him. He'd always been my boss at the Company—he'd hired me, supported me and treated me fairly all along, including at review and compensation time.

It was hard to tell if he cared about diversity for its own sake. We didn't discuss things like our personal views on diversity, women in the workplace or gender bias. Bill was as relaxed a person as Charlie was, but he was far less open. He and I had a much more businesslike and less personal relationship than Charlie and I had ever had, even when Charlie was my mentor and, on deals, my boss.

Whatever Bill's personal views may have been, he evaluated his direct reports on the bases of the results we produced and our work ethic. He had little tolerance for suck-ups and none at all for anyone who treated other people badly. He appreciated good work, too, although he had a more lenient grading scale than I would have imposed. Glad as I was to receive them, the kudos I got from Bill meant less to me than they might have, given the way he spread kudos around.

Still, he and I had an excellent relationship. There was nothing inappropriate or overly close about it, but my demeanor toward him was that of valued colleague rather than intimidated subordinate. This was less a choice on my part than my natural instinct—formed, no doubt, by the more autonomous, less hierarchical working relationships people at the Firm had with one another and with clients.

I was certainly under no misapprehension about Bill's power to fire me, but I never dreamed that the right way to avoid being canned was to toady to him. I figured if I did my job well, he'd want to keep me around to continue doing it well. Apparently, however, this (to me, eminently logical) approach to one's boss was revolutionary, even scandalous, in the world of corporate hierarchy.

More than one colleague marveled over how I didn't seem to be afraid of Bill or how I treated him like a peer instead of my boss. My team reveled in my "tight and special *in*" with our big boss. Other brand managers acknowledged the uniqueness of Bill's and my relationship in a variety of ways—from designating me to tell him "the things he won't want to hear" to making pointed, sometimes catty, little remarks about me being the teacher's pet or on the inside track.

It wouldn't have surprised me to learn there was speculation that Bill and I were sleeping together—the time-honored way to demean a woman's power or success—but, happily, no such nastiness reached my ears.

Bill himself appeared to be oblivious to the uneasiness our good working relationship was causing around us. Just as he valued the great job he said I was doing with my team and our brands, he also clearly valued my opinions and my willingness to tell him what I actually thought (as opposed to what I imagined he wanted to hear). He never made specific reference to these interpersonal characteristics, but he frequently sought my input and, more than a few times, I heard my thoughts or suggestions coming out of his mouth in group meetings. It was great to know I was having an impact on how he ran the unit.

I knew I had to be careful not to seem to be trading on our relationship or otherwise to show off or act as if I thought I was better than other people by virtue of it, but I was very pleased with the way Bill and I were working together. I also knew he was a staunch supporter of mine—a benefit that would only increase in value as his power and position expanded.

❖ ❖ ❖

JENNIFER AND I met for one of our regular lunches in the early summer. On the walk to the restaurant we'd decided on, she told me she'd finally thrown in the towel and terminated one of her assistant brand managers, a young woman named Ashley whom Jennifer had been trying for months to fire up instead of fire.

Ashley was bright enough, Jennifer said, but unable or unwilling to pay attention to what really mattered. There were a few things she liked to do and did well, but they were the entry level, working alone aspects of the job. When it came to pushing herself or working as part of a team, she wasn't interested.

This drove Jennifer nuts. She had explained to Ashley that no one could get ahead without leading projects, taking charge of teams, and otherwise handling next-level tasks and responsibilities. Jennifer had also pointed out that assistant brand manager was a self-limiting job, not one Ashley could stay in forever and expect to keep getting raises. Ashley had given it a halfhearted try and then started "acting out," Jennifer said scornfully, by taking sick days, missing deadlines, moaning about not wanting to take on stress in her life and engaging in other passive-aggressive resistance.

Jennifer was pissed off about the whole situation. She felt she'd wasted her time and, like me, she thought it was bad for every woman when someone like this assistant flamed out for reasons people would consider girly. I consoled her slightly by insisting that, despite the bad outcome, trying to mentor Ashley had been absolutely the right thing to do and the only justifiable choice.

We spent the short wait to be seated at the restaurant griping about how women seemed to take at least a couple steps back for every step forward, and how especially maddening it was when the steps back were caused by other women. Once we were seated, Jennifer was uncharacteristically quiet.

"Is there something else on your mind, Jen?" I asked.

"Yeah, there is." She sighed and pushed her hand through her hair, a sexy little habit that simultaneously drew attention to her hair and got it out of her face. "It's time for me to say so long to Charlie, but I'm having a hard time making myself do it." She frowned. "Is it OK if I talk to you about this?"

"Depends on what you're planning to say. Why don't you start and I'll tell you if you should stop."

"Deal," she said, with a nod. "I'll start with something I know you won't mind talking about. I agreed to go with him to a dinner thing that Firm of yours had. It was for big shots, group heads and mentors, he told me. The purpose was to celebrate the solid results they've had in the year since the insider trading scandal."

With a grimace, she continued, "I really didn't want to go. I hate being arm candy on general principles and, anyway, I'm not his girlfriend, you know? But he was very persuasive and against my better judgment, I said I'd go."

After we ordered, Jennifer said, "For the love of God, Jane, how in the hell did you ever work in that place? I've never felt so condescended to in my life! Other than checking out my cup size, very few people paid any attention to me at all! It was like they'd all decided in advance that I couldn't possibly have a brain in my head or anything worthwhile to say—or maybe that I couldn't even be counted on to speak English intelligibly!"

I couldn't help laughing. "Sorry, I'm not laughing at you. I'm laughing at your description and the look on your face. You're so right—those events are horrible for women, at least women other than wives. Actually, who knows? They're probably horrible for the wives, too."

I thanked the waitress, who'd just refilled my iced tea, then told Jennifer, "You were also suffering from two additional complications. First, if the crowd was just big shots, group heads and mentors, there can't have been more than two or three women there who *weren't* wives or girlfriends."

"Right you are," she said. "I met your friend Lynn—who asked me to say hello to you, by the way—but she was it in the way of women who worked at the Firm."

"Cheryl wasn't there?"

"No. Charlie mentioned her, but she couldn't attend for some reason." Jennifer shrugged. "What's the other complication?"

"That you were with Charlie. He always has a great-looking, sexy date at those things. A few of them have been quite interesting and intelligent, too, but the only thing the other guys notice—and the thing the wives resent—is what his dates look like."

"I knew I should have refused to go with him!" she said, giving the air a little punch with her clenched fist. "I hate that shit! It's bad enough if you actually are someone's girlfriend or wife, but it's fucking ridiculous if you're not!"

The waitress brought our salads, and Jennifer attacked hers as if the lettuce were responsible for the bad experience she'd had at the Firm's event.

"So why does this mean you can't keep seeing Charlie if you want to?" I asked. "Just tell him you won't go to any more Firm events."

She shook her head as she chewed and swallowed. "That won't solve the problem. I like these things with no strings, no obligations and no complications. He's a very nice guy and a great fuck, and that's plenty for me. Unfortunately, he doesn't seem to want to leave it at that. It's not just the Firm event. He's always wanting to *do things*."

I laughed again. "You say that as if he's demanding that you drown kittens or steal pencils from blind people in the subway!"

"Well, OK, it's nothing vile," she admitted with a smile, "but I don't want a 'relationship.' I just want to fuck when I'm in the mood."

"No offense, Jennifer, but surely you can see how he or anyone might feel a little used by that attitude."

"The using is mutual," she retorted, "and so are the benefits. Or at least that's how it is until they start insisting on relationships."

"I don't think wanting to do something with you besides have sex is necessarily insisting on a relationship," I said, reaching for the pepper. "But you must have been in this situation before. How did you handle it then?"

"I sent the guy on his way, of course," Jennifer said. "Nicely, but firmly. And it's what I have to do now, too. I know that. I just hoped it wouldn't happen so soon. I like Charlie, you know?"

"Yeah, sure I do. He's very likable." I grinned and added, "Although I guess what I find likable is precisely what you're trying to avoid."

Jennifer laughed. "And vice versa."

"No, no, no," I said, shaking my finger at her, "we're not going to have that conversation again. I told you before—I'm not trying to *avoid* sex with Charlie. I just like my relationship with him the way it is."

"Yeah, well, I like mine the way it is, too—or the way it was, anyway—but he seems to have a different view."

"He's hard to budge once he's made up his mind about something," I told her.

"So I'm seeing." She sighed. "Well, nobody's heart is going to get broken here, but I sure will miss him." The regretful expression that accompanied her sigh didn't last long. It had transformed into a leer by the time she finished the sentence.

"OK, this is where we change the subject," I said, smiling. "Who would have thought that you'd end up being yet another victim of the Firm's sexism? Apparently, no one is exempt from that bullshit! Tell me who else you met and all the ways they were awful."

❖ ❖ ❖

Charlie

Jim did my performance review in late July. HR required that these be done annually, a good enough idea, but Jim and I had been working together for so long that the reviews had become fairly perfunctory. His real feedback was always in real time. During the formal reviews, we spent more time on strategizing for the group and the Firm than on my performance, particularly after Jim was named head of Corp Fin and I took over M&A.

Every year, though, Jim did offer me a few business or career development ideas. Occasionally, he'd had a suggestion for improvement, too. He'd been a terrific supporter and coach for me over the years, so I always took his ideas and suggestions seriously. This year, he surprised me. Floored me, really.

This year's suggestion for improvement was that I get married.

As I sat in his office, listening to him make an out-of-left-field comment about my personal life, I started to get mad. Clenching my jaw reminded me of all the times Jane had stormed into my office, infuriated by just this sort of unacceptable, out-of-place mingling of personal status and professional progress. Fortunately, it also reminded me of the advice I always gave her.

I had nothing to gain by refusing to listen or getting on a high horse with Jim. He had always treated me honestly and in accordance with what he thought were my best interests, and he was entitled to the benefit of the doubt that he was still doing so. Also, information about what people were thinking, however offensive or out of place, was always useful intelligence.

Jim's line of reasoning was straightforward. I'd had a brilliant career at the Firm and I had a brilliant future. There was no reason I could not or would not continue directly to the top at the same accelerated pace so long as key senior people continued to view me as talented, stable and committed to the Firm.

There was no question about my talent or my commitment to the Firm, he reported, but there had been a comment or two about my stability. Nothing serious, no need to worry yet, but people tended to start wondering if there was cause for concern when men in their 30s did not settle down. Jim realized I was only 32, but because I had moved up so fast, people tended to judge me with reference to the older age men typically were when they reached my level.

Jim said the best way to quiet the rumbling about stability before it amounted to anything was to get married. He stopped short of saying that a marriage in form only was all that was necessary, but he made the point unmistakably.

He saw that I was seething and asked me to think it over before replying or making any decision about the suggestion. I agreed and we went on—after a few tense minutes, amicably—to other topics.

Later, back in my own office, I replayed the whole ridiculous and offensive suggestion. Neither I nor my personal life had ever done anything but benefit the Firm. Most of the people on the Executive Committee couldn't truthfully make the same claim. They had some nerve questioning *my* stability. And, married or not, I had already proved I could run things far better than those assholes—the M&A group was in great shape.

Again, I thought of Jane and wondered how she and other women routinely managed to handle this kind of intrusive, irrelevant horseshit with any equanimity at all. Would she be surprised to know that even "the white male template" was subject to conservative, traditional, heterosexual stereotyping?

I was willing to bet that at least as many of the married men at the Firm did fuck around as did not. Even a happy marriage was no guarantee of stability. There were a million ways for people to embarrass the Firm or run it poorly whether they were married or not. Character was the issue, not marital status. I could certainly manage not to embarrass the fucking Firm regardless of whether or not I "settled down."

I made myself relax. I reminded myself that Jim was on my side and, as always, trying to make sure I didn't trip over obstacles I could avoid.

As offensive as the suggestion was, it certainly wasn't beyond the realm of possibility that it was a good one. I decided to put the whole thing aside until I cooled off and developed a little perspective on it.

❖ ❖ ❖

A FEW DAYS LATER, I was still offended and disgusted, but I was no longer enraged. Jim was right—why face or try to skirt the obstacle when it was relatively simple to eliminate it altogether?

I decided to figure out how to go about getting married sooner rather than later. As I'd told Hannah, I had no objection to marriage. I'd always expected to get married. I also knew what I was looking for: someone I liked and admired and with whom I could feel a strong sense of mutuality, of partnership, of being equals together in something important.

I'd assumed I would eventually meet and fall in love with someone who would be that kind of partner and then we'd get married. But that hadn't happened. Thinking about why not, I realized that the women I knew fell into two categories—sex partners and friends—and neither category was likely to yield up a wife who fit that description.

For starters, I'd expected to fall in love with someone I was sleeping with. But I never seemed to have much in common with the women I slept with. Except in bed, there was never a feeling of mutuality or partnership or of being equals. I never felt enhanced or supported or *encouraged* by them. Sex with them was great, but that had been pretty much the extent of my interest in them.

With the possible exception of Jennifer, that is. I didn't connect with her any more completely than with any of the others, but with her it wasn't because I didn't find her interesting. Sexy as she was, I found her intelligence and her humor equally attractive. I tried to have a more complete relationship with her, but she was totally unreachable. Remarkably for someone with whom sex was so incredibly hot, Jennifer turned out to be essentially cold. She had no interest in intimacy or partnership—she seemed to see me as a means to a solely recreational end.

Actually, Jennifer probably felt about me the same way I'd felt about all the women I'd slept with *except* her. The only real difference was that it was she, and not I, who limited things to sex.

Hannah was right about my approach to sex and its chances of presenting me with the kind of partner I wanted. I was attracted to the women I'd slept with, including Jennifer, because they made it clear they wanted sex—not because of the kind of women they were or because they appealed to me, or I to them, in some other way.

I did have something like the partnership feeling with some of my female friends, but I'd never considered any of them as a potential wife either. There was obviously a sexual component to marriage, and sex with my friends was not something I'd thought about consciously or felt pulled to subconsciously.

But why not? Maybe Hannah was right on this score, too, and I never thought of my women friends sexually because they never threw themselves at me. As I thought about it, I recognized that they seemed self-contained and sexually remote to me, as uninterested and unreachable sexually as Jennifer had been in every other way. They never seemed to want or need anything from me *as a man.*

Freud's theories about Oedipus and incest aside, I didn't think this was because my friends reminded me of my sexually off-limits mother and sisters. It also wasn't because they intimidated me—they didn't. I liked the challenge they presented. I admired them and found their company very stimulating. My lack of sexual interest in them was probably part of why they liked my company, too. They appreciated being seen for who they were individually, instead of solely as women.

But what if, like Jane, they were all afraid that someone who wanted to take them to bed couldn't see them as anything other than a sex object? Maybe they all felt obliged to take their gender off the table—or at least to make it secondary—so as to make sure it wasn't the first and maybe the only thing men noticed about them. If so, it wasn't surprising that I never sensed they wanted anything from me as a man.

I wondered if I'd always had the wrong idea about all of this. Did love necessarily start with sex? Did marriage necessarily result from love? When I thought objectively about what I really wanted from marriage, love seemed more like a luxury than a requirement. It might be great, but wasn't the real requirement—the truly indispensable element—that feeling of mutuality and partnership with a woman I liked and respected?

I didn't want to marry someone I didn't feel I knew in any important way or by whom I felt burdened rather than supported. It would be crazy to marry someone I didn't find stimulating any way but sexually. And then what—look for partnership, intellectual fortification and career support somewhere else, all the while feeling faintly condescending toward my wife and, eventually, the mother of my children?

Waiting around to fall in love with someone I wanted to take to bed and could also consider a real partner started to seem crazy to me, too—way too random an approach to make a successful marriage likely. This was an important and, I hoped, long-term choice. Wouldn't a more logical, objective, *businesslike* approach make more sense?

Why not structure a marriage like a mutually beneficial merger of equals? Instead of business synergy between two companies, the goals would be partnership, intellectual chemistry and mutual career support between two people. A marriage like that would give me the kind of companion I really wanted—someone I found challenging and stimulating, someone who unquestionably brought as much to the table as I did, someone with whom I would be synergistic.

My choice would be far less hit-or-miss and my chances of success-fully achieving the kind of marriage I wanted would be far better if I got over traditional romantic notions like love and simply decided to marry someone I could legitimately consider an equal merger partner. And, obviously, the right place to look for someone like that was not among the women I had slept with, but among my women friends.

Jane, I thought. Jane would make a great merger partner. Her brilliance and business savvy were world-class. She had already been a first-rate adviser and a great asset to my career, directly and reflectively, for years. I admired and respected her enormously. She was strong and independent—unquestionably someone I would feel enhanced rather than burdened by. We enjoyed each other's company and had always gotten along easily and well, too. Wasn't all that plenty for a good marriage?

But then I thought about sex. Even in a marriage designed to be a mutually beneficial business arrangement, we'd have to have sex. For one thing, I wanted kids. Plus, I liked sex. I didn't want to get involved in a platonic marriage and be forced to look for sex elsewhere. And it wouldn't be right or fair to consign a woman I considered an equal to marriage with a husband who admired her brains and ignored her body. It probably wouldn't work either. To work, the solution had to be comprehensive.

It was very strange to think about having sex with Jane. We'd never been sexually attracted to each other. I wondered if I could find her attractive if I started thinking about her that way. Her looks were fine; in fact, she was adorable. And her energy, her intensity, her sharp sense of humor were all very attractive. It occurred to me that she might actually be great in bed.

There was her skepticism about sex, though. She really was very leery of it. She had said more than once that she suspected great sex was a fiction, a notion succumbed to by less realistic people, maybe even a pretense that permitted men to subjugate women. Also, she hated being viewed primarily as a woman, and it was hard to think of her role relative to sex any other way. Judging by what she'd said, her main problem with sex—and, for that matter, with marriage—seemed to be that both required her to "be the woman" in a way she mistrusted.

Jane was deeply cynical about men and our motives, too. Her cynicism was a result of all the sexist crap she'd had to deal with her whole life and it wasn't necessarily unreasonable, but it made her prickly, self-protective, even remote. I wondered if she would turn out to be any more receptive to an intimate relationship—or any more reachable—than Jennifer had been.

Even thinking logically rather than sentimentally, I wasn't sure I could be happy married to a woman who felt diminished and limited by being seen as female, let alone one who was determined to win and who viewed sex, love and marriage as power struggles in which she would inevitably be dealt the losing cards. And I wasn't sure Jane could be happy in any kind of marriage.

These problems seemed insurmountable at first. But I couldn't get the merger of equals idea out of my mind. It felt on target, right. Jane and I liked each other so much. If we could keep everything we had, changing just the context, and not the nature, of our relationship, we would have something incredible. It could be so great, so entertaining and mutually beneficial, so much better than a traditional marriage.

Why couldn't we make it work?

We already trusted each other and we already considered each other equals. This would be a career-enhancing business deal, not a conventional marriage, so the wife role wouldn't be limiting or diminishing in any way. Assuming we could develop some physical attraction to one another, sex didn't have to be a stumbling block either. Jane was smart and strategic—if she liked the other benefits of the deal, she could probably overcome her cynicism and her distrust.

I decided to float the idea past her and see how she responded.

❖ ❖ ❖

I CALLED HER the next morning. "Jane, hey, it's Charlie. I need your opinion on something. Want to have dinner with me?"

"Sure," she said. "I'm swamped today and busy tomorrow, though. How 'bout one day next week?"

"Actually, I was thinking of Saturday."

She was silent. I grinned as I pictured her calculating, assessing, mentally playing out the various angles, deciding on her next move. You had to love her.

Not surprisingly for someone as savvy as she, Jane decided to play it straight—the most reliable strategy for quickly learning more. "Charlie," she inquired, "are you asking me out on a date?"

"Sort of," I said and left it at that. Your ball again, Jane, I laughed to myself.

"Sort of?" she echoed, still sounding both bewildered and amused. "That's weird. But OK. You're on."

CHAPTER 12
A BRILLIANT AND INNOVATIVE SOLUTION

Jane

I was astounded and then perplexed by Charlie's call. A date? What the hell was he thinking?

In the six years we'd known each other, he'd never given the slightest indication that he was interested in me as a date. I was positive he hadn't been. Our relationship was so fundamentally a relationship of friends—honest, comfortable, mutually helpful and supportive, *collegial*. There had never been even an undercurrent of romantic tension or attraction.

So this was something new. What, had he just woken up this morning and decided to rethink all his relationships with women? Or just his relationship with me?

I felt a little like I had before I initially met him. Then, I'd worried about how to play our first meetings—specifically, how to sidestep him if he made a pass at me without blowing the chance to use him to further my career. Now, I couldn't even imagine that he would make a pass at me (interesting; I made a mental note to come back to that), but I had no idea what to worry about or how to play this new angle.

After pondering this for a few minutes, I realized there were too many possible alternatives. There was no way to develop strategies for handling all of them. My only realistic option was to rely on my instincts and play it by ear. And to trust Charlie (despite my uneasy suspicion that he might have lost his mind).

As for the idea of sex with him, it seemed both bizarre and wholly novel. Well, novel as anything other than a suggestion heartily proposed to me by practically every woman I knew who had also met him. Of course, like everyone else, I thought he was gorgeous, but I had never seriously considered him as someone to have actual sex with. That was why we got along so well. With the whole sex risk off the table, it was always easy and fun for me to work with him, debate things with him, be his friend—and trust his advice.

As stimulating as our relationship was, Charlie and I had never focused on each other as a man and a woman. This development made no sense. What could he be thinking?

I got up from my desk and walked over to the window, stopping, as always, a foot or so away from it. Floor-to-ceiling windows so far above the ground made me edgy. Knowing that Charlie was for some unknown reason thinking about me as a date made me edgy, too. But why? Wasn't I looking for a real relationship with someone I could really care about? Why did it make me nervous to think about sex in the context of a stimulating, collegial friendship based on mutual respect?

It didn't take me long to figure out the answer to that question—and once I did, I didn't much like it.

At some level, I had always known that sleeping with Tyler and Patrick presented no danger to me. Neither they nor my feelings for them were strong enough to diminish me or, as Tyler had understood, really even touch me in any important way. Although I'd been frustrated by my inability to let go with them, I had chosen Tyler and Patrick precisely because I *could* hold them at arm's-length.

God, was I just like the worst sort of man—only interested in fucking someone I could feel superior to?

I decided I wasn't quite that bad. My problem wasn't that I needed to feel superior, but that I needed to feel in control. Not of the man so much as of myself. I felt in my bones that sexual relationships were power struggles where someone had to be subordinate, and I'd be damned if I would willingly let it be me.

Sex—and love, too—plainly did have different impacts on women than on men. I remembered back to college, when Nina had become impossible for me to tolerate because she'd been transformed by lust and love from a sensible, practical person into a spacey, obsessed fool who cared about nothing but her boyfriend and would have followed him anywhere. I thought about Katherine giving up her job at the Firm, Cheryl planning to give up her career altogether, Liz worrying about losing her identity in the glare from Tyler's, my mother's life of hiding who she really was.

I didn't want any of that. Fear of those compromises had driven my decisions about sex for nearly a decade, and I had protected myself from them by limiting myself sexually to two men I knew I wouldn't fall for.

But even if my ability to control my feelings for Tyler and Patrick was why I had felt safe, it was almost certainly also why sex had been less than spectacular. Wasn't I now willing to consider that it might be possible to let go and really experience sex without feeling unacceptably vulnerable? Maybe even to fall in love without giving up too much or turning into an idiot?

Whoa, get a grip, I thought to myself with alarm. One out-of-the-blue invitation to go on a "sort of" date from a good friend and I was suddenly thinking about great sex and falling in love. I was transforming into a spacey, obsessed fool right in front of my own eyes!

I stopped pacing and sat back down at my desk. More calmly, I reflected on Charlie and my relationship with him. As a mentor, a boss, a colleague and a friend, he had without fail treated me wonderfully. I had trusted him with my career more than once. I admired him as a human being. I respected his talent, his determination, his adherence to achieving his goals, the *rightness* of those goals. He was a truly terrific person and I liked him immensely.

And that was precisely why the prospect of getting romantically involved with him scared me. Charlie *could* hurt me. I already cared more about both him and his opinion of me than I'd ever cared for Tyler or Patrick. I doubted I could control my feelings for Charlie if our relationship branched in this new direction.

I didn't kid myself that I could control him either. I'd had plenty of opportunities over the years to witness his steely side and his temper. Charlie was accustomed to having his own way and absolutely determined to get what he wanted. Decent as he was, he was also a golden boy who had always been on top. He was decidedly *not* someone I wanted to get into a power struggle against.

Possibly even worse, say I did manage to keep him and my feelings for him at arm's-length and have a "halfway" romantic/sexual liaison with him as I'd had with the others. Our great friendship would still automatically become less honest, less mutual, less equal.

I liked being Charlie's buddy. I liked that we treated each other as friends, colleagues, advisers, people. I wanted our relationship to stay the way it was, and a date—even a "sort of" date—had the potential to ruin things between us. I didn't see how it would be possible—for him or for me—to add the whole man/woman thing to our equation and stay level.

Wouldn't sex just mess things up? Wouldn't love, romantic love, be even worse?

❖ ❖ ❖

CHARLIE HAD SUGGESTED we meet Saturday night at an Italian restaurant we went to often. We liked it because the food was great and they never minded if you stayed for a long time. On the one hand, the choice of meeting place was reassuringly familiar; on the other, I kept remembering that it was also dark and private.

The restaurant had huge, comfortable booths, those tall, rounded ones that can seat three and are very roomy with just two. The booths were big enough for Charlie to stretch his legs under the table—a prerequisite where he was concerned for any chat over 30 minutes. I usually slipped off my shoes and curled my legs under me, one of my favorite ways to sit and something I rarely got to do, given that I spent most of my time at work where that sort of casualness wouldn't do.

I realized I was mulling over these irrelevancies as I walked to the restaurant because I was actually a little nervous.

I sighed. Charlie and I had been meeting and talking candidly for years. I had never once felt nervous about him, not even before our first meeting when I figured he'd be unbearable. What on earth did he have in mind, I wondered for the thousandth time.

I sighed again and, also for the thousandth time, hoped he wasn't going to do anything that would damage our friendship. He really was one of my favorite people, and one of the very few I felt completely supported by. His perspective was important to me, and I hated the thought of having to do without it or, to be honest, without him.

He was getting out of a taxi in front of the restaurant just as I walked up. He smiled when he saw me, closed the car door, and said, "Jane! Great to see you!"

"You, too," I said. We hugged in greeting. So far, completely normal. Relax, I instructed myself.

Small talk got us into the restaurant and seated in the booth I liked best by the now familiar maitre-d', who also took our drink orders. He seemed very glad to see us and welcomed us warmly. (I wonder what *he* thinks our relationship is, I thought to myself. Maybe he could explain it to me.)

"So, Jane," Charlie said, with a knowing sort of smile, "have you been thinking I've lost my mind?"

"Actually, yes," I told him. "I'm prepared to listen, but if you start showing signs of serious dementia, I'm assuming I can get help from our buddy, the maitre d'."

Charlie laughed. "No dementia, I promise. Do you always respond to the suggestion of a date by assuming the guy is demented?"

"Only when the suggestion comes from you," I retorted. "You have to admit it's not our deal. What did you do—just wake up one morning and decide to rethink all your relationships with women?"

"To tell you the truth, that's exactly what I did," he replied. "How about if we wait for our drinks and order some appetizers, then I'll tell you what's on my mind?"

"Sounds good," I agreed. "I'm sure it will be reassuring to have eggplant nearby while I listen to this."

Charlie laughed again. The flurry of activity surrounding drinks arriving, ordering food, and the waiter stopping by moments later with our *antipasti* made conversation unnecessary (not to mention impractical), so I studied Charlie instead. He looked completely normal and quite relaxed. I figured he would be at least a little agitated if he had something truly alarming to say, so I relaxed, too.

He waited until I really did have eggplant nearby, then he said, "OK. Have you ever thought about marriage in business terms instead of in traditional terms? Like a merger of equals—a career-enhancing deal between two people who admire and respect one another, who both bring great value to the table, who would be synergistic together?"

I think he was planning to say more, but he stopped and observed, "You look shocked."

"Well, I am shocked!" I exclaimed. "Marriage? We are talking theoretically, I hope."

"For now," he said blithely. "I've been thinking about why I'm not married, which got me thinking about all the problems you've expressed with marriage as an institution. It occurred to me that the real problem is that people get together for the wrong reasons or expect the wrong results.

"It seems to me that people could avoid all the traditional bullshit if they looked at the combination as a merger with the goal of synergistically enhancing their lives and their careers. If they did that, they would choose a true merger partner, not a husband or wife in any traditional sense, and that would greatly improve the chances of overall success."

He stopped talking, popped an olive in his mouth, and looked at me expectantly.

I stared back at him as if he really were out of his mind (which seemed like a genuine possibility) and said, "Leaving aside for the moment what 'people' you might be talking about and why you've suddenly developed this interest in marriage, I'll tell you that I suspect that's what people generally think they *are* doing. I mean, they don't usually talk like investment bankers about marriage, but I assume the goal is always to find a compatible partner and have a better life. Don't you?"

"That may be the goal," he said, waving away the waiter as I remembered my grilled eggplant and ate some, "but I think people hook up for reasons relating more to sex and then try to shoehorn that match into the merger model. Sexual attraction doesn't seem like a very reliable basis for choosing what is essentially a business partner."

"No," I conceded, astounded, "but it does seem like a necessary element in a marriage. Even one structured strategically to achieve the life and career benefits you described."

"We'll get to that," Charlie said calmly (We'll get to that? I thought in disbelief), "but stick with me on the structuring point. Don't you think choosing someone you considered a partner and an equal to start with would give you a real shot at a great marriage—one that would be stimulating and fun and mutually beneficial? Much better, in fact, than a marriage where the choice of partner was based on something as random as who you felt like having sex with at one point?"

"Sure I do," I said, hoping I didn't sound as thunderstruck as I felt. "Marriage as a merger of equals is a very cool idea. I imagine that good marriages are very much like that, whether they start out on such businesslike terms or just luckily end up that way after starting out with the more common random approach."

"That's my point exactly," he said. He looked impressed, as if I'd said something particularly intelligent. "I agree that good marriages must be like that. I'm positing that your chances of achieving a good marriage would be vastly improved if you chose your partner on the basis of partnership attributes, equality and mutual respect in the first place instead of sticking with the more common random approach and then hoping for the best."

Again, he stopped talking and looked at me expectantly.

"OK, buddy," I said firmly, "I need some context here. I feel like you're in possession of some undisclosed facts. What the fuck are you talking about?"

"I'm amazed you let me get this far without demanding that!" he laughed.

"I'm too busy trying to figure out who the hell you are and what you've done with the real Charlie!"

He laughed again. "Let's order some food before the waiter gives up on us completely, and then I'll tell you where all this is coming from."

I agreed, somewhat ungraciously, and we rounded up the waiter and ordered. "Talk," I demanded as I took the last slice of eggplant.

"Yes, ma'am," he said, smiling. "Jim made a suggestion to me last week. It was the kind of comment you hate—an offensive and inappropriate mingling of personal life and professional progress. I thought of you as I sat in his office seething and also, fortunately, of the advice I always gave you. I managed to stop myself from shouting at him or storming out of his office, but just barely."

"What on earth did he suggest? I can't imagine him making an offensive suggestion to you!"

"He wasn't trying to be offensive. It was just that kind of comment." Charlie looked at me intently. "Would it surprise you to know that even someone like me—as you would say—is subject to being pigeonholed negatively by conservative, traditional, heterosexual bullshit assumptions?"

I shook my head. "No, it wouldn't surprise me, I'm sorry to say. That crap is pervasive. I am surprised, though, that the *actual* you was subjected to it. Will you please tell me what Jim said?"

"He said I'd had a brilliant career at the Firm up to now and there was every reason to think it would continue so long as key senior people viewed me as talented, stable and committed to the Firm. No one questions my talent or my commitment to the Firm, but apparently when you get to be a 'man my age'—I'm quoting here—there can be 'rumblings' about stability if you don't 'settle down.'" Charlie said all the quoted words with deep disgust.

I put down my fork and took a deep breath. "Again setting aside for the moment precisely why we're talking about this under these Saturday night circumstances, I hope you won't have a fit if I tell you that doesn't surprise me either. I'm very sorry—I wouldn't wish this sort of negative assumption bullshit on anyone—but those Executive Committee bastards can't *stand* it when someone doesn't toe their line. It's what we've talked about over and over. They view any difference from the accepted norm, the status quo, as enormously threatening because without the status quo, they know they're dead in the water."

I sipped some water as I tried to figure out how to say the next part without further enraging Charlie. His face continued to look stormy.

"In your case, they're probably motivated by envy as well as by fear," I suggested warily. "Your father's prominence, beautiful women like Annemarie and Jennifer, your own gorgeous self, your dedication to leveling the playing field, the great job you're doing with M&A, their suspicion that you're better than they are. They probably *loved* the opportunity to knock you down a peg."

I frowned sympathetically, then took another deep breath and concluded, "But, Charlie, Jim is right—as I'm sure you've figured out. There's no percentage in leaving them room to think you're unstable."

Charlie's voice was controlled (if passionate) as he said, "Their 'concern,' their 'envy,' their definition of what's stable—it's *all* bullshit! My personal life is none of their fucking business! It's never had a negative impact on the Firm. It's been nothing but a big, lucrative positive for those assholes." After a short pause and a deep breath of his own, he added, "But, yes, I do know that Jim is right."

He pressed his palms on the table, leaned back, and stretched his shoulders and neck. Shaking his head, he asked, "How do you manage to handle this kind of crap routinely without wanting to smash something? Or do you want to smash something most of the time?"

"Why do you think I'm so irritable?" I asked him, trying to lighten things up, and he did smile, if reluctantly. "That wrong-headed focus on form instead of substance, on conformity or tradition instead of merit or even reality, is enough to make anyone wild. But I want to succeed so I've developed a heightened ability to cope with frustration and anger and unfairness without going completely crazy. There's no other choice in this game. You've told me this a million times—the goal is to win the game and take it away from those bastards. Coping with this crap is one of the prices even you have to pay."

"Apparently another of the prices even I have to pay is getting married on their timetable instead of mine." Charlie said this sarcastically, which startled me as much as what he said. He almost never sounded sarcastic.

"Are you kidding?" I asked. "Jim actually told you to get married?"

"He made it clear that dealing with an obstacle I could easily avoid was ill-advised, and also that getting married—sincerely or otherwise—would quiet the rumblings."

"That's disgusting!" I reached over and put my hand on top of one of his. "I *hate* that they've done this to you. It makes you feel totally powerless and pushed around, doesn't it?"

"Yeah," he muttered.

The waiter arrived with our entrées, refilled our drinks, and made himself scarce. Charlie and I both took a few silent bites. I noticed with interest that our silence wasn't tense. It was just a pause.

"So," I summarized soon after I perceived this, "you've been thinking about what to do next and you're too decent just to marry someone for the purpose of being married, so you've approached this like a business problem and come up with what you think is a brilliant and innovative solution."

"Exactly!" he said, looking much more like himself as he smiled. "And now I want to know what you think of my brilliant and innovative solution."

"In what capacity am I giving you my opinion?" I asked, as nonchalantly as I could manage. "Thoughtful friend or potential merger partner?"

"I adore you, Jane," he said, I think impulsively. "You are so direct and so fucking savvy. Your timing on that question is superb."

"Yeah, well, how about answering it?"

"I think you would make a perfect partner," he said comfortably. "Your brains and savvy are first-rate. You're a complete pleasure to talk to and brainstorm with. We already have a great relationship and a long track record of mutual support. I admire and respect you tremendously."

"Thank you. And I mean that. I like hearing that kind of thing, especially from someone whose opinion I value so much." I leaned forward a little and stared at him. "But, Charlie, have you gone crazy for real? Are you actually suggesting marriage to me?"

"I'm suggesting the idea of marriage on these terms to you. I know there's a lot more to consider and talk about, but how about if we put the concept on the table, spend a lot of time together over the next weeks or months kicking it around and trying it on for size, and see where we end up?" He asked this as if it were the most reasonable question in the world.

"I'm impressed with your approach," I teased him to buy some time to think. "Smooth presentation, the perfect amount of flattery to be complimentary but still believable, enough jargon to make you sound authoritative but not quite enough to drown in, and that closer's trick of behaving as if the deal is simple and already all but done. Really nice salesmanship."

"Don't be infuriating," he recommended, grinning. "I know you're just buying time to calculate your next move."

The astuteness of that comment, and the good-natured way he said it, tempted me to tell him I adored him, too, but it didn't feel like a safe thing to do.

"Unfortunately, that wasn't enough time," I said instead. "Look, you know I think you're terrific. I also think your idea is innovative and intriguing. But there's an enormous difference between a great friendship that involves ten or fifteen meetings a year, assorted phone calls, and the occasional crisis—and a marriage that involves living together and sleeping together."

A thought occurred to me. "You are talking about that sort of marriage, right? Not some ultra-modern thing where the 'people,' as you call them, live apart and don't have sex?"

"Right," he said crisply, leaning back and stretching his legs under the table.

"What do you mean, 'Right'?" I demanded. "You have to admit there's a huge difference between our relationship and a marriage."

"Figuring out if we could make that change is the point of what I'm suggesting we do for a few weeks or however long it takes. That is, spend a lot of time together with the goal of keeping our great relationship, but changing the context from friendship to marriage." Again, he said this as if it were a perfectly ordinary and unremarkable suggestion.

"Isn't that typically referred to as *dating*?" I asked, my eyebrows raised.

"It is," Charlie confirmed, unperturbed. He grinned. "If you prefer, you can think of it as negotiation or even due diligence instead."

I leaned against the back of the booth, feeling thoroughly nonplussed. It wouldn't have surprised me to suddenly wake up and realize I'd been dreaming. "You amaze me," I told him.

"In a good way?"

"I'm not sure." I paused, then put my hands flat on the table and said, "Here's my problem. I like being your buddy. I like that we're so comfortable with each other we can even have a bizarre conversation like this one. Our relationship has always been so collegial and honest— and so essentially a relationship of friends. Isn't that *because* we've never been attracted to each other? Wouldn't trying to focus on each other that way just ruin it?"

He started to reply, but I held up my hand. "Wait. Let me think this through. If it didn't work—you know, if we just don't appeal to each other and that's why we've never been attracted—wouldn't we start feeling all strange or awkward? And, if it did work, wouldn't sex change what we expect from each other—and how we feel about each other—too fundamentally and almost certainly in a bad way?"

I frowned at him, a little unnerved. "It's already feeling a bit peculiar, isn't it?"

"A bit," he acknowledged, still looking and sounding utterly relaxed. "I agree that sex is the tough question. I also agree that not having been attracted is part of why we have the friendship we have. But I don't think that's the basis of our friendship, Jane. Not after all this time."

He sat up and put his hands on the table near mine. "I know you hate being labeled a woman," he said, looking at me very directly. "I also know you think traditional relationships subordinate or subjugate women. But I'm not talking about anything traditional. I'm talking about continuing exactly as we are—equals who like and respect each other—and seeing if we can orchestrate a mutually beneficial merger that works for both of us. Even with sex as part of the deal, if we approach it that way and then see how it develops, I think we can avoid ruining anything."

I looked down at his hands, considering what he'd said. After a minute or so, he added mildly, "I'm not talking about falling in love or being crazy about each other or anything else you would find intolerable."

I couldn't help laughing as I looked back up at him. "I'm not speechless very often," I admitted, "but, really, I'm just stunned. Sitting over dinner on a Saturday night coolly discussing having sex with you as part of the consideration for a mutually beneficial merger of equals slash marriage—it's surreal! I couldn't have imagined such a thing if I'd tried!"

"Innovative ideas always strike people that way," Charlie said lightly. He looked at me inquisitively again and touched my hand (also lightly) as he asked, "So what do you say? Will you think about it?"

"Are you kidding? I doubt I'll be able to think about anything else! It's lucky it's Saturday and I don't have to work tomorrow."

He laughed. I shook my head, still flabbergasted, and asked, "Will I be as relaxed about this whole bizarre development as you seem to be after I've had as much time as you to think about it?"

"You'll never be as relaxed as I am about anything," he stated confidently. "Seriously, though, this isn't that bizarre. It really might work, too. Look at us now—we've been having this admittedly unusual and potentially awkward conversation and we're still OK."

"Yeah, I guess we are," I said, pleased to realize that it was true. "And there's really no turning back after this conversation anyway, is there? I sure hope you're right that we won't inevitably ruin things. I'd miss you."

Then, because that sounded more momentous than I'd intended, I asked, "Do you have a Plan B in case you're wrong about us?"

He rolled his eyes. "I asked you not to be infuriating, didn't I? Why would you say a nice thing like you'd miss me and then ask a truly insulting question?"

"Well, I don't want to start getting gooey so soon—or, for that matter, ever." I tried to sound firm even as I couldn't help smiling. "For God's sake, it's only 'sort of' a first date. We're in bad shape if I'm losing it already. Anyway, *do* you have a Plan B?"

"No, I don't have a Plan B, you cynic!" Charlie said. "I like Plan A and I think it will work. If I end up strangling you instead, I'll develop a Plan B then."

"You won't need one then," I told him. "Murder—even of a woman—probably qualifies as 'unstable' in the Executive Committee's definition."

"Not if it's justified," he said darkly, but he was grinning again. "How 'bout some coffee?"

"Dessert, too," I demanded, grinning back.

❖ ❖ ❖

Charlie

Well, that went well! Even better, everything felt so normal. From the second Jane heard the word "marriage," she looked disbelieving, shocked, but also intrigued—just the way I bet she would have looked if I'd told her I was from another planet instead. She didn't hide her amazement or her apprehension, but she never seemed to be uncomfortable or ill at ease. She was her usual self—sharp, clever, blunt and honest.

Her strategic sophistication never falters either, apparently not even when she's dumbfounded. She immediately understood and made the right call on Jim's thinking and his suggestion, offensive as it all was. Her timing on asking whether she was giving her opinion as a friend or potential merger partner—the question that had to have been foremost in her mind—was world-class, perfect, as were the words she used to ask it.

There were some great subtle signs, too. For years, Jane and I have been taking turns paying the bill when we go out to lunch or dinner. We have a business card—one of hers from when she was at the Firm—that we trade back and forth to remember whose turn it is. She had the card tonight, so she paid for dinner and then handed the card to me as usual.

I walked her home after dinner. By that time, we were arguing about the implications of the decreased revenue projections she had just seen for one of her group's recently introduced products. She called me—impatiently—on a mistaken assumption and some logic she considered flawed, but then she agreed with my recommendation for figuring out how serious a problem the revenue shortfall was likely to become. All exactly as usual.

At one point, Jane told me, a bit breathlessly, that I could run if I wanted to, but she preferred to walk. Of course, I wasn't running—I was just walking with the advantage of my much longer legs. I kidded her about being freakishly small and offered to carry her if she was having a hard time keeping up. She laughed very naturally and then said no thanks with exaggerated dignity, sounding just like herself.

We hugged and said good night just as usual, too, despite having immediately before made plans to get together again tomorrow night to continue the merger dialogue.

This whole idea is now striking me as completely brilliant. There's no doubt in my mind that Jane and I will make unbeatable partners. This is going to work—and it's going to be terrific.

CHAPTER 13
KICKING THE TIRES

Jane

After a week and a half of getting together with Charlie almost every evening, I am really starting to think this merger thing could work.

It's too weird to think of him (or anyone) as my husband, but it's surprisingly easy—and kind of exciting—to think of Charlie as my partner. I like thinking more proprietarily about him. And I seem to be noticing, in a very conscious way, the feeling, even the physicality, of being in his company. It's definitely not sexual. The thought of going to bed with him is still bizarre. But I like how it *feels* to be with him in this new couple mode.

I've always personally enjoyed his company, but now I'm noticing how effortless he makes everything. He has a natural lightness that seems to smooth interactions with everyone. People *like* Charlie. It's that whole golden boy thing, I suppose, but it's very relaxing to float through the world on his patient charm instead of slogging through it on my own impatient prickliness.

(Of course, it irritates me that people always assume *he's* the one they should pay attention to when we're out together socially. But that's a battle I learned not to fight a long time ago.)

I've also always enjoyed looking at Charlie, but in a good scenery sort of way—the same uncomplicated, detached, impersonal way I enjoy looking at mountains or a beautiful piece of art. Now, though, I keep noticing how spectacular he really is—and how physically imposing, but in a relaxed, easy way in this regard, too—and my appreciation is no longer detached or impersonal.

I'm relishing the combination of his gorgeous and impressive physical presence and his focus on me. It makes me feel singled out, select, flattered, fortunate. This isn't a new feeling for me. Tyler and Patrick are also golden boys to some degree, and their interest in me pleased me for this reason, too. It's a familiar feeling (as is my embarrassment at being pleased by such a thing), but I've never before had it with Charlie, despite all the time we've spent together over the years.

As surreal and unlikely as the merger idea continues to seem to me when I think about it on my own, it seems totally reasonable and doable when Charlie and I talk about it together. And to my amazement, adding the possibility of marriage doesn't seem to have damaged our relationship at all. We really appear to have added this new element without hurting any of the existing elements.

Even though we've added the possibility only conceptually so far, I'm still relieved that it hasn't changed how we think of or treat one another. Just as he was when he first floated the idea, Charlie is unruffled and comfortable about the whole thing. The nature of his interest in me seems entirely unaffected.

I'm still feeling and behaving like my regular self, too. I'm not distrusting him or feeling like prey, even though I know we will have to deal with sex eventually. I am watching him carefully for signs that he might be making negative assumptions or objectifying me, but I've always done that—with him and everyone else.

Charlie isn't showing any such signs. We still debate and disagree, often heatedly, without ending up at odds in any serious way. We still kid each other and laugh a lot. Even with sex and marriage on the table, there's no undercurrent of discomfort or awkwardness between us. And he's not trying to take over or *maneuver* me either. Charlie genuinely seems to think my independence is a plus. He likes knowing that I prefer to—and can—take care of myself. As far as I can tell, he really has no interest in assuming a dominant role relative to me or to us.

I'm not taking this on faith. I've tested his apparent lack of traditional motive or expectation every chance I've had or could create.

Money was an obvious potential sticking point, for both financial and control reasons. I certainly didn't expect him to demand an interest in my income or savings or to offer benevolently to take care of me. But I did think he'd probably make a pitch for the convenience of combining our assets or, at a minimum, reproach me for not trusting either him or the success of our venture sufficiently to do so. Instead, he cheerfully accepted my proposal that we keep our finances separate. (I wouldn't swear to it, but I think he was amused by my insistence on this point, probably because of the larger magnitude of his assets and earning potential compared to mine.)

The more I think about it, the more I like the idea of a marriage structured as a merger of equals, not just for Charlie's theoretical "people," but for Charlie and me. Only one tiny thing is troubling me. Ridiculously enough, at some deep and uncontrollable level I'm a little disappointed to be giving up on love.

But really, this is better—and a lot less dangerous.

❖ ❖ ❖

Charlie

Three weeks into the merger "negotiations," Jane and I are getting along as easily and as well as we always have—whether we're talking about work, debating the (allegedly) sexist aspects of a movie we just saw or negotiating merger terms. Despite her irritability (which I've always found entertaining), she's really a good sport. I love spending time with her.

But sex is starting to look like a deal-killer. The thought of taking her to bed is still odd, strange—as she would say, like a category mistake. I continue to feel, as I always have with her, that our relationship and sex exist in different spheres.

Jane seems self-contained and unavailable—unreachable, really. She's given no signals in the last three weeks that she might be interested in having sex with me (other than theoretically, as an intellectual matter relative to the merger) or that she might be feeling differently about being seen as a woman.

I've considered not waiting for attraction or some signal from her, and instead just suggesting we go to bed and give it a try as an experiment. That's so cold-blooded, though, so aloof and impersonal, that it's hard to imagine the result would be anything but awkward. I've never pushed sex on anyone and I certainly don't want to start with Jane. Nor do I want to introduce anything bad or awkward into our great relationship. I don't want to like her less or lose what we have. I don't want to force the issue at all without a clear invitation from her.

But I really don't want to give up on the merger. In every other regard, she's the right partner. I'm going to stick with the plan, hope for the best, and see what happens.

CHAPTER 14

THE POINT OF NO RETURN

Jane

Apparently, I'm going to have to seduce Charlie. Is this always the way it goes? I've often wondered. Even when men aren't afraid of being accused of harassment or rape, when it comes right down to it is it always the woman who risks the rejection and gets things going?

I have little doubt that Charlie's a wolf (albeit probably a gentle-manly one) with women, but he hasn't made any kind of a move on me after over a month of what can only be called dating. Why is he leaving this particular ball in my court? Could he be as skeptical as I am that we can really manage to have sex together and still consider each other equals?

Maybe he simply can't get past thinking of me as a person instead of as a woman. That probably would be a hard habit to break after all this time, especially since I've always made it clear how much I appreciate it.

But what if he's hesitating because he's simply not sexually attracted to me? If that's it, this deal is doomed. I don't want to get involved in a sham marriage, and I'm sure he doesn't either. We'd probably end up hating each other. And the potential for career embarrassment would be too high if we slept around.

Thinking about a modern "marriage of convenience" and mutual career enhancement, a true merger of equals, has been very cool. Very compelling, too. I love the idea of using the sexist old institution of marriage in a revolutionary way to bring our two sets of skills and abilities and ambitions together in a synergistic combination. Still, though, while we've approached the motivations, the rationales and the benefits as a business matter, we've always talked about a real marriage—one that includes, among other things, sex that we know in advance will be acceptable.

I have my doubts that sex will ever be anything but ho-hum for me inasmuch as I remain uninterested in losing my head or anything else important, but I'm not entirely cynical. I bet Charlie is terrific in bed. (Jennifer sure thought so and she can't have been easy to impress.) I'd like to give it a try with him and see if I could actually do better than ho-hum.

Well, to be honest, there's something else. Unexpected and improbable (not to mention un-businesslike) as it seems after all these years, I appear to have discovered lust. I no longer find the idea of sex with Charlie at all bizarre. Quite the opposite, it's something I find myself imagining. Frequently. I want him.

Of course, this terrifies as well as excites me. I feel very odd—agitated, jumpy, sort of buzzing. I'm in a tizzy, really, and I'm back where I started on the whole question of sex. What if it's fantastic and I lose myself the way I've always worried I might? What if it's not fantastic and we lose the easy comfort of our friendship as a result? It's hard to decide which would be worse.

Maybe there's an acceptable middle ground. I'd like to think we could add the reality of sex just the way we've added the idea as a concept—comfortably and without changing anything fundamental about how we think of and treat one another. We're both sensible adults. We ought to be able to have sex together without getting all ruffled.

I'd love to have great sex, assuming there really is such a thing and I can experience it without turning into an idiot. If that's not in the cards, decent sex will do. In either event, I want to close this merger with Charlie. If I have to seduce him to get the deal done, so be it. No problem. I'd like to retain as much control as I can of the situation anyway. The first move might as well be mine.

Do I have any idea how to seduce someone? Even assuming I can figure that out, can I do it and continue to be myself—in Charlie's mind and in my own? Maybe it would be better to talk to him directly about this. That seems like a clunky and potentially awkward approach to winding up in bed, but it would definitely be more in character for me than trying to pull off some half-baked seduction scene.

For God's sake—what a stupid and frustrating dilemma to have to face! Sometimes I *hate* being a woman. And I really hate feeling like I have no clue at all *how* to be one.

❖ ❖ ❖

Charlie

It's been the usual great evening with Jane. She's incredibly helpful; her ideas for dealing with my investment committee issue are genius, right down to the presentation slides she sketched out for me at dinner. She's also a lot of fun. She did a hilarious (if quiet) riff on the bizarre people at the next table, who were apparently strangers. They neither spoke to nor looked at one another, and they were dressed as if they'd had entirely different ideas about the evening's plans. As Jane said, he looked ready to move furniture and she evidently had a Victorian garden party in mind.

Jane looks particularly adorable tonight, too. She's fresh and exuberant, and she seems to be sparkling. Being with her is a complete pleasure. I may not be in love with her, but I do love her—easily enough to make the merger work. I'd love to spend my life with her. Why the hell can't we be physically attracted to each other?

She's invited me up to her apartment, which is not unusual, but she seems different tonight. She's revved up and she seems a little out of control. Jane always seems too small to contain herself, but tonight her "about to burst" effect is more pronounced than usual. I've asked her a couple times what's up, but she's evaded the question neatly (and almost imperceptibly) both times.

She calls me from the kitchen, where she's making drinks, and asks me to join her there. I do. Leaning in the doorway, I ask her if she needs some help. "No," she says, still focused on the lemon she's cutting, "but I want to ask you something."

"Shoot."

Putting the knife down, she turns to me and says, "Don't you think it's about time for us to go to bed together? We have to try sex with each other if we're going to make this deal happen."

"Jesus, Jane," I say without thinking. "Could you be any less seductive?"

For just an instant before she gets hold of herself and composes her expression, I see hurt and disappointment on her face. In that instant, I suddenly do want her. I want to reach that open, vulnerable, soft place she's buried under layers of self-protective cynicism to keep it hidden and unhurt. I want to show her that she is desirable and I want her, that she is lovable and I love her.

Before she can turn away or say anything, I've crossed the room, shoved the lemon and the knife aside, picked her up and set her on the counter. We are now eye to eye. I look frankly and seriously into her impassive eyes, trying to express in my own all the tenderness and desire, all the *sympathy*, I'm now feeling for her. "I do want you," I murmur. Then, my hands still holding her waist, I lean in and kiss her lips.

She's been oddly still during all this, but now she comes alive. She's a terrific and enthusiastic kisser. I feel ignited by her tongue in my mouth, her hands on my face, her open thighs around my hips.

I unbutton and take off her sweater, pull her shirt over her head, unhook and peel off her bra. Her breasts are a surprise. They're small, but very rounded, and the unexpected softness in the midst of her overall boniness is thrilling, erotic. I touch them, hold them while I kiss her mouth, then bend and kiss them and her neck and shoulders, too. Her skin is warm, and I can feel her heartbeat in my hands and lips.

Her voice—cool, dry, sarcastic—shocks me as, still kissing her shoulder, I slide my hand up her thigh, bare under her skirt. "You're very adept at getting clothes off women, aren't you?" she says.

I straighten up and look into her eyes, which are now mocking. She has put on her aloof, disdainful shell like a coat to cover her nakedness— and to hide the naked passion of her response. It's obvious that she's trying to hold on to her cynicism, shore up what she sees as her weakening position, regain her sense of control and, with it, the upper hand.

This incenses me. I want to wipe the smirk off her face. I want to *fuck* it off her face and make her moan with pleasure. I want to overcome her defenses, torpedo her sarcasm and smash through her cynical detachment. I want to transform her in a way she'll never be able to deny, to reach and then claim the vulnerable heart of her.

She looks alarmed as I lift her off the counter and carry her into the bedroom, without a word, but staring into her eyes and making no attempt to hide the intensity of the desire, the anger and the determination I'm now feeling. Laying her (gently, even as I imagine throwing her) on the bed, I strip off the rest of her clothes and all of my own, keeping my eyes locked on hers most of the time.

She stares back, and now she looks—could it be?—kind of eager and no longer either mocking or alarmed. I lie next to her, pushing one of my legs between hers, and pull her toward me. I caress her, the softness of my touch on her smooth skin at odds with the fierceness in our still-locked eyes. Jane holds my gaze as if to avert her eyes would be to lose something, to admit some weakness or even defeat, but she is melting, softening, responding, and her eyes are losing some of their determined focus.

After a little while, her eyelids do close as a soft moan escapes her lips. This inflames both my desire for her and my determination to blast through her control. I am inspired. We make love fervently, eloquently, powerfully. She is moaning without pause. So am I. We lock eyes over and over, and that continues to fuel our passion.

When she plants her feet, arches her back, grips my upper arms and screams, actually screams, I explode inside her and know I've done it. I've conquered her cynicism and her doubt. I've reached that buried and untouched place in her.

And it's the most intense experience I've ever had, too—way, way more than I'd ever dreamed of having with her. I feel a surge of pure triumph coursing through me.

❖ ❖ ❖

Jane

Now what, I marvel to myself, as I lie under Charlie, shaking with pleasure and amazement. I love the feeling of his strong body pressing on me, pinning me. I love the way that body—and his eyes, that challenging, penetrating, unfaltering stare—first demolished my resistance, then made my body hum and throb and vibrate to that astonishing, bone-rattling crescendo. Unbelievable. Thrilling.

I love *him*, actually. What an unexpected and wonderful realization. And what an amazing sensation. I feel so *with* him, so covered and firmly anchored to earth. At the same time, I'm flying—soaring and gliding over utterly beautiful, thrilling, dangerous and, until now, completely unknown territory. I feel open, known, possessed, overcome—and somehow it's all good.

Ah, sex—what a wild card! Here we were, orchestrating a merger with sex as part of the consideration. My definition of acceptability was that we'd be good enough together to keep us from concluding that our lack of chemistry was a deal-killer. Charlie's definition was probably similar. Mind-blowing sex wasn't even on the table. I hadn't really thought it was possible at all (unless you were simple or a man). He pretty clearly hadn't thought it was possible with me.

I want to close this deal immediately.

Wait.

I'm slipping into that mindset where you start wanting to offer a premium to get the deal done. I will not under any circumstances (including the current stunning, incredible and undeniably compromising circumstances) let myself turn into the sort of post-coital bimbo I've always been afraid of turning into. That is way too high a premium. Anyway, Charlie was convinced of the value of the deal before tonight and he seems pretty blown away now, too, so offering a premium shouldn't prove necessary.

I shift a little under his weight, but keep holding him tightly.

Here comes the acid test. Does he expect congratulations? Concession? Gratitude? Can I resist letting the huge and brilliant bubble inside me burst out in those clichés? I may be amazed and suddenly aware that I'm utterly in love, but I still feel like the real me, too—strong, razor-sharp and in full possession of my faculties.

I wonder if that will turn out to be what Charlie really wants after all. Will he still value the real me now that we've taken such a traditional step—and knowing, as he must, that he's gained the upper hand in a critical phase of the deal process by putting something new and unexpected and priceless on the table?

Here goes. Let's see what we're both made of.

❖ ❖ ❖

Charlie

Jane proved to be not just a worthy partner and a worthy challenge, but a worthy prize, too. Bowled over as she was, still she wasn't defeated or crushed or diminished, not even a little.

After a few minutes (during which, to my amusement, she was obviously analyzing alternatives and deciding on her next move), she kissed my collarbone and relaxed her hold. She nudged me over onto my back as she smoothly slid out from under me. Up on her knees, she looked into my face with wide-eyed amazement and then, completely unself-consciously, she whooped and shook herself all over like an ecstatic puppy.

I grinned up at her and said, "You've never fucked properly before, have you?"

"Properly?" she echoed, raising her eyebrows and making her eyes even wider. "Buddy, if that was properly, I've never fucked even adequately before."

Her bluntness and her honesty—her irreducible and apparently unshakable determination and ability to be herself, her whole strong-willed, equal self—pierced my heart like a real arrow. I knew in a flash and with certainty that she was my match, my merger partner, my love, my wife. "Marry me, Jane," I said, reaching up for her.

And she got even better. As she let me pull her close, Jane—small, naked, still trembling, her cynicism smashed, her tough shell in tatters around her, but her strategic sophistication working overtime as always—my Jane looked me in the eye and coolly said, "Not so fast. I don't bank on possible flukes. We'll have to do it again a few times first."

CHAPTER 15
CLOSING THE DEAL

Jane

Charlie slept peacefully next to me. No surprise there, I thought. He's probably used to sleeping in someone else's bed after having terrific sex. I was way too excited and shaken up to sleep, even in my own bed. What a night!

My emotions were a heated-up mixture of surprised delight, amazement, jubilation and disbelief. It seemed far-fetched, improbable, that Charlie and I could actually be naked in bed together. It seemed both perfect and impossible that we could have had fantastic sex with each other. And it seemed totally incredible—wonderful, but implausible—that our feelings for each other could have changed so easily and so fundamentally from the affection of friends to a love that felt, to me at least, identifying, possessive, elemental, profound, consuming.

My thoughts kept returning to the breathtaking moment in the kitchen when I saw the astonishing intensity in his eyes. Every time I got back to that moment, I shivered. The force of the desire and the resolve in those determined eyes froze my inclination to hold myself apart. Coupled with the gentleness of his touch, the power in his eyes was magnetic, irresistible. I couldn't take my eyes off his.

It was the moment I knew I had completely lost control over my feelings for him. My instinct had been to find some edge to grab on to and at least reclaim control of the situation—and I'd tried hard to do it, too. But I couldn't. The impulse to loosen my grip and let him sweep me away was as irresistible as he was.

I had never experienced that impulse to let go before—never. It was overwhelming and totally exhilarating. And it had been such a *relief* to indulge it. It was undeniably a surrender, but not the one I'd always feared. This was a good kind of surrender—acquiescence as opposed to capitulation. I didn't feel I'd lost anything. Just the opposite, actually. I felt I'd gained something priceless.

I shivered again and wondered why I'd had the impulse to surrender tonight and not on any of the other nights when I'd longed to be able to let go. Charlie stirred and I turned on my side to look at him. The answer was obvious. I trusted him. Perhaps unconsciously, but nevertheless instinctively and without doubt, I'd known that he wouldn't demean me or take advantage of me or exploit me.

And I'd wanted him, too, with an overpowering desire, a lust that was at last stronger, much stronger, than my desire to remain in control. The speed and purpose with which he'd crossed the kitchen, the ease with which he'd lifted me, kissed me, taken off my clothes, the sweetness of his touch, his taste—it all took my breath away, made my heart pound, changed everything. (How about that, I thought with cynical surprise. Those sensations had become clichés because they were accurate.)

Looking at Charlie's beautiful face while he slept, I understood that it was all real, despite how unlikely and surreal it felt and despite my instinctive skepticism. I was completely in love with him. I reached over and softly stroked his cheek.

But now the idea of marriage troubled me. The way he looked at me right before he said "Marry me"—his face lit up, like he'd just opened an amazing, fabulous present or discovered life on another planet. Had he really meant it? I knew he wanted to complete the merger, but were we now talking about the traditional love and marriage thing?

I thought I could handle marriage if I felt sufficiently in control and if, as we had been, we were talking business. I never seriously considered that I might really get swept away or that we might actually fall in love with each other. I wanted to be Charlie's friend and his merger partner. Could he possibly keep thinking of me as those things if I were also his wife in a traditional love and marriage sort of way?

I still had a very dim view of the way people in general, and husbands in particular, thought of wives. The whole societal approach to "wife," the very definition of the word, seemed to me to assign a distinctly subordinate, and also a sort of beside the point, status to the role. Would Charlie inevitably start thinking of me that way if I were to agree to marry him now?

And what about our amazing chemistry? I couldn't wait to do it again. I was his for the taking—and he knew it. I didn't want to deny that, and I wasn't sorry I'd admitted it to him, but it frightened me to know he had that much power over me. Wouldn't it have to change the way he thought about me?

He was too good a friend and too decent a person to relegate me to the status of conquest (Right? a little voice inside my head inquired unhelpfully), but would he still admire me, still think of me as an equal, still focus on me as a person with brains, when he knew he could make me shake and scream with pleasure? He was a man, after all. Wouldn't he gloat and, in the gloating, automatically think differently about me and who I was to him?

Thinking of that unbelievable crescendo made me shiver again. Charlie stirred in response, and I stroked his hair, then his shoulder and his arm. He didn't open his eyes, but he smiled and snaked his arm around me, cupping the back of my head in his hand and pulling me closer.

"Are you awake?" I whispered.

"I am now," he complained. "It's like being in bed with a Mexican jumping bean!" The words were irate, but his voice was drowsy and he was still smiling. "Did you wake me up to tell me you've decided to marry me?"

"No," I said, "but I'd like another demonstration of why you think it's such a great idea."

He laughed aloud. "You would, huh," he said, his sleepy voice full of amusement. "So this is how it's going to be with you."

He must have been more awake than his drowsy voice and all but closed eyes suggested because he swiftly kissed me and slid his hand between my legs. As before, he tasted wonderful, and his hand—well, very shortly, I was aware of little else.

We made love again, more calmly this time, but just as impressively. I came in a rush that shook me from head to toe. Charlie sat back on his haunches, gently turned me over and urged me up onto my knees. His hands bracing my hips, he pushed into me from behind. I caught his rhythm. My second orgasm came in an elongated wave, engulfing me. I felt his final few thrusts like little explosions deep inside me.

We collapsed onto our sides, Charlie still behind me and holding me tightly. "Jesus Christ," he said emphatically. I was trembling so violently that he asked me if I was cold.

"No," I whispered. "No."

He kissed the top of my head. "Now will you marry me?" he murmured, his lips in my hair.

"Are you trying to take advantage of my weakened state?" I wanted to demand, but my voice was hoarse and feeble.

"It would be foolish not to, wouldn't it?" he teased gently, his voice languorous. "Are you *in* a weakened state, Jane? Is such a thing really possible?"

"I think I am," I muttered.

"Not so bad, is it?" he crooned, the breath behind his words ruffling my hair.

A huge wave of love for him broke over me. I wanted to give him something, to thank him, to acknowledge the untouched place in me that he'd found and won, so I told him the truth. "It's wonderful," I admitted. "Completely wonderful."

He kissed my head again. Soon after, I fell asleep in his arms.

❖ ❖ ❖

I WOKE UP with the sun warmer on my face and higher in my window than it usually was when I awoke. The rich fragrance of coffee hung in the air and the shower was running. I felt sore and sticky and like ten million bucks. I wanted to laugh out loud. My limbs felt heavy, deliciously heavy, the way they did after a long swim. I stretched luxuriously. The sunlight in the room was thick and gorgeous, a presence I could feel as well as see. I felt afloat in it.

For God's sake, Jane, I said to myself sternly. Get a grip. You sound like a fucking romance novel. I turned my head to see the clock. 9:08 a.m.—a time I hadn't seen from bed since college. Luckily, it was Saturday. I did need to go into the office for a couple hours, but it wouldn't matter what time I got there.

It occurred to me that Charlie must have turned off the alarm. It was set for 7:00 and I kept it that way on weekends, too, since I didn't want to have to remember to set it on Sunday nights. I was usually awake by 7:00 anyway. Either he'd turned it off or I'd slept through it.

Look at us, I thought to myself—one great fuck (well, two) and I'm already slacking off, he's already taking over. I tried to think this sadly or admonishingly or furiously, but I still had that disturbing desire to laugh aloud.

The shower stopped. Charlie clattered around for a few minutes, and then appeared in the bedroom doorway. His hair was wet and slicked back, his skin was flushed from his shower, and he glistened from the little droplets of water that clung to his chest and legs. He had a towel wrapped around his hips, a mug of coffee in each hand, and a big grin on his face. He looked wildly happy and good enough to eat.

It was all I could do not to break into delighted laughter or maybe even song, but both struck me as poor tactical moves, so I contained myself. Instead, I raised my eyebrows and said, "Please. Make yourself at home."

"I already did," he said blithely. "Nice shower. Want some coffee?"

I continued to regard him with a look that I hoped was forbidding and maybe even a little chilling. He walked over to the bed and sat on the edge, putting the mugs down on the night table. "Give it up, Jane," he advised, still grinning. "Last night really happened. We're in a whole new place now."

I crawled into his arms, laid my head in the still-damp nook between his shoulder and his chest, and grinned back at him. "Wasn't it amazing?" I crowed. "I sort of can't believe that was really you and me."

"Oh, it was," he said, cradling me. "What a bonus."

"Yeah, this does sweeten the deal, doesn't it?" I teased. "Brains, savvy, adorability, my own hefty income, and now hot sex, too. You've hit the jackpot, Mr. Golden Boy."

"*I've* hit the jackpot—what about you, Ms. I Hate Having to Be a Woman?"

"OK, I admit it. It's not a completely shabby arrangement for me either." I grabbed the hand he raised in mock anger and kissed it. "But, Charlie, seriously, I really don't like the idea of being a wife."

"You won't be *a* wife. You'll be *my* wife." He touched my cheek gently, lovingly. "You seemed OK with the idea when we were talking merger. What's the problem now?"

I slipped out of his arms and sat up. "Which of these is mine?" I asked him, nodding at the coffee cups.

He pointed, then demanded, "Come on, let's hear it. What are you worried about?"

I sipped some coffee, which tasted great, then said, "I need to think about it more before I try to explain it to you. I'm going to take a shower, OK?"

I could have shot myself for the "OK"—I didn't need his goddamn permission to take a shower in my own goddamn apartment—but it had just slipped out.

"OK," he said lightly.

With as much dignity as I could muster, which sadly wasn't much, I got out of bed and walked toward the door. His shirt was on the floor at my feet and something made me put my coffee down, pick up the shirt and put it on, unbuttoned. It came almost to my knees.

Charlie groaned, then said, "You are so fucking sexy. I can't believe I never noticed it before."

I winked at him, but managed to restrain myself from skipping or dancing out of the bedroom. Get a grip, I reminded myself, as I picked up my coffee and left.

In the shower, I thought about what to say to him. How could I possibly explain my uneasiness about being his wife in a way he could actually hear instead of misunderstanding as a rejection personal to him?

As decent a person and progressive a thinker as he was, Charlie had always been a lucky white male. *And* he was the quintessential golden boy. ·He was accustomed to everything going his way, to getting what he wanted, to complete victory. Where both his life and his career were concerned (this recent marriage thing aside), he had never experienced the closed ranks, the outsider feeling or the personal sense of having been pigeonholed unfairly. He'd never had to climb uphill against negative assumptions that had nothing to do with him and everything to do with what people thought about others of his gender or his status, marital or otherwise. How could he possibly understand my qualms?

A little internal voice reminded me that *I* had pigeonholed him unfairly and made just such assumptions about him when we first met. I retorted (internally) that he hadn't known that or felt its impact and told the voice to shut up.

After my shower, I put his shirt back on (adolescent, to be sure, but I couldn't resist) and went into the kitchen to get more coffee. Last night's cut lemon was still on the counter. It was puckered and dried out, but the feeling it summoned up in me was anything but.

In the bedroom, Charlie had stretched out on the bed, the towel still more or less around him. His eyes were closed. He looked big and strong and beautiful and sure of himself. I knew he was going to think my worries were unfounded, my objections frivolous. Looking at him at home in my bed, I felt that way myself. I sighed.

He opened his eyes. "Come back to bed," he murmured.

I did, but I sat, lotus-style with my back against the headboard, and held on to my coffee mug. Charlie turned on his side, propped his head on his bent arm and looked at me expectantly. "Well?" he said.

Steady, Jane, I instructed myself for what seemed like the hundredth time already that morning. I sighed again.

"What?!" he insisted.

"It's hard to articulate," I said, looking down at my coffee. "You know I hate being seen primarily as a woman because of the assumptions people make about women that have nothing to do with me personally. You know, one woman doesn't do well or quits to take a different kind of job or has a baby and stays home with it, and the powers that be all start exclaiming about how uncommitted 'women' are, how 'women' don't have what it takes."

I paused, trying to figure out what I wanted to say. "It's not that I hate *being* a woman. I just hate my path being so cluttered with obstacles that aren't of my making and that I shouldn't have to deal with. And that I *wouldn't* have to deal with if I were in your shoes." I finally looked directly at him. "There's a kind of mass perception, a general noise, about women being less committed to their careers, less talented, less deserving that I always have to fight against. Even when people say, 'Oh, but not you, of course, Jane,' it's just a different way of saying the same thing."

Charlie kissed my elbow. "I understand that—you know I do," he said patiently. "I also understand that marital status is a double-edged sword for you. Stay single and people wonder about you. Get married and you're suddenly someone's wife instead of yourself."

"Exactly! And it's not the same for you. Jim's right—in the Firm's little Norman Rockwell world, you do need to get married soon or you'll appear unsettled or whatever he called it. But when you do get married, you won't become a 'husband,' will you? Not in the way I'd become a 'wife.' You'll still be you, the successful investment banker, who incidentally happens to be married. I'll be a wife—*your* wife—who incidentally happens to have a career. That would be true to some extent no matter who I married, but it will be true in spades if I marry someone like you."

I put my coffee mug on the table so I could gesture with my hands. "There's also that whole societal *thing* about wives. Will they move away if their husbands get jobs someplace else? Are their husbands' jobs more important than theirs—you know, if someone has to wait for a plumber, won't it likely be the wife? Isn't her career really more of a little hobby for her?

"And then, soon enough, will she have babies? If she doesn't, is she unnatural? If she does, will she stay home with them? If she comes back to work, will she be dedicated enough or able to concentrate or the same A-plus player she once was? And, really, wouldn't the world be a better place if mommies *did* stay home and raise their babies? Etcetera, etcetera, etcetera. Someone's always trying to define us or dictate what it means or should mean to be a woman! It's exhausting—and it never stops!"

"You're ducking your real problem, whatever it is," Charlie said, still calm. "I know all that. Marriage does have a bigger potentially negative impact on women than on men. And it's unfair. No argument."

He laid his hand on my thigh. "But you had all that to deal with before last night. Whether we get married for business benefit reasons or because we're crazy in love with each other, married is married. And I didn't get the impression that you were going to say no to the merger for these reasons."

"Sometimes I hate it when you're perceptive," I complained, frowning at him (and resisting my strong impulse to kiss him).

He grinned and rubbed my leg.

"You're right," I admitted, with another sigh. "I'm concerned about 'crazy in love.' I don't feel in control of this situation at all. Frankly, if you asked me to do your laundry right now, I feel like I might actually say yes—and then lovingly fold your fucking clothes with a dreamy expression on my face."

Narrowing my eyes menacingly at his smile, I said, "Also, signs so far are positive, but I'm not convinced you can keep seeing me and treating me the same way after last night. Don't you have to gloat or feel superior or something?" I saw his exasperated eye roll, but kept talking. "And even if we manage to make being lovers work, which I'm not at all sure is possible, I really, *really* don't know that you'll be able to keep thinking of me as your friend, your adviser, your equal if I become 'the little woman.'"

"You already are the little woman, you idiot. Look at you—you're practically a midget!

"OK, sorry, couldn't resist," he apologized as I scowled. "But, Jane, this is you and me, not some sociology experiment. Nothing about your—or my—brains or personality or attitude is required to change if we get married or, for that matter, if we fuck. And no, I don't have to gloat or feel superior. How insulting! Am I doing that? Do you think this is all some act to reel you in and then demand that you do my laundry?"

"No, of course not."

"So why do you think I'll start treating you differently, try to turn you into some sort of bimbo? Are you *planning* to become a different person now that we've had sex or if we get married?"

"I don't think you'll do it on purpose or for some specific reason. I'm worried it will just happen, that it's inevitable or unavoidable or something. I don't know very many men who consider their wives equals. Do you?"

Charlie absently stroked my thigh while he considered this. "No, I guess I don't," he finally said. "But you *are* my equal, and then some. You know I think that. Can't you trust me? If you don't become someone different, there's no reason for me to admire or respect you any less."

I dragged my attention away from the way his hand felt on my skin and said, "That's not the point. I already *am* someone different. Now I'm not just smart, successful Jane, your brilliant friend and former colleague. I'm also someone you've had sex with."

"So?" He took his hand off my leg. "Do you think I'm a complete pig? Unable to think of someone I've had sex with as anything but body parts to fuck?"

"No, I don't think you're a complete pig. But how the hell should I know how you think of someone you've had sex with?" I glared at him. "You seem to have discarded the others pretty effectively! Why didn't you marry any of them?"

Charlie sat up and put his hands on my knees. "That's just it," he said passionately. "I didn't feel about any of the others the way I feel about you. I didn't admire them to start with like I do you. I didn't think they could hold their own or help me get ahead. I didn't *want* to marry any of them. I didn't love any of them."

He looked at me very intently, his eyes as commanding and mesmerizing as they'd been the night before. "Please listen to me," he insisted. "You are going to have to trust me on this. I said it before—amazing sex is a great bonus. You've bowled me over, too, you know. But I love you and I want to marry you *because* of who you are, *because* you're my equal. I want you to be my partner. I wanted that before last night."

This gave me a lump in my throat, but I swallowed it and said, "That's very nice—no, I mean it; don't look at me like that, I'm practically crying here! It *is* nice. It's wonderful. I love that you feel that way about me. And I *do* trust you. But I'm really skittish about the whole love and marriage thing. Couldn't we leave the marriage decision on the table for a while?"

Trying to lighten the mood, I winked at him and suggested, "Maybe just add lots of sex to our relationship and see how that works out first?"

Charlie's face relaxed a little, but he still looked determined. "OK," he said reluctantly, "but I'm not going to give it up. I want to marry you."

He moved his hands to my face and held it gently, although he looked (and sounded) like he wanted to strangle me when he said, "And you'd be nuts not to marry me! Where are you going to find someone else who thinks so highly of you and is also willing to put up with all your crap, you infuriating little midget?"

"And who's so big and strong and handsome and rich and successful, too," I said sweetly, batting my eyelashes at him.

He gave me a look of complete disgust, and then he leaned forward and kissed me.

❖ ❖ ❖

I WAS RELIEVED to have gotten out of that conversation before Charlie focused on the control issue. I didn't know how to articulate my problem even to myself, let alone to him. It had something to do with the newfound intensity of my feelings for him and my deep discomfort with putting myself in a position where I cared enough to change for a man, where I might end up compromising in some fundamental way to please him or to avoid losing him.

I recalled Lynn referring to Charlie (sarcastically) as "the perfect man." I was starting to think of him that way for real, and it scared me. How could I tell him that? He would think I didn't trust him, but it wasn't that. It didn't have anything to do with him personally or, if it did, it was positive, not negative.

But, really, it was about me and about what loving him might mean for me. I was *way* too crazy about him. My comment about feeling like I might be willing to do his laundry hadn't been entirely in jest. I felt *girly*—a new, weird and rather alarming feeling. I didn't want to love him in a way that would diminish me. And I was afraid to need him.

At the same time I was worrying about what all this meant and where it would lead, I also felt fantastic. The sky seemed bluer, food tasted wonderful (although I seemed to need very little of it), I felt super-competent and productive at work, and also sort of fizzy, effervescent.

Even as I scoffed at these clichés and sharply warned myself against turning into a fool, I danced through my days.

Charlie and I were both busy that first week and we didn't have much time together, but we made the most of the time we had. We spent every night together, making love until the wee hours, then sleeping next to each other for a few hours before heading back to work. The lust I felt for him was every bit as vivid as its literary and cinematic counterparts. We were both rapt with lust, spellbound, and sex continued to be spectacular. I completely understood what the big deal was about. And I was continually surprised and totally thrilled that we could feel so *physical* about each other.

One night, he walked into his apartment around 8:00, and I went to meet him in the front hall. Our eyes met and we were instantly in each other's arms. Later, I smiled and shook my head in happy resignation at the out-of-control picture we made: most of our clothes still more or less on us, the key items strewn around us on the floor, our skin flushed and glowing.

"I'm so crazy about you!" I said softly, looking into his eyes, which weren't more than six inches from mine. I smoothed back his hair with both my hands. "Jennifer once asked me how I could possibly hang with you for over five years and not want to have sex with you. I told her I just didn't—and I felt rather superior about it, too, as I recall." I laughed. "The joke's on me, isn't it? Now I can't even spend five *seconds* without thinking about it!"

After initially looking disconcerted (I presumed either by my mention of Jennifer at such an intimate moment or at the thought that she and I had talked about him in this context), Charlie smiled and teased, "And you thought sex would mess everything up!"

I kissed him before I said, "That wasn't a totally unreasonable worry. I was afraid I might lose myself—and I *have* lost myself. But it's some great kind of lost. It amazes me that we can be so single-minded, so *obsessed*, but also still so normal. With each other, I mean."

I kissed his neck, then rested my cheek just above his collarbone and breathed him in. I loved the smell of his skin, its feel, the taut strength of the muscles underneath it. He wrapped his arms more tightly around me and I felt enclosed—not trapped, but embraced. "I told you we wouldn't ruin anything," he murmured.

It was true—we hadn't ruined anything. That first Monday, I found a messenger package from his office on my desk when I got back from a morning meeting. Inside were the investment committee presentation slides he'd had someone prepare over the weekend based on the suggestions I'd made to him on Friday. Charlie had scribbled a note on the top slide; it read, "I hope you'll have time to review these today. Think they'll do the trick?"

I was on the lookout for signs that he was seeing or thinking about me differently, but there were none. He was completely normal.

❖ ❖ ❖

WE ORDERED INDIAN FOOD Wednesday night and had been peacefully eating it for a while when I said, "And another thing."

"What?" Charlie asked warily, as if fairly sure he wouldn't like what was coming next.

"You know how you're always picking me up and carrying me around? I was thinking about that today..."

"Light day?" he interrupted, reaching for the lamb curry.

"Shut up," I advised him. "I was thinking about how it really turns me on."

Now he smiled. "Me, too."

"Yeah, but that bugs me. It's so stereotypical. So *biological*. Why would either of us be turned on by the big man-small woman thing if we really consider each other—and ourselves—to be equals? Isn't it just another warning sign that we're inevitably going to fall into those bad traditional patterns?"

"Jane. You *are* a small woman. I *am* a big man. Why is it a problem if that makes both of us hot? It's not like you have to announce it in your boardroom."

"Hah! Can you imagine if I did? Fat cats would be having heart attacks all over the place. Our whole deal is that the only whiff I bring into the boardroom is the sweet whiff of profits. They look at me and see dollars, not a woman. They overlook my dubious gender precisely *because* I don't make them think about sex."

"Don't I know it?" He grinned at me. "Look how long it took me to catch on."

"OK, but wait." I chewed the last piece of naan slowly, trying to put into words what was bugging me. "If *you* announced something like that in your equivalent of the boardroom, your position wouldn't be diminished—well, assuming everyone got past how inappropriate it is to announce something like that. Do you see what I mean? People wouldn't think less of you or start thinking of you in a subordinate or weak way. If anything, they'd be impressed. Like so many other things relating to sex and gender, us liking your bigness and my smallness is positive for you and negative for me."

Charlie rolled his eyes. "I do see what you mean, and I get the point, but who cares? Neither of us is going to announce it in the boardroom. And where just the two of us are concerned, it's positive for us both."

"But is it? Is it really? I don't like what my being turned on by your ability to manhandle me implies."

Seeing his suddenly ominous face, I amended this. "By your size and strength, I mean. And I don't like what you relishing my smallness might imply. Might it not reveal that under our façade of modern thinking and equality we're basically cave people, too? Will I inevitably become overly dependent on you? Will you inevitably start thinking of me as weaker instead of equal?"

"Jesus Christ! Do you *ever* give this topic a fucking rest?" Charlie's voice was thick with exasperation. "Don't you trust me at all? Don't you trust yourself at all? Are you suddenly one of those 'biology is destiny' morons? Think about it! Sex itself is traditional—and biological. Cave people fucked the same ways we do, too. Do you mean to be suggesting that we also have to do that differently to avoid falling into cave person mentality?"

(Good point, I thought to myself admiringly, really good point! I might have to raise that A-minus grade I gave your intelligence all those years ago.)

Aloud, I said, "I hope not. I'm extremely happy with the way we're doing it now. But that's exactly it! That's the question I'm trying to ask. My instincts have always made me suspicious of situations where I seem to be required—simply by virtue of being female—to take on a subordinate role or even an arguably subordinate role. Now here I am, totally turned on whenever my he-man lover demonstrates that he's stronger than I am and can carry me around."

Charlie started dumping the food debris into the delivery bag. His tone adamant, he declared, "I think you and I in our personal situation get to decide whether or not to fall into traditional ways of thinking about each other. I do not think it's inevitable that having sex together will force either of us to change our opinion of each other—or of ourselves—as equals." He stood up. "No matter what makes us hot."

He stalked off to put the bag in the kitchen trash. When he came back, he loomed over me. I looked up and into his eyes.

"You're going to pick me up, aren't you?" I asked, resigned (and not at all resistant).

"Oh yeah," he said, nodding as if that had been a foregone conclusion for quite a while.

❖ ❖ ❖

ON THURSDAY, I had to fly to the Midwest for an afternoon meeting, followed by a dinner. It seemed simpler to stay out of town overnight and fly back Friday morning than to cram everything into one day. Friday looked as if it would be a light workday, as Fridays in the early fall often were. A whole night's sleep sounded inviting, too.

When I finally walked into my hotel room Thursday night, I found a beautiful bouquet of flowers from Charlie, along with a note that said "I'm missing you." To my amazement, I burst into tears.

I sat on the bed and cried for a while, something I couldn't recall ever having done before. It felt surprisingly good—cathartic, I guess—to sit alone and weep. When I started to feel less good and more like some sort of would-be tragic heroine, I decided it was time to pull myself together and figure out what the hell was wrong with me.

Luckily, the hotel had a pool. I always traveled with swimming things, so I went for a swim. Throughout my life, I had solved problems while swimming. Something about the combination of physical activity, counting laps, and not otherwise being able to control my thought process led to answers. I frequently got out of the pool and found myself in possession of the solution to a problem, sometimes a problem I wasn't even aware I was thinking about.

It worked that time, too.

I had stayed alone in hotel rooms many times before, and I'd never once felt isolated or solitary. I'd always enjoyed the break from routine, the stop in the action, the fresh sheets and towels, the chance to sleep. I'd always felt I had everything I needed.

I still felt I had everything I needed, but now everything was entirely different. Those flowers—that beautiful gesture and the way it flooded my heart—had made it plain to me that I was no longer self-sufficient. Whether I wanted to need Charlie or not was irrelevant. I did need him.

Surprisingly—it was a night of surprises—this realization did not upset me as much as I would have expected it to. I felt overloaded with feelings, numb even, and too tired to think or sleep. I dozed on and off for the rest of the night in a bed that felt strangely (and wrongly) huge and empty, then flew home in the morning.

I spent a few hours in my office, and was barely this side of comatose by late afternoon. Since nothing critical needed to be done before Monday, I left early.

I suddenly wanted to see Charlie immediately, so I went to his apartment instead of mine. I was basically living at his anyway. It was bigger and closer to both our offices, so I'd packed up and moved some clothes and other essentials (and contained my uneasiness over this unambiguous further dent to my autonomy).

His apartment was quiet and peaceful. I turned off the phone, kicked off my shoes and curled up on the sofa. I woke up an hour or so later when Charlie kissed my cheek. "Welcome home," he said softly.

I stared at him for a minute or two, and then felt tears start to drip from my eyes. He looked shocked. "Are you OK?" he asked urgently. "What's wrong?"

I felt so strange. The whole scene felt unreal. I felt disconnected from it, too, not only as if I were watching from afar, but as if it were all happening to someone else entirely. I had no idea what to say. I sat up and reached for Charlie. He sat down next to me and we held each other.

After a minute, he stroked my hair and murmured, "Please tell me what's wrong."

I heard myself say, "It was the flowers."

"The flowers? What fl—oh, the flowers I sent you at the hotel? What about them?"

"I saw them," I said slowly, "and I realized I'm not self-sufficient any more. I've lost control of my life. I didn't want to be dependent on anyone but myself—ever—but now I am. I would feel incomplete and alone without you. Now I need you, too."

"Oh, Jane, Jane, Jane," he crooned, still holding me and stroking my hair. After another moment or two, he leaned back a little, held my face in his hands, and looked into my eyes. "It's not bad for you to need me, darling. You have me—always. I need you just as much."

This made me want to cry harder, which, in turn, really pissed me off. I shook my head in annoyance, sniffled, and tried to smile at him through the tears sliding down my cheeks and into his hands.

"This is exactly what I didn't want to become, exactly the kind of gooeyness I was worried about," I protested. "I *hate* being all vulnerable and needy. Look at me—I've cried more in the last twenty-four hours than in the last twenty-four years! I'm a complete mess."

"You're not a complete mess," he said (more kindly than truthfully). "You're exhausted and at the end of your rope. And vulnerable and needy aren't feelings you have any experience with, are they? No wonder they've opened your tear ducts."

And then, gently brushing away the tears under my eyes with his thumbs, he said very softly, but distinctly, "It's actually reassuring to know you have tear ducts."

I laughed, just as he'd intended. "The perfect man," I muttered to myself.

"What did you say?"

"Nothing—just raving." I sniffled again. "I think I need a Kleenex, a hot shower and a long night's sleep. With any luck, after all that I'll once again be someone we can both recognize."

"Would you like company for all but the Kleenex?"

"Yes, I would."

❖ ❖ ❖

I DID FEEL MORE NORMAL in the morning. I had always handled sleep deprivation fairly seamlessly in the past. But, as Charlie pointed out (making me laugh again), it had never before been accompanied by relinquishing control, falling in love or a week of world-class sex, let alone all three.

He didn't seem to think my meltdown was alarming nor did it affect how he treated me. He was gentle, but he had always been gentle when it was warranted—during the Ian business, for example. And, as he had done then, Charlie managed to be gentle without making me feel as if he were thinking less of me.

The weekend was great. There was no real reason for me to go into the office, so I broke my years-long habit of logging Saturday office time. I spent the whole day at Charlie's, wearing nothing but one of his shirts and (my own) socks. He had a golf thing with a client in the afternoon; while he was gone, I accomplished nothing but catching up on sleep. It was a soothing and peaceful day, and I felt more like myself with each passing hour.

Charlie brought food home with him. While we ate, he outlined the deal his client wanted to do and then argued with me at length about how best to get it done. That was all very stimulating, so we went back to bed—not, this time, to sleep. I could get used to this, I thought, as my body started to hum and throb. I really could.

We spent the whole day together on Sunday, something we'd never done before. I was amazed by how comfortable it was, how easy. Sometimes we talked; sometimes we sat together, doing our separate things, in perfectly companionable complete silence; sometimes we were in different rooms altogether. Charlie was on a conference call for an hour or so. I continued to make progress toward believing the whole love and marriage thing might actually work.

Partly for fun and partly to reassure myself that I still had some control over where this love story was going, I continued to resist Charlie's frequent marriage proposals. I could no longer imagine putting a real stop to things, but this phase—the chase, if that's what it was— couldn't have been more perfect. I was loath to bring it to an end.

❖ ❖ ❖

A FEW DAYS after that idyllic weekend, one of the Company's new products headed south in a serious way. I participated on the crisis management team and worked nearly constantly for four days. I missed Charlie during those long, intense days (a new and not entirely welcome distraction) and so, despite my fatigue, I went to his apartment around midnight each of those nights. We were sensational together—talking to him, touching him, making love, waking up next to him; it was all wonderful—but I started to feel sleep-deprived and doubtful again.

The fifth evening, after a particularly trying day, I called his office to tell him things were fucked up and I would be home even later than usual. I was tired and irritable; as we talked, I found myself blaming him. I told him, not very nicely, that maybe I'd just go to my actual home and get a decent night's sleep for a change. Perhaps I was trying to provoke an argument or a display by Charlie of temper or muscle that I could resent and then use as a means of regaining some control over what felt like my increasing need for him. In any event, I could not have been more taken aback, or more electrified, by his response.

It would be hard to imagine a better response or one further from the "I'm the man and I want things my way" demand I'd been half hoping to hear. His only reaction to my nastiness was to sound sympathetic. After he agreed that a whole night's sleep sounded good, he said he'd also love to see me and whatever I decided was fine with him.

I was galvanized. I suddenly understood that this wasn't a contest that would, of necessity, ultimately end with a winner and a loser. Charlie and I wouldn't be at odds at all. We had the same goals for marriage and we would pursue them as equals. It wasn't about control or loss of control either. Control, I realized, was antithetical not only to passion, but also to love.

Charlie had been right all along. This was about trust—the prerequisite for passion and love. Trust was what made it possible to understand and to believe that the surrender I had always feared was a *good* thing when it was truly reciprocal. I did love Charlie and I did need him—both way beyond my ability to control—but neither of those things spelled anything dangerous for me if I believed that he loved and needed me just as much. In short, if I trusted him.

And I did trust him. He had never in all our years together done even one thing—not the slightest little thing, despite plenty of opportunity—to give me any reason not to trust him. I trusted him as much as I wanted him, as much as I loved him.

I almost told him right then and there on the phone that I would marry him. Luckily, I caught myself in time—I wanted to be there to see his face when he learned the deal was finally a go.

❖ ❖ ❖

Charlie

For a week or so after what she called her meltdown, Jane and I continued to spend every spare moment together, mostly in bed. We were incredible together. After all those years of not noticing her sexually, then all those weeks of wondering if I would ever scrape up even a whisper of desire for her, I couldn't stop marveling over our pyrotechnic chemistry.

I was crazy about her, totally in love with her. My sense of having discovered, reached and claimed a buried and fundamental place in her had coalesced with my enormous respect for her brains, her savvy and her unshakable sense of self into a potent stimulant, the likes of which I'd never before experienced. It was intoxicating. It was also addictive and I couldn't get enough of it—or of her.

I kept asking her to marry me—when we woke up together, in the middle of conversations about something else, whenever she had a particularly intense orgasm (which happened gratifyingly often). She remained noncommittal, but we had progressed from the original "Not so fast" to the promising "I might; it could happen" and, once, to a gasped "How could I not?"

Jane was having a great time and she was also getting more relaxed about needing, and having to trust, someone other than herself. I knew she loved me and I was pretty confident that sooner or later she would agree to marry me.

She had a crisis at the office that week. After working pretty much nonstop for several days, she called my office around 7:00 one night to tell me things were not going well and she would be even later than usual. She sounded exhausted and grouchy, and I wasn't surprised when she said she might just go to her own apartment and get a good night's sleep. Sleep sounded good to me, too, but so did being with her, so I told her I'd be home and she could let me know one way or the other when she decided.

At 10:45, she let herself into my apartment and sang out, "Honey, I'm home!" She sounded sarcastic, but totally jazzed—no longer either exhausted or grouchy. I met her in the front hall with my usual question: "So have you decided to marry me yet?"

She grinned, then gave me the once-over. Holding out her arms, she shook her head and said in a very resigned, almost dejected way, "You are too gorgeous."

"You say that like it's a bad thing," I objected as I picked her up. She wrapped her arms and legs around me; I held her and nuzzled her neck.

"Well," she said, "I don't love the idea of spending the rest of my life having people wonder the minute they see us what a gorgeous, successful hunk like you is doing with the likes of me."

I looked up and into her smiling, sarcastic eyes. "What crap, Jane. What total crap. You know you're adorable and brilliant. There's no mystery to what I'm doing with you. Also, you're totally conceited and you don't give a shit what anyone thinks anyway, so who do you think you're fooling with *that* line?"

"Fuck you," she whispered, gently rubbing the back of my neck with her fingers.

"Just what I was thinking," I murmured.

Despite our exhaustion, we outdid ourselves. When eventually we lay, calmed and worn out, on the bed, her back was pressed against me. After a few minutes, I felt her turn in my arms to face me and she said, "Charlie?"

"Mmm," I breathed, hugging her, but not opening my eyes.

"Look at me?" she requested, with a surprising and very uncharacteristic note of shyness in her voice.

I dragged my eyelids open and found her eyes right in front of mine, filling up my sight. Jane's eyes were shiny. I couldn't tell for sure in the dark, but I thought they might have tears in them.

"I will," she said softly.

"You will what?" I asked, trying completely without success to contain the jubilant grin that was spreading across my face.

"You idiot," she said tenderly. "I will marry you. I'd love to marry you. I love you."

I knew then that I hadn't been at all sure she would eventually agree, and also that I'd wanted her to marry me more than I'd ever wanted anything in my life. I found myself too overcome to speak, so I just kept grinning at her while a lump developed in my throat. A tear or two might have sprung up in my own eyes.

After a while, we crawled under the covers together and slept until morning.

CHAPTER 16
POST-CLOSING MATTERS

Jane

And so Charlie and I married each other. We didn't follow the conventional wedding format. I wanted nothing to do with the usual public display of sexism and subordination of women. And the notion of appearing as a bride in front of colleagues from the Company and former colleagues from the Firm was about as appealing to me as inviting them all into our bedroom.

Charlie didn't care how we did it as long as we got it done. So we decided to marry privately, take an extravagant honeymoon trip, and then have a big reception when we returned.

We were married in early December by a judge Alex recommended. She performed the ceremony in her chambers with her clerk and her secretary as witnesses. Charlie loved it. He was the only male present, and he said he felt like part of some Amazonian matriarchal ritual. (He only hoped human sacrifice wasn't involved.)

He arranged the trip, which began our tradition of extravagant (if infrequent) vacations. He decided on a lush resort on a tiny island off the coast of Venezuela. The island wasn't reachable by air, not being large enough for a landing strip, so we had to fly to a nearby island and take a boat to the resort. After encountering some frustration as he attempted to book commercial flights, Charlie decided to book a private plane.

A private plane is shockingly expensive, but it may well be one of those few indulgences that are worth every penny of the cost. A private plane travels on your schedule, not the other way around. You depart from an "executive" section of the airport, within ten minutes after you show up. No intrusive security, no lines of any sort, incredibly pleasant and helpful people. Ditto with customs and baggage handling when you arrive.

On the plane, you have astonishingly comfortable seats (even if you're the size of my husband), as well as food, drinks and movies you have chosen and ordered for yourself. You giddily feel like a character in a movie the whole time.

You also have an incredibly pleasant and helpful pilot and copilot. These delightful gentlemen (I haven't yet seen a woman in this role, but I remain hopeful) run through the safety info as if you are an intelligent and valued customer rather than a disobedient toddler for whom they are not very graciously doing a favor. They couldn't care less how much you move about the cabin, and they go out of their way to make sure you're comfortable and happy.

Honestly, the contrast between a private plane and a commercial flight is one of the most distinct I know. The private plane makes the transportation one of the best parts of the vacation.

And the resort was fabulous. No telephones, no television, no fax machines, no mobile phone coverage and no newspapers. Guests don't have rooms so much as their own wholly private wedges of the island, each complete with a private beach and deluxe living quarters. The bedroom and bathroom were enclosed, but the sitting room was partially covered and essentially open-air. There was a communal dining room with excellent food; even better, there was room service 24/7.

Best of all, the resort had a clever little flag system. If you wanted something—food, the maid—you raised the green flag at the end of the short path outside your front door. A charming person quickly appeared to find out what you wanted and then provided it. They used golf carts to get around the island, there being no cars and no real roads.

If you wanted to be left alone, you raised your red flag. Red flags were respected utterly. Charlie and I stockpiled some food and spent two whole days and nights totally by ourselves. For people whose work required constant involvement with other people, many of them irritating, this was paradise.

Most days, we walked once or twice around the island, swam in the ocean, lounged together in the double hammock on our beach or in bed, and ate lobster and fruit. We read books, we got tan, and we made love whenever and wherever we felt like it. Day and night stopped having their usual meanings—we napped frequently during the sunny afternoons and had many chats and debates in the wee hours.

One afternoon, I awoke from a gentle doze and contemplated my beautiful husband as he slept next to me in our hammock on the beach.

It seemed miraculous to me that we could have arrived at this place, this moment in time, this point in our relationship with each other. I thought about how it had happened.

We started as colleagues, despite the inherent power imbalance in a mentoring relationship. We continued that way, despite the inherent power imbalance in a senior/junior working relationship. We became friends. We needed help from each other and provided help to each other in a variety of situations, always using our own and one another's talents and power for mutual benefit.

We admired, respected and came to love one another as friends. Sex and romantic love were the last pieces we added to the mosaic of our relationship; their inherent—or perhaps societal—power imbalance also failed to damage our sense of equality. Where had that apparently impervious sense of equality come from, I wondered?

It was obvious that Charlie and I had always had a strong attraction to each other. But, despite our different genders, it hadn't until recently been a sexual attraction. Had we maybe avoided the typical man/woman pitfalls by being colleagues and friends for a long time before we were lovers? Had I been at least partly right in thinking for so long that sex and romance created inequality—either by their nature or by the layers of repressive bullshit they had been swathed in by centuries of so-called civilization?

I thought of those silly admonitions about saving sex for marriage that I and the other embarrassed girls in my high school "health education" class were force-fed. What a ridiculous notion *that* was. It was hard to imagine anyone stupid or optimistic enough to promise a lifetime of love and fidelity without first doing at least a little due diligence.

I'd always assumed those admonitions were designed primarily to keep us from having sex in high school—and winding up distracted, pregnant or diseased—rather than actually to preserve our virginity for marriage. Could they possibly have been partly right, too? Was it a better plan to love or at least care non-sexually for each other first?

No, I decided. That wasn't it. The problem wasn't sex. It was what drew people to have sex with each other.

The problem was lust—specifically, the forms sexual attraction typically took and the reactions it typically engendered. There was the hormonal daze that made people impulsive and non-strategic and drove them together, often against their better judgment. There was the predatory urge that transformed people into aggressor and prey. And there was the approach I'd favored—the overly strategic and self-protective calculation that brought people together more for physical contact and something to do than anything else.

My certainty that sex and love were power struggles with, of necessity, a winner and a loser had blinded me. I hadn't been able to see that the real enemies were control and detachment, not surrender and passion. I hadn't understood that trying to stay in control in an intimate relationship missed the point and was completely counterproductive.

Once Charlie and I actually had sex, I knew that my pretensions toward handling the whole thing coolly and as essentially a business transaction were ridiculous. I couldn't deny the power of my passion for him nor could I pretend it hadn't changed me. But my lingering fears over what it meant to love him, to want him, to be crazy about him couldn't begin to trump the exhilarating reality—or the irresistibility—of those feelings.

The point for us wasn't that we hadn't had sex with each other until recently. It was that we hadn't *wanted* to have sex with each other until recently. Our friendship had been free to grow and unfold naturally and with mutual respect for over six years. And it had, as a result, grown into something extraordinary—a truly complementary relationship that sex, love and marriage only made better.

A breeze stirred the trees our hammock hung from and sent a few leaves fluttering down as I recalled a conversation I'd had with my new sisters-in-law. Charlie's family was wonderful. He and Alex were not atypical; Andy, Claire, Hannah and Kate were all charmers, too. Andy's wife and Claire's and Hannah's husbands also seemed great. (They were also—every single goddamn one of them—way too tall. Andy's *children* were practically my size. Apparently, I was doomed to spend the rest of my life feeling like poor Gulliver among those Brobdingnagians.)

I particularly loved the way Claire treated Charlie as if he were still eight years old to her eleven and also still smaller than she. He told me he grew taller than Claire right around the time he actually was eight, but she'd never been willing to break her older sister habit. I felt sure that her persistence in calling him "small fry" and "baby brother" was part of why Charlie, even with all his golden boy advantages, was neither self-important nor overbearing.

Claire informed me that the whole family was hugely relieved by my appearance on the scene. They had been deeply worried, she confided in a voice pitched to be sure he could hear her, that Charlie planned to disgrace himself and destroy the family tradition of intelligent and inclusive discourse—as well as witty and satirical repartee—by eventually marrying one of his babes instead of someone suitable for introduction into the family circle.

Hannah, who frequently sounded exactly like Charlie, was also pleased to see him with me. She was more serious than Claire, but she made a similar point. She told me both her brothers had found their paths strewn with willing women from the time they were teenagers. While Andy had enjoyed this as much as the next guy, Hannah said, he was never limited by it. Nor was he distracted from thinking about what he wanted in a mate over the long term and then choosing his girlfriends and ultimately his wife with that in mind. (*Strategically*, I thought to myself.)

Charlie, on the other hand, had applied all his brain power to his career ambitions. Where women were concerned, he had been content simply to choose among the ones who jumped in his lap (as Hannah put it). She had found it interesting—and of some concern—that while he always had women friends, he never slept with any of them, opting instead to fuck around with women he had very little in common with, and as an activity only loosely connected with the rest of his life.

(Obviously used to his sisters, Charlie's response to all this had been stoical and humorous. He rolled his eyes, shrugged in a "What are you gonna do?" sort of way, and suggested we change the subject.)

Remembering this, I bent my arm, which was already resting on his chest, and curled my palm around the side of his neck.

It occurred to me that our early relationship had been protected from the dangers sexual attraction might have posed by the very combination of character traits that could have kept us from ever becoming lovers—that is, my distrust where sex was concerned, coupled with my cynical and self-protective need to choose partners I wouldn't fall for, and Charlie's probably unconscious strategy (and golden boy luxury) of limiting himself sexually to women who made it clear to him that they were available and interested.

So what had brought us together as lovers? I laughed aloud as I recognized the irony of the answer. What had brought us together was Jim telling Charlie to get married in order to quiet irrelevant, inappropriate rumblings—simply another instance of the same conservative, traditional, heterosexual white male *bullshit* that had created our character traits in the first place.

Well, and also an instance that Charlie had responded to with flair, intelligence and creativity—rather than only with anger, frustration or resignation.

My laugh woke my remarkable husband. "What's so funny?" he asked sleepily.

I settled into his arms to tell him.

❖ ❖ ❖

AFTER ANOTHER WONDERFUL private plane experience, we returned home from the island feeling rested, euphoric—and married. It was a great feeling, and a surprising one. I kept finding it suddenly top of mind, in the same way I kept unexpectedly noticing the platinum band on my ring finger or on Charlie's.

Coming home was also jarring. The time difference between the island and home wasn't enough to produce jet lag, but we found ourselves with lifestyle lag. The island's lush vegetation, brilliant sunshine and nearly total absence of other people and technology, automotive and otherwise, could not have been more different from our wintry, crowded and loud lives back in the city. We felt as if we were returning to earth from a different planet.

Neither of us went back to work before our reception, which was three days after we got home. We spent the first day holed up in Charlie's apartment, pretending we were still on the island, and the second day finalizing arrangements for consolidating our lives. Surprisingly, the island pretense worked pretty well and the consolidation looked as if it would go relatively smoothly. It also irritated me far less than I (or Charlie) expected it to.

I was not particularly looking forward to the reception, but it turned out to be a lot of fun. My mother and sister, who excelled at these things, had taken on all the planning and coordination details as a wedding gift to Charlie and me. I told them I wanted a lot of really good champagne, food and music, and no speeches or silliness, and then left it in their hands. I counted on my sister's desire to impress Charlie to keep her sillier party-planning tendencies in line.

Twenty-four at the time, Laura had developed a colossal crush on my husband-to-be within ten minutes of meeting him. She and the rest of my family seemed thunderstruck that I was marrying someone like Charlie—or, perhaps more correctly, that someone like Charlie was marrying me. I would have been offended if I hadn't been so tickled about shocking them. They had always found the path I chose for my life to be unfeminine and incomprehensible. The notion that I had followed that path *and* snagged what appeared to be their dream husband blew them away.

Laura and my mother did a great job with the reception. It was beautiful and elegant, and nearly everyone was there. Our families, friends from work and elsewhere, college friends—I kept seeing people I hadn't seen in way too long, and I was amazed by how many people we knew and liked.

Even the Firm muckety-mucks we'd felt obliged to invite were no trouble. Most of them spent their time in a feeding frenzy over Alex (retired, but serving on several prominent corporate boards), Walker (still august and powerful), Tyler (still related to his father), and the two or three other real players in attendance. After greeting and congratulating us, the muckety-mucks were way too busy to pay much attention to Charlie or me, which suited me perfectly.

Jennifer was no trouble either. Charlie and I had a little discussion about including her on the guest list. He felt strange about it because it had been barely six months since they were an item. I wanted her on the list because she was a good friend of mine—and she would certainly not be the only ex-lover in attendance. Charlie's hesitation apparently had more to do with my feelings than his own. Once he saw I had no problem with inviting her, he said OK.

She was quite funny when I told her about Charlie and me. Jennifer thought she was entitled to the credit for waking me up to the notion that he was someone I might consider as a lover. She also thought her relationship with him had alerted him to the possibility of looking in my direction. She gracefully reiterated both these points when she congratulated us at the reception, and I was very glad we'd invited her.

I also got a kick out of the surprised looks her presence prompted on the faces of the Firm people who'd originally met her as one of Charlie's sexy dates. And I was amused to see that she spent more than a little time talking with Patrick.

I had tried to assemble my girls' club a couple months before to tell them my surprising news, but Anna was still in London and it had proved impossible to find a date that Katherine, Lynn, Cheryl and I could all make. I'd ended up telling all but Cheryl on the phone, and so I was anxious to talk to the others in person. I was also looking forward to seeing Cheryl again—she was by then in her eighth month of pregnancy.

Katherine and Jordan arrived relatively early. As usual, they looked as if they were thinking about the ice cream incident every time they looked at each other. Since they'd been married for nearly four years, I found their ongoing enraptured delight with each other very encouraging.

Jordan told Charlie and me that it would have been more thoughtful of us to have taken romantic advantage of our mentoring relationship sooner, preferably in time to have deflected some of the criticism he got for having done the same thing. Katherine, naturally, saw a business opportunity in recasting the Firm's mentoring program as a marriage brokerage.

"What the hell, Jane!" she said with her usual verve. "Why not? It could be a very lucrative new business line and a great way to get more women recruited into the place! The dopes at the Firm who don't get the joke won't ever take women seriously anyway. And, with any luck, those dopes will soon be displaced by our lawful wedded husbands, who, I'm reasonably sure, *do* get the joke. And who, of course, take women terribly seriously."

She looked amorously at Jordan, her eyes sparkling, then gestured to include both Jordan and Charlie. "Really," she crowed, "imagine marketing materials with these two poster boys plastered everywhere. It could be huge!"

While Charlie and I laughed, Jordan smiled at Katherine, kissed her bare shoulder, and said, "Come on, beautiful. Let's go get more champagne and rough out some numbers for the business plan."

After congratulating us again, they moved away arm-in-arm, presumably to do just that.

"Suppose we'll still be that crazy about each other four years from now?" I asked Charlie.

"I'm certain of it," he said, smiling. "Suppose you'll let me kiss your shoulder in front of a roomful of people you work with by then?"

"Katherine doesn't work with these people," I retorted. A new group of well-wishers was bearing toward us, but I had just enough time to stand on tiptoe and confide in a low voice, "I know this will shock you, but I'm sort of tempted to let you kiss it right now."

Charlie raised his eyebrows suggestively, but contented himself—and me—with putting his arm around me and resting his hand warmly on my shoulder as we greeted the new well-wishers.

Shortly after that, we got separated by people coming at us from both directions. After finishing with my contingent, I decided to use the opportunity to find Cheryl and Lynn, neither of whom I'd yet spotted in the crowd.

I hadn't seen Cheryl during her pregnancy except when I told her about Charlie and me. She was then six months' pregnant and still at the Firm, but not sure how much longer she would continue working. Because of the nature of my news that day, we hadn't spent much time on her career plans. I was curious to know what she was thinking.

She and Richard proved to be harder to find than I expected because they were sitting down. As soon as I did find them, they both stood and I saw why. Cheryl was hugely pregnant. "Look at you!" I exclaimed, hugging her. "You're so pregnant—and lovely as ever. That whole business about glowing must be true!"

"That's a nice thing to say," she said, smiling. "I think 'appalling' is a more apt word than 'glowing.' I feel like a whale—a beached one, most of the time now. We've been trying to make it over to congratulate you and Charlie, but I can barely move and Richard won't carry me."

Richard laughed and said very fondly, "Honey, it's not that I won't carry you. I doubt that I *can* carry you." He caressed her cheek, then turned and hugged me. "Congratulations, Jane! You look terrific—and very happy—yourself."

"You really do!" Cheryl concurred as she sat back down (with obvious relief). "I have such a hard time believing that you and Charlie have married each other! It's wonderful—and so wonderfully unexpected. I was telling Richard that, as far as I know, you're the only woman who ever worked at the Firm who *didn't* have a crush on Charlie at one time or another. I know I sure did."

"She still refers to him as 'the perfect man' from time to time," Richard told me, smiling and caressing her cheek again.

"Well, you won't get any argument on that from me. I have a serious crush on him now," I said, grinning. "Cheryl, what are your plans?"

"I'm officially on an indefinite leave of absence as of just before Thanksgiving. The Firm was amazingly accommodating. At this point, I'm not willing to commit to going back to work at any set time, so I had planned to quit altogether. They suggested the leave of absence, which works for me. No reason not to leave the door open."

She gestured to her bulky middle. "I really can't move much, so I'm glad I don't have to get up and into the office every day, but I'm very bored. Who knows? Maybe I will go back to work some day. My original life plan may require further refinement." She smiled. "Since I exchanged the investment banker for a lawyer and worked into my seventh month of pregnancy, the plan's already covered in red ink anyway."

"'Diversified' from the investment banker to a lawyer, you mean," Richard corrected, with a smug look. "But for the fact that I'm surrounded by investment bankers, I would even say 'upgraded.'"

"Careful," I warned him, smiling, before I turned back to Cheryl. "I'm so glad the Firm was accommodating. They should be—you've done a great job for them for a long time. Speaking of the Firm, do you know if Lynn's here somewhere?"

Cheryl pointed me toward where she'd last seen Lynn. After Richard helped Cheryl struggle back to her feet, they headed off to find Charlie and I went looking for Lynn.

I had not thought Lynn's "I am who I am" strategy would work, but she was still doing very well at the Firm. Charlie reported that she was very highly thought of, thanks in part to being unusually good at originating and handling clients. (His decision to reassign responsibility for John's company and one of his other clients to her, and to designate her as one of M&A's mentors, hadn't hurt either.)

I kept getting sidetracked on my way to find her; luckily, she finally found me. She tapped me on the shoulder and when I turned in response, I was enveloped in a very sincere hug.

"I'm so happy for you, Jane!" Lynn said. "I remain unconvinced about marriage, but I always thought you were out of your mind to have such a great relationship with Charlie and not take it the rest of the way. I wondered more than once if it would ever occur to either of you. I'm so glad you finally wised up!"

I laughed and thanked her as she took a goblet of champagne from the tray a circulating waiter offered. I gave him my empty glass and told Lynn, "We got the nicest note from Anna, congratulating us. But she didn't say anything about what she's up to. What do you hear from her?"

"She's still in the London office, slaving away. She prefers living there to here, but she dislikes the regional office environment and would much rather work in a headquarters office." After a sip of champagne, Lynn said, "I hope she won't leave the Firm altogether, but she may have to if she really wants to stay in London."

"I hope she stays at the Firm, too. I'm sure it's all right in line with some demographic trend, but I hate to think of you ending up being the last woman standing. It's strange to think you and Anna are the only ones from our little group still at the Firm, isn't it?"

"Not so strange, really." She smiled. "Even leaving your glorious husbands out of the equation, you and Katherine got the best of what the Firm has to offer analysts and associates and you're both using it to have great careers where you are. And Cheryl never planned to stay."

"She looks great, doesn't she? I wonder if she'll decide to go back to work after all. Did she tell you she's bored?"

"Yeah, we had lunch not too long ago. She figures she'll see what life is like once the baby is born, then decide."

"Do you think it would be hard for her to get back in at the Firm?"

"Not if I have anything to say about it," Lynn declared. "If necessary, I'll get you and Katherine to pressure those husbands of yours, too. Cheryl is very good at the job and I could use a *compadre*. I hope she does want to come back."

"You know," I said, grinning, "I have no idea how to go about pressuring a husband effectively. Think I can pull off a trick like that with Charlie?"

Lynn snorted. "Having observed the way he now looks at you, I doubt there's anything you couldn't get him to agree to."

I laughed. "For a while, maybe," I demurred. "But he has a strong mind of his own. And don't forget that steely side."

"True," she said, "but my money's still on you. So when are you free for lunch or dinner? As I said, I'm short girlfriends at work. I'd also love to know what your bosses are thinking about in the way of acquisition activity for next year."

I promised to call her to set something up as soon as I got back to the office and finished digging through the piles that had no doubt accumulated while I was away.

Later, after chatting with some Firm people I hadn't seen in the two years since I'd left, I turned and found myself in a little pocket of solitude. I stood alone for a minute or two, recharging, then looked up to see Charlie across the room, listening intently to someone.

Suddenly, the room seemed to go silent. Contemplating my dazzling husband, I marveled as I had on the island over our having arrived together at this moment, this place, this kind of relationship. It still seemed extraordinary, unimaginable, fantastic, perfect. The huge wave of love I'd felt for him our first night together poured over me again—I felt drenched in it, saturated, buoyed.

As if signaled by the strength of my feelings, Charlie looked up and directly at me. I don't know what he saw in my face, but his face lit up in response. He looked for a moment like he had discovered something utterly fabulous, utterly out of this world, then he smiled tenderly and slowly winked at me.

"I saw that," Tyler's voice said softly. "You should see your face, Jane. You've really fallen in love, haven't you?"

I tore my eyes away from Charlie's and saw that Tyler was standing next to me with a very soft expression on his own face.

"I really have," I heard myself say dreamily, dazed from the intensity of the last few moments. The room still seemed quiet and blurry.

"See what I've been trying to tell you all these years?" Tyler teased. "It's an incredible feeling, isn't it? Really incredible, I mean, as in beyond belief."

I shook my head to clear it. Sound and clarity returned to the room in a rush and I focused on Tyler. "Beyond belief is right!" I said. "It's supernatural, actually. I seem to be losing my grip on the here-and-now altogether!"

He laughed. "I knew you had it in you. I'm really glad you finally discovered it."

"Tyler, is this how you felt about me?"

"Not quite," he replied. "I might have if you'd loved me, too, but I think the real deal requires both people to feel that way. I did love you—still do—but when Liz and I fell in love with each other, it was a whole new thing. It was amazing—its power took me completely by surprise."

"Those are the words for it," I agreed. "Who knew? I really had no idea at all."

I shook my head again, realizing how indebted I was to Tyler for his steadfast love and support over the years. Still feeling very emotional, I hugged him tightly and said fervently, "I owe you so much. I don't know how you put up with me and my detachment for so long. You've been a terrific friend—thank you!"

He hugged back, murmuring, "You're so welcome. I really couldn't be happier for you—or for Charlie."

Liz appeared and rescued us from this scene before it spiraled into total gooeyness. "Unhand my husband, Jane!" she commanded. After pausing briefly for effect, she said, "I want to hug you again myself."

And she did—while her husband and I both blinked away a few happy and grateful tears.

❖ ❖ ❖

Charlie

In the limo on our way home from the reception, Jane rested against me, her cheek on my lapel. I held her tightly, something I'd wanted to do for hours. Watching her be exactly the kind of impressive partner I knew she would be when I came up with the merger idea, and knowing she was also so much more, had filled me with happiness, satisfaction and the strong desire to hold her close.

"Are you awake?" I asked her.

"Barely," she said drowsily. "I'm worn out. That was really fun, though. Much better than I expected."

I kissed the top of her head and breathed in the faint scent. She didn't like perfume, but she used some product that made her hair smell great. "You're incredible, Jane," I told her. "Really amazing."

She looked up, pleased surprise in her eyes. "I am? Why do you say that?"

I thought about how to express what I'd been feeling all night, and some words of my mother's came to mind. Both my parents thought Jane was terrific. My mother had also said she was proud I'd chosen a woman like Jane to be my wife. In my mother's opinion, one's choice of spouse spoke volumes about one's character, and she thought Jane and I had both distinguished ourselves by choosing each other.

"You really are the perfect partner," I said. "You're brilliant and accomplished and impressive, and tonight you were obviously incredibly happy, too. It all reflects so well on me and makes me feel great. I feel distinguished by your choice of me as a husband."

"Are you *trying* to make me cry?" she demanded. "That is about the nicest thing you've ever said to me."

I smiled and touched her cheek. "I'm not trying to make you cry, but I'm not done either, so you're not out of danger yet. Can you take more?"

"If I have to," she smiled.

"I kept thinking tonight about how much more we've accomplished—already—than we set out to accomplish." I kissed her forehead. "We've been together for less than three months, married for less than three weeks, and it's already exceeded our merger expectations by miles. I feel like there's no limit to what we can accomplish together. And I'm happier than I've ever been in my life."

Jane buried her face in my coat and hugged me hard. After a couple minutes, she looked up and said, "I feel distinguished by your choice of me, too. You're in every way so much more than I imagined it was possible to have. You just dazzle me."

She paused, gazing at me, and I bent to kiss her lips.

A little while later, she said, "I don't mean that you dazzle me just because you're so beautiful. You've always given me so much, too. You've been helping me succeed from the moment we met. You've never doubted me or my abilities. You've shown me what trust is. And if not for your brilliant and innovative merger of equals idea, we wouldn't be where we are now—and I wouldn't know how great it feels to love some-one in this amazing over-the-top way."

She sniffed and added, a little hoarsely, "I'm happier than I've ever been, too, but I have to tell you that my poor tear ducts could really use a rest."

"Yeah, they aren't used to all this activity, are they?" I stroked her hair. "Have I ever mentioned that I love you?"

"Once or twice," she said softly, smiling.

We rode in happy silence for a few minutes, then Jane said, "Jim was funny, wasn't he? He seemed stunned. I bet he's wondering how you managed to pull off what appears to be a real marriage within a few months of his suggestion. Suppose he thinks you've had me as a fallback position all along?"

I laughed. "Knowing how familiar he is with your prickliness, I doubt it. But, yeah, I thought he was funny, too. He probably didn't think he had so much influence, especially given my initial reaction to that offensive suggestion."

"Will that be weird for you at work—having so many people know me, I mean?"

"Not at all!" Her question surprised me. "It will be great. The people who know you all think you're brilliant. They'll envy me my privileged access to your brains just the way they did when we worked together."

"Quite a few of those people don't particularly like me, you know."

"Maybe not, but even those dopes know you're smart. I'm sure it won't be weird. I'll get kidded about it for a while, but that won't bother me."

"You're such a big shot now—they wouldn't dare kid you in a way that would bother you," Jane said, stroking my cheek with her knuckles.

"What about you?" I asked, smiling. "Will it be weird for you to have to come to the Firm's social events again, but now as a wife?"

"Oh, God—it will be totally weird! I really thought I'd left those horrible things behind. I can't imagine finding even one thing to say to the wives, and they'll hate me if I spend all my time with you and the other Firm people." She sighed. "They'll probably hate me no matter what I do."

Then she brightened up and said, "I suppose I could even the scales a bit by paying lots of attention to the younger women and maybe even treating the younger men as if they're out of place."

"Come on. It wasn't that bad for you—not after you rounded up Tyler to smooth your way."

"He sure did a great job of that, didn't he?" Jane laughed. "You know, it always irritated me to be treated like an insider at the Firm because the bigwigs thought I might marry well instead of because I *was* an insider. How ironic that I'll be back because I *did* marry well." She shook her head. "That's one negative you bring to the table, buddy."

She smiled and caressed my face again as she said, "It's the only one so far, though."

"It will be offset by how well I'll reflect on you at the Company's events," I promised her, grinning. "People will be amazed."

She rolled her eyes. "Sadly, they probably will be. Just another example of how sexist the world continues to be. I can hear their thoughts already: How in the world could Ms. All Business, Ms. Barely a Woman, have bagged a guy like that?"

"And here I've been thinking I was the one who bagged you! Have you outplayed me as usual?"

Jane winked. "I'll never tell," she said.

❖ ❖ ❖

MID-AFTERNOON on Jane's and my first day back at work after our honeymoon, I found myself missing her. It was strange—kind of like at the reception, I longed to talk to her, touch her, hold her, and I could feel the longing physically, in my chest and my fingertips. I figured talking to her would be better than nothing and I had some free time before my next meeting, so I called her.

Jane's secretary, Beth, answered the phone. I identified myself and said hello to her; before I could say anything else, Beth said she knew Jane wouldn't want to miss my call and, if I could hold on, she would find her for me.

Jane picked up the phone a few minutes later and said, "I understand 'my husband' is holding for me?"

"That's right," I answered, smiling at both the words and the sound of her voice. "Apparently, that's a privileged status over in your world. Beth never offered to find you for me before. Are you busy?"

"Yes, dear," she said sarcastically. "You've called me at work. But it's nice to hear your voice. What's up?"

"I'm sitting at my desk, missing you terribly. I think this is the longest I've gone in the last three weeks without your tongue in my mouth."

She gasped. "I'm shocked!" she exclaimed. "Are we having phone sex? At work? How inappropriate!"

"No, darling," I said, laughing. "This isn't phone sex. It's just a statement of fact. I got used to having you around 24/7. I guess I'm suffering through withdrawal."

"I'm not even going to dignify that with a response, you animal. What time are you coming home tonight?"

"Unfortunately, I have another meeting here this afternoon, then I have to meet a client for drinks. I'll be home around eight. Want me to bring food?"

"Nope," she said smugly. "I'm on that. And, sorry, but I have to go. Thanks for calling me. I love you."

The first thing I noticed when I walked into our apartment a little after 8:00 was that it smelled fantastic. I called to Jane. She called back that she was in the kitchen. The wonderful aroma was obviously coming from there, too. To my amazement, she was standing at the sink washing things, a pile of unfamiliar-looking cooking tools already drying in the drainer. Some pots were bubbling on the stove, and there was also something baking.

"Who are you and what have you done with my wife?" I demanded, standing in the doorway in shock.

Jane turned and smiled at me, a smudge of something red on her cheek. Otherwise, the kitchen was immaculate. She obviously approached cooking with the same organizational and strategic planning skills she used to approach everything else.

"Hi, honey," she said, drying her hands on a towel.

"Are you actually cooking?"

"I love to cook," she said coolly. "If you tell anyone, though, I'll deny it."

"Are the results edible?"

"Fuck you!" she said, laughing. "I wouldn't do it if I couldn't do it well!"

I walked over to her and wiped the smudge off her cheek with my thumb, then offered her the thumb. She licked it, then asked, "Not willing to taste it yourself? Don't you trust me?"

"I'm not sure. This is shocking. What other hidden talents are you planning to spring on me?"

"Only good ones—don't worry. And don't make a big deal out of this, OK? So I can cook—just like anyone else who can read."

"Relax," I said soothingly, putting my arms around her. "I'm not going to start pigeonholing you. This is like your toes, right?"

Jane laughed. When we first slept together, I had been astonished to discover that her toenails were painted red. It had seemed so unlike her—so ultra-feminine. She got prickly when I said so and very defensively told me that pedicures were simply a matter of good grooming. I couldn't resist pointing out that, while that might be true, red polish was still quite a statement for someone like her—and not one I objected to in any way.

For a moment, she had looked like she might explode, but she laughed instead and told me she did have a few feminine features in addition to the ones I'd already discovered. She then looked very fierce—which was actually pretty intimidating, despite her small size—and stated ominously that if I planned to make negative assumptions about her or pigeonhole her as a result, I would be extremely sorry.

Now, she said, "It is sort of like my toes, I guess. Certainly not something I was likely to mention to a work colleague. As for cooking, don't expect me to do it very often—it takes too much time—but I thought it would be nice for our first day back at work."

"It's very nice," I said, bending down to kiss her.

Over Jane's dinner (which was really good), I decided to find out exactly why she'd never mentioned that she could cook or done any cooking during the last three months, when we'd basically lived together.

She scowled at me. "I asked you not to make a big deal out of this! I'm already a little freaked out by my desire to cook for you. Do you want me to decide never to do it again?"

"Don't get prickly. I'm not making a big deal out of it. I'm just trying to understand why it never came up."

"Habit, I guess," Jane said, eyeing me suspiciously. "I like to cook because it's so orderly and precise, and the results are so fast and tangible. You know, you decide what you want, assemble ingredients, apply some simple techniques, and then you quickly have what you wanted. It's something I do because it's relaxing—not something I need to advertise to other people."

She quickly added, "I'm sorry. I didn't mean to lump you with other people. I just meant that it's not an important thing about me. It *is* like my red toenails—not something I'd talk about or display in a work context, and so something I'm just not in the habit of mentioning."

"OK, I'll buy that, but if it's something you like to do, why haven't you done it even once since we've been together?"

She smiled. "We've been busy doing something I like even more," she said, her eyebrows high.

"Fair enough," I said, grinning.

A few bites later, she said, "It's not like I *decided* not to mention it to you, Charlie. It really is a habit for me to keep things like cooking or the toes or swimming to myself. Ditto with my personal life in general. Those things don't define me, but they're the kind of thing that always ends up having too defining an impact on how people perceive me. It's just easier to leave them out of the picture and let people perceive the kinds of things that help me instead of hurt me."

"Do you ever think you withhold too much of yourself? Now that you're past those rookie years with some solid successes behind you, don't you think you'd be just as successful if you let people see more than such a small part of who you are?"

"To what end? Why take the risk?"

"To the end of not isolating yourself and not having to feel like you have to be so careful all the time," I suggested.

"Do you think I'm isolated?"

"I think you're very careful with other people, and pretty distrusting of most of them, and I'm assuming that's isolating—and also more work for you than is really necessary."

Jane looked thoughtful as she chewed and swallowed a mouthful of eggplant. "You know, I've always assumed that people respond so well to you because you're so clearly the very picture of what men want to be and women want to have." She smiled and clarified, "I mean that in a nice way," before she said, "But maybe that's too surface a way to look at it. You're so trusting and you do let people in, way more than I do. I remember being surprised by that when I first met you. Do you think that's the real reason people always like you so much?"

"I don't know that people always like me so much," I said, smiling. "But if they do, that could be why. The surface stuff obviously helps, too. It's like my mother's always telling Andy and me—the big, handsome, easy-to-get-along-with white guy costume is a useful one to have. But I think the 'easy-to-get-along-with' part comes more from being open with people than because I'm a 'type' that people like or want to suck up to."

"I *have* noticed since we got together that it's very relaxing to float through the world on your golden boy charm," Jane said, sounding serious despite the "golden boy" label she usually used sarcastically. "Some of that has to be because you're a more favored type in the world, but I suppose my lack of it could be at least partly because people sense I'm closed to them—just the way I feel when circles are obviously closed to me."

"Good point. That's probably right." I smiled again. "We're where we always end up when we talk about this kind of thing. I do have unfair advantages over you in the game you've chosen to play, but that doesn't mean my approach is the wrong one."

Jane looked at me, her expression very soft. "I don't think I'll start wearing open-toed shoes to work or broadcasting that I can cook, but I will take your approach under consideration. It might be restful to be less careful all the time—you know, to give myself a little more room, a bigger range to operate in."

"I bet it would be restful, and I really don't think it'll hurt you." I put my hand on her shoulder and rubbed her collarbone. "Look at us right now, for example—I've just learned you can cook and I haven't started disdaining or pigeonholing you at all!"

She laughed. "Or expecting food to be on the table when you get home every night either, right? You'll still be picking up plenty of takeout!"

"No problem," I assured her. "Hey, Jane?"

"What?"

"You're a wonderful wife."

"I'm not sure how I feel about hearing that," she said, frowning. "Especially in light of your troubling delight with my ability to cook."

She got up, walked the couple steps to my chair and looped her arms around my neck. "But if I had to be a wife at all," she said, "I'm glad I'm your wife. I like your marriage as merger concept—and you—quite a bit."

I pushed my chair away from the table and she climbed into my lap.

❖ ❖ ❖

ON SATURDAY, we slept late, went out to breakfast and then spent a few hours in our respective offices. Jane wanted to cook again, so we met at home late in the afternoon. I watched football and kept her posted on developments in the game while she made another terrific dinner.

While we ate, we argued about whether or not it was the right time for John's commercial finance company to acquire one of the vendors handling its outsourced infrastructure functions. As usual, debating with each other was very arousing, so we made love. Later, as we lay side by side, catching our breath, Jane murmured, "So good, so unbelievably good."

"We are amazing, aren't we?" I turned on my side to look at her.

"Yes, we are," she said, looking up at the ceiling, "but I didn't mean just this. The whole day—it's been completely perfect. I've loved everything about it. In fact, being married has been completely perfect. This has been the most amazing month of my life."

"Mine, too." I laid my arm on her warm body, my hand cupping her shoulder.

"Charlie?" she said hesitantly, still not looking at me.

"What?"

"Would you have gone through with the merger if we hadn't fallen in love?"

"I think so, yeah. That's an odd question. Why do you ask?"

"This—us—feeling the way we do, it's all so intense and—I don't know—significant and spectacular and worth everything. If we hadn't fallen in love, but we'd gone ahead with the merger anyway, it would have been fine, probably, but we would have missed out on all this." She frowned. "If I'd known it could be like this, I wouldn't have wanted to settle for anything less. But I didn't have any idea. I would have settled for a lot less."

She turned on her side and looked into my eyes. "You, though—you always thought something like this was possible. Would you really have settled for less?"

"That's an impossible question to answer now," I said, resting my hand on her hip. "We did fall in love, we do have this. Knowing that now is what makes what we were planning seem like less. I had more faith that something amazing was possible, but I didn't know what it would be like until it happened either. Maybe this is what was inevitable for us, and the merger idea was just our way of getting here. Who knows? What difference does it make?"

She looked frustrated. "I don't really know what I'm trying to say. I guess it's that things ended up being sort of random anyway. I feel a little like we dodged a bullet or were incredibly lucky. It horrifies me to think we might never have known."

"But we do know, honey. Whether it was random or not, we do know."

"But we might not have."

"You're extrapolating too negatively again," I said, smiling. "Any number of different things might have happened or not happened. If Tyler or Jennifer—or people we don't actually know—had been different people or done different things, we might have ended up with them instead of with each other. If we hadn't fallen in love or sex together hadn't been terrific, the merger might have been fine anyway, and we'd still have a lot of what we have now. If a meteor had crashed into earth, we might be dead. But who cares about any of that? None of it happened and this did. We did hit this jackpot, whatever the reason."

"Yeah, OK, but I *hate* the thought that we might have settled for less simply because we didn't aim high enough or imagine this was possible!"

I caught the hand she was waving emphatically and kissed it before I said, "It wasn't a matter of aiming high or having this particular expectation. We didn't do either. This is just how it happened for us. It's probably not possible for everyone—or at least not the same. Different people must experience love differently. And it wouldn't necessarily be settling if their experience made them happy."

I remembered a conversation I'd had with Hannah right after she decided to marry Jason. "Hannah and I talked about something like this once," I told Jane. "She wasn't originally sure if she loved Jason. She realized she did when she focused on the fact that she was expecting love to feel the way it would to a fireworks person, as she said, even though she's not that kind of person. The way it felt to her was much quieter, but just as real."

"I'm not a fireworks person either," Jane said, putting her arm around me, her palm open on my back, "but here I am, experiencing major fireworks."

"Are you joking?" I looked at her in disbelief. "You are absolutely a fireworks person! You're hot all the time about one thing or another! You're one of the most vehement and passionate people I know. The only things you weren't passionate about were sex and love—until recently, that is."

"I guess," she said doubtfully. "Maybe the thing I should be horrified about is the randomness of our whole history together. What if I hadn't come to the Firm? What if I hadn't been assigned to you in the mentoring program? What if we hadn't worked together and gotten to be friends?" She smiled. "What if there hadn't been so many sexy women jumping in your lap all the time that you'd had to consider women at work as possible sex partners?"

I grinned. "That would certainly have been the end of our friendship, huh?"

"Maybe not," she said, her expression very sarcastic. "You wouldn't have come after me. Judging by your dates up to now, I wouldn't have been your type."

"That's faulty logic and you know it," I protested. "You can't turn me from someone else back into myself in the middle of your example!" I kissed her, then suggested, "How about if you decide not to be horrified at all? You can't organize and control everything. Some things just happen. And it really doesn't matter if it was all random or all inevitable. We got here—we are here—that's all that matters."

"Surely you're not suggesting I go with the flow," she said, her eyes sparkling. "Aren't I much too vehement and passionate—not to mention controlling—for that?"

"Let's find out," I said, gently pushing her onto her back and enveloping her in my arms.

CHAPTER 17

BACK TO BUSINESS

Jane

The gooey phase of my feelings for Charlie lasted for only a month or so after we got married. I was still deeply in love with him, and I still felt intense lust for him, too. But to my immense relief, I stopped feeling girly in that weird and alarming way, and my tear ducts went back to their normal inactive state.

I learned a lot from him career-wise during those first months of marriage—nearly as much as during our mentoring year. What had always struck me as his practically Pollyanna-ish view of the world was even more startling at close range. Charlie was irrepressibly optimistic. He effortlessly, and apparently unconsciously, assumed that everything would work out the way he wanted it to. He never seemed to doubt or second-guess himself, and he blithely expected the best of other people. To my ongoing amazement, he seemed to *get* the best from other people and for himself nearly all the time, too—much more consistently than could be explained solely by his enviable golden boy status.

I wasn't quite sure how—or if—to apply his example to managing my own career. I was obviously not in the same golden position as my untroubled and self-assured husband. The business world was nowhere near as welcoming to me or as likely to work naturally in my favor. Skeptical vigilance continued to seem like the most sensible approach for someone in my shoes.

Nevertheless, I had noticed that most people were followers looking for a lead to follow. Whether they understood it consciously or not, followers seemed to want to be told what to think or believe in or do. I already had plenty of examples of how setting high performance expectations made people work harder to satisfy them and, in the process, pleasantly surprise both themselves and me. Watching Charlie's example, I wondered if this same phenomenon would hold true more broadly.

Was it possible, I wondered, that I was actually *creating* some of the downsides and disappointments I'd experienced by considering them as possibilities and preparing in advance to handle them? Was it all more of a cause and effect circle than I'd imagined? Would reducing the *level* of skepticism and pessimism with which I approached my career and my colleagues also reduce the *need* for skepticism and pessimism?

At first, these questions struck me as silly. After living with Charlie for a while, though, I had to reconsider whether his "you get what you give" attitude was righter and more effective than I was disposed to give it credit for being. There were too many instances of luck and success that couldn't be explained solely by who he was on the surface no matter how skeptically I thought about them. As example after example piled up, I started to think that maybe his combination of optimism, trust and inclusive thinking was working together with his compelling (and much-favored) presence to create a powerful influence over other people and the way they behaved.

New clients fell into his lap (just as easily and frequently as the sexy women he no longer took up with). He'd decided to get married, plotted his course, come after me, and struck gold for both of us. The two more likely candidates to succeed Jim as head of M&A conveniently took themselves out of the running at the perfect time to benefit Charlie— any sooner and he would have been judged too young, no matter how capable and well-liked he was. And when he'd given M&A's thugs the benefit of the doubt, all but two or three of them had transformed into contributing members of the group.

It was this last example that forced me to rethink. I'd been sure that giving those assholes the chance to reform and play fair was an unwise, short-sighted and potentially dangerous waste of time, but I was wrong. And, try though I did, I couldn't persuade myself to believe their reformation was a bizarre and inexplicable anomaly.

Charlie made the point about most people being followers when he originally described his reasons for not firing all the thugs the minute he took over M&A. He also said he knew morale would suffer if he summarily fired anyone (no matter how reviled). He wanted the group solidly on his side before he took any action with the potential to scare or intimidate people, and he was sure the way to get people on his side was to offer everyone a chance to play and win.

In his opinion, giving everyone that chance moved the burden for performing where it belonged—on each individual to execute rather than on him to punish. With the responsibility so shifted, Charlie had been confident that if he did ultimately fire a thug, the action would be perceived as more about the thug's non-performance than about Charlie's exercise of power and, thus, much more palatable to the rest of the group.

I couldn't dispute that he'd been absolutely right. Most of the thugs had reformed, and M&A was ahead of where it would have been without them. Lynn told me she'd gone on a three-day business trip with one of the worst of them and hadn't felt the desire to kill or maim him even once. He'd actually behaved like a colleague (and a decent human being)—no underhanded machinations on the deal, no attempts to close her out or undermine her with the client, no condescension.

Charlie had unquestionably been lucky as well as savvy, but, even so, the decision to lay out the new rules and then give everyone a shot was a decision I would never have made. It required an optimism and a willingness to believe people would change (or at least go with the flow) that I simply didn't have.

We'd had a consultant at the Company who talked during a marketing presentation about how your most dangerous blind spots weren't what you didn't know, but what you "didn't know you didn't know." I had been tempted, as I always was with consultants, to roll my eyes and dismiss that comment as so much slick doubletalk, but the concept stuck in my mind.

Viewing things with less skepticism was starting to look to me like a way to diminish what I didn't know I didn't know. Charlie's having made and benefited tremendously from a decision I wouldn't even have considered got my attention. I decided to incorporate at least some of his optimism and trust into my own approach.

I didn't plan to get carried away. The last thing I wanted to become was a fool, over-optimistic or otherwise. Just as I was still keeping quiet about my ability to cook and my red toenails even as I made an effort to relax a little and not withhold so much of myself from other people, I was also not about to turn into Pollyanna. But I did look for and find opportunities to lighten up my thinking, broaden my starting point perspective, and consider the worst as more of a possibility than a likelihood.

All of this made Charlie very happy. He always thought I made things harder for myself than necessary, and he was glad to see me moderating my cynicism (as he insisted on calling it). In his usual generous way, he also seemed to be genuinely pleased on my behalf—as opposed to pleased because I was following his lead. (Not being an idiot or even all that optimistic, I did wonder if *anyone* could really be as generous and non-egotistical as my new husband seemed to be. I recognized that I might well be seeing him through the dazzled eyes of someone too in love with him to see straight.)

I was more gratified by his delight with my "improvement" than I would have expected—and than I was initially comfortable with. I felt rather like a throwback to a more traditional era. My gratification was a too stereotypical "I've pleased my husband" sentiment for me to like it or feel easy about having it. And it wasn't the only one either. Despite my fiercely held and modern views of what it meant to be a married woman, once I actually became one I started experiencing a few atavistic and, I worried, alarmingly *female* reactions.

Some of these struck me as minor, if surprising. Things like continuing to take pleasure in cooking for us, gleefully buying new sheets and towels, and uncharacteristically relishing other nesting behaviors (for lack of a less domestic term) amused me more than they concerned me.

But certain other unexpected reactions were actually quite disturbing. For example, I'd always enjoyed arguing with Charlie, and I still did—now partly because arguing was invariably wonderful foreplay for us. But sex wasn't the only new result of our debates. Charlie never pulled any punches or cut me any slack when we debated. He was direct and plainspoken, and he didn't hesitate to tell me when he thought I was wrong or nuts. This wasn't new, but my reaction to it had become more complex.

I still appreciated his candor and his assumption that I could take it. I would have felt patronized if he'd done anything different. At the same time, though, I sometimes felt wounded by his bluntness and his exasperation. I never doubted his love (I knew he was as crazy about me as I was about him), but more than once I felt that perhaps a tad less frankness would have been nice.

Of course, this irritated the hell out of me. I sharply warned myself against turning into a *wife* who had to be managed or treated with kid gloves—"handled" as if she weren't strong or resilient or smart or important enough to be treated as an equal. My husband admired me and considered me a peer instead of demeaning me as an inferior, and that was exactly what I wanted.

Nevertheless, I couldn't deny that I occasionally felt insufficiently coddled. Several times, the words "You could be a little nicer to me" were on the tip of my tongue. This ridiculous reaction to being treated the way Charlie had always treated me was surprising and worrisome—just like the delight I felt over having pleased him by deciding to moderate my skepticism. I chalked both reactions up to insidious social conditioning and tried not to let them affect my behavior.

Insidious social conditioning reared its sexist head in other ways, too. Marriage gave people a whole new dimension of demeaning assumptions to make about me. Just like when I was a rookie at the Firm, I often felt caught inside an ill-fitting and insulting mistaken identity with no viable way out.

Maddeningly, Charlie's day-to-day life didn't change at all in this regard. Marriage really was completely incidental to the way other people perceived him. For me, though, there was the predictable, but still infuriating, "Why are you hassling with work when you have a rich husband?"—a question that not only belittled me, my career motives and my reasons for getting married, but also sold short my work, my husband and the institution of marriage.

There were also the weird little throwaway statements that seemed to come from every direction. They stuck in my head and niggled until I recognized them for the emblems they were. My pedicurist, for example, loved to recommend fancy lotions and for years I'd been buying more than one at a time to try out. But the first time I said I'd take three after I was married, she frowned and said she didn't want to get me in trouble with my new husband—as if it went without saying that he had acquired supervisory authority over what I bought or how much I spent.

This kind of sexism drove me nuts and made me feel hostile, sometimes wildly so. It forced me into an inaccurate political and economic box that I resented both on my own behalf and on general principles. And as usual with sexist bullshit, I had no realistic recourse.

If I pointed out and attempted to address every instance, people would think I was a tiresome, obsessed crackpot with no sense of humor or perspective whatsoever. I had to get along with people, particularly at work. Being a vocal, hard-nosed activist would reduce (if not destroy) my chances of making it up to a position where I could influence some real change. But being a good sport was equally wrong. Sexism is like any other prejudice. Letting it go lends it an acceptability, even a validity. It amounts to tacit approval and inures people to the harm.

Given what I wanted to accomplish, there was no good response to most of the day-in, day-out sexism I encountered. So I had to swallow my outrage and cope with chronic frustration, not to mention the discomfort that came from knowing that my silence effectively constituted consent and made me a collaborator.

On the plus side (conventionally speaking), I discovered that being married was a good thing in the Company's culture. Unlike the Firm, the Company had far more married women than single ones in its employee ranks.

When I left the Firm, it still had virtually no institutional experience with married women. The secretaries were a relatively young crowd, youth, shapeliness and lack of an inconvenient husband evidently being three of the important criteria by which administrative hiring decisions were made. Professional women were also young and unmarried. The Firm had only recently hired us at all, and then only at the entry levels.

Since I was by no means the only woman to have hightailed it out of there while still well under 30, the average age of professional women at the Firm wasn't getting higher very quickly. Being a married woman was still both unusual and an extra minus. When a woman got married, senior types immediately started wondering when she'd show her true colors and do something "unprofessional" or "more seemly for a woman" (depending on the senior type) like quit to devote herself to her husband or reproduce.

Senior people at the Company may well have worried about the same thing, but their concern was offset by the comfort they took in being able to classify someone in the nice, normal category of "married." I was only 26 when I started working at the Company, but, even so, people responded with widened eyes and other subtle signs of surprise when I answered "No" to the question "Are you married?"

This may have been more for ease of continuing conversations than anything else. Two years later, once I started answering "Yes," people very naturally went on to ask what my husband did. (If I really wanted to warm someone up, I confessed to being a newlywed. This uniformly produced smiles and congratulations. Apparently, all the world loves a newlywed, despite its jaded attitude toward marriage more generally.)

I suspected, however, that the happy reaction to my "Yes, I'm married" was more likely an expression of pleasure or comfort at being able to file me in the "toes the line" category. The Company was a culture of conformity, and I was bucking enough norms as it was by being a woman in my position. People were likely relieved, I thought, to learn I wasn't unnatural in some way they considered troublesome or threatening.

Helpful though this was, it disgusted me for the same reasons the Firm's Norman Rockwell fantasy world pretense had disgusted me. I wondered if we would ever evolve to the point where difference was just different, as opposed to better or worse or frightening.

I also fervently hoped that the nice, normal file people were tucking me into wasn't labeled "Wife—Ignore and Overlook."

❖ ❖ ❖

CHARLIE AND I went to visit Cheryl and Richard in the suburbs three weeks after their daughter, Amanda, was born.

The Sunday we went was a clear, crisp, cold February day, and the suburbs looked clean and sparkling after the gray slush of the city. I laughed the minute I saw the house Cheryl and Richard had bought. It was exactly the kind of stately, white picket fence house called for in Cheryl's original life plan. Evidently, she'd stuck with a few of that plan's requirements, despite having changed more than one of its major features.

Cheryl looked great, and both she and Richard were totally ecstatic over the baby. Amanda was beautiful—tiny, with creamy skin, alert eyes, and just the faintest dusting of dark hair. I had a hard time taking my eyes off her as we toured the house, Richard holding the baby and Cheryl doing most of the tour-guiding.

When we got back to what Cheryl called the family room, Richard offered Amanda to me. Not having been the kind of teenage girl who babysat for pocket money, I had almost no experience with infants. My attitude toward babies and children also wasn't the slightest bit romantic or sentimental. For both reasons, I took Amanda with some trepidation and was very surprised to find that holding her was delightful.

I loved having her in my arms. She weighed practically nothing, she smelled wonderful, and she snuggled into me as if she couldn't imagine a more comfortable place to be. After a few minutes of staring at nothing in particular while the four adults talked around her, Amanda closed her eyes and fell asleep. I slipped off my shoes, curled my feet under me and settled back on the couch against Charlie, one of whose fingers was grasped tightly in Amanda's fist. Richard joked that I was a natural, but I told him his exemplary baby deserved the credit.

Even more surprising to me was my reaction to Charlie and Amanda. Thanks to his brother's kids, he was more experienced than I with babies, and he was very taken with Amanda. After half an hour or so of sleeping in my arms, she woke up and squawked a bit. Charlie said it had to be time for his turn, and I handed her over. He was the natural; he had her happy and entranced within seconds. Cheryl laughed and said that result was no surprise—Amanda was, after all, female.

I was entranced, too. Amanda fit into Charlie's hands. After holding her upright and cooing to her for a few minutes, he rested her on his legs, one of his hands securing her entire body. He smiled and made faces at her while we chatted. She gazed at him intently. Occasionally, he touched her cheek or held her feet.

Watching the two of them, all I could think about was how good it would feel to have his hands on me. This was not an unfamiliar feeling. I had it pretty much daily, to be honest, but not usually when we were with other people and never before in the context of babies. I didn't know whether to be amused or horrified.

When Cheryl asked Richard to refill our drinks, Charlie said he wanted to stretch his legs and would help. Cheryl offered to take Amanda, but he refused to give her up. He got up, holding her against his shoulder with one bent arm, and followed Richard out of the room.

Cheryl looked at me and smiled. "It's astounding how sexy they are with babies, isn't it?" she said knowingly.

"How did you know that's what I was thinking?" I exclaimed.

"Just a guess from the expression on your face. And from the way I've been feeling. I'm still way too sore even to consider sex, but practically every time I see Richard holding her, I want to take him directly to bed."

"Whew! I couldn't agree more. I was wondering if it was getting a little warm in here or what," I said, fanning myself. "Suppose it's some sort of biological imperative? Or just how big men are relative to babies or how gentle they look holding them?"

"All of the above, probably. Does holding Amanda or seeing Charlie with her make you want one of your own?"

"No, I'm not ready for that yet." I smiled as I acknowledged, "I bet Charlie would give you a different answer, though."

"No bet—I'm sure you're right about that," Cheryl said, smiling very warmly. She rearranged the pillows on her chair and nestled cozily into them. "You two seem so happy, Jane, and so in love. But you also seem just like you always did when you worked together—like great friends."

"We are. It amazes me, but love and marriage really haven't changed the basic nature of our relationship at all."

"Remember when we talked with Lynn and Anna about the nature of marriage—back when Katherine and Jordan got married? I often think it was thanks to Katherine's example that I figured out the real requirements for a happy marriage are mutual regard, mutual lust and two people who are their actual selves with one another. You know, as opposed to all that stereotypical crap we grew up with about the husband's role being smart, strong provider and the wife's sweet, dim nurturer."

"I do remember that conversation," I nodded, "but I didn't believe then—or for a long time afterward—that it was possible for marriage to be like that other than theoretically."

"Really?" She grinned. "Took the perfect man to turn you into a believer, I guess."

I laughed. "Apparently."

Charlie and Richard rejoined us, Charlie holding a beer in one hand and cradling Amanda, who was again asleep, against his chest with the other. "This is a fantastic baby!" he told Cheryl.

"Yeah, I can see you two have bonded," Cheryl said, smiling up at him. "She does have her disgruntled moments, though."

"Usually between two and four in the morning," Richard griped, but with a very indulgent expression. "Maybe you'd like to come over some night and work your magic on her then. We could use the sleep."

Cheryl smiled tenderly at Richard, then asked Charlie what was up at the Firm. When it was clear that Cheryl was getting tired, I said we should get going and Charlie reluctantly relinquished Amanda to Richard. We promised to visit again soon and left them looking the very picture of domestic bliss (just as described in Cheryl's life plan).

Back in the car, I said to Charlie, "So you like babies, I see."

"Yeah, I do," he said, grinning. "You seemed to like her too, Ms. All Business."

"I did—more than I expected to." I laughed, then confessed, "I was also surprised by how it made me feel to watch you with her. It was very sexy."

He raised his eyebrows. "Yeah?"

"Yeah." I leaned over to kiss his cheek. "Don't get any ideas, though. I'm not ready for that whole experience yet, even if you can charm them into angelic behavior."

"No problem," he said serenely. "I'll get you there eventually, just like I got you this far."

"Awfully sure of yourself, aren't you?"

"Think I'm wrong?"

"No," I admitted, smiling.

❖ ❖ ❖

BY EARLY SUMMER, I started to feel some impatience with my job at the Company. The actual work was interesting enough, and I still felt solidly on track for continuing up the corporate ladder, but the inefficiency—and, in some cases, stupidity—of the day-to-day experience was maddening.

There were the omnipresent and time-consuming politics that frequently made it necessary to go from A to Q to G to B instead of directly from A to B. There was administrative bullshit like HR requirements that took a ton of time and didn't even begin to assure that people were hired, reviewed or compensated intelligently. Or security procedures that had no hope of actually securing the premises but made it a daily ordeal for legitimate employees to get to their offices. (You practically needed a separate wallet for all the ID and key cards, and it was incredibly frustrating to line up every morning to show the right one to the *same* security guard.)

And there was the more important problem of colleagues who seemed to have a very hard time keeping their eye on the ball. From senior management handing down unrealistic or uninformed decrees (the air up at the top was apparently very thin indeed) to rank-and-file people who were indifferent to the big picture, just about everyone seemed to be making it harder than it had to be to get things done.

This was more than a work ethic or attitude issue. My coworkers seemed to me to be flailing—awash in a sea of activity, with no clear connection between the activity and the desired results.

As always, there were the people who never looked up or around, but instead simply came to work and did as many of their to-do list items as they could. They never prioritized, never asked themselves (or anyone else) what the purpose of their work might be, and never seemed to care much one way or the other if what they were doing made sense. They responded to the loudest or scariest voices, and seemingly devoted no time at all to planning either their day-to-day work or their careers.

There were also the blowhards—those guys so in love with the sound of their own voices that they never missed an opportunity to hold forth. They were easy to recognize (and way too easy to hear), but difficult to forestall. In meetings, they felt obliged to repeat what others said, usually opening with "As John described..." and then telling us again what we had all just heard from John. In one-on-one conversations, they had to start pretty much at the beginning of the world and bring you up to date before they could get to the point.

I frequently felt as if I'd spent my entire workday smiling politely and trying not to scream while these bores pontificated. I often wondered if they thought they were living alone in the world. Or maybe they believed their own time constraints were the only ones of consequence.

Unnecessary repetition wasn't the only way in which people showed a truly breathtaking lack of consideration for other people's time. Meetings were another constant irritant. Not only were there too many of them, but no meeting at the Company ever started on time. (In the apparent belief that instantaneous arrival was possible, participants habitually left their offices at 2:00 for a 2:00 meeting on another floor.) We actually had a concept called "Company Time," which ran about ten minutes behind real time. This was a standing joke, but we all tolerated it. Some people even set their watches behind to compensate for it.

Everyone complained about the late meeting issue, but virtually no one dealt with it effectively. One group imposed a $10 fine on latecomers—as if timeliness were a requirement only for the poor. It became routine in that group for people to show up late and further disrupt the proceedings by flinging a ten-dollar bill on the conference table as they sat down.

Worse still was our corporate tendency to recap what stragglers had missed when they waltzed in well after meetings finally did get underway. Not only did this repetition reward latecomers and punish timely arrivers (in a staggering reversal of logic), but it caused many meetings to conclude without covering all their agenda items, let alone accomplishing their objectives. Naturally, this made it necessary to have *more* meetings.

Thanks to my long-standing intolerance for slackers, blowhards and the irritations of inefficiency, I had learned years before to deal more or less effectively with all of them. But that summer, two new factors were contributing to my increasing impatience and making it harder for me to cope.

The more obvious of these was my ongoing delight with my new husband and my strong desire to be in his company. Being married had given me some new goals and wrought some adjustments in my priorities. This change was very different from the change I'd feared marriage might cause. I didn't lose my desire to make it big at work nor did my ambition falter. In fact, having Charlie and everything he represented in the picture in this new, married way actually fueled my zeal (and my ability) to succeed career-wise.

But at the same time and with equal zeal, I also wanted to spend time with him and to help him succeed. Suddenly, I had three big goals instead of just one. Since I had previously devoted virtually all my energy and attention to my own career, it took some doing to spread that energy and attention around. This was a time management as well as a focus issue for me. Timewasters like the ones I'd begun to resent at work made my balancing act harder.

I was also beginning to think it was time for a new challenge at the Company. I'd been in my brand manager position for over two-and-a-half years by that summer. I wasn't bored, but the job was starting to feel too familiar to me. I rarely had to do anything I hadn't done before or didn't know how to do.

One of the things I'd particularly enjoyed about my work at the Firm was that every deal offered a chance to learn something new. I liked being challenged and having to exert myself to figure something out. I was the polar opposite of the guy who'd told me his goal was to get to the point where he could do his job in his sleep. I felt rather as if I *were* doing my job in my sleep, and I didn't like the feeling.

I needed more, and so I decided to develop a game plan for moving sooner rather than later to the next rung on the ladder.

❖ ❖ ❖

Charlie

There was a message to call Jane on top of the pile of messages on my desk when I got back from lunch one hot July day. She was always happy to talk when I called her for no reason in particular, but she didn't call me at work unless she needed something. I had about 20 minutes before the first of an afternoon of meetings, so I called her back right away.

Neither of us spent much time at our desks answering our phones, and it usually took a round or two of phone tag before we connected. I was lucky that day. I reached her on the first try.

"Hey, honey," I said. "Were you looking for me?"

"I thought this might be you! That's why I picked up the phone." Jane sounded both pleased and hassled. "But I can't talk right now—I have to get to a meeting in a few minutes. It shouldn't last too long—can I call you back in an hour or so?"

"Sorry, no. I've got the last of the comp committee meetings this afternoon. They'll take the rest of the day. What's up?"

"I've been offered an interesting—and potentially very exciting—opportunity that I wanted to tell you about." She sighed. "It'll have to wait until tonight, I guess."

"Is that OK? Can it wait?"

"Yeah, sure. I just felt like telling you so you could think about it before we talk tonight."

"Want to give me a hint? I could use something interesting to think about during these meetings."

"I've been invited to be part of a new executive leadership develop-ment program the Company's starting—damn!" After a short pause, she said, "Sorry. I'm not swearing at you. The program's still confidential and there's now a crowd of people waiting for me outside my office. I have to go. You're not coming home late, are you?"

"No," I promised, smiling. "No one can stand too much more of this comp stuff. I might even be early."

After I said goodbye to Jane, I walked over to the window. My office had a spectacular view—building tops and sides, streets far below, water in the distance—but, after noticing that everything was blurred by the heat, I didn't pay attention to the view. Staring out, I organized my thoughts for the upcoming battle.

The Firm's compensation committee meetings were incredibly important, if equally dull. Because of the sensitivity of the information—or so people were told—the proceedings were always cloaked in secrecy. Three months after I took over M&A, I was disappointed to find out that the secrecy was in fact more about protecting unjustifiable decisions. The sensitive information being kept confidential was the self-serving horse-trading that characterized the comp committee's deliberations and determinations.

Notwithstanding my wife's view to the contrary, I was not overly trusting or unrealistically optimistic. I had no illusions about the greed and willingness to self-deal of many of the Firm's senior people. And I understood that bonus compensation at our professional levels depended on a host of relatively ill-defined criteria in addition to measurable client origination and revenue production numbers. It didn't trouble me that one of those ill-defined criteria was a very nebulous "star quality" and another was a similarly imprecise "how much can he hurt us?" fear factor, both of which were highly subjective, with no clear tie to actual performance.

Nevertheless, my first experience with the comp process as a group head had shocked me. Despite the Firm's painstaking annual performance review rigmarole, the performance reviews were largely irrelevant. I hoped the other group heads were trying, as I was, to keep actual performance in mind at least as a guideline, but the process didn't make this easy. It was essentially a matter of getting as large a pot of compensation dollars for your group as you could—and then trying to get the right results for each of your people—all by bullying other group heads with any ammunition you could lay your hands on.

There was some tie to reality. The best ammo you could possess was strong revenue numbers for the year and the next best was highly regarded people. Basically, though, it was a free-for-all usually won by the people whose fortunes were flying high in July when the process occurred.

The deliberations played out over a series of meetings in which each group head had to justify his bonus recommendations, person-by-person. We explained our reasoning during the short period we each got for interruption-free presentation. Then, we fielded and parried angry statements like: "Your guy doesn't deserve ninety percent of what my guy is getting—I worked with your guy once and he's a fucking moron!" or "You can't pay her X! That would make her the highest-paid associate in that class!"

The stated reason for this comparison/justification baloney was the need for compensation across the Firm to make both absolute and relative sense within and among the various groups. Jane thought it was really a defensive thieves' accord. She was sure that most of the group heads were too slimy to be trusted to allocate dollars fairly among their people, both on the high side and the low side, and also that no one trusted anyone else. Whatever the real reason, the result was an excruciatingly boring two-week-long annual ritual.

After as much "discussion and deliberation" as the comp committee could stand, its members handed down final decisions based on who in the room they wanted to suck up to or mollify or punish. The actual merit of the individuals under discussion was, if not inconsequential, certainly not the decisive factor in what they ended up getting paid.

Even if we'd all read all the performance reviews (which no one did), it wouldn't have helped. Savvy group heads made sure their people's reviews said what they needed to say. You also had to decide each year how you were going to approach presenting your recommendations.

If you inflated numbers (which required some tricky math, given the fixed amount of the total pool), you left yourself room to concede graciously (down to your real numbers) in response to objections from people whose support could prove useful to you later. If you were too obvious about this, however, it could blow up in your face. Going with your real numbers was equally risky, if more aboveboard (and easier). If everyone else started with inflated numbers and then came down, you'd inevitably have to do the same in at least a few cases, thus underpaying some of your people.

How your people fared during the meetings was also affected by other ridiculous things: how long you were willing to fight; who backed you up; whether you'd won or lost earlier rounds. It was as if the goal were to ensure that we all backed winners or that group heads all came out more or less even and didn't feel excessively abused—rather than to reward the Firm's employees fairly for their contributions.

I'd even used my height to M&A's advantage. I was one of the tallest people at the Firm, and the tallest by a wide margin among the senior ranks. During the meetings the year before, a combination of frustration and the need to stretch my legs caused me to stand up while I was arguing in favor of one of my bonus recommendations. Since I was talking, I didn't walk around; I just stood, stretched and continued to talk.

The next thing I knew, my two principal opponents decided they could live with the recommendation I was making. Still standing, I went on to my next recommendation. There was very little argument in response, and I realized I might be on to something. Not sure if the advantage was for real and not wanting to dilute its potential impact by overuse if it was, I sat back down. The next time I ran into significant objections to a recommendation I felt strongly about, I got back on my feet. Again, the objections faded. I didn't know why the hell this worked. I couldn't imagine people were really afraid of me, but they obviously felt intimidated and I had no problem using that to my group's advantage.

The first year I was involved in the comp process was not a good one for Corp Fin. We were only a few months past the scandal. Revenues were solid, but the future wasn't. Jim and I didn't have a leg to stand on vis-à-vis the other groups during the comparison and justification part of the process, so we didn't object too strenuously when their people fared marginally better than ours.

By my second year as a group head, M&A was doing very well, Corp Fin was doing pretty well, and the Executive Committee was pleased with the job Jim was doing. As a result, we had a lot of dough to allocate. This actually complicated the process. In comparison to groups with less money to work with, my recommendations for my people looked high. By then, I was also using different performance review criteria, which the other group heads both distrusted and disdained.

We had worked with HR (using some very helpful materials from Jane's company) to develop a performance review matrix for M&A that included all the types of contribution I really cared about, not just originations, revenues and other easy-to-measure metrics. I was determined to reward people the way I'd promised I would when I reorganized the group. All the lip service in the world about things like leadership and teamwork meant nothing if people couldn't see a clear connection between demonstrating those qualities and getting a bigger bonus.

Both the term "performance matrix" and the actual form we used were met with contempt by most of the other group heads. I couldn't blame them for the sarcastic remarks about the term. I thought it was stupid, too. But the form really helped M&A's people focus their efforts on the kinds of behavior and contribution that were making us successful. Despite the sarcastic reactions, my group had come out very well in the comp meetings the year before.

As I stood by the window after talking to Jane that hot afternoon a year later, I planned my approach for what was left of the current year's process. M&A had delivered its second consecutive year of excellent performance. New client originations were up, revenues were up significantly, as were profit margins, and the group was tightly knit and stable, despite my having let go the last of the unreformed thugs a couple months before. Our good morale in particular was being noticed around the Firm, thanks to the top marks M&A had recently received in a bi-annual analyst satisfaction survey conducted by a business magazine.

Thanks to my group's strong performance, my own star was higher than ever. I had gone into the comp process planning to get exactly what

M&A needed and deserved. For the first time, I had departed from the usual lockstep way employee bonuses were determined. I saw no reason to pay close to the same bonus to people the same number of years out of school when one was outperforming the other. I wanted to use our money to make significant contribution-based distinctions among M&A's people.

While this shouldn't have been hard for other group heads and the comp committee to understand—it was how partner compensation worked—it had already caused problems. The Firm's comp structure for professional employees emphasized parity. My recommendations were based more on performance and potential than on when people happened to get out of college, so some looked too high for their "classes" and others looked too low.

I knew I had to handle the upcoming meeting carefully to achieve the right balance of persistence and diplomacy. Corp Fin had a history of being perceived as arrogant by the rest of the Firm, and we weren't that far past the scandal that had knocked us off our pedestal. I had to present my recommendations as reasonable and all but unassailable without appearing to be overconfident or unwilling to bargain.

I was determined to prevail, but it wouldn't be enough to wield my power and influence simply to get my own recommendations approved. I also had to generate current and future support for myself and for Corp Fin—and to avoid creating any powerful enemies.

❖ ❖ ❖

I WAS EXCITED about getting home earlier than usual to see Jane. I wanted to hear more about her opportunity and I was looking forward to telling her how well M&A had done in the comp meetings. But I always wanted to see her, whether or not there was any specific news to talk about. I craved her company, her opinions, her body, even her mere proximity. Our nearly eight months of marriage had been terrific. I loved being married to Jane.

For the first time in months, I got home before she did. Our apartment felt disappointingly empty to me when I walked in, called her name, and got no answer. I realized, not for the first time, how quickly I'd gotten used to living with her. After years of not thinking one way or the other about living alone, I now felt lonely at home whenever she wasn't there.

I had time to take off my jacket and tie, roll up my sleeves, and open a cold bottle of beer before she showed up. When I heard her come in, I went to meet her in the front hall. She had dropped her briefcase on the floor, kicked off her shoes and, looking very overheated, was in the process of peeling off her clothes.

"Want some help with that?" I asked.

She grinned, but said, "No, thanks. Nice idea, but I'm too hot to be touched right now. It's disgusting out! You look cool—have you been here long enough to cool off?"

"No, I just got here a few minutes ago, but I took a taxi. It was too hot to walk."

"I would have done the same thing if I could have found one. It ended up being faster to walk, but now I'm boiling! I hate hot, humid days like this!"

I handed her the beer, which she swigged. Then she touched the bottle to each of her flushed cheeks. I told her she looked very sexy.

"Thanks," she said, smiling. "But I'm still too hot to be touched."

"You're too hot not to be touched, toots," I said, putting my hands on her face and kissing her.

She kissed me enthusiastically, but briefly, and then said, "OK, enough. Really. I'm already too sweaty as it is." She looked up at me and smiled again. "You look quite triumphant. Did you get everything you wanted at the comp meetings?"

"Sure did," I told her, grinning and reclaiming my beer.

"That's great—congratulations!" She picked up her clothes and shoes, and bundled them in her arms. "Will you tell me all about it while I take a quick shower?"

"Sure. Or do you want me to go get something for dinner?"

"No, stay with me. It's too hot to go out. Unless you're starving, I'll make us something later."

"Sounds great."

I leaned against the wall and recapped the afternoon's meetings for her while she showered. Jane was always good at doing more than one thing at a time—she listened intently and asked intelligent questions despite being busy with soap and shampoo. It was a pleasure (and a relief) to talk frankly and without editing my thoughts after my afternoon of diplomatic tact.

We were still talking about the comp meetings when she got out of the shower. She dried herself off and started putting lotion on her arms and legs, all the while asking me questions about how various people had behaved. With a few choice comments about people she didn't like, she finished with the lotion and handed the bottle to me.

"So tell me about your new opportunity," I said as I rubbed lotion on her back.

"I've got a letter and a packet of information about it in my brief-case. Basically, it's a new program called 'Building Executive Leadership.' Fifty people at my level or above have been invited to be in the first group that will go through it. The idea is to help the best of the people in middle management develop the skills—and, I suppose, the visibility—necessary to become executives. It's part of the Company's 'promote from within' strategy."

Drying her hair with the towel, she continued, "It's a year-long program and it's very intense. We start with a battery of psychological tests to determine personality type, learning style and that kind of stuff, then we get divided into groups designed to maximize learning potential—if you'll forgive the expression." Our eyes met in the mirror; she rolled hers, and we both smiled. "Anyway, for a year we attend workshops, both on- and off-site. Some of that will probably be bullshit; some of it will be useful. The one thing that's worrying me is what happens to our jobs during the program."

"What happens to them?"

"We don't have them any more," she said, frowning as she combed her hair. "As part of the program, we rotate through several of the Company's corporate departments—treasury, corporate development, internal audit and a couple others—and through the principal business divisions."

"Why does that worry you?" I asked, following her into the bedroom.

"Wait. Let me put something on, and I'll get you the packet. It'll be easier to explain once you've read it."

She put on one of my shirts. Jane wore my shirts all the time, but I still smiled every time I watched her roll each of the sleeves up five turns so they wouldn't hang past her wrists.

She gave me a quick hug on her way out of the bedroom and suggested I get comfortable in the living room. She said she'd get me the packet, then organize what we had in the way of dinner ingredients while I read it.

The packet was quite a production. Jane's description wasn't wrong, but the program was evidently a much bigger deal than she'd made it sound. The cover letter was from the Company's CEO, personally addressed to Jane and hand-signed. The packet itself was actually a slim, leather-covered binder emblazoned with the logo (based on the acronym "BEL") that had been developed for the new program. It contained some very professional-looking materials, all printed on letterhead with the same logo.

The whole thing looked fancy and expensive. The materials were well-written and obviously the result of a lot of thought and advance preparation. I'd seen enough of this kind of corporate communication on my father's desk over the years and from clients since I'd been at the Firm to know it signaled an initiative the Company was taking very seriously. Both the slickness of the packet and the content of the CEO's letter made it plain that the Company was committed to (and had already invested plenty of money in) the success of the "Building Executive Leadership" program.

The Company had thousands of employees, only 50 of whom had been invited to participate. The 50 included people in Jane's salary grade and the three salary grades above it, so she would probably be one of the youngest people in the program. The corporate-speak in the packet was comical, but there was no mistaking the selectivity of the invitation process or the exclusivity of being a participant. It was a huge kudo for Jane, and a terrific opportunity.

"Honey, this is incredible!" I called to her. "They're obviously grooming you for senior management by inviting you into this thing. Congratulations!"

"You think?" she asked, joining me in the living room.

"Yeah, absolutely! They've already spent a fortune on structuring the program, lining up speakers, preparing these materials and selecting the 'best of the best,' as the CEO's letter calls you. And you know they're committed to the 'promote from within' strategy. This is fantastic!"

Jane looked doubtful as she sat in the oversized chair she'd brought from her apartment when we consolidated our stuff in mine after we got married. She sat off-kilter, her legs crossed lotus-style and her back leaning against the place where the chair's plush arm and back intersected. It was her favorite way to sit and, as usual, she looked tiny and enveloped by the chair, an effect compounded by the size of my shirt on her.

"I know it's impressive, and I am pleased and flattered to be invited," she said, "but I'm hearing a few warning bells, too. There's something about the way they're plucking us out of our real work so we can be in this program that's making me nervous."

"Are you nuts? This will be a big leg up. They've isolated what they think are the key skills for executive leadership, chosen the people around your level they think are the best prospects, and built you a program to give you those skills. You'll get to the top faster than you would if you stuck with your current job *and* you'll be better prepared when you get there."

"Yeah, I guess," Jane said. "That's what Bill said when he told me about the program and gave me the packet. He's the one who recommended me."

"So what's your problem? You're being recognized as a superstar and singled out as a future leader by the people who matter. You should be overjoyed about this."

She tried to explain her "bad feeling," but it made no sense to me at all. She seemed to be cynically and pessimistically determined to find a problem with something completely fantastic. When I told her this, she got angry and her position hardened. Her warning bells seemed to solidify into serious misgivings as we talked.

I got nowhere with her as I tried to make the positives as obvious to her as they were to me. Ditto with trying to relieve or explode her misgivings. Our voices got louder as we grew increasingly frustrated with one another. We also started interrupting each other, something we rarely did when we debated.

The whole disagreement was unlike our usual debates. It developed an antagonistic and hostile tone, and it felt like a fight. Jane's comments took on a cutting harshness that I'd never heard from her before. I stopped trying to soothe her concerns or encourage her to understand and started arguing with her in earnest.

After this went on for a while, Jane launched herself out of her chair and stormed around the living room. I had stretched out on the sofa when we first started talking, but had long since sat up. Once she started moving around, I sat forward and followed her with my eyes. She looked coiled and about to burst, which was exactly how I felt.

At one point, she told me there were only five women among the 50 participants. I reminded her of her desire to be a scarce resource back when she decided to move to the Company, and said I assumed she thought being one of those scarce five was a good thing. She did, but her paranoia extended to that, too. She wondered if she would really be competing for the whole range of executive positions in the future or if the Company was planning to designate one "girl job"— and thus effectively relegating her to a ghetto of five who would ultimately compete for that lone spot.

I gave that distrustful theory the reaction it deserved. "That's absurd! You have no reason other than cynicism to think anything like that. You've told me over and over that the Company doesn't have the same problem with women as the Firm. Are you now fabricating problems just to prove everyone's out to get you?"

"Could you not yell at me?" she said, her tone scathing. "I'm trying to play out all the angles! I need to feel comfortable that this isn't a trap."

"No, you need to think the worst about it!" Exasperated, I got up and walked over to the window. Turning to face her (and trying not to raise my voice), I said, "You're being pessimistic to a spectacular degree. It's irrational to think this is a trap. Why would the Company go to all the expense of developing a program like this to trap you? This is a privilege, an honor. It's a fucking *gift*, for Christ's sake!"

"Remember the Trojan horse?! Gifts aren't always good."

"What the hell is the matter with you? You're being ridiculous! This is a painfully obvious white boy break. Now you can't even recognize one of those?"

Her eyes widened. "Don't you dare patronize me!" she said, her voice taut with rage. "I've been trying to explain my concerns to you for the last hour, and you're not even trying to understand. You're not even listening to me! You're only trying to convince me I'm wrong!"

"I'm listening to you, I'm just not agreeing with you. You haven't said anything intelligent for most of the last hour! You *are* wrong. You're being foolish—and your concerns are laughable. They're not based on anything other than cynicism and your determination to find sexism and hostility everywhere!"

Jane marched over to me and stood about a foot away. She was trembling and her hands were balled into fists at her sides. She looked livid.

"Stop minimizing!" she shouted, glaring up at me. "You don't know what you're talking about! You have no idea what it's like to be anything other than everyone's epitome of perfection! Just because everything is easy in your perfect life and one triumph after another falls in your goddamn lap doesn't mean problems aren't real for the rest of us!"

I was suddenly furious. "Stop blaming me!" I shouted back at her. "This isn't about me! It's not my fault your path isn't as smooth as mine or that I don't make everything so fucking complicated! I'm not the one creating problems for you! I've never done anything but support you! And I've worked plenty hard, too. I'm sick of listening to you demean what I've accomplished!"

Jane opened her mouth, but said nothing. She looked stricken—still mad, but also dismayed, surprised and maybe a little scared. I was torn. I wanted to put my arms around her, but I was also very angry. I realized that I wanted to drive my point home more than I wanted to touch or comfort her. After glaring at her for a few seconds, I walked past her and out of the room.

I strode down the hall and into the room we used as our office, banging the door open on my way in. It felt strange, unsettling, to be furious with Jane. She often exasperated me, but fury was not something she'd provoked before. I wasn't sure what to do next. My temper usually got people's attention and intimidated them into doing what I wanted, but I didn't feel right about using it like that with Jane. And my anger was already dissipating, which was also strange. It normally took more time and an act of will to get over it.

I paced around the room, thinking about Jane still standing in the living room, probably feeling frightened and alone—and hating those feelings. I knew she would be overreacting as usual, sure she had gone too far and that I would never forgive her or things would never be OK between us again. I was very, very tempted to stride right back to where she was and tell her that everything was OK and I understood— whether she did or not—that her harsh comment hadn't really been about me at all.

But she had to wise up. It was long past time for her to knock that chip off her shoulder and develop a little optimism and trust. Her knee-jerk inclination to distrust blinded her, and it was still strong after years of success and other evidence to the contrary. It would probably slow down her success, if it wasn't already doing that. And although I didn't doubt that she respected my accomplishments, I *was* pretty fucking sick and tired of hearing her complain about how easy life was for me.

I was still undecided about what to do when she appeared in the doorway to our office. I stopped pacing and met her eyes, but didn't say anything. She looked apprehensive, but determined.

"I feel pulled in two different directions," she said carefully. "I feel terrible about attacking you and saying something so unfair, and I hate it that you're mad at me. I kind of want to beg you to forgive me. And I want to hug you and feel your arms around me very badly. But, at the same time, I am really, really mad at you."

"That's exactly how I feel," I said, surprised that she had voiced the identical feelings.

"I apologize for attacking you," she said, walking into the room and closing about half the distance between us. "I truly didn't mean to demean your accomplishments. I do respect them, and your efforts, very much. But I need you to understand and to quit minimizing how much harder and more complex things are for me. I know you think I should just relax and be more trusting, but I'm not an insider in the same way you are. I never have been and I never will be. I *have* to be more vigilant."

"Being vigilant is not the same thing as always assuming the worst," I said, leaning back against the wall, my hands in my pockets.

"I don't always assume the worst," she insisted. "I just don't automatically assume the best. I consider that the worst might be a possibility. I'm not in a position to take it on faith that the worst *isn't* a possibility."

As I thought about this, I realized my jaw was clenched and unclenched it.

Perhaps Jane noticed my face relax. She stood a little less stiffly and said in a conciliatory tone, "It's like the business world is a circle with a thick, boldfaced circumference. You're inside the circle. It was drawn, delineated, by and for people like you—like you on the surface, I mean—and you *can* assume that what goes on inside it will generally be favorable for you."

She looked at me anxiously. Evidently encouraged by what she saw—or didn't see—on my face, she continued, "I'm outside the circle—by definition. The circumference looks pretty impenetrable from afar, but I know there are all sorts of openings once you get up close. The problem is that some of the openings don't really lead to the inside. They're blind alleys, little pockets to get stuck in or shunted aside by."

She paused and then somewhat hesitantly she asked, "Could we sit down? And could you please stop glaring at me?"

"I'm sorry," I said, walking to the couch and sitting down at one end. "I didn't realize I was glaring at you."

She walked over and sat sideways at the other end, her back against the arm of the couch and her legs folded in front of her. She looked very serious and still worried.

Leaning toward me, she said, "Thank you, that's better. What I'm trying to say is that even when no one is intentionally trying to keep me out of the circle or treat me unfairly, there's always the possibility that I'll end up disadvantaged. What goes on in the circle doesn't operate naturally in my favor—often, it doesn't even operate in a way that makes sense to me. That's why I have to consider all the possibilities, play out all the angles, before I can be sure I'm not going to get screwed."

"That seems ridiculous and unnecessary to me," I said. "After seven years of success, you could have a little trust that you're not going to get screwed instead of always assuming it's a possibility."

"I know that's how it seems to you," she said, looking at me steadily. "If I *were* you, it *would* be ridiculous and unnecessary. But I'm not you. Getting screwed really is always a possibility for me. I understand that it's less of a possibility now than it used to be, but it's not enough less that I can afford to assume it away or let down my guard."

"Even if that's true, it doesn't make sense in this case. It's counter-productive and dumb. You're being singled out for an exclusive executive leadership program! How can you look at that as anything but an honor, a privilege? Proof that you're highly regarded and on your way up?"

"Because it's just the kind of thing that looks good, but might easily be a pretty façade that hides a trap or a blind alley. The typical path to senior management at the Company has always been up through the line business ranks. This is a detour off that path, so it makes me suspicious."

I was no longer furious or even all that angry with her, but I felt like shaking her. "For Christ's sake, Jane, you're the last person in the world who should be insisting on doing things the typical way!"

"It drives me so crazy when you say things like that!" she exclaimed, and she did look wild-eyed as she slammed her palm down on the couch. "You're missing the point! I'm *not* insisting on doing it the typical way! I'm trying to explain to you why I'm suspicious of this detour. When someone suggests that I take a detour from the usual way people succeed, I naturally wonder why!"

She took a deep breath. Then she put her head in her hands, shook it in a discouraged way and said in a muffled voice, "You have *no* experience being an outsider, *no* idea what it feels like to have people and circumstances lined up against you, no *concept* of what it's like not to have every assumption working in your favor. How am I ever going to explain this to you in a way you can understand?"

Before I could respond, she looked up and said vehemently, "You're just wrong about this! Not for yourself, but for me! You and I are not on the same footing! It would be stupid—foolish, to use your mean word—for me to take it on faith that I'm operating in a benign world where things are more likely to work out well than badly. Because I'm not! And the success I've had so far is because I haven't been foolish enough to forget it! Can't you see that?"

"Sure I can see it," I said, trying to sound—and stay—calm. "And I can agree that vigilance is a good approach in response to it, too. But you take it way too far. What you're calling vigilance looks more like pessimism, cynicism and distrust to me."

"That's because you *are* operating in a more benign world! I know you're sick of hearing that, but it's true!"

She took another deep breath before she added in a more reasonable tone, "You don't have to agree with my approach. You don't have to take it yourself. You don't even have to approve of it—although I wish you did. All you have to do is understand why I think it's the right approach for me. And you have to stop discounting my concerns."

Jane was now looking at me in a pleading way. I considered not saying what was on my mind, but decided she needed to hear it.

Trying to speak patiently, I said, "I only discount your concerns when I think you're over-valuing them. I don't think your knee-jerk inclination to distrust is any different, any less strong, than it was when you were a rookie at the Firm. You're going to hurt yourself and slow down your success if you don't moderate that and start demonstrating some real optimism and trust. You might already be hurting yourself—your level of pessimism and cynicism is way too high for someone in your position."

She started to say something, but I silenced her with a look and kept talking. "I'm not finished. My perspective has always been useful for you because it's different from yours. That's the point. You need to listen to what I'm telling you, not try to convince me that you're right and I'm wrong. And I'm not wrong about this leadership opportunity. If you don't go for it, you'll get left behind. You'll end up regretting it and you'll mark yourself as someone who's not with the program, who can't recognize a good thing when she sees it."

"But what if it really does turn out to be a detour?" she asked, almost in a whisper.

"Then you'll find a way to get back on the main road—along with forty-nine other superstars. Jesus, Jane, you must be able to see how irrational it is to think the Company would intentionally send fifty known superstars off on a detour!" I realized I was glaring at her again and tried to stop.

"Lots of well-intentioned things end up causing more problems than they solve," she said. "The mommy track, for instance? Or sabbatical programs where the people never really get back in the loop? Or harassment policies that end up operating to hurt the people they're supposed to help?"

"And lots of things turn out fine or even better than expected. Look at the Firm's mentoring program. That was originally a real joke and it turned into a badge of honor."

Thinking of the mentoring program reminded me of Jane when she was my mentee. I'd had several mentees since, but she'd been the best. So smart and fierce and loyal—and, despite her distrust, in the end so open to suggestion, too. I'd always thought our mentoring relationship was the most successful and mutually beneficial of the ones I'd had. I suddenly wondered if falling in love with her had been in the cards all along.

"Honey," I said, "we're going around in circles. I'll always think your approach is too pessimistic and you'll always think mine is too optimistic. We don't have to agree. It's enough to listen to each other and consider the other perspective. That's always helped both of us make good decisions up to now, right?"

I held out my arms and she immediately crawled across the couch and into them. "Right," she said, hugging me. "Absolutely."

She climbed onto my lap and put her hands on my shoulders as I put mine on her waist. Her eyes looked more confused than angry as she said, "But it's different now. I used to be able to listen to you in a more detached way."

"What do you mean?"

"Before I loved you, I could listen to what you said and factor it into my decision. It didn't upset me when we didn't agree. It just gave me food for thought. But tonight I felt like I had to make you see it my way and think I was right. When you didn't, it scared me and made me doubt what I was saying, and that pissed me off. So I attacked you." She frowned apologetically. "You know I didn't mean it, don't you?"

"Of course I do," I said, smiling. "I'm the one who does know how to trust, remember?"

"Please don't make me feel worse. I already feel terrible about what I said."

"Don't feel terrible. All kidding aside, I don't doubt that you respect what I've accomplished—whatever you might be shouting at me." I kissed her cheek. "I do have one question, though."

"What?"

"How did you manage to restrain yourself from calling me 'golden boy' even once?"

"Well, I'm not an idiot," she said, not yet smiling. "You look annoyed when I call you that even when you're not furious. It was on the tip of my tongue a couple times, but, to be honest, I was afraid to say it."

She shivered. "You looked so scary! It's been terrifying enough to see that directed at other people over the years, but I had no idea how it would feel directed at me. I have a whole new level of sympathy for poor Frank—remember him?—and everyone else who's been on the receiving end of your temper. Do you have any idea how ferocious and barely contained—and large—you look when you're mad?"

"Yeah, I have an idea. I've seen the reactions." I moved my hands from her waist to her face. "But you're not afraid of me, Jane."

"Not physically, no." She paused and looked at me a little anxiously. "Still, though, I couldn't help feeling it wasn't a good idea to goad you when you were already so angry." She clasped my wrists. "And I *am* afraid of losing your good opinion of me. I can't stand the idea that you might start thinking less of me. So I can't stick to my guns the way I used to. I can't stop myself from taking your opinion into account."

"That's a good goddamn thing for you. Taking my opinion into account has saved you from making more than one stupid mistake."

"Yeah, yeah, yeah," she said, finally smiling. "Where would I be without you and your brilliant ideas?"

She kissed me, then moved off my lap onto the couch where she again sat sideways, her legs folded and her knees touching my leg. She took my hand in both of hers and massaged it.

"Seriously, though," she said, "I guess this is another example of what scares me about love and marriage. I care so much what you think—maybe too much. I'm still afraid of getting weak or overly dependent on you. I don't want to stop being able to figure out what I think without knowing what you think or worrying about what you *will* think or caring more about your opinion than my own. I don't want loving you to mean I'm losing my ability to think for myself or to develop an opinion and hold on to it."

"There's no chance of that, honey. Your prickliness alone is more than enough to protect you. And you're still plenty stubborn, too." I smiled and squeezed her hand. "Anyway, caring what I think doesn't mean you're getting weak or too dependent. Neither does wanting to take my opinion into account. I always consider what you say before formulating my opinion or making a decision, and I never think that makes me weak. It's just a matter of two heads being better than one."

"But you're standing on firmer ground to start with where power is concerned," she said, but halfheartedly.

"I'm also standing on firmer ground to start with where instinctively knowing how to play the corporate game is concerned," I pointed out. "Honestly, this BEL program is totally fantastic. You should be very proud of yourself and very excited about it."

"I am. Really. I was before, too—I was just hearing some warning bells." She sighed. "My concerns were pretty vague, actually, and not too serious, but when you dismissed them, I felt like I had to defend them. Then, when you ridiculed them, I felt like I had to make you see they were real. My problem wasn't as much with the program as it was with you thinking I was being foolish."

She sighed again. "This love thing is so complicated. Are we OK?"

"We're fine," I said, hugging her.

She nuzzled my neck, then said, "Interested in a more intimate reconciliation?"

"I would be if I weren't weak from hunger. Weren't you supposed to make dinner?"

"Wasn't I *supposed* to make dinner?" she echoed, her eyebrows high.

"You did say you'd make something. Are you trying to weaken me and my influence on you by deliberately starving me?"

Jane laughed. "You idiot," she said. "How could I do that? It's not up to me whether you starve or not. You're perfectly capable of getting yourself something to eat."

"But you'll save me the trouble tonight, won't you?"

"Of course I will," she said, getting up and pulling me to my feet. "Come keep me company while I do. You can tell me again how amazing I am and how great it is that I'm going to be a BEL."

CHAPTER 18
NUANCES OF IDENTITY

Jane

In mid-September, Charlie and I joined the rest of his family for the weekend at his parents' summer home. I loved spending time with his family. Everyone was smart and interesting, and the conversation was often eye-opening. It was usually entertaining, too, thanks to Claire's over-the-top personality and Andy's and Kate's senses of humor.

The conversational dynamic also interested me. Different people dominated the conversation on different subjects, but everybody participated in his or her own way. Most of us contributed on most topics. Andy and Claire were always talkers. Claire's husband, Stephen, and Hannah rarely said anything, but they too spoke up when they felt like it and never seemed ill at ease.

I was particularly intrigued by the way Alex participated. He was always engaged and willing to answer a direct question, but, like Stephen and Hannah, he tended to observe rather than speak, no matter the topic, and he was content to fade into the background. It was quite a contrast with his powerful business persona. I wondered whether he was deliberately holding himself back so as to leave room for everyone else or just taking it easy. I planned to ask him about it some day.

Charlie was also a little different. He was his usual relaxed self, but he too tended to be quieter when his older siblings were around. He thought this was simply birth order habit. Laughing, he'd said it was a miracle he and Hannah had ever spoken at all, given that Andy and Claire never shut up.

I suspected his quietness was also a reflection of how restful he found his family. He wasn't competitive with his siblings, so the leadership skills he instinctively demonstrated in other settings simply took a rest when he was with them. I felt especially close to him then—both identified with him (in a good way) and like he was even more mine than usual.

We had a relaxing and lazy day on Saturday, and then a wonderful dinner, which everyone got involved in cooking. It was beautiful that Saturday night—almost fall weather, but not yet too cold to sit outside, and still light until fairly late. After Andy and Chris got their boys settled in the house with a video, all the adults grabbed sweatshirts and strolled down to the small private beach.

The beach was within shouting distance of the house; a little wall of rocks separated the lawn from the sand. We arranged ourselves in a loose circle, just right for conversation. Alex and Kate had beach chairs, as did Claire and Stephen. Everyone else stretched out on blankets on the sand or used the smoother areas of the rock wall—or, in the case of Hannah and me, our husbands—as backrests.

Charlie sat on a blanket, his back resting against the wall. Every now and then, he kissed my head or stroked one of my arms. I felt embraced and supported—a good physical metaphor, I thought with a smile, for our whole relationship.

Claire and Stephen had arrived after dinner, so we hadn't yet had a chance to talk with them. Claire was pregnant for the first time at (in her words) "the antediluvian age of thirty-six." She'd been entertaining us all summer with her take on pregnancy. She was finally over the bad morning sickness she'd had early on, but she still thought being pregnant was primitive, ridiculous and barbarian—not to mention something she should have refused to become.

As soon as we were all settled on the beach, she said, "Stephen and I have an announcement to make."

"We all know you're pregnant, Claire," Andy said.

"Oh, you don't know the half of it," Claire retorted.

"Literally," Stephen said, grinning broadly.

"Hey!" Claire punched him gently on the arm. "This is your fault, but it's *my* announcement. I'm the one doing all the work." Turning to the rest of us, she said flatly, "We found out today that we're having twins. Can you believe it? Twins!"

There was a hubbub of exclamations and congratulations, followed by an excited chorus of questions. Stephen continued to grin and Claire continued to look put out. She held up her hand, palm out. When we were quiet, she said, "Here's what we know. They're fraternal twins, a boy and a girl, both healthy. My profligate weight gain in the last three months, despite the nearly constant vomiting, is now explained."

Looking dourly at Hannah and me, she added, "You two will be glad, I'm sure, to learn that twins do not run in our sensible family. You too, Chris, if you're thinking of having any more. It turns out there *is* a little run of them in Stephen's family—a crucial fact that my cagey husband saw fit to hide as he hoodwinked me into this absurd adventure."

"I honestly didn't know about the twin thing," Stephen said, still beaming, "but she's mad because she knows I wouldn't have told her even if I had. It took me over five years to talk her into this as it was—and persuading people to do things is what I do for a living!"

"It's lucky your clients and opponents aren't as intractable as your wife," Chris said, laughing.

Chris was a biologist by training, in addition to being a very capable mother (with very nice kids). Like Andy, she was athletic, and they had a teammate sort of relationship—they always seemed easy and in tune with each other. They'd had the first of their two children ten years before; since then, Chris had worked as a freelance editor of textbooks and articles in her field. That way, she said, she stayed up to speed without having to hassle with the day-to-day of an actual job.

Andy had a big personality and an inspired sense of humor to go with his good looks. Like Charlie, he was a world-class golden boy, but he cared far more than Charlie did about being the center of attention. Andy was the very model of a talented and much-loved first-born child. He stopped just short of being off-puttingly full of himself, perhaps in part because Claire was a natural star and he'd been battling with her for center of attention status since he was a toddler. (Given the positive impact I also thought she'd had on Charlie's character, I wondered if growing up with a strong-minded sister was somehow essential to the development of a man who understood that the world didn't revolve around him.)

Chris, with her intelligence and her independent strength, struck me as a very cool choice of wife for someone like Andy. Every time I saw them together, I was reminded of what Hannah had said about Andy choosing his wife strategically and what Charlie had said about being distinguished by one's spouse.

Now Andy said, "No one on the planet is as intractable as Stephen's wife."

"Yeah?" Claire growled. "You try growing two children in your abdomen simultaneously, then we'll talk. This system is moronic. If men had to do it, we'd have had a more streamlined way of reproducing centuries ago. So far, it's been mostly about nausea and vomiting. For the next six months, I have excessive weight gain, general discomfort, and the increasing inability to be taken seriously as a physician to look forward to. Then, I get to cap the whole thing off with appalling pain and oceans of blood."

"Jesus, Claire," Charlie said. "Could you lighten up a little? I don't want to have to spend the next five years persuading Jane that having kids is a great idea."

"I'm not telling Jane anything she doesn't already know," Claire said tartly. "Anyway, pretty boy, Jane's a tough customer. You'll never be able to persuade her to do something she doesn't want to do. The smart money's on her."

"Thanks for the vote of confidence, Claire," I said, laughing, "but you might want to hold onto your money. Your brother is used to getting what he wants. And complicating matters further, I find him completely irresistible."

Charlie and I kissed each other while the rest of them made gagging sounds. Well, maybe not all the rest of them—when I turned back to the group, Alex and Kate were smiling at us fondly.

"Newlyweds!" Andy griped. "You're revolting! Isn't it about time for the two of you to be done with this sickening phase?"

"Apparently not," Charlie said cheerfully.

"Maybe more talk about babies will cool them off," Jason said, grinning. Hannah's husband was a sculptor, with exceptionally beautiful and expressive hands (perhaps as a result) and a very informal and agreeable manner. He also taught art at the university he'd graduated from, and he and Kate were fascinating to listen to when they discussed academic politics. (These were evidently not that different from corporate politics, but even more cutthroat.)

Turning to Alex and Kate, Jason said, "I don't know whether to congratulate you or be mad at you, but how did you raise two sons who love the idea of kids and two daughters who view it so suspiciously?"

"That's easy," Kate replied. "We raised four kids able to think clearly and for themselves. Any man who can think straight knows his part in the process will be the easier part, so he focuses on the upside. Any woman thinking straight knows she's going to bear the lion's share

329

of the burdens and so she focuses on those. Everyone likes the idea of creating a legacy, but from pregnancy and birth to juggling parenthood and career, the woman has the harder part.

"Dare I say," she added, smiling in a way that made her look young, "that conception is the only time the man has the harder part—and not in the same sense of the phrase at all?"

"Mother!" Andy exclaimed as if scandalized. "Behave yourself! And unlike the rude little pun at the end of it, your explanation isn't solid. It's belied by your having had four kids yourself. Obviously, you weren't as dubious as you've made Claire and Hannah."

"Give me a break, please," Hannah said quietly. "I'm only thirty. I get to be not yet ready for a while longer without being characterized as dubious."

"OK," Andy said, smiling at her. "Not yet ready it is."

"What the hell *were* you thinking, Mom?" Claire demanded. "So far, this experience is more of a nightmare than anything else. I can't believe you willingly did it four times! And don't tell us Alex made you do it. No one will believe that."

Alex chuckled. "Actually, daughter of mine, after Andy and you, I thought we had enough children on our hands. Your mother thought otherwise and she used her 'lion's share of the burdens' argument to persuade me to agree that a third and then a fourth were good ideas."

"And they were," Jason said, massaging Hannah's shoulders.

"Definitely," I murmured.

"Glad the newest in-laws are happy," Claire said. She laid her hands on her slightly swollen abdomen. "But, Mom, really. Four?"

"Darling," Kate said, "the point isn't the pregnancies. It's the children and the resulting family. You'll see."

"If you try to think about it logically in the abstract before you have kids, the cons far outweigh the pros," Chris said. She and Andy had been lying side-by-side on their stomachs; she sat up as she spoke. "And pregnancy is burdensome—if also a remarkable thing to be able to do. But once the abstract becomes a real kid, the cons are insignificant, almost meaningless. You stop being able to imagine *not* having the kid, and the pregnancy fades to a fairly abstract memory."

Andy nodded and said, "And in your case, Claire, you won't have to do it again if you don't want to. You'll already have two."

"Are you convinced, honey?" Stephen asked Claire. He was grinning again (or maybe he'd been grinning the whole time). Stephen's attitude toward Claire reminded me of Jordan's toward Katherine. They both seemed enchanted by their wives and similarly happy to play second fiddle without seeming at all intimidated.

"Provisionally," Claire grumbled. "I still can't imagine why I let you get me in this state."

"You're crazy about me," Stephen told her.

"I know," Claire said sorrowfully. "You're my Achilles heel. Watch yourself, Jane—being a sucker for an irresistible man who knows how to get what he wants can lead you down some very questionable paths."

Charlie laughed, and Andy said, "We didn't think it was actually possible to influence Claire's behavior until Stephen came along. They're all the proof you'll ever need that the irresistible force is stronger than the immovable object."

"And look where not being able to resist him has gotten me!" Claire wailed.

"Don't pay any attention to her, Jane," Jason said. "I highly recommend finding your spouse irresistible."

"Since I don't seem to have much of a choice, I'm glad to hear that," I said, squeezing Charlie's legs where my hands were resting on them. "But, Kate, what about what Claire said earlier about being taken seriously as a doctor? I think she's right that being pregnant makes it harder to be seen as a professional. You must have experienced that—how did you handle it?"

Kate shook her head. "I didn't experience that—not the same way your generation seems to. Being a woman was a minus, if not an automatic disqualifier, for most professions, but no one had a problem with women being wives or mothers. It's a paradox, isn't it? Now it's much easier and less irregular for women to pursue professions, but career women of my generation were far less behaviorally constrained."

She laughed. "When I was twenty-five, I was a married, female, much too tall graduate student studying mathematics. That was already the height of peculiarity in too many ways to count. I imagine the conventional people around me thought being pregnant was one of the more normal things I did. In any event, at the university, people interacted with me on the basis of what I did in the classroom, not what I did outside it."

"And what you did in it," Alex said, "was terrify them. They were too busy trying to keep up with you to pay attention to your gender or your pregnancies."

"That might be the reason pregnancy wasn't more of an issue for me," Kate said. "Or perhaps it was because it hadn't yet occurred to the narrow-minded to try to condition a woman's professional status on her willingness to deny part of her identity. But being a professional wasn't as limiting then as it seems to be today. I never felt obliged to pretend I wasn't a woman so I could have a career—or to limit my personal options because I did have one. You younger women aren't oddities in the professional world the way I was, but you seem to feel your professional status will be compromised if you do anything considered traditionally feminine."

"That's because our opportunities have a tendency to narrow or disappear when we do traditionally feminine things like have babies," I said. "We're not oddities in terms of being as few and far between, but we are absolutely still considered oddities. And the way we succeed includes being careful not to give those in power reasons to consider us different in a bad way."

"Well said!" Claire nodded approvingly.

"I wonder why that's happened," Kate said. She shook some sand out of her shoe, then slid the shoe back on her foot. "In my case, no one—including me—thought it was necessary for me to forgo motherhood or any other traditionally feminine behavior I felt like engaging in simply because I'd decided to pursue a career. The choice to pursue a career was itself deemed odd, but once I made it, I was no more constrained than the men around me from becoming a parent. As I said, pregnancy was considered one of the more normal, even reassuring, things I did."

"But, Mom," Claire said, "wouldn't it have been more of an issue if you hadn't been so stellar? I'm sure your aptitude and your brilliance made it easier for people to overlook your gender and your four pregnancies."

"I think being stellar was the reason I had the opportunities I did. Forty years ago, there weren't opportunities at all for women who were anything less than stellar, in terms of both brilliance and determination." Kate held up an emphatic finger as she said, "Don't misunderstand. I was a rarity by reason of my gender, and I had to be far better than my male counterparts to succeed at the level I did. I also had to have a thick skin. But given all that, being female was more or less beside the point. Honestly, I don't believe I hurt myself or was viewed by anyone at work as less capable or valuable because I also chose to have four children."

"So it was harder to get in, but once you were in, you got to be who you were and do what you wanted," Andy said.

"I got to be who I was and do what I wanted all along," Kate declared, looking severe. "There was never a need to do otherwise. The narrow-minded had no power over me. They weren't in charge of how I pursued my career or ran my life. It would have been ridiculous to let someone else's view of how I should live take precedence over my own knowledge of who I was and what I wanted to do."

Kate's comments were familiar (the third of her four children having said similar things to me about a million times), but they surprised me coming from her. Women in her generation had so much less freedom to pursue professional goals. I knew she must have faced sexism and negative assumptions of a nature that made my uphill battle look minor by comparison. Yet, throughout her life, Kate had apparently done exactly as she pleased without much in the way of discomfort or second thoughts.

I had wondered before how she could possibly have been so determined and thick-skinned—even as a young woman, so sure of herself both personally and professionally. As far as I could tell, she was—and had always been—basically impervious to conventionality and other external pressures to conform to a more customary mold. That night, I decided to see if I could find out why.

Leaning forward slightly, I rested my hands on Charlie's knees and said, "I don't disagree with your point, Kate, that we, rather than other people, get to determine who we are and what we want. But when getting what you want depends on the decisions of people inclined to dictate behavioral terms, you have to pay attention to what they think you should be and do."

"Define 'pay attention,' please," Kate said. Her shoulders seemed to square and her tone was subtly different. I felt suddenly like a student sure the professor was going to be able to shoot down anything I offered up.

"Well," I said, "at the Firm, for example, I always felt like an interloper who was allowed into the game grudgingly and would be closed out of it in a heartbeat if I didn't toe the expected lines. There was a very small range of acceptable behavior for someone like me. I succeeded there because I learned how to operate in that range whenever I could and to look like that's what I was doing the rest of the time. I couldn't have done that if I hadn't paid attention to what others thought I should be and do."

"That was a very effective and powerful approach to getting what you wanted," Kate said. "That kind of paying attention isn't the same as allowing other people to determine who you are or what you achieve. You didn't yield your power—you used it. That's why you succeeded at the Firm."

Her expression went from approving to stern. "But 'allowed into the game'? 'Closed out of it'? Those are expressions of defeat, Jane. It's your game as much as it is theirs—that is, unless you yield it to them. Why are you giving them the power to run it?"

"I'm not giving them the power to run it," I protested, feeling defensive. "They already have that power. I'm trying to get to the level where I have it, too."

"By letting them dictate who you are and what you do? That won't gain you power. It will merely prove they're right in thinking they can manipulate you. By virtue of your talents, your ability to pay attention to how the game is played and your desire to win it, you already have all the power you need to succeed. To reach the level you're aiming for, all you have to do is wield your power effectively and yield it to no one."

"You can't win this," Charlie murmured into my ear. "Not only is she right, but you can't sidetrack her like you can me."

I went from wanting to smack him to wanting to kiss him when he sat up straighter and said aloud, "Jane is right about the Firm being an environment that demands toeing certain lines if you want to succeed. To be fair, it's hard on men, too—it's not an easy place for anyone to succeed. But the range of acceptable behavior was determined and is maintained by men, and it's absolutely less hospitable to women. And to get back to the original point, pregnancy is way out of the mainstream. It calls into question in many minds whether the woman can be a real player and it often limits her opportunities."

"And not only in stodgy places like the Firm," Claire said. "Every environment where the professionals are traditionally men raises issues like these for professional women. *We're* what's out of the mainstream, and pregnancy gives people yet another reason to doubt our commitment or our suitability to be doing what we're doing."

"Let me ask a series of questions," Kate said calmly. All four of her children groaned.

Alex laughed and turned to me. "Kate always constructs proofs this way," he explained, "and the kids hate it. They always end up speechless."

"They don't just end up speechless," Chris laughed. "They always lose!"

"The questions are so fucking innocuous," Andy said as he sat up. It was getting too dark to distinguish facial expressions, but he sounded both mystified and miffed. "You answer them innocently and then, suddenly, you realize you've proved her point. It's diabolical!"

Thus warned, my heart sank when Kate said, "These questions are for Jane. Let's stay within the construct of the Firm. Jane, how would you handicap Charlie's chances of succeeding in that environment?"

"It's a certainty," I said, leaning back against him. "He's smart and determined, great at the job, and he knows how to get along well with everyone—clients and colleagues." I was tempted to add that he also perfectly fit the profile, but I thought I knew where Kate was going and I didn't want to fall into her trap if I could help it.

"Has he hurt his chances of succeeding by getting married?"

"No. He's probably helped them." I smiled and clarified, "I'm not just patting myself on the back. The Firm's culture of conformity prefers men in their thirties to be married."

"Noted," Kate said smoothly, not even momentarily distracted from her questions. "Will he hurt his chances of succeeding in that environment if the two of you have children?"

"No."

"All other things being equal, would he be more capable or more suited to succeed if he had stayed single or if you two were to decide not to have children?"

"No," I said again—this time slowly, not because I had any doubt about the answer, but because I couldn't tell where she was headed. I also had a strong sense that Charlie was grinning.

"Taking into account, if you like, the difference in your ages and experience," Kate asked, "are you as good at the job as Charlie is?"

"She's better than I am," Charlie said. He put his arms over my shoulders and his hands over mine on his knees.

Kate smiled at him indulgently, then said, "Jane, would you agree that you are at least as good at the job as Charlie is?"

"Yes."

"Has being married negatively affected your skills or your ability to do that job?"

"No."

"Do you believe that women who stay single or elect not to have children are more suited to succeed at the Firm or more capable of doing so, all other things being equal?"

"No, of course not."

"Is being married or having children grounds for termination at the Firm?"

"No," I said, with a sinking feeling that the coup de grâce was coming, but completely in the dark about how to defend against it. Everyone else seemed to think so, too—the group had an expectant air.

"As between you and the Firm, who decides if you get married or stay single?" Kate continued inexorably.

"I do."

"As between you and the Firm, who decides if you have children?"

"Still me."

"As between you and the Firm, who decides if you want to succeed there?"

"I do," I said, finally seeing her conclusion.

"And so," she said, "as between you and the Firm, whose responsibility would it be if you failed to succeed there solely because you married or had children? Whose responsibility would it be if you decided against marrying or having children in order to make it easier to succeed? Unless you affirmatively give it up, in whose power are your success and your ability to make whatever choices you like on marriage and children?"

Charlie hugged me as the rest of the group seemed to relax. I smiled and said to Kate, "OK, I see your point and I have no idea how to dispute it, but the conclusion doesn't feel right to me. Why is that?"

"I'll tell you why," Claire said, planting her feet and sitting up straight. "You're living in the real world, not in Mom's cerebral world of equations and abstractions and elegant proofs. Mom, it's fair enough to put the responsibility for succeeding on us, but you're not taking into account how incredibly difficult and draining it is to fight against the status quo."

"That line of argument is beneath you, Claire," Kate said. "The status quo is what it is, but what you choose to prioritize is completely up to you. No matter how difficult and draining the fight may be, you have no one to hold responsible but yourself if you choose to give up something you care about so as to make it easier—or, for that matter, if you choose not to fight."

Gesturing to include all of us and sounding very professorial, she declared, "That goes for every one of you. The status quo is perpetrated and perpetuated by people without the courage or the confidence to think for themselves. There is no reason for you to let yourself be dictated to by such people. You're in charge of your life and what you decide to make of it. Your duty is to use your abundant talents and advantages to suit yourself—personally and professionally—and thereby to set the kind of example that will change the world for the better. You are all more than powerful enough to do so, regardless of the inequality and unfairness around you."

Kate shared Charlie's knack for making uncommon and debatable views seem obvious, reasonable—and beyond debate. Alex could do it, too. The trick was as hypnotic as it was eye-opening.

Charisma was part of their magic. I frequently found myself unable to argue with their positions while in their presence, as if their personal magnetism were spinning cobwebs that fogged my ability to think straight. But there was more to it than charm or personality. Charlie and his parents consistently espoused views that had a certain irresistibility of their own. The world *should* operate the way they thought it did.

As far as I could tell, the three of them felt utterly at home in a world they perceived as both fundamentally benign and also bendable to their personal and altruistic will. And they believed without reservation in their own inherent goodness. Their comfort in the world and their trust in themselves gave them strength and power and also shaped their perceptions and opinions.

While their outlook was not hard to reject as unrealistic optimism (once you got out of their personal magnetic fields), it was extremely difficult to challenge the positions they took without resorting to the kind of distrustful, zero sum game comebacks suitable only for thugs. Not only did it feel churlish to offer up thuggish counterarguments, it never worked either. Charlie, Alex and Kate were all expert at shooting them down.

I had no trouble understanding (and dismissing as more or less irrelevant to me) how golden boys like Alex and Charlie could maintain this perspective. The world did operate almost without exception in their favor. They could typically bend it to their will, whatever their purpose, and there was every reason for them to feel relaxed and comfortable in it.

But Kate was in the same boat I was in—possibly an even leakier boat, given our generational difference. Her self-assurance stumped me, as did her strong sense of personal power. I recognized the point of view she offered—again, because Charlie had been offering it to me (with varying degrees of patience) for years—but coming directly from her, the mindset was impossible to dismiss. It would have been foolish to ignore her example, and I felt I had to reconsider my own outlook.

We were all quiet after Kate finished speaking, leaned back in her chair, and looked up at the stars. For a while, the sound of the waves rolling onto the sand was the only noise.

It had grown very dark by then and a little colder. I smiled to myself and pressed back against Charlie when he moved his hands under my sweatshirt, pushed my T-shirt out of the way and caressed the bare skin just above the top of my jeans. I was still thinking about what Kate had said (and luxuriating in the sensation of Charlie's warm hands on my skin) when Chris said to Andy, "We should go check on the boys." She got to her feet and pulled him to his.

Andy pleasantly surprised me when he turned to me and said, "You're a good sport, Jane. And Claire's right—you are a tough customer. You gave the Grand Inquisitor here a decent run for her money."

"Thanks!" I smiled up at him. "But she clearly won."

"Oh, she always wins," Andy said, waving his hand dismissively. "That's unavoidable. But she had to resort to her 'series of questions' M.O. and work harder for it than she's had to with any of us in years."

Kate laughed. Chris hugged Claire and murmured a few words to her. Then, linking her arm through Andy's, Chris said, "Good night, all," and the two of them walked back to the house (stepping up on the rock wall in unison as if it were merely a stair step).

Unexpectedly, the voice that broke the silence was Hannah's. "Your conclusion is liberating, Mom," she said, "but it's also very demanding. I think, for many people, the burden of responsibility may look like too high a price to pay for the freedom. A lot of people seem to find both personal responsibility and freedom very frightening."

Despite my interest in the points Hannah raised, I let the resulting conversation go on around me instead of participating in it. For one thing, it was educational to listen to everyone else. For another, I needed a breather after my first experience with Kate's interrogatory technique. And, for a third, I was distracted from critical thinking by lust.

I smiled to myself again. For me at least (and I knew I wasn't alone in thinking so), part of Charlie's potent magnetism was most definitely sexual. Just about everything he did made me want to take off my clothes and leap into bed with him (a reaction that still came as a bit of a surprise to me after my six years of obliviousness to his allure). I was frequently sidetracked by my desire for him and by the recollected experience of sex together—sometimes explosive, sometimes gentle, always sizzling.

Getting distracted like this didn't trouble me in the slightest. It felt too good. It would have upset or angered or worried the person I'd once been, but the person I'd become had no such qualms. There was no harm in letting myself slide when I felt like it. I could still concentrate and think clearly whenever I wanted to, and I still wanted to plenty of the time.

Pleasure and satisfaction had turned out to be additive, not depleting. I knew there was no need for even a flicker of concern, and so my distractibility did nothing but make me happy.

❖ ❖ ❖

THE BUILDING EXECUTIVE LEADERSHIP program was great right from the start. Along with the other BELs, I spent the first three months transitioning out of my regular job, taking psychological tests, reviewing the results with an executive coach, and attending workshops on leadership, management, teamwork and the like.

The results of the psychological tests were quite instructive and helpful. This came as a surprise to me, particularly given how peculiar the test questions were. (Would I rather teach a deaf child to sing or a blind child to read? Could I read if the TV was on? Did I prefer to work in bright light or in soft light?) Despite the strange questions, the resulting reports were startlingly accurate—as if whoever had written them had done in-depth interviews with me and everyone I'd ever met. Reading the reports was oddly disquieting; they were so valid, so reflective of both my own experiences and the comments others had made to me over the years, that I almost wondered if someone had been spying on me for the last decade.

Similarly, I got exceptionally constructive coaching from my rigorous and plain-speaking executive coach. In addition to offering a great deal of useful insight, she resolved one of my long-standing performance improvement questions. Reviewers had often told me I would benefit from improving my listening skills. Given the inordinate amount of time (and energy) I felt I spent patiently listening to other people, this comment always rankled.

My coach asked me if I'd been told I could be a better listener. When I said yes, she said she was sure I found the comment off-target. She told me my problem wasn't with listening, but with acknowledging. In her opinion, people likely couldn't tell I'd listened to them and incorporated what they'd said into my thinking before I went on to the next thing because I processed information too quickly and invisibly for most people to follow.

She thought this also explained some of the interpersonal issues I'd experienced over the years. Her suggestion for improvement was that I take the time to acknowledge other people's comments before moving forward. This seemed sensible (if yet another consumer of time), so I tried it the next day. It was incredible how readily, even hungrily, people responded to it and how eagerly they offered additional good ideas.

The BEL workshops were also terrific. With only two exceptions, the speakers and instructors were anything but lame (despite being consultants). A few of them were truly inspirational as they talked about leadership, ambition and organizational performance. The sessions were often interactive and, unexpectedly, that aspect was excellent, too. I wasn't usually a fan of group discussions—other people's efforts to keep up bored and frustrated me—but my fellow BELs were far from boring.

They were an impressive bunch. All the people in my sub-group were new to me (Jennifer was also a BEL, but she was in another sub-group and I rarely saw her). There seemed to be no one in my group who couldn't keep up, and there were several people who frequently raced ahead. Our discussions leapt from person to person in what felt to me like real or even double time, and they were very stimulating.

Within our groups, we often worked with a partner for role-playing or other hands-on exercises. The program's architects evidently believed it made sense for us to work with the same partner throughout the training, so we were each assigned to one for the duration of the program. My assigned partner was a wonderful guy named Sam, whom I liked almost from the moment I met him.

Sam was a smallish, intense guy with an unfortunate resemblance to Ian. But he was not visibly over-muscled the way Ian had been and, to my relief, he didn't seem to be overcompensating in any other way either. Unlike Ian, Sam was neither aggressive nor in my face. Despite the physical resemblance, it became clear pretty quickly that he didn't have any of Ian's negative characteristics.

Sam was also a brand manager, but in a different division of the Company. He was a year older than I (and in a bit of a state about being 30), as well as brilliant, self-confident and ambitious. As befitted a future CEO (his plan), he was also the soul of affability. He was friendly and generous, and he smiled all the time. Even during our first one-on-one exercise—always an awkward situation—Sam was fun and unflustered.

We quickly discovered that we had a strong facility for learning from one another. Although our learning and working styles were similar and we related easily and well (no doubt the reasons we'd been partnered), our perspectives were very different. We had a lot to offer each other. Working with Sam was one of the big reasons I was enjoying the program.

❖ ❖ ❖

CHARLIE AND I celebrated our first anniversary exactly the way we wanted to: quietly and alone with each other. Our married year together had been incredible. It had exceeded my wildest expectations, merger-related and otherwise. I felt full of happiness, surrounded by love, flooded in contentment. I also felt buttressed, nurtured, inspired—and stronger than ever.

At the same time, Charlie and I were both learning through trial and error that a spouse was a very different animal than a friend. As spouses, we had acquired the power to upset and wound each other, an unexpected phenomenon that caught us off guard. It turned out that I wasn't the only one in whom marriage had prompted some new reactions to familiar stimuli.

This became painfully evident one night when I inadvertently (and totally unexpectedly) triggered Charlie's temper. I was complaining about the sexist crap that came along with being a married woman. We'd discussed sexism countless times over the years; while Charlie got exasperated pretty regularly, he'd never before gotten offended or angry. He so rarely took *anything* personally that it never occurred to me he might be hurt by my comments.

That evening, he agreed that assumptions about married women were often inapt, but he couldn't understand why they made me so angry. In his view, I had two choices: I could ignore sexist crap or I could buckle under it and let it exclude me from situations that provoked it. Letting it get to me when I knew it was unfounded made no sense to him.

In an attempt to describe how desperate I sometimes felt when I had to smile and eat shit in response to other people's limiting pronouncements about what marriage meant for women (however wrong I knew them to be in my case), I made the mistake of saying I felt trapped in a category I didn't belong in. With a suddenly icy expression that made me feel like a repellent stranger, Charlie demanded, "So you're saying you'd rather not be married?"

I tried to explain that my point was an entirely different one—not about him or our marriage at all—but it was too late. He felt rejected and blamed by my comments and enraged by what he saw as my callous disregard for his feelings. He told me (loudly) that he was sick of feeling like he had to justify marriage to me and if I didn't think its benefits outweighed the mindless assumptions of a bunch of fucking Neanderthals, I was as obtuse as they were. He then stalked out of the room and was icily civil, but basically impossible to reach, for the next couple hours.

Charlie's boiling point was unusually high and he lost his temper very rarely, but when he did, he was terrifying. His anger made me feel besieged, sub-par, scared and anxious to mollify him. He didn't exploit this—his rage was genuine, not manufactured—but he was well aware of its impact and he didn't hesitate to use it. The same blithe simplicity that made him so generous and unself-centered most of the time was a lot like arrogance when he felt crossed. The flip side of self-confidence, I discovered, was high-handedness and my husband had no shortage of either characteristic.

I hated making him angry. He always recovered pretty quickly and apologized for losing his temper, but being its target made me miserable (even as my craven instinct to placate him pissed me off). I also had no desire to hurt him, and knowing I had the power to do so made me want to be more careful. I didn't stop talking to him about sexism or any other subject, but I tried hard not to abuse—or inadvertently trip over—my newfound ability to get under his skin.

❖ ❖ ❖

IN MID-DECEMBER, the Company hosted a combination holiday party/kick-off event for BEL participants. The party marked the end of the program's introductory phase and the start of the real deal.

We were scheduled to begin the rotational part of the program in January. My first rotation was to be in Corporate Development, which pleased me. It was an area I knew a lot about thanks to my four years at the Firm. And the strategic thinking and planning aspects of projects were always more interesting and fun for me than the tactics (although I did take a certain pleasure in the meticulousness of getting the details right, too). I was also hoping I could influence the Corporate Development decision-makers to send some investment banking work to the Firm. The Company hadn't historically used the Firm, but I was sure the relationship would be a great one if I could get some M&A work referred to Charlie and Lynn.

It was possible that the Corp Dev guys would listen to my recommendation on this. The BEL designation was a big deal at the Company, and the visibility aspect was already proving valuable. BELs were noticed and congratulated in nearly every setting, from the board-room to the cafeteria. The congratulations no doubt stuck in the craws of those of our colleagues who resented us, but just about everyone had enough sense to want to stay on the good side of people who could end up in charge.

To my surprise (and feeling rather unlike myself), I was excited about the kick-off party. I liked and admired the other members of my BEL group and I was looking forward with pleasure to seeing them in a social context with their "guests" (as the invitation coyly put it).

I was also interested to see how the Company handled social events of this type. The Company had turned out to be more sensitive than the Firm to the pressures that all couples events placed on employees, particularly younger employees. Or perhaps the Company was just too big (or its party-planners too cheap) to host events like the Firm's horrible proms. Whatever the reason, the Company's social events were normally for employees only.

I suspected (and expected ultimately to find out) that the executive ranks functioned more like the Firm—that is, that a presentable spouse was *de rigueur*. While the culture of conformity aspects of this conven-tional requirement still angered and disgusted me, its potentially negative impact on me personally was no longer a concern: I had a spectacularly presentable spouse.

Charlie and I had attended a few dinner parties and small receptions for one corporate thing or another since we'd been married, but he hadn't yet had the experience of attending a large function in his capacity as my spouse. I was curious to see how he handled it and how he felt about it. I knew he wouldn't embarrass me or be inappropriate in any way (I doubted he knew how; good manners and easygoing charm were as natural to him as breathing). But I did wonder if he would experience any of the aggravation I'd experienced at being pegged as "Charlie's wife" rather than as a person with an independent identity.

At the few Company-related events we'd attended as a couple, it had never taken more than a few minutes of conversation for Charlie to transform from "Jane's husband" into his independent identity as an investment banker and the head of the Firm's M&A group (as well as my spouse). People always asked him what he did, which made it easy for him to talk about his work without making a big deal of it.

I'd noticed that it was easier for male spouses to do this. No one expected them *not* to have careers. This was in sharp contrast to the experiences I'd had as a working woman at social events, both as Charlie's wife and, before that, as Tyler's date. People seemed to assume that a woman didn't have a career or, at any rate, not one worth talking about. Very few people at social events asked me what I did. If I wanted to assert my identity as something other than a wife or date, I had to insert it forcibly into the conversation—not an easy thing to do gracefully.

This had always been true at events where I was the "guest" rather than the employee. At Firm events, it had happened several times even when I *was* the employee. Wives (perhaps innocently, perhaps not) and Firm people who didn't know me had simply assumed I was the guest (and thus beneath notice).

To my surprise, I hadn't felt this way at the Firm events I'd attended with Charlie. They were actually fun in a weird way. I saw lots of people I knew (and who already knew I wasn't only a wife), including quite a few I liked very much and didn't get to see often enough otherwise. It was a pleasure to spend time with Lynn, Katherine, Jordan, Patrick, Jim and several of the other M&A guys I'd liked working with. And I never felt I had to hide behind Charlie or assert my own identity with any of them.

Even the awful Firm people weren't so awful. Their recollection of my tenure at the Firm was more glowing than our actual experience together (as least in my memory). They seemed to remember me as a superstar and a real player, and they treated me very nicely. This pleased me, but it also irritated me. More than once, I was tempted to remark that the red carpet treatment would have meant more to me when I actually worked at the Firm.

I knew the flattering treatment had more to do with my escort than with me—just as it had when I'd attended events with Tyler. Charlie was a favorite at the Firm for all the reasons he'd always been golden. As head of M&A, he was also quite a big shot. Muckety-mucks, their wives and most of the younger people (the ones who'd figured out how to play the game) went out of their way to make sure I noticed them favorably, I presume in the hope that I'd say something positive about them to my powerful and charismatic husband.

I wasn't entirely comfortable with all this, based as it was on my identity as Charlie's wife rather than as my independent self, but it really didn't bother me much. Katherine helped me articulate why when she said something about considering it her job to promote Jordan at the Firm's events.

I was back at the events for a different reason than I'd originally attended them. It was no longer *about* me the way it was when I worked at the Firm. As Charlie's wife, I had a unique opportunity to help him succeed, both by being the kind of spouse people thought well of and by observing and listening carefully and gathering intelligence he could use. Together, we covered more ground and saw from more angles than either of us could alone, and this was enormously valuable to Charlie as he continued his climb to the top.

Although my experience as a wife at Firm events was a pleasant surprise, I'd had a few other opportunities to feel pushy, gauche and out of place in that capacity. The most abysmal of these was at one of Charlie's softball games. It was the third or fourth game he'd played. He'd asked me to all of them, but some work conflict or other had arisen for the first few.

At least I thought I'd had a legitimate reason for not going. I wasn't aware of any disinclination to go. I liked watching sports, and it was fun to go anywhere with Charlie. Also, I was getting used to thinking of myself as his wife in a way that didn't mask or take precedence over the rest of my identity. I figured I could handle being part of a group of wives watching their husbands play softball without getting prickly.

I was wrong. The experience was so unsettling, and I ended up feeling so ashamed of myself, that I couldn't help but wonder if the seemingly legitimate conflicts had been a premonition or even an unconscious self-protective instinct. I somehow managed to feel exactly like a wife in the worst sense imaginable while at the same time feeling like I was completely abnormal—neither a wife nor a woman in any sort of customary way.

We arrived just as the guys were getting organized to play and the wives were settling into the little stand of sideline bleachers. The first person we saw was Charlie's friend, Jeff, whom I liked a lot. He teased me about the corporate rat race and confirmed that he still loved teaching, then said he would have talked Susie into coming if he'd known I was going to be there. (It was actually fine with me that his wife hadn't come. I always had a hard time finding things to talk about with her.)

Charlie also introduced me to a few other guys. They all seemed nice, if preoccupied with getting ready to play. After a few minutes of chatting with them, I gave Charlie a squeeze, wished him luck, and turned to face an undifferentiated mob of aging prom queens, all sporting carefully coordinated outfits and high-pitched voices.

This was a casual summer softball league in the park, but none of these ladies was dressed, as I was, in jeans and a T-shirt. They wore belted shorts outfits, capris and twin sets, sundresses with little sweaters—and the amount (if not the kind) of makeup and jewelry that I considered appropriate for one of Tyler's family's fancy dress events.

I contained both my knee-jerk inclination to disdain them and my strong desire to flee. Women like these had always frightened me. They never seemed to talk or care about anything that interested me (or about which I knew anything), and I never knew what to say to them.

I was further put off by how clique-ish they appeared to be. They all seemed to know each other and they had arranged themselves in conversational clumps that looked awkward to join. Once the high-pitched cacophony became recognizable as individual voices, my heart sank another couple notches. The bits of conversation I could pick out related to kids, a new couch and a bestseller that I was sure was sexist drivel and wouldn't have dreamed of reading.

Suppressing a sigh, I climbed up a couple bleacher levels and sat down gratefully next to a woman who smiled at me. We introduced ourselves; her name was Sandy. She told me they'd all wondered what Charlie's wife was like—he was such a doll, didn't I think?—and then turned to introduce me to the others. I suddenly found myself the center of attention.

How had we met, they wanted to know. Cringing internally over my inability to say simply that we'd worked together, I heard myself telling them I'd been an investment banker at the Firm before my current job at the Company, and that Charlie and I had been friends for years. I kind of wanted to describe our marriage as merger model, too, but I managed to stop myself. Instead, I answered their questions about our wedding, where we'd gone on our honeymoon (it took some doing, but I left out the private plane), and where we lived.

After the barrage of questions, some of them startlingly personal, I was relieved when the conversation turned to other people's weddings and honeymoons and I could listen and comment instead of having to be on the hot seat. Commenting suitably wasn't much easier than being the center of attention, but at least I had extra time to think before I had to speak.

I felt so out of step. The other wives had been attending games together long enough to have developed a shorthand way of talking. And they had a lot more in common with each other than any of them had with me. Their interests were pretty stereotypical: kids (although no one had any kids in tow), clothes, decorating, diets. I doubt they meant to be exclusive, but effectively they were.

They kept doing weird things, too—things that made me feel contrary. They talked about their husbands' jobs possessively, as if the jobs were also theirs. ("The new sales quotas are brutal!" "We really don't like working for this boss.") When one of the husbands got a hit or caught a fly ball, his wife was cheered and high-fived, as if his prowess reflected well on her or she had done something worthy of congratulations herself. (What could this be? I wondered. Marrying him? I doubted any of these women ran softball practice drills with their husbands.)

Charlie hit a double in the second inning. After I fielded the obligatory chorus of congratulatory praise (feeling very fake and self-conscious), a woman named Judy smiled brightly and said to me, "We all *love* Charlie! He's *so* handsome and such a sweetie, too. That's a rare combination, isn't it? And, boy, is he hot! To tell you the truth, I've always had a little thing for him—I bet he's *great* in bed. If I'd ever thought I had a chance with him…"

She and several people around us looked at me expectantly after this bizarre speech. I wondered uneasily what they wanted. Was I supposed to confirm that he was indeed great in bed? Offer to find out if Judy had ever had a chance with him? Blush? Thank her? Scratch her eyes out?

My instinctive response was a very definite "He's mine!" but I knew that wasn't right. A sarcastic or cutting remark also seemed wrong, and it clearly wasn't the time for a lecture on appropriate conversational topics for strangers. Bereft of these possibilities, however, I had nothing.

I was speechless. I smiled in what I hoped was a friendly and non-gloating way and turned back to the game in response to a well-timed upsurge in noise.

Half-watching the game, I told myself—sharply—to get a grip. I had no idea who these women were or what they did. Despite the little outfits and the clanking jewelry, for all I knew they were CEOs. (Well, OK, probably not CEOs, but still.) It was short-sighted and beneath me to damn them as stereotypes or pigeonhole them with negative assumptions. I resolved to stop acting like an ill-mannered adolescent. Sandy was talking to someone behind her, so I took a deep breath, turned back to Judy, and asked her how old her kids were. She happily told me all about them, others soon joined in, and I at least felt polite.

But I couldn't seem to stop trying to set myself apart. At one point, the conversation turned to manicures. My pedicurist was great and she would probably have loved the referrals, but I didn't offer her up. There was no chance my fingernails would give me away, so I pretended to be unacquainted with things like manicures and manicurists.

I was at the game to watch Charlie, but I didn't get to do much of that. The other wives seemed to have come more to socialize with one another than out of interest in what their husbands were doing. They paid scant attention to the game after the first innings, and they and the men had very little to do with each other. I found this odd in light of the women's blatant (and, to me, overdone) classification of themselves as wives, but their husbands didn't seem to mind. A few of them offered victorious thumbs up or smiles in response to cheering, but most of them paid no attention to the stands at all.

Further setting us apart, Charlie came over to say hi about halfway through the game. Putting one of his feet on the bleacher step below me, he reached up and cradled my face in both his hands as he asked me if I was having fun. Knowing the eyes around me were on us, I leaned forward and kissed him, something I rarely did in public and never for the benefit of an audience. He was oblivious—after the kiss, he spent a few minutes being charming in response to the flirting he drew like a magnet from the women surrounding him—but I was mortified by my showy fakeness.

After he went back to the field, Sandy and I chatted. She had been an office manager for a good-sized medical practice before she got married. We talked entertainingly about how inefficient most people were and what a difference good organizational skills could make. She also said, with an ironic laugh, that while men had driven her crazy when she was working, she'd sort of missed them since she quit. Apparently, her married life included very few men other than her husband.

I was tempted to ask her why she'd quit her job, but my contrariness had shaken me and I wasn't sure I could do it without being offensive. I also thought that for someone who claimed to be happy with her lifestyle choices, she was pretty quick to throw her former job into the conversation. (Later, it occurred to me that she may well have brought it up graciously so as to provide a topic of interest to me. Unlike me, she might not have felt compelled to deny all commonality—or to behave like a brat.)

Charlie and I walked home after the game. I knew that talking to him would help me sort out my confusing array of unpleasant emotions, but I was too embarrassed to describe how I'd felt and behaved. He was all excited about the game, the way participants always are afterwards, so he didn't notice my discomfiture or my preoccupation.

He jumped in the shower as soon as we got home. Later, when I went to see why he hadn't reappeared in the living room, I found him in bed, sound asleep. That night, we went out to dinner with Tyler and Liz. I still felt shaken and preoccupied, but I couldn't seem to find the right opportunity to bring up the topic with them either, even though I knew that they, like Charlie, would be sympathetic and helpful.

I couldn't stop wondering why I'd felt so defensive, so combative, simultaneously both superior and inferior. I'd felt the way I did when I ran up against some business world "truth" that made no sense to me—that is, excluded and at a bit of a loss, as if someone had maliciously ripped a few pages out of my copy of the how-to manual before giving it to me. Or the way I did at work when people undervalued me or treated me like I didn't belong—like it was necessary to demonstrate my differentiating skills and accomplishments, to compete, to prove my fitness, to win.

But what was I trying to prove to the softball wives? I disdained their game, didn't I? Why did I also feel the need to beat them at it?

The wives were rather shallow, and they certainly exemplified the conventional—and limiting—view of women that so often unfairly damned women like me, but the wives weren't the enemy. They were as entitled to their lifestyle choice as I was to mine. Why had I felt and acted as if it were necessary to demean the wife lifestyle altogether, as if it and my lifestyle couldn't co-exist? Even more perplexing, why had I at the same time hedged my bets and also tried to make it clear that I could out-wife them if I wanted to?

I fell asleep that night struggling with those questions. Fortunately, my subconscious was more adept than my conscious mind at answering them. I woke up suddenly and quite completely while it was still very dark, with some words Jennifer once said as present and clear in my mind as if they were written in light on the air in the room. The words felt revelatory, so much so that I suspected they were what woke me up.

A glance at the clock told me it was 3:26. Charlie was sleeping, his back to me. I kissed his shoulder blade gently, then lay back and contemplated Jennifer's words: "It's not a contest, Jane. You're not trying to get ahead of them or take anything away from them. You're trying to do something fun together with them."

Jennifer had been talking about sex, but the words seemed equally applicable to my softball wife dilemma. And she'd been right about sex. It wasn't a contest or a power struggle or a political statement. It didn't require me to prove or hedge anything in order to maintain who I was or control who I became. It didn't have the power to diminish me unless I gave it that power.

The same, I realized, was true of the wife lifestyle. I'd always had a sense that women like the softball wives possessed a mindset I lacked, but I didn't regret lacking their mindset or find myself wanting as a result. There was no need for me to compete with them, no matter how weird I felt around them. Anyway, the wives had been *nice* to me. They hadn't treated me like I didn't belong; I had done that to myself. It was just a Saturday afternoon softball game in the park—the competition was on the field, not in the stands.

Really, I thought, I had behaved just as badly as traditional men with their negative assumptions about women (or anyone else unlike them). And far less explicably: at least the mediocre, scared guys at work *were* competing with me to get ahead and *were* finding themselves wanting.

I remembered when Liz had surprised me with her comment about how sad it was that women weren't natural allies instead of combatants warring with each other over what was "more feminine." There were certainly societal reasons for us to find ourselves at odds (including, significantly, discrimination and scarcity of opportunity), but women had a much better chance of changing the status quo united than we did divided.

The softball wives deserved the same civility and respect from me that I deserved from the men at work. They were entitled to the same freedom, in general and from unfair negative assumptions. Our lifestyles could co-exist. They *did* co-exist. The fact that some women chose to be traditional wives was absolutely not the right thing to blame for the sexism I'd encountered at work and in the world. Nor was being a traditional wife something I needed to feel duty-bound to belittle (or to prove I could do). It wasn't necessary for one lifestyle to win and all others to lose. One size did not—and did not have to—fit all.

These conclusions pleased me. I was still embarrassed by my behavior, but having figured out where it came from and how unnecessary it was made me feel better. I was reasonably sure that the next time I went to a softball game or some other wife venue I could avoid an encore of both the bad behavior and the unpleasant emotions that triggered it.

I also sensed that I had learned something important about myself, the discovery of which gave me more space and more freedom. When, still asleep, Charlie turned over and reached for me, I tucked myself under his arm and nestled into his warmth, delighting as I always did in how big his body was. My last conscious thought before I fell asleep was that I was becoming a bigger person, too—not physically, but in terms of perspective and outlook.

I thought often about my discovery during the months between that June softball game and the December BEL kick-off party. After sex and wives turned out to have less inherent power and "truth" about them than I had thought, I started to wonder how many other rules I felt I had to live by, how many other lines I felt I had to toe, were, in reality, limitations I imposed on myself rather than strictures required by others as the price for the personal identity and career success I wanted.

My reluctance to talk about the softball behavior with Charlie didn't last. I gave him an only slightly bowdlerized version of the actual events, and described my newly discovered sense that maybe I was the person drawing the lines of the box I'd always felt I had to contain myself in— and, if so, that maybe I could draw them more expansively without making my way unreasonably harder.

He was delighted. He'd always thought I withheld too much of myself and worried too much about conforming to external views. He repeated his opinion that external truths and rules were only advisory, not mandatory or even directive. He granted that they were influential and couldn't be ignored, but insisted that no one had to be ruled by anything external.

Like his mother, he was certain that the best behavioral guides were who you were, what you wanted to accomplish, and what you believed was good and right. He was equally certain that these internal standards were top priorities that rightly took precedence over external rules and opinions. In his view, winning wasn't winning at all if it required the sacrifice of a greater priority for a lesser one. The only true victory was one that squared with your top priorities.

As we talked, I began to understand what self-esteem really was. A strong and solid belief in your own decency and merit was what made it possible to take in external opinions, whether negative or positive, without letting them reign or prompt either pangs of self-doubt or delusions of grandeur.

I recognized that lack of respect for what most of them thought wasn't the only reason I held people at arm's-length. Another was self-protection. My sense of identity, of self-belief, was too vulnerable. Perhaps unconsciously but nevertheless persuasively, I'd always known I had the potential to be overly influenced by other people's opinions of me.

Charlie's model was incredibly helpful as I figured this out. He believed in himself utterly and effortlessly. He wasn't egotistical or over-bearing, but his self-esteem was impregnable. Other people's views of him had no power to dent him or his sense of who he was. He didn't resent people who thought badly of him, nor did he feel obliged to prove them wrong. If someone thought he was an asshole, he considered why that might be and whether he could alter his behavior so as to get a better reaction, but it didn't occur to him to worry that he might actually *be* an asshole. He knew he wasn't.

His self-esteem was what made him so charismatic and also so unguarded, open-minded and unafraid to take chances. Self-esteem is itself appealing. The confidence and "why not?" optimism with which Charlie's endowed him often made his ideas and opinions seem irresistible. And not only to me. People not head over heels in love with him also responded beautifully to the combination of his unassailable self-assurance, his unreserved willingness to put skin in the game, and his unambiguous readiness to trust and listen to them.

His self-esteem also gave him courage. He wasn't afraid of failure— as a possibility or a reality. It didn't rock or discourage him in the slightest, and so he took more chances than other people. He ventured more and he gained more.

The way he had gone about pitching the marriage as merger idea to me was a perfect illustration. Someone with less innate self-esteem would have worried that I might laugh in his face or otherwise react badly to such a bizarre idea. He might have shied away from feeling awkward or embarrassed or wondered uneasily if I would consider him a worthy merger partner. The potential for a bad reception—and the risk of feeling sub-par as a result—might well have caused someone else to decide against making the pitch altogether (or at least to have thought it over for more than a day).

But Charlie never let the possibility of a bad reception or any other sort of failure foreclose the possibility of success. When he wanted something or thought it was the right thing to do, he went for it. Bad receptions didn't make him feel insecure or wounded or sub-par. He was rarely embarrassed, and he never took failure personally. He just dealt with it and learned from it, his internally generated sense of himself as a good and deserving person intact.

It was actually quite ironic: Charlie thought much more highly than I did of other people and he always gave them the benefit of the doubt, but their opinions of him personally had no power to rattle him. He didn't need to hold people at arm's-length, distrust them or otherwise seek to protect himself from potentially hurtful attitudes or situations. His self-respect was his protection.

I had enough self-respect to believe in my right and my ability to succeed, but hostility and negative assumptions—real or anticipated— had always had the power to dent my self-esteem and make me feel unwelcome, unsure, combative, even bratty. I resented people inclined to undervalue or dismiss me, and I felt obliged to prove them wrong— on *their* terms.

Despite my self-respect and my success, the negative assumptions of the narrow-minded (as Kate had called them) had always shaped my sense of who I was and how I had to behave. I hadn't let them eliminate me from too many games, but their attempts to define and label me, to limit and restrict my demeanor, had without a doubt circumscribed my path.

What I was learning was that other people could do this to me only if I let them.

❖ ❖ ❖

Charlie

I really enjoyed the BEL reception. Jane was right about her fellow BELs—they were impressive and interesting. The Company's CEO and most of his executive team were there, too. Everyone seemed to admire Jane (and to want to tell me so), and I had quite a few chances to cast the Firm in a good light for people in a position to send us work.

The CEO and I hadn't met before, although of course I knew him by reputation. As soon as Jane introduced me, he told me he knew my father and asked me to convey his regards. Smiling, he smoothly complimented me on my choice of family members and said he was a big fan of both my wife and my father. Jane beamed, and they talked briefly before we moved away to let the next people greet him.

We mingled for a while, having a series of brief and pleasant conversations, many of them much more interesting than the usual business event small talk. Jane was incredible—smart and quick and fun. I knew she didn't particularly enjoy doing it, but she had always been good at making small talk and keeping conversations lively. She was also a superstar, which made her someone others sought out.

This had been true of her at the Firm, too, but by the time of the BEL event she had two more things going for her. Because she was more senior and thus more powerful, she had more admirers. And she was far less prickly than she'd once been. I kept being surprised and impressed by her comfortable, humorous manner, and I saw that her colleagues at the Company didn't just admire her, they also liked her. She still wasn't open, exactly, but she had much easier relationships with them than she'd had with most of the people at the Firm.

Jane had really relaxed over the previous year. She was still very intense—and that was still one of the things I loved most about her—but her intensity was comprised much more of passion and determination and much less of wariness and distrust.

She had been brave enough to loosen up and stop withholding so much of herself from other people. When that didn't hurt her, she was perceptive enough to recognize it, honest enough to admit it, and strong-minded enough to push herself even farther. She stopped worrying so much about steering clear of anything with the potential to stereotype her as a woman. And she worked hard to check her instinctive distrust and approach people and situations more optimistically.

All of this made her interactions with other people a lot easier. It also made me very proud of her. I admired her self-awareness and her courage. And at the reception I felt like the husband of a real player.

In addition to being gratified by everyone's admiration of my wife, I was glad to have the chance to do for her what she'd done for me at Firm events since we started going to them together. Having her at my side at those things had been incredibly helpful. Jane was so adept at reading people, and so astute, that she often saw things I missed.

It wasn't only a matter of two heads being better than one. Jane wasn't just any extra set of eyes and ears—her inside knowledge of the Firm, even if somewhat obsolete, made her a very perceptive observer. Her natural skepticism was also a big plus. The Firm's environment was an antagonistic one in many respects. I had no problem recognizing knives when they were drawn and coming at me, but Jane's more pessimistic perspective was adroit at sensing sheathed knives. She was usually right when she warned me of potential hostility from someone I considered completely benign. Thanks to her advice, I had sidestepped or prevented more than one lurking fiasco.

Jane didn't need any help sensing sheathed knives (at the BEL event or anywhere else), but I figured meeting her colleagues would help me pull her back from the cynical ledges her instinctive pessimism still occasionally pushed her out on. She hadn't stopped teasing me about being way too trusting, but ever since I'd been right about the BEL program, she'd moderated her inclination to discount my perspective as unrealistically optimistic.

She'd also gotten over her concern that listening to me would make her weak. She described work situations and problems and asked for my opinion all the time, and—just like before we were married—she had no trouble taking it into account as she figured out her best approach. Meeting her colleagues in person could only make my suggestions better.

After nearly an hour of mingling, Jane spotted her friend Sam and we headed his direction. I liked him right away. He was just as she'd described—smart and ambitious, levelheaded and very friendly. I could see why he and Jane made good work partners. They had a similar intensity and their respect for one another was plain. They were also very informal and comfortable with each other, and it was obvious that they liked each other a lot.

Sam was with his girlfriend, Julie. Jane was curious about Julie, in part because she thought it was strange that Julie and Sam had been living together for several years, but weren't married. (Hearing this, I'd kidded Jane about her sudden traditionalism where marriage was concerned. In her new relaxed mode, she didn't get mad. Instead, she pointed out that Sam was no more immune than I'd been from corporate pressures to settle down, and stuck out her tongue at me.)

Julie turned out to be very nice. She told Jane it was good to finally meet someone she felt she already knew. With a smile, she asked me if I had heard as much about Sam as she'd heard about Jane. I laughed and said I thought I probably had.

As Julie and I talked, I noticed that Jane looked at me closely, her eyes slightly narrowed, before turning to Sam, who had asked her something about a workshop they'd attended the previous week. That answered, the four of us spent quite a while together, talking very enjoyably, until Jane and Sam decided it was probably a good idea for them to mingle with someone other than each other.

Before I had a chance to ask Jane about the look, Jennifer came over to say hello. Jane was completely untroubled by my past with Jennifer, so I had gotten over the reservations I'd initially felt at having any kind of continuing contact with her after Jane and I got together. Jennifer tried to make me uncomfortable—or, at any rate, she flirted more overtly than I thought a friend of Jane's should have—but since it didn't bother Jane, it didn't bother me.

Jennifer hugged us both and told us we looked great. Waving in the direction of the bar, she told us her date had gone to get drinks, then said she'd been dying to talk to Jane. They started talking about how great the BEL experience was and how surprisingly relaxing it was to be "off line" in terms of actual job responsibilities.

Half-listening to them, I looked around the room. At one point, I caught Julie's eye. She was apparently doing the same thing while Sam talked animatedly to someone. When our eyes met, she smiled and shrugged.

It occurred to me that this must be what Jane meant when she talked about the "beside the point" feeling she sometimes got while standing at my side at Firm events. Jane disliked the feeling, but it didn't bother me at all. I didn't feel beside the point or ignored. I liked being next to my wife, listening to people tell me how brilliant she was or observing that for myself. I also found it very relaxing to coast along, not having to be the center of attention.

Jane and Jennifer were still talking when I saw Carol, a lawyer I had worked with on a deal not too long before. She was across the room and she'd seen me, too—she was waving. I waved back, then lightly touched Jane's shoulder and told her I was going to go say hello to Carol while she and Jennifer talked. She nodded and said she'd come find me in a while.

"Bye, handsome," Jennifer said, grinning.

"That's my husband you're flirting with, Jen," Jane said mildly, smiling. I wanted to kiss her, but doubted she'd think that was a good idea, given the surroundings, so instead I put my hand on her neck and rubbed her cheek gently with my thumb. We smiled into each other's eyes in one of those nice moments of wordless agreement. Then I turned, said so long to Jennifer, and walked across the room to talk to Carol.

Half an hour or so later, the reception was winding down and Jane and I left. It was a clear and not too cold winter night and the air felt very fresh, so we decided to walk home. Jane initially looked doubtful and said her shoes were not really walking shoes, but when I told her I'd be happy to carry her if the shoes got too uncomfortable, she laughed and agreed to walk.

We did a general debrief as we walked. I'd introduced her to Carol, who turned out to be married to another BEL, but there hadn't been much time for them to talk. Carol had been astonished to see me at the reception; apparently, she'd been planning to call me the following week to let me know she'd recommended the Firm to one of her clients and suggested he give me a call.

Jane shook her head in resigned wonder when she heard this. "Only you," she said, "could go to an event as a spouse and have a new client fall into your lap thanks to another spouse. Your lucky star never takes a break, does it?"

She was very revved up and happy. She'd had a terrific time at the reception; being Jane, of course she wanted to analyze why.

"I feel like I belong in that group, you know?" she said. "Not just that I have what it takes, but that no one's questioning my right to be there. I don't feel like I'm *inserting* myself or like I'm an unwelcome party crasher. It's so much easier to relax and have a good time when you feel welcome."

"Yeah, I'm sure it is."

"Do you think that's just the difference between being almost thirty instead of twenty-two and having the confidence that goes along with that? Or is the Company really as different from the Firm as it seems? Or have I really changed that much—you know, would I feel this way by now if I were still at the Firm, too?"

"All of the above, to some extent. Also, the BEL designation helps— for the obvious reasons and because it puts you with people less likely to be intimidated by you and so less likely to resent you."

"Good point." She looked up at me and grinned. "I can't believe I'm going to admit this, but being married to someone like you really helps, too."

"Why? And why don't you like admitting it?"

"Relax. I don't mean that in an insulting way. I just think people at work should see me and evaluate me for who I am and what I do, not for who I married."

"Who you married is part of who you are."

"I know, but it shouldn't be that relevant a part at work." We had linked arms when we started walking, and now she tugged on mine. "Could you slow down, please? I may seem taller because of these damn shoes, but I'm still walking with my usual legs."

"Sorry," I said, slowing down. "Sure you don't want me to carry you?"

"You'd love that, wouldn't you?"

"So would you!"

She laughed. "Probably—once I got over the indignity of having to admit I couldn't keep up! Anyway, stop trying to sidetrack me. What I was trying to say was that being at this thing with you was really good for how people saw me. It's like a whole new wrinkle of identity for me. People don't think of me as someone who'd have such a spectacular and charming husband."

"Thanks, but aren't you being a little hard on them—and on yourself?"

"I don't think so. People perceive me as very serious and businesslike, and they draw conclusions based on that. The stereotypical view seems to be that women like me aren't attracted—or attrac*tive*—to guys like you. It's the same thing going the other way. Guys like you are supposed to have wives more like the softball wives than like me, right? Anyway, I'm sure the people at work assumed I was pretty one-dimensional. You surprised people, and it made them rethink their perception of me."

"You're OK with that?"

"Well, yeah. Who wouldn't be? You're all handsome and charming and friendly, and so people start thinking, 'Hmm, there must be more to Jane than I thought. She can't be all business after all.' It's very sexist, but the sexist assumption works in my favor for a change. I still get to behave like myself instead of in a way that people would find less threatening"— she said "less threatening" very sarcastically—"but they find me less threatening anyway because of what they presume to be true of me now that they've met my charming and handsome husband."

"So you're using me," I teased her.

"I'd love to," she said shamelessly. "Why are we *walking* home when we could already be there—in bed?"

"We could pick up the pace if you weren't so damn small! And stop trying to sidetrack *me*!" I said, laughing. "You know I'm about to ask why it's OK for you to use your husband to broaden and maybe improve how people perceive you when you have nothing but contempt for women who define themselves only as wives."

"Hey, give me a break!" she exclaimed, bumping me indignantly. "I knew I was out on a ledge. That's why I said I couldn't believe I was going to admit it! But it's not the same. Really. It's not that I have *no* identity except what I can lift from you. This is a whole different thing. I have my own identity, but it's one that typically triggers negative assumptions. By being together, we rebut a few of those and that helps me a lot."

I thought about this. Before I could say anything in response, Jane asked, "Did you feel sort of objectified? I think *everyone* commented on your looks, quite a few of them in this very surprised tone that made me wonder if I should be offended." She mimicked someone saying, "That tall, unbelievably good-looking guy over there? *That's* your husband?!"

I laughed. "Honey, it's a compliment! I'm sure no one meant to offend you. And, no, I didn't feel objectified."

"Must be nice to have the stereotyping work in your favor all the time," Jane grumbled. "Or to be able to ignore it so easily. Even Sam gave me a hard time! He said he would never have figured me as a sucker for a pretty face."

"He must be a brave man to risk saying something like that to you," I said, only partly kidding. "Did you take him apart?"

"Not really. I told him your looks were a side benefit and not even close to the best thing about you, gorgeous though you are. He looked crestfallen and said he didn't want to hear it." She sounded satisfied. "Did you like him?"

"I did. I liked Julie, too. That reminds me—you gave me a look when Julie asked me if I'd heard as much about Sam as she'd heard about you." We stopped at a corner to wait for the light to change and I looked down at her. "Do you remember? What was that about?"

She nodded as she turned up her coat collar. "I thought Julie's comment had an edge—like she wasn't all that pleased that Sam talked about me so much or she had some concern about him and me or something. Her comment struck me as pointed, maybe even antagonistic, and I wondered if you thought so, too."

"Nope. You do talk about Sam a lot. That's why I was looking forward to meeting him. Julie probably felt the same way."

"Maybe," Jane said as we stepped off the curb. "But I got the definite impression that she was less than pleased. What she said also made me wonder how you were feeling about being a spouse instead of yourself. Did you get the 'beside the point' feeling?"

"I did, but I liked it," I told her. "It was relaxing. Besides, it's not a matter of being a spouse instead of myself. I *am* a spouse."

"You know what I mean," she said impatiently.

"Yeah, but I don't agree. It was great to be at your side, watching you shine. It always is. It makes me proud of you and gratified that you chose me."

Jane sighed. "OK, just so you know," she said, "now I feel bad for arguing with you after you've said something so nice and supportive, but don't you have to admit that it's easy for you to feel that way because you know no one is dismissing you as *only* a spouse?"

"Maybe. But you can do the same thing. You can just ignore the possibility that people might be dismissing you. You aren't only a spouse—what do you care if some dope mistakenly assumes otherwise at a Firm event or a softball game or anywhere else?"

"I know—I probably shouldn't care. I do get less frustrated than I used to. But it irritates me when people figure I can't possibly be interesting or there's nothing to me other than my spouse just because I'm a woman. I *hate* to be pigeonholed unfairly and then ignored."

"I didn't feel pigeonholed or ignored. I just felt like I wasn't the center of attention. I was basking in your reflected glory instead of having to be 'on.'" I squeezed her arm. "I'm used to that feeling, you know. I get labeled as my dad's son all the time. That's never bothered me either. It's always been a plus."

"Being labeled your father's son is hardly the same thing as being labeled my husband. He's in the stratosphere!"

"I'm just as proud to be labeled your husband. More so, in some ways. My connection to him is just luck, but you and I chose each other."

Jane stopped walking, stood stock still and looked up at me, an expression of complete incredulity on her face. "I cannot believe you actually said that!" she exclaimed. "You really mean it, too, don't you?"

"Of course I do."

"You are completely wonderful," she said, still looking astonished. "Best husband imaginable!"

She pulled on my coat lapels and reached up to kiss me. I'd been wanting to kiss her for hours; she obviously felt the same way, and we got a little carried away.

After a couple minutes, she murmured, "Maybe I should let you carry me after all."

"Any time," I said, moving to pick her up.

She skipped away. "Not quite yet," she smiled. "We're almost home."

She finally let me pick her up in the elevator on the way up to our apartment. Actually, I had no choice—she jumped into my arms and passionately kissed my face and neck. After we got home and made love, she curled up next to me, her head resting on the arm I had circled around her. She was so quiet for so long that I thought she had fallen asleep.

I was nearly asleep myself when she said, not sounding the slightest bit sleepy, "Can I tell you two things?"

"If you have to," I said, without opening my eyes.

She shoved me gently. "I don't have to, but I really want to. I think I just recognized an interesting parallel and it's led me to a paradox."

I groaned. "Your brain's like my lucky star, isn't it? Never takes a break."

"Oh, my brain took a break. Didn't you notice?"

I opened my eyes and smiled at her.

"Anyway," she said, sounding frighteningly alert, "I was thinking about how strange it was that Julie seemed threatened by how much Sam and I like each other. It never occurred to me that you might feel that way. Now that she's brought it up and I've had to think about it, I'm certain you don't. Then, that reminded me of Jennifer flirting with you. She just can't help herself, can she?" Jane rolled her eyes. "But the point is, when I thought about why stuff like that doesn't bother either of us, I realized it's because we trust each other."

"Right."

She smiled and kissed my arm. "So I started feeling bad for Sam that he and Julie may not have the kind of trust that makes you sure about where you stand with someone, and that made me wonder how anyone could be in an intimate relationship at all without that kind of trust. But then I realized it's not only intimate relationships. Being approached with distrust makes people uncomfortable under any circumstances. The reason Julie's comment bugged me was the implication that she didn't trust *me*, not that she didn't trust Sam. And so I felt awkward with her, and a little put off. There's the parallel."

"Huh?"

"Intelligent question," she said sarcastically. "You are groggy, aren't you?"

"Very. Is there any chance you can contain this until tomorrow?"

"I don't think so," she said, looking slightly apologetic as she sat up. "I want to get it said and see where it goes. Can you stick with me for a few more minutes? Please?"

"I'll try, but I have to tell you, all this being spectacular and wonderful is wearing me out."

"Don't think I don't appreciate it." She rubbed my chest softly. "OK, here goes. The truth is that there's nothing inappropriate about Sam's and my relationship. If Julie's concerned, it has to be because she's making assumptions due to lack of trust.

"Leaving aside why she doesn't trust Sam, she's also assuming something negative about me—I imagine because 'conventional wisdom' says men and women don't have close relationships that aren't intimate or sexual. She also doesn't know me, so she doesn't know I would never cheat on my husband or try to steal someone else's. Her distrust is understandable, if unwarranted, and she was civil, but I resented being distrusted. That's part one of the parallel. Are you with me?"

"Yes, darling." I sat up and leaned back against the headboard. "I don't think she's actually all that concerned, but I see what you mean. What's part two?"

"Part two starts in the same place. Julie's lack of trust made me feel prickly and like maybe I should defend myself, even though I know I have nothing to apologize for. Just like I feel prickly and hostile around strangers who demean or dismiss me because I'm a woman or serious or smart or whatever."

She looked at me keenly. "Here comes the paradox. Are you ready?"

"Well," I said, running my hand down the front of her body, "I am a little distracted."

She grabbed my wrist. "Concentrate!" she said sharply, but she was smiling. "I've always believed that my instinctive distrust—and my vigilance—were warranted because experience tells me chances are good that people will make negative assumptions about me, given my gender and my career choices. Just like your instinctive trust is possible largely because you can be pretty certain people will think well of you.

"But, in fact," she continued excitedly, giving my wrist an emphatic little squeeze, "you could actually get away with more distrust precisely because of your golden status, and I'd actually be better off if I were more trusting. When I act like I don't trust people, the ones who don't deserve it probably feel as prickly and uncomfortable with me as I felt with Julie. And that creates yet more negativity for me to deal with!"

"That's not just a paradox. It's an epiphany!"

"Glad you like it," she said, grinning. "I'm sure it sounds familiar to you. Can you wait a little longer before you tell me to just wise up and trust everyone unless and until they prove they don't deserve it?"

"A minute or two, maybe."

"Thank you." She kissed my hand, then let go of it. "I realize that your 'you get what you give' thing is part of this. And I've wondered before if trust is all more of a cause and effect circle than seems obvious."

"I think it is."

"Of course you do, Mr. Way Too Trusting," she smiled. "You're a perfect example of someone who trusts instinctively. But I'm different. Absent evidence that I can trust people, I assume they're thinking the worst—or at least something not wholly positive. I do feel ignored or belittled. Whether it's justified or not isn't the point—just like the truth about Sam and me has nothing to do with Julie's feeling threatened."

Jane made a summarizing motion with her hands (a businesslike gesture so at odds with her nakedness that it made me smile) and said, "So. Both my nature and the sexism I've spent my life battling make me more inclined to distrust, but doing so probably worsens my situation. Distrust breeds distrust. And it punishes everyone, including me, for small-minded attitudes."

"Well said! So what are you going to do about it?"

"That's the big question. I don't have a clue how to go about doing it, but I'd like to change my default from distrust to trust. My usual approach is backwards. The narrow-minded are going to think what they think no matter what I do, but that's not a reason to distrust everybody. The group of people *not* actually out to make things harder for me may not be the biggest group in the world, but it's the wrong group to punish. It would be smarter to apply the selectivity to distrusting than to trusting."

"Much smarter," I said, nodding. "And changing your default is just a mindset. Assume the best instead of the worst while you're looking for evidence. You can always circle the wagons if distrust proves to be the right response for someone, but it's a lot harder to undo if it's the wrong one."

"We can wait until tomorrow to argue about tactics, Pollyanna," she said, grinning.

"Thank God!" I completed my slide back to horizontal. "Can we go to sleep now?"

"There's one more thing," she said, lying down beside me. "Don't look at me like that! It's shorter and easier. I just want to thank you."

"For what?"

"For everything. For staying awake and listening to me. For being the perfect accessory and actually enjoying the 'beside the point' feeling. For not pointing out that the revelation I've just had is something you've tried to tell me a thousand times. For constantly saying—and meaning—incredibly supportive and beautiful things. For being proud of me. For always being someone I could trust. For being the best husband imaginable. I love you so much."

She had started out sounding ironic, but by the time Jane finished her list, she looked and sounded serious, even emotional. I felt pretty touched myself. I couldn't think of any words that seemed adequate, so I hugged her tightly and told her I loved her, too. Several times.

❖ ❖ ❖

CLAIRE'S TWINS were born in February, about a month early. They were small, but otherwise healthy and after just a week in the hospital Claire and Stephen were able to take them home.

Along with the rest of my family, Jane and I visited Claire and the babies in the hospital. She looked tired and kind of depleted, but she and Stephen were flying high. They seemed both shell-shocked and deliriously happy. Claire was maintaining her wise-cracking "can you believe this has really happened to me" attitude, but it was obvious that she had fallen for the twins (if not for certain of the realities of motherhood) in a big way.

Her description of the delivery was hair-raising. I knew from talking to Stephen on the phone that there had, in fact, been a few frightening hours, but I chalked the grislier aspects of Claire's account up to her flair for the dramatic (and hoped Jane was doing the same). Claire was also theatrical (and pretty funny) on the mechanics of trying to breastfeed two babies, a logistical nightmare she gave up on a few weeks later.

A couple months after the twins were born, Claire called to ask if Jane and I would be willing to come over the following weekend and babysit with them overnight. She said she could not be responsible for the consequences if she and Stephen didn't get a night off, a chance for some uninterrupted sleep, and five minutes to reintroduce themselves to each other as people rather than parents.

We'd all been concerned about how Claire would handle motherhood. She'd resisted having kids for a long time and, throughout her pregnancy, she'd made it clear that she was apprehensive. It didn't seem likely that she'd fall apart, but she liked her professional life as a doctor and she was used to being the center of attention.

She'd said many times before Sean and Mia were born that she didn't relish the notion of being at the beck and call of a couple of boring, needy newborns instead of at work where she called the shots. Stephen had always lavished his attention on her, too. It wasn't hard to foresee that she might resent being pushed aside, even by her own kids.

She seemed to be doing fine—a conclusion verified by Hannah, who was spending a fair amount of time with her—but giving her a break still seemed like a good idea. Somewhat to my surprise, Jane agreed with me that taking care of the babies sounded fun. When I told Claire she had a deal, she said with great excitement that she felt just like a teenager before her first date—and was, accordingly, taking her head out of the oven.

She and Stephen had a roomy vintage apartment in the city. Before the twins, there was never much around the apartment other than the furniture, the art on the walls, and lots of books. When Jane and I showed up for our weekend of babysitting, I was amused to see that there was clutter everywhere. Baby paraphernalia and gifts for the twins, both opened and still wrapped, were all over the place.

In the midst of more disorder than I would have guessed she could tolerate, Claire sat on the couch cooing to Mia. Stephen, with Sean, had come to the door to let us in. The babies had changed a lot in the three weeks since we'd seen them. Mia looked more like Stephen than ever and she also seemed to have his thoughtful, observant personality. Sean was bigger and very interactive. I was willing to bet that he would prove to have Claire's personality as well as her looks.

Claire handed Mia to me as soon as I was close enough to take her. "I feel like I'm being released from jail," she said. "I'm tempted to get up, grab Stephen and race out of here right this minute, but I can't quite make myself do it without giving you some instructions first."

"Don't let her fool you," Stephen said, grinning. "Now that today's actually here, she's not sure she can leave them after all."

"Oh, I can leave them," Claire said. "I just want to be sure these two rubes know what they're doing before I do."

"Come on, Claire," I teased. "How hard can it be? You feed them, change them and put them in their cribs—oh, and try not to drop them, too, right?"

"Yeah, that's it, smart ass," Claire said, standing up. "Good luck."

I would have called her bluff, but Jane took pity on her and said, "I could use some instructions, Claire. I promise I won't drop anyone, but I really am a rube."

With a triumphant sneer for me, Claire took Jane off to the nursery. I sat on the couch, rested Mia on my legs, and asked Stephen how things were going. He said he and Claire were having a great time, except for needing sleep badly. The twins were sleeping for longer stretches than they had in the beginning, but he said there still weren't many occasions when everyone in the apartment was asleep.

Stephen was worried about Claire going back to work, which she planned to do in another two weeks. He'd taken almost a month off right after Sean and Mia were born, and he said he'd actually been less tired then. Despite the chaos and at least one of the twins being awake nearly all the time, he and Claire had been able to nap for an hour or two whenever things were quiet. He said the nighttime squalling was much harder to handle after he went back to work. He doubted Claire would handle it calmly.

He was hoping she'd be willing to scale back from full-time if it proved to be too much for her. She could easily do this—she ran her own practice and could always schedule fewer patients. Stephen laughed ruefully and said someone was going to have to scale back unless Mary Poppins suddenly appeared. Apparently, the process of interviewing nannies was not going well.

Claire and Jane came back into the living room just as Stephen said this. Claire rolled her eyes. "Really, you wouldn't believe it," she said. "You wouldn't hire most of these people to water your plants, let alone to take care of your children! Despite our cultural reverence for mother- hood, we evidently don't take child care seriously at all! Anyone who thinks it has any real status should interview nannies. There are no screening criteria and everyone is considered qualified based on nothing more than the willingness to do the job."

"Aren't you using agencies to screen candidates?" Jane asked. She sat on the edge of the couch next to me and stroked Mia's little head.

"Sadly, yes," Claire said. "I can't even imagine what we'd be seeing if we'd put an ad in the paper." She shook her head. "The ones we're interviewing next week better be more like it! I'm dying to get back to work! You two aren't interested in taking care of these kids permanently, are you?"

We assured her that we weren't, but promised to do our best for the next 24 hours. Claire and Stephen left a few minutes later, after an elaborate process of saying goodbye to the twins that included a lot of hugging and kissing, instructions to be good and a detailed itinerary (all as if the babies actually had some ability to take in the advice or use the information).

Jane, who had taken Sean from Stephen, looked at me and said, "Yikes! Now what do we do?"

"Don't look so shocked," I told her, smiling. "We don't have to do anything as long as they're quiet."

"Claire mentioned so many eventualities. I kind of got the impression there was always something you had to be doing."

"She's just hyper. Look at them—don't they seem fine?"

Jane agreed that they did, then said, "Do you remember that conversation we had a few years ago about marriage? When we argued about its disproportionate and disproportionately defining impact on women?"

"Seems to me we argued about that more than once."

"Yeah, we did," she smiled. "Before we married each other anyway. I'm remembering the one at the seafood place. I was sure marriage, love, sex, etcetera were a bad deal for women because of something inherent about them, and you were sure it was more a matter of choosing well and making a good deal."

"Yeah, I remember that. Are you bringing it up to admit I was right and you were wrong?"

"Not exactly," she said, giving me a sarcastic, amused look. "You were right about marriage, at least for us, but I was just thinking that where kids are concerned, the impact on women really is much greater. And it's not something you can diminish much by choosing well and making a good deal."

Jane put Sean down on the blanket Claire had spread on the floor and then slid off the couch and sat next to him. "Look at Claire and Stephen," she said, looking up at me. "A lot has changed for him, obviously, but he's still physically the same person and he's still the same person at work. In his own mind and everyone else's. But for Claire, things aren't just suddenly different at home the way they are for Stephen. And it's not just a matter of having to adjust to thinking of herself as a parent in the same way he does either. Claire *is* physically different. I bet she feels much more changed than Stephen does."

Jane glanced down at Sean, then, to his delight, played with his legs while she talked. "Claire's also the one who seems to be managing everything—you know, where the bottles are, where the diapers are, the twins' schedule, that kind of thing. She's in charge. If they can't find a nanny, she's the one who won't be able to go back to work, don't you think?"

"Probably, but that's as much because she takes control as because she's the mother."

"I don't think so." Jane shook her head. "I really think the responsibilities fall more on the mother. Stephen is great, and he's obviously very involved—I'm not criticizing him at all—but I think the big changes affect Claire more. It's what your mother said last summer. Like pregnancy, child care seems to fall more in the mother's camp than the father's. Even for someone like Claire and even leaving aside work issues and what other people may think."

"Are you trying to tell me something?" I asked, giving her my version of the sarcastic, amused look.

She laughed. "Relax," she said. "I'm just thinking aloud. Having kids is what it is. I'm just trying to understand it, to know how to think about it."

"That's the most positive thing you've ever said about having kids! I'm very encouraged."

"Don't get excited. I don't see us doing it any time soon."

I put Mia down next to Sean and joined Jane on the floor. "There's no rush, honey," I said, touching her leg.

"Good. It all seems very complicated to me and definitely something for later. Much later." She smiled at the babies, then looked back at me and said, "Oh that reminds me. I meant to tell you that I told Cheryl to call you. She and I had lunch yesterday. Amanda's nearly a year-and-a-half old, can you believe it? Cheryl wants to come back to the Firm, but she doesn't want to commit to the normal double-time schedule. We talked about it for a while and came up with kind of a cool idea."

"Something part-time?" I asked, frowning. "That hasn't worked for the few people who've tried it."

"The few *women*, you mean," Jane retorted. "It hasn't worked because people are too rigid about it. The Firm thinks you have to do everything the 'normal' way and the part-time people get very inflexible about working certain days and being off certain days. Obviously, that doesn't work in a transactional business. But Cheryl and I were thinking, what if you looked at it in a more macro way?"

"What do you mean?"

"What if instead of agreeing to work certain days each week, she committed to work a certain number of hours per year or do a certain number of deals, whichever makes more sense for the Firm. When she's working on a deal, she'll work nights and weekends like everyone else, but she'll do fewer deals each year. That way, the clients she works with will still get what they need and she'll still be back in the loop, but she'll also have more flexibility and more time off."

"How would the money work?"

"I assume you'd figure out the percentage of what the Firm considers full-time she'll be working, then pay her that percentage of what you'd pay a full-time person with her skills and seniority." Jane put the rattle back in Sean's hands. "She's very efficient, so the Firm would probably get more than it was paying for that way, but she'd be OK with the 'extra' discount because she'd have more control over her time."

"That is a cool idea!" I looked up from the babies, who were wriggling happily on the blanket. "I doubt we would agree to do it for just anyone, but, with her, we'd know we were getting someone great. And someone we could trust to take good care of clients even if she isn't working full-time. But she wants to go back to the IPO group, doesn't she? Why'd you tell her to call me? Owen runs that group—it'll be his decision."

Jane rolled her eyes. "Don't be naïve, darling. Owen doesn't know Cheryl from a hole in the wall. He seems like a good guy, and I know you think he is—which I told her—but if you were to coach her on how to approach him and put in a good word for the idea, she'd have a much better chance of getting him to agree."

"Sure, I'd be happy to. I can let him know that Jim thinks highly of her, too."

"See?" she said happily. "I knew you'd make it happen!"

"I appreciate your confidence," I said, laughing, "but it hasn't happened yet. The Firm will have all kinds of objections—from the overhead still being full-time to setting a dangerous precedent."

"But if you and Jim and Owen want it to happen, it will," she declared. "Who's going to stand up to the three of you and tell you you can't do what you want in your own group? And their objections about setting a bad precedent are bullshit. This will set a great precedent! Cheryl will make it work and every other woman who thinks having a baby means giving up her career at the Firm will have another option. The Firm will probably retain a few women it wouldn't otherwise and actually benefit from the investment it's made in them instead of wasting it!"

"Good point. Maybe you should come argue in favor of the idea to the Executive Committee."

"Who, me?" Jane said, grinning. "I'm just a wife. Who's going to listen to me?"

As if she disapproved of Jane's comment, Mia started crying. In an apparent show of solidarity, Sean joined her. Suddenly, it was incredibly noisy. Jane scrambled to her feet and said they were probably hungry. I got up too, picked up Sean, and asked Jane to hand Mia to me. While Jane heated up some bottles, I walked around with both twins. They were quiet as long as I kept moving, but they wouldn't let me stand still or sit. Every time I tried, they started howling again.

The next few hours flew by. Jane was amazing. She had evidently taken in Claire's instructions and she handled everything in her usual organized and capable way. After we fed the twins, we played with them for a while and then got them ready for bed. This included bathing them, a process that involved a lot of laughing and splashing as we held on to their slippery little bodies.

Once everyone was dry, Mia fell asleep right away, but Sean needed some coaxing. Jane sat with him in Claire's rocking chair and rocked him to sleep. The nursery was peaceful and dim. I leaned against the wall and enjoyed the view.

After a minute or two of rocking, Jane looked up at me. She smiled and shook her head. "Get that look off your face, OK?" she said softly. "It's coercive."

"What look?"

"That sappy, sentimental, 'this is so beautiful' look. You're pretending this baby is ours, aren't you?"

"Sort of," I admitted, grinning.

"Please don't push me."

"I'm not pushing you, honey," I promised. "But this is fun, isn't it?"

"It is, actually," she said, gently stroking Sean's head. "They're very lovable. And taking care of them hasn't been hard at all. I know you were teasing Claire before, but other than needing to have a lot of stuff and knowing where everything is, there really doesn't seem to be much more to it than feeding them, changing them and putting them in their cribs."

She laughed quietly. "Of course, one night probably isn't very representative of the real deal. You know, being responsible for all this day-in and day-out until they're eighteen and also trying to make sure they become happy, productive, independent people."

"No, probably not. It isn't hard to see how it could get tiring and even a little overwhelming."

"Are you actually admitting there might be more to it than romance and a few diapers?"

"I know there's more to it, a lot more, but I really am enjoying this. It's fun to do it with you."

"It's fun to do it with you, too," she murmured, looking down at Sean with a very soft smile.

❖ ❖ ❖

LYNN CALLED ME in mid-May from Chicago, where she was closing a deal for one of our best clients.

After assuring me that the closing was going well, she said, "I think you should come out here tomorrow for the closing dinner. We're having some trouble with the new General Counsel. I don't think he's a bad guy, but he has strong ties to another investment bank. He's making noises about cost and top-level commitment to the company. Luckily, Tom isn't paying much attention to him, but a well-timed visit by our magnificent head of M&A couldn't hurt."

Tom was the client company's CEO. I had originated the company's business for the Firm, and Tom was my original contact. I knew he was happy with Lynn in the relationship manager role I had given her when I took over M&A. I doubted the Firm's relationship with the company was in any serious danger.

But CEOs always paid at least some attention to the opinions of new members of their senior team. There was no reason to bring in a new person if you weren't going to listen to what he had to say and try to benefit from his fresh perspective. And the Firm's relationship with the top lawyer at a company was often iffy. Many companies seemed to view the General Counsel more as an impediment to the deal process than as a member of the deal team. Even in those situations, though, the lawyers weren't without power, so we had to approach them carefully.

We couldn't ignore them, which wouldn't have been politic anyway. Given the movement from company to company in the corporate world, they could end up anywhere and there was no reason for us to make enemies. Also, whatever his or her relative power in the company, the General Counsel often had the CEO's ear.

This was probably true in Tom's case. He'd been relieved when his former GC decided to leave, and he'd told me he was looking for a replacement with business acumen who could be a real counselor to the executive team (as opposed to a stuffy legal expert like the old guy). Judging by the press release announcing the new GC's arrival a couple weeks before, the new guy appeared to fit that bill.

It also didn't surprise me that the new GC was recommending another investment bank. That often happened when new people came on board; they usually had loyalties to someone they'd worked with before. I appreciated Lynn's sensitivity to the issue and her suggestion that we use the closing dinner as a smooth way to bring me into the picture and let me work the GC. My calendar was clear enough for a trip to Chicago the following day and night, so I got my secretary started on rescheduling a few meetings and making travel arrangements.

That underway, I put my feet up on my desk and spent half an hour on the phone with Lynn. She brought me up to speed on the deal's specifics and players, and gave me her take on the best approach to the General Counsel.

"Basically," she said, "we have two problems with this guy—in addition to his desire to use a firm he's already comfortable with and that would owe its access to him. I'm sure he would love to have bankers who viewed him, rather than Tom, as their principal contact. But our particular problems stem from the kind of guy he is."

"Which is?"

With a derisive laugh that reminded me of Jane, Lynn said, "The kind who doesn't take women seriously and finds associates like Colin too unprepossessing."

Colin was a terrific associate—smart and creative, and an incredibly hard worker—but he was a small, quiet, balding guy whom clients and, occasionally, colleagues overlooked. Jane had put it well: Colin was impressive in substance, but not in form. His reticent demeanor and rather humorless focus on getting the job done were disadvantages in a business where glad-handing was essential, if not paramount.

It was as important in our business to be personally impressive—and an enjoyable dinner companion—as it was to have the required expertise. Lynn was great on these fronts. I'd asked her to staff Colin on the deal in part to give her a chance to coach him and to give him a good example to study and follow. I asked her how he was doing.

"Better," she said, "but he's no world-beater. Definitely not someone who can wow this particular GC. I'm not really getting anywhere with the guy either. He doesn't consider me a peer, despite the fact that Tom and the rest of the team obviously do. In his world view, I can't possibly be a big shot. He has a tendency to look around for someone more important whenever we talk."

She sounded like she was smiling as she added, "You'll wow him, Mr. Perfect."

"I'll do my best," I promised, laughing. "Let Tom know I'm coming, would you?"

"Will do," Lynn said. "I'll also tell him why. He'll appreciate the gesture."

I told Jane about the trip and the reasons for it at dinner that night. After she ranted about men who couldn't see past someone like Lynn's gender to her impressive skills, Jane had some great ideas for dealing with the new GC. In particular, she advised against identifying myself too plainly with the CEO. Based on what Lynn had said, Jane thought the more effective approach was to the General Counsel directly. She was sure he would be flattered—and swayed—if he knew I'd made the trip on his account.

She pointed out that my involvement could backfire if the GC viewed my arrival as a power play designed to defend the Firm's position by trying to thwart his connections or competing with him for the CEO's attention. By playing to the GC instead—and thereby acknowledging *his* importance at the company—Jane felt I could not only defend the Firm's position, but also create a new supporter.

I thought about how best to do this on my way to the airport the next day. I was really looking forward to it. It was good to get out of the office and out of the city, particularly to meet the challenge of "wowing" clients, all things I didn't get to do as often after I took over M&A.

When I got to the airport, I was taken aback to find Annemarie waiting for the same plane. We hadn't seen each other in years. She was as gorgeous as ever and as unmindful of the stares and murmurs she generated in the waiting area and then on the plane, where we sat together after she sweet-talked the ticket agent into reassigning seats.

I had forgotten how intense the scrutiny was when Annemarie was around. As we caught up with each other, I kept noticing people staring at us. According to my wife, I generated a fair amount of the same kind of scrutiny myself, but I never noticed it. It seemed to be Annemarie's obliviousness that brought it to my attention. She continued to wear her beauty like a shield, with the curious result that it was even more notice-able to everyone but her.

As it turned out, she was also as available and as interested as she'd been on our first plane trip together. Neither my wedding ring nor my description of myself as very happily married deterred her. As before, she was looking for no-strings sex and she reminded me, subtly and then more directly, of how good we'd been together. I remembered that well (and with pleasure) and Annemarie was just as hot as she'd been on that first trip. I spent a couple minutes considering the possibilities.

Later, alone in my hotel room, I thought about why I'd turned her down. The obvious reason was that I loved and respected Jane and wouldn't have slept with someone else even if I'd wanted to. What inter-ested me was that I *hadn't* wanted to. Annemarie was sexy and insignificant, and Jane would never have known, but I wasn't even tempted.

I already had everything I wanted.

CHAPTER 19

CONSOLIDATION AND EXPANSION

Jane

The rotational part of the BEL program turned out to be fun, if unrepresentative of real work. Dropping into and then, soon after, out of departments and divisions had a transactional project feel to it that reminded me of working on deals at the Firm.

I learned a lot about the personalities of the various areas of the Company—and of the people who worked in those areas—but I never felt really connected with any of them. People were nice enough to me, and they were very respectful (something I heard from other BELs was consistent across the board), but I always felt like a guest rather than a working member of the group.

It was interesting to recognize how much I'd changed since I'd left the Firm. I could now see the drawbacks of the "renter" (versus "owner") style that I'd enjoyed so much at the Firm. I still enjoyed the rhythm and the challenges of moving from one project to another. And never being bored was fantastic. But it had become very important to me to accomplish something more lasting than the corporate equivalent of closing a deal.

A deal is self-contained. It has a defined result, a well-understood process and a short timeline. That all creates certain pressures and it isn't for everyone, but for those of us who like working under the gun and knowing quickly and indisputably whether we've succeeded or failed, it's an exciting and gratifying way to work.

It wasn't easy to make the change to a slower pace and more incremental results. Charlie and I talked about this a lot. Like me, he was inclined toward deal work and he tended to get bored when he had to contend with the same people and the same issues for more than a few months. Also like me, however, he wanted to be more than a gun for hire.

Most of our friends loved being guns for hire. Lynn, Jordan, Katherine, Patrick, Cheryl (who was now happily and successfully working part-time at the Firm along the lines I had helped develop and Charlie had helped implement), among many others, all flourished on deal work. They certainly set examples that were beneficial to their employers, but none of them was interested in taking on a formal leadership role.

Charlie told me that Jim had sounded out Jordan on running the IPO group before he'd hired Owen. Jordan had decided the role was too administrative for his taste. Charlie found this decision surprising and short-sighted, but it didn't surprise me. Jordan was a perfect example of someone who thrived on pressure. Also, while he was very loyal to the Firm, he had no particular zeal for owning or managing it.

He and Katherine had this in common. They weren't organizationally focused. They continued to be absorbed in one another, and the busy, stop-start pace of transactional work provided them with a frame for their life together that they found pleasurable and stimulating. Jordan didn't view turning down the IPO group head job as a career-limiting decision. Quite the opposite, he viewed accepting it as a life-limiting decision.

In my opinion, the difference between his approach and Charlie's and mine was what one of the BEL workshop speakers called "organizational ambition." The speaker's thesis was that all effective leaders, no matter how personally ambitious, were at heart motivated by the desire to make great something bigger than themselves. Those who became true leaders, he asserted, were not content with personal power, glory or wealth. They might well welcome those rewards, but they couldn't and didn't consider themselves successful unless they had also changed their surroundings—be those a company, a country or the world—for what they considered to be the better.

I thought Charlie was a great example of this kind of leader. He was a very successful investment banker at the deal level. He could easily have continued in that role and still had plenty of power; ditto with making plenty of money. And he affirmatively disliked many aspects of heading M&A. He was frequently annoyed by administrative requirements and frequently frustrated by the too-familiar bureaucratic stodginess of the Executive Committee, which he largely ignored while doing deal work, but had to cope with all the time as a group head.

But Charlie was driven by his desire to make the Firm a better place, to realize his vision of a Firm that, by virtue of benefiting inclusively from all the resources available to it, was a wildly successful force in the marketplace and a great place to work (no matter what you looked like). For him, this vision was pressing and compelling—he *had* to work to make it a reality. It wasn't his nature to be obsessed, but his desire to transform the Firm shaped every work-related thing he did.

I was sure this desire was what made him so successful as head of M&A. It may well have been what got him into the job in the first place. His charisma, his personal success on deals and with client development, and (I teased him) his pretty face didn't hurt, but people—particularly deal junkies like the majority of the people who worked at the Firm—would never have gotten behind him and enthusiastically followed his lead if they'd thought personal triumph was all he cared about or even what he cared about most.

The speaker at our leadership workshop verified that most people were followers rather than leaders, but he made the additional point that even followers wouldn't follow just anyone. He said followers expected leaders to have feet of clay and were always on the lookout for the evidence that would prove their leaders were really more interested in personal glory than in the kind of organizational glory that benefited everyone.

According to the speaker, this gloomy combination of examination and pessimism was one of the key reasons real leadership was rare. Not only was the constant scrutiny disturbing and off-putting to would-be leaders, but the constant expectation that you would fall short often proved hurtful, disillusioning and even depressing. You had to be made of pretty stern stuff and have a very strong sense of vision and commitment to withstand these downsides of leadership—and to steer clear of doing anything that would be perceived as solid evidence that you were, as a leader, the usual disappointment rather than the real deal.

In Charlie's case, it seemed to me that his relaxed nature made these leadership downsides relatively trivial. His golden boy advantages obviously didn't hurt either—because he looked the part, plenty of people gave him the benefit of the doubt. But even when people were watching him to see if he would trip (and, in at least a few cases, hoping for the stumble), he rarely noticed it. When it did catch his attention, it didn't bother him. Nor did he find upsetting, nerve-wracking or even annoying any expectation that he would prove ultimately to be a selfish opportunist. He just blithely and self-confidently went about the business of doing what he believed was right.

As always, I mulled over how to apply his example to managing my own career. I didn't have a relaxed nature and I was about as far from being a golden boy as it was possible to be. The downsides of constant scrutiny and negative assumptions had already been driving me crazy for years.

It also seemed to me that my organizational ambition was itself more personal than Charlie's. I wanted to prove that talented, skilled women and, by extension, others who didn't fit the traditional profile were every bit as valuable and could be just as successful in the business world as the white men who typically succeeded and who still ran that world.

Charlie thought our organizational ambitions were of the same nature and that mine was no more personal or less organizational because I happened to be one of the disadvantaged people who would benefit from the changes I sought to bring about. He accused me of thinking too conventionally when I suggested that his ambition looked— and maybe was—more altruistic because of his starting point.

He believed the benefits he would reap personally from realizing his vision were just as significant as the benefits I would reap, despite the advantages he enjoyed under the system we were trying to change. He pointed out that exclusionism, inequality of opportunity and slavish adherence to the status quo hurt everyone, including the people perpetrating them. The essence of the problem with the narrow-minded, he insisted, was their short-sighted inability to see that what looked to them like self-preservation was in actuality what would ultimately wipe them out, given its limiting and destructive impact on the organizations they counted on to sustain them.

I couldn't argue with this (and I admired him hugely for believing it), but I felt instinctively that the desire that motivated me was less altruistic and more personal. This troubled me and made me reconsider my goal and my reasons for wanting to achieve it. I had wanted to be a huge success in the business world practically since I was a child. Now I asked myself why. What was the purpose behind what I was trying to accomplish?

I knew that part of what fueled my determination to succeed was my desire to prove I could to all the people who seemed to think otherwise or to want to stop me. Closed ranks drove me nuts. I hated being kept out or categorized or thwarted by expectations that had nothing to do with my personal competence or dedication. More than once, I had responded to "What motivates you?" by saying, "Because it's there and because I can."

Was I still trying to prove to my father that girls weren't second-class citizens? If so, who was that about? The world needs women among its leaders, and my successes would continue to have a positive impact on the availability of opportunities for other women, but wouldn't that be merely a side benefit of having proved that I, at least, didn't deserve to be overlooked?

I decided I had to recast my goal and my own sense of what motivated it. I had to sift out goals that were too personal, too exclusively about me. I wanted to become the kind of example that inspired other people and opened their eyes, not the kind they could effortlessly reject as self-serving or inimitable or out of the mainstream. It wouldn't be enough to carve out a foothold for myself or even to ascend to the top if the path I took erased itself behind me.

I wanted to throw my foothold and my path into high relief, to make them evident, difficult to reject and part of the regular fabric of business life. The changes I sought to bring about would become a reality only if and when people generally—other women to be sure, but, equally importantly, men—believed as a matter of course that a career like mine was just one more of many options routinely available to anyone with the talent and desire to pursue it—as opposed to something unusual for anyone other than a certain kind of man.

I wanted the women who came after me to have it easier, to feel a sense of comfort and welcome and belonging. I wanted them to have a better map and to experience less frustration along the way. I wanted them to feel less pressure to conform by renouncing part of the unique value they brought to the party—and, thus, denying the very differences that, used effectively, were their advantages.

The point I wanted to drive home was that you *could* be different and still succeed. Diversity—whether of gender, working style, personality, background or perspective—was the positive, the desirable business benefit, not something to be homogenized into invisibility.

I decided my real goal had to be to broaden the traditional profile, to make it more "normal" for someone other than the customary white male to roam the halls of corporate office buildings, be part of the official power structure and set the tone for business activity and cultural "truth." My vision was of a meritocracy where people could freely be who they were and succeed (or not) based on what they contributed. This, it seemed to me, was where the individual and organizational benefits of diversity intersected. And it was the altruistic crux of what was driving me.

Thanks in part to what Kate had said about priorities and suiting oneself, I had also come to believe that it wouldn't do to give up anything important to achieve my success. Enormous personal sacrifice was neither necessary nor appropriate. Denying who I was or forgoing something I wanted or thought important so as to ease my climb to the top was a sucker bet.

What were the odds—really—that I would still be my whole self and capable of suddenly behaving as such if I'd spent decades pretending to be someone else? I was much more likely to become what I was pretending to be. And even if it were possible to remain whole while conforming to narrow-minded dictates, if I succeeded that way my message would effectively be "Pretend to be something you're not or you can't succeed." With that message, I wouldn't be much of an example—and I certainly wouldn't be a leader.

I wasn't looking to create yet another restrictive profile. I wanted to change the rules of the game by opening the doors. The only way to do that effectively was to succeed *by* being a whole person, my whole self— and, significantly, a woman.

Taking my gender off the table as an issue had served me well, but it was time to worry less that people *would* notice it and more that they would not.

❖ ❖ ❖

MID-SUMMER, just after we had started a new rotation, Sam and I sat in his office late one Friday afternoon, talking about leadership and how to go about demonstrating it effectively to jaded and cynical people who assumed that everyone did, in fact, have feet of clay. We were surrounded by people who seemed to believe it was human nature to have a personal agenda, and that no one really cared as much about making the Company great as about being personally powerful or revered or wealthy.

We were facing the usual mixed reception in our new groups. People were glad for the extra help BELs provided, and they were always anxious to make a good impression on someone who'd been anointed a future big shot. At the same time, though, they were defensive about what they did, as if the Company's real purpose in rotating us through their groups were to expose them as incompetent slackers. In the time-honored (and, to me, still illogical) traditions of interpersonal interaction, *they* worried about not being up to snuff and blamed *us* for their anxiety.

"What *is* their problem?" I railed to Sam after I'd pushed off my shoes and tucked my legs under me. "I feel like I've spent my whole life being blamed for other people's sense of their own shortcomings! If they don't think the way they're operating is good enough or right, why don't they fix it instead of worrying that I might point it out?"

Sam brushed this off. "You're missing the point," he said, "and taking it too personally. It's not about you. It's also not a question of them thinking what they're doing isn't good enough. Or, for that matter, thinking it *is* good enough, but worrying that someone of your superior intelligence will think otherwise. They just don't know. You're someone new looking at what they do. Naturally, they wonder if you're going to criticize it or see a better way to get it done."

"But I don't understand reacting to that so defensively. Don't they have any pride? Why don't they welcome suggestions or even constructive criticism if it will make things better? Seems to me they're the ones taking it personally—not me."

Sam shook his head. "You know people aren't confident. Most of them also don't think in a particularly big picture way. Criticism, suggestions, change—it's all the same to them: essentially, a negative review. Why *wouldn't* they take that personally?"

Before I could answer, he added, "That's one of the reasons we're BELs and they're not. They may not understand that distinction, but they sure as hell feel it. Of course they're going to resent us or be nervous around us. You're right that it has more to do with them than with us, but they're not blaming you for their shortcomings. They're just reacting. And they're the people you have to enroll in your vision if you're going to lead."

I laughed. "Enroll? You've been spending too much time with consultants."

"Sorry," Sam said, smiling, "but I'm right." He turned his chair slightly, opened one of his desk drawers and put his feet up on it as he said, "There are only two ways to get to the top. By being a ruthless, unscrupulous asshole and stepping on the backs and necks of other people or by enrolling them and getting them to hoist you on their shoulders willingly and enthusiastically. If you do it the first way, you'll probably get there, but you'll have to watch your back all the time because everyone will want to knock you down. The second way is not only more justifiable, it's safer and more dependable, too. With the support of the people you're leading, you're basically..."

"Bulletproof," I finished. "I understand that."

"So what are you whining about? You need these people, whether you admire or understand their reactions or not."

"You sound like my husband," I said, grinning. "I'm not whining. I'm venting my frustration with interpersonal bullshit and what a pain it is to have to deal with it all the time." I put my feet down and slouched in the chair, my legs out straight, ankles crossed on the floor. I'd picked up the habit of sitting this way from Charlie. I wasn't tall enough to do it comfortably for long, but it stretched my back and legs and always felt great at first.

"Who exempted you from having to deal with interpersonal bullshit?" Sam demanded, with a pointed look that also reminded me of Charlie.

"Hey, I surrender!" I held up my hands. "I don't expect not to have to deal with it. It just irritates me. It's always the same old story. It bores me. And the inefficiency drives me nuts."

"Get over it. It's the price you pay for being exceptional. Would you rather be one of the insecure masses?"

"Spoken like a true man of the people," I teased. "You're going to have to show a little more respect for those masses if you expect them to carry you to the top on their shoulders."

He laughed. "I have tremendous respect for them. However insecure or lame, they—collectively—have way more power than I do. I need them. So do you. And don't forget that change is incremental. You can't expect everyone to immediately grasp and welcome every good suggestion. Even if they could, it would still take time for them to implement it. You have to have a longer-term view. And more patience."

"Now you sound like my father-in-law." I sat up straighter and told him what Alex had said about having a long-term view of both results and cultural transformation, and how he'd put that kind of view to work at his former company.

"Wait." Sam looked thunderstruck. "He's your father-in-law?"

"Yeah," I said, surprised. "I assumed you knew that."

"No, I didn't. I guess I never focused on Charlie's last name. Wow! He's a legend! He transformed that company. I have a friend who works there, and he says your father-in-law is really smart, incredibly compelling and charismatic, and known by everyone to be a man of complete integrity and dedication to doing the right thing."

"He is all those things. He's also kind and funny and an independent thinker—and unbelievably helpful to other people, including virtual strangers." I told Sam how I'd met Alex while working on a deal and how graciously he'd helped me think about moving from the Firm to a corporate job, all long before I married Charlie.

"Do you think you could introduce me to him?" Sam asked. "I'd like to meet a legend."

"Sure. He and I get together for lunch every now and then. You could join us. Or we could do a whole evening thing sometime. Charlie's mom is great, too, and Alex is fun to see in a more personal setting."

"I'd rather have lunch with just you and him." Sam paused, looked away, then looked back at me with a discouraged expression. "Julie's still not comfortable with how great I think you are, and I'd rather not rub her nose in it."

I was sorry to hear this. He had mentioned it before, confirming my sense of Julie's concern, but not for a while. I decided to ask what I hadn't felt comfortable asking the first time. "She's not worried that we're having an affair, is she?"

"No, she knows I wouldn't cheat on her." Sam smiled sardonically and added, "Even if she had been worried about that, one glimpse of your husband was more than enough to convince her otherwise. She's still talking about how good-looking he is. She also thought he was unusually nice to her at that reception last year."

"So she doesn't trust me, but she figures no one who has Charlie would want to fool around?" I rolled my eyes. "His looks and his charm always improve how people think of me. It kills me! I never know whether to be more grateful or more offended!"

"You should be more grateful. Whatever works."

"I guess. But, Sam, if Julie knows we're not having an affair, what's her problem?"

"Her problem is our intellectual connection. And that we have so much in common." He took his fountain pen out of its fancy desk holder and flipped it back and forth through his fingers. "I made the mistake of talking too much and for too long about how smart you are and how much I like working with you. She got sick of hearing it."

"You must have talked about people at work before. You must have felt a few strong connections before, too. Why the problem with me?"

"You're the only woman."

Pretty sure I knew where we were headed (and already irate about it), I went ahead and asked, "So? If the problem is our intellectual chemistry, why should it matter that I'm a woman?"

"Don't be stupid, Jane. You know why it matters. There's no chance I'd want to leave Julie for a male colleague I really like and admire."

"I knew you were going to say that! That kind of thinking makes me crazy! It presumes that, in men's minds, women are primarily for sex or romance. It's one of the conventional excuses for keeping women out of the workplace, too. It's so unfair and *it's* what's stupid! There's no requirement that men and women consider each other romantically or sexually, nor does that inevitably happen."

"Get off your high horse, OK?" he said, with a small smile. "You just presumed the same thing when you asked if she was worried about us having an affair."

"Touché." I couldn't help smiling, despite my annoyance. "I'm apparently not exempt from thinking conventionally either. But, Sam, really, there's absolutely no reason for Julie to be threatened by your relationship with me."

"Isn't there? Not because we are something other than colleagues and friends, but theoretically?" He sat up and put the pen back in its holder, then put his elbows on his desk and massaged the back of his neck with his fingers. "It's certainly not beyond the realm of possibility that a man and a woman with a lot in common who work fantastically together might decide to take the relationship up a level. Doesn't Charlie worry about that with you? Hell, don't you worry about it with him? Judging by Julie's reaction to him—and yours—he must have smart women falling all over him."

I resisted my urge to object to the term "falling all over him" and said instead, "I'm sure he does, but I trust him. And he trusts me. Besides, it's hard to imagine either of us finding someone we have more in common with than we do with each other. We've been sounding boards and advisers for each other since a few weeks after I started working at the Firm. I told you we were colleagues and friends for a long time before we ever talked about marriage."

"So isn't that an example of exactly what Julie's worried about? You were colleagues and friends who fell for each other and took the relationship up a level."

I smiled (much less reluctantly this time). "Not exactly. We were colleagues and friends who decided collegiality and friendship were the right foundation for a marriage." I explained our marriage as merger model and how it had come about.

"Well, that's unusual," Sam said. "I see why you aren't worried about extramarital intellectual connections. But I don't believe you and Charlie got married just for those reasons. You're obviously in love with each other."

"We are, but that was an unexpected development. Seriously. It happened after we'd hammered out most of the merger terms." I grinned. "We both think of it as a bonus."

"Nice bonus," he said, his eyebrows high. "I still think your example may do more to validate Julie's concern than to negate it. But maybe I'll suggest the merger concept to her. She's the one who didn't want to get married. She thought it was institutional and sexist and unnecessary." He smiled. "I'm quoting, obviously."

"I used to feel the same way, and I still do think marriage tends to subjugate women. But Charlie turned out to be right about the downsides not being inevitable."

"You won't mind if I present the concept to Julie without attribution, will you?" Sam joked. "I don't like my odds if I start talking to her about marriage and you at the same time."

"No problem at all," I said, laughing. "Whatever works."

❖ ❖ ❖

MY OLD FIRM GIRLS' CLUB got together for drinks toward the end of the summer. Thanks to Lynn and Cheryl working at the Firm, and Katherine and I attending most of its social functions, we now saw each other more than we had since our rookie year. But we all had roles to play at Firm events. We still needed girls' club sessions to really talk.

Lynn and Cheryl already had drinks and were seated at one of those high bar tables when I arrived. I hugged them both, then climbed onto one of the two empty chairs.

"You look great, Jane!" Lynn said. "Is it work or marriage that's so clearly agreeing with you?"

"Both," I said, smiling. "This leadership development program at work is fabulous. The rotational part we're in now feels a lot like doing deals did. I love it! I'm learning about different parts of the Company, and it's also really nice to be able to say goodbye to the annoying aspects of each group after just a month."

"What comes after the rotational part?" Cheryl asked.

"Good question. There's this whole corporate production over the next step. It's kind of a matching thing. We have to rank our top three interests in terms of job type and area of the Company, then a committee of our old bosses, our executive coaches and the program directors will place us where they think is best. We're all stressing now over how to do our rankings so we don't end up someplace awful."

"What would be awful?"

"Well, there are a few groups that are total pits of despair. You know, they have an asshole manager or the people are all morons or the work is boring. We all think line jobs in the business units are probably preferable to staff jobs in the corporate groups, but we could end up with more senior positions—and in higher salary grades—in the staff groups. It's all very political, and kind of a crap shoot."

"You'll end up with something great," Lynn declared. "You always do. Speaking of that, is the perfect man still the perfect husband, too?"

"I'm embarrassed to sound so besotted," I said, grinning, "but, yeah, he pretty much is."

"Don't worry about it, Jane." Cheryl touched my arm gently. "I think it's great that you're besotted. And, if it's any consolation, Charlie sounds the same way whenever he mentions you."

"Which is often," said Lynn. She raised her eyebrows sarcastically, but she was smiling.

"OK, stop. You want me to start blushing, too?" I looked around for the waiter.

"Too late," she said crisply. "But I will change the subject slightly. I'm working on another deal for Charlie's and my Chicago client—you remember, the one with the pompous, sexist GC? Well, that jerk still wants nothing to do with me, but he's now your husband's best friend. Charlie's doing a great job of taking him off my hands, but leaving me in charge of the deal and the relationship with the CEO. He's the perfect boss, too."

"So, Lynn, are you finally willing to concede that the best thing about him is something other than the way he looks?" Cheryl teased, with a wink for me.

"I'll concede that it might be a tie," Lynn said as if she were offering a major concession.

Cheryl and I laughed, then she said to Lynn, "Let's tell her Anna's news."

"Oh, yeah, we heard from Anna last week!" Lynn paused while I ordered a tequila gimlet, then said, "Do you remember that German guy she was seeing while he was working in his company's London office? Well, they've decided to get married and move to Berlin! Anna has a new job in corporate development with a German technology company."

"We're bummed that she's leaving the Firm," Cheryl said, "but the job sounds great and Anna is really happy."

"That's so cool!" I said. "What else did she say?"

They told me what they knew about Anna's fiancé and her new job until Katherine strode up to the table a few minutes later.

"I'm so sorry," she said. "Jordan called just as I was leaving." Exchanging her apologetic look for one of irritation, she growled, "Sometimes he is such an idiot!"

"What?" Lynn said, her eyebrows high again. "Is there trouble in paradise? I thought it was all wonderful all the time for you and the ice cream man."

"Hardly," Katherine said, hopping onto a chair. "There've been plenty of times it was lucky we weren't on the roof because if we had been I'd have shoved him off it. This was one of those times."

"What's going on?" Cheryl asked.

The waiter finally remembered my drink—or perhaps it was Katherine's arrival that reminded him to bring it. She always got noticed and attended to immediately. We'd commented more than once that it was a shame she was so often the last to arrive.

After she ordered her usual Scotch (neat), she said, "Jordan's got this pushy little analyst on one of his deals who's making a play for him in a big way, and he's totally unable to deal with it effectively. He's all uncomfortable and awkward around her—totally freaked out. She's done just about everything but strip and stretch out on his desk."

"Something you've done, as I recall," Lynn drawled.

Katherine grinned. "Not quite. I was slightly more circumspect when we actually worked together."

"This is one of the Firm's analysts?" I asked.

"Yeah, the little slut!" She named the analyst, then gave the waiter (who'd of course brought her Scotch in record time) a dazzling smile.

While Katherine and the waiter negotiated a schedule for keeping our drinks refilled, I watched Lynn and Cheryl note the analyst's name and thought about how different things were when the power structure included women as well as men. The analyst was hurting herself, probably more than she imagined, by making a play for Jordan, but now there was a chance she'd get the advice she needed and wise up.

In the minds of men who learned of it, she would irrevocably be branded a plaything. That would hurt her chances of getting ahead, but most of the men at the Firm were more likely to try to exploit the situation than to address it. Even the ones who weren't interested in a fling weren't likely to take her aside and give her the frank advice she needed.

I had no doubt that Lynn or Cheryl would do just that. They were both mentors with an interest in the success of the Firm's younger women. And they were both more than familiar with the negative repercussions for all the women at the Firm of behavior like the analyst's. They would see to it that she understood the nature of the hole she was digging for herself and, unless she was a complete idiot, she would stop digging.

"Jordan is incapable of telling her straight out that he's not interested," Katherine continued, her expression now one of exasperation (which contrasted sharply with the totally infatuated look on the waiter's face as he walked away). "He'd be so much better off if he weren't so goddamn genteel! He doesn't want to hurt her feelings or embarrass her, so he's been trying to fend her off politely. That's not working, so he's running out of options. He called today to see what I thought about getting her reassigned." She rolled her eyes. "How stupid is that?"

"What did you tell him?" Lynn asked.

"Most of it isn't repeatable in polite company. Basically, I told him to stop letting her play him and to start acting like the person in charge, not to mention someone with balls. I seem to recall hissing something about being in danger of losing all respect for him, too." She sighed. "I do feel sorry for him—situations like this suck—but what is so fucking hard about looking her in the eye and telling her it's never going to happen?"

"I agree—that's his only option," Cheryl said. "But it will make finishing the deal pretty awkward."

"Please," Katherine said, waving her hand. "She's an analyst! He can ignore her completely and let the manager deal with her. So she won't get the benefit of his superior attention and coaching. After the way she's behaved, she doesn't deserve it anyway!"

"This reminds me of a question I got from my current mentee," Cheryl said. "She's got a boyfriend who's very jealous—of her and also, I think, of her career. He gets suspicious whenever she works late and crazy whenever she travels with men."

Lynn wrinkled her face in disgust and said, "She needs a new boyfriend."

"Yeah, she does," Cheryl said, smiling. "But here's what interested me. When she asked me if my husband and I had the same problem, I realized we never have. Like you, Kath, my problem with Jordan's mess would be with how he's handling it, not with any doubt about where his interests lay. So to speak."

"It's a matter of trust, don't you think?" I said. "I'm sure Charlie still has most of the opportunities he had before he started wearing a wedding ring, but I don't worry about it because I trust *him*. He knows where he stands with me, too. I can't imagine him doubting me."

"Come on, married ladies," Lynn said, pointing at us with a swizzle stick that still had one olive impaled on it. "Are you for real? Do you honestly think you're exempt from cheating or being cheated on? That your husbands will never revert to type and decide an uncomplicated fling with a bimbo might be refreshing? What about when you're fighting? What about those times when you can't remember exactly what it was you ever liked about each other?"

"Honestly, I haven't wanted anyone else since I met Jordan," Katherine said. "I love the guy, you know? No matter how moronic he's being, it's never even close to enough to outweigh that. And I know he feels exactly the same way about me."

"I agree," Cheryl said, nodding. "Richard and I go through stages where we don't like each other much at all." She smiled good-naturedly. "I know you all think I'm so mild, but Richard knows better. He's had plenty of opportunities to see my shrewish side. And he has plenty of blind spots that drive me nuts, too. But the positives of our relationship are fundamental and they completely outweigh the transient negatives."

"Also—and I trust this is true for you guys, too," Katherine said, grinning, "one of those fundamental positives is great sex. I might worry or be tempted to stray myself if sex ever got boring. But neither Jordan nor I is missing anything we need to go looking for in that department."

Lynn laughed. "Given where you started, it's hard to imagine what you're up to now to keep it from being boring!"

"What can I say?" Katherine shrugged happily. "We're hot together. Seriously, though, our marriage is tight. I honestly don't think it's susceptible to cheating. It's not just the heat. Jordan gets me. I get him, too. We're very, very content with each other."

"You know," Cheryl said, turning slightly so she could cross her legs, "the kind of man who'd marry women like us in the first place is probably not the kind who'd run rashly or cavalierly into someone else's arms anyway. No matter how ticked off with each other we were or how tempted he might be. It seems to me a man would have to have sort of a fundamental disrespect for women to cheat like that."

"I think that's the real key," I said. "Unlike your mentee and her boyfriend, we and our husbands respect each other. And we have strong intellectual connections, too."

I told them about Julie's concern with Sam's and my intellectual chemistry, then said, "When you think about it, sleeping around is just tawdry—not something men like Jordan, Richard or Charlie are really very likely to do. And certainly not something they'd do lightly. Ditto for us. But someone intellectually stimulating, with whom you felt a real connection? That would be a serious worry if we didn't already have it in our marriages."

"Yes, it would." Cheryl nodded. "That's exactly what's wrong with my mentee's relationship with her boyfriend."

"Well, this is all very inspiring," Lynn said, "if also a little nauseating. You were all awfully lucky."

"It wasn't only luck," I disputed as Lynn pulled a mirror and her lipstick out of her briefcase. "We also chose men who wanted to be partners and made a different kind of deal with them."

"Right," Cheryl said. "None of us got married for security or protection or because it's expected or for any other traditional reason that's inherently disrespectful to women. We're capable of taking care of ourselves and making our own decisions, and we married men who think that's what's great about us. They don't consider us inferior nor are they threatened by us. That's also why we're comfortable going after what we want instead of feeling constrained like my mentee."

Lynn stopped mid-application and looked disbelieving. "So you really think you can have it all, as they say?"

"Why not?" I demanded. "If by 'it all' you mean a happy marriage, a rewarding career and, eventually, kids, why the hell not? Men routinely have that so-called all. Why shouldn't we?"

"Yeah!" Katherine cheered. "Although I don't know about the kids." She smiled at Cheryl. "With all due respect to Amanda, who's adorable, kids seem like more than I want to take on."

"They do require a lot of accommodations in the rest of the 'all' we're trying to have," Cheryl smiled. "But, so far, she's been totally worth it."

"Some of those accommodations aren't so bad," Lynn said. She closed her mirror with an emphatic snap. "Your work schedule is the envy of just about everyone who knows about it. And I think it would be basically impossible for anyone but a woman with kids to get the Firm to agree to anything like it."

"Hmm," Katherine mused, "maybe I'll reconsider. Wait, Lynn—let me see that lipstick before you put it away. The color is gorgeous!"

"You know," I said as Lynn handed the lipstick to Katherine, "accommodations, good or problematic, are just part of the game. They don't make our successes less real. There's no requirement that we do things the same way men do. Women don't all have to succeed the same way either. Isn't the point to succeed while you suit yourself, to quote my inspiring mother-in-law?"

"Good Lord, Jane!" Lynn protested. "Is there *anything* wrong with that man? He even has a mother you like?"

Katherine looked up from admiring the streak of lipstick on her hand. "Now that would be having it all," she said longingly as I smiled (and probably blushed). "My mother-in-law is a fucking nightmare. She's part of the reason I don't want kids. I adore Jordan, but he's obviously an anomaly in that awful family. What if I ended up with a kid more like the rest of them than like him?"

"Much as I'd like to follow up on that point, I should go," Cheryl said. "I've got a busy day tomorrow and a trip out of town the day after that." She stood and took some money out of her bag (a gorgeous soft leather thing she'd used in place of a briefcase for years). "And after this discussion, I'm anxious to get home. I want to give Amanda a big hug and tell Richard how much I appreciate having a husband like him."

I knew exactly how she felt. I couldn't wait to see Charlie and tell him how very exemplary I thought he was.

❖ ❖ ❖

A MONTH LATER, I couldn't wait to get home to talk to Charlie for a different reason. Thanks to a mid-afternoon meeting with Bill, my old boss, I'd had the most thrilling day of my career. I'd spent the two hours since the meeting in a frenzy of excitement—totally unable to concentrate on work and, in fact, barely able to breathe normally.

I'd decided against calling Charlie because I really wanted to see his face when he heard the news, but I was dying to talk to him. Nothing ever seemed complete to me until we'd talked about it. This phenomenon was very different from the "husband first; wife second" experience I'd once worried marriage would be. I didn't need Charlie's approval or even his awareness of my news to make it important or great—it was already both. But our lives had become so linked that a whole layer of meaning and pleasure was simply missing from any news until we talked it over with each other.

He wasn't home when I got there. This wasn't unusual, but it frustrated me anyway. There was no interesting mail, I was much too wound up to be able to pass the time cooking or reading, and I didn't want to call anyone else with my news before I told Charlie. After changing out of my work clothes into jeans and a sweater, I basically flitted around the apartment, all but bouncing off the walls, until he walked in 45 minutes later.

The instant I heard the door open, I ran into the front hall. "The most amazing thing happened this afternoon!" I crowed.

He kissed me, then smiled and said, "You look like you're about to burst! What happened?"

"Bill called me into his office and told me he's been promoted to head the division our unit is in, which is great for the Company and something he totally deserves. He promoted this guy Steve to his—Bill's, that is—old job heading up our unit. It's a big promotion for Steve, too. He used to head one of the smaller units in the division and our old one is one of the biggest. And—here's the thrilling part!—Bill offered me Steve's old job! My post-BEL position is going to be unit head! Can you believe it?"

Charlie's face lit up. "Of course I can believe it. You're a great choice for that job! Congratulations, honey—that's fantastic!"

He lifted me off the floor as he hugged me (thus matching my actual elevation with where I already felt I was floating). After a few kisses, he put me back down and said, "I'm really impressed! You've got to be one of the youngest unit heads there, if not the youngest!"

"Yeah, probably! I'll definitely have direct reports who are older than I am. You'll have to give me tips on how to handle them."

"Happy to," he said, and he did look extremely happy.

"Are you dying to say 'I told you so' about how the BEL program's already boosted me past at least a rung or two on the ladder?" I asked, grinning up at him.

He laughed. "The thought never crossed my mind. Come on, let's go out and celebrate over dinner. I'll buy you a lobster and you can tell me all the details."

"That's a deal. But change first and let's go somewhere casual for it, OK? I don't feel like getting back into real clothes."

I put my arms around his neck; he picked me up and carried me with him to the bedroom. As he walked, he teased, "You couldn't sit still long enough to do anything fancy anyway, could you? You feel like you're going to jump out of my arms any second!"

"Never," I said, snuggling into them. "There's no place I'd rather be."

"You and me both. This is really exciting news, Jane. I'm so proud of you!"

"Me, too! I did manage to be excited in a professional way while I was with Bill, but just barely. I practically skipped back to my own office! I was so worried about ending up with a job that would be dull after the BEL year. I never dreamed I'd get something like this. And with Bill as my boss again, too!"

I kissed Charlie's cheek. "And thanks! I couldn't wait to tell you. I didn't want to tell anyone else until you knew, but I've been dying to talk about it!"

"I bet," he said, putting me down on the bed, then taking the stuff out of his pockets and putting it next to me. "This is a major promotion. You're going to be in the stratosphere sooner than you thought!"

As I basked in the glow of that thrilling prediction, I watched Charlie take off his clothes and wondered how serious I was about going out. His long legs, his broad, strong, smooth upper body, his beautiful face alight with happiness for me—it all had quite an effect. I didn't like to think I objectified him or was overly focused on his looks, but my appreciation of his splendor was keener than ever. I indulged in a possessive little internal bout of gloating. It was beneath me, I knew, but how could I resist congratulating myself on having made someone like him mine?

"You are so gorgeous," I told him as he pulled on a pair of jeans.

He grinned. "I'm all yours. Sure you want to go out?"

"You read my mind," I said, laughing, "and you make a very strong case, but, yeah, I'm starving. Let's go out soon and get back soon, OK?"

"You got it, Ms. Unit Head."

"God, I love the sound of that!"

"You should. It's very impressive. Did I mention that I'm very impressed?"

I smiled at him. "Did I mention that I love you?"

Over dinner, I told him about the new unit—my unit!—which consisted of about 35 people managing four related products. I didn't know much yet about the people or the products, but I would be learning about them fast. Bill wanted me to start right away so I could overlap with Steve for a week or so before he moved into Bill's former unit head job. Bill, obviously, was in a hurry to put his old job in capable hands so he could focus on his huge new one.

My BEL year was ending after another week, and I'd originally scheduled some time off right after the program ended. Charlie and I hadn't been planning a real vacation—it wasn't a good time of year for him to get away—but it looked like even the long weekend we'd arranged would have to wait. With only a little disappointment, we decided to plan a replacement weekend when we could, and went back to talking about my new job.

Charlie was so interested in all the details. It was exhilarating to tell him what I knew and speculate with him about what I didn't. Thanks to his experiences as head of M&A, he was also really helpful. He had great ideas for how I could get started on the right foot and up to speed quickly.

The generosity and depth of his interest and his excitement took my breath away. He couldn't have been more pleased if the promotion had been his instead of mine. As I sat across the table and, full of joy, observed how happy, exuberant and *involved* he was, I felt a new understanding of what our marriage really meant.

My accomplishments *were* also Charlie's, just as his were also mine. I realized again how very much I had gained when I relinquished my self-sufficiency in favor of trust and partnership. Just as Charlie had promised, our merger gave each of us someone to share the burdens with and made self-sufficiency unnecessary.

That night, as we cracked lobsters, toasted each other with champagne and barely stopped talking long enough to eat and drink, life did not feel burdensome. It felt far more like a confection, an enchantment, a bubble filled with lift and effervescence. But life was unquestionably a load to shoulder—it took effort and energy and attention. Magically, alchemically, marriage had both doubled the load and made it lighter.

When we got home after dinner, the night doorman greeted me, as he always did, using Charlie's last name. I had tried a couple times politely to correct him before I realized that he knew my name. He was just an older gentleman who believed married ladies ought to be addressed as such as a matter of respect. Ordinarily, this mildly irritated me, suggesting as it did that my identity had been subsumed into Charlie's.

That night, it didn't bother me a bit.

❖ ❖ ❖

Charlie

Jane's new job kept her incredibly busy. I was happy for her, but I missed the pattern of our lives before she became a unit head.

In our nearly two years of marriage, we'd settled into a very satisfying life together. I hadn't given it much thought until it changed, but, for both of us, everything seemed to revolve around being together. Work was always important, too, but it had brought us closer. It had never before distracted us from each other, no matter how busy we got.

Nothing big or significant changed when she took over her unit. What changed was the day-to-day feel of our life together. Jane seemed less present somehow.

For one thing, she was working longer hours. Before her promotion, she was always up and out before I was in the mornings, but she got home earlier too unless she was traveling. As a unit head, she decided she could quit worrying so much about conforming to the Company's normal hours, and she started staying later at the office.

I loved coming home to her, and I disliked coming home to a dark, empty apartment night after night. After a couple weeks of this, I got in the habit of calling her office as I was leaving mine to see what her plans were. Usually, she had lost track of time and was glad for the reminder to leave. A few times, when she still had work to finish, I joined her in her office and hung out there, reading, until she was ready to go.

This turned out to be a great way to recapture evening time with her. Jane's office was comfortable and quiet, and she had no problem working with me there. She liked the company—she always complained about how deserted and creepy the Company's offices were after hours. Whenever she got up to get a file or put something on her secretary's desk, she hugged or kissed me. I was happy to have her nearby, even if she was working.

And she was always working. She pored over focus group reports, financial results and revenue projections late into the nights. She paid nearly as much attention to structuring her unit, which she thought was set up inefficiently. The unit was performing and she didn't want to make rash changes or disrupt things unnecessarily, so she was taking her time conceptualizing the org design she wanted. Our dining room table was regularly covered with her latest configuration of the note cards on which she'd written the names of the people in her group.

We still talked all the time. Jane often wanted to brainstorm and she was very interested in my opinions and ideas as she went about settling into her new job and dealing with her people. She didn't ask what was going on at the Firm as often as she once had, but she was usually available to talk about my work issues if I brought them up. Even so, things felt different. I didn't feel abandoned or ignored, but I frequently felt as if she were just beyond my reach.

One night, we went out to dinner together, then came home and spent an hour or so working. I was reviewing the presentation book for a pitch to a prospective client the next day; Jane was preparing for her standing meeting with her boss. I finished my work first and turned on the TV (something that never bothered Jane when she was reading—her powers of concentration were impressive).

After about ten minutes, she stuffed her papers back in her briefcase and joined me on the sofa, nestling into the arm I circled around her. She didn't say anything, but she didn't seem to be watching TV either. I figured she was organizing her thoughts for her meeting and would probably run something or other past me. Instead, a few minutes later, she climbed onto my lap and, after a very hot kiss, she started unbuttoning my shirt. "Want to make love to me?" she murmured.

I gladly agreed. And I noticed, as she continued to kiss and undress me, that I had her full attention. It felt great, and it hadn't happened much, except when we were making love, in the weeks since she'd started her new job. Most of the rest of the time, she seemed to have something unspoken on her mind.

I realized I was no longer alone in my place at the top of the priority list for her attention. I was now sharing her with her job in a way that hadn't been necessary before. Her attention to me, to our life together, hadn't been diminished so much as divided.

This was OK with me, if not ideal. I admired Jane's commitment to her career and her passionate determination to excel in her new job. I was very proud of her and wouldn't have wanted her to be any different—I loved her as she was. If that meant I had to share the number one spot in her day-to-day focus, I could handle it.

I assumed the distraction was temporary. Jane was a quick study. I had no doubt that before long she would once again be doing her job as usual—brilliantly and with intensity, but without preoccupation.

❖ ❖ ❖

I ORIGINALLY PLANNED to celebrate our second anniversary in December with a vacation along the lines of our honeymoon. Other than a few long weekends and occasional days off, we hadn't taken a vacation since that terrific trip. It was more than time for the real thing.

It was also more than time for a break from the Firm. I was tired. Running M&A continued to be rewarding and we'd had another good year, but it had been a hard one. Clients were less loyal than in the past and we'd had to participate in a lot more beauty contests to keep our repeat business numbers up at prior years' levels. For me, this had entailed more travel and more hands-on involvement with existing clients.

Selecting new associates for M&A that year had also been more difficult for some reason, and July's compensation process had been contentious and exhausting as usual. All in all, my group seemed to have presented a constant parade of deal and staffing issues, interpersonal squabbles and other competitors for my attention.

On top of all this, the Executive Committee was proving to be a bigger pain in the ass all the time. A number of the younger leaders at the Firm, including me, had begun to meet with the goal of figuring out how we could more effectively influence—or perhaps take over—the Commitee.

The old guys hanging on to their EC positions with all their might were not best-suited to preserve the Firm's success or to take us the directions we had to go to ensure an even more successful future. They seemed to get more entrenched—and apparently deafer to new ideas—by the day. Many of them had not originated any new clients for years, and their privileged social connections no longer yielded as much in the way of annual revenue dollars. They were out of touch with what clients expected; that and their obsolete ideas about recruiting and management were hurting the Firm.

The time had come for a change. But those of us planning the change were all over the map in terms of the best way to bring it about, and so our meetings were also draining.

One thing we did agree on was to take a break in December and focus on year-end deals, then relax over the holidays and reconvene in January (with, we hoped, some new ideas and an improved shot at reaching a consensus). That out of the way, I decided M&A could do without me for a week or so while I took a long-overdue vacation and had my wife to myself for a change.

But Jane had only been in her unit head job for a little over two months by then, and she wasn't ready to take any time off. She was still working long hours, getting to know people and making her presence felt. Her unit was also having a robust year and she thought she had a pretty good handle on its operations and on what was good (and not so good) about the way it was set up and staffed. Even so, she felt sure it would be a mistake to go away so soon, even for a week, and I couldn't persuade her to change her mind.

By the end of February, I wasn't willing to postpone the vacation any longer. We'd had a nasty winter and I was sick of the cold, gray weather. Getting away from the city to soak up some sun with Jane sounded like a dream and felt like a necessity. She was still working hard, but things were more or less back to normal, so I talked her into picking a week (and both surrounding weekends), and then made the plans.

I chose another secluded resort, this one on the west coast of Mexico, and booked a villa with a private pool. I also booked a private plane. Jane had loved that, and the thought of not having to deal with the usual airport irritants—not to mention too-small airplane seats—appealed to me, too, particularly after all the business travel I'd done in the past few months.

With great excitement, we ordered food and movies for the plane, packed the few clothes we'd need and headed out of town. When we landed in Mexico, we had to laugh—we hadn't gotten much benefit from anything but the comfortable seats on the plane. We were both so tired that we'd slept the entire time. On the plus side, we arrived more or less in synch with the local time and we felt very refreshed.

The surroundings were rustic, but the resort was spectacular and our villa was surprisingly luxurious. Our pool looked inviting, too. It was too small for Jane to swim laps in, but bigger than I'd expected, and the maids had scattered fresh flower petals in it when they made up the room (something we discovered they did every day). Resisting the temptation to jump right in, we went out to dinner instead.

It was wonderful to be away from everything and alone with Jane. Despite her initial resistance to leaving the office, she seemed to have left work completely behind. She was her old self—not preoccupied or distant at all.

She wanted to hear all about the latest "mutiny meeting," as she called the EC restructuring initiative, and she was gleefully evil about the fate soon to befall the old guys whom she blamed for the

Firm culture she had found so unwelcoming. She was also helpful. The most recent coup suggestion had been striking me as off the mark for reasons I couldn't articulate, and she ably put into words exactly what was wrong with it as soon as I described it to her.

Talking with her was such a pleasure. I'd just about forgotten how exceptionally sharp, funny and passionate she was when she wasn't buried in work. It was incredibly gratifying to have her undivided attention.

Before I could say so, she read my mind and said, "This is so fun! I've missed you! I feel like I've had a million things on my mind for months. It's great just to talk to you, without anything else pressing to do or think about."

"I was just thinking the same thing! You *have* had a million things on your mind. It's nice to have you back!"

"Have I been neglecting you, husband?" she asked, a smile playing around her lips and eyes.

"No, not really, but you have seemed preoccupied. Far away. I've missed you, too."

Jane put her hand on mine. "Having second thoughts about choosing a career woman to be your wife?"

"Not at all, but it is nice to be back in first place. I was getting a little jealous of your job," I confessed. "I'm glad you're finally at the point where you don't have to focus on it 24/7."

"Finally?" she echoed. "Give me a break, would you? It's a big job and it's only been five months!"

"I know, honey. I'm teasing you. I'm sure I was the same way when I first took over M&A."

"You think?" she said, her eyes now definitely twinkling. "You always seemed pretty relaxed to me. Of course, you didn't have a spouse to pay attention to then, did you? Man, *everything* is easier for you!"

I laughed. "So, now you want me to believe that getting a big promotion when you've got a spouse to pay attention to is yet more proof that the world is out to make things hard for you?"

"Quite the opposite, actually," she said cheerfully. "It's been wonderful to have your help and your support—and your patience with my inattention, too. I *was* preoccupied. But now I feel like I have everything pretty much figured out and under control. Haven't I been better in the last month or so?"

"Much better. I wouldn't even have tried to talk you into a vacation otherwise." I squeezed her hand. "But don't worry about it. You were

OK before, too. I don't need to be front and center with you all the time. I know how important your career is to you. It's important to me, too. I can share you with it."

"What a beautiful thing to say!" she said, leaning over to kiss me. "Do you suppose I did something really stupendous in a prior life to deserve someone like you in this one?"

"Could be," I smiled. "Come on, let's get this bill paid and go check out our pool."

After its day under the sun, the water in our little pool was still warm. The also balmy desert air was refreshingly dry and pure. The resort was very dark—with that deep darkness cities never get—but the sky was bright with stars. Lazing in the pool with Jane in my arms was fantastic—calming, soothing, fulfilling and exactly what I'd needed for months.

We held each other, tried to name the constellations (and discovered that very little from our long-past astronomy classes had stayed with us), laughed and talked about nothing in particular. The din and all the clutter that normally surrounded us seemed far, far away. Jane said it felt like the rest of the world had retreated and left us floating together in paradise, carefree and perfectly alone. I felt like I was experiencing life boiled down to its best essentials.

Later, in bed, I gazed at her as she lay next to me and felt full of love for her—suffused and shot through with it. I rubbed her cheek with my thumb and softly said her name.

"Mmm—what?" she purred.

"Let's have a baby."

Her eyes snapped open and she looked at me as if I'd lost my mind. She also stiff-armed me, as if to keep me at a safe distance, but her palm on my breastbone felt more like a caress than a barrier. "Why do you always suggest crazy, outrageous, out-of-the-blue ideas as if they're the most ordinary and reasonable things in the world?" she demanded.

I laughed. "Honey, having a baby with a spouse you adore *is* one of the most ordinary and reasonable things in the world."

"For you, maybe," she said grumpily, but her eyes were twinkling again. She gently scratched my chest. "And what's with this disturbing habit you have of bringing up stuff like this after we've made love until I can't think straight and would do anything for you? Are you trying to outfox me?"

"I wouldn't dream of trying to outfox you. I doubt I could. I'm just trying to take advantage of your weakened state, as I believe you once called this strategy."

She smiled, tucked her hand back under her cheek and said, "I love you, Charlie."

"I know you do," I said, pushing her hair out of her eyes. "And I love you. So have a baby with me, OK?"

"Yikes! I sort of feel like saying 'I'd love to.' You've bamboozled me! I think we better table this conversation until I'm not all trembly and satisfied."

"No way! I'm planning to prevail—no reason to make it harder on myself."

Jane laughed. "You mean 'prevail' in the nicest possible way, of course."

"Of course," I said, grinning. "Seriously, though, wouldn't it be great to have a baby together? A real joint production? I know there are career implications for you, but we can handle those."

"Motherhood-related implications are a whole new level of complicated," she said, but she still sounded happy and dreamy, not at all concerned, and her body felt very relaxed. "It wouldn't be our first joint production, you know. Although I guess it would be our first traditional one."

"Marriage being our previous non-traditional one?"

"That is one, but it wasn't the first either. The first was my career, then there was your spectacularly successful M&A group."

"Fair enough on the group, but I think your career is more a matter of your own efforts."

"Oh, really," she said, her eyebrows high. "In a way pregnancy won't be?"

"I walked right into your trap, didn't I?" I said, smiling. "I guess you're not the only one in a weakened state. Damn!"

She grinned and looked very smug. Then she surprised me by saying, "Let me think about it, OK? This doesn't seem like the best timing in the world for a baby, but I'm not sure that will ever change. If the idea keeps feeling as comfortable and appealing as it feels right now, you might have yourself a deal."

"This is too easy!"

"Well, I didn't say how long I'll need to think about it."

"You've only got the rest of the week. I want a definitive 'yes' from you before we go home."

"And of course you always get what you want, don't you?"

"Always," I murmured, moving toward her.

"Don't tempt me to prove you wrong," she warned just before our lips met.

❖ ❖ ❖

THE SO-CALLED BLACKOUT SHADES in our villa turned out to be more of a good intention than a reality, but it didn't matter. Jane never had a problem sleeping with too much light, and I slept soundly and dreamlessly despite it. I was vaguely aware of brightness and of Jane moving around before I opened my eyes, but I didn't really wake up until she kissed my cheek and said softly that she was going down to the main pool to swim laps.

After she left, I ordered some breakfast from room service, figuring it would show up around the same time she got back. Then I lounged in bed, feeling totally relaxed, until it occurred to me that it would feel even better to lounge outside.

Our pool was sunk into the ground a few feet from the villa's door. It was about ten feet square, but irregularly shaped, and around five feet deep. As I'd discovered the night before, it had been designed with a thoughtful ledge at just the right level for me to sit, mostly in the water, with my arms resting on the bright blue edging tiles. I sat there, flower petals floating around me and the sun warm, but not yet blazing, on my skin. The fatigue I'd felt all winter seemed to drift out of my bones and muscles and mind and evaporate into the warm, dry air.

The room service guy who brought breakfast was very jovial, and accommodating, too. He insisted that I stay in the pool as he organized the coffee, fruit and croissants (Jane's favorites) on the little poolside table. Jane showed up a few minutes after he left. She grinned when she saw me luxuriating in the pool and clapped her hands together in delight when she saw the food. "I was hoping you'd get breakfast!" she exclaimed. "I'm starving. Thanks, honey!"

"Sure. How was swimming?"

"Great!" she said, eating chunks of pineapple with her fingers as she assembled a plate of food. "The pool is gorgeous. The inside tiles are that same cobalt blue as the ones your arms are on, so the whole thing looks navy blue. It was beautiful to swim in, and it was practically empty, too. God, this pineapple is unbelievable! Do you want some?"

"Please." I crossed the pool and took the fruit from her. "Pour me some coffee too, would you?"

She nodded, her mouth full, and poured two cups of coffee. Handing one to me, she put the other at the edge of the pool with her plate, then sat next to them and dangled her legs in the water. "This is the life, isn't it?" she said happily. "Want a croissant?"

"Yeah." I put my coffee cup down next to hers and took one. "And I want to know what's on your mind, too."

"What makes you think there's something on my mind?"

I grinned at the put-on innocence of her expression. "You always have something on your mind after you swim. And you have your about-to-burst look. And I know you—there's no way you don't have something to say about having a baby."

Jane smiled. "That's what I thought about the whole time I was swimming."

"And?"

"It's hard to believe, but I really kind of love the idea. I can't stop thinking about how cool it would be for us to have a kid—we'd have a cool kid, don't you think?—and how much I'd like to raise kids with you."

"Me too, honey." I stroked her leg. "And, yeah, I think we'd have a very cool kid. So is it a plan?"

"Not quite." She brushed croissant crumbs off her hands, then sipped her coffee. "I love the idea in theory, but I've identified several stumbling blocks. I have two primary areas of concern."

I thought I'd kept my face neutral, but she scowled and said, "Don't laugh at me!"

"I'm not laughing at you," I said, taking more pineapple off her plate. "It's just funny to hear you sound so businesslike when you're talking about having a baby."

"Not unlike the way you approached marriage, as I recall," she retorted. "And I don't remember laughing at you!"

"I think you suggested I'd lost my mind, but OK, I'll be serious. What are your two primary areas of concern?"

"Wait a sec." She reached for the coffeepot and refilled both our cups. "I know you're going to shoot these down and, to tell you the truth, I can't get too worked up over them either—at least not here in paradise. But, really, they are legitimate concerns."

She put her cup down, no doubt so she could wave her hands around. "The first is the timing issue I mentioned last night. I don't imagine the timing ever seems particularly good, but this seems particularly *bad*. I've only had my job for five months. Getting pregnant now sort of makes it look like I'm not serious about my career. I can't help thinking that it isn't a very fair thing to do to Bill, either. No, don't say it—I know it's not about Bill, but he's running the whole division and he's counting on me to do my part! I keep picturing how his face would look if I told him I was pregnant so soon after he gave me this opportunity."

Before I could say anything, she touched my shoulder in a pacifying way and said, "It's obvious from the way *your* face looks that you're about to tell me there are a million things wrong with what I just said. Be kind, OK?"

"OK," I said, smiling. "But do you really need me to tell you what's wrong with what you said? Come on, Jane, you know this. If you and I want to have a baby, nothing else matters. That's the end of the conversation. We don't need input or approval from anyone else. No one but us has any right to weigh in on the decision."

"Well, I wasn't suggesting we get Bill's permission. I'm only thinking about the impact making the decision will have on my career. And on my relationship with Bill."

"Even assuming it would ruin your relationship with Bill— which isn't a very trusting assumption to make about someone who's been great to you—would that be reason enough for you to decide not to do it?"

Jane scowled at me again. "No," she grumbled.

"OK, then. As for the impact pregnancy will have on your career, isn't that up to you?"

"Charlie, please. Could you just lay it out for me instead of doing this interrogatory thing? You sound like your mother."

I laughed and sat back down across the pool from her. "Sorry— force of habit. The bottom line is that you *are* serious about your career. There's no doubt about that, regardless of whether or when you get pregnant. There's also no reason you can't do your job while you're pregnant. I'm sure you'll continue to do it brilliantly. And, finally, even if you got pregnant today, you'd still have nine more months before you went on leave. By the time we actually have a baby, you'll have been in your job for well over a year—probably longer. That's not too soon to take a maternity leave."

"Might I get pregnant today?" she asked, clearly trying not to smile.

"Are you trying to distract me?"

"Obviously." She shrugged off the shirt (one of mine) she was wearing over her bathing suit, slid into the pool, and swam over to where I was sitting.

Floating in the water, her hands on my knees, she said, "I don't feel like debating this with you. For one thing, I'm not very wedded to my position. It's more of a knee-jerk feeling of anxiety, I think, than a real problem for me. For another, I know I don't have a leg to stand on. Unless I'm willing to argue that pregnant women either can't do, or shouldn't be allowed to have, important jobs—which I most certainly am not—there's no reason but narrow-mindedness to think pregnancy will hurt my career."

"Well said. So what's your other area of concern?"

"Now that you're warmed up? I'll warn you—this one will be harder to demolish. Even for you, Pollyanna."

"Let's hear it." I put my empty coffee cup on the blue tiles behind me.

Jane tried to sit next to me, but she was too short to do it comfortably with her nose and mouth above the water. Instead, she half-floated, half-sat on my lap, with her feet on the ledge. She smoothed some water on my face, which felt great—the sun was getting hotter—and then put her cool hands on my shoulders.

Looking much more serious, she said, "I'm worried that taking care of a child will fall more on my shoulders than yours. Don't be insulted—I don't mean that you'll dump it on me or be bad at it. It just seems to happen. And not only with parents like Cheryl and Richard or Chris and Andy, where the deal is that the wife will take the bigger part. It's just as true of Claire and Stephen, even though Claire's like she is."

"In what ways do you think the responsibility would fall more on you?"

"The working mothers I know need to feel sure their kids are in good hands or it's impossible for them to feel right about working. That's very distracting for them. Men don't seem to worry about child care in the same way. It's not so much the responsibility as the anxiety."

"You don't think men worry about their kids being in good hands?"

She gently squeezed my shoulders. "Please don't have a fit, but I really don't think it's the same. I don't know any men who wonder if they're doing the wrong thing by working instead of staying home with small children."

"That's a different point," I argued. "That's not about having more responsibility. It's about how you view being a parent. You and

I both believe we can be good parents without giving up our careers, right? Pursuing your career is a priority for you, just like it is for me, so that's what you'll do. And we'll make sure—together—that we have the right kind of child care so no one has to be anxious or distracted."

"That's easier said than done. And I'm not so sure it is a different point. Women seem to *feel* the responsibility more acutely. I suspect men aren't distracted by child care issues because they count on their wives to be the main line of defense, so to speak. And also, obviously, because no one judges them harshly for not staying home with their kids."

"I think you're extrapolating from generalities to us again. This is the same as love and sex and marriage. You get to make whatever deal you want to—and ours will be to share the responsibility equally."

Jane sighed. She went back to floating, leaving her hands propped on my shoulders. "Somehow, I don't think it's that easy," she said. "It's not just that women have to cope with societal pressures or narrow-minded attitudes or oblivious husbands. I have a strong suspicion there's an internal component, too."

"So where does that take you? Is it enough to make you decide not to have kids at all?"

"Hey, fight fair!" She shoved a little wave of water toward me. "You know that's not where I'm headed. I already said I love the idea."

"But, honey, that's the only real question. Unless you're going to decide against having kids altogether because it might make people think you're not serious about your career or because you're worried it will be too hard to have a career and a family, those things are irrelevant to making the decision. They're just things to deal with assuming you *do* decide to have kids."

"I guess," she said, looking unconvinced. "But I'm trying to understand what I'd be taking on. You know, to get a better feel for what it would be like."

"From everything I've seen and heard, including a lot from Claire, there's no way to know that in advance." I reeled her back into my lap and put my arms around her before I said, "You're just going to have to trust that I'll be a real partner and also that, like me, you can be both a good parent and good at your job."

"Again with the trust," Jane complained, but she was smiling. "Why does it always come down to trust?"

"I know—the hardest thing in the world for you."

"It seems to be getting easier all the time," she said, a little to my surprise and much to my delight.

❖ ❖ ❖

A COUPLE MONTHS after that great vacation, I got a lunch invitation from one of the two most senior members of the Executive Committee. This was unusual in its own right, and the conversation that took place over our lunch was even stranger.

Victor was nearly 70. He had worked at the Firm for over 40 years, and he had been on the EC forever—since long before I joined the Firm. He was smart and very shrewd, but he was a complete dinosaur. He seemed unable to understand that times and clients had changed, and that investment banking was no longer essentially an outgrowth of conversations among members of gentlemen's clubs.

Whatever he may have felt about women and minorities personally, he continued to believe they had no place in the management or owner-ship of the Firm. He may well have felt they didn't belong at the Firm at all, but, if so, he had enough sense to keep that opinion to himself. Nevertheless, thanks in part to his strong influence, the EC continued to view diversity with suspicion—and as a fad that would pass.

Victor had taken an interest in me when I joined the Firm, largely, I assumed, because he considered it politic to be seen as someone interested in helping my father's son succeed. Our thankfully infrequent meetings during my rookie years were very awkward. We had nothing in common. This wasn't due to our large age difference; he had nearly as little in common with my father. Politically, culturally, ideologically and in just about every other way, Victor and I were at opposite ends of the spectrum.

Jane thought he was evil incarnate. That was extreme, but she wasn't too far off. Victor was certain that his view of the world represented not only objective reality, but also the way things should be. Unlike many bigots, he wasn't afraid or uncomfortable around people who didn't share his gender, his socio-economic status or his world view. He simply believed such people were misguided and inconsequential inferiors.

When we first met, he behaved as if I shared not just his gender and his privileged background, but also his narrow-minded belief that we were the world's only rightful players. I was political enough to treat him respectfully (and to restrain myself from calling him a pompous asshole), but our conversations were full of (his) offensive pronouncements followed by (my) unpleasant and uncomfortable silences.

When the relationship he tried to build with me didn't take, Victor sought me out less and less. He never tried to slow or stop my progress, but I understood from Jim that he considered me a loose cannon, if also a talented investment banker. Over the years, as my own standing rose, I took Victor on whenever he said something I considered unacceptable. Probably as a result, our one-on-one meetings had become rare. I hadn't had lunch with him in years.

Victor had aged, but he was still a fairly impressive example of the tall, sleek, "master of the universe" type investment banker of the past. At our lunch (which was, of course, at his stuffy club—I couldn't wait to tell Jane she'd been right about what she'd called the "inevitable locale"), he behaved as if we were old friends and genuine colleagues.

He flattered me for a while, told me he'd always known I would become one of the Firm's brightest stars and then, apparently randomly, starting talking about working abroad. He said most of the Executive Committee members had spent a year or two in one of the Firm's European offices. He actually had the nerve to state that this provided a valuable broadening of one's perspective—or perhaps the irony of such a statement coming out of his mouth escaped him.

Just as I was wondering what exactly he might be getting at, he offered me the opportunity to move to London and run the Firm's office there. He said the EC was very impressed by M&A's performance "on my watch" and they were certain I was just the man for London. He implied that the foreign posting (as he called it) was a prerequisite for eventual EC membership and smoothly suggested that after two or three years abroad, I could expect to return to a seat on the EC.

The Firm was not a hierarchical place, but there was enough of a chain of command culture for it to be abnormal for this conversation to have occurred without Jim. In the normal course, people didn't get plucked out of a position like mine via an end run around the powerful and highly respected head of Corp Fin.

The whole thing—Victor's out-of-the-blue lunch invitation, the London offer, Jim's absence—struck me as fishy. The Firm had always been a sieve for information. I figured the EC must have gotten wind of the restructuring initiative. That had to be what prompted the sudden renewal of Victor's interest in my career.

I bought time by letting him think I was pleased by both his attention and the offer he made, and told him I would think over the London opportunity.

As soon as I got back to the office after lunch, I went to see Jim. He didn't look surprised as I told him what Victor had offered. The first thing he said when I finished was, "What did you tell him?"

"About London? I told him I'd think it over and let him believe I'd consider it."

"Will you consider it?"

"No." I shook my head. "I'm not in a position to move nor do I want to. The action is here, especially with the EC up for grabs."

Jim smiled. He was in the generation between the then-incumbent EC members and the coup planners. Although he wasn't on the EC, he always knew what went on there, thanks to a tight relationship with one of the few good guys on the Committee. The restructuring initiative was confidential, but our plans included putting Jim on the EC (and keeping his buddy there), so I'd brought him into the loop and kept him informed.

"They wanted me to make you the offer and convince you to accept it," Jim said. He made a minute adjustment to one of the already neat stacks of paper on his desk. "I told them you'd do the Firm more good in M&A than in London. I also told them you wouldn't go even if you didn't recognize what they were up to, but I guess they decided they knew better. You did see through Victor's offer, I presume?"

"It made me suspicious, yeah. I assume it's somehow in response to the restructuring initiative. What's going on?"

"According to Cam"—Cam was Jim's EC buddy—"the EC's very worried about the initiative. They don't have many details, but they know it's serious. They see you, Evan and Jack as the ringleaders and they think neutralizing the three of you will put down the insurrection."

"That's probably true," I said, a little amazed by what the EC knew and wondering where they got their information. I walked over to the window, looked out briefly, then turned back to Jim. "Not a very impressive plan for neutralizing me, though. Did they really think I would agree to move to London?"

"For a plum position and along with the promise of an EC seat when you returned? Absolutely. They were sure that was impressive enough to lure you over to their side and make you forget about the revolution."

"So, basically a bribe."

Jim smiled again. "I told them you wouldn't take it."

"I don't know which offends me more. The assumption that I could be bribed into abandoning what I think is right and selling my fellow revolutionaries down the river or the assumption that I'd be gullible enough to believe it for real. And they totally forgot to account for Jane's job."

"They didn't forget." Jim looked amused. "It never occurred to them that you'd consider your wife's job a reason to turn down their offer."

"Unbelievable." I shook my head again, this time in wonder. "Are they making similar offers to Evan and Jack?"

"To Jack, yes. Like you, he controls a lot of clients, so they don't consider him expendable. Evan's power base comes more from his exceptionally strong leadership of that group. The EC isn't worried about losing him. Once they got you and Jack on their side and/or out of the office, they were planning to find a reason to fire Evan."

This made me angry for a variety of reasons, not the least of which was that the EC's plan would probably have worked had Jack and I been corruptible (as the EC assumed). Evan was a strong enough leader that he might have been able to keep the initiative alive even with us on the other side. But with Evan gone, too, the others would never have stayed committed. They would have figured you couldn't fight city hall and, demoralized, gone back to believing the Firm would never change.

That this result struck the EC as optimal, desirable or even tolerable was horrifying. It strengthened my resolve to put our plans into action as soon as possible.

I thanked Jim, told him in response to his question that I was sure Jack would react to any proffered bribe the same way I had, and went back to my office deep in thought. Before I got started on my full afternoon of meetings, I asked my secretary to arrange for Jack and Evan to meet me that evening, and stressed that it was urgent. I also asked her to let Jane know I'd be home late.

The EC had eleven members. Three, including Cam, were good guys—exactly the kind of loyal, Firm-focused and forward-thinking people we wanted running the place. Three more were spineless puppets who tended to follow prevailing winds. The remaining five were what Jane called the evil cabal—men, like Victor, who saw no reason to change anything and were dedicated to preserving their own positions above all else.

With that breakdown of EC members, it was essentially impossible for new ideas to gain ground or for change to occur. The cabal needed the support of only one of the puppets to win the day, whereas the good guys needed the support of all three. Given the dominance of the cabal and their ability to make anyone's life hell if they felt like it, they were nearly always the ones pulling the puppets' strings.

We mutineers (as Jane called us—a swashbuckling term we all rather liked) had contemplated a number of paths to reconstituting the Committee. Its members were elected and we knew a majority of the Firm's voters would be in favor of a more progressive slate. The problem was how to get such a slate up for a vote.

The slate was ordinarily developed by a nominating committee. Unfortunately (from our standpoint), the nominating committee consisted of the previous CEO, the current CEO and two or three other people chosen purportedly to assure broad enfranchisement and "new blood." In reality, these others were usually so flattered to have been included, or so cowed by the CEOs, that they went along with whatever they were told.

We had considered staging a classic proxy battle. But proposing an alternate slate and putting it up for a vote against the "official" slate posed significant risks. We might lose, particularly if the incumbents used their power to twist voters' arms. Also, that sort of internal power struggle would inevitably become known outside the Firm. No one but our competitors would benefit from the disruption the resulting talk would cause among clients and employees. Our goal was to reconstitute the EC, not to damage the Firm.

We were in agreement that the most effective approach was to get the nominating committee to propose our slate in place of whatever the CEOs had planned. That way, the battle would occur entirely behind the scenes. For the election, there would be one slate, the vote would proceed normally and, to the world and the rest of the Firm, the shakeup would look like progressive action on the Firm's part instead of like a power struggle.

We'd also agreed that the right EC membership would include the three good existing members, Jim and two other broadly-respected people with similar seniority, three of us, and two of the bad existing members (preferably the ones with lucrative client relationships). That composition was far more representative of the Firm's people. And it would ensure genuine discussion and debate, as well as rational and fair-minded decision-making.

The decision to keep two of the bad guys came only after a great deal of argument, but there were compelling reasons for it. For one thing, the bad guys were not without followers. As a practical matter, it would be much easier to accomplish our goals—and less disruptive, internally and externally—if we didn't attempt to unseat all five of them.

Moreover, asking them to decide among themselves who stayed and who stepped down gave them a measure of control that was real as well as face-saving. It would make the change more palatable to them and to their followers. We hoped it would also pit them against each other and diminish the energy with which they fought us.

Just two weeks earlier, the planning group had voted for Jack, Evan and me to be our representatives on the slate. The existing EC had to have learned that news almost immediately in order to have developed counter-measures and swung into action when they did. This—and what we should do about it—was what I wanted to discuss with Jack and Evan.

There wasn't much we could do about a leak other than get the coup accomplished as soon as possible. The only sticking point had been our disinclination to stoop to the cabal's level and use strong-arm tactics to induce the nominating committee to propose our slate.

The old guys weren't hard people to collect dirt on, and we had plenty. (Advantageous investments in clients, preferential treatment for their cronies, sexual indiscretions—the cabal had always behaved as if the rules didn't apply to them.) The mutineers, in aggregate, also controlled a significant percentage of the Firm's client base, most of which would follow us if we left the Firm. We were confident that the twin threats of exposure and departure, coupled with our magnanimous willingness to retain two of their number (five, if you counted Cam and the other good guys), would be enough to persuade the cabal to support the proposal of our slate.

The EC's disgusting countermeasures, particularly their plan to fire Evan—one of the Firm's few truly extraordinary leaders—swept away my discomfort with using unscrupulous tactics. Although I wasn't wholly comfortable with the idea, it seemed to me that the end of taking power away from people willing to abuse it so odiously justified going ahead with the means we'd hesitated to use. I was hoping Jack and Evan would feel the same.

Jack did feel the same. Evan remained concerned that using dirty tactics would haunt us, both as a personal conscience matter and because, having used them, we wouldn't be much better than the people we were trying to replace. He argued forcefully against doing anything we or our followers would find repugnant or improper.

Jack and I admired him for it, but we had no better plan. Also, as Jack pointed out, if we didn't accomplish the restructuring, no one would and things at the Firm would stay the same. Finally, Evan tentatively agreed, but said he wanted to sleep on it.

On my way home, I found myself thinking about the conscience issue he'd raised. It was a fair point. I decided to talk it over with Jane.

She was curled up in her oversized chair, reading, when I got home. She took one look at me, put down her book and said, "Tough day?"

"More strange than tough."

"Do you need something to eat before you tell me about it?"

"No, we ordered in some dinner. Thanks, though." I kissed her, then sank onto the sofa. I pulled off my already-loosened tie and tossed it on the coffee table. "You were right about the lunch locale, by the way. Victor's club looks the same as it did ten years ago."

"I'm sure the prince of darkness thinks it's too bad the same can't be said about the Firm and the rest of the world," Jane said, settling back in her chair. "What did he want?"

"He wanted to tell me he'd always known I'd be a bright star at the Firm and spin some other 'we're both masters of the universe' crap, then he offered me a job as head of the London office and suggested there would be an EC seat waiting for me when I came back."

"So he tried to bribe you."

I smiled at her. "Right. The EC knows about the mutiny. They also know the fastest way to crush it is to turn, or at least neutralize, Evan, Jack and me."

Jane contemplated me for a few seconds before she said, "What about the London thing? That's a pretty sweet offer. I'm not suggesting you take the bribe, but is the position something you should consider?"

"No. The only place I can make the difference that has to be made is here as part of the EC. Also, your job is here, and I'm not going anywhere without you."

She smiled. "OK, then. Good. So where the hell did the EC get its info on the mutiny?"

I told her what I knew and what I'd talked to Jack and Evan about. Jane admired Evan's high-road position and his courage, too. She went off on a little tangent about genuine leadership and how Evan's unwillingness to compromise his integrity even to assure the right result for the Firm was a great example of that, especially since assuring that right result was the only way to save his own skin. (Cynic that she was, she also noted that no one had offered him any sweet bribes, so his integrity remained to be fully tested.)

Despite her admiration for Evan's position, Jane's advice was to go ahead and use the threats of exposure and departure. She was certain there was no way to get the EC restructured other than to force the incumbents to see that things were going to change one way or another—and that it was in their best interests to support the change we proposed and keep the Firm healthy.

She argued that the evil cabal consisted of bullies who wouldn't budge unless they felt threatened. Unless we bullied them, she said, they'd continue to believe they could beat us by playing dirty while we insisted on playing fair. If, on the other hand, they believed that sticking to their guns meant they would be left presiding over a decimated Firm, and possibly forced to step down anyway, she thought they'd figure supporting us was the lesser of two evils.

I thought she was right and I was glad we had the same view. "But what about Evan's question?" I asked her. "Do you think stooping to their level will haunt us personally or dilute our ability to accomplish our goals?"

"I think you have to distinguish between threatening to do something dirty and actually doing it," she said, leaning toward me. "You guys don't intend to damage the Firm nor will you. Your goal is to improve it. So why not use the bluff to get the EC structured the way it should be?"

I frowned. "That's kind of a dubious distinction, isn't it?"

"No, I don't think so. A bluff is not an inherently sleazy tactic, even if what you're bluffing about is questionable."

"I'm not so sure. Think about those despicable whiners we get every year who threaten to leave and take their clients with them unless they get more money."

"They're not despicable because they're bluffing. They're despicable because they're threatening to harm the Firm to get something for themselves. They'd probably do it too, if anyone ever had the balls to call their bluff. But you guys can feel good and right about using your bluff. You won't harm the Firm and you aren't being self-serving."

"OK. Good point."

"Thanks," she said, with a small smile. "I'm glad you like my distinction, because I really don't think you have a choice. The threat is the only way to get the EC's attention and convince them you mean business. It's the strong move. It'll work, too, because even if they suspect it's only a bluff, they still can't risk calling it. It's like with Ian, remember?"

"I remember. But our evil cabal is probably made of sterner stuff."

"Possibly, but they also have more to lose. They'll do what bad guys always do, which is assume everyone thinks the way they do. The evil cabal would decamp with clients in tow in a heartbeat if they thought they could do better for themselves somewhere else. They also wouldn't hesitate to use dirt to further their ends. They'll assume the same is true of your group."

She yawned and stretched. "Sorry. I'm tired, not bored. Go for it, honey, and don't worry about being sleazy. You guys have honorable, organizationally focused goals and motives. You're not sleazy and you're not going to do anything sleazy. All you're going to do is talk to assholes in the only language they understand, beat them at their dirty game and then change the game for the better."

"Thank you—that helps," I said, standing up. "I don't think this will be my finest hour, but I can live with it. I hope Evan comes to the same conclusion." I smiled down at her. "I'm glad you're on my side. I wouldn't want you as an enemy."

She grinned, raised her eyebrows and pointed to my tie. I picked it up, then took her hand and pulled her to her feet. "Come on, let's get some sleep."

❖ ❖ ❖

EVAN CAME MOST of the way around, and the modifications he suggested to our plan made it both easier to live with and better. He wanted to stick to facts—to describe ourselves to the EC as representatives of a group that controlled a significant percentage of the Firm's business, and then to state that as a condition of staying at the Firm, the group wanted a bigger say in management and would only support our EC slate.

He wasn't willing to expose any of the dirt we'd collected nor was he willing to threaten to do so. In addition to believing these tactics were unacceptable, he didn't think either would prove necessary. If the departure threat didn't seem to be working, he thought we should leak to Cam (via Jim) that we had dirt (which was another simple statement of fact) and stop there. Like Jane, Evan was sure once the cabal knew we had dirt, they would assume our intent was to use it.

Grinning, he admitted he was splitting hairs, but the difference was enough to make him to feel comfortable that we weren't compromising our integrity.

The plan worked. It took four meetings (the first three of them brutal), and we did have to disclose the existence of our dirt stockpile, but by the third meeting the cabal's smug, arrogant complacency was nowhere in sight and, by the fourth, they were obviously scared stiff.

It was hard to know exactly what did the trick. The old EC may have been disarmed by our slate's inclusion of five of their number. They may have been terrified by the volume of business the mutineers represented; despite their access to any numbers they wanted relating to the Firm's operations, they seemed shocked by our spreadsheets. Or perhaps they were shocked by the number and identities of the people who had joined the restructuring initiative. They may even have considered themselves unconquerable and counted on that to dissuade or vanquish us. In any event, they didn't put up much of a fight.

It turned out to be a great summer. The new EC overcame its initial awkwardness and got down to business pretty fast. Some real and very positive changes were already underway, with plenty more to come. (Victor remained on the Committee. He was still a force to be reckoned with, but a much diminished one. This wasn't thanks purely to the revised EC membership. In Victor's world view, what had happened couldn't have happened, and the success of the coup shook his self-satisfied smugness badly.)

M&A was also clicking along. Even July's compensation process wasn't as excruciating as usual. My EC position was a big help. I knew it was an unfair advantage, but I tried hard not to exploit it, figured what the hell, and let it work for me.

And by August, Jane was pregnant.

❖ ❖ ❖

I WOULDN'T HAVE GUESSED it was possible for me to love or admire her more than I already did, but once she was pregnant, I discovered that it was. I felt very possessive of her, too. Jane told me frequently that she loved the idea and the feel of our baby growing inside her—a remarkably moving thing to hear.

I was impressed (and a little surprised) by the way she handled being pregnant. Apparently effortlessly, she incorporated it into her and our lives. She didn't flip out or find it ridiculous the way Claire had. She had nearly as much energy as usual. And she didn't make a big deal about physical discomforts. Jane complained about the few she had, but in a funny "wait until you hear this" sort of way—almost as if she were telling a cute story about someone else.

At work, she took all the effort she had once expended on making her gender irrelevant (not an option, she said sarcastically, while she did something as female as be pregnant) and redirected it toward making her pregnancy, if not invisible, then a non-issue. She reported that it was actually functioning as kind of a beneficial cushion. Apparently, her coworkers were very solicitous of her comfort and very nice to her, as well as interested in the baby in a way she found supportive and gratifying.

She lost her cool only once during the entire pregnancy. Her meltdown puzzled me. Triggered by something insignificant, it seemed out of character for her. She was shaken and a little frightened by it, and it ended up demonstrating to both of us how insidious cultural conditioning could be—and how dangerous, given that it evidently had the potential to bubble up out of the blue even in someone as progressive and wary as Jane.

"Charlie?" she had called from the bathroom one Sunday morning. "Can you come here a minute?"

"Sure," I called back. "Be right there."

In the bathroom, she was sitting on the edge of the tub, wrapped in a towel, her feet on the floor and her head in her hands.

"What's wrong, honey?" I asked. "Do you feel OK?"

She looked up. I was worried when I saw that her eyes were wet and a little swollen. Jane was not a crier. Except for the overactive tear duct phase, as she called it, around the time we got married, I couldn't recall ever having seen her cry.

I sat next to her and put my arm around her shoulders. She didn't relax and melt into me the way she normally did when I held her; instead, she held herself separate and looked at me with an expression composed of equal parts anger and alarm.

"Please tell me what's wrong," I asked again.

"I can't do this!" She gestured at herself and then around the room, and she sounded panicked. "I'm not going to be able to handle it!"

"Do you mean the baby?"

"The baby and doing my job and running a household. It's too much! I'm not equal to it."

"Of course you are," I said, I hoped soothingly. "You're equal to any challenge, darling. You're incredibly capable."

"Yeah?" she said angrily, wiping her eyes. "Then why don't we even have decent towels?"

"Towels?" I'm sure I looked as confused as I felt. "What are you talking about?"

"I got out of the shower and started drying myself with this goddamn towel and realized it's practically threadbare! These towels should have been replaced weeks ago!"

"Yeah," I smiled, "now that you mention it, getting dry with them is more a matter of friction than absorption lately. But who cares? It's not a big deal."

"Not to you!" she said, her voice shaky. "You don't have to notice and take care of things like replacing towels. You think it's my job!"

"I don't think it's your job. Why would it be your job? I meant it's not a big deal that the towels should have been replaced before now. Let's just replace them now."

She looked impatient even as tears trickled down her cheeks and she again wiped them away. "You don't understand! Somebody has to feel responsible for things like this and make sure they get done, and that somebody is me. You could have used these towels until they were strings and not thought about replacing them. You do think it's my job! I know you do!"

"You can't know that because it's not true. I don't think it's your job any more than I think it's my job. It's just *a* job, something that has to be done. Now that you've noticed it, we'll get it done."

Jane put her head back in her hands. "You never understand," she moaned. "You think everything's easy and things just work out. But they don't! They don't!"

I rubbed the back of her neck. "Honey, calm down. This is a very small and easily fixable thing. There's no reason to get so upset about it."

She jerked her head back up. "But it's indicative of a big thing, which is that there's no way I'm equal to all this. How am I going to manage a baby when I can't even make sure we have decent towels around here?"

"Give yourself a break, would you? You're more than equal to the important things. It's not a character flaw to fail to notice threadbare towels—for either of us. And, Jane, really, I don't think this kind of thing is your job. Why do you?"

"I don't *think* it is," she said, almost in a whisper. Her eyes were wide, and she looked horrified. "I *feel* it is. I feel like I'm failing—like there are probably a thousand things I'm not doing well around here. I feel like I can't possibly stay on top of everything I'm supposed to be responsible for."

I pulled her onto my lap and put both my arms around her. She didn't quite melt into me, but she did feel a little less stiff. "You know you don't have to feel responsible for traditional wife things," I told her. "You know that's not our deal. I certainly don't expect you to. I couldn't care less about most of that shit. You don't have to care about it either."

"But apparently I *do* care about it! *I* expect myself to!"

"Well, stop!" I said, brushing the tears off her cheek, then kissing it.

She turned in my lap to face me and wrapped her arms and legs around me, her feet now dangling inside the tub. (She was only about halfway through her pregnancy, so this was still possible.) Laying her forehead on my chest, she muttered, "I want to be you. Everything is so easy for you!"

"Partly because I don't make everything hard, right?" I kissed the top of her head. "Listen, if things like the towels start to make you nuts, just tell me. I'm pretty sure I can handle buying new towels. Even if you can't stop feeling so responsible, you can always deploy me on the actual errands. OK?" I rubbed her back. "Does that make you feel better?"

"A little, I guess," she said doubtfully, sniffling. "Except it's not really the errands I don't feel equal to. It's the thinking."

"But, honey, if neither of us thinks of something, we don't have to worry about it. Who cares whether household things live up to some standard as long as they don't bother us? Just lighten up, can't you?"

"I don't know," she said tremulously. "I'm not sure I can. The words 'I'm not equal to this' keep echoing in my head."

"You don't have to be equal to it by yourself," I reminded her. "We'll be equal to it together."

She finally looked up. Although her voice was still shaky, she sounded much more like herself when with an unmistakable touch of irony she said, "You really are the perfect man, aren't you?"

"I do what I can," I smiled, tightening my arms around her as her body finally relaxed.

CHAPTER 20
DIVIDENDS

Jane

Being pregnant was, surprisingly, not too bad. I didn't totally love it, but it was OK.

I was lucky: I felt fine most of the time and everything went smoothly, health-wise and at work. And it would be difficult to imagine a better partner with whom to experience it. Charlie was amazing. I wondered more than once if he had some secret manual that spelled out all the right words and moves. (On further thought, I decided the perfection of his demeanor was more likely thanks to lifelong exposure to his mother and sisters.)

Pregnancy was great in some ways. It was exciting and I also felt important, as if I were involved in a highly significant and remarkable undertaking. I was particularly elated to have created a baby with Charlie; I loved that it was *our* baby who was growing inside me.

At the same time, though, I had to agree with Claire that our system of reproduction has its primitive and ridiculous aspects. Growing another human being in one's body is a strange thing to do. I often felt like a character in a science fiction movie who'd been taken over by a tyrannical alien life force. I disliked feeling like an incubator, particularly for a peremptory stranger with whom I couldn't reason. I felt co-opted and even a bit used.

Pregnancy affected everything I did—not always in a bad way and sometimes insignificantly, but unremittingly. Practically from day one, I found myself no longer solely in control of my body or my day-to-day life. From sudden food sensitivities to altered sleep and energy patterns to the eventual changes in my shape, balance and posture, I was essentially at the whim of a microscopic, but utterly domineering, collection of splitting cells.

My admittedly perverse inclination to put a little wrinkle in my husband's smooth, perfect life turned out to be far weaker than my desire to have a baby with him. Well before the end of that great vacation, Charlie got the definitive "yes" he wanted and expected. But I was glad it had taken a few months for me to conceive.

Making love with the goal of getting pregnant was exceptionally fun. It seemed both momentous and illicit—a very arousing combination. After over a decade of being careful to assure that sex did not result in pregnancy, it felt unauthorized in an exciting, flouting the rules sort of way to be trying to assure just the opposite. It would probably have become depressing had too many months gone by without conception, but, as it was, we had a lot of fun.

And by the time I got pregnant I'd been running my unit for nearly a year. I knew I was doing my job well, and I felt pretty confident that being pregnant wouldn't change anything about that.

I wasn't as optimistic about how my colleagues would react. I didn't happen to hear any discriminatory bullshit about pregnancy while mine was still secret, but I knew that quite a few people who thought I was a star employee were skeptical about pregnant women in the workplace. This was entertaining while I was the only one in on the secret, but I did wonder what would happen when my pregnancy became obvious.

I needn't have worried—or squeezed into my normal clothes for two extra weeks. Bill and my group met the news of my pregnancy calmly and with congratulations. No one seemed to question either my dedication to my job or my ability to keep doing it.

I continued to feel like myself, too, even with the ever-present (and rather electrifying) sense that I was utterly different. One of the weirder aspects of pregnancy was that despite being constant—and nearly always front of mind—it didn't make much of a difference in my work life. In the later months, I tired easily and found it harder to sit through long meetings, but that was about it. In day-to-day terms, going to work pregnant was rather like going to work with a really great new haircut. People kept noticing and mentioning it (with smiles), and it pleased me every time I thought about it or was reminded of it, but it was irrelevant to actual working.

The only significant difference I experienced was the humanizing effect pregnancy had on me in other people's eyes. Just as meeting Charlie always made people revise their opinions of me, my pregnancy had a similar impact. Apparently, my serious, businesslike demeanor and my ambition caused many of my colleagues to assume I was uninterested in a "regular" life (and, therefore, unlike them in a scary way).

The fact of my pregnancy, just like the fact of my handsome and charming husband, made me seem less driven, more mainstream, more "normal" to other people. The positive effect this had on their attitude toward me arose from sexism, to be sure, but the effect itself was very helpful and quite pleasant. I occasionally ranted about the sexism on general principles, but I recognized that it was working in my favor (for a nice change).

I also permitted a little sexism at home. When I agreed to have a baby, I made Charlie promise that he wouldn't objectify me, either as a pregnant woman or as the mother of his child. He kept that promise, but he did pamper and baby me—and I let him. It would have bothered me if he'd been condescending or patronizing, but he wasn't.

He never suggested that I take it easy at work or any other belittling thing. We still debated things heatedly, and he never cut me any slack. He still sought and paid serious attention to my opinions on Executive Committee and other Firm issues. (I loved knowing that I was having a bigger impact on changing the Firm as a wife than I would ever have had as someone working there. Talk about hoisting the narrow-minded on their own petard!)

What Charlie did do was fuss over me. He was solicitous and attentive. As I got bigger, I got lazier (at home, anyway) and he indulged that. He was always easygoing, but he achieved a whole new level of patient, tolerant equanimity while I was pregnant. No errand was too much trouble, no annoying household duty too much extra work.

If anything, I felt *more* equal rather than less. I still had everything I loved about our marriage—and then some. Charlie joked that the extra effort on his part was necessary to even the scales for the extra effort pregnancy required of me, but the truth was that he couldn't help himself.

He was jubilant about my pregnancy and completely overjoyed at the prospect of being a father. He was also much more sentimental than I was about the whole thing—I had to tell him quite a few times to quit looking at me in such a sappy way. Notwithstanding the gushing, however, he never made me feel as if I had become, in his mind, primarily a carrier vessel for our child. He left no room for doubt that he still saw me as myself and thought of me as his partner.

Once the baby started to kick, Charlie loved to have his hands on my abdomen so he could feel the movements. While I was equally fascinated by the sudden appearance in my body of knees and fists that didn't belong to me, Charlie's fascination would have bugged me had he not also continued to want to put his hands on me for non-fetus-related reasons. But I had no complaints in that regard.

It was a wonderful time in our married life. The jointness of our production enchanted and delighted us both, and made us very grateful in a new way for each other. Nothing fundamental changed, so I forgave Charlie for the sappy, sentimental looks and I didn't worry too much about the alarming ramp-up in my own nesting instincts.

I did occasionally feel as if things were close to slipping out of my control, and I got totally panicked once, but on the whole I wasn't overly concerned about incorporating an actual baby into our lives. I felt pretty sure we could handle it without ruining anything for ourselves.

The actual baby arrived in early April. The less remembered about the labor and delivery, the better. I was familiar with the basic principles of biology and reproduction, and I should have realized long before the eleventh hour that mating with a very large man had the potential to create a very large baby. I wouldn't have decided not to do it for that reason, but I might have been better prepared.

After a few hours of annoying discomfort and a couple more of astonishing pain, I ended up having a Caesarean section. Learning that this would be necessary disappointed me, and it was frightening, too, but the immediate and complete relief from pain via anesthesia was heavenly.

Until the pain got shocking, our time in the hospital was rather fun. Charlie entertained me and kept me calm. (It stopped working, but he tried to do the same once things got bad. His hand and forearm were bruised for nearly a week afterwards from where I gripped them.) It was easy to forget about work and the rest of the world—knowing we were about to have a baby was all-encompassing. The process was insistent, too. Once it began, I would gladly have done it anywhere, without regard to who was around, both to get it over with and because there was a peremptory inexorability to it.

We had a lot of company in the early hours. Everyone had told me that OB nurses were the best—capable and comforting and encouraging. That turned out to be true, and we had an unusually large sample on which to base our opinion. Word of my gorgeous husband spread quickly through the labor rooms, and just about every nurse on duty came to check him out.

It was very amusing to watch them do it. Unlike other women on whom Charlie had this effect, the nurses paid attention to me. They stole glances at him and answered his questions with obvious pleasure (and a little flirting), but I was their main concern. I felt coddled. This may have been due to their innate compassion and empathy or perhaps they thought lavishing care on me was the best way to impress him. Whatever the reason, the attention was nice.

I was used to becoming invisible to other women once they beheld Charlie. This always irritated me, both because I disliked being ignored and because it drove me crazy when women acted as if men were more deserving of their attention. In Charlie's case, the phenomenon had as much to do with his beauty as his gender, but I'd also noticed it in a variety of other settings with a variety of other (far less beautiful) men.

It wasn't limited to social situations, where it was understandable, if still unforgivable. At work, groups of professional women often started accommodating or pandering to a man the minute he walked into the room. This occurred even on the (sadly rare) occasions when he didn't outrank them. I'd also seen it in the context of a nonprofit board of directors I'd joined at Liz's suggestion. The board was comprised mostly of women, all very competent and distinguished, but several of them nevertheless routinely deferred to, or went out of their way to flatter, the few male board members.

It seemed to me that all this was the grown-up equivalent of standing up your high school girlfriends if a boy asked you out. It also reminded me of a documentary I'd once seen on lions, which included a truly brutal (and uncomfortably familiar) segment on competitive mating behavior among females. Treating men as if they were by definition more important, more interesting or otherwise more deserving of attention yielded power to them and implied a belief that they were superior. Whether the result of cultural conditioning or biological imperative, as far as I was concerned the behavior was deplorable.

The OB nurses didn't suffer from this syndrome. They clearly appreciated Charlie's looks and his charm—and I'm pretty certain he was the reason we had such a throng of them in and out of our room— but I was the focus of their attention.

In fact, the whole obstetric experience was in sharp contrast to most of the rest of my experience. Women reigned, while men were more or less extraneous and certainly beside the point. (This effect was somewhat negated by the preponderance of male doctors, but not for us—my doctor was a woman.) It was bizarre and rather delightful to be engaged in an important endeavor, however traditional and biological, that was indisputably all about—and achievable only by—women.

In his usual blithe way, Charlie wasn't bothered by this reversal of the status quo. He didn't even notice it until I pointed it out. When I did, he said it reminded him of our wedding, where he'd also been the only male present (albeit with a more equal role). Later, as my labor intensified, he said it was like the "beside the point" feeling, but with a negative twist. He didn't expect anyone to pay attention to him, but he felt helpless, in the way, and irrelevant.

He was superfluous to the process, but, as I assured him, he was far from irrelevant to me. He stayed where I could see him and touch him at all times. Never seeming to tire, he kept up a comforting stream of conversation and, later, supportive murmuring. He fed me ice chips and frequently kissed my hand or stroked my head.

Once the room got crowded, he stayed right beside me. He sat still, his long legs cramped (and, I'm sure, itching to be stretched), and did his best to stay out of everyone's way. He held my hand and arm between his two hands and he didn't flinch no matter how hard I clutched. I could have done it without him, but I was very, very glad I didn't have to.

What with the surgical drape blocking my vision and the anesthesia blocking my nerve endings, the C-section was a very disconnected way to give birth. I continued to feel disconnected when the doctor announced that the baby was a boy. I had truthfully told everyone who asked that I didn't care if we had a boy or a girl, but I had always assumed it was a girl. I'd loved the idea of a girl having parents like Charlie and me—what a strong and self-confident woman she would have become.

I was shocked that the baby was a boy. I had a few minutes to think about this while they did whatever they do to newborns before they hand them over, but I seemed to be unable to think complete thoughts. Charlie squeezed my hand, then kissed it, and we gazed at each other wordlessly, his face tired but alight with joy, mine (I suspect) full of amazement mixed with confusion.

Despite my shock and a lingering sense of incredulity, I fell in love with our son the second I had him in my arms. (Another clichéd but irresistible reaction, I thought to myself.) He was beautiful—partly in that way new babies must always look beautiful to their parents, but also because he was less banged-up and misshapen than babies delivered the regular way. He was bright red when I first held him, but it was clear that he would have Charlie's coloring once he got over the trauma of birth.

He was also very long ("off the charts" for length, as I later learned one was supposed to say), and kind of lanky for a baby. Evidently, my DNA hadn't counteracted the excessive height trait in his father's gene pool. More like me than like his easygoing father, however, the baby was sporting a narrow-eyed, suspicious sort of look. It was easy to imagine him thinking, "What the hell is *this*?" as he breathed air, experienced light and felt our hands on his skin.

Charlie and I counted his fingers and toes, let him grasp our fingers in his fists (with surprisingly strong pressure), and stroked his unbelievably soft and smooth head and limbs. I asked Charlie if it felt as weird and unlikely to him as it did to me that we were this child's parents. He grinned and said, "More so, probably, given how he got here," then, with a questioning look which I answered with a nod, he took the baby from me.

Seeing the two of them together (a better sight was impossible to imagine), it occurred to me that, in some ways, it would be even better for a boy to have parents like us. Sexism and inequality continued to thrive just about everywhere, and a boy would have an easier path and a clearer shot at making things better. I liked the idea of unleashing into the world another fair and open-minded man with all the protective coloration necessary to become powerful and make a difference.

I also realized, as I watched Charlie hold our baby, that tears were running down my face. I decided to consider them tears of relief that the whole labor and delivery process was over and chalk them up to exhaustion rather than sentimentality. Unfortunately, I was still emotional in a weepy sort of way after we left the hospital and settled in at home.

This would have concerned me more than it did had I not also found myself wondering cynically whether my propensity to cry in response to things like love, marriage and childbirth was trying to tell me something. (I figured if I could still be sarcastic, chances were good I wasn't becoming irrevocably gooey.) I also took some comfort from the fact that Charlie was even worse. He only had actual tears in his eyes once or twice, but he looked like they were a possibility pretty much all the time.

We decided to name the baby Nicholas, which had been Kate's father's name. We called him Nick right from the beginning—part of the reason we liked the full name was that it had such an excellent nickname. We felt a little fake and strange calling him by name for a couple days, but then it started feeling right and we decided it suited him.

Kate thought it suited him, too, and she was very pleased that we'd chosen her father's name. She produced some baby pictures of Charlie that looked startlingly like Nick and told me that Charlie had always reminded her of her father. Then she laughed and said looks weren't what Charlie and her father had in common. Kate was sure Nick was going to end up looking like Charlie, but she doubted he was going to have the even temperament Charlie and her father had shared.

Apparently, of her four kids, Charlie had been the easiest infant. Kate claimed, Alex verified, and it was easy for me to believe that he had been a calm, go with the flow sort of baby. The same could not be said about his son.

Charlie was kind enough to say he hoped Nick had my brains as well as my prickliness, but there was no doubt about the prickliness. He had very definite ideas about what he wanted and how things should be, and he didn't hesitate to make his displeasure known in the only way available to him. I had thought he was tyrannical *in utero*, but that paled in comparison to what he could coerce by using his lungs.

He wasn't an awful baby. He was often peaceful, he loved to be held and played with, and he got more beautiful every day, which had its own appeal. But he was most assuredly the one calling the shots. Every parent we knew told us that babies sometimes cried for no fixable reason, but Charlie and I leapt to Nick's aid whenever he so much as whimpered. I worried that something might be wrong with him; Charlie couldn't stand the thought that he might be unhappy.

His needs were pretty easy to meet. When the standard fixes—feeding him, changing him, cuddling with him—didn't work, movement was a good second wave response. Rocking with him often calmed him. And he loved it when Charlie held him and walked around. Like Claire's twins when they were infants, Nick usually relaxed the minute Charlie started moving, but wouldn't let him stop. As a result, Charlie did countless laps around our apartment, the baby's little head lolling on his shoulder.

Every so often, Nick got inconsolably cranky. After trying everything to no avail, we deduced that he might just want to be left alone. Doing so was terribly hard on us (and taught us a thing or two about the nature of control), but by the time we were done wringing our hands and asking each other what he could possibly want and whether we were the worst parents in the history of the world, he had usually cried himself to sleep.

A few times, he got totally hysterical. His face bright red, his fists clenched tight and his limbs shaking with apparent fury, he would scream at a decibel level it was hard to believe such a small thing could produce. Nothing soothed him; we simply had to wait these fits out. Luckily, they never lasted too long. They would actually have been funny if they hadn't been terrifying (and horribly noisy): Nick looked massively pissed off and wild with frustration, as if he were raging over the misfortune of having gotten stuck with two such boneheaded and useless parents.

Charlie didn't work much while Nick and I were in the hospital, and he didn't go to work at all for a week after we got home. I felt OK, but it was great to have someone else around to take care of all the non-baby-related things that needed doing. Charlie also handled plenty of the baby care, and he continued to pamper me. I felt very loved and, despite my weepiness and some pain as I healed, very happy, too.

We spent most of that first week at home lounging with the baby, sleeping when he slept and interacting very little with the outside world. We didn't have too many visitors—Charlie's various family members came and went in a helpful, non-intrusive way, and my parents weren't coming until the following week. We marveled over Nick's existence and his perfect little body, and exclaimed to each other about how utterly and wonderfully our lives had changed.

It was like having a fabulous new toy. Nick was endlessly fascinating to us and our only real topic of conversation (although we frequently said "I love you" to each other, too). He didn't seem quite real to us—every time we woke up, we raced over to his bassinet to see what he was doing and, to be honest, to make sure he was still there. It was hard to tear our attention away from him.

It turned out to be a good thing I'd decided to take a three-month maternity leave from work. Before Nick was born, this had seemed unnecessarily long, but it was the Company's standard leave for people in my salary grade and I wanted to support the policy.

Although I didn't plan to be wholly absent, I thought it best to arrange for interim management of my group while I was on leave. I couldn't run it effectively from afar, and I doubted I'd want to go into the office for the first month or so after I had the baby. I also didn't want Bill to have to worry about the unit or run it himself, and I liked the idea of offering a controlled leadership opportunity to one of my direct reports.

Four brand managers reported directly to me. I had inherited all four of them, but they were pretty good and, over time, they'd become loyal to me. They were all men; three were older than I and the fourth was younger. Mike (one of the older ones) and Paul (the youngest) demonstrated the best leadership potential. My original thought was to name them co-interim unit heads.

Bill persuaded me that it was a bad idea to put two people in charge. He argued that effective management required a strong sense of both ownership and accountability that would be hard to come by with co-managers. Not only could they be divided and conquered by their troops, they could easily wind up being so careful to take each other's opinions into account that decision-making would become torturous, if not impossible.

In all honesty, I thought Paul had the best long-term leadership potential. But after a lot of deliberation, I decided to name Mike interim unit head. Paul was so much younger that naming him would demoralize my other direct reports. They would have to wonder if they had any chance at all of future promotion—a disruption I saw no need to create simply because I needed to take a maternity leave. Paul, on the other hand, wouldn't be demoralized or even disappointed by not being named, and I could continue to nurture his development via the normal compensation and review processes.

I'd also decided to split my leave into two phases. I didn't plan to call in or otherwise stay in the loop during the first month, but I told Mike to call me if any emergencies arose or he otherwise needed my input. I asked my secretary to collect the regular financial and management reports and any other important mail I received and send me a package at the end of the first month and weekly thereafter.

During my second and third months off, I figured I'd read the reports and talk with Mike a few times. My goal was to get myself back in the loop, not to reassume control early. I wanted him to have a legitimate chance to run the unit without me looking over his shoulder. I also wanted to preserve my own ability to be at home with the baby without distraction—and to continue to avoid setting the kind of example that could make it harder for other women to take the Company's standard leave.

After Nick was born, I was very glad I'd set up my leave this way. For the first three weeks, I wasn't even remotely interested in what might be going on at the office. In addition to feeling tired and a little weak as

I recovered from the C-section, I felt somewhat overwhelmed by the responsibility of caring for an actual baby. I was relieved that I hadn't put myself in a position where I also had to worry about my unit.

I was still very emotional, too. My feelings for Nick and for Charlie were often quite overpowering. I loved both of them more passionately than I'd once imagined it was possible—or safe—to love anyone. It would have been wrenching to feel obliged to pay attention to anything else.

I knew Mike or Bill would call me if there was anything I really needed to know, so I calmly forgot about the office and focused on life at home.

❖ ❖ ❖

I WENT SWIMMING one Saturday afternoon about a month after Nick was born. I'd been longing to swim for several days, but the logistics of organizing a trip to the gym without him seemed too complicated. On Saturday, though, Charlie was home. After I fed Nick, I felt energetic and in the mood for swimming laps, so I left the two of them and went to the pool.

It was wonderful. The combination of physical activity, being by myself for the first time in weeks, feeling like myself, and letting thoughts (mostly about my baby) meander through my mind was incredibly refreshing. On the way home, I felt recharged—and very eager to get back to Nick and Charlie.

I heard the excited voice of some sports announcer on TV as soon as I walked in. I didn't call to Charlie in case Nick was sleeping, which turned out to be a lucky thing. A picture-perfect sight awaited me in the living room. Charlie was lying face up on the sofa, his head on a pillow at one end and his calves and feet hanging over the other end. Nick was lying face down on Charlie. One of Nick's little arms was stretched upward and his fist was lightly touching Charlie's neck. One of Charlie's hands covered the whole of Nick's back, anchoring him in place. Their heads were both turned toward the TV and, despite the announcer's keyed-up ranting, they were both sound asleep.

They looked so beautiful and so appealingly *male*. I knew it was a sight I'd never forget. Even as tears popped (yet again) into my eyes, I also knew I'd never been happier.

❖ ❖ ❖

MY SISTER LAURA came to visit when Nick was six weeks old.

I'd originally thought it was odd that she hadn't come with our parents right after he was born. That was an unusually enjoyable visit. My parents ordinarily found everything I did incomprehensible, but they adored Charlie and, not surprisingly, they had no problem with the idea of me as a mom. They were thrilled to be grandparents, and they thought Nick was the most wonderful baby in the world. For a nice change, their visit pleased rather than irritated me.

There was really no good reason for Laura to have come with them. She was nearly 28 years old. And as an adult, she'd demonstrated both an independent streak and more backbone than I would have given her credit for having.

After she graduated from college, Laura surprised me and shocked our parents by getting a job instead of marrying her college boyfriend. She started as a receptionist at a local bank. (This had amused me when I first heard about it. I'd never run across a receptionist who wasn't attractive, and my sister fit that mold perfectly. Companies must think a pretty woman at the front desk is good for business.)

Laura had not historically aspired to be anything but a cosseted wife, but she had never been stupid. At the bank, her intelligence evidently drew as much attention as her looks, and she was quickly promoted to a career-track job in the lending division. Further shocking our parents, she dumped the college boyfriend, who wanted her to quit working and marry him, and got a second promotion. She loved her job and was evidently quite good at it.

A few months before Nick was born, Laura got engaged to a man she'd met at a business conference. The fiancé was great—a big improvement over the college boyfriend, whom I had always found conventional and condescending. Laura was planning a huge, traditional wedding for the fall. Although I was somewhat reassured by her decision to keep working after she was married, I still worried that she might be relapsing into our mother.

I decided it couldn't hurt to assemble my girls' club while she was in town and expose her to a diverse group of strong, self-directed women. I wanted to see them all, too, and to introduce them to Nick. I'd talked with everyone on the phone, but except for Cheryl, who'd come for a visit with Richard and Amanda soon after Nick was born, no one had yet seen him.

I invited them over to our apartment on a Saturday afternoon when Charlie had a golf outing with a client. While I was at it, I included Liz and Jennifer. Laura wanted to handle food and drinks, and she'd decided that an "afternoon tea party with sweet and savory tidbits to eat" would be just the thing. (I resisted rolling my eyes. Instead, I marveled over our being sisters, suggested we also have alcoholic beverages on hand, and thanked her for being willing to do all the work.)

Only Jennifer couldn't make it. She was going away for the weekend with her latest lover. To my amazement, she had sounded quite smitten when I talked to her on the phone. I wondered if she might actually have fallen in love. She'd promised to call me to set up a time to visit when she got back, and I planned to cross-examine her when I saw her.

The Saturday of the party was a beautiful day, more like summer than winter. Charlie and I were both relieved. May weather could be so iffy and he hadn't liked the idea of having to play golf in the rain (or worse). I'd been worried that his outing might get cancelled altogether. The girls' club wouldn't have been the same with him at home, but I hated the thought of asking him to make himself scarce.

My post-partum weepiness was gone, but I was still emotional, even sentimental, and I was feeling especially close to him. We were so happy about Nick and so elated to be living life as a little family. Also, we had just started having sex again, and it was as fantastic as before the baby (to our mutual delight and a little to my relief). I felt as giddily in love with Charlie as I had the first time we slept together. The last thing I wanted to do was suggest I didn't want him around.

Cheryl was the first to arrive on Saturday. She and Laura hit it off right away and were chatting easily when I came back into the living room with Nick. Cheryl took him from me and cradled him in her arms in that expert way experienced mothers do.

"Jane, he is absolutely beautiful!" she exclaimed. "The new pictures in Charlie's office are cute, but they don't do him justice!" She tapped the baby's nose lightly. "You're going to be as glorious as your daddy, aren't you?" she cooed. Then she looked up and said, "His daddy isn't lurking around here somewhere, is he?"

"No, he's at a golf outing. Why?"

"I'm not telling the Firm for another couple weeks, but I'm dying to tell you. I'm pregnant again! The baby's due in November."

"Congratulations!" Laura said. "How exciting!"

"Yeah, that's wonderful!" I hugged Cheryl (inelegantly since she still had Nick), then grinned and asked, "Don't I recall that you're just inside the timing window you wanted? November's a couple months before Amanda's four, right?"

"Exactly," she smiled. "Richard and I originally liked the idea of kids three years apart, but work's been great and the time just flew by! Late last year we realized we better get serious if we didn't want Amanda to be in high school before we had a sibling for her."

"I'm so happy for you! Is it just Charlie we shouldn't tell or are we keeping quiet about it with everyone else today, too?"

"Lynn already knows, and I'd love to tell the others. Katherine won't tell Jordan if I ask her not to, will she?"

"I'm sure she won't."

Cheryl looked apologetic. "I hope you won't mind not telling Charlie for a while either, but I don't want to put him—or Jordan—in a potentially awkward position with Owen."

"No problem," I assured her as I played with Nick's toes. "I remember how carefully the whole disclosure had to be managed at work. But I'm glad we don't have to pretend we don't know this afternoon."

"That would be hard," Laura said, smiling. "There's bound to be plenty of talk about babies with my little attention magnet of a nephew here."

"There's also bound to be some talk about pregnancy," I said. "Did you know Liz is pregnant, too? She's due in September."

"I didn't know! That's great!" Cheryl giggled. "I can just imagine Tyler as a father-to-be. He's so soft-hearted and starry-eyed—he must be completely delirious!"

"He is. Liz has been rolling her eyes at him for months," I said as I left in response to the doorbell.

Lynn and Katherine were at the door, having run into each other in the lobby. They both hugged me and told me I looked wonderful. I was glad to have a chance to talk to them without Nick. I knew the conversation would have turned immediately to him if I'd had him with me. Laura was right—babies were magnets for people's attention, even people like Lynn and Katherine who didn't have much personal interest in them. It was nice to talk about other things.

After a few minutes, I took them into the living room and introduced them to Laura. They said hello to her, then turned to Cheryl, who was still holding Nick. There was a lot of exclaiming over how cute he was (which, embarrassingly enough, I found very gratifying), and then Cheryl told Katherine her news, prompting more excited congratulations.

I noticed that Laura was listening with interest and taking everyone in, no doubt trying to remember who went with which background story. Nick also seemed to be paying attention. Obviously, he wasn't listening, exactly, but he was very relaxed in Cheryl's arms and his eyes were darting around. He seemed quite happy with all the hands patting him.

I smiled to myself and thought how like a man it was to relish being the center of attention in a group of women. I wondered if this was how it started for all of them—being petted and cooed over by their mother's friends when they were infants.

As I went to answer the door again, Lynn sat down next to Laura and they started talking. Katherine sat next to Cheryl and took Nick. She held him less expertly than Cheryl did, but with more enthusiasm than I would have thought likely.

At the door, Liz and I hugged each other and said, practically in unison, "You look great!" She really looked amazing. She'd told me her personal shopper had gone nuts buying maternity clothes and then having them tailored, and the results were obvious. Liz looked incredibly chic, a remarkable feat for a woman who was nearly six months' pregnant. She also looked healthy and happy.

After the introductions and hellos, Liz said, "I'm so sorry to be late! It was all I could do to get here without Tyler. He follows me pretty much everywhere these days and he's also dying to see Jane's baby. It took forever to talk him into staying home, and I'll warn you all now that he's certain to show up later to pick me up!"

"We were just speculating about how delirious he'd be over becoming a father," Cheryl said, smiling.

"'Delirious' doesn't begin to cover it," Liz griped. "What with his hovering and my in-laws behaving as if I'm producing some sort of heir to the throne, I'm going crazy!"

As Liz talked, Laura watched her closely. Before I married Charlie, Laura had considered me the greatest of fools for not wrapping up Tyler when I had the chance. She'd liked him a lot and, of course, she'd thought he was ideal husband material. I knew she'd be curious about Liz. (I also knew she wouldn't fail to notice Liz's elegant clothes or the simple flawlessness of her jewelry.)

"Men are unbelievably sentimental about impending fatherhood, aren't they?" Cheryl said. She leaned back on the sofa and crossed her legs. "Richard is nearly as bad this time as he was when I was pregnant with Amanda."

"It goes along with their general egotism," Lynn said. "I'm sure they're quite overcome at the thought of their magnificence continuing into the next generation."

"With good reason in this case," Katherine said, indicating Nick. "This is one good-looking baby! And he seems to be a charmer like his father, too."

I laughed. "You're seeing him at his best. So far, his personality is more like mine than like Charlie's. He can be very prickly."

"He's been pretty charming since I've been here," Laura said, with a smile. "They must learn early how to play to an audience." She looked from Nick to Cheryl and Liz, then to me. "I'd like to ask a question about this so-called male sentimentality. Do you think your husbands are the way they are in part because they're surprised that you wanted to have babies? You know, because you're so devoted to your careers?"

"I like this sister of yours, Jane!" Lynn nodded approvingly at Laura. "What a direct and interesting question!"

Laura's question interested me, too—not the substance of it so much as the fact that she was asking it. She no longer found me as inexplicable as she once had (and as our parents still did), but she continued to make assumptions about me based on my long-standing zeal for a serious career. My marriage, Charlie's and my love for each other (which she'd characterized as "unmistakable and inspiring"), and my having had a baby demystified me to some degree in her eyes, but apparently my sister still considered these things somewhat out of my character.

"I think our husbands know us better than that," Cheryl said in her usual gentle way. "Their sentimentality has more to do with them than with us. Despite what people always say, it's been my experience that men are much more emotional than women about most things."

"I agree that it has more to do with them than with us," Liz said. "I'm also inclined to agree with Lynn that there's a fundamental egotism to their sentimentality."

"You guys aren't answering Laura's question," Lynn said. "I know you think your husbands are exempt from the bad male behavior we spend our lives dealing with, but isn't it possible that at some level they're simply amazed and grateful that you're willing to be wives and mothers at all?"

"That's one of those either/or assumptions that make me wild!" I said. "Wanting to have a career and wanting to be a wife and mother aren't inconsistent. They're not mutually exclusive either. There's nothing 'unwomanly' about working or being ambitious and there's nothing unprofessional about getting married or having kids!"

"Then why do so many people—men and women—think otherwise?" Lynn pressed.

Liz was shifting in her chair and I pushed the ottoman toward her. She smiled gratefully and put her feet on it as I said, "Who knows why these things get so polarized? Maybe this is the personal equivalent of women having to work twice as hard to get to the same place as men do at work. You know, maybe we think we have to be twice as good as they are at being parents, too. Whatever the reason, lots of women seem willing to believe—and lots of people seem hell-bent on convincing us— that you can't do both, as if they're essentially paths that start in the same place and go in entirely opposite directions. I believed that myself until..."

Feeling my cheeks grow warm and unsure whether I wanted to say out loud why I'd changed my mind, I paused. Katherine rescued me. "Until you fell in love with one of the hottest guys on the planet," she said, "and found that neither wanting him nor being with him changed your ambition for your career in the slightest."

"Basically," I said, smiling. "Ditto with having a baby. And, really, why should it surprise anyone that a woman might want to have this kind of personal life and our kind of career at the same time? Men do it all the time! No one thinks they have to choose one path over the other. Why should we?"

"That's the real question!" The gusto in Katherine's voice startled Nick, but she put her hand on his chest and he relaxed. "Also, I don't think devotion to career is all that relevant to wanting to be a parent, either as a qualifier or a disqualifier. The two things don't necessarily have anything to do with each other. There are lots of reasons to want or not want kids that have nothing to do with whether you have a career. I, for example, don't want kids, but not because I'm committed to my career. That's just my preference regarding kids."

"You seem to like babies well enough," Cheryl said, smiling in Nick's direction.

"I like kids, too," Katherine said. "But I also like my life the way it is, and I don't want to share it or my husband with anyone else."

"Speaking of the hottest guys on the planet," Lynn said, grinning. Katherine smiled and shifted Nick to her other arm.

"Do you want me to take him?" Liz asked her.

"Nope. We're doing fine over here."

"You have to share him at some point—I need the practice!" Liz said, smiling. "You know, Laura's question also raises a definitional problem. If you define being a wife and mother to mean subordinating your interests to your husband's and children's, then no career woman is going to be interested. But it's certainly possible to get married or raise children without subordinating or negating your own identity or value. Somehow in our society we've muddled the two definitions."

"I'm not sure we've muddled them so much as elevated the traditional definition to an exclusive, 'only way to go' status," Cheryl said. "But that's not the only way to go. In my opinion, it's actually the wrong way to go. No one benefits—not really—when someone's interests have to be subordinated. Men don't need that to be happy, children don't need it to thrive, and it's affirmatively harmful for the women who do it."

"It's a pretty good deal for men and children, though," Lynn said, gesturing with the shrimp puff she'd just taken from the colorful array of food Laura had arranged on the coffee table.

"Yes and no," Cheryl said. "My mother was a martyr type. She was always accommodating us or my dad, but she made sure we all knew how much she was 'sacrificing' for us. That was a load to carry in and of itself."

"Women have really been sold a bill of goods," I said, feeling indignant. "We seem to think we have to be either *über* career woman or *über* mom and that it's not possible to compromise on either side without, essentially, failing. That's the real reason the two paths seem mutually exclusive to us."

"What do you mean?" Laura asked.

I slipped off my shoes, folded my legs and settled back into the corner of my favorite chair as I explained. "If we want a serious career, there's an implicit assumption that we have to be devoted one hundred percent to it and that motherhood will be a distraction or even a disqualifier. If we want to be mothers, there's an implicit assumption that we have to stay home and devote ourselves one hundred percent to *that* to do it properly. So choosing to do both makes us feel like we're not doing either one well or right."

"It's ironic, isn't it?" Cheryl said. "Women are known to be good multi-taskers, but the status quo assumption is that we can't possibly do these two things well at the same time—even though they're two things that most men do simultaneously without giving it a second thought."

"We haven't only been sold a bill of goods," Liz said. She put her feet back on the floor and leaned forward. "Women have also been way too willing to buy into inflexible definitions and to force them down one another's throats. Not that long ago, being a wife and mother was considered the only valid option. Then, being a high-powered career woman became the requirement. Now, we're seeing backlash to that."

Her diamond glittered as she put her glass on the table next to her chair. "It's all so unnecessarily restrictive! The world is a sexist place, but this stuff is more diffuse when it comes from men. It's women who make one another feel like failures. We're incredibly hard on each other. Jane and I have talked about this before. It's like we have rival camps."

"That's what makes *me* wild," Lynn said. "I'm sure the feeling is mutual, but I can't stand those fascist suburban mothers who seem to feel they can't rest until they've driven every woman alive to her knees and made her admit that the only true achievement for women is what they do. I have a sister-in-law like that. You know the type—well-educated, holier-than-thou and determined to justify their own parasitic existence by insisting that marriage slash motherhood *is* a career. It may be politically incorrect to say so, but marrying and raising your own children is not a career!"

"I'd like to temper that a little," Cheryl said, with a tolerant smile. "I agree that 'woman' is not a synonym for 'wife' or 'mother.' I also agree that raising kids isn't a career. In fact, treating it as if it is causes a lot of problems. Kids don't need to have schedules that are booked solid with activities and they shouldn't be regarded as trophies for their parents. That said, though, raising kids is both a completely justifiable way to spend your time and a very important responsibility."

"OK," Lynn said, "but as far as I can tell, my sister-in-law and her gang don't spend much time actually raising kids. They shop and play tennis and decorate their homes. And quite a few of their kids are real disasters."

She held up her hands. "But whatever. They're entitled to live their lives the way they want to. What they're not entitled to do is impose their choices on everyone else or try to cut other women off at the knees. And their reasoning is so fucking specious! If they're so sure motherhood is the quintessence of being a woman, why do they need to insist that it's a *career*?"

I'd noticed that Nick had been fussing a little. Katherine had been jiggling him and murmuring to him, which was why she'd been uncharacteristically quiet. Now he started to cry—to my relief, not very seriously.

"Does your baby object to the use of the word 'fucking,' Jane?" Katherine asked.

I laughed. "I hope not. If he does, he'll have to get over it. This isn't the first time he's heard it and it certainly won't be the last. It's weird how you notice it when he's around, though, isn't it?"

"He's probably hungry," Laura said, looking at her watch. "I'll go warm up a bottle."

I thanked her as she headed for the kitchen and I took Nick from Katherine. It felt good to hold him and he seemed glad to be back with me, too, especially after I put the knuckle of my index finger in his mouth and let him suck on it.

"Have you stopped breastfeeding?" Liz asked.

"Yeah, a couple weeks ago. It was great in the beginning, but after about a month, it started driving me crazy to have to get undressed every time he had to be fed."

"Oh, thank God!" she said. "Everything you read suggests you're some kind of monster if you don't breastfeed until the kid goes to pre-school. I assumed that was just more herd mentality fascism, but I'm glad to know you've left the herd."

"So to speak," Katherine said. "Didn't you do it for longer?" she asked Cheryl.

"Yeah, about five months," Cheryl said, smiling. "I know what you mean, though, Jane. It was great and then, one day, I just couldn't wait to be done with it."

Katherine had started assembling a plate for herself. "What's the deal on this beautiful food you've all been eating while I've been baby-sitting?" she said. "It looks fantastic!"

"It's delicious!" Liz said. "Don't tell me you did all this, Jane. I'm already feeling intimidated by how easily you're handling the baby and how calm you seem."

"Don't worry," I assured her, smiling. "Laura did all the food, and my calmness is highly situational. If Nick starts howling, chances are good you'll see me do the same."

"Anybody need anything from in here?" Laura called from the kitchen.

After the chorus of "No, thanks," Katherine said, "Laura, your food is great!"

"I'm glad you're enjoying it!" Laura said as she came back with Nick's bottle. "It was fun to put it all together." She held up the bottle and asked me, "Want me to feed him?"

"Oh, can I?" Liz asked.

"Sure." I waited until she was settled with the bottle and one of Nick's blankets to protect her clothes, then handed him to her. As I sat back down, I said, "I'm not sure I can rant and feed him at the same time anyway."

"I'll get you started," Katherine said. "Here's what I've been dying to ask during this whole conversation. Why do we give a fuck what anyone else thinks of the choices we make for our own lives?"

She ate another of Laura's savory tidbits with a little murmur of pleasure, then she said, "Twenty-four is much too young to get married, did you know? If you do it anyway, you're really supposed to have produced a kid or two by the time you're thirty-one. Lynn can verify that not getting married is also highly questionable. Where working is concerned, we all know plenty of men who think we don't belong anywhere near their offices in anything but an unmarried secretarial capacity. We all know plenty of other people who think the term 'working mother' is—or should be—an oxymoron. That attitude isn't limited to fascist suburban mothers."

Katherine grinned in delight. "I love that phrase, Lynn! It's like a whole demographic group! But those ladies aren't alone. Lots of people think that women who go back to work after having babies aren't doing the right thing by their babies or, for that matter, by their jobs either now that they have babies.

"There's no way to win. The decision not to marry or not to have kids is considered peculiar or even fishy. The decision to be a working mother is more common, but it's not much more respected or applauded than it ever was. The decision to be a non-working mother, once perfectly acceptable, has fallen into total disrepute—make it and you can count on being considered weak-minded even by people who claim great reverence for motherhood. No wonder some of those dames turn into fascists!"

Gesturing emphatically with a cookie, she concluded, "No matter what choice you make, there's someone to criticize it. It's all misogynistic bullshit, designed to hamstring women and make us feel bad! And, probably, to make things easier for men. You can't win, so why not just tune out all the noise and do whatever the fuck you want?"

"Wow!" I said with sincere admiration as Katherine popped the cookie into her mouth. "I couldn't do a better rant than that! Can I change just one thing? You can't win in everyone else's eyes, but so what? Winning in your own eyes is what matters. Tuning out the noise and doing whatever the fuck you want is exactly how you *do* win. That's what men seem to understand instinctively. Maybe it's egotism, maybe it's arrogance, maybe it's because society's expectations aren't as hard on men, but most of them do exactly as they please with their personal and professional lives and they couldn't care less whether other people approve of their choices."

"That's so true! It doesn't even occur to them to wonder whether other people approve," Liz said, looking up from Nick, who was enthusiastically draining his bottle. "And, you know, this 'career versus motherhood' issue is actually pretty effete. Most of the women in the world—and probably even in this country—would consider it a luxury to be in a position to worry about what to choose. They have *no* choice. They're having babies because women are the only ones who can do that and they're working because it's the only way to make ends meet."

"That's a really good point," I said. "Ever since Nick was born, I've felt like all this crap doesn't have anything to do with how things really work. It *is* effete, and it's more political and intellectual than real, too. The reality is that doing both isn't that complicated or even that conscious. Yesterday, for example, I reviewed financial reports and made some suggestions to the guy I put in charge of my unit while I'm gone. I also took care of my baby. One didn't affect the quality of the other at all."

"That's exactly right," Cheryl said. "Speaking as someone who's been doing both for nearly two years, it's just not that hard. Managing the logistics can get stressful and it does require some accommodations, but it's not even close to impossible. And it's incredibly rewarding."

"That must be the secret all the criticizers don't want anyone to know," Lynn said. "Particularly the suburban fascists." She grinned and turned to Laura. "So, Laura—have we answered your question?"

"And then some!" Laura said. She looked a little wide-eyed, but she smiled warmly.

Later, over dinner, Laura and I recapped the afternoon for Charlie. Dinner itself was a new mother's dream—it was totally delicious and it was produced without any involvement whatsoever on my part. Charlie grilled thick steaks to rare perfection; Laura assembled the perfect variety of tea party leftovers, along with a salad of ingredients I didn't even know we had.

My sister's recap and her take on what she'd heard surprised me. I realized that she had turned into a woman I admired. Despite her ultra-feminine demeanor and her predilection for tea parties and big weddings, she was neither silly nor weak. She really did have a backbone, and she also demonstrated an unexpected facility for clever and insightful frankness.

For one thing, she made Charlie blush—not an easy thing to do. Laura told him he had quite the fan club among my friends and repeated the comment about him being one of the hottest guys on the planet. Then, she wittily but unambiguously implied that he must really be something as she congratulated him on having so effectively domesticated someone like me.

Much as I was enjoying seeing my normally unflappable husband blush, I had to object to Laura's use of the word "domesticate." She coolly replied that, whether I was willing to admit it or not, I'd clearly and irrefutably stopped believing that marriage and motherhood were sexist traps best avoided by women with other options, a "truth" she reminded me I'd tried to force down her throat more times than she cared to remember.

Then she said, "It's really good that you've opened yourself up, Jane, and I love that it's made you so happy! I love your friends, too. You're all so different from stereotypical career women. Do you think there even *are* stereotypical career women? And you're not clones of each other either. It was inspiring to be with all of you!"

"Inspiring how?" Charlie asked her (his cheeks back to their normal color).

"It was a great illustration of how arbitrary—and unwarranted—it is to think women have to be any particular thing or make any particular choice," Laura said. "There's not a right way to be a woman. Just like men, we are who we are. And no apologies are necessary."

❖ ❖ ❖

I WAS EXCITED about going back to work.

I missed being my business self. Maternity leave was a nice break, but after the flurry of the first few weeks, it got boring. There was plenty to do, but not enough to occupy my mind. And there was too much unmanageable emotional turmoil.

It wasn't that I resented being at home with a baby. I enjoyed the time with Nick. Once Charlie and I stopped being so jumpy around him, he calmed down considerably and was often a lot of fun. He continued to engross us, and I felt that I had become a fairly capable and comfortable mother (a somewhat unexpected and very gratifying development).

But isolation with an infant was emotionally challenging and frustrating in ways work wasn't. There were times—usually the seemingly interminable afternoons toward the end of the week—when I almost hated Nick. Well, not Nick exactly, but his pushy neediness and his utter dependence. I knew he wasn't deliberately beleaguering me, but he seemed perverse when he fussed for hours or refused to sleep or screamed at the top of his lungs. And my inability to do anything effective about it made me feel desperate, even angry.

I could calmly and capably put together billion dollar deals, launch new products, manage recalcitrant people. How was it possible, I wondered (near tears), that I couldn't keep a fucking *baby* happy? But with the baby it wasn't a matter of using expertise to achieve a logical result. And there wasn't a clear definition of success either—it was unrealistic to expect an always content, always healthy, always adorable baby. Sometimes Nick was simply out of sorts, and my only option was to try not to go crazy while I waited him out.

There also wasn't much intellectual stimulation involved in taking care of an infant. Whether Nick was playing happily with me or howling, my intellectual capabilities weren't the ones I used to deal with him. I talked to him all the time, but he said nothing intelligible in return. I had almost no one to converse with during the daylight hours. Charlie and my friends were all at work, and we didn't live among other families with young children (even assuming I could have found things to talk about with stay-at-home moms).

I did a lot of reading, including of the materials being forwarded from my office, and I talked to Mike weekly about my unit. Both Sam and Jennifer called occasionally to gossip about the Company or get my opinion on something, and my girls' club and other friends stayed in touch, too. But none of that engaged my brain the way working did.

I also missed being with other people, which came as a surprise. I'd spent so much of my adult life finding other people irritating that I didn't expect to feel isolated without them. Taking a break from interpersonal interactions was another of the reasons I'd decided on a full three-month leave.

It turned out that I was apparently more social than I'd thought. When I took Nick for walks in his stroller, I found myself chatting with all sorts of random people—salespeople in stores, librarians, other pedestrians. Even in a busy city, a baby is a good conversation starter. I enjoyed quite a few pleasant chats I would never have had without Nick to capture people's attention and break the ice. These conversations were mostly small talk, but I was thirsty even for that after the relative silence of spending my days in the company of an infant.

I still had Charlie to talk to in the evenings, of course, and we still talked the way we always had—a lot and on a variety of topics. (Despite our continuing fascination with our offspring, after the first few weeks we did manage to fit in a few other topics of conversation.) Charlie cut back on his travel schedule while I was on leave and he was home by 7:00 or 7:30 almost every night. By that time, I was often literally starving for adult company. As I asked him hungry questions about every aspect of his day, he joked that he felt like an emissary from the outside world to a remote outpost.

I understood how women tended to get overly dependent on their husbands once they had children. In my case at least, this had nothing to do with weak-mindedness. It was the result of being removed from the quotidian world of business and commerce and charged instead with the care and feeding of a needy and dictatorial, but non-verbal, baby. I didn't feel involved with the world. Instead, I felt cocooned with Nick. This was great in many ways, but it wore thin as an exclusive pursuit.

Charlie was my pipeline to the outside world and the only other adult I saw on a daily basis. I counted on him for everything I had once gotten from my work and the many other people who surrounded me there. He did a terrific job, but I didn't like being dependent on him in this way. It created an imbalance in our relationship that I doubted would be healthy for very long. I was eager to rejoin the game, both to feel like my real self again and to get back on a more reciprocal footing with Charlie.

I knew I was going to feel insanely busy when I first went back to work, so I decided to put our home in order while I was still on leave. One of the tasks I set for myself was to cull through a few boxes of papers I'd moved from my old apartment when Charlie and I got married. I hadn't needed anything in them (or even touched them) for well over three years, and I suspected the financial records and whatever else they contained were probably no longer worth keeping.

That turned out to be true, but under some old tax records, I found my paper calendars from my first years at the Firm. I was surprised that I'd kept them. I'd never been a packrat and I rarely kept things I had no further use for. I couldn't recall, but I must have thought the record of my old appointments and projects would somehow prove useful.

Flipping through the calendars offered a surprisingly good history of my early career. I was happily reminiscing (and wishing I had someone more interested than Nick to exclaim to) when I came upon the notation of my first mentoring meeting with Charlie.

To my amazement, the date of our first meeting was ten years to the day before the date I was going back to work. I knew this was merely a fluky calendar coincidence, but it felt meaningful, like a portent. I liked the symmetry of a decade bookended by those two events. They were so connected, and in some ways so linear, but they nevertheless represented points on a path that was beyond the imagination of the person who made the original calendar notation.

I could still remember the Jane I had been when I made that note. I still felt like her occasionally, too, although her inflexible certainty about what the world required of her as the price of success had felt foreign to me for some time. She had been so sure that control and detachment were vital to achieving career success—and equally sure that love and babies were antithetical to it. She could not in a million years have guessed (and she would never have believed) that on the tenth anniversary of the meeting she was calendaring, she would be returning to her job as head of a corporate business unit after having had a baby with the mentor she was about to meet.

Nick wriggled excitedly and gurgled at me when I told him this. Smiling at him and thinking about his father, I had another of the epiphanies that characterized my relationship with Charlie—those striking moments of insight that had occurred luminously and consistently, like mile markers along a dark road, ever since that date ten years before.

Love hadn't tamed or broken me. It had unlocked my life. My life before I fell in love was in the same category of constrained as my life on maternity leave. There was nothing wrong with the features of either life, but they were both incomplete, partial. Work without love and love without work were equally fractional.

It was neither necessary nor desirable to choose one over the other. Like Charlie's and my merger, the combination of love and work was enhancing and multiplicative. It created a whole that was more, alchemically more, than the sum of its parts. It had propelled me to a much more open attitude as well as to my husband, my pregnancy and my baby—all things that humanized me not only in other people's eyes, but also as a matter of actual fact.

❖ ❖ ❖

Charlie

I was unprepared for the intensity of my feelings once Nick was born. Being excited about becoming a father in theory turned out to be nothing compared to the passionate exhilaration—and the powerful sense of responsibility—I felt in response to the reality.

From the moment I saw Nick in Jane's arms, I loved him fiercely, protectively. All I wanted was to keep him safe and make him happy. And when I held him in my own arms, the enormity of my responsibility to him hit me forcefully. He deserved nothing less than the best person I could be, and I felt inspired, as well as determined, to live up to that standard for him.

My fierce and protective feelings weren't only for Nick. I felt them for Jane, too. It seemed to me that I'd had no idea what she was capable of or how strong she was. Her courage and her grit knocked me out. I felt overpoweringly grateful to her, too.

Her labor horrified me. She was white-faced and breathless, but so resolute, so stoical, so *concentrated*. She simply clenched her teeth (and my hands) and handled it, not even aware of the tears that trickled down her cheeks. I understood her "beside the point" feeling with a vengeance. I felt useless as well as of no consequence. I hated not being able to relieve the pain or do the work for her.

My mother had been so right—just like pregnancy, the burdens of childbirth fell squarely and basically exclusively on the mother. Even as the realities of labor and delivery faded in the exultant, fervent joy we felt at Nick's birth, Jane's huge effort stayed very fresh in my mind. I doubted there was anything she couldn't handle, but I resolved many times during the first days of our son's life that the burdens of raising him would not fall so unequally on her shoulders, however powerful.

Jane and I were both dazed with happiness, amazement and some lingering disbelief. Nick's existence was remarkable to us at first, even a little implausible. And we felt like the rubes Claire had called us when the twins were infants—there seemed to be a tremendous amount to take in and to learn. As Jane joked when we left the hospital, it seemed surprising—not to mention ill-advised—that the proper authorities would so casually relinquish an innocent baby into our inexperienced and essentially clueless clutches.

Nick seemed mysterious, complex, even a little frightening when we first got him home and were faced with having to take care of him without the expert help of the incredible nurses at the hospital. He often looked judgmental to us as well. When he gazed at us mutely or screamed in apparent outrage, it was as if he simply could not believe we were too incompetent or lazy to get him what he needed.

Feeding him, changing him, holding him and so forth were straightforward and easy enough, but they were all we had. Whenever they failed to make him happy, we felt like blunderers. We weren't at all sure of our parental instincts, so everything that didn't work instantly felt wrong. We agonized over his distress and searched for the reasons behind it.

The reality, of course, was that he was just doing what babies do. Late one night, I suddenly understood that taking care of him was never going to be a matter of finding one right combination of actions or fixes. Nick wasn't a problem to be solved; he was an independent human being with a personality of his own and needs that would no doubt change frequently. There was bound to be plenty of trial and error over the years, even after he was better able to communicate with us.

Jane realized this quickly, too. She just needed enough experience to feel confident that we weren't missing or failing to do anything important. By the time he was three weeks old, we were having a great time with him. And we felt like we'd done something incredibly significant.

Having children with Jane had appealed to me from the moment I fell in love with her, and I found it very moving to see the two of us blended in Nick. The general consensus was that he looked like me, but I saw Jane in his face, too—and not only because he often looked irritated. It was something about his eyes. His expression suggested a skeptical, observant appraisal of what was going on around him that was very reminiscent of Jane. He also had an intensity that reminded me of hers. Whatever the reason, I felt full of love for his mother every time I looked at our son.

The week I stayed home right after he was born was fantastic. I liked being as involved as Jane was in taking care of him. Once I went back to work, I envied her ever-increasing expertise and the additional time she got to spend with him. It occurred to me that one of the reasons mothers so often seemed to have tighter connections than fathers with their kids might be that they spent more time at home in the beginning and, accordingly, became more adept caretakers.

It was very hard for me to leave Jane and Nick each day. And while I had no trouble concentrating on work while I was there, by late afternoon I was always anxious to get back to them. Nick was often cranky when I got home, but he usually responded pretty well to me and it was gratifying to be able to soothe him. (Jane joked that he was probably just as hungry for different companionship as she was after they'd spent the better part of twelve hours together.) She thanked me often for arranging my schedule so that I was almost always home by 7:30 while she was on leave, but the truth was that I did it as much for myself as for her. I loved being at home with my wife and our baby.

I thought often about the kind of person Nick would become and all the things we'd do together as he grew up. This was terrific enough before he offered much in the way of reaction, and it got even better once he started responding. Smiles, gurgles, squeals, excited movements of his arms and legs—they all made me unbelievably happy. Jane rolled her eyes at me and teased me about gushing, but I couldn't help it. Nick touched and inspired me, and I knew it was only the beginning.

❖ ❖ ❖

SHORTLY AFTER Jane went back to work in July, Victor's remaining crony on the Executive Committee announced that he was retiring at the end of the year and would step down from the Committee as soon as we named a replacement. That created the first vacancy since the EC coup, and I felt strongly that we should fill it with a woman.

At the time of the coup, I had regretted that our slate didn't include any women. But there were none of sufficient seniority at the Firm and we'd decided we had enough to manage without adding the effort of identifying and recruiting someone from outside, then selling her to the rest of the Firm. One step at a time, we'd told ourselves.

There was something about Nick's birth and the straightforward, capable way Jane went back to running her unit after her maternity leave that made me feel our "one step at a time" approach, however practical, had been essentially a rationalization. Women seemed to me to be able to handle just about anything, and it started to strike me as shabby that we hadn't yet managed to handle getting even one into the Firm's management.

The Firm still had no women positioned for appointment to the EC, although we had made good progress in the last year. We'd moved women up via both the mentoring program and the creation of a group operations manager job. In addition to streamlining group management, the GOM position was a feeder job for group head. Two of the GOMs were women and both of them were stellar. I had no doubt that in another year or two they and several of the mentors would be good candidates for the EC.

We considered naming one of these women to fill the EC vacancy even if it was premature. A couple of them, including Lynn, were probably strong enough to make their voices heard even without a more established power base. But we weren't looking to put a woman on the EC just so we could say we had one. The goal was to realize the actual benefits, financial and otherwise, of inclusivity and diversity—and to demonstrate that it wasn't necessary to relax standards in order to include women.

Putting a token woman on the Committee satisfied neither of these goals. We needed someone with proven leadership skills and either a client base or some other equally credible value to bring to the Firm. All the EC members had strong client relationships; most were (or had once been) group heads and also chaired important Firm committees or held other administrative leadership positions. Naming a woman without these qualifications would undercut both the purpose behind our stated diversity goals and her ability to feel and act like a full-fledged member.

Because we'd have to look outside to fill the immediate vacancy with a woman, there was a fair amount of discussion at the EC about waiting for the next opening or seeking a woman for the open spot but filling it with the best candidate we found, irrespective of gender. As far as I was concerned, this was just so much bullshit designed to put off diversifying the Committee. I argued hotly that there was no reason we couldn't find a qualified woman unless we failed to look seriously for one and that we shouldn't settle for filling the vacancy with another man. As a result, I ended up in charge of the search committee.

Jane was very pleased about this. She also joked that it was evidently my year to be seeking qualified women for one position or another. I told her I hoped I'd be as lucky with the EC search as we'd been in finding a nanny.

We'd worked together to conceptualize what kind of person with what kind of skills we wanted to care for Nick, and I'd handled the logistics of identifying and contacting agencies. Jane disliked making cold calls and explaining what she wanted to people too uninterested or unintelligent to pay attention. She also thought we might stand out with the agencies, and perhaps get better results, if they thought of us as the unusual couple where the husband had called. I doubted that was enough to make us stand out, but I was happy to make the calls.

I remained determined to share the responsibility of raising Nick equally with Jane. I knew she would take the lead on arranging and conducting interviews with prospective nannies, both because she liked to control things and because she was home, but I wanted to be as involved in the process as she was. I also wanted whoever we hired to consider both of us her boss—not just Jane.

Just as we were beginning to arrange interviews with agency candidates (none of whom looked very promising on paper), Claire called. One of the medical residents she worked with at the hospital was asking around to see if anyone was interested in talking to her mother about a child care position. Lena, the mother, was in her early 50s. She had four children, the oldest being Claire's resident. The youngest had left for college the year before, and Lena was looking for something to do.

Jane and I liked her right away. We also liked the fact that Claire spoke highly of her daughter—we figured Lena probably knew what she was doing if she had intelligent, responsible kids. She and her husband had emigrated from Eastern Europe 20 years before. He had always worked long hours, which he continued to do, and she had devoted her time to raising their kids. She was overjoyed at the idea of being a nanny for a baby.

Her situation was perfect for us, too. We didn't have room for a live-in and we weren't ready to move, but we needed someone who could come early and, when necessary, stay late. Jane and I both planned to get home early most nights—we knew we'd want to see Nick and each other—but we frequently had evening events to attend and we had no illusions about how unmanageable work hours could be. We didn't want to have to watch the clock or turn down opportunities because we had a nanny who had to leave at a set time every evening.

Lena didn't need a place to live and she had no problem staying late, even on short notice. She also kept our apartment very neat, which was a nice bonus, and she liked to shop for groceries and cook for us. (Jane asked her to cook only occasionally. Lena was big on heavy meals. She was sure American women in general and Jane in particular were iron-deficient, and she didn't consider a meal to be adequate if it didn't include, as Jane put it, huge hunks of roasted meat.)

Lena was terrific with Nick, if a little over-protective, and he always seemed happy to see her. Jane and I felt very good about leaving him in her care and very lucky to have found her.

The EC search turned out to be more complicated. Victor's retiring crony was not a group head, so the pending EC vacancy would not create a simultaneous group head vacancy. The best candidates—women or men—were not likely to be interested in coming to the Firm if we had nothing to offer in the way of a leadership position (or internal power base) other than the EC spot. Accordingly, we had to move someone aside.

This was not as difficult or potentially awkward at the Firm as it would have been in a more hierarchical culture. More than one group head had already made noises about wanting to be relieved of the job. People at the Firm were deal junkies, the vast majority of whom viewed group head jobs as bureaucratic distractions from what really counted. To most of our people, the challenges of originating business and structuring deals were much more appealing than the challenges of managing the Firm, and the power that came along with a group head position didn't look worth the aggravation. (I had my own occasional doubts along these lines.)

We decided that Public Finance offered the best opportunity. The field was one with a lot of women in it, quite a few of them senior and experienced, and the Firm's group was in need of stronger leadership. The incumbent was a good enough guy, but not a particularly forceful or effective leader. He was also tired—he'd been in the job for a long time. While there were a couple younger guys who'd indicated some interest in the position, neither was ready for it and neither, we thought, would be seriously affronted by not getting it. The best people in the group— the ones we didn't want to lose—had no interest at all in the group head position. Obviously, they cared who we put in the job, but they didn't object as a matter of principle to our going outside to fill it.

By late August, we had developed a short list and put out feelers. After the first round of interviews, it was clear that the best candidate was Renée, a woman in her late 40s who was at the time the treasurer of a large, publicly held transportation company.

Renée had started her career as a lawyer. After ten years of representing municipal finance clients from that end, she'd moved to a competitor of the Firm's and done deals as an investment banker. The company she was with when we approached her had been her client at her law firm and her banking firm. Her company did a steady stream of large and visible financing projects, using both public and private money. Renée had executive management responsibility for those projects as well as for investments and cash management.

She would bring her company's business to the Firm, which was a big plus. Because she had only been out of investment banking for five years, it was likely she would also be able to bring in some of her other former clients.

Renée had an entrepreneurial spirit and a strong personality to go along with her on-the-money background, experience and client base. She aced the interviews—we all thought she was impressive as well as someone who would easily fit into the Firm's culture. She was well aware that she wouldn't be roundly welcomed in all quarters, but that didn't faze her. She said she'd faced and overcome similarly wary receptions twice before and was confident she could do it again.

I had no reservations about her. She was smart as hell, a straight talker, highly self-confident and charming, too. She knew the business inside out, which gave her a lot of credibility. She also had years of leadership experience at both the deal and departmental levels; that, along with her informal and extroverted personality, would be more than enough to win over (or at least let her hold her own with) naysayers like Victor, people in Public Finance unsure about their new boss, and anyone else inclined to give her a hard time.

After overcoming some delaying tactics on the part of a few reluctant EC members (who voiced no problem with Renée in particular, but were still hoping they could forestall adding a woman to the Committee), we offered her the job. She was, as we expected, pleased and interested, but she had compensation requirements that took longer than expected to iron out.

If we'd had any doubt about her savvy or her negotiating skills, they would have been completely eradicated by the finesse and well-mannered stubbornness with which she approached structuring her compensation package. She was neither greedy nor unreasonable, but she accurately perceived that we needed her more than she needed us and she didn't hesitate to use that imbalance to her advantage. As frustrated as I was with both the Firm's relatively inflexible comp structure and Renée's intransigence, I also had to hand it to her. She clearly knew how to handle herself and how to get what she wanted.

She liked the opportunity the Firm offered, but she saw no reason to give up her company's much greater wealth-building opportunities for nothing. We could match her salary without creating parity issues for other group heads. We could also allocate points to her that would equate to her corporate bonus target, assuming the Firm continued to perform at historical levels. Not being a public company, however, we couldn't match her annual stock option grants.

Renée understood this and was willing to take the job without compensation of this kind, but she wanted both a significant signing bonus and monetary protection against arbitrary termination or other unjustifiable actions on the Firm's part for at least two years. Even after we agreed in principle on terms (which required taking the Firm's HR director out of the loop), Renée's lawyer and ours argued at length before they finally hammered out an unusually complex contract.

To celebrate the successful conclusion of that overlong process, Jane and I took Renée and her husband, Phil, to dinner one evening. I was curious to know what Jane would think of Renée and also to see how the two of them interacted.

Jane had given me a hard time about not having any women on the Firm's interview team, both on general principles and because she thought a woman interviewer was more likely to be able to smoke out what she called a queen bee—that is, a woman who would not be supportive of other women. I saw her point, but the interview team was the interview team. I was no more interested in undermining our eventual decision by modifying the team than I was in filling the vacancy with a token woman who didn't meet our standards.

Their interaction at dinner was fascinating. Jane's intelligence and demeanor in business situations—social or substantive—always impressed and entertained me, and Renée was masterful. She reminded me of my father—she was sincere, friendly, confident and clearly the one pulling the conversational strings.

After the introductions, congratulations and some small talk, Renée complimented Jane on having reached such an impressive level at such a young age. She spoke highly of both Jane's company and a couple people she knew in its treasury group and asked a few questions that let Jane talk about her career path and her unit. Then, with a smile, Renée asked, "Do you find corporate politics suffocating in comparison to your investment banking experience?"

Jane smiled, too. "I don't find them suffocating," she said, "but they are definitely more cumbersome. Is that one of the reasons you were interested in joining the Firm?"

"Indirectly, yes," Renée said. "I preferred my law and banking firms to the corporate environment. They were much less predictable and stultifying, and I never felt I had to contain myself to the degree that's necessary to get along well at a company. I also like new challenges. The logical next step for me at the company would have been to throw my hat in the ring to succeed the CFO. But the CFO job didn't appeal to me enough to make it worth the effort to take on the politics entailed in getting it."

"That's a very high profile next step to leave behind," Jane said. "It would really be something for a woman to hold the CFO job at your company. It must have been difficult for you to walk away from that possibility."

"Not really." Renée shook her head. "The Firm offers me a less high profile, but I think more meaningful leadership opportunity—and in a much less rigid, more self-directed environment." She sipped some wine, then smiled pleasantly. "I've never been overly swayed by the 'big step forward for women' aspect of jobs. As far as I'm concerned, just because I *can* do something splashy in that regard doesn't mean I have to—or even that I should. My career is for me. I've always rather resented being considered a flag bearer for womanhood."

Phil, who was quite a bit older than Renée, had, like me, been following the conversation with interest. He seemed as aware as I was that these comments might provoke Jane—we both swiveled our heads toward her to see what she would say.

"Really," she said (rather flatly, I thought). "I'm not sure exactly what you mean by that."

"Don't get the wrong impression," Renée said, with another of her pleasant and self-possessed smiles. "I realize that I'm a role model and an example. I know I'm in a spotlight, and I do my best to perform in a way that reflects well on women. I also seek to hire and promote women, particularly for positions where we're under-represented. I've had a lot of success with that, too. Like most senior women, I find other women are drawn to my groups. A good role model is easier to recognize when it looks like you, isn't it?"

"Just like talent," Jane said.

"Exactly." Renée nodded. "But I don't believe that the goal of achieving workplace equality for women should govern my career decisions simply because I am a woman. That's a lot of pressure to put on a career—unnecessary pressure, in my opinion. I believe I'm a better role model, a better example, and more successful, too, when I let my interests and my skills govern my career decisions."

"That's fair enough, Renée," I said. "And I'm very glad you're coming to the Firm instead of going after the CFO job, but that would be a very high visibility job for a woman to hold. How do you expect companies to become more diverse and more inclusive if women like you don't consider yourselves flag bearers and go after jobs like that?"

Renée looked amused. "Before I answer that," she said, "I'd like to ask you why in the world I should have any greater personal responsibility than you do to bring that change about. One might more easily argue that *you* should have the greater responsibility, given that men still write the rules."

After a brief pause (clearly to let that sink in), she continued, "But, be that as it may, my point is that women shouldn't let sexism and inequality of opportunity force us to pursue goals that *don't* excite us any more than we should let them stop us from pursuing the goals that do."

"You'll get no argument from me on that," I said. "I'm also not going to argue that I have less responsibility than you do to bring about change. But don't you have to admit that you're better positioned to set the high profile example?"

"Sure," Renée said, shrugging her shoulders, "but that doesn't outweigh my personal preferences." She leaned forward and spoke to both Jane and me. "Look, I believe in the end result of achieving equality, and I hope it's one of the outcomes of my work, but it is not—nor do I think it should be—the *raison d'être* or governing principle of my career."

Turning to me, she said, "I imagine that's exactly how you think about your own career. And surely you don't want to contend that I should have less freedom to formulate and pursue my personal career goals simply because men still own the business world?"

Phil chuckled. "I think she's painted you into a corner, Charlie."

"I think so, too," I said, laughing.

"Men tend to serve up softballs on questions like these," Renée said, grinning. "But I bet Jane has a harder ball to throw."

"I'm not sure I do," Jane said. She looked puzzled, but not on guard the way she had before. "I'm certainly not going to disagree that the powers that be have as much responsibility to work toward equality as women do. I also agree that no one's personal career goals should be limited by anything other than his or her talents and interests. That said, though, someone has to take on the responsibility for blazing trails. And who better to do it than women like you with the track record to prove you have what it takes?"

"The question is what trails and at what personal cost?" Renée said. "Being the first woman on the Firm's Executive Committee and in charge of its Public Finance group is certainly blazing a trail. And it suits my interests." She leaned back in her chair, her wineglass in hand, and Jane leaned toward her, as if pulled. "Who's to say it's a less meaningful or significant trail to blaze merely because it won't put me on the list of women who are one of the top five executives at a public company? That's a visible and easily measured sign of progress, but it's by no means the only important one."

"OK," Jane said, "but isn't the ingrained sexism at your company one of the reasons leaving suits your interests? If so, and if women keep leaving for that reason, then the change that women at the top would bring will continue to elude us. It's a catch-22—and one that can't be broken through without us, no matter how well-intentioned the men in power may be."

"Good point," Renée said, "but still not enough to justify taking the position that women should sacrifice their personal interests to 'the cause.' Also, that isn't the reason leaving the company suits my interests. I doubt I'm leaving ingrained sexism behind. Do you think the Firm is any better in that regard?"

"Hardly," Jane laughed. "If anything, it's worse."

"That's what I'm assuming. But the more autonomous culture suits me better. As I remember it, even an obnoxious lunatic can flourish if he has lucrative clients or enough power of some other kind." Renée smiled. "I'm not endorsing obnoxious lunatics, but I do like the behavioral freedom, which I've had relatively little of as a senior corporate executive. I often feel hamstrung and as if I have to take the longest way possible to get to the right result—and for reasons having nothing to do with sexism."

"That's so true!" Jane exclaimed. "Even at my level, it's already obvious that, while both are important, how your colleagues feel about what you accomplish is more important than what you actually accomplish. That's always seemed backwards to me. I think the top priorities should be results and good faith collegiality, but keeping colleagues comfortable and not intimidated tends to have more sway, at least at my company."

"Mine, too," Renée said. "I doubt the Firm is totally free from that, but I expect both my position and the looser environment to diminish its influence on what I do day-to-day. I'm very excited about the move! My impact as a woman and a leader at the Firm may be less visible to the outside world than that CFO job I'm leaving on the table, but I'm betting it will be much bigger."

"You sound very passionate about that, and it's great to hear." Jane raised her wineglass to Renée. "You'll be a wonderful influence at the Firm!"

"Thank you!" said Renée. Their glasses clinked.

"You speak very passionately about your work, too, Jane," Phil said. "And with a line job like yours at a more prominent company, you may well be a better candidate than Renée to break into those high profile top ranks."

"I hope so," Jane said. "And I know there are other good candidates, too—at my company and any number of others. But it drives me crazy that we *still* have to have this discussion!" She shook her head impatiently, then smiled and asked Phil what kind of work he did.

He was interesting. After knocking around, as he put it, at a number of jobs for a few years after college, he decided he wasn't interested in being an employee. He and three friends scraped together enough money from other friends and family to invest seed capital in a start-up company. That investment did OK and they parlayed the results into other start-ups, the third of which was a home run.

From then on, Phil had been a venture capitalist. Sometimes he invested with the three friends, who'd established a private equity firm; more often, he invested on his own. He said he was a loner where business was concerned. His dislike of being an employee had only grown stronger over the years, and while he enjoyed counseling the executives at his portfolio companies from the board seat he insisted on having, he had no interest in building a company or managing infrastructure of his own.

He'd met Renée when she represented his friends' private equity firm. She was his second wife, and it was obvious that he thought she was terrific. He beamed at her pretty much nonstop and he nodded frequently, in apparent admiration, while she talked. He also seemed to get a huge kick out of her, and it didn't surprise me to learn that his first wife, who was also the mother of his two daughters, had been more traditional.

One of Phil's daughters had been working with him on deals for several years. He was very proud of her and told us he was in the process of passing "the family business" on to her. Then he said, "Now my other daughter has no interest in business. Like her own mother, she's a mom."

"Phil!" Renée looked and sounded affectionately exasperated. "Business and motherhood are neither comparable nor mutually exclusive." She turned to us. "You'll have to forgive Phil. He can be a little old-fashioned."

"I'm not old-fashioned!" Phil protested. "If I've learned anything from you and the girls, it's not to underestimate women. But, judging by Barb and my first wife, raising kids is a full-time job."

"Not necessarily for their mother!" Renée said sharply. Then she smiled and said, "Right, Jane?" Phil looked confused and she told him, "Charlie and Jane have a baby."

"You do?" Phil said, now looking surprised.

"We do," I said, smiling. Jane's hand was resting on the table and I took it in mine. "Our son Nick is almost six months old."

"Well, congratulations! That's wonderful! We have a grandchild not too much older than that—great age!" He smiled. "I have a feeling I'm about to be even more impressed by you than I already am, Jane. How on earth do you handle it all?"

"Not by myself, that's for sure!" She squeezed my hand. "Charlie is a wonderful partner, and we have a great nanny, too."

"But the mother is still the mother," Phil declared. "An infant, plus your big job, is a lot to take care of. I know I'd find it daunting."

"There is a lot to manage," Jane said, with an indulgent smile for Phil. "But I'm used to complexity and I'm very organized."

"Complexity characterizes women's lives, doesn't it?" Renée said. "Whether or not we have children. I wonder if that's because men run the world or if there's something more intrinsic about it."

"Both, I think," Jane said. "But, honestly, even though being a parent has added logistical complexity—there's definitely a lot more to pay attention to and feel responsible for—for me, it's also had a simplifying effect."

She twined her leg around mine under the table as she said, "I think having Nick has actually made me calmer about work and probably more effective, too. I seem to have a better perspective on what's important. My time is at more of a premium, so I tend not to waste it on things that don't really matter. And I have a mandatory break every night—Nick demands my attention and I love to see him. It's impossible to brood about work when I'm with him, and that's turned out to be very refreshing and helpful." She grinned. "It surprises me, too, Phil, but the combination has turned out to be accretive."

Phil laughed and patted Jane on the back in an appreciative, one player to another kind of way. "Hang on to this one, Charlie," he said. "She's a winner."

❖ ❖ ❖

A COUPLE WEEKS LATER, I got home about an hour later than usual after attending a reception. Jane had just finished feeding Nick. When I walked in, she kissed him and told him she loved him, then handed him to me and asked me to change him and put him to bed. I was glad to do this. I'd been worried that I might be too late to see him at all. I gave her a quick kiss and took him to his room.

I sat and rocked with him for a while before I put him in his crib. I disliked days when I didn't get to spend more than ten minutes with him or see him when he was actually awake—they made me feel deprived. He was pretty sleepy, though, so after not much longer than ten minutes, I put him down and went to find Jane.

She was standing at the dining room table, sorting through some of Nick's clothes. The minute I appeared in the doorway, she said, "Would you go get something for dinner?"

"Sure. What would you like?"

"What I'd like," she said furiously, "is not to have to be responsible for making every fucking decision that has to be made around here!"

"What is that supposed to mean?"

"It means," she snapped, "that while you blithely think swashbuckling thoughts about how you'd take a bullet for Nicky or me, I'm up to my neck in mundane decisions about whether we need diapers and when he'll have outgrown all his clothes and what time we should go to Liz and Tyler's to see the baby on Saturday and a million other fucking details, including—evidently—what we're going to eat for dinner tonight!"

I walked over to her. She looked wild-eyed, but tired, too, and hassled. I tried to hug her, but she wouldn't let me. She blocked my arms and moved back a couple steps, one of Nick's little shirts in her hand.

"What's wrong with you?" I asked, feeling provoked.

She glared up at me, her body stiff. "I'm sick of *everything* being my responsibility!" she shouted. "Why can't *you* decide what to get for dinner?"

"I'll be happy to decide what to get for dinner. I was just asking what you'd like, not making you responsible for the decision! And what do you mean everything is your responsibility? Don't you think I'm doing my share?"

"That's not the point!"

"What is the point?"

She shook her head dismissively. "I don't want to talk about it! You'll never understand!"

"Try me."

"Just forget it!" She turned to walk away, but I blocked her this time and took hold of both her arms, just below her shoulders.

"What the hell are you doing?" she demanded. "Let go of me!"

"No," I said, holding on to her. "Not until you stop shouting and tell me why you think everything is your responsibility."

"I said I don't want to talk about it! I already have a million things to do—the last thing I need to add to the list is trying to explain something you'll never understand!" She squirmed angrily again. "Let go of me this instant!"

I shook my head. "Stop shouting and tell me what's wrong."

She looked livid, but she took a deep breath and said in a slightly more reasonable tone, "I'm drowning in logistics and decisions—that's what's wrong! It's not that you're not doing your share, but your share is easier. I wish I had your share instead of mine! You get to think grand thoughts and cheerfully do everything I ask and feel like a wonderful husband and father all the time, while I'm stuck with a million day-to-day logistical decisions! I feel constantly bombarded!"

She continued to glare at me, but I kept my voice level as I said, "What else should I be doing?"

"That's the whole fucking problem! Why is it up to me to decide what else you should be doing? Why do I have to be in charge? I don't want to have to think of everything! I *hate* having to be the mother!"

She looked so furious and so miserable that I wasn't even tempted to argue with her. "Do you really?" I asked her instead. "Hate being a mother, I mean?"

"I don't hate *being* a mother," she said, sounding both angry and frustrated. "I hate having to be the mother as opposed to getting to be the father. It's all so much easier for you—and not just because you're a more relaxed person. Your role doesn't include feeling responsible for a million logistics!"

"No, I guess it doesn't, but you know I'll gladly do anything that needs to be done. You don't have to feel responsible for doing everything."

Jane sighed impatiently. She still looked mad, but it no longer felt like she was going to turn away and refuse to talk to me the minute she thought she could, so I let go of her arms. She stayed put and said, "I knew you'd say that and I know you mean it, but that's not the point. None of the things that need doing are that difficult or even that burdensome, but there are *millions* of them. And I always feel like I'm responsible for staying on top of them and making sure they get done, whether by doing them myself or deploying you or Lena or whatever! It's exhausting!"

"Can you give me an example of the kind of thing you mean?" I asked as gently as I could.

"I can give you a hundred fucking examples! I've got examples coming out of my ears!" She crushed the soft little shirt in her hands. "You know the cleaning people were here today, right? Well, that required the dispatcher guy to call me at work to set the time, then I had to call Lena to let her know when they'd be here. Then, I spent twenty minutes when I got home putting all the things they rearranged back where they belong. Lena told me Nick was outgrowing his clothes—she was all excited about how big he's getting, and so am I, but now I'll have to get him more clothes. Liz called to confirm for Saturday, but we couldn't settle on a time because I didn't know your schedule, so I have to figure that out and call her back."

She took an overdue breath, then sighed again. "No particular item is a big deal. It takes less time to do most of it than it would to tell you about it and ask you to do it. But that's part of the problem— it's all so menial. And it's just never-ending. It adds up and overwhelms me. It's been over two hours since I got home and I haven't stopped moving for a second, but I haven't even made a dent. And dinner is nowhere in sight!"

I wanted to smile—both at how outraged she looked over something as minor as dinner and because she seemed a little calmer and I thought she might be ready to take things down another notch or two. But then she added, "And you're oblivious! It's all happening at a level you never worry about, a level you don't even see!"

"Honey, I'm sorry you feel more burdened than I do, but I'm not your problem. We're not adversaries—we're in this together."

"You're *part* of my problem!" she insisted. "I'm horribly envious of you, and I resent the inequality of our roles. *I* want to be oblivious! I wish being a parent were as easy for me as it seems to be for you!"

"It could be easier than it is for you. For one thing, you could ask for help more often. You don't have to do as much yourself."

"But I'd still be organizing everything! I'd still feel like everything was my responsibility!"

"You organized and started handling a lot of things while you were on leave," I reminded her. "The reason I don't think about them is because you've already taken care of them, not because I can't see them. But it doesn't have to stay that way. The cleaning service dispatcher can call me instead of you, for instance. Actually, why can't he talk directly to Lena?"

She shook her head. "I need to know what's going on. I feel like I'm at the center of things—and the one keeping all the plates in the air. I'm worried that if I let go of anything, it will all swirl out of control."

"You can't have it both ways, Jane. If you have to control everything, then you're going to feel in charge. You can't insist on that and then resent it."

"I know," she moaned, looking defeated. She dispiritedly tossed Nick's shirt back on the table, then she walked over to the sofa and sat down.

"You're doing an incredible job, you know," I said, sitting with her. I put my hand on her neck and ran my thumb back and forth across her cheek. "You're a fantastic mother. Nick's happy and healthy, and he adores you. I adore you, too, and I'm really impressed by how smoothly and expertly you're handling things."

"Thanks, I guess, but..."

"Wait, let me finish what I was saying before, OK? In addition to asking for help more often, you could let go of some things—trust that they'll get handled and stop worrying about them. Diapers, for instance. Do you really think Lena or I would use the last few without taking care of buying more? That's never happened and it's not going to. You could also lighten up and let a few things go altogether. You're holding yourself to an incredibly high standard. I know it drives you nuts when the cleaning people rearrange stuff, but did it have to be fixed right away when you were already feeling overwhelmed?"

"It did if I had to look at it!" After snapping this, she closed her eyes and leaned her head back against the sofa. "I know I'm being irrational," she said quietly. "I just feel completely ruffled."

I stroked her hair. "I see that, and I'm sorry. I also understand that feeling responsible for keeping a million plates in the air is a heavy load. But I honestly think you could lighten it just by putting less pressure on yourself."

"Maybe." Her eyes were still closed, but she sounded more optimistic when she said, "It doesn't always seem too heavy. It just crashes down on me sometimes. But your ideas are good ones. I can try them."

"Good. I think they'll help."

"Yeah, they will. I can think of other ways to be more strategic about all this, too." She opened her eyes and looked at me. "But I'm pretty sure I'll still melt down every now and then."

That did make me smile. "You can melt down any time you have to."

Jane smiled back. "You know," she said, "when Nick's old enough to pay attention to us, you're going to have to stop doing things like grab me and refuse to let go when I'm trying to walk away from you. It's undermining."

"It's not my intent to undermine you, darling," I said, grinning. "I was only trying to get your attention and remind you that we're in this together. You don't get to blame me when something's bugging you. I'm not the bad guy."

"I know, and I'm sorry about blaming you, but grabbing me and refusing to let go until I talk to you is a pretty high-handed way to remind me that we're partners!"

"It worked, didn't it?"

She laughed. "That's hardly the point! And when exactly did you stop feeling obliged to fight fair with me? You know how demonstrations of your size and strength make me feel!" She kissed me meaningfully.

"I love you very much, Jane," I said the next time I had a chance to speak.

"I love you, too, you manipulative bastard," she said softly.

❖ ❖ ❖

JANE AND I celebrated our fourth anniversary by taking a long weekend trip to Maine. We left Nick with Claire and Stephen, after the same comically elaborate process of saying goodbye to him that I had mocked

Claire for right after Sean and Mia were born. We also extracted a promise from the twins (and a more reassuring guarantee from Stephen) that they would not use their cousin as a football.

We stayed at a hotel I'd been to with my family on summer vacations. It was more a lodge than a true hotel, with a long, low central building and surrounding cabins. Like other north woods vacation destinations, the accommodations were old and worn—nothing fancy. The cabins were small, no doubt to make them easier to heat in the freezing winters, and they all had fireplaces, which had come in handy even on summer trips when the nights were often cold.

We'd gone to the lodge three or four times when I was a kid. My parents always booked the same two adjacent cabins, a two-bedroom for the four kids and a one-bedroom for themselves. We usually stayed for a week, and the vacations were always good ones.

We spent the days in the pool or on the shore or playing softball and the nights star-gazing or playing board games in front of the fireplace. In contrast to the threadbare surroundings, the food had seemed exotic. We started every day with blueberries and heavy cream (a fantastic substance) and every meal but breakfast offered lobster in one form or another.

Mom and Dad paid very casual attention to us. They put Andy nominally in charge, but Claire refused to recognize his authority, so the two of them spent most of their time fighting with each other. That left Hannah and me free to do as we liked. Hannah was a great vacation buddy—fearless, agile, energetic and closemouthed. (Our more hazardous tree-climbing and ocean-related exploits remain known only to the two of us.) Since she was younger, I got to push her around a little, too, which was a refreshing change from my usual experience as Andy's and Claire's flunky.

When Jane and I arrived at the lodge in December, it looked both familiar and strange to me. The pool was covered and surrounded by piles of snow instead of sparkling and surrounded by swarms of mosquitoes. The sky and the ocean were gray and forbidding instead of blue and inviting. Even with the change in season, though, it was amazing how little seemed to have changed. The only big difference was that everything looked much smaller than I remembered.

I couldn't stop reminiscing as we walked around. We kept coming across tangible reminders of my childhood trips, including the tree Hannah had fallen out of with a sickening thud (scaring the hell out of me, but fortunately not breaking anything) and the strangely enticing walking trail through the woods that every few yards had odd little calisthenics stations marked by boards picturing stick figures exercising. The grassy area between the cabins and the shore that we'd used as a softball field seemed in its snow-covered state to be nowhere near big enough for four bases, let alone an outfield.

Jane's and my cabin was across from the two I remembered and on the opposite side of the main lodge. Otherwise, it was identical, right down to the speckled mirror above the bureau in the bedroom that distorted our faces and the faded paintings of ducks and seagulls hanging crookedly on the sitting room walls. Seeing the lone good-sized upholstered chair by the fireplace made me laugh aloud. Night after night, my siblings and I had fought furiously over the like chair in our cabin until our parents finally wised up and instituted a one child per night schedule for sitting in it.

Jane and I decided to eat at a casual diner. There weren't any fancier options near the lodge and neither of us was in the mood for anything formal, anyway. We sat across from each other at a banged-up old picnic table about equidistant from the fireplace and the lobster tank. The fire heated the room very unevenly. Jane said her right side was glad for the thick sweater she was wearing and her left was sorry for it. Laughing, she wondered if we were in danger of having a thunderstorm right over our table.

As she always did on vacations, she had left work completely behind. She was relaxed and happy and animated, which matched my mood perfectly.

"Isn't it weird," she said at one point, "how you can feel two totally inconsistent ways at the same time? I love being alone with you and I've missed that since Nick was born, but I also miss him. I feel sort of like I've left my wallet somewhere. I keep feeling startled and wanting to look for him."

"Yeah," I smiled, "it does feel like we've forgotten something. I'm sure he's fine, though."

"Me, too. I'm not worried about him—I just keep thinking about him." She smiled tenderly. "We'll probably feel like this for the rest of our lives. He's permanent!"

"It's been a great experience so far, hasn't it?"

"Yeah, it has—surprisingly so, actually." She raised her eyebrows. "Are you just going to keep offering up experiences that are way better than I imagined forever?"

"That's not very hard to do, Ms. Cynic," I said, grinning, "but, yeah, that's my plan. That reminds me—do you remember when I told you at our wedding reception that we'd still be crazy about each other in four years? Well, now it's been four years. Was I right?"

"Yes, of course, dear, you're always right." Then she looked serious and said, "I was thinking about that, too, on the way up here. I think I have to say something sappy."

"No kidding! Is the occasion actually getting to you?"

She gave me a narrow-eyed look, but then she smiled and in a rush of words she said, "I have a hard time believing the last four years have really happened! They're like a dream! Being with you has made me so happy, and it's really opened me up, too—Laura was right when she said that. I see *everything* less rigidly now. Nothing seems set in stone, and just about anything seems possible. It still horrifies me to think I could so easily have settled for so much less simply because the reality of this was beyond my imagination. I'm so grateful to you."

"I'm grateful to you, too, honey." I covered her hand with mine. "Our marriage has been just as great for me."

"I know—that's part of what makes me so happy. But I really do think you risked more."

"You do? Why?"

"Because of the kind of person you are. Before you, I didn't want to be head over heels in love. I really didn't. I doubted it was possible at all and, in any event, it seemed more like something to avoid than something to long for. I liked your merger concept largely because it was so unemotional and businesslike." She widened her eyes and held up her hands in a gesture of resigned disbelief. "I just had no idea, you know? But you're a total romantic. You believed this kind of love was possible— in fact, you expected it. And yet you risked missing it all by approaching marriage the way you did. You took a hell of a chance on me—and you didn't even love me then!"

"I might have loved you then," I said, voicing something I'd thought about occasionally before. "I formulated the merger idea with you in mind, and I never considered pitching it to anyone else."

Jane tilted her head and looked at me thoughtfully. "I've wondered about that, too," she said. "Maybe we've always loved each other at some level. That might explain why you didn't feel you were risking too much by looking for a merger partner instead of waiting to fall in love." She smiled. "Or maybe it didn't seem like too big a risk because you blithely assumed marriage would work out wonderfully for you just like everything else in your golden life. You know, regardless of how you approached it or with whom."

"I didn't think about it as a risk at all. I wanted a partner and I knew you'd make a great one. That's as far as my thinking or my expectations went. I figured that would be great enough. I'm not surprised that we fell in love or that it's all even better than what I was proposing, but this wasn't what I thought I was aiming for—or risking missing."

"That shows such confidence and such trust!" She shook her head admiringly. "It still amazes me! Anyway, what I wanted to say was that the last four years have been incredible. I wouldn't have wanted to miss one second of them. Spending them with you hasn't only been wonderful, it's also turned me into the kind of person who truly *can* love and appreciate them. Thank you so much!"

I reached across the table and cradled her face in my hands. "You're welcome, darling. And right back at you. I may have taken a hell of a chance on you, but it has paid off beyond anything I could have imagined."

We gazed at each other for a minute or two, my hands on her face and hers clasping my wrists. She looked (and I felt) a little teary. Then, she sniffed and rolled her eyes. "Sappy enough for you?" she demanded.

"I like it that you're sappy about me," I told her, stroking her cheek.

She turned her head slightly and kissed my palm. "Yeah," she said. "It's not so bad."

Although we'd turned on the heat in our cabin before we left for dinner, there was still a distinct chill in the air when we returned. Jane asked me to light the fire, said she'd be right back, and disappeared into the bedroom. All the makings of a fire had been laid in the fireplace grate—all I had to do was open the damper and light the kindling. That done, I moved the good chair closer to the fireplace and sank into it (smiling as I relished not being hauled immediately out of it by Andy or Claire).

Jane reappeared, having exchanged her boots for thick socks and her jeans for flannel pajama pants. She curled up in my lap and rested her head on my chest. Her forehead grazed my neck as she took a deep breath and sighed softly. The fire was building nicely; we listened to it crackle.

"Are you OK?" I asked her after a few minutes of uncharacteristic silence.

"I'm so far past OK," she said. "I might be the happiest person in the world."

"That's quite a statement!"

"I know! Amazing, isn't it?" She hugged me. "You know what I want to do?"

"I can guess."

She smiled. "You're right, but not this minute. Right now, I want to sit here quietly and stare into the fire and enjoy all the blissful thoughts running through my head. Would that be OK for a while?"

"Sure," I said, kissing the top of her head.

I felt blissful, too—intensely in love and full of good memories. The now blazing fire recalled countless past fires in similar fireplaces. I imagined bringing Nick and his eventual siblings up to the lodge for summer vacations in the future (and could practically hear Jane saying, "Siblings? Plural?!"). It was odd enough—both jarring and cool—to be an adult in a place I'd known well as a child. It would be even odder to visit as one of the parents instead of one of the kids.

I had a moment of disbelief that I really had a child of my own. It didn't seem quite possible, as a concept or in terms of time. The room seemed to echo with the childhood voices of my brother and sisters and the sounds of cards shuffling, pieces slapping down on game boards, play money crinkling. Time warped—our family vacations seemed both long-past and very recent. Even as I thought about Nick and the future, I could easily remember being my ten-year-old self.

My life had always been great. I'd expected no less, but it was still very sweet to recognize what a pleasure life was and how lucky I'd been.

Jane shifted her position slightly, which brought my thoughts back to her. My happiness with our life together went so far beyond what I had anticipated. Notwithstanding my high expectations and my optimism, she had provided a depth and a richness that were totally unexpected.

Loving each other, living together, learning from each other's experiences, admiring and wanting to impress each other—it was all transforming. Jane had always challenged me. She never coasted and she didn't let me coast either. Her honesty, her brilliance, her skepticism and her grit had pushed and inspired and improved me for ten years. She had made me a better person.

I was also succeeding far more spectacularly than I would have without her. Before we met, I was more oblivious than I'd recognized to the true impact inequality had on people unlike me. The very advantages that made me powerful enough to achieve my goals also limited my point of view and made those goals harder to achieve. Knowing Jane, watching her struggle, listening to her, and caring what she thought had given me a more complete picture of the full shape and depth of both inequality and opportunity.

It was gratifying to know that I was as significant to her success as she was to mine. She would have done fine on her own, but she would have made a few unnecessary missteps and felt much more uneasy and in the dark, as well as much more frustrated. I was tremendously proud of what she was accomplishing and of the contributions I'd made to her ability to accomplish it.

Nick brought another kind of mutuality to our relationship. He bound us together, obviously, but I hadn't focused before he was born on all the ways a baby would require Jane and me to count on each other. Having a child together really was a joint leap of faith, and I couldn't imagine anyone I'd rather depend on than Jane. Raising Nick with her was a very satisfying additional pleasure. And I loved him all the more because she was his mother.

I'd wanted a marriage that gave me the sense of being together with someone in something important. I'd gotten that in spades, but my original conception had missed the mark. I'd envisioned marriage as a matter of adding someone to my life and being added to hers, like adding a prominent new color to each of two unfinished paintings. I'd imagined complementing our existing lives, not creating an entirely new work-in-progress.

As it turned out, our relationship was itself the "something important" we were in together. Our merger increased and supported us. It created possibilities and lit up opportunities. Exactly like the constituent parts in a successful business merger, Jane and I were better together than we'd been separately. Our lives had deeper meaning and purpose with each other in them, and we were achieving more.

When I formulated the merger concept, I had the idea that love was a luxury. And it was a luxury, too, but not in the sense of being superfluous. Love was an extravagant wonder that provided immense pleasure, joy, comfort and satisfaction. It wasn't necessary, I supposed, at least not strictly speaking, but I wouldn't have wanted to live without it.

Gazing into the fire, these thoughts in my head and Jane in my arms, I couldn't imagine being happier. I smiled as I recognized that I'd felt the same way many times before, but somehow things kept getting better and better.

EPILOGUE

Jane

Today was the first anniversary of my promotion to division head at the Company. I had filed the announcement of the promotion, together with a sheaf of the congratulatory messages that followed it, in my tickler file for today. I can't remember why I thought I'd want to look at them a year later, but it turned out to be a nice walk down memory lane.

The announcement was flush with promise and enthusiasm. It had come from Bill, who lived up to expectations and made the leap to executive management a few years ago. He's now President and Chief Operating Officer of the Company and on the short list to succeed the CEO. I've always liked working for him, and he's continued to value and promote me over the years. After my post-BEL unit head job, which I stayed in for six years, he named me to head one of the larger units in the division. When Bill's successor as division head moved last year to run one of the Company's European operations, Bill moved me into the division head job.

He had asked me to draft the announcement memo for him, and the finished product was in hindsight a rather clunky amalgam of ill-fitting elements: my "just the facts" attempt at corporate focus (sincere enough) and self-deprecation (totally fake); the tinges of personal pride and satisfaction that bled through this politically correct mash; Bill's addition of the complimentary, congratulatory sentiments that justified his having elevated me to the position; the letterhead that wasn't quite right because each secretary did letterhead on the computer with a template and his secretary (big shot that she was by virtue of working for him) couldn't be bothered to do hers correctly.

Double-speak, the zeal to get ahead, achievement, fake self-deprecation, "policies" that don't have to be (and aren't) followed, the constant and never-ending double helix of appearance and reality coming together and zooming apart—all the elements of corporate life embodied in one little memo.

The business world hasn't lost very many of its negative aspects over the years I've been in it. It's still more of a boys' club than it should be, and it's still perceived by most of the people in it as a zero sum game. How comfortable colleagues are with you continues to take precedence over the results you accomplish. Partly because of this, mediocrity continues to rule. It's still laughably easy to be a superstar where results are concerned and highly problematic to be one where other people are concerned. A thick skin and an ability to pull arrows out of your back without sustaining serious injury remain key requirements for anyone who strives for excellence.

Still, there has been progress. I am the only female division head at the Company, but there are now several female unit heads and veritable crowds of women in middle management. The women coming up behind me seem to spend far less time questioning their welcome or their right to participate. And while "working mother" continues to be a loaded phrase (and "working father" continues, annoyingly, not to be a phrase at all), many of the women in leadership positions are, like me, mothers who have taken multiple maternity leaves.

Yes, I let Charlie talk me into not one, but two siblings for Nick, even though our second child was a girl and we could really have considered our family complete at that point. To tell the truth, it didn't take much persuading. I liked having babies with Charlie and I liked the impact that excelling at my job while pregnant had on the people around me. Being a working parent has its challenges and I still sometimes wish I could be the father instead of the mother, but the joys far outweigh the added complexity.

We have a lot of fun as a family. I love the kids' curiosity, the open intensity of their emotions, the way they can crawl into my arms and cling like monkeys, their instinctive certainty that Charlie and I will take care of them and be able to solve any problem. We're always tickled (and relieved) by their abrupt shifts from being at each other's throats to being thick as thieves, and charmed by the way they occasionally gang up on us like a band of determined little revolutionaries. Nick's brilliance and burgeoning independence, Amy's passion for sports and her comfort in her own skin (temperamentally, she's the child most like Charlie), Joe's sunny disposition and exuberant disregard for rules and limitations of every kind—it's all so *interesting*.

As for work, I no longer feel like an interloper. I'm still the only woman in the conference room disappointingly often, but now no one who works with me doubts that I have what it takes. The current buzz on me is that I'm a shoo-in to follow Bill into the top executive ranks. My career is extremely rewarding and I'm proud of the contributions I've made to improving the corporate culture—actively as well as by example. I'm wholly committed to staying in the game and continuing to make a difference that counts.

I haven't lost my inclination to distrust or my instinctive cynicism as I've gotten older and more successful, but I, too, have made progress. I no longer hide, withhold or repudiate big chunks of who I am. I routinely give people the benefit of the doubt (without having to exert superhuman effort to do so). And while I'm still sarcastic, still frequently angered by sexism, and still more than a little frustrated and irritated by other people, I've learned to contain my impatience. People no longer find me as intimidating or as prickly as they once did.

I'm not sure whether this is progress or not, but I have also become utterly and unabashedly gooey about Charlie. I love him with an unrestrained intensity that I would once have found disturbing, even menacing. My passion for him remains quite uncontrollable, but in a good way that continues to amaze me—and that has, among other things, taught me the relative place and value of control where feelings are concerned.

It hasn't all been perfect. There have been plenty of times over the years when I could cheerfully have strangled my blithe, easygoing and innately high-handed husband. I'm sure there have been even more times when he could cheerfully have strangled me. (Or maybe not: I'm undeniably more irritable as well as more irritating.) But there has never been a time—not one single moment—when I've had any doubt that without Charlie both my life and my career would have remained cramped and small-time.

I suppose everyone needs a catalyst to experience life fully. I don't think it has to be another person. It could as easily be a quest or a talent or anything else that ignites passion. Detached as I once was, I would have guessed that my own catalyst would have been something more abstract (both less animate and less sentimental) than another person. Ambition, perhaps, or zeal to change the business world seemed more likely. I had plenty of both, and they did indeed motivate and inspire me. But Charlie was my catalyst.

I once worried about caring so much for a man that I might compromise something fundamental about myself in order to please him or avoid losing him. As it turned out, but for compromising the self-sufficiency and detachment I once held inviolate, I would have lost myself—personally and professionally. Love and marriage facilitated my career success as effectively as they opened up my life. In fact, I think they facilitated my career success *by* opening up my life.

I don't mean this in a sexist way. It's not that I was an incomplete person without a spouse or that love and marriage were somehow necessary to me as a woman. (Ugh!) Charlie didn't give me something I lacked without him. What he did was prompt feelings in me—powerful and unexpected feelings—that compelled me to recognize the whole of who I was and what I could achieve. My feelings for him broadened my sense of what's possible and taught me to take risks.

I was already a complete person (like everyone else, man or woman), but I wasn't experiencing life like one. I had walled off too much of myself—sometimes self-protectively, sometimes in response to what I thought the dictates of the narrow-minded mandated, sometimes inadvertently or unconsciously. Because my sense of who I was and what I wanted was overly influenced by what other people seemed intent on blocking me from being and doing, I had an incomplete picture of myself and I was doing an incomplete job of formulating and achieving my goals.

I'd certainly seen plenty of other evidence proving that it was not necessary for a woman to deny any particular part of her identity or personality to succeed at work. Lynn's "I am who I am" strategy, Jennifer's sexy free agent approach, Cheryl's patent intelligence and ambition coupled with her commitment to marriage and motherhood above all, Liz's success at folding herself into Tyler's world without losing her independent strength or her individuality, Katherine's professional expertise flourishing right alongside her big personality and her ongoing passion for Jordan, even my sister's surprising combination of traditional femininity and a real job—they were all examples proving that career success and "woman," however defined, were not mutually exclusive.

But I didn't recognize these examples for what they were until I wanted—irresistibly—to experience things that I had up to then considered resistible and not all that big a deal, not to mention detrimental to achieving my career goals. Falling in love with Charlie changed everything for me. The strength of my feelings for him aroused the need and triggered the ability for me to have a bigger life, one that includes trust, love, marriage, children, self-direction—and career success.

Charlie served as a guide for me from the day we met. His advice, his example, his optimism and his trust all accelerated my success. It was as if I'd captured a member of the enemy forces—and not just any member, but a high-ranking, influential member, one who had the handbook, the training manual, the maps and the game plan. He was always willing to share what he knew with me, so I got a lot of useful knowledge and insight from our mentoring relationship and from our friendship. But love and marriage gave me the chance to observe my captive up close and the desire to pay attention to his example in a deeper and more effective way.

I learned what makes him tick and how he thinks, what he understands instinctively and where his blind spots are. Charlie is exceptional in many ways, but he is also a card-carrying representative of the powers that be. Knowing him intimately has taught me to understand those powers, to anticipate their reactions and maneuvers, to play their game like an insider. For me, our life together neutralizes the home field advantage by which white males maintain their hegemony in the business world.

Charlie's example also alerted me to the limitations of my own outlook. He didn't *decide* to live a complete life or to be self-confident and optimistic. Nor does he think he's entitled to disregard other people's opinions. He doesn't think or worry about these things at all. He simply goes about the business of living his life as he sees fit and he deals with the fallout, good and not so good.

The narrow-minded have never had any power over Charlie. His golden boy status obviously helps—people attempt to exert far less influence over him and his choices than they do over me and mine. But what Alex and Kate taught their children was absolutely right. The determining factor is not how much influence other people attempt to exert, but rather how much power one yields to them. Charlie yields none.

I, on the other hand, yielded far too much. Behaviorally speaking, this offered some advantages; the less I flaunted the differences people found threatening, the smoother my career path. But I'd miscalculated both the costs and the benefits of confining my identity to the small range that the narrow-minded considered (more or less) acceptable. The true benefits did not begin to justify the costs. You can't win the game by letting the opposition call the plays.

Even as I thought I was beating the narrow-minded, I was in fact well on my way to becoming yet another victimized woman willing to live a half-life as the price of career success. Nowhere was this more evident or more damaging to me than in my fears relating to intimacy. I was certain that it was necessary to forgo full-blown lover, wife and mother experiences to have the kind of career I'd always craved—and that was a bargain I'd been willing to make. So I'd drawn myself a tiny little box in which to feel comfortable with sex and romance.

If not for Charlie and the non-traditional, innovative and utterly respectful way he proposed the idea of marriage to me (and what that proposal, in turn, led me to experience), I might never have discovered that feeling untouched and in control was not, after all, my priority. I had no idea I was capable of overwhelming passion, but once I experienced it, the constraints of the tiny box I'd created for myself became intolerable.

Exploding out of that box began the process of understanding that I had drawn a like, but less visible, box around the rest of my life. Detachment and distrust weren't helping me anywhere. The world is full of other people, and there's no choice but to interact with them. Participation, passion, trust, connection—intimacy, if you will—are as essential to living fully out of bed as in it.

I've always understood that I am my own actor and also the director of my own personal play. What Charlie's example and my love for him have made plain to me is that I am also the playwright.

It is most definitely improvisational theatre. Other actors appear and do what they do, and what they do can take scenes, even whole acts, in directions and to places very different than my original script contemplated. I have to deal with them, but other actors do not have the power—unless I give it to them—to change my role or my character. Other people will no doubt try to contain or impede me, whether inadvertently or otherwise, but the power and the responsibility to decide who I am and what I do are mine. Now I understand that the way to get out of the box is simply to get out of the box.

I still count on Charlie for full-fledged optimism—and I'm sure I always will—but I, too, now look toward the future with confidence and hope and enthusiasm. And I know two things with absolute clarity: trust is worth the risk and passion is worth everything.

❖ ❖ ❖

ABOUT THE AUTHOR

DEBRA SNIDER is an author and speaker. She retired in 2001 from a distinguished twenty-year business career. As a transactional lawyer, she handled corporate and securities deals with two large law firms and a real estate syndication company, and she was a senior executive at a $20 billion publicly held commercial finance company. Her short story, "The Day Lust Left the Room," was awarded Honorable Mention in the Mainstream/Literary Short Story category of the 74th Annual *Writer's Digest* Writing Competition (2005). *A Merger of Equals* is her first novel.